The Snow Queen

The
Snow Queen

Joan D. Vinge

The Dial Press
New York

B-2

A QUANTUM NOVEL
Published by
The Dial Press
1 Dag Hammarskjold Plaza
New York, New York 10017

Manufactured in the United States of America

First printing

Library of Congress Cataloging in Publication Data

Vinge, Joan D
The snow queen.

(A Quantum novel)
1. Title.
PZ4.V78Sn   [PS3572.I53]   813'.5'4   79-20555
ISBN 0-8037-7739-6

"... strait is the gate and narrow is the way which leadeth unto life, and few there be that find it."

—New Testament, Matthew 7:14

"You shall have joy, or you shall have power, said God; you shall not have both."

—Ralph Waldo Emerson

To the Lady, who gives, and who takes away.

I would like to gratefully acknowledge the inspiration and artistry of Hans Christian Andersen, whose folk tale "The Snow Queen" gave me the seeds of this story; and Robert Graves, whose book *The White Goddess* provided me with the rich Earth in which it grew. And I would like to thank those people who helped me weed, and tend, and harvest the fruits of my labor: my husband Vernor, and my editors Don Bensen and Jim Frenkel, without whose perceptive and sensitive suggestions this book would not have grown as strong or as truly. I would also like to thank my father, for his love of science fiction; and my mother, for teaching me a woman's strength and giving me the freedom to become.

The Snow Queen

Prologue

The door swung shut silently behind them, cutting off the light, music, and wild celebration of the ballroom. The sudden loss of sight and hearing made him claustrophobic. He tightened his hands over the instrument kit he carried beneath his cloak.

He heard her amused laughter in the darkness at his side, and light burst around him again, opening up the small room they stood in now. They were not alone. His tension made him start, even though he was expecting it, even though it had happened to him five times already in this interminable night, and would happen several times more. It was happening in a sitting room this time—on the boneless couch that obtruded into a forest of dark furniture legs dusted with gold. The irrelevant thought struck him that he had seen a greater range of styles and taste in this one night than he had probably seen in forty years back on Kharemough.

But he was not back on Kharemough; he was in Carbuncle, and this Festival night was the strangest night he would ever spend, if he lived to be a hundred. Sprawled on the couch in unselfconscious abandon were a man and a woman, both of them deeply asleep now from the drugged wine in the half-empty bottle lying on its side on the rug. He stared at the purple stain that crept across the sculptured carpet-pile, trying not to intrude any more than he must on their privacy. "You're certain that this couple has also been—intimate?"

"Quite certain. *Absolutely* certain." His companion lifted the white-feathered mask from her shoulders, revealing a mass of hair almost as white coiled like a nest of serpents above her eager, young girl's face. The mask was a

1

grotesque contrast to the sweetness of that face: the barbed ripping beak of a predatory bird, the enormous black-pupiled eyes of a night hunter that glared at him with the promise of life and death hanging in the balance. . . . *No.* When he looked into her eyes, there was no contrast. There was no difference. "You Kharemoughis are so self-righteous." She threw off her white-feathered cape. "And such hypocrites." She laughed again; her laughter was both bright and dark.

He removed his own less elaborate mask reluctantly: an absurd fantasy creature, half fish, half pure imagination. He did not like having to expose his expression.

She searched his face in the pitiless lamplight, with feigned innocence. "Don't tell me, Doctor, that you really don't like to watch?"

He swallowed his indignation with difficulty. "I'm a biochemist, Your Majesty, not a voyeur."

"Nonsense." The smile that was far too old for the face formed on her mouth. "All medical men are voyeurs. Why else would they become doctors? Except for the sadists, of course, who simply enjoy the blood and the pain."

Afraid to respond, he only moved past her, crossed the carpet to the couch and put his instrument kit on the floor. Beyond these walls the city of Carbuncle climaxed its celebration of the Prime Minister's cyclical visit to this world with a night of joyous abandon. He had never expected to find himself spending it with this world's queen—and certainly not spending it doing what he was about to do.

The sleeping woman lay with her face toward him. He saw that she was young, of medium height, strong and healthy. Her gently smiling face was deeply tanned by sun and weather beneath the tangled, sandy hair. The rest of her body was pale; he supposed she kept it well protected from the bitter cold beyond the city's walls. The man beside her was a youthful thirty, he judged, with dark hair and light skin, and could have been either a local or an offworlder; but he was of no concern now. Their Festival masks looked down in hollow-eyed censure, like impotent guardian gods resting on the couch back. He dabbed the

2

woman's shoulder with antiseptic, made the tiny incision to insert the tracer beneath her skin, doing the simple procedure first to reassure himself. The Queen stood watching intently, silent now that he needed silence.

Noise concentrated beyond the locked door; he heard slightly slurred voices protesting loudly. He shrank like an animal in a trap, waiting for discovery.

"Don't worry, Doctor." The Queen laid a light, reassuring hand on his arm. "My people will see that we're not disturbed."

"Why the hell did I let myself be talked into this?" more to himself than to her. He turned back to his work, but his hands were unsteady.

"Twenty-five extra years of youth can be very persuasive."

"A lot of good it'll do me if I spend them all in some penal colony!"

"Get hold of yourself, Doctor. If you don't finish what you've started tonight, you won't have earned your twenty-five years anyway. The agreement stands only while I have at least one perfectly normal clone-child somewhere among the Summer folk on this planet."

"I'm aware of the terms." He finished with the small incision and sealed it. "But I hope you understand that a clone implant under these circumstances is not only illegal, it's highly unpredictable. This is a difficult procedure. The odds of producing a clone who is even a reasonable replica of the original person are not particularly good under the most controlled conditions, let alone—"

"Then the more implants you perform tonight, the better off we'll both be. Isn't that right?"

"Yes, Your Majesty," tasting self-disgust. "I suppose it is." He rolled the sleeping woman carefully onto her back and reached into his kit again.

3

1

Here on Tiamat, where there is more water than land, the sharp edge between ocean and sky is blurred; the two merge into one. Water is drawn up from the shining plate of the sea and showers down again in petulant squalls. Clouds pass like emotion across the fiery red faces of the Twins, and are shaken off, splintering into rainbows: dozens of rainbows every day, until the people cease to be amazed by them. Until no one stops to wonder, no one looks up. . . .

"It's a shame," Moon said suddenly, pulling hard on the steering oar.

"What is?" Sparks ducked down as the flapping sail filled and the boom swept across over his head. The outrigger canoe plunged like a wingfish. "It's a shame you aren't paying attention. What do you want to do, sink us?"

Moon frowned, the moment's mood broken. "Oh, drown yourself."

"I'm half-drowned already; that's the trouble." He grimaced at the water lapping the ankles of their waterproof kleeskin overboots, and picked up the bailer again. The last squall had drowned his good nature, anyway, she thought, along with the sodden supply baskets. Or maybe it was only fatigue. They had been at sea on this journey for nearly a month, creeping from island to island along the Windward chain. And for the last day they had been beyond the Windwards, beyond the charts they knew, striking out across the expanse of open ocean toward three islands that kept to themselves, a sanctuary of the Sea Mother. Their boat was tiny for such far ranging, and they had only the stars and a rough current-chart of crisscrossed sticks to guide them. But they were children of the Sea as

5

truly as they were the children of their birth-mothers; and because they were on a sacred quest, Moon knew that She would be kind.

Moon watched Sparks's bobbing head catch fire as the pinwheeled binary of Tiamat's double sun broke the clouds, to kindle flame in the red of his hair and his sparse, newly starting beard; throw the soft-edged shadow of his slim, muscular body down into the bottom of the boat. She sighed, unable to keep hold of her irritation when she looked at him, and reached out tenderly to finger a red, shining braid.

"Rainbows . . . I was talking about rainbows. Nobody appreciates them. What if there was never another rainbow?" She brushed back the hood of her mottled slicker and tugged loose the laces at her throat. Braids as white as cream spilled out and down over her back. Her eyes were the color of mist and moss agate. She looked up through the crab-claw sail, squinting as she sorted tumbled cloud from sky to find vaulting ribbons of fractured light, dimmed here to nothingness, brightening there until their banners doubled and redoubled.

Sparks dumped another shellful of water overboard, sending it home, before he lifted his head to follow her gaze. Even without its sun-browning, his skin was dark for an islander's. But lashes and eyebrows as pale as her own tightened against the glare, above eyes that changed color like the sea. "Come on. We'll always have rainbows, Cuz. As long as we have the Twins and the rain. A simple case of diffraction; I showed you—"

She hated it when he talked tech—the unthinking arrogance that came into his voice. "I know that. I'm not stupid." She jerked the coppery braid sharply.

"Ow!"

"But I'd still rather hear Gran tell us that it was the Lady's promise of plenty, instead of hearing that trader turn it into something without any point at all. And so would you. Wouldn't you, my starchild? Admit it!"

"No!" He beat her hand away; anger blazed. "Don't make fun of that, damn it!" He turned his back on her, splashing. She pictured his knuckles whitening over the corroded crosses-inside-a-circle: the token his offworlder father had given to his mother at the last Festival. "Mother of Us All!"

It was the one thing that drove between them like a blade—their awareness of a heritage that he did not share with her, or with anyone they knew. They were Summers, and their people rarely had contact with the tech-loving Winters who consorted with the offworlders—except at the Festivals, when the adventurous and joyful from all over this world gathered in Carbuncle; when they put on masks and put off their differences, to celebrate the Prime Minister's cyclical visit and a tradition that was far older.

Their two mothers, who were sisters, had gone to Carbuncle to the last Festival, and returned to Neith carrying, as her mother had told her, "the living memory of a magic night." She and Sparks had been born on the same day; his mother had died in childbirth. Their grandmother had raised them both while Moon's mother was at sea with the fishing fleet. They had grown up together—like twins, she often thought: strange, changeling twins growing up under the vaguely uneasy gaze of the stolid, provincial islanders. But there had always been a part of Sparks that she was shut off from, that she could not share: the part of him that heard the stars whisper. He bartered surreptitiously with passing traders for mechanical trinkets from other worlds, wasted days taking them apart and putting them back together, finally throwing them into the sea in a fit of self-disgust, along with propitiating effigies made of leaves.

Moon kept his tech secrets from Gran and the world, grateful that he at least shared them with her, but nursing a secret resentment. For all she knew her own father could have been a Winter or even an offworlder, but she was content with building a future that fit under her own sky. Because of that it was hard for her to be patient with Sparks, who was not, who was caught in the space between the heritage he lived and the one he saw in starlight.

"Oh, Sparks." She leaned forward, rested a chilly hand on his shoulder, massaging the knotted muscles through

7

the thickness of cloth and oilskins. "I'm not teasing. I didn't mean to; I'm sorry," thinking, *I'd rather have no father at all than live with a shadow all my life.* "Don't be sad. Look there!" Blue sparks danced on the ocean beyond red sparks gleaming in his hair. Wingfish flashed and soared above the swells of the Mother Sea, and she saw the island clearly now, leeward, the highest of three. Serpentine lace marked the distant meeting of sea and shore. "The choosing-place! And look—mers!" She blew a kiss in awed reverence.

Long, sinuous, brindle-colored necks were breaking the water surface around and ahead of them; ebony eyes studied them with inscrutable knowledge. The mers were the Sea's children, and a sailor's luck. Their presence could only mean that the Lady was smiling.

Sparks looked back at her, suddenly smiling too, and caught her hand. "They're leading us in—She knows why we've come. We've really come, we're going to be chosen at last." He pulled the coiled shell flute out of the pouch at his hip and set free a joyous run of notes. The mers' heads began to weave with the music, and their own eerie whistles and cries sang counterpoint. The old tales said that they lamented a terrible loss, and a terrible wrong; but no two tales agreed on what the loss or the wrong had been.

Moon listened to their music, not finding it sad at all. Her own throat was suddenly too tight for song: She saw in her mind another shore, half their lifetime ago, where two children had picked up a dream lying like a rare coiled shell in the sand at the feet of a stranger. She followed the memory back through time. . . .

Moon and Sparks ran barefoot along the rough walls between the shallow harbor pens, and net slung swaying like a hammock from shoulder to slim shoulder between them. Their deft, callused feet slapped and splashed along the piled-stone pathways, immune to bruises and the lapping icy water. The klee in the pens, usually as sluggish as stones on the weedy bottom, surfaced with ungainly haste to watch the children pass. They blew spray and grunted with hunger; but the net was empty, its burden of dried seahair already dumped into the family stock-pens for the midday feeding.

"Hurry up, Sparkie!" Moon, in the lead as usual, pulled the netting taut between them, hauling her shorter cousin along like a reluctant load of fish. She swept the white fall of her bangs back from her face, eyes on the deep-water channel that drove straight in to shore beyond the fish-yards. Already the tall tops of the cloven sails—all she could see of the fishing fleet from here—were sweeping ahead. "We'll never get to the docks first!" She pulled harder, in frustration.

"I'm *hurry*ing, Moon. It's almost like *my* mother coming home, too!" Sparks found an extra burst of speed; she felt him catch up behind her, heard him panting. "Do you think Gran will make honeycake?"

"For sure!" Leaping, she almost stumbled. "I saw her getting out the pot."

They ran on, dancing over the stones toward the gleaming noonday beach and the village beyond. Moon pictured the brown, smiling face of her mother as they had last seen her, three months ago: thick sand-colored braids piled on her head, hidden under a dark knit cap; the thick high-necked sweater, slicker, and heavy boots that made her indistinguishable from her crew as she tossed them a last kiss, while the double-hulled fishing boat leaned into the winds of sunrise.

But today she was home again. They would all go down to the village hall with the other fishing families, to celebrate and dance. And then, very late at night, she would curl up in her mother's lap (although she was getting too big to curl up in her mother's lap), held close in the sturdy arms; watching Sparks through heavy lids to see if he fell asleep first, in Gran's arms. There would be the warm snap and whisper of flames on the hearth, the smell of sea and ships that clung to her mother's hair, the hypnotic flow of voices as Gran reclaimed her own daughter from the Sea, who was Mother to them all.

Moon leaped down into the soft, golden-brown beach

9

sand. Sparks thumped down from the wall behind her, their shadows tangling in the noonday glare. With her eyes fixed on the cluttered stone houses of the village and the boats dropping sail in the bay, she almost darted past the stranger who stood waiting, watching, as they came. Almost—

Sparks collided with Moon as she slid to a stop. "Look out, fish brain!" A cloud of sand exploded around their ankles.

She threw her arms around him for balance, squeezed the indignation out of him as her own amazement tightened her hold. Sparks pulled free, subsiding; the net dropped, forgotten, like the village, the bay, their reunion. Moon tugged at the hem of her hand-me-down sweater, knitting her fingers into the heavy rust-red yarn.

The woman smiled down at them, the radiant oval of her face touched with windburn above her ancient gray parka, the thick pants and clumsy boots worn by any islander. But she was not from Neith, not simply from any island. . . .

"Did—did you come out of the Sea?" Moon gasped. Sparks gaped beside her.

The woman laughed; her laughter broke the spell of otherworldliness like window glass. "No . . . only across it, on a ship."

"Why?" "Who are you?" Their questions ran together.

And in answer to both, the woman held out the medallion she wore on a chain: a barbed trefoil like a bouquet of fish hooks, glittering with the darkly sinister beauty of a reptile's eye. "Do you know what this is?" She went down on one knee in the sand, her black braids dropping forward. They shuffled closer, blinking.

"Sibyl . . . ?" Moon whispered timidly, seeing Sparks clutch his own medal out of the corner of her eye. But then her gaze was wholly the woman's, and she knew why the dark, compelling eyes seemed to open on infinity. A sibyl was the earthly channel for supernatural wisdom, chosen through the Lady's Own judgment, who by tem-

10

perament and training had the strength to withstand a holy visitation.

The woman nodded. "I am Clavally Bluestone Summer." She set her hands against her forehead. "Ask, and I will answer."

They did not ask, dazed by the knowledge that she would—could—answer any question they could imagine; or that the Lady Herself would answer them with Clavally's lips, while the sibyl was swept away in a trance.

"No questions?" Formality fell away again, held at bay by her good humor. "Then tell me who you are, who already know everything you need to know?"

"I'm Moon," Moon said, pushing at her bangs. "Moon Dawntreader Summer. This's my cousin, Sparks Dawntreader Summer . . . and I don't know enough to ask about anything!" she finished miserably.

"I do." Sparks pushed forward, holding out his medal. "What did this used to be?"

"*Input . . .*" Clavally took it between her fingers, frowned faintly, murmuring. Her eyes turned to smoky quartz, moved wildly, like a dreamer's; her hand fisted over the disc. "Sign of the Hegemony—two crosses bound within a circle symbolize the unity of Kharemough and its seven subordinate worlds . . . medal awarded for valorous service, Kispah uprising: 'What all may strive for, this one has found. To our beloved son Temmon Ashwini Sirus, this day, 9:113:07.' Sandhi, official language of Kharemough and the Hegemony . . . *No further analysis.*" Her head dropped forward, let go by an unseen force. She swayed gently on her knees, sighed, sat back. "Well."

"But what does it *mean?*" Sparks looked down at the disc which still danced against his parka front, and his mouth formed an uncertain line.

Clavally shook her head. "I don't know. The Lady only speaks through me, not to me. That's the Transfer—the way it is."

Sparks's mouth quivered.

"The Hegemony," Moon said quickly. "What's the Hegemony, Clavally?"

11

"The offworlders!" Clavally's eyes widened slightly. "The Hegemony is what they call themselves. So it's an offworld thing, then. . . . I've never been to Carbuncle." Her glance went to it again. "How did this get here, so far from the starport, and the Winters?" And back to their faces, "You're merrybegots, aren't you? Your mothers went to the last Festival together, and were lucky enough to come back with you . . . and also this keepsake?"

Sparks nodded, as much in awe of adult logic as he was of the Lady's trances. "Then . . . my father isn't a Summer; he isn't even on Tiamat?"

"That I can't tell you." Clavally stood up. Moon saw a strange concern cross her face as she looked back at Sparks. "But I do know that merrybegots are specially blessed. Do you know why I'm here?"

They shook their heads.

"Do you know what you want to be when you grow up?"

"Together," Moon answered without thinking.

Again the bright laughter. "Good! I'm making this journey through the Windwards to urge all the young Summers, before they settle into life, to remember that they can dedicate themselves to the Sea in another way than as fishers or farmers. They can serve the Lady by serving their fellow human beings as sibyls, as I do. Some of us are born with a special seed inside us, and it only waits for the Lady to touch us and make it grow. When you're old enough, maybe you two will hear Her call, and go to a choosing-place."

"Oh." Moon shivered slightly. "I think I hear Her now!" She pressed cold hands against her leaping heart, where a dream seed sprouted.

"Me too, me too!" Sparks cried eagerly. "Can we go now, can we go with you, Clavally?"

Clavally pulled up the hood of her parka against a sudden buffet of wind. "No, not yet. Wait a little longer; until you're certain of what you hear."

"How long?"

"A month?"

12

She rested her hands on the two small shoulders. "More like years, I think."

"Years!" Moon protested.

"By then you'll be sure it isn't just the crying of sea birds you hear. But always remember, in the end it won't be you who will choose the Lady, but the Lady Who will choose you." She looked again, almost pointedly, at Sparks.

"All right." Moon wondered at the look, and straightened her shoulders resolutely under the hand. "We'll wait. And we'll remember."

"And now—" the sibyl dropped her hands—"I think someone is waiting for you."

Time began to flow forward again, and they fled, running—with many backward glances—toward town.

"Moon, remember the last thing she said to us?" The silver play of notes dissolved as Sparks lowered his flute and looked back, breaking in on Moon's memory. The mers stopped their own song, looking toward the boat.

"Clavally?" Moon guided the outrigger around the point of land that jagged inward at the mouth of the bay. The shoreline of the Choosing Island was as spiny as the trefoil the sibyls wore. "You mean, that my mother was waiting for us?"

"No. That the Lady chooses us, not the other way around." Sparks glanced toward the surf line, made his eyes come back to her face. "I mean . . . what if She only chooses one of us? What will we do?"

"She'll choose us both!" Moon grinned. "How could She do anything else? We're merrybegots—we're lucky."

"But what if She doesn't?" He fingered the packing of moss where the halves of the wooden hull had been lashed together. *Inseparable* . . . he frowned slightly. "Nobody *makes* you become a sibyl, do they, just because you pass the test? We can swear to each other now, that if only one of us is chosen, that one will turn it down. For the sake of the other."

"For the sake of us both." Moon nodded. *But She will choose us both.* She had never doubted, since that moment

13

years ago, that she would come to this place and hear the Lady call her. It had been her heart's desire for half a lifetime; and she had made certain Sparks always shared it, not letting his hopeless stardreams lead him away from their common goal.

She put out her arm and Sparks took it somberly; they shook, hands clasping wrists. The clasp became a hug before she knew it, and the doubts in her heart burned away like morning fog. "Sparkie, I love you . . . more than anything under the sky." She kissed him, tasting salt on his lips. "Let the Sea Mother witness that you hold my willing heart, only you, now and forever."

He repeated the words, clearly and proudly, and together they sipped sea water from their cupped hands to complete the vow. "Nobody can say we're still too young to pledge after this journey!" They had pledged their love for the first time when they were barely old enough to recite the words, and everyone had laughed. But they had been true to each other ever since; and through the years they had shared everything, including the hesitant, yearning inevitability of lips touching, and hands, and flesh. . . .

Moon remembered a hidden cranny among the rocks on a leeward bay; warm callused hands of stone cupping their shivering bodies as they lay together in love under the bright noon, while the tide whispered far away down the beach. Now, as then, she could feel the strength of the need that bound them together: the heat they made between them that held the cold loneliness of their world at bay. The union of souls that overcame them in the final moment—the height, the wholeness, that nothing else in their world could ever give her. Together they would enter this new life, and at last they would belong to their world as completely as they belonged to each other. . . . Sparks's lips brushed her ear; she leaned forward, her arms going around him again. The boat nosed toward shore, untended.

"Do you see anything?"

Sparks checked the boat a last time where it lay beached firmly in shells and storm wrack, beyond the high-tide line.

The family totem carved at its prow regarded him with three staring painted eyes. The tide was still going out, but it had already exposed enough wet-mirrored sand so that dragging the canoe up the beach had taken away their breath. One of the mers had actually come out onto the shore with them, let them stroke its wet, slick, brindle fur with timid hands. He had never been close enough to touch one before; they were as large as he was, and twice as heavy.

"Not yet—here!" Moon's voice reached him, along with the frantic waving of her hand. She had followed the mer's floundering progress as it moved on up the beach. "Here by the stream, a path. It must be the one Gran told me about!"

He started across the littered beach slope toward the freshwater outlet, abandoned shells crunching under his feet. The stream had laid down a wide band of red silt in the ochre, cut into the red with channels of moss-green water flow. Where it left the shore, Moon stood waiting to start into the hills.

"We follow the stream up?"

She nodded, following the swift blue-green rise of the cloaked land with her eyes. Naked peaks of raw red stone soared even higher. Those islands were new on the measure- less time scale of the Sea; their spines still clawed the sky, undulled by age.

"Looks like we climb." He jammed his hands into his pockets, uncertain.

"Yeah." Moon watched the mer start back down the beach. Her hand tingled with the feel of its heavy fur. "We'll dance in the rigging today." She looked back at him, suddenly very much aware of what their presence here meant. "Well, come on," almost impatiently. "The first step is the hardest." They took it together.

But it was a step that had been taken before, Moon thought as she climbed . . . *how many times?* She found the answer engraved in the hillsides, where the passage of feet had worn down the airy volcanic pumice until some- times they walked in narrow tracks eaten away to the height of their knees. *And how many have climbed it just*

15

to be refused? Moon thought a quick prayer, looking down as the trail became a narrow ledge running ankle deep above a canyon of evergreen fern and impenetrable bush. The day was utterly silent when the wind died; she had not seen a trace of any living thing larger than a click beetle. Once, perhaps, the distant cry of a bird. . . . The stream winked at her from cover hundreds of feet below, and on her left the green-coated wall vaulted another hundred into the sky. Though she was used to the precarious footing of sailors and the narrow paths among fish pens, these contrasts made her giddy.

Sparks clutched at a protruding bush, scratching his face. "This isn't for weakhearts," not really meaning to say it out loud.

"Probably the point," she mumbled, and wiped her own face on her sleeve.

"You mean maybe this is the test?" They pressed gingerly past a crumbling patch of eroded wall.

"Lady!" half curse, half prayer. "It's enough for me!"

"How far does this go? What if it gets dark?"

"I don't know. . . . The valley's closing, up there."

"I thought you said Grandpa did this, when he was young? I thought you *knew*."

Moon swallowed. "Gran told me he gave up and turned back. He never even found the cave."

"Now you tell me!" But he began to laugh. "This isn't what I thought it would be, somehow."

The stream curved back on itself below, and beyond the next turn of the wall the ledge widened and the trail widened with it. Here in this inland valley cut off from the sea wind, the heat of the sun echoed and re-echoed from the heated rock. Moon pulled off her heavy parka as she walked; Sparks already wore his knotted around his shoulders. The breeze pressed her damp linen shirt against her chest. She unlaced the shirt down to her belt, scratched herself, sighing. "I'm hot, you know that? I'm really hot! What do people do when they get too hot? You can always put on more clothes, but you can only take off so many." She loosened the waterskin from her belt and drank. Some-

16

where ahead she heard a rushing sound, but she only thought of fat sizzling in a kettle.

"We probably won't have to worry about it." Sparks shrugged with good-natured reasonableness. "High summer's still a long way off. We'll probably be dead before it gets that hot." His foot slipped; he went down on one knee with a grunt. "Maybe sooner."

"Funny." She helped him up; her own feet were as clumsy as stones. "You can already see the Summer Star. I saw it through my fingers a few days. . . . Oh—" whispered. She rubbed her stinging face with the back of her hand.

"Yes." Sparks slumped against the outcurving wall. Beyond the final turn of the trail the rushing became the roar of water flung over a precipice, battered by rocks, a silvered sacrifice falling eternally to its death. And there the trail ended.

They stood breathless and confused in the cacophony of sound and spray beside the falls. "It can't end here!" Sparks struck at the falling water. "We know this is the right path. Where is it?"

"Here!" Moon crouched, peering over the edge beside the water curtain, loose strands of hair falling forward in dripping fingers. "Handholds in the rock." She stood up again, wiping her hair back. "Suddenly this isn't . . ." She shook her head, the words lost as she looked back at him and saw the anger on his face.

"What is this, anyway?" Sparks shouted down the valley toward the sea. "What more proof do You want? Do we have to kill ourselves?"

"No!" Moon pulled at his arm, his temper grating like sand on her fatigue. "She wants us to be sure. And we are." She crouched down again, pulling off her boots, and put a foot over the edge.

She began to climb down, letting the roar and the spray fill her senses, batter down her fear. She saw Sparks begin the climb above her; telling herself that countless people had gone down before her, through countless years . . . (foot fumbling over wet rock) . . . she would do it, too . . . (another step! her fingers clutched a lip of stone) . . . this

17

wet climb was no more than the rigging of a ship, which she had climbed without thought countless times . . . (and once more) . . . always trusting in the Sea Mother to place her hands and feet surely . . . (fingers cramping; she bit her lip). . . . She concentrated on belief, in the Lady, in herself; because only if she doubted either one would she . . . (her foot beat against the wet-slimed wall, finding no crevice, no step, no—)

"Sparks!" Her voice scaled up. "It just ends!"

". . . *ledge!* . . ." She heard the word, distorted by the roaring and her own terror; clung to it desperately, as she hugged the cliff face. "*Go right!*" She kicked right, opening her eyes as her foot found the ledge of stone. Blinking hard, she saw it disappear behind the falling water. She reached out, with a quick twist of her body pulled herself over and into the cleft. Sparks came after her; she put out her hand to help him across.

"Thanks." He shook himself, shook his stiffened hands.

"Thank *you*." She took a long breath. They moved deeper into the cleft together, realizing, as their eyes adjusted to the green dappling of light, that it pushed on into the side of the valley. "This is it—this must be it! We're here, the choosing-place. . . ."

They stopped again, their hands reaching out for each other instinctively. They stood breathless, waiting. Nothing called them but the voice of the falls. Nothing touched them but the random drift of spray. "Come on," Sparks tugged at her, "let's go deeper."

The cleft peaked in shadows far overhead, making Moon think of praying hands, as they followed the serpentine shaft into the rock face. Sparks collided abruptly with a sharp turn. "I knew I should've brought a candle."

"It's not dark." Moon looked at him in surprise. "It's strange how the light keeps getting greener . . ."

"What are you talking about? It's like being buried alive —I can't even see you!"

"Come on." Unease began to stir in her. "It's not that dark—just open your eyes. Come on, Sparkie!" She pulled on his arm. "Can't you feel it? Like music . . ."

"No. This place gives me the creeps."

"Come on." She pulled harder, straining now.

"No—wait . . ." He gave a few steps, and a few more.

The music filled her now, centered at her head and spreading through her body like the rhythm of her blood. It touched her like silk, with the taste of ambrosia and the green light of the sea. "Don't you *feel* it?"

"Moon." Sparks grunted as he came up against another wall in the darkness. "Moon, stop! It's no good. I can't see anything, I don't hear anything . . . I'm—failing, Moon." His voice wavered.

"No, you're not! You can't." She turned distractedly to the truth in his eyes, unfocused like a blind man's, the confusion on his face. "Oh, you can't . . ."

"I can't breathe, it's like tar. We've got to turn back, before it's too late." His hand tightened over her wrist, pulling her back toward him, away from the music and the light.

"No." Her free hand closed over his, tried to break his grip. "You go back without me."

"Moon, you promised! We promised—you *have* to come."

"I do not!" She jerked loose, saw him stumble back, surprised and hurt. "Sparks, I'm sorry . . ."

"Moon . . ."

"I'm sorry . . ." She backed away, into the arms of the music. "I have to! I can't stop now, I can't help it—it's too beautiful. Come with me! Try, please try!" getting farther and farther away from him.

"You promised. Come back, Moon!"

She turned and ran, his voice drowned by the song of her breaking heart's desire.

She ran until the cleft widened again, spilling her out into an unnatural space lit by the perfectly ordinary flame of an oil lamp. She rubbed her eyes in the sudden gold, as if she had come out of darkness. When she could see again, when the shining song fell away and released her, she was not surprised to find Clavally waiting, and a

19

stranger . . . Clavally, whose smile she could never forget, through years, or even a lifetime.

"You're—Moon! So, you did come!"

"I remembered," she nodded, radiant with the joy of the chosen, and wiping away tears.

2

The city of Carbuncle sits like a great spiral shell cast up at the edge of the sea, high in the northern latitudes on the coast of Tiamat's largest island. It breathes restlessly with the deep rhythms of the tide, and its ancient form seems to belong to the ocean shore, as though it had actually been born of the Sea Mother's womb. It is called the City on Stilts, because it wades on pylons at the sea's edge; its cavernous underbelly provides a safe harbor for ships, sheltering them from the vagaries of the sea and weather. It is called Starport because it is the center of offworld trade; although the real starport lies inland, and is forbidden ground to the people of Tiamat. It is called Carbuncle because it is either a jewel or a fester, depending on your point of view.

Its resemblance to a sea creature's cast-off home is deceptive. Carbuncle is a hive of life in all—or at least many —of its varied forms, human and inhuman. Its lowest levels, which open on the sea and are home to laborers, sailors, and island immigrants, rise and merge into the Maze, where the interface of tech and nontech, local and offworlder, human and alien, catalyzes an environment of vibrant creativity and creative vice. The nobility of Winter laugh and argue and throw away their money, experimenting with exotic forms of stimulation elbow to elbow with the offworld traders who brought them. And then the nobles return to their own levels, the upper levels, and pay homage to the Snow Queen, who sees everything and knows everything, who controls the currents of influence and power that move like water through the seashell convolutions of the city. And they find it hard to imagine that a pattern which has lasted for nearly one hundred and fifty years, guided by her same hand, will not go on forever.

". . . Nothing lasts forever!"

Arienrhod stood silently and quite alone, eavesdropping as the voices poured out of the speaker in the sculptured base of the mirror. The mirror was also a viewscreen, but dark now, showing her only her face. The unseen nobles were discussing a broken-stringed selyx, and not the future; but they might as well have been, because the breaking of the former and the ending of the latter were ultimately interrelated, and her own mind was absorbed with the future—or the lack of one.

She stood at the wall, which was also in this chamber a window rising up to the star-pointed pinnacle of the roof. She stood on top of the world, for she was the Snow Queen and she stood in her sanctuary at the city's peak. She could gaze down its folded slopes, the undulations of a mountain's side cracked from the mass of land, or out across the white-flecked, iron-gray sea. Or, as she did now, up into the sky, where the night was a glowing forge fired by the incandescence of fifty thousand suns: the stellar cluster into which this footloose system had blundered eons ago. The stars like flaming snow did not move her—had not, for more years than she could remember. But one star, insignificant, unremarkable, moved her with another emotion darker than wonder. The Summer Star, the star whose brightening marked their approach to the Black Gate, which had captured the roving Twins and made them its perpetual prisoners.

The Black Gate was a phenomenon the offworlders called a revolving black hole, and among the things they did not share with her own people was the secret of using such openings on another reality for faster-than-light travel. She only knew that through the Gate lay access to seven other

21

inhabited worlds, some so far away that she could not even comprehend the distances. They were bound to each other, and to countless uninhabitable worlds, because the Black Gate let starships through into a region where space was twisted like a string, tied into knots so that far became near and time was caught up in the loop.

And they were bound together too as tributary worlds of the Kharemough Hegemony. Autonomous worlds—she smiled faintly—thanks to the relativistic time lags ships acquired in transit to and from the Gates. But she was a loyal supporter of the Hegemony, because without it the Winter clans would not have access to the offworld technology that gave them dignity and purpose and pleasure . . . that raised them above the level of the Summers, superstitious fish-farmers reeking of seaweed and tradition.

In return Tiamat offered offworld voyagers a stopover and a haven, a resting place or meeting place to ameliorate the long passages between other Hegemony worlds. It was unique as a kind of crossroads, because it alone orbited its Gate: Even though its orbit was long, it was still closer and more accessible by light-years than any other world.

Arienrhod turned her back on the stars and moved silently across the sensuous synthetic pile of the pastel carpet to the mirror again. She confronted her own reflection with the same porcelain lack of expression that she used on the offworld trade representatives or delegations of the nobility, assessing the elaborate piling of the milk-white hair behind the snow-starred diadem, the flawless translucency of her skin. She ran a hand along her cheek, down her jewel-stranded throat and over the glittering silk of her shirt in what was almost a caress; feeling the firm youthfulness of her body, as perfect now as it had been almost one hundred and fifty years ago, on the day of her investiture. Or was it—? She frowned faintly, leaning closer to her own face. *Yes.* . . . Satisfaction, in the eyes that were the colors of mist and moss agate.

There was another reason why the offworlders came to Tiamat bearing gifts: She held the key to growing old without aging. The seas of this world were a fountain of

22

youth, from which the richest and most powerful paid to drink, and she personally controlled the source—the slaughter of mers. Hers were the calculated judgments that determined which offworld merchant or official would serve Winter's interests best in return for this unique commodity . . . hers were the not-quite-casual whims that gave her favored nobility rights of exploitation in the ranges of the sea, or the right to a precious vial of silvery fluid. It was said that the closeness of a given noble to the Queen's favor could be estimated by the noble's apparent youth.

But nothing lasts forever. Not even eternal youth. Arienrhod frowned again; the gilded atomizer twitched as her hand tightened. She lifted it, opened her mouth, and inhaled the heavy silver spray. It turned the back of her throat to ice, making her eyes water. She sighed with relief, a release from anticipation. The ideal state of preservation was maintained by a daily renewal of the "water of life," as the offworlders euphemistically named it. She found the term amusing, if only for its hypocrisy: It was not water, but an extract from the blood of an indigenous sea creature, the mer; and it had as much to do with death—the death of the mer—as it did with the long life of a human being. Every user was as aware of that fact as she was, on one level or another. But what was the life of an animal, compared to the chance for eternal youth?

So far technology had failed to reproduce the extract, a benign virus that enhanced the body's ability to renew itself without genetic error. The virus died after a short time outside the body of its original host, no matter how carefully it was maintained. Its half-life in any other mammaloid creature was just as limited, so a constant supply was needed, for a constant demand. And that meant prosperity for as long as Winter reigned.

But the Summer Star was already visible in the daytime sky; spring was official, the Change was coming, even the Summers would be aware of that by now. This world was moving into its high summer at last, the time when the unnatural stresses created by their approach to the black hole caused a flare-up of the Twins' own energy, and Tiamat became insufferably hot. The Summers would be forced to move north from their ranges in the equatorial islands, and their influx would disrupt Winter's status quo as they filled the interstices of its territory.

But that was only a part of the greater change that would overtake her people. Because the Twins' approach to the black hole would also make Tiamat a lost world to the Hegemony. . . . She looked back out the window, at the stars. As the Twins neared the Black Gate, as its other tormented captive, the Summer Star, brightened in Tiamat's heaven, the stability of the Gate itself deteriorated. The passage from Tiamat to the rest of the Hegemony and back was no longer simple or certain. Tiamat ceased to be a meeting place and stopover for Hegemony travelers, the outflow of the water of life and the inflow of technology ceased together. And Tiamat was an embargoed world; the Hegemony allowed no indigenous technological base to be developed, and without the crucial knowledge of how their imported goods were made, the machinery of Winter's society would quickly, irrevocably decay. Even without the Summers moving north at the Change to hurry it along, the world as she knew it would cease to exist. She detested even the thought of life in such a world. But then, that would scarcely concern her, would it? *They say death is the ultimate sensory experience.*

Her laughter sounded in the quiet room. Yes, she could laugh at death now, even though she had been withholding payment from it for one hundred and fifty years. Soon it would claim its debt; and the Summers would take payment from her at the next, the final Festival, because that was the way of things. But she would have the last laugh on the Summers. At the last Festival, nearly a generation ago, she had sown among the unsuspecting Summers the nine seeds of her own resurrection: nine clones of herself, to be raised among them and accepted by them as their own; who would learn their ways and, being the children of her mind, know how to manipulate them when the time came.

She had kept track of the children as they grew, always believing there would be at least one among them who

24

would be all that she herself was . . . and there had been one. Only one. The offworlder doctor's pessimism almost twenty years ago had not been purely spite; three clones had been lost in spontaneous abortions, others were born with physical deformities or grew up retarded and emotionally disturbed. Only one child was reported to be perfect in every way . . . and she would make that child the Summer Queen.

She reached down, picked up the small, ornate picture cube from the tabletop beside her. The face within it might have been a picture of herself as a girl. She rotated the cube, watched the laughing face change expressions through three dimensions as it moved. The island trader who kept track of the child's progress had taken the hologram for her, and she found herself moved by strange and unexpected emotions when she looked into it. Sometimes she found herself longing to see more of the child than just this picture . . . to touch her or hold her, to watch her at play, watch her grow and change and learn: to see herself as she must have been, so long ago that she could not really remember it any more.

But no. Look at the child, dressed in coarse, scratchy cloth and greasy fish skins, probably eating out of a pot with her hands in some drafty stone hovel. How could she bear to see herself like that—to see in microcosm what this world would be reduced to in a few more years, when the offworlders abandoned it again? But it might not have to happen again, at least not so completely, if only her plan could be carried through. She looked more closely at the face in the picture, so like her own. But when she looked this closely, there was something that was not the same, something—missing.

Experience, that was all that was missing. Sophistication. Soon she would find a way to bring the girl here, explain things to her, show her what she had to look forward to. And because she would be explaining those things to herself, the girl would understand. What little technology the offworlders left to them must not be allowed to die again. This time they must preserve and nurture it; at least

25

try to meet the offworlders as something more than barbarians when they returned again. . . .

She crossed the room abruptly, switched the endless courtly banalities into oblivion by twisting a pearl on the mirror's base. She changed the audio and brightened video to pick up images from another hidden eye. The inconspicuous incorruptibility of mechanical spies and the sheer pleasure of manipulating them had led her to have installed a network of thousands throughout the levels of the city. Omniscience and license were blossom and thorn on the same vine, both fulfilling their separate needs while feeding from the same source.

She looked now on the image of Starbuck; watched him striding impatiently inside the mirror's heart. The muscles knotted and flowed as he moved, under his dark offworlder's skin. He was a powerful man, and he seemed too large for the confinement of the chamber's intimacy. He was nearly naked; he had been waiting for her to come to him. She stared with frank admiration, her memory a kaleidoscope of images of passion, forgetting for the moment that he had come to bore her like all the rest. She heard him mutter a profanity, and decided that she had kept him waiting long enough.

Starbuck was many things, but he was not a patient man; and knowing that Arienrhod knew that, and used it against him, did nothing to improve his mood. He might have spent the time she kept him waiting contemplating the fine line between love and hate, but he was not particularly introspective, either. He swore again, more loudly, aware that he was probably under observation, knowing it would amuse her. Keeping her satisfied, in every way, was his chief function, as it had been that of the Starbucks before him. He had the mental facility of an intellectual, but it was guided by the inclinations of a slave dealer and no morality at all: qualities that together with his physical strength had freed the youth known as Herne from a futureless life on his homeworld of Kharemough to follow a successful career of trading in human lives and other profit-

26

able commodities. Qualities ideally suited to his current life as Starbuck.

"Who is Starbuck?" He posed the rhetorical question to the mirror-inlaid bottle on the small cabinet by the bed, laughed suddenly, and poured himself a drink of native wine. (Gods! the things these stinking backwater worlds could find to get high on. He almost spat. And the things a man got used to. . . .) Even now he spent a part of his time inside his old Herne-persona, drugging and gaming with casual offworld acquaintances, sampling the diversions of the Maze. And as often as not they would turn, looking him straight in the face with bleary eyes, and ask him the same question: Who is Starbuck?

And he could have told them that Starbuck was a traitor, the offworld advisor for this world's Queen, who worked to protect her interests against the Hegemony's. He could have told them that Starbuck was the Hunter, who called up his alien Hounds and led the pack on the Queen's orders to a grim harvesting of mers. He could have told them that Starbuck was the Queen's lover, and would be until some quicker, shrewder challenger brought him down and became the new Starbuck—for the Queen was traditionally the Sea Mother incarnate; she had many lovers, as the sea had many islands. All of those things would have been true, and several more besides. He could even have told them that he was Starbuck, collecting the confidences he needed to keep the Queen's position in negotiations firm—and they would have laughed, as he did.

Because Starbuck could have been any one of them, and as easily none of them. He merely had to be an offworlder. And he merely had to be the best. Starbuck's anonymity was assured by ritual and law; he existed above and beyond all authority, all retribution except the Queen's.

Starbuck turned, gazing over the rim of his drink at the incongruous clothing laid out on a shelf along the mirrored wall by the mirrored door: the calculated black silk and leather of his formal court attire, and the traditional hooded helmet that masked his real identity, that made Herne interchangeable with a dozen other ruthless and power-hungry predecessors. The helmet crested in a set of curving, steely spines like the antlers of a stag—the symbol of all the arrogant power any man could ever want to wield, or so he had thought when he first settled it onto his head. Only later had he come to realize that it belonged to a woman, and so did the real power—and so did he.

He sat down suddenly on the turned-back covers of the long bed; watched his endless reflections in the walls mimic him mindlessly into infinity. *Seeing the rest of his life?* He frowned, pushing the image away, running a hand through the thick black curls of his hair. He had been Starbuck for better than ten years now, and he was determined to go on being Starbuck . . . until the Change. He wielded power and enjoyed it, and it had never mattered to what end, or where the real source of the power lay.

Didn't matter? He looked down at the heavy strength of his arms, his body still hard and youthful, thanks to privilege. And the butchering of mers . . . No, the slaughter didn't matter at all, as an end it was only the means to a greater end. But the source, yes, that mattered. She mattered—Arienrhod. All the things that had the power to move him were hers—beauty, wealth, absolute control . . . eternal youth. In the first moment he had seen her at audience in the palace, with her former Starbuck at her side, he had known that he would kill to possess her, to be possessed by her. He imagined her body moving against his own, the bridal veil of her hair, the red jewel of her bitter mouth . . . tasting power and privilege and passion incarnate.

And so it did not strike him as incongruous that he moved unthinkingly from the bed to his knee, as the door opened and made the vision reality.

3

"... *The time of Change is upon us! The Summer Star lights our way to salvation....*"

Moon stood hugging herself on the dock in the shrouded dawn, shivering with a chill born of cold mist and misery. The breath she had held in until she ached puffed white as she exhaled, dissipated into the gray fog breath of the sea like a spirit, like an escaping soul. *I will not cry.* She wiped at her cheek.

"*We must prepare for the End, and the new Beginning!*"

She turned, looking back past Gran along the fog-wrapped tunnel of the pier as the insane old man's roaring broke like a wave over the sand castle of her self-control. "Oh, shut *up*, you crazy old . . ." She muttered it, her voice quivering with the helpless frustration that made her want to scream it. Gran glanced over at her, sharp sympathy etched on her weather-worn face. Moon looked away, ashamed at feeling resentful, resentful at having to feel ashamed. A sibyl didn't say those things; a sibyl was wisdom and strength and compassion. She frowned. *I'm not a sibyl yet.*

"*We must cast out the Evil Ones from among us—we must throw their idols into the Sea.*" Daft Naimy threw his arms up, shaking fists at the smothered sky; she watched the ragged sleeves of his stained robe tumble back. Dogs barked and bayed around him, keeping a cautious distance. He called himself the Summer Prophet, and he roamed from island to island across the sea, preaching the word of the Lady as he heard it, distorted by the echoing of divine madness. When she was a child she had feared him, until her mother had told her not to; and laughed at him, until her grandmother had told her not to; and been embarrassed

29

by him, until her own growing understanding had taught her to endure him. Only today her endurance was already tried beyond all reason . . . *and I'm not a sibyl yet!*

She had heard that Daft Naimy had been born a Winter. She had heard that he had once been a tech-loving unbeliever . . . that he had scorned natural law by shedding the blood of a sibyl. That he had been driven mad by the Lady as punishment; that this was how he served his penance. The trefoil symbol the sibyls wore was a warning against defilement, against trespass on sacred ground. They said it was death to kill a sibyl, death to love a sibyl, death to be a sibyl . . . and they meant a living death. *Death to kill a sibyl . . .*

"There is the Sinner who worships false gods! See him!" The gnarled hand flew out like an accusing arrow.

Sparks's face rose up past the end of the pier into its line of flight as he climbed the laddered gangway. His face hardened over with hateful resolution as his eyes focused on the old man in the distance, and then on her own face. *Death to love a sibyl . . .*

Moon shook her head in denial, answering another unspoken accusation. But his eyes were gone from her again, looking at Gran instead; showing her with that look all the things she had loved, and was losing. At last she understood what they meant when they said that it was *death to be a sibyl.*

"But I'm not a sibyl yet." The whisper caught on her teeth.

Someone called up to Sparks from below; he threw back an answer before he came toward them, tall and pale and determined. The tide was ebbing; the water of the bay lay far below the pier. All she could see from here of the Winter trader's ship that would take him away was the tip of its mast, like a beckoning finger. "Well, I guess that's about it. All my things are on board; they're ready to sail." He looked down at his feet as he stopped before them, suddenly awkward. He spoke only to Gran. "I guess—I guess I'm saying good-bye."

"Prepare for the End!"

30

"Sparks . . ." Gran put out a hand, reached up to brush his cheek. "Must you go now? At least wait until your Aunt Lelark gets back from sea."

"I can't." He shook his head against the touch. "I can't. I have to go now. I mean, it's not forever—" as if he were afraid that if he waited, tomorrow could become forever too easily.

"Oh, my beloved child . . . my beloved children." She stretched her other arm stiffly, brought them both together in her embrace, as she had done since time past remembering. "What will I do without you? You've been all my comfort, since your grandfather died. . . . Must I lose you now, and lose you both at once? I know Moon has to go, but—"

"Repent, sinner!"

Moon felt the tightening of Sparks's mouth more than she saw it, as his head came up and he glared at Daft Naimy. "Her destiny's been calling her all her life—and so's mine, Gran. I just didn't know they'd lead us separate ways." His hand pressed his offworld medal like a pledge; he pulled away from them.

"But to Carbuncle!" more like an oath than a protest. Gran shook her head.

"It's only a place." He grinned, gripped her scarf-wrapped shoulder in reassurance. "My mother went there; and she came back with me. Who knows what I'll come back with. Or who."

Moon turned away, clutching the sleeves of her parka as though she were strangling something. *You can't do this to me!* She moved to the edge of the pier, looked over the rail and down along the sheer, seaweedy face of the stone-built jetty, at the trader's ship rocking patiently far below. She took a long breath of damp-heavy air, and another, sucking in the harbor smells of seaweed and fish and salt-soaked wood . . . listening to the murmur of voices below, the creak and slap and whisper of the moorage in the restless tide. So that she wouldn't hear—

"Your world is coming to an End!"

"Good-bye, Gran," his voice muffled by an embrace.

31

Suddenly all that she saw and heard, that was so terribly familiar, took on an overlay of alienness, as though she saw it all for the first time ... knowing that it was not reality, but her own perception that had changed. Two saltwater tears slipped down the sides of her nose, and fell thirty feet into the bay. She heard him pass behind her toward the gangway without slowing.

"Sparks!" She turned, putting herself in his way. "Without a word ... ?"

Sparks backed up slightly.

"It's all right." She straightened her face, managed with some pride to speak as though it were. "I'm not a sibyl yet."

"No. I know. That wasn't why—" He broke off, pushing back his knitted cap.

"But it *is* why you're leaving." She couldn't tell, herself, whether that was a statement or an accusation.

"Yeah." He looked down suddenly. "I guess it is."

"Sparks—"

"But only partly!" He straightened. "You know that it's true, I've always felt this pulling me, Moon." He faced northward, toward Carbuncle at the back of the wind. "I have to find out what I'm missing."

"Or who?" She bit her tongue.

He shrugged. "Maybe."

She shook her head desperately. "After I come back from my initiation ... it won't be different, we can still be together!" *I can have both, I can*— "It can be like it always was again. Like we always wanted it to be—" not even convincing herself.

"Hey, boy." The voice rose from below, breaking into echoes off the jetty wall. "You coming? The tide won't wait all day!"

"In a minute!" Sparks frowned. "No, it won't, Moon. You know that. 'Death to love a sibyl ...' " His voice faded.

"That's just superstition!" Their eyes locked. And in that moment she knew that he shared her understanding of the

32

truth; as he had always known, and shared, everything: It would never be the same again.

"You'll be changed. In a way that I can never change, now." His fingers whitened on the rail. "I can't stay here, stay the way I am now. I have to change, too. I have to grow, and learn ... I have to learn who I really am. All this time I thought I knew. I thought—becoming a sibyl would answer all my questions." His eyes darkened with the new emotion that she had seen first as she came back to him there in the hidden cave, on the Choosing Island. The thing that envied her, and accused her, and shut her out.

"Then go, if that's really why you're going." She challenged the darkness, afraid to retreat. "But don't go out of bitterness, because you're hurt, or because you're trying to hurt me. Because if you do you'll never come back." Her courage broke. "And I don't think I could stand that, Sparkie—"

His hands came up, but as she reached out to him they dropped to his sides again. He turned away, shaking his head, with no forgiveness or understanding or even sorrow. He moved to the gangway, started down the ladder.

Moon felt Gran come up beside her, watch with her as Sparks dropped to the boat's cross-deck where it rose on the water to meet him. He disappeared into the cabin on the broad platform that joined the double hulls, and though she kept watching he did not come out on deck again. The deckhands cast off the mooring ropes, the crab-claw sails fell jingling down the masts and filled with moist wind.

The fog was lifting as the world brightened. Moon could see as far as the channel leading to the open sea, and she watched the trader's catamaran grow smaller as it angled out into the bay, reaching for the gap. She heard its engines start, once it was well away from the Summer docks. At last it reached the channel entrance and merged with the wall of fog, snuffed out in an instant, like a ghost ship. Moon rubbed at her eyes, her face, wetting her hands with mist and tears. Like a sleeper waking, she turned to look at

33

her grandmother, small and stooped with sorrow beside her. She looked beyond her at the silhouetted nets and winches along the dockside; the ancient, seaworn storage house at the foot of the steep village street. Somewhere further on was their own cottage . . . and her outrigger lying on the beach, waiting to carry her away from all that she had left in the world. "Gran?"

Her grandmother patted her hand firmly; she saw a determination to keep hope and belief foremost fill the deep-set gray eyes. "Well, child, he's gone. We can only say a prayer that he finds his way home to us again. Now the Lady's waiting for you, too. The sooner you go, the sooner you'll come back to me!"

She took Moon's arm and started along the pier. "At least that motherlorn old crackbrain won't be around to see you off." Moon glanced up, realizing with some relief that Daft Naimy had gone his way. Gran remembered herself and made the triad sign, "Poor soul that he is."

Moon's mouth twitched up briefly, made a firm line as she felt her strength come back. Sparks had gone to Carbuncle to spite her . . . damned if she'd drift with the tide. She had her own destiny lying across the water, one she'd waited half a lifetime for; the calling beauty of it filled her again. She began to walk faster, hurrying her grandmother along.

Sparks stood on the deck, pressed against the mast by the force of the frigid wind from behind him, listening to the ship's engines strain against the heavy seas. Gazing straight ahead, he saw Carbuncle lying at the sea's edge like the incredible fragment of a dream. They had been approaching it for an eternity across the white-flecked sea, as they had sailed north forever along the boundary of this endless island's shores. He had watched the city grow from the size of a fingertip into something beyond the range of his comprehension. Now it seemed to spread like a stain across the sky, filling his awareness until there was nothing else in the world.

"Hey, there, Summer." The trader's voice broke open his reverie; a gloved hand cuffed his shoulder lightly. "Damned if I need another mast. If you can't find anything useful to do on deck, get inside before you freeze." Sparks heard the high laughter of a deckhand; turned to see the smile on the trader's heavy face that took the smart out of the words.

He pulled back from the mast, felt the crackle of resistance as his gloves broke away from the ice film. "Sorry." His breath rose up in a cloud, half blinding him. He was bundled in heavy clothes until he could barely bend his arms, but still the northern wind cut him to the bone. Carbuncle was protected from being totally ice locked only by the presence of a warm sea current following this western coastline. There was no feeling left in his face; he couldn't tell whether his own smile still worked or not. "But by'r Lady, it's all one piece! How could anyone even imagine a thing like that!"

"Your Lady had nothing to do with it, boy. And She's had nothing to do with the people who live there, ever since. Always keep that in mind while you're there." The trader shook his head, looking at the city, and pressed his wind-chapped lips into a line. "No . . . nobody really knows how Carbuncle came to be. Or why. Not even the offworlders, I think—not that they'd tell us, even if they did."

"Why not?" Sparks glanced around.

The trader shrugged. "Why should they tell us their secrets? They come here to trade their machines for what we have. We wouldn't want them if we knew how to make our own."

"I guess not." Sparks shrugged, flexing his fingers inside his mittens. The Winter trader and his crew ate, talked, and slept trade, as they sailed from island to island; it had

35

worn thin very quickly. The only thing that had impressed him—until now—during this interminable voyage was the fact that they dealt as freely with Summers as with Winters, as though the differences between the two were unimportant. "Where are all the starships?"

"The what?" Laughter shook the trader. "Don't—don't tell me you were expecting a skyful? By all the gods! Did you think there was one for every star? And after all the tech stories you've wormed out of me over the years. You Summers really must be as thick-headed as everyone claims!"

"No!" Sparks frowned, humiliation prickling his numb face. "I just—I just wanted to know where the starport was, that's all."

"Sure you did," the trader wheezed. "It's inland, and forbidden territory to us." He sobered abruptly. "Are you sure you know what you're doing, Sparks, going to Carbuncle? Are you sure you understand what you're getting into?"

Sparks hesitated, glanced out over the water. Moon's face at parting drove the distance out of focus; he heard her voice in the calling of seabirds, in the air. *Death to love a sibyl.* Cold pain lodged suddenly in his chest, like a dagger of ice. He shut his eyes, shivering; the voice, the vision were gone. "I know what I'm doing."

The trader shrugged and turned away.

The trader's ship nudged the floating pier where Sparks stood; a skater on the calm, dark water. It was dwarfed on every side by larger, taller, longer ships, dwarfed in turn by the expanse of the moorage like a mat of floating weed. And reducing it all to insignificance, Carbuncle itself, crouching like a great sheltering beast overhead. Pylons whose girth would swallow a house rose barnacled from the sea, a strange forest crowned by the city's underbelly, trailing festoons of chain and pulley and incomprehensible appendages. The smell of the sea mingled with stranger and less appealing odors; the city's underside dripped and oozed unnameable effluence. A broad causeway bristled

36

with more alien shapes, rising from the artificial harbor's floating docks into the city's maw. . . . He thought suddenly of a great beast's waiting hunger.

"You stick to the lower levels, boy!" The trader had to shout to make himself heard over the shouting of a hundred others, the clanking and groaning and shifting that reverberated in this strange underworld caught between land and sea. "You look for Gadderfy's place in the Periwinkle Alley; she'll rent you a room!"

Sparks nodded absently, lifted his hand. "Thanks." He swung the sack of his possessions up onto his shoulder, and shuddered as the cold wind off of the water wrapped itself around him.

"We'll be here four days, if you change your mind!"

Sparks shook his head. Turning, he began to walk, and then to climb. The trader watched until the city swallowed him up.

"Hey, out of the road, you! What're you, blind?"

Sparks threw himself aside into a pile of boxes as the house on treads loomed above him at the head of the ramp, then tipped slowly over the lip and down the way he had come. High up in a tiny windowed room he saw the face, too small to belong to the warning voice, with eyes that did not even look back to see whether he had gotten clear. He picked himself up numbly, thinking, *It is true . . . it's all true!*, suddenly only half-glad.

Afraid to let his thoughts settle, he began to move, following the main street as it started its long, slow spiral upward; keeping to the edges now, warily. The street went on forever, gently rising, gently circling, tunneling upward through canyon walls of gaping-eyed warehouses and stores, apartment hives hung with railings. There was no sky, only the underside of the next spiral, gleaming dully with a kind of striated phosphorescence. Spurs of alleyway like centipede legs scrabbled at daylight—at the true sky of the world that he had always known, dim and unreachable at the alley-ends beyond the shuttered storm walls.

He picked his way past piled goods and piled rubbish,

37

the vacant storehouses and the vacant faces of the mob, trying to keep his own face expressionless. There were fisherfolk among them, in clothing enough like his own; but there were shopkeepers, laborers, others whose clothing matched their occupations and whose occupations he couldn't even imagine. And everywhere there were what seemed to be sexless semihuman beings doing with mindless precision tasks that no two humans could have done. He had approached one of them timidly; asked, inanely, "How do you *do* that?" The thing had gone on loading crates, not dignifying the question with an answer.

He began to feel as though he had been walking forever along the Street, that he had only been going in circles. Every alley was like every other, the noise and the crowds and the stink of fumes clogged his senses to overload. Makeshift buildings cluttered the cracks of the city's hive form, sand and plaster, sagging and peeling; aging scabrously, ungracefully, against the support of far more ancient buildings as eternal as the sea itself. Nothing happened singly here, but in twos and threes and dozens, until every impression became a beating. The crushing weight of the city bore down on the fragile ceiling above his head, on his own shoulders. The catacomb of walls converged on him, closed in around him, until. . . . *Help me!* He stumbled back against the unnatural warmth of a building side, cowered in a nest of cast-off wrappers, covering his eyes.

"Hey, friend, you all right?" A hand nudged his side tentatively.

He raised his head, opened his eyes, blinked them clear. A sturdy woman in laborer's coveralls stood beside him, shaking her head. "No, you don't look all right to me. You look a little green, in fact. Are you landsick, sailor?"

Sparks grinned feebly, feeling the green go red over his face. "I guess so," grateful that his voice didn't shake. "I guess that's what it was."

The woman bent her head with a faint frown. "You a Summer?"

Sparks shrank back against the wall. "How'd you know that?"

But the woman only shrugged. "Your accent. And nobody but a Summer would dress up in greasy hides. Fresh from the fish farms, huh?"

He looked down at his slicker, suddenly embarrassed by it. "Yeah."

"Well, that's all right. Don't let the big city beat you down, kid; you'll learn. Won't he, Polly?"

"Whatever you say, Tor."

Sparks leaned forward, peering past her as he realized that they weren't alone. Behind her stood one of the metal half-humans, its dull skin dimly reflecting light. He had no idea whether the thing was male or female. He realized that it had lowered a third leg, almost like a tail, on which it was now sitting, rigidly at ease. Where its face should have been, a clear window showed him the sensor panels set into its head.

Tor produced a small flat bottle from a sealed pocket in her coveralls and unstoppered it. "Here. This'll stiffen your spine."

He took the bottle, took a swig from it . . . gasped as a cloying sweetness burst into flame in his mouth. He swallowed convulsively, eyes watering.

Tor laughed. "You're a trusting one!"

Sparks took another mouthful deliberately, swallowed it without gagging before he said, "Not bad." He handed the bottle back. She laughed again.

"Is . . . um . . . is—" Sparks pushed himself away from the wall, looking at the metal being, trying to find a way to ask the question without offending.

"Is that a man in a tin suit?" Tor grinned, pushing a finger of drab-colored hair behind her ear. He guessed that she was maybe half again as old as he was. "No, he just thinks he is. Don't you, Pollux?"

"Whatever you say, Tor."

"Is he . . . uh—"

"Alive? Not in the way we think of it. He's a servo—an

automaton, a robot, whatever you want to call it. A servo-mechanical device. He doesn't act, he only reacts."

Sparks realized that he was staring, glanced up, down, uncertain. "Doesn't he——?"

"Mind us talking about him? No, he doesn't mind anything, he's above all that. A regular saint. Aren't you, Polly?"

"Whatever you say, Tor."

She slung an arm over his shoulder, bumping against him familiarly. "I do his maintenance myself, and I can guarantee he's got *no* missing parts. He's got a short circuit somewhere, though—tends to limit his vocabulary. You may have noticed."

"Well, yeah . . . kind of." Sparks shifted from foot to foot, wondering if it was catching.

Tor laughed. "At least he isn't stuck on 'screw you.' Say, where'd you get that, anyway?" She reached out abruptly toward the offworld medal on his chest.

"It was my——" Sparks pulled back, keeping it out of reach. "I—uh—got it from a trader."

Tor looked at him; he had the sudden feeling that his skull was made of glass. But she only let her hand drop. "Well, listen, Summer—why don't you stick with me and Polly here, until you get used to the way we do things in Carbuncle? As a matter of fact, I just got off shift; we were heading down to check out a little subterranean action. Have a good time, a little excitement, maybe pick up a bet or two on the side. . . . Got any money on you?"

Sparks nodded.

"Well, this could be your chance to double it! Come on along with us. . . . I've got a feeling this's going to be a real education for him, Pollux."

"Whatever you say, Tor."

Sparks followed them down the alleyway, toward the twilight fading beyond the storm walls. Somewhere along the way Tor stopped at an unobtrusive door in a paint-thick warehouse front, rapped twice, then three times, with her fist. The door slid open a crack, then wider, to let them into a cavernous darkness. Sparks hung back, went forward again at Tor's impatient gesture as he heard the rising murmur of sound and realized they were not alone.

"How much are you betting?" Tor called back at him through the noise from across the vast room. She was already passing a fistful of coins to a shrunken man drowned in a cloak. She stood on the edge of a crowd of watchers who kneeled, squatted, sat, their attention fixed on the small arena closed off in their midst. Sparks joined her, trying to see through the pall of throat-catching smoke that lay in the stifling air. "Betting on what?"

"On the bloodwart, of course! Only a fool would bet on a starl against a bloodwart. Come on, how much are you good for?" Her eyes flashed the eager electricity that he felt rising around him everywhere, like the tide.

"Lot of people are fools, then." The man in the cloak stretched his mouth, and jingled the markers in his fist.

Tor made a rude noise. Behind her the crowd murmur crested and broke, the echoes flowed away into cracks and shadows; the room waited. Sparks saw two beings—one human, one not—step into the empty space carrying oblong boxes. The alien's skin had an oily gleam, its arms were fingered with long tentacles. "Are they going to—?"

"Them? Gods, no! Those are just the handlers. Come on, come on, place your bet!" Tor pulled his arm.

He rummaged in his sack of belongings, fished out two coins. "Well, here's—uh, twenty."

"Twenty! Is that all you've got?" Tor looked crestfallen.

"That's all I'm betting." He held them out.

The shrunken man took his coins without comment, and flowed away into the crowd.

"Hey, this isn't illegal or anything, is it?" Sparks hesitated.

"Sure is. . . . Clear us a path through these highborns, Pollux. We want a front-row seat for the last of the big spenders here."

"Whatever you say, Tor." Pollux pressed forward with

singleminded purpose. Sparks heard curses and sudden yelps of pain marking his progress through the crowd.

"But don't worry, Summer, it's not the death sport that's illegal." Tor pulled; Sparks found himself somehow halfway to the ring already. "It's just the importation of restricted beasts."

"Oh. Sorry—" as he stepped on a gemstoned hand. About half of the crowd seemed to be laborers or sailors, but the other half glittered with jewels in the dim light, and some of them had skin the color of earth, or hair like clouds. He wondered whether they had stained themselves on purpose. Tor jerked him down at ringside; he folded his long legs under. Beside him Pollux towered back on his support leg; there were useless shouts of "down in front." Tor pulled out her flask and drank, handed it to Sparks. "Finish it off."

The changing flavor of the smoke was already weaving a soft cocoon around his head, separating him from himself and everyone else. He put the bottle to his mouth and drank recklessly; there was plenty to finish. His throat hurt, making him cough.

Tor patted his knee. "That puts you in the mood, doesn't it?"

He grinned. "For anything," hoarsely.

She took her hand away. "Later, later."

Gulping, Sparks turned back with her to look out over the low partition; the movement made him giddy, like the sudden drop of a sea swell. The potential energy of the place was singing in him now, and the crowd's long sigh of indrawn breath was his, as the handlers threw open their cases and leaped clear.

If the whip-fingered alien in the arena had stunned his eyes (although suddenly nothing surprised him), it had been no more than a promise. Now, over the rim of the container in front of him spilled a mass of lashing, fleshy tentacles; groping, slipping downward, drawing after them a flaccid pouch of body mottled like a bruise. "The bloodwart," Tor whispered. It had no head that Sparks could see, unless its head and body were all one, but ragged pincers scissored among the tentacles. He heard them click in the waiting silence. Abrupt movement at the other end of the square pulled his eyes away—"The starl," Tor muttered—to a liquid shadow of black on black: the dappled hide of a sinuous creature as long as his forearm. He caught the spear of light from a bared tusk as the starl whined far back in its throat. All light was centered on the square now, and every eye. The starl circled the bloodwart, oblivious to the crowd, still keening far back in its throat. The bloodwart's tentacles lashed the air but it made no sound—even when the starl struck, ripping a flap of skin from its heaving pouch-body. Its tentacles whipped frantically, caught and wrapped the starl's narrow head. "Poison," Tor hissed gleefully. The starl began to scream, and its scream was lost in the hungry roar of the crowd.

Sparks leaned forward, drawn like a wire, knowing a dim surprise as the cry of protest he had expected came out of his throat as a hunting cry. The starl pulled free, snapping and ripping in a frenzy of pain at the bloodwart's tentacles and its soft, flabby body. The bloodwart floundered, its oozing tentacles flailed again . . . and exulting in his own lost innocence, Sparks threw open his heightened senses to take in the ballet of death.

An eternity later, but all too soon, the starl lay with sides heaving as the bloodwart wrapped it in strands of broken tentacle and closed in for the kill. Sparks saw the whiteness of the starl's wild eye, the white-and-red-flecked straining mouth; heard its strangled moan in the sudden silence as the pincers found its throat. Blood spurted; drops spattered his slicker and his sweating face.

He jerked back, rubbing his face, stared at his hand freshly bloodied. And suddenly he had no need to look back again, no need to watch the flattened bladder fill and flush red or the redness seep out through its torn sides as the bloodwart drained its victim. . . . Suddenly he had no voice either, to join the clamoring dirge of curses and cheers. He turned his face away, but there was no escape from the gleaming insanity of the crowd. "Tor, I—"

And turning, he discovered that she was gone, that Pollux was gone . . . and that the sack filled with his belongings had gone with them.

"I'm telling you, sonny, we got no city work available for a Summer—you can't handle machinery, you don't know the social codes; you got no experience." The posting clerk looked at Sparks over the sill of the tiny office window the way he might have looked at a backward child.

"Well, how can I get experience if no one'll hire me?" Sparks raised his voice, frowned as it beat back on his aching head.

"Good question." The clerk gnawed on a fingernail.

"That's not fair."

"Life ain't fair, sonny. If you want work here you'll have to change your clan affiliation."

"Like hell I will!"

"Then go back where you belong with your stinking fish skins, and quit wasting the time of real people!" The man behind him in the line pushed him aside; the gloved hand was studded with metal.

Sparks turned back, saw the gloved hand make a fist twice the size of his own. He turned away again, away through the laughter, and went out of the hiring hall into the street. A new day brightened at the alley's end beyond the shuttered walls, after a night when storm clouds had blackened the stars but darkness had never fallen here in the streets of the city. There had been no way to hide his rage or his humiliation, or the misery of the vomiting that had purged what he had drunk, and seen, and done. He had slept like a corpse on a pile of crates afterward, and dreamed that Moon stood looking down on him, knowing everything, with pity in her agate-colored eyes . . . *pity!* Sparks pressed a hand over his own aching eyes to pinch her face away.

Down the long slope of the street lay the harbor beneath the city, and the trader's small boat waiting to take him home. His stomach twisted with fury and sick hunger. In not even a day he had thrown away everything—his belongings, his ideals, his self-respect. Now he could creep home to the islands, having lost his dream, and live with Moon's pity for the rest of his life. His mouth pulled back. Or he could admit that he had learned the real lesson: that Carbuncle had only stripped him naked of his illusions, taught him that he had nothing, he was nothing ... and that he was the only one in this motherlorn city who cared. Whether that ever changed or not was in his hands only.

His empty hands ... He moved them helplessly, brushed the pouch hanging at his belt, the one thing that Tor and Carbuncle had left him: his flute. He drew it out gently, possessively, put it to his lips as he began to walk; letting melodies from the time he had lost ease the loss of everything else.

He moved aimlessly up the street, shutting out the restless motion that never ceased even through the night. Strangers looked at him, now that he had become oblivious to them. He did not notice, until at last something rang on the pavement in front of him. He stopped, looking down. A coin lay at his feet. He bent slowly, picked it up, flexed his fingers over it in wonder.

"You'd make more if you worked the Maze, you know. The listeners there have more to throw away ... and more appreciation for an artist."

Sparks glanced up, startled; saw a woman with dark, plaited hair and a band across her forehead standing before him. The crowd separated and flowed around them; he had the feeling that they stood together on an island. The woman was his Aunt Lelark's age, or older by some years, wearing a long dress of worn velvet and bands of feather necklace. She held a cane with a tip that glowed like a brand. The tip rose along his body to his face; she smiled. She was not looking at him. There was a deadness around her eyes, something missing, as though a light had been snuffed out.

"Who are you?" she asked.

Blind. "Sparks ... Dawntreader," he said, suddenly not sure about where to look. He looked at her cane.

She seemed to be waiting.

"*Summer.*" He finished it almost defiantly.

"Ah. I thought so." She nodded. "Nothing I hear in Carbuncle is ever so wild or wistful. Take my advice, Sparks Dawntreader Summer. Move uptown." She reached into the beaded pouch hanging from her shoulder and held out a handful of torus coins. "Good luck to you in the city."

"Thanks." He reached out to meet her hand, took the coins hesitantly.

She nodded, lowering her cane as she started past him. She paused. "Come to my shop sometime, in the Citron Alley. Ask for the maskmaker; anyone can tell you where it is."

He nodded too; remembered, and said quickly, "Uh—sure. Maybe I will." He watched her go.

And then he moved uptown. Into the Maze, where the building fronts were painted with lights, in strings and whorls and rainbowed pinwheels; where the colors, the shapes, the costumes that peered from windows or moved on bodies along the street never repeated twice; where the flash of signs and the cries of hucksters promised heaven and hell and every gradation of degradation in between. Finding a half-quiet street corner under fluttering flowered banners, he stood and played for hours to a jingling harmony provided by the coins of passersby—not as many as he had hoped, but better than the nothing he had started with.

At last the fragrance of a hundred separate spices and herbs pulled him away, to spend a few of his coins filling his empty stomach with a feast of strange delights. Afterward he shed his slicker for a shirt of red silk, chains of glass and copper beads; the shopkeeper took the rest of his money. But as he started back through the evening alleys to his corner, to try to earn keep for the night, he sang a silent prayer of thanks to the Lady for the gift of his music that She had sent with him into Carbuncle. With his music he could survive, while he learned the rules of his new life—

Four offworlders in spacer coveralls without insignia,

who had walked the alley behind him, closed around him abruptly and dragged him into the dark crack between two buildings.

"What do you want—?" He twisted his head, freed his mouth from a hand that reeked of machine lubricant. Blinking frantically in the dim light, he saw the three others, not sure he really saw white teeth bared in the grin of a closing hunt, but sure of the gunmetal gleam of something deadly held by one, and the restraining cuffs, more hands reaching out for him as the crushing grip tightened across his throat.

He threw back his head and felt it impact in the face of the man behind him, heard a grunt of pain, then used his elbow and his heavy boots. The man fell back, cursing unintelligibly; and Sparks stumbled free, opened his mouth to shout for help.

But the shadow with the gunmetal gleam used his weapon first. The shout went out of Sparks in a gasp as black lightning struck him. He fell forward on his face, a string-cut puppet, helpless to keep his head from cracking on the pavement. But there was no pain, only dull impact, and the dry rattle of a thousand synapse lines gone dead in a body that could not respond. A band of steel was tightening around his throat, he heard the ugly sound of his own strangling.

A foot rolled him. The shadow men closed over him, looking down; he saw their smiles clearly this time, as they saw the terror on his face.

"How much did you hit him with, lardfingers? Looks like he's choking."

"Let him choke, the wormy little bastard. Brain damage won't hurt his price offworld." The man he had hit in the face wiped blood from a split lip.

"Yeah, he's a pretty one, ain't he? Not just mine fodder, nosiree. We'll get a load for him on Tsieh-pun." Laughter; a boot settled on his stomach, pressed. "Keep breathing, pretty boy. That's the way."

One of them knelt, locked his useless hands with the metal cuffs. The man with the bloody face dropped down

47

beside him, pulled something from a pocket, flicked a switch at its base. A narrow blade of light flamed, the length of the man's hand; fingers of his other hand probed Spark's mouth, found his tongue. "Last words, pretty boy?"

Help me! But his scream was silent.

"Gods, I hate this duty!" Police Inspector Geia Jerusha PalaThion jerked the end of her scarlet cape free of the patrolcraft's doorseal. The car trembled lightly, hovering on repellers in the palace courtyard at the high end of Carbuncle's Street.

Her sergeant looked at her, an ironic half-smile crumpling the pale freckles on his dark, fine-boned face. "You mean you don't enjoy visiting royalty, Inspector?" innocently.

"You know what I mean, Gundhalinu." She jerked the cape roughly around to open from one shoulder, hiding the utilitarian dusty-blue of the duty uniform beneath it. A brooch with the Hegemonic seal pinned its folds. "I mean, BZ—" she gestured—"that I hate having to dress up like something out of a costume strobe to play spaceman's burden with the Snow Queen."

Gundhalinu tapped the flash-shield at the front of his flaring helmet. Her helmet had been sprayed gold; his was still white, and he was capeless. "You should be glad the Commander doesn't put a potted plant up there, Inspector, to make you more impressive.... You have to look the part when you go to lay down universal law before the Mother lovers, don't you?"

"Manure." They began to walk toward the massive doors of the ceremonial entrance, across the intricate spiral

patterns of pale inlaid stone. At the far side of the courtyard two Winter servants scrubbed the stones with long-
handled brushes. They were always out here, scrubbing,
keeping it flawless. *Alabaster?* she wondered, looking
down, and thought about sand, and heat, and sky. There
were none of those things here, not anywhere in this cold,
spun-stone confection of a city. This courtyard marked the
beginning of the Street, the beginning of the world, the
beginning of everything in Carbuncle. *Or the end.* She saw
the frigid sky of the upper latitudes glaring at them helplessly beyond the storm walls. "Arienrhod is no more taken
in by this charade than we are. The only possible good that
could come out of this would be if she believes we're as
stupid as we look."

"Yes, but what about all their primitive rituals and super-
stitions, Inspector? I mean, these are people who still believe in human sacrifice. Who deck up in masks and have
orgies in the street every time the Assembly comes to
visit——"

"Don't you celebrate, when the Prime Minister drops in
on Kharemough every few decades to let you kiss his feet?"

"It's hardly the same thing. He *is* a Kharemoughi."
Gundhalinu drew himself up, shielding himself from contamination. "And our celebrations are dignified."

Jerusha smiled. "All a matter of degree. And before you
start throwing around cultural judgments, Sergeant, go
back and study the ethnographies until you really understand this world's traditions." She turned her own face into
a mask of official propriety, letting him see it while she
presented it to the Queen's guards. They stood stiffly at
attention, doing their own costumed imitation of the offworlder police. The immense, time-gnawed doors opened
for her without hesitation.

"Yes, ma'am." Their polished boots rang on the corridor
leading to the Hall of the Winds. Gundhalinu looked aggrieved. He had been on Tiamat for a little less than a
standard year, and had been her assistant for most of that
time. She liked him, and thought he liked her; she felt that
he was on his way to becoming a competent career officer.

But his homeworld was Kharemough, the world that dominated the Hegemony, and a world dominated by the technocracy that produced the Hegemony's most sophisticated hardware. She suspected that Gundhalinu was a younger son from a family of some rank, forced into this career by rigid inheritance laws at home, and he was Tech through and through. Jerusha thought a little sadly that a hundred replays of the orientation tapes would never teach him any tolerance.

"Well," she said more kindly, "I'll tell you one man in a mask who probably fits all your prejudices, and mine too—and that's Starbuck. And he's an offworlder, whoever or whatever else he is." She looked at the frescoes of chill Winter scenes along the entry hall, tried to wonder how many times they had been painted and repainted. But in her mind's eye she already saw Starbuck standing at the Queen's right hand, wearing a sneer under that damned executioner's hood while he looked down on the hamstrung representatives of the Law.

"He wears a mask for the same reasons as any other thief or murderer," Gundhalinu said sourly.

"True enough. Living proof that no world has a monopoly on regressive behavior . . . and that scum tends to rise to the top." Jerusha slowed, hearing the sigh of a slumbering giant deep in the planet's bowels. She took a deep breath of her own against the Trial by Air that was a part of the ritual in every visit to the palace, and shivered under her cloak with more than the growing chill of the air. She never got over the fear, just as she never got over her amazement at the thing that caused it: the place they called the Hall of the Winds.

She saw one of the nobility waiting for them at the brink of the abyss, glad that for once the Queen had seen fit not to keep them waiting. The less time she stood thinking about it, the less trouble she would have getting across. It might mean that Arienrhod was in a good mood—or simply that she was too preoccupied with other matters to indulge in petty harassments today. Jerusha was thoroughly informed about the spy system the Queen had had

50

installed throughout the city, and particularly here in the palace. The Queen enjoyed setting up minor ordeals to demoralize her opposition . . . and it was obvious to Jerusha that she also enjoyed watching the victims sweat.

Jerusha recognized Kirard Set, an elder of the Way-aways family, one of the Queen's favorites. He was rumored to have seen four visits of the Assembly; but his face, below the fashionable twist of turban, was still hardly more than a boy's. "Elder." Jerusha saluted him stiffly, painfully aware of the crow's-feet starting at the corners of her own eyes; more aware of the moaning call of the abyss beyond her, like the hungry laughter of the unrepentant damned. *Who would build a thing like this?* She had wondered it every time she came to this place, wondered whether the crying of the wind was not really the voice of its creators, those lost ancestors who had dreamed and built this haunted city in the north. No one she knew knew what they had been, or done, here, before the collapse of the interstellar empire that made the present Hegemony seem insignificant.

If she had been anywhere else, she might have sought out a sibyl and tried to get an answer, obscure and unintelligible though it probably would have been. Even here on Tiamat, in the far islands the sibyls wandered like traveling occultists, thinking they spoke with the voice of the Sea Mother. But the wisdom was real, and still intact even here, though the Tiamatans had lost the truth behind it, just as they had lost the reason for Carbuncle. There were no sibyls in the city—by Hegemonic law, conveniently supported by the Winters' disgust with anything remotely "primitive." Calculated and highly successful Hegemonic propaganda kept them believing it was nothing more than a combination of superstitious fakery and disease-born madness, for the most part. Not even the Hegemony would dare to eliminate sibyls from an inhabited world . . . but it could keep them unavailable. Sibyls were the carriers of the Old Empire's lost wisdom, meant to give the new civilizations that built on its ruins a key to unlock its buried secrets. And if there was anything the Hegemony's wealthy and powerful didn't want, it was to see this world stand on its own feet and grow strong enough to deny them the water of life.

Jerusha remembered suddenly, vividly, the one sibyl she had ever seen in Carbuncle—ten years ago, only a short time after her arrival here at her first post. She had seen him because she had been sent to oversee his exile from the city, had gone with the jeering crowd as they led their frightened, protesting kinsman down to the docks and set him adrift in a boat. There had been a witch-catcher of iron studded with spikes around his neck; they had pushed him along at pole's length, rightfully afraid of contamination.

Then, down the steep dropoff to the harbor, they had pushed him too roughly, and he had fallen. The spikes bit into his throat and the side of his face, laying them open. The sibyl's blood that the crowd had been so afraid of spilling had welled and run like a necklace of jewels under his chin, patterning down his shirt (the shirt was a deep sky blue; she was struck by the beauty of the contrast). And stricken with fear like the rest, she had watched him sit moaning with his hands pressed against his throat, and done nothing to help him. . . .

Gundhalinu touched her elbow hesitantly. She looked up, embarrassed, into the faintly scornful face of the Elder Wayaways. "Whenever you're ready, Inspector."

She nodded.

The elder lifted the small whistle suspended from a chain around his neck and stepped out onto the bridge. Jerusha followed with eyes looking fixedly ahead, knowing what she would see if she looked down, not needing to see it: the terrifying shaft that gave access for the servicing of the city's self-sufficient operating plant, servicing that had never been needed as far as she knew, during the millennium that the Hegemony had known about it. There were enclosed elevator capsules that gave technicians safe access to its countless levels; there was also a column of air, rising up this shaft at the hollow core of Carbuncle's spiral the way an updraft formed in an open chimney. Here was the

52

only area of the city not entirely sealed off by storm walls; the bitter winds of the open sky ran wild through this space, sucking the breath out of the subterranean hollows. There was always a strong smell of the sea here high in the air, and moaning, as the wind probed the irregularities of cranny and protrusion in the shaft below.

There were also, suspended in the air like immense free-form mobiles, transparent panels of some resilient material that flowed and billowed like clouds, that created treacherous cross-currents and backflows in the relentless wind. And there was only one way across the hall to the upper levels of the palace: Here the corridor became a draw-bridge vaulting the chasm like a band of light. It was wide enough to walk easily in silent air, but it was made deadly by the hungry sweep of the winds.

The Elder Wayaways sounded a note on his whistle and stepped forward confidently as the space around him grew calm. Jerusha followed, almost stepping on his heels with the need to include herself and Gundhalinu in the globe of quiet air. The elder continued to walk, at a calm even pace, sounding another note, and a third. Still the globe of peaceful air surrounded them; but behind her Jerusha heard Gundhalinu take some god's name in vain as he lagged a little and the wind licked his back.

This is insane! She repeated the litany of fear and resentment that always went with her crossing. *What sort of a maniac would build this sadist's funhouse?* ... knowing that the technology that had designed it could easily have circumvented it, if it had simply been meant as a security measure. At the tech level permitted the Winters on Tiamat now, it was effective enough. Whatever nerveless madman had had it put here in the first place, she suspected that it suited the purposes of the present Queen all too well.

They were midway across already. She kept her eyes fixed on the elder's back, hearing the atonal wind-charmer's notes that held back death shrill above the groaning pit. It was not the weaving of some magic spell, but the activation of automated controls that diverted the wind curtains to the traversers' protection instead of their destruction. Knowing that was no great comfort to her when she considered the potential for human error, or for a sudden failure in such an ancient system. There had been control boxes once that did what the whistle player did now; but as far as she knew the only one that still worked hung on Starbuck's belt.

Safe. Her boots found the security of the far rim. She controlled the overwhelming desire to let her legs melt out from under her and sit down. Gundhalinu's sweating face grinned at her gamely. She wondered whether he was trying not to think about the return trip, too. Looking ahead again, she read triumph in the Elder Wayaways's walk as they followed him on into the audience hall.

Even here, so near the pinnacle of Carbuncle, the hall was overpowering in its vastness; she imagined it could hold an entire villa from Newhaven, her homeworld. Fiber hangings in chilly pastels drifted down from the geometric arches of the pillared ceiling, winking and chiming with the exotic song of a thousand tiny handmade silver bells.

And across the expanse of white carpet—an offworld import—the Snow Queen sat back on her throne, a goddess incarnate, a taloned snow hawk in an ice-bound aerie. Unconsciously Jerusha drew her cloak closer around her. "Colder than the Karoo," Gundhalinu muttered, and rubbed his arms. The Elder Wayaways motioned them to wait where they were, went ahead to announce their presence. Jerusha was sure that the dark, distant eyes beneath the crown of pale hair were already more than aware of them, although Arienrhod did not acknowledge them, but gazed out across the hall. As usual Arienrhod had struck Jerusha's eye first; but now, as she followed the Queen's gaze into the nearer distance, a searing line of light, the *hum-snap* of an energy beam striking home, wrenched her attention away.

"*Schact!*" Gundhalinu hissed, as voices cried out and they saw the knot of nobles split open as the bolt knocked one sprawling onto the rug. "Dueling—?" His voice was incredulous. Jerusha's hand tightened on the empire-cross of her belt buckle, barely controlling her sudden outrage.

54

Did the Queen mock police authority to the degree of staging murder in her presence? Her mouth was open to protest, to demand—but before she could find words, the victim rolled over and sat up, not blistered or charred, with no blood staining the snow-field purity of the rug. A woman, Jerusha saw; the fads in clothing affected by the nobility sometimes made it hard to tell. There was a faint distortion of air as she moved; she had been wearing a repeller field. She climbed gracefully to her feet with an elaborate bow toward the Queen, the rest clapping and laughing their amusement. Gundhalinu swore again, more softly, in disgust. As the nobles shifted, Jerusha caught sight of the black figure, the cold gleam of metal, and realized that the one who had playacted the murderer had been Starbuck.

Gods! What sort of jaded halfwits would try to burn each other down for laughs? They treated a weapon that could maim and kill like a toy—they no more understood the real function or significance of technology than a pampered pet understood a jewelled collar. *Yes—but whose fault is that, if not ours?* Arienrhod's gaze caught her suddenly in mid-expression. The strangely colored eyes stayed on her; the Queen smiled. It was not a pleasant expression. *Who says the pet doesn't understand its collar?* Jerusha held the gaze stubbornly. *Or that the savage doesn't see through the lie that makes him less than human?*

The Elder Wayaways had announced them and was backing from the Queen's presence as Starbuck came to stand beside her throne. His hidden face also turned toward them, as if he were curious about the effect of his play-acting. *We're all savages at heart.*

"You may approach, Inspector PalaThion." The Queen lifted a desultory hand.

Jerusha removed her helmet and walked forward, Gundhalinu treading close behind her. She was certain that no more than the bare minimum of respect showed on either his face or her own. The nobles stood off to one side, striking poses like so many hologrammic traders' dummies, watching with sincere disinterest as she made her salute.

She wondered briefly why they found playing at and with death so amusing. They were all favorites, young-faced— the gods only knew how old in reality. She had always heard that users of the water of life became pathologically protective of their extended youth. Could it be that there really came a time when you had experienced everything you could possibly desire? No, not even in a century and a half. Or could it be that they simply didn't know, that Starbuck hadn't warned them of the danger?

"Your Majesty—" She glanced up, half at Starbuck, then back at Arienrhod enthroned on the dais. The sweet girlish face was made into a mockery, a mask like Starbuck's, by the too-knowing wisdom of her eyes.

Arienrhod raised a finger, the slight motion cutting off her words. "I have decided that from now on you will kneel when you come before me, Inspector."

Jerusha's mouth snapped shut. She took a moment, and a long breath. "I'm an officer of the Hegemonic Police, Your Majesty. I have sworn an oath of allegiance to the Hegemony." She gazed deliberately at the rising back of the Queen's throne, through her, around her. The blown-and-welded surfaces of glass, the shining spirals and shadowed crevices dazzled her eyes with the hypnotic spell of the Maze; the bizarre artistry that catalyzed out of Carbuncle's volatile mix of cultures.

"But the Hegemony stationed your unit here to serve me, Inspector." Arienrhod's voice startled her attention back. "I ask only the homage due any independent ruler," putting a slight emphasis on *independent*, "from the representatives of another."

"Ask and be damned!" Jerusha heard Gundhalinu breathe the words almost inaudibly behind her; saw the Queen's eyes flash to his face, marking him in her memory. Starbuck moved down one step from the throne, almost lazily, the gun still swinging from a black-gloved hand. But the Queen lifted her own hand again and he stopped, waiting wordlessly.

Jerusha hesitated, too, feeling the stunner that weighed heavily at her side, and Gundhalinu's quivering indignation

56

behind her. *My duty is to keep the peace.* She turned slightly, toward Starbuck, toward Gundhalinu. "All right, BZ," as softly as he had spoken; not softly enough. "We'll kneel. It's not such an unreasonable request."

Gundhalinu said something in a language she didn't know, his pupils blackening. On the dais Starbuck's fist went tight over his weapon.

Jerusha turned back to the Queen, felt the eyes of the onlookers, no longer indifferent now, pressing hard on her shoulders as she dropped to one knee and bowed her head. After a second there was a rustle and a creak of leather as Gundhalinu dropped down heavily behind her. "Your Majesty."

"You may rise, Inspector."

Jerusha pushed herself to her feet. "Not you!" The Queen's voice struck past her as Gundhalinu began to get up. "You kneel until I give you permission to rise, off-worlder." As she spoke, Starbuck moved like an extension of her will to his side, the heavy arm in fluid black closing over Gundhalinu's shoulder, forcing him back to his knees. Starbuck muttered something in the unknown language. Jerusha's hands fisted beneath her cloak, slowly opened again. She said brittlely, "Take your hands off him, Starbuck, before I run you in for assaulting an officer."

Starbuck smiled—she saw his eyes crinkle, insolently, the face alter beneath the smooth surface of his mask. He did not move until the Queen gestured him away.

"Get up, BZ," Jerusha said it gently, keeping her voice together with an effort. She put out her hand to help him to his feet, felt him trembling with fury. He didn't look at her; the freckles stood out blood red against the darkness of his skin.

"If he were my man, I would discipline him for such arrogance." Arienrhod watched them, expressionless now.

Punishment enough. Jerusha glanced away from his face, lifted her head. "He is a citizen of Kharemough, Your Majesty; he's nobody's man but his own." She looked pointedly at Starbuck still standing at her side.

The Queen smiled, and this time there was a trace of

57

appreciation in it. "Maybe Commander LiouxSked sends you to me as more than just a token female, after all."

That proves you're not omniscient. Jerusha's mouth pulled into a tight half-smile of her own. "If I may ask your indulgence, then, I would like to make the point that—" she moved suddenly, and with a hidden nerve-blocking pinch, took Starbuck's gun away from him, "these weapons are not toys." The blunt metal grip settled in her hand, the tube pointed like a cautionary finger as he started toward her; she heard the excited twitter of the onlookers. "An energy weapon should never be aimed at anything unless you're willing to see it blown apart." Starbuck froze in mid-motion, she saw his startled muscles tense and twitch. She lowered the gun. "A repeller field will fail under a direct hit one time in five. Your nobles should keep that in mind." The Queen made an amused noise, and Starbuck's head twisted toward the throne, light dancing through the spines of his helmet.

"Thank you, Inspector." Arienrhod nodded, making a curious motion with her fingers. "But we're well aware of the limits and liabilities attached to your offworld equipment."

Jerusha blinked her disbelief, held the gun out again silently, butt first, to Starbuck.

"You'll regret this, bitch," for her ears only. He twisted the gun out of her hand, bruising her palm, and strode back to the dais.

She grimaced involuntarily. "Then . . . with your permission, Your Majesty, I'll present the Commander's monthly report on the status of crime in the city."

Arienrhod nodded, leaning out to lay a possessive hand on Starbuck's arm, as one might soothe a hackled dog. The nobles began to drift away, backing out of the Queen's presence. Jerusha suppressed a smile of pained empathy. This report was no more significant than a hundred others before it, or any that would follow; she would sooner be elsewhere herself. She reached down and switched on the recorder at her belt, heard her commanding officer's voice reciting the statistics on the number of assaults and robberies, arrests and convictions, offworld or domestic crimes and victims. The words ran together into a meaningless singsong in her mind, raising all her familiar frustrations and regrets. Meaningless . . . it was all meaningless.

The Hegemonic Police were a paramilitary force stationed on all Hegemony worlds, to protect its interests and its citizens . . . which usually involved protecting the interests of the local onworld power structures. Here on Tiamat, with its low technology and sparse population (half of which barely even entered into the Hegemony's consideration) the police force was only a single regiment, confined to the starport and Carbuncle for the most part.

And its activities were confined, hamstrung, restricted: the breaking up of drunken fights, the arresting of petty thieves, an endless cycle of nose wiping and futile prosecutions, when right under their own noses some of the most blatant vice in the civilized galaxy went unchallenged, and some of the Hedge's most vicious abusers of humanity met openly in the pleasure hells where they were so much at home.

The Prime Minister might symbolize the Hegemony, but he no longer controlled it, if he ever had. Economics controlled it; the merchants and traders had always been its real roots, and their only real lord was Profit. But there were many kinds of trade, and many kinds of traders. . . . Jerusha looked up at Starbuck, slouching arrogantly at the Queen's right: the living symbol of Arienrhod's peculiar covenant with the powers of darkness and light, and her manipulation of them. He was all that was rotten, venal, and corrupt about humanity, and Carbuncle.

Crime and punishment on Tiamat—in effect, in Carbuncle—as on other Hegemonic worlds, had been split into the jurisdictions of two courts, one presided over by a local official chosen by the Winters and acting under local laws, and one by an offworld Chief Justice, who passed judgment on offworlders under the laws of the Hegemony. The police provided the grist for both mills, and to Jerusha's mind the harvest should have been bountiful. But Arienrhod tolerated and even encouraged the presence of the

Hedge's underworld, creating a kind of limbo, a neutral ground convenient to the Gates. And LiouxSked, that pompous, boot-licking imitation of a man and a commander, didn't have the guts to stand up against it. If she only had the rank, and half an opportunity—

"Do you have any comments to make about the report, Inspector?"

Jerusha started, feeling stupidly transparent. She switched off the recorder, an excuse to keep looking down. "None, Your Majesty." *None that you'd want to hear. None that would make the slightest difference.*

"Unofficially, Geia Jerusha?" The Queen's voice changed.

Jerusha looked up at Arienrhod's face, open and compelling, the face of a real woman and not the mask of a queen.

She could almost trust that face . . . she could almost believe that there was a human being behind the ritual and deceit who could be reached . . . *almost.* Jerusha glanced back at Starbuck standing at the Queen's side, her henchman, her lover.

Jerusha sighed. "I have no unofficial opinion, Your Majesty. I represent the Hegemony."

Starbuck said something in the unknown language; she translated the crudeness of the insult from his tone.

The Queen laughed: high, incongruously innocent laughter. She gestured. "Well, then, you're dismissed, Inspector. If I want to listen to a canned recitation of loyalty, I'll import a coppok. At least their plumage is more imaginative." The Elder Wayaways appeared, bowing, to lead them out of her presence.

Jerusha stood in the palace courtyard at last, staring fixedly at the patrolcraft. A starburst of exploded cracks rayed out from the slagged impact point on the ruined windshield. *So it's come to this?* "I'm sure there must be a lot of heavy remarks I could make about this." Her hand jerked out at the vandalism, dropped away to the doorlatch instead. "But I'm goddamned if I'm going to put on a show here." She slid into the bobbing seat as Gundhalinu got in on the driver's side. "Besides—" she pulled down the door, "all I can think of to say is that I'm tired, and I feel like I've been spat on. Sometimes I wonder if we're really in charge of anything on this world." She dug into her pocket for the pack of iestas, tapped a couple into her palm. She put them into her mouth and bit down on the leathery-tough pods, felt the sour tang begin to ease her nerves. "Finally . . . Want some?" She held out the pack.

Gundhalinu sat rigidly behind the controls, staring out through the wild tendrils of destruction. He had been silent through their journey back, crossed the Hall of the Winds as though he were crossing an empty street. He began to punch in the ignition code, and didn't answer.

She put the pack away. "Are you capable of driving, Sergeant, or shall I take the controls?" The sudden goad of officiousness in her voice made him flinch.

"Yes, Inspector! I'm capable." He nodded, still looking straight ahead. She watched more words struggle in his throat; he swallowed hard, like an angry child. The craft began to nose slowly back and around, edging toward the city.

"What did Starbuck say just before the Queen sent us away?" She kept the tone impersonal. She could recognize some of the Kharemoughis' ideographic writing—the operating instructions on most of their exported equipment—but she had never bothered to learn spoken Sandhi. The force used the speech of the place where they were stationed as a linguistic common ground.

Gundhalinu cleared his throat, swallowed again. "Begging your pardon, ma'am, the bastard said . . . 'If you're what the Hegemony sends to represent itself, it must be short on balls these days.'"

"Is that all?" Jerusha made a sound that was almost a laugh. "Hell, that's a compliment. . . . I'm surprised the Queen thought it was funny. Wonder if she really understood. Or maybe she understood that it only reflected on us."

"Besides," Gundhalinu mumbled viciously, "she's got his."

61

She did laugh this time. "Yeah. And welcome to them. So Starbuck is from Kharemough."

Another nod.

"What did he say to you?"

He shook his head.

"There's nothing you could possibly say that I haven't heard by now, BZ."

"I know, Inspector." He looked back at her finally, away again with his freckles reddening. "That is, I *can't* tell you. It wouldn't mean anything, unless you'd been raised on Kharemough. A matter of Honor."

"I see." She had heard him speak of Honor before, heard the capital H, the peculiar emphasis.

"I—thank you for taking my part against Starbuck. I could not have responded on my own to his insults without further losing face." The ceremony of the words and the sudden gratitude in his voice caught her by surprise.

She looked out at the nobility and servants gaping back at them through the shattered windshield as they drifted past the mansions of the upper city. "There's no honor lost in being insulted by a man who never knew the meaning of the word."

"Thank you." He swerved upward to avoid a child floating golden hoops in their path. "But I brought it on myself; I know that. And I caused trouble for you, and embarrassment to the force. If you want to dismiss me as your assistant, I'll understand."

She leaned back in the padded concavity of the seat, flexed the hand that Starbuck had bruised. "Maybe it would be just as well if you didn't go with me to pay any more calls on the Queen, BZ. Not because I really disapprove of what you did. Simply because Starbuck has a weapon he can use against you now; and that will only make it hard on you, and harder on me by association, and harder to keep them from dragging the Hedge's good name in the mud. Other than that—frankly, I like you, BZ, and I'd be damned disappointed if you were that eager to get away from me." *Though you probably wouldn't be the first.*

62

A feeble smile of relief stirred on his face. "No, ma'am. I'm content . . . more than content. As for staying behind when you visit the Queen—that's just cream." The smile spread, infectious.

She nodded. "If I could get away with sending you instead of going myself, don't think I wouldn't do it." She grinned; felt it pull down again. She unfastened her heavy cloak and shrugged it off, removed her helmet, looking at the gold-painted eggshell curve. "Somebody ought to hang that on a tree. Gods, I'm fed up with this! I'd give anything to be doing an honest job, somewhere where they want a real police force and not a laughingstock."

Gundhalinu glanced back, not smiling now. "Why don't you get a transfer?"

"Do you have any idea how long it takes to get a transfer?" She shook her head, resting the helmet across her knees as she loosened the high collar of her uniform jacket. She sighed. "Besides, I've tried. No luck. They 'need me here.' " The bitterness in her voice burned like acid.

"Why don't you quit?"

"Why don't you shut up?"

Gundhalinu looked back at the controls dutifully. They were in the Maze now, moving more slowly along the congested street. Evening stained the sky beyond the storm walls already. Jerusha watched the tatterdemalion alleyways, the garish hells along the street front, pass by like a mockery of her own dreams and ambitions. . . . And would she really give anything to be doing a better job? Would she take the risk of losing the rank she knew LiouxSked had given to her simply to make her a respectable offering to the Queen? She pulled an auburn-black curl over her left ear. After all, in another five years it would all change anyway. The Hegemony would be leaving Tiamat, and it would send her somewhere better—*anywhere* was better. Patience, patience was all she needed. The gods knew it was hard enough for a woman to survive in a career as a Blue at all, even now—let alone rise to a position of any authority.

She glanced down another alley as they passed its en-

63

trance. This one was predominantly blue-violet—painted walls, lights, banners: Indigo Alley. . . . She'd been sent to Tiamat in the first place, she was almost sure, because she was a woman; and at first the idea had appealed to her. But it had soured soon enough. She was a Blue because she liked the job, and the job wasn't getting done. . . .

Half-glimpsed movement set off an alarm in her unconscious. "BZ, back up! Hit the flasher, I saw something down that alley." She clapped on her helmet, jerking the strap under her chin as she hit the door open. "Follow me down." She was out, running, as the patrolcraft jounced to a stop at the dim alley entrance. Cooking smells hung heavy in the air; the narrow cul-de-sac was lined with hole-in-the-wall eateries, and dinnertime empty. The few bodies who were out in it seemed to melt into the walls at the sight of a red light and a dusty-blue uniform. Halfway, it had been just halfway. . . . She slowed, reaching for the light button on her helmet, angling toward the black crevices that pitted the three-story makeshift building face on her left. She switched on her headlamps; it showed her nothing in the first one but piled metal drums, nothing in the next. She was aware of Gundhalinu's footsteps coming after her down the pavement . . . *voices.*

Her lamp flooded the next break in the wall, deeper than the others. It pinned three figures—no, four—five—one squatting over a prostrate victim, something alive with its own light in his hand. "Freeze!" Her stunner was in her hands and pointing.

"Blues!" A confusion of movement, like insects dazzled in the light; one movement that struck her wrong.

She fired, saw a weapon fly free as the man went down. "I said freeze! Get up, you with the blade; switch it off and throw it out here. Now!" She felt Gundhalinu stop beside her, stunner out, all her own attention focusing on the fourth man as he obeyed her order. The light-pencil slid across the pavement and struck her boot. "Now flat on your bellies, scum, and spread-eagle. BZ, pull their teeth. I'll cover you."

Gundhalinu went forward quickly; she watched while he

crouched down by one and then another and checked them for weapons. While she waited, her gaze wandered to their victim lying helpless to one side; she frowned, moved closer to look down at his face. "Uh-oh . . ." She caught a blurred image of youth and red hair in the harsh light; saw the terror whitening his eyes and heard the raw noise of his crippled breathing. She dropped to her knees beside him. Gundhalinu was searching the last of the slavers. "BZ, find the key for the cuffs they put on this boy. He took a bad jolt, I think he needs some antifreeze." She snapped open the aid kit at her belt, removed a prefilled syringe of stimulant. "I don't know if you can see my face, boy, but picture a big smile. It's going to be all right." Smiling, she pulled open the boy's shirt and injected the medication directly into the muscles of his chest. He gave a small grunt of pain or protest. She lifted his head, let it rest on her knees as Gundhalinu moved in with jingling keys to take the handcuffs off him. The boy's hands dropped limply at his sides.

"I know where I can put these to good use." Gundhalinu grinned, holding up the cuffs.

She nodded. "Good. Do it." She unhooked her own binders and passed them across to him. "Here you go. Equal treatment under the law." Gundhalinu got up again. She watched him handcuff the three mobile slavers. A tremor ran through the boy's body; glancing down, she saw him begin to gulp air with desperate relief. The lids drooped closed over his wild, sea-colored eyes. She smoothed the wet tendrils of red hair back from his face. "Better radio in, BZ; we'll never get this crowd into the back seat. I think our young friend is coming out of it all right."

Gundhalinu bobbed his head. "Right, Inspector." The slaver he was straddling raised his face and then spat. "A woman! A fucking woman Blue. How the hell do you like that! Busted by a woman." Gundhalinu nudged him ungently with a boot; he grunted.

Jerusha leaned back against the wall, propping her stunner on her knee. "And don't you ever forget it, you son of a bitch. Maybe we can't get at the heart of what's rotten in this city, but we can sure as hell cut off a few fingers."

65

Gundhalinu stepped out into the alley and started back to the patrolcraft. If anyone else out there wondered what had happened, they weren't stopping to ask. She was certain that anyone with any real interest knew already. The boy made a tentative sound that was half a moan, and his hands came up onto his chest. He opened his eyes, squinted them shut again against the glare of her lamp. "Think you're ready to sit up?"

He nodded, put his hands out again to push as she shifted him back against the wall. Blood oozed from his nose and a scrape along his chin; his face and his shirt were smeared with oily stains. He fumbled among the strings of gaudy broken beads hanging around his neck. "Hell. Oh, *hell* . . . I jus' bought these!" His eyes were glassy looking.

"Never mind the packaging, as long as the goods are intac—" She broke off as she saw the tarnished medal of honor swinging among the beads. "Where did you get that?" She heard the unthinking demand in her voice.

His fist closed over it protectively. "It belongs to me!"

"Nobody's saying it doesn't— Hold it!" Movement caught the corner of her eye; her gun came up. The slaver nearest the alley entrance swayed, halfway to his feet with his hands locked behind him. "Flatten, creep; or you'll do it the hard way, like the boy did." He flopped onto his stomach, glaring obscenities at her.

"He . . ." the boy began, and pressed a hand against his mouth. "He was gonna—cut me. They were gonna sell me! They said they . . . I'd . . ." He shivered; she watched him struggle to control it.

"Mutes tell no tales . . . though where you were going they wouldn't have understood a word you said anyway. And they sure wouldn't have cared. . . . No, it's not a pretty thought, is it?" She squeezed his thin arm gently. "But it happens all the time. Only these big-hearts won't be making it happen again. You're from offworld?"

His hand tightened over the medal again. "Yeah . . . I mean, no. My mother wasn't. My father was." He squinted fiercely into the light.

She kept the surprise off of her own face. "And the medal belonged to him." She made it a statement of accepted fact, not caring where he'd gotten the medal, more interested now in the possibility of bigger crimes. "But you were raised here? You consider yourself a citizen of Tiamat?"

He rubbed his mouth again, blinking. "I guess so." A trace of hesitation, or suspicion.

Gundhalinu reappeared from the alley; the beam of his light overlapped her own to drive the shadows back. "They'll be here for a pickup any time, Inspector." She nodded. He stopped by the boy. "How you doing?"

The boy looked up at Gundhalinu's dark freckled face, almost staring, before he seemed to remember his manners. "All right, I guess. Thanks . . . thanks." He turned back to Jerusha, met her eyes, looked down, away, back again. "I don't know how . . . I just . . . thanks."

"You want to pay us back?" She smiled; he nodded. "Be more careful where you walk. And be willing to swear in a monitored testimony that you're a citizen of Tiamat." She grinned at Gundhalinu. "Not only kidnapping and assault, but attempting to take a citizen of a proscribed planet offworld." She stood up. "I'm feelng better all the time."

Gundhalinu laughed. "And somebody else is feeling worse." He bent his head at the prisoners.

"What does that mean?" The boy climbed to his feet, leaning heavily on the wall. "Do you mean I can't ever go to another world, even if I want to?" Gundhalinu put out a hand, steadying him.

Jerusha glanced at her watch. "In your case, maybe you can. If your father was an offworlder that makes a difference—if you can prove it. Of course, once you leave here you can never come back. . . . You'd have to take it up with a lawyer."

"Why?" Gundhalinu asked. "Were you planning to ship off?"

The boy began to look hostile. "I might want to, some time. If you come here, why won't you let us leave?"

67

"Because your cultures haven't reached an adequate degree of maturity," Gundhalinu intoned.

The boy looked pointedly at the offworld slavers, and back at Gundhalinu. Gundhalinu frowned.

Jerusha switched on her recorder. "If you don't mind, I'll just get a few facts for the record. Then we'll see about taking you down to the med center for—"

"I don't need it. I'm all right." The boy straightened up, pulling at his clothes.

"You're probably not the best judge of that, you know." She looked at him sharply, met embers in his gaze. "But that's up to you. Go home and get a good night's sleep instead, if you want. In any case we need to know where to reach you when we want you. Please state your name."

"Sparks Dawntreader Summer."

"Summer?" Belatedly she registered the burr in his speech. "How long have you been in the city, Sparks?"

He shrugged. "Not very long." He glanced away.

"Hm." *Which explains a lot of things.* "Why did you come to Carbuncle?"

"Is that against your laws too?" sarcasm dripping.

"Not as far as I know." She heard Gundhalinu's sniff of disapproval. "Are you employed, and if so, doing what?"

"Yes. Street musician." The boy's hands began to grope suddenly, searching his shirt, his belt, the air. "My flute . . ."

Jerusha lit the corners of the darkness with a sweep of her helmet light. "Is that it?"

The boy dropped down on hands and knees beside one of the slavers, and picked up the pieces. "No—no!" His face and his hands tightened with pain. The slaver laughed, and the boy's fist hit him in the mouth.

Jerusha moved forward, pulled the boy up and away. "That's enough, Summer. . . . You've had a hard time of it here, because nobody's told you the rules. And nobody can, that's the problem. Go back to your quiet islands where time stands still, while you're still able to. Go home, Summer . . . and wait another five years. You'll belong here after the Change."

"I know what I'm doing."

Like hell you do, she thought, looking at his battered face and the broken flute still clutched in his hands. "In that case, since you now lack a means of earning a living, I'm going to charge you with vagrancy. Unless, of course, you leave the city within the next day period." *Anything to get you back on a ship and away from here, before Carbuncle ruins another life.*

The boy looked incredulous. Then his anger came back, and she knew that she had lost. "I'm not a vagrant! The—the maskmaker's, in the Citron Alley. I'm staying there."

Jerusha heard the sound of another patrolcraft arriving, and booted feet in the alleyway. "All right, Sparks. If you have a place to stay, I guess you're free to go home." *Only you won't go home, you fool.* "But I still need your monitored victim's deposition, to put these leeches away for good. Stop in at police headquarters tomorrow; you owe me that much at least."

The boy nodded sullenly, and stepped out into the alley. She didn't expect to see him again.

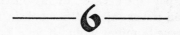

"What do you mean, you don't know what happened to the boy?" Arienrhod leaned out of her seat, glaring at the bald dome of the trader's bent head. Her fingers sank into the soft arms of the lounging chair like talons.

"Forgive me, Your Majesty!" The trader glanced up at her with the eyes of a terrified rodent. "I didn't think you were interested in him, only in the girl. I told him to go to Gadderfy's in the Periwinkle Alley, but he didn't go there. If you want me to search the city . . ." His voice wavered.

"No, that won't be necessary." She managed to produce

a placating tone of voice, not wanting the old man to keel over dead at the thought of it. "My methods are much more efficient than yours. I'll find him myself if I decide that I need him." *And I think that perhaps I was meant to find him.* "You said that he decided to come here because ... Moon ... has become a sibyl, while he was rejected?" *How hard it is to call yourself by another name.* "What does he expect to find in Carbuncle?"

"I don't know, Your Majesty." The trader wrung his tooled leather belt-end between his hands. "But like I told you, they were pledged to each other; they were always together. I guess it hurt his pride, that he couldn't join her in the hocus-pocus. And his father's an offworlder, he always wears that medal ... I guess he's curious."

She nodded, not looking at him. Over the years he had brought her stories of the two children growing up together, childhood sweethearts bound by some invisible cord of loyalty ... which perhaps could be used to draw the girl here to Carbuncle, and get her away from her superstitious sibyl-fixation. She couldn't blame the girl for aspiring to the highest honor in her limited world; that only proved how surely they were the same woman. But Moon's obsession had kept her unreceptive when the trader had tried to interest her in Winter technology, though it had caught the boy's interest, perhaps because of his offworlder father. At least Moon had never rejected her cousin for being a tech lover, as any true Summer would have. That had prompted Arienrhod to tolerate their relationship, in the hope that even such diluted contact with technology would help make Moon ready for her destiny. At least she hadn't gotten pregnant by him—even the Summers grew childbane, and knew how to use it. If he were here in the palace, waiting for her ...

"You're sure that Moon is 'studying' with these sibyls on their island now? Will she be safe there?"

"As safe as anywhere in Summer, Your Majesty. Probably safer. She may even be back on Neith by the time I put in there again."

70

"And you say the sibyls you've seen aren't actually deranged—?" Her voice tightened. She had hoped to bring the girl here before she had the chance to contract the sibyl disease; but now it was too late.

"No, Your Majesty." He shook his head. "They control their fits completely; I've never seen one who couldn't." His own lack of fear reassured her.

Arienrhod studied the mural on the wall behind his head. As long as the girl was sane, that was all that really mattered; the disease could even be an asset, a protection, if it made the Summers trust her. She looked back at the trader. "Then you'll bring her a message from her cousin, which I will supply. I want her to come to Carbuncle." Moon would have to come of her own free will; the Summers would never stand by and let someone kidnap a sibyl.

The trader kept his head bowed; she could not tell what his expression was, although he twitched slightly. "But, Your Majesty—if she's become a sibyl, she may be afraid to come to the city."

"She'll come." Arienrhod smiled. "I know her; she'll come." *If she thinks her lover is in danger, she'll come.* "You've served me well—" she realized that she had forgotten the man's name, and did not use it, "trader. You deserve to be well rewarded." *Gods, I must be getting old.* The smile altered slightly. She pressed a sequence of lighted keys on the chair arm. "I think you will find that the debts for your new cargo of trade goods have all been canceled."

"Thank you, Your Majesty!" She watched his sagging face jiggle as he made obeisance, hating the sight of the ugliness that age inflicted, even while she took pleasure in the awareness of her own invulnerability.

She dismissed him, not even cautioning him to keep this meeting to himself. He was a distant but loyal kinsman; no matter what he might wonder about his strange guardianship or the stranger object of it, she knew that he would never ask, or betray. Particularly not when he was paid so well.

She rose from her seat in the small private room when he had gone, and went to the doorway, drawing the white inlaid panels aside. She found Starbuck waiting there, not quite expected, in the wider hall beyond it. With him were his Hounds—the amphibian hunters from Tsieh-pun, ideally suited to the work of outwitting mers. The Hounds stood in a cluster at the far side of the chamber, tentacled arms waving as they grunted at each other in desultory conversation.

But Starbuck stood leaning with his usual public insolence against a massive Samathan side table very close on her left . . . very close to the door. She wondered whether he had been listening; decided that he probably had, decided that it probably didn't matter.

He was hooded and still in black, but instead of his court costume it was a utilitarian thermal suit hung with equipment for the hunt. Light caught on his sheathed killing knife as he straightened up. He bowed to her with rigid propriety, but not before she saw the searching look and the questions in his dark eyes.

"Are you leaving already?" She gave him nothing but the coldness of her voice.

"Yes, Your Majesty. If it pleases you." She detected the faint assumption of a ritual repeated between equals.

"It pleases me very much." *Yes, flinch, my overconfident hunter. You are not the first by many, and you may not be the last.* "The sooner you go, the better. You hunt the Wayaways preserve this time?"

"Yes, Your Majesty. The weather is clear there and should hold." He hesitated, came toward her. "Give me luck in the hunt—?" His hand caressed her arm through the film of cloth.

He lifted his mask, and she drew his face toward hers with her hands, giving him a kiss that was a promise of greater rewards. "Hunt well."

He nodded and turned away. She watched him gather the Hounds and go looking for life and death.

72

7

"Input—"

An ocean of air . . . an ocean of stone. She was flying. Moon gaped with a stranger's eyes at the vaulting walls of striated rock that funneled her out into the canyonlands, an immeasurable vastness of eroded stone like scrimshaw lace, stained violet, green, crimson, gray. She was trapped in the maw of a transparent bird, an airship in flight; dials and push buttons and strange symbols blinked and clicked on the panel before her. But she was held in stasis by her trance, and she could not reach them, as the ridge of purple stone rose like a wall into her headlong flight.

The ship banked steeply on its own, clearing the ridge and plunging into a deeper chasm, leaving her giddy. Something on the panel flashed red, bleeping critically as her altitude stabilized once more. Where she had come from, where she was bound, where this lithified sea existed, where mysteries she would never be able to answer; along with who, and how, and why . . . Overhead the sky was a cloudless indigo, blackening toward the zenith, lit by only one tiny, silvery sun. She could not see water anywhere. . . .

"Input—"

An ocean of sand. An infinity of beach, a shoreless dune-sea whose tides flowed endlessly under the eternal wind. . . . Her ship moved over the sand in rippling undulation, and she was not certain from where she sat, helmeted against the furnace of light, high on its armored back, whether it was truly alive or not. . . .

"Input—"

An ocean of humanity. The crowds surged around her on the corner of two streets, pushing and dragging at her like treacherous undertow. Machines roared and clattered

73

past her, clogging the roadways, filling her nose with their bitter reek and battering her ears. . . . A dark-faced stranger dressed all in brown, peaked hat, shining boots, caught at her arm; raised his voice in an unknown language, questioning. She saw his face change abruptly, and he let her go. . . .

"*Input—*"

An ocean of night. An utter absence of light, and life . . . a sense of macrocosmic age . . . an awareness of microcosmic activity . . . the knowledge that she would never penetrate its secret heart, no matter how often she came back and came back to this midnight void of nothing, nothing at all. . . .

". . . *No further analysis!*" She heard the word echoing, felt her head drop forward in release, caught her breath as the end of another trance wrenched her back into her own world. She sat back on her knees, relaxing the muscles of her body consciously, in a rising wave . . . breathing deeply and aware of each tingling response.

She opened her eyes at last, to the reassuring presence of Danaquil Lu smiling at her from the rough wooden chair on the other side of the chamber. She controlled her own body now during the Transfer; they no longer had to hold her down, tying her to the real world. She smiled back at him with weary pride, shifted to sit cross-legged on the woven mat.

Clavally ducked in at the doorway, momentarily blotting out the puddle of sunlight that warmed Moon's back. Moon twisted to watch her enter the second pool of light below the battered window frame; Clavally dropped her hand absently to smooth Danaquil Lu's always-rumpled brown hair. Danaquil Lu was a quiet, almost a shy man, but he laughed easily at Clavally's constant whimsies. He struck Moon as being somehow ill at ease or out of place here on this island, in these rooms chipped from a wall of porous rock. Where he did belong she couldn't guess; but sometimes she saw a longing for it in his eyes. Sometimes she caught him looking at her, too, with an expression on his face that she couldn't name—as though he had seen her somewhere before. There were ugly scars on his neck and the side of his face, as though some beast had clawed him.

"What did you see?" Clavally asked the question that was almost a ritual in itself. To help her learn to control the Transfer, to master the rituals of body and mind that guided a sibyl, they asked her questions with predictable answers—questions they had been asked themselves as a part of their own training. Moon had learned that she never knew what words she would speak in response to a seeker's questions. Instead she was swept away into a vision: into a pit of blackness as vast as death...into a vibrant dream world somewhere in the middle of another reality. A mystical strand bound each question to a separate dream, and so Clavally or Danaquil Lu could guide her Transfer experience, lessen the terrifying alienness with predictions of what she would see.

"I went to the Nothing Place again." Moon shook her head, throwing off the maddening echoes of the dream, shaking out the shadows that still rattled in her memory. The first things they had taught her after her initiation were the mental blocks and disciplined concentration that would keep her sane, that would keep her from overhearing all the thousand hidden thoughts of the Lady's all-seeing mind, or being swept away into the Lady's rapture every time anyone around her spoke a question. "Why is it that we go there more than anywhere else? It's like drowning."

"I don't know," Clavally said. "Maybe we are drowning —they say that those who drown have visions, too."

Moon moved uneasily. "I hope not."

Laughter. Clavally crouched down beside Danaquil Lu, rubbing his shoulders with absentminded tenderness; his necklace of shell beads rattled musically. The damp cold at night in these stone rooms left him stiff and aching, but he never complained. *Maybe this is why*...Moon's hands tightened over her knees as she watched them together.

"Your control is fine, Moon." Danaquil Lu smiled, half at her, half at Clavally's hands. "You improve with every Transfer—you have a very strong will."

Moon pushed herself to her feet, "I guess I need some air," her voice suddenly sounding feeble and thin even to her. She went quickly out the doorway, knowing air wasn't really what she needed.

She half ran down the path that led toward the inlet where their boats were; took the branching track that rose along the blue-green, windy headland above the blue-green sea. Breathing hard, she threw herself down in the long, matted salt grass, pulling her feet in as she looked back toward the south-facing cliff where she had lived like a bird in an aerie for the past months. She gazed out over the sea again, seeing in the blue-clouded distance the ragged spine of the Choosing Island, whose small sister this was ... remembering with all the vividness of a Transfer dream the moment of the Lady's decision that had torn her life and Sparks's apart. *I'm not sorry!* Her fist struck hard on the damp grass; opened, strengthless.

She lifted her arm to look at the thin white line along her wrist where Clavally had cut it, as she had cut her own, with a metal crescent long months ago. Danaquil Lu had pressed their wrists together as their blood mingled and dripped down, while he sang a hymn to the Sea Mother, here on this very spot. Here, overlooking the Sea, she had been consecrated as they hung the barbed trefoil around her neck; welcomed into a new life as they all sipped in turn from a cup of brine; initiated with that bond of blood into this holy fellowship. Shaking with fear, she had grown suddenly hot and cold and dizzy as she felt the Lady's presence come over her ... collapsed in a faint between them, waking the next day still weak and feverish, filled with awe. She had become one of the chosen few: From the scars on their wrists, it was clear that Clavally and Danaquil Lu had initiated only half a dozen others before her. She cupped the trefoil in her hand, remembering Sparks holding his own symbol of the distance between them; cupping hers warily, for its barbed points. *Death to love a sibyl . . . to be a sibyl . . .*

But not to love, and be, a sibyl: She looked back at the cliffs jealously, imagined Clavally and Danaquil Lu sharing love in her absence. Sparks's bitter words at parting were only a thin white line on the surface of her mind now, like the white line along her wrist. Time and the memories of a lifetime had swept away her hurt like a wave sweeping footprints from the sand, leaving a bright mirror, a reflection of love and need. She had always loved him, she would always need him. She could never give him up.

Clavally and Danaquil Lu were pledged, and the knowledge was like a small demon trapped inside her chest. To islanders sex was a thing as natural as growing up, but they were private about their private lives; so she had spent many hours in dutiful, solitary meditation, that too easily bled into daydreams of envious longing. And one of the things she had learned about sibyls was that they were not more than human: Sorrow and anger and all the petty frustrations of life still grew from the seeds of her dedication, wrong still came out of the best intentions. She still laughed, and cried, and ached for the touch of him. . . .

"Moon?"

She twisted guiltily at Clavally's voice behind her.

"Are you all right?" Clavally settled beside her on the grass, putting a hand on her arm.

Moon felt a sudden surge of emotion, beyond the surge of energy any question set free in her mind now—misery craving company. She controlled it, barely. "Yes," gulping, "but sometimes I . . . miss Sparks."

"Sparks? Your cousin." Clavally nodded. "Now I remember. I saw you together. You said you wanted to be together forever. But he didn't come with you?"

"He did! But the Lady—turned him away. All our lives we planned to do this together . . . and then She turned him away."

"But you still came here."

"I had to. I've waited half my life to be a sibyl. To

matter in the world." Moon shifted, hugging her knees, as a cloud abruptly darkened the sun. Below them the sea turned sullen gray in its shadow. "And he couldn't understand that. He said stupid things, hateful things. He—went away, to Carbuncle! He went away angry. I don't know if he'll ever come back." She looked up, meeting Clavally's eyes, seeing the sympathy and understanding that she had hidden from for so long, and realizing that she had been wrong to hide—to carry the burden alone. "Why didn't the Lady choose us both? We've always been together! Doesn't She know that we're the same?"

Clavally shook her head. "She knows that you're not, Moon. That was why She chose only you. There was something inside Sparks that isn't in you—or the other way around—so that when She struck your hearts there in the cave She heard a false note from his."

"No!" Moon looked out across the water toward the Choosing Island. The sky was massing with clouds for another rain squall. "I mean—there's nothing wrong with Sparks. Is it because his father wasn't a Summer? Because he likes technology? Maybe the Lady thought he wasn't a true believer. She doesn't take Winters to be sibyls." Moon fingered the lank grass, searching the tangled strands for an explanation.

"Yes, She does."

"She does?"

"Danaquil Lu is a Winter."

"He is?" Moon's head came up. "But—how? Why? I always heard . . . everybody says that they don't believe. And that they're not . . . like us," she finished lamely.

"The Lady works in strange ways. There is a kind of well at the heart of Carbuncle, that opens down to the sea from the Queen's palace. On his first visit to court, Danaquil Lu crossed over the bridge that spans the well—and the Sea Mother called up to him, and told him that he must become a sibyl."

Clavally smiled sorrowfully. "People are sweet and sour fruit together, wherever you find them. The Lady picks the ones that best suit Her tastes, and She doesn't seem to care whether they worship Her, or anyone." Her eyes turned distant; she glanced up at the rooms in the cliff face. "But few Winters even try to become sibyls, because they're taught that it's madness, or superstitious fakery. They rarely even see sibyls, sibyls are forbidden to enter Carbuncle. The offworlders hate them for some reason; and whatever the offworlders hate, the Winters hate too. But they believe in the power of the Lady's retribution." Lines deepened in her face. "They have a pole, that ends in a collar of spikes, so that no one is 'contaminated' by a sibyl's blood. . . ."

Moon thought of Daft Nairy . . . and of Danaquil Lu. Her hand touched the trefoil tattoo at the base of her neck, beneath the ivory wool of her sweater. "Danaquil Lu—"

"—was punished, driven out of Carbuncle. He can never go back; at least while the Snow Queen rules. I met him during one of my circuits through the islands. I think, since we've been together, he's been happy . . . or at least content. And I've learned many things from him." She glanced down—suddenly, unexpectedly, looking like a girl. "I know it's probably wrong of me, but I'm glad they sent him into exile."

"Then you know how I feel."

Clavally nodded, smiling down. She pushed back her parka sleeve, exposing the long-healed scars on her wrist. "I don't know why we were chosen . . . but we weren't chosen because we're perfect."

"I know." Moon's mouth twitched. "But if it's not because he's interested in technology, how could Sparks be less perfect than I am—"

"—when you think there couldn't be anything more perfect than the lover you remember?"

A sheepish nod.

"When I first saw you together, I had a feeling—after a while you do—that if you came here you would be chosen. You felt *right* to me. But Sparks . . . there was an unsettledness."

"I don't understand."

"You said that he left angry. You think he left as much

79

for the wrong reasons as for the right ones—that he did it to hurt you? That he blamed you for your success, and his failure."

"But I would have felt all those things too, if he'd been chosen instead—"

"Would you?" Clavally looked at her. "Maybe any of us would . . . all the good will in the world can't keep us from swallowing the fishhook baited with envy. But Sparks blamed you for what happened. You would only have blamed yourself."

Moon blinked, frowned; remembered their childhood, and how rarely he had tried to disagree with her. But when they did argue, he would run away and leave her alone. He would hold his anger for hours, even days. And in the lonely space he left behind, she would turn her own anger in on herself. She would go to him every time, and apologize, even when she knew he was wrong. "I guess I would have. Even though it's nobody's fault. But that's wrong, too."

"Yes . . . except that it hurts no one but you. And I think that's the difference."

Two sudden drops of rain pelted Moon's uncovered head; she looked up, confused and startled. She pulled up her hood as Clavally got to her feet and gestured toward shelter.

They ducked under a stand of young tree-ferns. The rain smothered all other sound for a space of minutes. They stood silently, blinded by a field of molten gray, until the rain squall moved off across the sea on the back of the wind. Moon stirred away from the fern's dark, pithy trunk; watched the pattern of droplets stranded like pearls in the fragile lacework of its canopy, watched them fall. She put out a hand. "It's stopped already." Her anger at Sparks had passed as swiftly as the rain, and had as little effect on the greater pattern of her life. But when they met again, so much would be different between them. . . . "I know people have to change. But I wonder if they know when to stop."

Clavally shook her head; they began to walk back together along the path, sidestepping the sudden stream that it had become. "Not even the Lady can answer that. I hope you'll find that Sparks has answered it for himself, when you see him again."

Moon turned in the track, walking a few strides backwards as she looked out across the restless sea toward home.

—————— 8 ——————

"... And then a part of the wealth from the last Festival was put into a new fund for me, so that I could begin work without interruption on the masks for this one ... almost nineteen years ago. How time slips past, masked in the rhythm of the days! That's the rhythm of creation for you—individual creation, universal creation. Red-orange feathers, please." The maskmaker held out her hand.

Sparks leaned forward on the stoop, reached into one of the trays scattered in the doorway between them and passed her a handful. Malkin, her long-limbed gray cat, poked a surreptitious paw among the feathers still in the holder. Sparks pushed him away, went back to separating strands of beads, dropping them into their appropriate cups. He looked up and down until it made him dizzy, trying to watch her work while he worked himself. "I don't know how you do it. How can you create so many masks, and every one different? When you can hardly—" He stopped, still unsure of his words in spite of her reassurances.

"—tell a red feather from a green one?" She smiled, lifting her head to look at him with the dark windows of her eyes, and the light sensor on the band across her forehead. "Well, you know, it wasn't easy in the beginning. But I had a desire to learn—a need to create something beautiful myself. I couldn't paint or draw, but this is more like

81

sculpture, really, a creation of touch and texture. And the craft is hereditary in the Ravenglass family, you know; like blindness. Being born blind, and then being given half-sight —sometimes I think that combination creates a heightening of imagination. All forms are vague and wonderful . . . you see in them what you want to see. I have two sisters who are both blind too, and who have their own shops here in the city. And many other relatives as well, all doing the same, though not all blind. It takes a lot of creative energy to make certain that there's a mask for every reveller who will be dancing in these streets at the next Festival time. And you know something?" She smiled, the pride shining through it. "Mine are the best of all. I, Fate Ravenglass Winter, will make the mask of the Summer Queen. . . . A piece of red velvet, please."

Sparks passed her the piece of cloth, letting it slither sensuously between his fingers. "But all this work—half a life's work—it's only for one night! And then it's gone. How can you bear that?"

"Because it's so important to Tiamat's identity as a separate world—our heritage. The rituals of the Change are a tradition that reaches back into the clouded times before the Hegemony and its rulers ever set foot on our world . . . some of it into the time when we were offworlders here ourselves—"

"How do you know?" interrupting. "How do you know what anybody did before the firstships sailed down out of the Great Storm?" He slipped absentmindedly into the language of myth.

"All I know is what I hear on the threedy." She smiled. "The offworlders have archaeologists who study the Old Empire's records and ruins. They claim we came here as refugees from a world called Trista, after some interstellar war near the end of the Old Empire. These fantasy faces I make began as real creatures; once they were on the standards of the firstship families that ancestored Summer and Winter. You probably recognize some of them—in Summer they still have meaning. Your shipname, Dawntreader, is one of the original dozen names—did you know that?"

Sparks shook his head. "But when the Hegemony came, they made us ashamed of our 'primitive' traditions; so now we only bring them out at the Festival, not really celebrating the Prime Minister's visit, but our own heritage."

"Oh." He was still confused and disturbed by the Winters' Ladyless view of history, although he would never admit it.

"Anyway, some things are more beautiful simply because they are ephemeral. Think of a flower opening, or a song as you play it, or a rainbow . . . think of making love."

"*What if there were no more rainbows . . .*" Sparks thought of those things, and bit his lip. "I guess it's stupid to look back and be sorry they're gone, then."

"It's human." She tilted her head quizzically, as though she were listening to his thoughts. "But for the artist the real joy is in the creation of the thing. When you feel something growing under your hands, you grow with it. You're alive, the energy flows. When it's finished, you stop growing. You stop living. You only live for the next act of creation. Don't you feel that, when you play your music?"

"Yes." He picked up his flute, running his fingers along the hair-fine seams left like scars on the wounded shell, where she had put it back together for him. She had done her work so well that even its sound had scarcely been altered. "I guess so. I never thought about it. But I guess I do."

"The blue-violet beetle's wing, please . . . thank you. I don't know how I got along before you came." Malkin sidled along Fate's hip and crept up into her lap, kneading the cloth of her loose skirt.

Sparks laughed; a pinched, self-deprecating sound that told her truth was flowing upstream. In spite of her prediction to him the first time they met, the competition of the Maze's numberless delights was too much for his fragile island music; he barely earned enough with his street-corner songs to put food in his mouth. He inhaled, breathing in the confusion of exotic smells from the Newhavenese botanery next door and the Samathan restaurant across the alley. If she hadn't given him the shelter of her back room,

83

instead of sleeping under the watchful gaze of a thousand spirit facemasks, he would be sleeping in the gutter . . . or worse.

He looked back at her, grateful at last that she had forced him to go to the offworlder police to make his accusation against the slavers. He remembered the surprise on the face of the Blue who had saved his life when she saw him again, and the guilt that had reflected on his own. He sighed. "Are the offworlders really all going to just pack up and leave Tiamat after the next Festival? Abandon everything they have here? It's hard to believe."

"Yes, almost all of them will go." She twisted a tassel from golden cord. "Their preparations have already begun, just as ours have. You could sense the changes if you'd grown up here. Will that make you sad?"

He looked up, because it wasn't the question he had expected. "I—don't know. Everybody in Summer always said it was a day to look forward to, the Change; that we'd come into our own. And I hate how the offworlders blind Winter with a lot of glory while they take what they want, and then think they can just forget about us." His hand closed over his medal; he twisted his fingers through the openings. "But—"

"But you've been blinded by the glory, just like all of us Winters." She broke off her knot tying to stroke Malkin's silvery, sleeping back.

"I—"

She smiled, watching him with her third eye. "What's wrong with that? Nothing. You asked me once whether I resented not being able to leave our world, when I might have my blindness cured somewhere else. You were thinking that I must resent being given these sensors instead—having to settle for half-sight instead of full vision. If I looked at it with perfect eyes, that's what I might have seen, too. But I looked with blind eyes . . . and to me they look wonderful."

"Wonder-full." Sparks leaned back against the wall of the shop, looking away down the alley. "And after the Festival it all ends."

"Yes. The last Festival. Then the offworlders will abandon us, and the Summers will have to move north again, and life as I've always lived it will cease. This time the choosing of the Queen for a Day will be in earnest . . . the Summer Queen's mask will be my last and best creation."

"What will you do after the Festival is over?" He realized suddenly that the question was more than rhetorical.

"Begin a new life." She tightened a final knot. "Just like everyone else in Carbuncle. That's why it's called the Change, you know." She held the finished mask up like an offering to the people passing in the alleyway. He saw some of them stare and smile.

"Why did they call you Fate? Your parents, I mean."

"My mother. Haven't you guessed? For the same reason you were called Sparks. Merrybegots have special names."

"You mean, two Festivals ago—?"

She nodded. "And it's been a heavy load, to carry a name like that around for a lifetime. Be glad you don't have to."

He laughed. "It's hard enough to carry 'Summer' around, in Carbuncle. It's like an anchor, it keeps me from getting anywhere." He picked up his flute again and put it to his lips; put it down, looking toward the alley entrance as a murmur of surprise traveled from person to person toward them.

"What is it?" Fate put the mask aside, her forehead wrinkling in an unconscious squint.

"Somebody's coming up the alley. Somebody rich." He could see the fineness of the clothing before he could make out the faces as the strangers came up the narrow way. There were half a dozen women and men, but his gaze caught on the one who clearly led the rest. The richness of her exotic clothing suddenly meant nothing, as he saw her face clearly—

"Sparks?" Fate's hand found his arm and tightened around it.

He didn't answer. He stood up slowly, feeling the world draw back until he was left alone in a private space with only . . . "Moon!"

She stopped, smiling recognition at him, and waited while he crossed the space to her.

"Moon, what are you—?"

Her attendants closed around him, catching his arms, holding him back from her. "What's the matter with you, boy? You dare to approach the Queen?"

But she lifted her hand, signaling them to let him go. "It's all right. I remind him of someone else, that's all. . . . Isn't that right, Sparks Dawntreader Summer?"

They all looked at her, but none of them could match his own disbelief. She was Moon, she *was* Moon . . . but *not* Moon, too. He shook his head. *Not Moon. The Queen.* . . . Then this was the Snow Queen, the Queen of Winter, who stood before him. Embarrassed, half-frightened, he dropped to his knees before her.

She reached down, took his hand, and drew him to his feet. "That isn't necessary." He raised his head, found her studying his face with an intensity that made him blush and look away. "How rare to find a Summer with any respect. Who is it that I reminded you of so much that you saw her instead?" Even the voice was the same; and yet something in it mocked him.

"My—cousin, Your Majesty. My cousin Moon." He swallowed. "H-how did you know who I am?"

She laughed. "If you were a Winter, you wouldn't ask that. Nothing in this city escapes my attention. For instance, I've heard about your unusual talent as a musician. In fact, I've come here today just to meet you. To ask you to come to the palace and play for me."

"Me?" Sparks rubbed his eyes, suddenly not sure whether he was awake. "But, nobody even listens to my music—" He felt the day's few coins rattle in his half-empty pocket.

"The right people listen." Fate's voice reached him from behind. "Didn't I tell you they would?"

The Queen's gaze followed as he glanced back. "Well, maskmaker. How is your work proceeding? Have you begun the Summer Queen's mask yet?"

"Your Majesty." Fate bowed her head solemnly. "My work has been going better than usual, thanks to Sparks.

But it isn't time yet for the Summer Queen." She smiled. "Winter still reigns. Take care of my musician. I'm going to miss him."

"The best care imaginable," the Queen said softly.

Sparks moved to the stoop, picked up his flute and slipped it into the pouch at his belt. Then, impulsively, he took Fate's hands in his own, leaned across the trays to kiss her cheek. "I'll come and see you."

"I know you will." She nodded. "Now, don't keep your future waiting."

He stood up, turned back toward the Queen, blinking as reality and illusion blurred his vision. Her attendants closed around him like the petals of an alien flower, and she took him away.

"I'm going to ask him for a ride. I can't wait here any longer. Too much time has passed already." Moon stood at the window of her grandmother's cottage, looking out through the rippled glass toward town. Her mother sat at the heavy wooden table where her grandmother was cleaning fish; Moon kept her back to them, ashamed at needing that crutch to support her resolution. "That trader won't be back again for months. Think of how long it's been since Sparks sent for me." And she had been too late, by a month, coming home; the trader who had brought her the message had already gone on his way again. Her hands whitened on the wooden window ledge, among the shells she and Sparks had gathered on the beach together when they were children. There would not be another ship coming to these remote islands from Carbuncle for too long; the closest place where she could hope to find one was at

Shotover Bay, on the edge of Winter, and that was too long a journey by sea for her to make alone.

But in the fields above the village now a stranger worked to repair a ship that flew, like the ship she had seen in one of her trances; not a Winter, but an actual offworlder, the first one who had ever set foot on Neith, a man with skin the color of brass and strange, hooded eyes. His flying ship had made a forced landing, she had watched it come out of the sky while she stood among the villagers' eager questions this morning. She had been relieved and a little proud to tell them from her own knowledge what the thing was, and that it was nothing to be afraid of.

And the offworlder had looked relieved, too, that the villagers had known enough about technology not to panic. Listening to him speak, Moon had realized that he was just as uneasy about his presence among them as they were. They had all gone away at his brusque urging, leaving him to work in peace, hoping that if they ignored him he would disappear again.

And she had to act now, before he did disappear. He must be on his way to Carbuncle; all the offworlders were from there. If he would only take her, too . . .

"But Moon, you're a sibyl now," her mother said.

Angry with half-guilt, she turned back to them. "I won't be abandoning my duty! Sibyls are needed everywhere."

"Not in Carbuncle." Her mother's voice strained. "It's not your faith I'm questioning, Moon, it's your safety. You're the Sea's daughter now. I know I can't forbid you to lead your own life. But they don't want sibyls in Carbuncle. If they learned what you were—"

"I know." She bit her lip, remembering Danaquil Lu. "I know that. I'll keep my trefoil hidden while I'm there." She picked it up on its chain, cupping it in her hands. "Just until I find him."

"It's wrong for him to ask you to go." Her mother stood up, walking restlessly around the table. "He must know that he's putting you in danger. He wouldn't ask that if he was thinking of you. Wait for him to come to you, wait for him to grow up and stop thinking only of himself."

Moon shook her head. "Mother, it's Sparks we're talking about! He wouldn't say that he can't come home unless he's in trouble. He wouldn't ask me to come unless he needs me." *And I've already betrayed him once.* She looked out the window again. "I know him." She picked up a shell. *I love him.*

Her mother came to stand beside her; she sensed the hesitation that kept even her own mother a little apart from her now, when they stood together. "Yes, you do." Her mother glanced back at Gran, who still sat at the table with concentration fixed on her scaling. "You know him better than I do. You know him better than I know you." Her mother touched her shoulder, turned her until they faced each other; she saw a brief instant of awe and sorrow in her mother's gaze. "My daughter is a sibyl. Child of my heart and body, sometimes I feel as though I don't really know you at all."

"Mama—" Moon bent her head, pressed her cheek against her mother's callused hand. "Don't say that."

Her mother smiled, as though an unspoken question had been answered.

Moon straightened again, took her mother's hand carefully and lowered it in her own. "I know I've only just come home. And I wanted so much to have this time with you." Her hands squeezed tight; she looked down. "But at least I have to talk to the offworlder."

"I know." Her mother nodded, still smiling. She picked up the slicker that lay at the foot of Moon's cot and handed it to her. "At least I know the Lady goes with you now, even if I can't."

Moon pulled the slicker on over her head and went out of the house. She followed the stony track to the terraced village fields, half running with the fear that she would see the offworlder's ship rise into the drizzling gray sky before she reached it. And as she climbed the parapet onto the terrace where the flying ship sat, a high whine filled the sodden air around her, the unearthly sound of a power unit engaging.

"Wait!" She began to run, seeing the handful of curious

89

children who lurked at the field's perimeter point at her and wave, thinking she waved at them. But the man in the flying ship stuck his head out the door opening to look at her, too, and the whining died.

He stepped out of the craft and straightened up. He wore the clothing of an islander, but it was made from a material she had never seen before. She slowed as she realized that he was not about to leave without her. He put his hands on his hips, glaring down at her as she approached; she saw suddenly how very tall he was, that she barely reached his shoulder. "All right, what's the crisis, missy?"

She stopped, reduced by the tone of his voice to another childish nuisance in a mucky field on a rocky, godforsaken island. "I—I thought you were taking off."

"I will be, just as soon as I get my tools aboard. Why do you ask?"

"That soon." Moon looked down at her slicker, tightening her resolution. If it had to be now, it had to be. "I'd like to ask you a favor before you go."

He wasn't looking at her; he slid a compartment shut beneath the window curve at the craft's front and rapped on it with a hand. "If you want an explanation about how the magic ship flies, I'm afraid I just haven't got the time. I'm late for an appointment."

"I know how they fly, my cousin told me." Her own irritation chewed the words. "I just want you to take me to Carbuncle."

He did look up this time, in mild astonishment. She forced the smile that said she had every right to ask. Several responses almost got past his lips, before he stooped to pick up his tool kit. "Sorry. I'm not going to Carbuncle."

"But—" She took a step, putting herself between him and the door opening as he started toward it. "Where are you going?"

"I'm going to Shotover Bay, if it's any business of yours. Now if you'll just—"

"That's all right. That's fine, in fact. Will you take me there instead?"

He pushed back his black, reed-straight hair, leaving a muddy track through it; he was beardless, but a black mustache draped his downturned mouth. "Just why in the names of a thousand gods should I do that?"

"Well . . ." She almost frowned at his lack of generosity. "I'd be glad to do anything you ask, to repay you." She hesitated, as his expression changed for the worse. "I . . . guess I've made a mistake, haven't I?"

He laughed unexpectedly. "That's all right, missy." He thrust the tool kit past her into the space behind the seats. "But you shouldn't be so ready to run off with the first stranger you see. You might just wind up in a worse situation than the one you think you're in."

"Oh—" Moon felt her cheeks burning in the cold air. She put a hand up, covering her face. "Oh, no, that's not what I meant! Here in the islands, when someone wants to go somewhere, and you're going, you just—take them. . . ." Her voice disappeared. "I'm sorry." She started away, stumbling over a rut, suddenly feeling like precisely the foolish child she had seen in his eyes.

"Well, wait a minute." The sand of annoyance was still in his voice, but its sting wasn't as sharp. "Why do you want to go there?"

She turned back again, trying to remember the trefoil hidden beneath her slicker, and that she had a right to a sibyl's dignity. "I want to find a ship at Shotover Bay to take me to Carbuncle. It's very important to me."

"It must be, to make a Summer willing to get into a flying machine with an offworlder."

Moon's mouth tightened. "Just because we don't use offworld technology, that doesn't mean we turn pale at the sight of it."

He laughed again, appreciatively, as though he enjoyed being paid in kind. "All right, then. If all you want is a ride, missy, you've got it."

"Moon." She put out her hand. "Moon Dawntreader Summer."

"Ngenet ran Ahase Miroe." He took her hand and shook it, not clasping wrists as she was used to; said, as an

91

afterthought, "Last name first. Climb aboard and strap in."

She climbed in resolutely on the far side, looking no further than the present moment, and fumbled with the safety harness. The interior of this craft was different from the one she had seen in her trance; she thought that it looked simpler. She held tight to the straps, and its false familiarity. Ngenet ran Ahase Miroe got in behind the controls and sealed the doors; the whine began to build in the space around them, muted this time, no louder than the rush of blood in her ears.

There was no sensation of movement when they lifted from the field, but as she saw Neith and her village fall away below she felt a sourceless wrench of pain, as though something inside her had been pulled apart. She pressed her hands against her chest, feeling the trefoil safely beneath her clothes, and sang a silent prayer.

The hovercraft banked sharply, heading out over the open sea.

Jerusha PalaThion stared out at the endless mirroring blue seeded with green island hummocks. She pictured it flowing past beneath the patrolcraft like waters under the earth, pictured herself caught in an endless loop of time, freed from the suffocating futility of her duty.... She blinked her eyes back into focus, glanced over at Gundhalinu where he sat reading behind the autopilot-locked controls. "How much longer till we get to Shotover Bay, BZ?"

He glanced up, down at the chronometer on the panel. "Still a couple of hours, Inspector."

She sighed, and shifted her feet again.

"You sure you don't want to read one of my books,

Inspector?" He held up one of the battered Old Empire fantasies that he spent half his off-duty time wallowing in. It was in Tiamatan; she read the title: *Tales of the Future Past.*

"No thanks. Being bored is more interesting." She flicked an iesta pod discreetly into the waste container. "How can an honest technocrat like you stand to read that crap, BZ? I'm surprised it doesn't cause brain damage."

He looked indignant. "These are based on solid archaeological data and analysis of sibyl Transfers. They're——" he grinned, the vacant bliss crept back into his eyes—"the next best thing to being there."

"Carbuncle's the next best thing to being there; and if that's any sample, good riddance to the good old days."

He made a disgusted noise. "That's exactly what I'm trying to get away from when I read. The real Carbuncle was——"

"Whatever it was, was probably just as bad. And furthermore, nobody gave a good goddamn about changing things then, any more than they do now." She settled back in her seat, frowning out at the blue water. "Sometimes I feel like a bottle thrown into the sea, carried endlessly on the tide, never reaching a shore. The message I carry, the meaning that I try to give my own life, is never realized . . . because no one is ever interested."

Gundhalinu put his book down, said softly, "Commander really knows how to try your sainted ancestors, doesn't he?"

She looked back at him.

"I could hear every word both of you said yesterday, clear out in the ward room." He grimaced. "You have more nerve than I have, Inspector."

"Maybe just a shorter fuse, after all these years." She pulled absently at the seal of her heavy coat. "Not that it made any difference." They were still on their way to Shotover Bay on the edge of Summer, as near to the antipodes of LiouxSked's universe as he could arrange on short notice. "A quarter around the planet in a patrolcraft, after a 'possible' smuggler report!"

93

" 'While the real criminals deal openly in Carbuncle and laugh in our faces.' " Gundhalinu quoted the end of it, from yesterday, with a sorrowful smile. "Yes, ma'am, it stinks." His hands tightened over the wheel. "But if we really can knock down somebody running embargoed goods to the locals . . . We've gotten a lot of heat about that lately."

"From the Queen." Jerusha's mouth twitched, remembering the royal display of hypocrisy that she had endured during her most recent official visit.

"I can't understand that, Inspector." He shook his head. "I thought she *wanted* all the high technology she could get her hands on for Tiamat; she's always talking up technological independence. She wouldn't care whether it was illegal. Hell, I expect she'd prefer it that way."

"She doesn't care about Tiamat or technology or anything else, except in relation to how they affect her own position. And some of the contraband goods have been getting in her way lately."

"Hard to imagine how." Gundhalinu changed position carefully behind the controls.

"Not all the customers of the trade are harmless cranks." She had read reports on smuggling in the Winter outback with interest and more than a little sympathy: The few independent smugglers' ships that managed to penetrate the Hegemony's planetary surveillance net could make a small fortune on a cargo of information tapes and tech manuals, power cells and hard-to-come-by components. There were always wealthy Winter nobles with an obsession about what made things shine and hidden labs on their island estates; self-styled mad scientists trying to crack the secrets of the atom and the universe. There were others privately stockpiling technology against the coming offworlder departure, too; planning to set up their own little fiefdoms, and never realizing that the Hegemony had its way of making sure they didn't. There were even a few offworlders who had gone native living out here in this wilderness of water, and not all of them liked the restrictions the Hedge put on their adopted home.

94

"Somebody's been harassing Starbuck and the Hounds when they go mer hunting, and I gather they've been having too much success. The mer population must be pretty well depleted by now; it must be cutting into the Queen's profits . . . and her measure of control over us. The interference involves some sophisticated jamming devices and comm gear, and there's only one place that it could be coming from."

"Hmm. So if we arrest any smugglers, we might get a lead on who's doing the harassing?" He shifted restlessly again.

"Maybe. I'm not holding my breath. This whole trip is a waste of energy, as far as I can see." *And that's just what LiouxSked intended it to be.* "Frankly, I hope we don't find anything. Does it shock you, BZ?" She grinned briefly at his expression. "You know, I hate to admit it, but sometimes I have trouble convincing myself these techrunners are doing anything wrong. Or that anybody who objects to cutting one species' life short so that another species can stretch out its own abnormally is in the wrong, either. Sometimes I think that everything that disgusts me about Carbuncle is tied to the water of life. That the city draws rottenness and corruption because its survival depends on a corrupt act."

"Would you still feel that way if you could afford immortality, Inspector?"

She looked up, hesitated. "I'd like to think I wouldn't feel any different. But I don't know. I really don't know."

Gundhalinu nodded, and shrugged. "I don't suppose either one of us will ever get to find out." He changed position again, glanced down at the chronometer.

"What's the matter, BZ?"

"Nothing, ma'am." He gazed out at the sea with stoic Kharemoughi propriety. "Something I should have done before we left the city." He sighed, and picked up his book.

95

11

"You travel awfully light. You sure you're going to get all the way to Carbuncle from here, with nothing but the clothes on your back?" Ngenet pressed a long finger into the lock on the hovercraft's door while Moon stood looking out over the harbor. They had covered the distance from Neith in hours instead of days. Her knees were weak with the unbelievable fact of her presence in this distant place.

"What? . . . Oh, I'll be all right. I'll crew with some trader from here—there must be a hundred ships in this bay!" Shotover Bay would have swallowed the harbor at Neith, and the village, and half of the island, with no trouble. The setting suns broke through clouds, scattered chips of ruby across the water surface; ships of all sizes rode high on the tide's flow. Some had an alienness of form that she couldn't put a name to. Some were mastless; she wondered whether they had been caught in a storm.

"A lot of Winter ships use engines, you know. A lot of them don't even use sail at all. Will they take you on?" Ngenet's brusque questioning tapped her on the shoulder again, as she suddenly understood why there were no masts. During their arrow's flight across the sea she had not learned much about him except that he didn't like to talk about himself; but his curt inquiries about her journey told her more than he knew.

"I'm not afraid of engines. And the work will be the same; there's only so much you can do on a ship." She smiled, hoping it was true. She ran her hand along the hovercraft's chill metal skin, struggling against the fresh awareness that it could have taken her to Sparks in less than a day. . . . Her smile faded.

96

"Well, you just make sure you find yourself a ship run by females. Some of the Winter men have picked up bad habits from the starport scum."

"I don't— Oh." She nodded, remembering why her grandmother had told her to stay off the traders' ships. "I'll do that." Even though she was certain that Ngenet was an offworlder, he spoke as if his people meant no more to him than Summers or Winters seemed to. She hadn't asked him why; she was no longer afraid of his surliness, but she wasn't ready to impose on it. "And I want to thank—"

He frowned across the harbor at the sunset. "No time for that. I'm half a day late for this meeting as it is. So you just—"

"Hey, honeycake, ditch that old man an' let us show you a *good* time!" One of the two Winter males who had been weaving toward them along the quay angled closer, grinning appreciatively, arms out. But as she reached for a biting reply Moon saw his expression change. He pulled his companion into a precarious veer away, muttered something close to the other's ear. They hurried on, looking back.

"H-how did they know?" Moon's hands pressed against her slicker front.

"Know what?" The frown was still on Ngenet's face, etching deeper, as he watched them go.

"That I'm a sibyl." She reached down inside and brought the trefoil out on its chain.

"You're a what?" He turned back to her, actually took the trefoil into his hands as if he had to prove its reality. He dropped it again, hastily. "Why didn't you tell me that?"

"Well, I didn't . . . I mean, I—"

"That settles it." He wasn't listening. "You're not staying here alone overnight. You can come with me; Elsie'll understand." His hand closed around her upper arm; he pulled her after him across the expanse of paving toward the quay's townside.

"Where are we going? Wait!" Moon stumbled after him with impotent anger as he strode toward the nearest street entrance. She saw light blossom at the top of a slender pole, and then another and another ahead of them, im-

mense flameless candles. "I don't understand." She dropped
her voice, "Do you believe in the Lady?"

"No, but I believe in you." He guided them onto a
sidewalk.

"You're an offworlder!"

"That's right, I am."

"But, I thought—"

"Don't ask, just walk. There's nothing strange about it."
He let go of her arm; she kept up with him.

"Aren't you afraid of me, then?"

He shook his head. "Just don't fall down and skin your
knee, or I might worry some." She looked at him blankly.

Behind them another hovercraft, with the markings of
the Hegemonic Police, drifted down toward a landing on
the quay. But he did not look back, and so he did not see it
settle beside his own.

"Where are we going?" Moon maneuvered around a
cluster of laughing sailors.

"To meet a friend."

"A woman friend? Won't she mind—"

"It's business, not pleasure. Just mind your own when
we get there."

Moon shrugged, and pushed her numbing hands into
the pockets of her pants. She could see their breath now, as
the temperature followed the sun down. She peered curiously into the assortment of one- and two-story building
fronts, more buildings than she had ever seen in one place,
but stolidly familiar in form. Mortared stone and wood
planking leaned on each other for support, and among
them she saw an occasional wall made of something that
was not really dried mud. Multiple layers of exotic noise
reached out to catch at her ears as they passed by one
tavern after another. "How *did* they know what I was, if
you didn't, Ngenet?"

"Call me Miroe. I don't think they did. I think they
probably just noticed that I was a lot bigger and a hell of a
lot more sober than either one of them."

"Hm." Moon fingered the scaling knife at her belt
thoughtfully; she felt the knots go out of her back muscles

as she realized that the eyes of everyone passing were not staying on her too often and too long.

Ngenet turned down a narrow side street; they stopped at last before a small, isolated tavern. Light rainbowed out onto the cobbles through colored glass; the peeling painted sign above the door read The Black Deeds Inn. He grunted. "Elsie always did have a peculiar sense of humor." Moon noticed a second sign that read Closed, but Ngenet pulled on the latch; the door opened, and they went inside.

"Hey, we're closed!" An immense balloon of woman pouring beer into a mug for no one glowered at them from the bar.

"I'm looking for Elsevier." Ngenet moved into the light.

"Oh, yeah?" The woman put the mug down and squinted at him. "I guess you are at that. What took you so long?"

"Engine trouble. Did she wait?"

"She's still in town, if that's what you mean. But she's out looking into—other arrangements, in case you decided not to show." The woman's buried eyes found Moon; she frowned.

Ngenet swore. "Damn her, she knows I'm dependable!"

"But she didn't know if maybe you'd been permanently delayed, if you take my meaning. Who's that?"

"A hitchhiker." Moon felt Ngenet's hand on her arm again, moved forward at his urging, reluctantly. "She won't make any trouble," cutting off the woman's indignation. "Will you?"

Moon looked up into his expression. "Me?" She shook her head, caught a whisper of a smile.

"I'm going out again to look for my friend. You can wait here until I get back." He pointed with his chin toward the room full of tables. "Then maybe we'll talk about Carbuncle."

"All right." She chose a table near the fireplace, went to it and sat down. Ngenet turned back toward the door.

"You know where to look?" the fat woman called. "Ask around the Club."

"I'll do that." He went out.

Moon sat in uncomfortable silence under the innkeeper's

dour gaze, running her fingers along the scars in the wooden tabletop. But at last the woman shrugged, wiping her own hands on her apron, picked up the glass of beer and brought it to the table. Moon flinched slightly as it came down in front of her, froth spilling out onto the ring-marked wood. The woman billowed away again without speaking, did something to a featureless black box behind the bar. Someone began to sing abruptly, in the middle of a song, the middle of a word, with pieces of the same rhythmic stridency Moon had heard in the streets as accompaniment.

Moon started, glanced back over her shoulder to find the room as empty as before. Emptier—she watched the innkeeper disappear up the stairs, taking another mug of beer with her. Moon's eyes came back to the black box. She had a sudden smiling image of it stuffed full of sound, like a keg or a sack of meal. She took a swallow of her beer, grimaced: kelp beer, sour and badly brewed. Setting down the mug, she pulled off her slicker. In the fireplace a solitary chunk of metal glowed red hot like a bar of iron in a smithy's forge. She twisted in her seat, her fingers exploring the animal faces capping the chair back while she absorbed the heat and the music. Her foot began to tap time as a kind of pleasant compulsion moved her body. The harmonies were complicated, the sound was loud and throbbing, the voice trilled meaningless noise. The effect was nothing like the music that Sparks made with his flute ... but something in it was compelling, distantly akin to the secret song of the choosing-place.

Moon closed her eyes, sipping beer; let her mind separate out the memory of all that had gone wrong from all that was right between herself and Sparks, as she listened to the music that he had always heard with a different ear. *They would talk about Carbuncle*, Ngenet had said. Would he take her there, then? Or would he only try to change her mind? No one would change her mind ... but she thought she could change his. She could use his concern about her to make him take her there, she was sure of it. She could be there tomorrow. ... She began to smile.

100

But was it right? Some part of her mind stirred uneasily. *How was it wrong?* Ngenet wanted to help her; she knew he did. And she didn't even know why Sparks needed her: She imagined him sick or hungry, moneyless, friendless, starving. A day, an hour, could make a difference.... Lady, every minute that she could spare him any sorrow or pain was important, more important than anything else.

A noise at the back of the room made her open her eyes. She looked toward the doorway at the rear of the room, felt her eyes widen, and widen again, as her mind refused to accept the information they took in. It was alive, and moving. It stood on two legs like a human being, but it's feet were broad and webbed, its motion was the fluid shifting of sea grass in the underwater swell. The gray-green, sexless body, glistening with an oily film, was naked except for a woven belt hung with unidentifiable shapes; the thing's arms split into half a dozen whiplike tendrils. Nacreous, pupilless eyes fixed on her like the eyes of a sea spirit.

Moon stood up, her mouth too dry for the sounds she was trying to make; she put the chair between herself and the nightmare thing as she reached for her knife. But at her motion the creature gave a guttural cough and darted back through the doorway, disappearing from her sight before she could really believe that it had ever been there.

Standing in its place was a man she had never seen before, half again her own age, with a stiff crest of blond hair falling over one eye. He was wearing a fisherman's parka, but his pants were a lurid green in the flameless brightness of the room. "Don't go for it, young mistress, I've got you marked." He stretched out his arm, she saw something unidentifiable in his hand. "Toss it out onto the floor, now, gently does it."

She finished drawing her knife, uncertain about the threat. He moved his hand impatiently, and she tossed the curved blade out. He came forward far enough to pick it up.

"What do you want?" The shrillness of it told her just how afraid she really was.

"Come on out, Silky." The man glanced toward the

101

doorway, instead. Unintelligible hissing sounds were the response; the man smiled humorlessly. "Yes, precisely as delighted to meet you as you were to find her here. Come out and give her a better look."

The creature came cautiously through into the room again; Moon's hands tightened over the animal heads on the chair back. The thing made her think suddenly of a family crest come to life. "I—I don't have any money."

The man looked at her blankly, laughed. "Oh, I see. Then we're all in the same boat, at the moment. But not for the same reason. So just stay calm, and you won't get hurt."

"Cress! What in the world is going on here?" A third stranger entered the room behind him, human again, but just as unexpected. Moon saw the small plump woman with blue-black skin and silvery hair stop, hands clasping in surprise. "My dear, you'll never get a date by holding the girl at gunpoint," not quite smiling as she studied Moon back.

The blond man didn't laugh this time. "I don't know what she knows, but she shouldn't be here, Elsie."

"Obviously. Who are you, girl? What are you doing here?" The words asked her to answer as a simple courtesy, but the voice was steel.

"Friend—I'm a friend of Ngenet Miroe. Are you Elsevier, are you the one he came to see?" Moon took the initiative as she saw the answers start to register. "He went to look for you. I can go find him—" She glanced toward the door.

"That won't be necessary." The woman waved her hand; the man lowered his weapon, pushed it into the pocket where her knife had gone. Both their faces eased a little. "We'll wait with you." The spirit-thing hissed an almost human-sounding question. "Silky would like to know what kept him."

"Engine trouble," Moon repeated mechanically, shifted her weight, still keeping the chair between them.

"Ah. That explains it." But she thought something in the old woman's voice was still not entirely satisfied. "Well, no need for us to stand up while we wait, is there? My old bones creak at the thought. Sit down, dear, we'll all just sit by the fire and get acquainted until he comes back. Cress, bring us some beers too, won't you?"

Moon watched in dismay as the woman and the nightmare came toward the table. But the creature crouched on the hearth just out of kicking range, looking down, its body glistening in the heater's radiance. Its flat tentacles traced the patterns of the hearthstones with rhythmic, hypnotic motions; some of the tentacles were maimed, distorted by old scars. The woman pulled out a chair and sat down beside her with a smile of seeming encouragement. She unfastened a slicker several sizes too large, revealing a plain one-piece garment, its orange color as vivid as the green of the man's pants. "You'll have to excuse Silky if he doesn't join us at the table; he's not very fond of strangers, I'm afraid."

Moon moved slowly around her own chair and sat down. The man came back with three mugs of beer and set one down on the hearth. Moon watched the tracing tentacles of the sea-demon caress the mug, wrap it, and lift it to drink. She picked up her own mug and drank, in long gulps. The man sat down on the other side of her, grinned. "You sure put away the brew, young mistress."

The old woman clucked disapprovingly, sipping at her own mug. "Never mind. Tell us about yourself, dear. I don't think you've told us your name. I am Elsevier, of course, and this is Cress. And that is Silky, my late husband's—business partner. Silky is not his real name, obviously. We simply can't say his real name. He is a dillyp, from Tsieh-pun; from another world, as we are," with quiet reassurance. "Are you one of Miroe's—colleagues?"

"I'm Moon. I . . ." She hesitated, aware of their hesitations; still not sure of them, not sure whether a lie or the truth would be a worse choice. "I just met him. He gave me a ride."

"And then he brought you here?" Cress leaned forward, frowning. "Just like that. What did he tell you?"

"Nothing." Moon drew away from him, toward the old

103

woman. "And I don't care, really. I'm just going to Carbuncle. He—said that you'd understand." She turned to Elsevier, met the astringent indigo eyes set in a web of age lines.

"Understand what?"

Moon took a deep breath, pulled the sibyl sign out of her sweater. "This."

Elsevier started visibly; Cress sat back in his chair. The thing on the hearth hissed a question, and Cress said, "She's a sibyl!"

"Well . . . !" Almost a sigh. "We are honored." Elsevier glanced at the others, Cress nodded. "I understand that this half of Tiamat is not the best place for a sibyl. That would be like Miroe, to go getting involved." She smiled suddenly, deeply, but with great weariness. "No, it's nothing—simply that seeing you who are so young and so wise makes me feel old and foolish."

Moon looked down at her fingers twisting on the wood. "I am only a vessel for the Lady's wisdom." She repeated the traditional words self-consciously. These were offworlders, and yet their reaction, like Miroe's, was the respect-that-was-almost-awe a Summer would feel. "I—thought that no offworlder believed in the Lady's power. Everyone says you make the Winters hate sibyls. Why don't you hate me?"

"You don't know?" Cress said, incredulous. He looked at Elsevier, around at the alien on the hearth. "She doesn't know what she is."

"Of course she doesn't, Cress. The Hedge wants this world kept in the technological dark, and sibyls are beacons of knowledge. But only if someone knows how to use their light." Elsevier sipped her beer thoughtfully. "We could bring our own little Millennium, our own golden age, to this world. You know, Cress, we may just be the most dangerous people ever to visit this planet. . . ."

Moon half frowned. "What do you mean, I don't know what I am? I'm a sibyl. I answer questions."

Elsevier nodded. "But not the right ones. Why are you

going to Carbuncle, Moon, if you only expect to be met by hatred there?"

"I—have to find my cousin."

"That's the only reason?"

"It's the only thing that matters." *He belongs with me.* She looked down at the trefoil.

"Then it's not just a kinsman you're looking for, is it?"

"No."

"A lover?" very gently.

She nodded, swallowing to ease the sudden cramp in her throat. "The only one I'll ever love. Even if I never find him . . ."

Elsevier put out an age-stiffened hand, patted her own. "Yes, dear, I know. Sometimes you find one that you'd walk barefoot through the fires of hell for. What makes that one so different from all the rest, I wonder . . . ?"

Moon shook her head. *And what made him different from me?* "Are you from Carbuncle?" She looked up. "Maybe you've seen him there. He has red hair . . ."

Elsevier shook her head. "No, alas. We're not from the city. We're just—visiting, temporarily." She glanced toward the door, as if she suddenly remembered why they were waiting.

"Oh . . . What did you mean, about not asking the right ques—"

The door of the inn burst open with enough force to slam it back against the wall. Moon looked up with the others, her question left hanging in the air.

Two figures came in out of the darkness: a slender man of medium height, and a tall sturdy woman, both offworlders; heavily dressed in matched clothing, wearing helmets. Holding weapons.

"Blues!" Cress muttered, his mouth barely moving. Elsevier's hand rose to her throat, drawing the slicker together over the orange beneath it. She looked down at the darkness of her skin, let the hand drop.

"What is it?" Moon controlled a desire to leap up as Silky took refuge beside her. "Who are they?"

"No one you should know any better," Elsevier said mildly. She picked up her mug before she looked back at the intruders. "Well, Inspector. This is unexpected. You're a long way from home tonight."

"Not half as far from home as you are, I expect." The woman moved forward, searching them with her eyes, the weapon still showing in her fist.

"I'm afraid I don't know what you mean." Elsevier glittered with controlled indignation. "This is a private party of responsible Hegemony citizens, and I consider your bursting in like this highly—"

"Spare me, techrunner." The woman gestured with her gun, her mouth set. "Your ship was spotted coming in, you're on this planet illegally. I charge you further with suspicion of smuggling contraband items. Stand up, all of you, and put your hands on top of your heads."

Moon sat frozen, looking from Elsevier to Cress and back; but their eyes were only for the strangers. The trefoil cut into her tightening hand; understanding just enough to be afraid, she stuffed it into her sweater.

But the uniformed woman spotted the motion and came forward; as she came Moon saw the frown on her face change into the same incredulity that had shown on the faces of the two Winters on the quay. The man behind her began to move watchfully to the side, as Elsevier and Cress got to their feet together. Moon felt Elsevier nudge her elbow and rose awkwardly, her chair grating on the floor.

"Now, Silky!" Elsevier murmured, jerking Moon back as the alien bolted away from the table, scrambled toward the doorway they had all come through. Moon came up against the chimney wall as the two officers wavered between targets, as Cress swept a mug from the table and hurled it, as the mug struck the light fixture suspended from the rafters and smashed it. A shower of electric sparks and foam rained down in the sudden darkness.

"Run for it!"

"BZ! Nail him!"

"Moon, stay out of this!" Moon felt Elsevier shove her

ungently away, stumbled blindly over her own chair and fell against the table. There was noise and a cry behind her; dimly she saw the woman officer leap to catch Elsevier by the slicker. Moon's hand closed over another mug on the tabletop; she brought it around and down with all her strength on the woman officer's arm and heard a gasp of pain. Elsevier broke free, herded her ahead toward the way out. "Never, never hit a Blue, my dear—" breathlessly, next to her ear. "But thank you. Now run!"

Moon bolted through the doorway, her mind a white blur like the brightly lit room beyond, then through another door into a dark alley.

"This way!" Cress materialized beside her, pointing left. "That's a dead end. Elsie?"

"Here." The door banged behind them. "Don't talk about it, get to the LB!"

They ran; Moon caught the old woman's hand, lending her strength and speed. Up ahead she saw the alien in a band of reddish-gold starlight, disappearing into a bolt-hole of shadow; behind them she heard the door fly open and a shout of discovery. Her free hand went dead suddenly up to the wrist; panic gave her wings.

Cress slid to a halt where she had seen the alien disappear. She saw a night-gilded board fence, saw him duck through the space between two rotten planks. She followed him through, pulling Elsevier with her, and almost fell over a peninsula of piled driftwood on the other side.

"Get to the LB!" Cress waved them on frantically. "I'll plug the gap."

"This way." Elsevier pulled at her arm, started away through the stacks and mounds of salvage and flotsam. Moon went with her, looking back as Cress dragged the spiny-armed corpse of a tree-shrub up against the gap. A limb caught in his parka as he turned away and jerked him back; she saw him struggle free before a pile of moldy sails cut off her view. Elsevier stumbled over some obstacle in the shadows beside her, and she put out a steadying arm.

Before them now across the shadow and gold of the star-washed yard she saw a lens of battered metal lying in the midden. A hatch stood open in its side, and a ramp extended to the ground. "What is it?"

"Sanctuary," Elsevier gasped. They reached the ramp and went up it together to find Silky waiting at the top. "Switched on?"

The alien grunted affirmation, gestured with a tentacle.

"Then strap in, we're getting out of here." Elsevier leaned against a bulkhead, a hand pressed against her heart. "Cress?" She looked toward the hatchway, but it showed them only junk and smoldering sky.

Moon turned back, leaned out to look down the ramp. Cress came running; but as she watched he tripped and fell, lay stunned on the ground for a space of heartbeats. When he pushed himself up at last and came on, she thought of a man running underwater, with every motion resisted. "Here he comes!"

He reached the foot of the ramp, stopped, and looked up it for a long moment with his arms wrapped across his stomach before he began to climb. Behind him she saw one of their pursuers round the heap of sails. "Cress, hurry!"

But even as she called to him he slowed, midway up the ramp, his eyes glazing with despair.

"Come on!"

He shook his head, swaying where he stood.

Across the lot she saw both police officers now, saw one of them taking aim at him, heard a voice shout "Hold it!"

Moon pushed out and down the ramp, grabbed the flapping sleeve of his parka and dragged him forward through the hatch. The ramp telescoped upward behind them, and the door hissed shut, hurting her ears with pressure-change. Cress clutched at the frame of the inner doorway as Moon found her balance, letting him go. Her hand was still crippled with a strange paralysis; she looked down at it and gave a small, disbelieving cry as she saw it smeared with blood.

"Cress, get up front and—" Elsevier stopped as Cress

crumpled to the floor. Moon saw the vivid stain on his jacket and knew that the blood was not her own.

"Oh, my gods, Cress!"

"What happened?" Moon dropped to her knees beside him, reaching out.

He struck her reddened hand aside. "No!" She saw the hilt of her own scaling knife protruding from the pouch pocket at the center of the jacket's spreading stain. "Don't touch it . . . I'll gush." Moon pulled back, folded her hands against her sides. "Elsevier?" He looked past her.

"Cress, *how* did it happen?" Elsevier let herself down stiffly on his other side, laying her hand against his cheek. Silky appeared in the doorway behind her.

Cress laughed through white lips. "Should've let the young mistress keep her dagger . . . fell on the goddamn thing, running. Put me in the freezer, Elsie, I'm h-hurting . . ." He struggled to push himself up, groaned through clenched teeth as they hauled him to his feet.

"Silky, get to the controls."

Silky moved ahead of them as they guided Cress through into the next chamber and let him down onto a level couch in the cramped space.

"Putting her knife in your pocket! Dear boy, that was incredibly stupid, you know." Elsevier kissed her fingers and laid them lightly above his eyes.

"I'm an astrogator, not . . . not a hired killer. What do I . . . know about it?" He coughed; a trickle of blood appeared at the corner of his mouth, ran down his cheek toward his ear.

Elsevier stepped back as a smoke-colored translucent cone lowered over the couch, shutting him away from their view. "Sleep well." It had the sound of a benediction; but she shook her head, looking up into Moon's unspoken question. "No. This will keep him alive until we can get him to help." Her face changed. "If we can even get out of the atmosphere before those Blues call down heaven's wrath. Strap in, dear, the acceleration may be unpleasant your first time." She pushed past, settled into a padded,

109

upright seat before a panel of controls. The alien was settled in a second seat, tentacles suspended above a board of lights. In front of them a wide, thickly glassed port showed her another view of the junkyard. Moon took the third upright couch and fastened the straps uncertainly. The alien made a guttural query.

"Well, what else am I going to do?" Elsevier said sharply. "We can't leave her to the police; not a sibyl. Not after she fought to save me—you know what they'd do . . . Lift!"

Moon leaned forward, listening, was driven back into the seat by the crest of an unseen wave. She gasped in surprise, gasped again as the pressure went on increasing, squeezing the air out of her lungs. She fought against it like a drowner, with no more success; collapsed into the cushioning curves with a whimper of disbelief. Between the forward seats she could no longer see the junkyard or any ground at all, but only stars. As she watched, the moon fell like a stone past the window and disappeared. She shut her eyes, felt herself being sucked down into a whirlpool of nightmare, bottomless and black.

But among the tumbled waters of dark panic she found the memory of another blackness, more utter, more absolute than any she would ever know—the black heart of the Transfer. *The Transfer* . . . this was like the Transfer. She clung to that anchor, felt the solid weight of familiarity slow the spiraling of her fear. She centered her concentration on the disciplined rhythms of mind and body that kept the narrow thread of her awareness tied to reality . . . slowly she settled into enduring.

She opened her eyes again, saw that the stars were still outside; rolled her head to look over at the wall of blinking lights and dials beside her own seat. She did not try to touch them. She became aware of Elsevier's voice, strained, almost inaudible, and the alien's responses; one was as unintelligible to her as the other.

". . . Checking. No tracking alerts going out yet. Hope that they hadn't relayers . . . by the time they call it in we may clear. . . . Are the shields green?"

110

Silky responded, in unintelligible alien speech.

"I hope it too . . . but stay ready to shift power."

(Response.)

"Affirmative, we're damped. They look for inbound runners, anyway . . . they don't look behind them enough . . . I pray they don't."

(Response.)

A weak chuckle. "Of course . . . Time elapsed?"

Moon closed her eyes again, comforted, letting the words go on by. They were flying, somehow, in this metal-bound cabin; but it was nothing like her flight with Ngenet. She wondered why, and how, wondered dimly whether this was anything like being on an offworlder starship. . . . Her eyes came open suddenly. "Elsevier!"

"Yes. . . . Are you all right, Moon?"

"What are we doing? . . . Where are we going?" She gasped for air.

"We're leaving. . . . Time elapsed?"

(Response.)

"Out of the well!" A squeezed laugh of triumph. "Cutting energy . . . we'd better save what we've got left for rendezvous."

The pressure vise dissipated around her, as abruptly as it had come. Moon stretched her arms in release. With the crushing weight gone from her body, she felt as though she had no substance at all, rising like a bubble through the waters of the sea . . . rising from the padded couch against the restraining straps. She looked down at herself wildly, clutched the straps with her hands.

"Ohh, Silky. I'm getting too old for this. This is no way for a civilized person to make a living."

(Response.)

"Of course it's been the principle of the thing! You don't think I would have carried on TJ's work just for money? And certainly not for the thrill of it." She *tsk*ed. "But there won't be any more trips, anyway. We won't make a brass cavvie from this one, we've still got all the goods on board. . . . Ah, poor Miroe! The gods know what's become

111

of him." There was the sound of a catch releasing; Moon saw Elsevier's silvery head begin to rise up past the seat back. "But we never shall, now." Elsevier turned to look back at her. "Moon, are you——"

"Don't be afraid!" Moon raised wondering eyes. "It's the Lady's presence. The room is full of the Sea, that's why we're floating. . . . It's a miracle."

Elsevier smiled at her, a little sadly. "No, my dear—only the absence of one. We're beyond the reach of your goddess, beyond the grasp of your world. There's simply no gravity this far out to hold you down. Come forward and see what I mean."

Moon unstrapped uncertainly, and pushed herself up. Elsevier lunged and caught her by the leg before she crashed into the cone that hung, like the one that protected Cress, above her own couch. "Gently!" Elsevier drew her forward to the window and pointed down. Below them lay the curve of Tiamat's sphere, a foam-flecked swell of translucent blue breaking against the wall of stars.

In her heart she had known what she would find; but as she drifted to the window, the vision surpassed anything she had imagined, and she could only breathe, "Beautiful . . . beautiful . . . ." She pressed her hands against the cold transparency.

"Wait until you pass through the Black Gate, and see what lies on the other side."

"Oh, yes . . ." A dark seed of doubt sprouted in her mind. She pulled her eyes away, turning her head. "The Black Gate? But that's how the offworlders go to other worlds. . . ." She looked back and out, at her entire world that had seemed so immense and so varied lying below her feet like a blue glass fishing float. "No . . . no, I can't go through the Gate with you. I have to go to Carbuncle. I have to find Sparks." She pushed firmly away from the window, caught herself on the back of Silky's seat. "Will you take me back down, now? Can you, would you put me—ashore at the starport?"

"Take you back down?" A frown creased the space between Elsevier's blue-violet eyes; she pressed her hands against her lips. "Oh, Moon, my dear . . . I was afraid that you hadn't understood. You see, we can't take you back down. They'll track us, and we're low on charge besides— there's no way we can go back now. I'm afraid that when I told you about the Gate I wasn't offering you a choice."

——12——

"You're the owner of this vehicle?" Jerusha stood beside the hovercraft on the quay, her breath frosting in the frigid night air. She frowned her bad humor at the big man who leaned against it with the same false self-possession the techrunners in the bar had displayed. Gundhalinu stood beside her, rising and settling on his heels with barely controlled frustration.

"I am, as I plainly have every right to be." His voice was like crunching gravel. The man gestured abruptly at his face; the light was poor, but he was obviously an off-worlder—from D'doille, she guessed, or maybe Number Four. "Have you come all the way from Carbuncle just to give me a parking ticket, Inspector?"

Jerusha grimaced, using her irritation to disguise her discomfort. She kept her arms crossed tightly against her heavy coat, nursing the one that the girl in the bar had struck with a mug. Her right forearm was a white-hot star, burning furiously at the center of her body's shivering universe; the pain nauseated her, only the intensity of her anger kept her mind clear. An old woman and a handful of misfits had made an ass of her, and eating at her was the suspicion that it was because she'd wanted them to. Damn it, her place was to enforce the law, not rearrange it to suit herself! And at least this one hadn't gotten away. "No, Citizen Ngenet, we've come to accuse you of attempting to buy embargoed goods."

His face was the picture of resentful surprise. *Gods,*

what I wouldn't give to just once see one of them put up his hands and say, "I admit it"!

"I'd like to know on what evidence you're making the accusation. You're not going to find—"

"I know we won't. You didn't have time to make the deal. But you were seen in the presence of one of the offworlders who escaped us."

"What are you talking about?"

She could almost believe that he didn't know. "Female, age roughly seventeen standard years, pale hair and skin."

"She's no smuggler!" Ngenet pushed away from his craft, glaring.

"She was with them when we went to make the arrest," Gundhalinu said. "She struck the inspector, she ran with the rest."

"She's a Summer from the Windwards, her name is Moon Dawntreader. I gave her a ride, and I left her at the inn because—" He broke off, Jerusha wondered what he was afraid to say. "She wouldn't know anything about it."

"Then why did she help them escape?"

"What the hell would you do, if you were fresh from Summer and two offworlders burst in on you with guns?" He paced two agitated steps between them. "What in the name of a thousand gods would you think, if you were her? You didn't hurt her—?"

Jerusha grimaced again, twisted it into a smile. "Ask it the other way around." She wondered with more interest why he was trying to protect the girl. *His mistress?*

"You said they all escaped?"

Gundhalinu laughed sourly. "For a man who doesn't know anything, you're damned concerned about what happened tonight."

Ngenet ignored him, waiting.

"They all escaped. Their craft cleared Tiamat space without damage." Jerusha saw the expression on his face turn into something that was not relief.

"All? You mean she went with them?" The words came out as though each one was alien on his tongue.

114

"That's right." She nodded, tightening her good hand over her other elbow, pinching off the nerve paths. "They took her off. You mean to tell me she really was an innocent bystander, a local?"

Ngenet turned away, struck the frost-rimed windshield of the hovercraft with a gloved fist. "My fault—"

"And mine. If we'd held onto them she would have been all right." *And that's what happens when you start trying to change the rules.*

"What was she to you, Citizen Ngenet?" Gundhalinu asked. "More than a passing stranger." Not a question.

"She's a sibyl." He looked back at them. "It doesn't matter if you know that now."

Jerusha raised her eyebrows. "A sibyl?" The wind off the bay clutched her in icy talons. "Why—would that make a difference to us?"

"Come now, Inspector." His voice turned bitter, like the wind.

"We're law officers. We enforce the law"—*liar*—"and the law protects sibyls, even on Tiamat."

"Like it protects the mers? Like it protects this world from progress?"

She saw Gundhalinu stiffen like a hunter scenting his prey. "How long have you been living in the outback, Citizen Ngenet?"

"All my life," with a kind of pride. "And my father before me, and his father. . . . This is my homeworld."

"And you don't like the way we're running it?" Gundhalinu made it a challenge.

"Damn right I don't! You try to choke the life out of this world's future, you let a maggot like Starbuck wipe his boots on you while he slaughters innocent beings for the gratification of a few filthy-rich bastards who want to live forever. You make a mockery of 'law' and 'justice'—"

"And so do you, Citizen." Gundhalinu stepped forward; Jerusha could see everything that had locked into place inside his head. "Inspector, it seems likely to me that this man is involved in more serious criminal activities than just smuggling. I think we ought to take him back to the city—"

115

"And charge him with what? Behaving like an arrogant fool?" She shook her head. "We have no evidence that would justify that."

"But he—" Gundhalinu gestured, accidentally struck her arm.

"Damn it, Sergeant, I said we're letting him go!" She lost his startled face in a burst of painstars. Blinking, she refocused on Ngenet instead. "But that doesn't mean I'm letting you off completely, Ngenet. Your presence here and your attitude are questionable enough to warrant my revoking your permit to operate this hovercraft. I'm impounding it. We're taking it back to the city." A trickle of perspiration crept down the side of her face, burning cold.

"You can't do that!" Ngenet straightened away from the hovercraft's door, towering over her. "I'm a citizen of the Hegemony—"

"And required to obey me." She lifted her head to glare back at him. "You're a citizen of Tiamat, by your own choice. If that's what you want, then you can live like one."

"How am I supposed to run my plantation?"

"Just like any other Winter. Use a ship, deal with traders. You'll get along fine, if that's all you really need it for. . . . Or would you rather take the trip to Carbuncle with us, and have your plantation electronically searched for contraband?" She watched him struggle against speech, and was gratified.

"All right. Take the vehicle. Just let me get my things."

"That won't be necessary."

He looked back at her.

"I'll drop you off at your plantation before I take the craft to Carbuncle. . . . BZ, you'll pilot the patroller home."

Gundhalinu nodded; she saw some of his disappointment shaken loose in the motion. "You want me to tandem you, Inspector?"

"No. I don't think Citizen Ngenet is going to do anything stupid. He doesn't strike me as a stupid man."

Ngenet made a sound that was not really a laugh.

"We might as well get started." She bent her head grimly at the patrolcraft. *It's going to be a long trip.*

"Yes, ma'am. See you in Carbuncle, Inspector." Gundhalinu saluted and walked away.

She watched him get into the patrolcraft, watched it rise from the stone terrace of the quay. The sky was clouding over again; she shivered more violently. *At least Carbuncle has central heating* . . . suddenly longing for the touch of a warm wind fragrant with sillipha, the endless summer afternoon of her childhood on Newhaven. "Well, Citizen Ngenet—"

Ngenet reached out, his hand closed gently but firmly over her aching arm. She gasped, stiffening with surprise and sudden alarm.

"Ah," as he held up his other hand in a cautionary gesture. He let her go. "I just wanted to be sure. The Summer girl hurt you, Inspector. Maybe you better let me see how badly."

"It's nothing. Get in." She looked away from him, jaw tight.

He shrugged. "Feel free to be a martyr if you like. But it doesn't impress me. As you say, I'm not a stupid man."

She looked back. "I prefer to wait until I can see a medic at the starport."

"I am a qualified medic." He turned, pressed his hand against a seal on the side of the hovercraft. A storage compartment opened, but in the poor light she could not see what was inside. He removed a dark satchel, set it on the ground and pulled it open. "Of course," he glanced up with a sardonic smile, "you'd probably consider me to be a vet. But the diagnostic tools are the same."

She frowned slightly, not understanding, but let him take her hand and run the scanner along her arm.

"Hm." He released her hand again. "Fractured radius. I'll splint it temporarily, and give you something for the pain."

She stood silently while he tightened and sealed the rigid tube of the splint around her arm. He pressed a small,

117

spongy pad into the palm of her ungloved hand; she felt blissful nothingness begin to extinguish the fires up her arm, and sighed. "Thank you." She watched him put the bag away, wondered suddenly whether he saw her as a gullible female. "You know this isn't going to change my mind about anything, Ngenet."

· He resealed the compartment, said brusquely. "I didn't expect it to. I was indirectly responsible for your getting hurt; I don't like that. Besides"—he faced her again—"I expect I owe you something."

"What do you mean?"

"For offering me a choice of the lesser of two evils. If that overeager sergeant of yours had his way, I expect I'd end up a deportee."

She smiled faintly. "Not if you have nothing to hide."

"Who among us really has nothing to hide, Inspector PalaThion?" He unsealed the hovercraft's door, watching her with a faint smile of his own. "Do you?"

She circled the craft, waited until he unlatched the far door and settled in carefully. "You'll be the last to know, Ngenet, either way." She fastened the straps one-handed.

He said nothing, but went on smiling as he started the power unit. And all at once she was not so certain that he would be the last one.

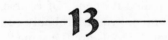

"... So his presence there gives us reason to think the man may be involved in the interference with the mer hunts. I personally confiscated his hovercraft, though; I don't think he'll give your hunters much trouble without it."

Arienrhod rested her head against the flower-fragrant pillow that protected her from the cold back of the throne; listened to the inspector give her tight-lipped report with much more interest than she allowed herself to show. She read the look the woman gave Starbuck as she finished speaking, and sensed more than saw his reaction to it. He had driven off the arrogant boor who was PalaThion's assistant some time back, much to his amusement; she had enjoyed his graphic fantasies of what he would do to the woman if he had the chance. She had no particular interest in Starbuck's past, but it intruded into the present in ways that sometimes surprised her . . . though he rarely surprised her in any way at all any more. "Who is this man, Inspector? Why didn't you arrest him, if you knew he was guilty?" Her voice was sharp with the need to uncover a deeper mystery that shrouded Shotover Bay.

"'I didn't have sufficient evidence," PalaThion said ritually, as though it was something she had repeated over and over. "Since he is an offworlder, he's under Hegemony jurisdiction in any case, Your Majesty, so his identity wouldn't be of use to you." Her expression became a shade more stubborn.

"Of course, Inspector." *And I can find it out easily enough, offworlder.* She glanced down at the foot of the dais, at the bright, burnished head of Sparks Dawntreader where he sat uneasily on the steps. She had sent the crowd of jabbering nobles away on the inspector's arrival, and for the same private reasons had ordered the boy to stay. Pala-Thion had stared at him with astonishment showing. And Arienrhod had seen Sparks's body stiffen with what might have been pride as PalaThion bent her head in a brief acknowledgement of his new station. "Did you also see the Summer girl to whom this offworlder of yours gave a ride?"

PalaThion started visibly; she had not mentioned the girl. "Yes . . . I did, Your Majesty." Her left hand moved unconsciously to press the thin sheath of cast on her right arm. "But she didn't stay to be questioned. She ran off with the smugglers when they made their break. They—got away from us, as you know," she glanced down, "and they took her off-planet with them."

"No!" Arienrhod pushed forward, the one word escaped between her teeth before she could trap it. *Gone, gone . . . ?*

119

She loosened her fists, sat back again fluidly as she felt three sets of eyes move to her face. The inspector's brown, deep-set ones narrowed with calculation; Arienrhod realized that she must have noticed the remarkable resemblance. But PalaThion only looked down again, as though she were unable to follow the suspicions through to any logical end.

"Do you know the girl's name? I have reason to believe that she may have been a—kinswoman." Let PalaThion make of that what she wished.

"Her name was Moon Dawntreader, Your Majesty."

Expecting it, she kept her reaction under control this time, felt the surge of emotion sing inside her body. But below her the boy, hearing the name and understanding at last, dropped his flute. It rolled down from the step onto the carpet at PalaThion's feet, soundlessly, leaving the silence of the hall perfect. PalaThion looked at the boy for a long moment before she looked up.

"I'm sorry this happened, Your Majesty." She glanced at the boy again as she said it, as though she had realized there was some tie between them. "I—don't think anybody meant it to happen that way."

Not half as sorry as I am. Arienrhod twisted a ring with her thumb. *And not half as sorry as you will be, offworlder.* "You are dismissed, Inspector."

PalaThion saluted and walked quickly away toward the Hall of the Winds, her red cape flaring behind her. Arienrhod's hands tightened again, trembling. Sparks stood, picked up his flute, struggling with grief and bewilderment. "Your Majesty, I—may I go . . . ?" He kept his leaf-green eyes downcast; his voice was barely a whisper.

"Yes, go. I'll call you when I want you." She lifted a hand. He left the dais without making the proper bow. She watched him leave, forgetting her, with his hair like new blood against the snow-white carpet: a wounded thing needing a hole to hide in, hurt, abandoned, vulnerable . . . beautiful.

Ever since he had come here she had felt something asleep within her stir. A freshening, a renewal, a desire . . .

But not desire in the way she knew it for Starbuck, or any of a hundred other lovers past or present—for that soulless flesh hungry to answer power's insatiable needs. When she looked at Sparks Dawntreader, yes, she ached to have that slender, supple body beside her on the bed, longed to touch it and feel it against her own. But when she looked at him she also saw his face, the freshness of his wonder, the innocence of his gratitude... those things that she had learned to despise in others and deny in herself through her long Winter's reign. He was the beloved of Moon—her otherness, the daughter of her mind—and half-man, half-boy, his presence breathed on the dim embers of her own long-forgotten girlhood and stirred a warmth in the cold halls of her soul.

But he had not responded when she had let him know subtly, and then not so subtly, that she wanted him. He had retreated, mumbling and seeming half-afraid, behind the shield of his pledge to her other self. There he had remained, unyielding as stone against all temptation, while the heat of her unexpected frustration fed the fires inside her. But now, now that they had both lost their future.... She willed him to turn back, to look at her once.

He stopped, a lonely figure on a field of snow, and looked back. A kind of haunted realization filled his face as she held him there with her eyes, thinking, *We have both lost her....*

He turned away again at last, went on to the spiraling stair that led to the upper levels.

"Now that you've lost the fish, maybe you'll throw the bait back."

She twisted to look at Starbuck, feeling the razor edge of envy that was always on his voice when he was talking about the boy.

"Get rid of that Summer weakling and his damned whistle, Arienrhod. The sight and sound of him makes me want to puke. Throw him back on the Street where you found him, before I—"

"Before you what, Starbuck? Are you commanding *me* now?" She leaned toward him, lifting her scepter.

121

He drew back slightly, dropped his eyes. "No. Just asking, Arienrhod. Just asking you—get rid of him. You don't need him, now that the girl's—"

She brought the scepter down sharply on the hand that rested on the throne arm; he gave a yelp of startled pain. "I told you never to speak of it." She pressed a hand against her eyes, shutting him out of her view. She had lost the gamble; she had lost it! Her plan, her future, all were gone, on this one final miscasting of fate. Nine seeds that she had succeeded in planting, one flawless blossom that had grown up from them . . . and now that one was gone. Because of the interfering incompetence of those same offworlders whose cycle of tyranny she had hoped to break. If they had known what she was planning they could not have ruined her plans more neatly. And now—what was she going to do now? She would have to begin again, with a new plan, and one that would have to be less subtle, less fragile . . . and so potentially more dangerous to her own position. But it would take time to search out the possibilities. . . .

And in the meantime she could have her revenge on the ones responsible. Yes, she could. "LiouxSked. I want him to pay for this, I want the Blues to suffer. I want him taken care of, gotten rid of."

"You want the Commander of Police killed, over this?" Starbuck's voice betrayed a small astonishment.

"No." She shook her head, shifting her rings on her fingers. "That's too easy. I want him ruined, I want him utterly humiliated, I want him to lose everything: his position, the respect of his friends, his respect for himself. I want the police degraded. You know the kind of people who can make it happen to him . . . go into the Maze and arrange it."

Starbuck's dark eyes filled the slots in the blackness of his mask with darker curiosity. "Why, Arienrhod? Why all this over a Summer brat you've never even seen? First the boy to get her here; now this, because she's gone— What in seven layers of hell could she possibly be to you?"

"She is something to me—" she took a breath, held it, "*was* something to me, that I could not begin to explain to

122

you, even if I wanted to." She had given him only the skeleton of the matter, no flesh on the bones, when his jealousy of the boy's presence had begun to make him unmanageable. As long as he was certain her interest in other lovers was superficial, he was content; but Sparks was something more, and she was not the only one who realized it. She disliked Starbuck's possessiveness, but like his other weaknesses it had its uses. And so she had told him of the girl's existence, but not the reason behind it. . . . "Since she's gone now, there's no reason for you to know what she was, in any case. Forget about her." *As I must.* . . .

"And the boy?" resentfully.

"Forget about him, too, if it makes you feel better." She saw him frown. *The more one withdraws, the more eagerly one is pursued.* She thought of Sparks Dawntreader. "Concentrate on LiouxSked, and you'll make me feel much, much better." She reached out, touched his arm lightly.

He nodded, easing under her touch. "What about Pala-Thion? It was her fault the smugglers got off-planet at all. You want me to—arrange something for her, too?"

"No." She glanced away toward the Hall of the Winds. "I have other plans for her. She'll pay her debt . . . believe me, she will. Now go. I want it to happen soon."

He bowed, and left the hall. She sat alone in the vast white silence.

Sparks lay spread-eagled across the bed in his private suite of rooms, his fingers tracing the tendrils of an alien vine across the elaborately carven headboard, and retracing them. *Gone. She's gone* . . . repeating the words as he repeated the pattern, over and over. But he had no strength to believe—no strength to react, to move, to feel. No tears.

How could she be gone—gone˙ from his world as irretrievably as if she had died? Not Moon, who had been a part of his life from the day he was born. Not Moon, who had pledged herself to be a part of him forever. . . .

Moon who had broken her pledge, and become a sibyl. Why? Why had she done that to him? Why had she done this to him now? Because she'd believed he was never coming back? Then why hadn't he gone back to Neith long ago! If he'd been there when she came home, this wouldn't have happened.

But he hadn't gone back. First because of all that had gone wrong, and then, after the Queen had come to find him, because of everything that had gone right. And always, because of Carbuncle. Neith and the whole of Summer's world seemed as distant and gray as a bank of fog now; the only reality was the kaleidoscope of city images that had expanded his senses and his awareness until he would never be content in that narrow world of islands and sea again. The Sea . . . the sea was no more than a film of water on a ball of stone to the people of the city. They swore by a thousand gods, and prayed to them rarely—and the answers they really wanted they got from their machines.

He had an outlet for one of those machines here on a table in the next room. He had filled up the absurd amount of space the Queen had set aside for him with instruments that talked and sang and even listened, that took pictures and showed pictures, that told him the time or the distance to the nearest stars. Sometimes he had tried to take them apart, only to find that their workings crumbled to dust in his hand, or that they were empty, except for flakes of metal painted with insect tracks and furred with filaments. But the Queen had encouraged him to do it, let him explore the tech devices of the palace; even sent him out into the labyrinth of shops in the Maze to choose more.

He still wondered why she had chosen him, and why she had rewarded him so greatly for the little he had to offer. Although he no longer wondered about it as much as he had in the beginning. He had first grown aware of the way the Queen watched him while he played for her—the intensity that had nothing to do with his music, that made his fingers begin to stumble, and left him feeling as though he stood before her naked. And later there had been a touch, a whispered word, a kiss, a chance encounter in a private place. . . . And she was so like Moon that he had found it hard to keep his own eyes off her, hard not to meet her gaze, hard not to match the emotion and answer the demand he found there.

But she was not Moon, she was the ageless Queen of Winter, and as he watched her deal with the offworlders and nobles who came before her at court that truth was made plain to him over and over. There were things she was that Moon lacked the years for—the wisdom, the calculating judgment, the depths of experience that lay behind her knowing smile. And there were things she was that Moon would never be, things he found harder to name . . . like the nameless things that were Moon which he never saw in her. And she could never become the memories, never be the one he had shared everything with.

Yet they were so alike, and it had been so long . . . until sometimes, like the city, Arienrhod became the reality, Moon only an afterimage. And that made him afraid; the fear of losing his own reality stopped his tongue when he would have taken her invitation.

But now the string had been cut that kept him bound to the Summer half of his life. Moon was gone. She was gone. There was no reason now for him ever to go home . . . they would never unravel the tangle they had made of their future now. He would never see her again; he would never lie beside her again, as he had lain beside her for the first time on the braided rug before the hearth, while the wind rattled and wailed through a midnight blackness beyond the walls and Gran slept peacefully in the next room. . . . The tears came at last, he rolled onto his side and buried them in the soft darkness of his pillow.

He did not hear so much as feel someone enter the

room, a chill draft as the door opened and closed again silently. He sat up, wiping at his face, started to rise as he recognized the Queen.

But Arienrhod put a hand on his shoulder, forced him gently back down onto the bed. "No. Tonight we aren't subject and queen, but only two people who have both lost someone they loved." She sat down beside him, the pleated fluidness of the robe she wore baring one shoulder. She was dressed almost plainly, with no jewels but a necklace of beaten metal leaves on a knotted silk cord.

He wiped his face again, wiping away his embarrassment but not his confusion. "I—I don't understand . . . Your Majesty." Seeing her beside him here, it occurred to him at last to wonder. . . . "How did you know? About Moon. About Moon and me?"

"You're still asking me how I know things, after all the time you've been here?" She smiled.

He looked down, pressed his hands over his knees. "But . . . why us? Out of everyone in the world—we were just Summers."

"Haven't you guessed even a little of it by now, Sparks? Look at me." He looked up again. "I reminded you of someone . . . I remind you of Moon, don't I?" He nodded. "You thought I didn't understand," she touched his arm. "But I did; I know it—bothered you. She is my kin, my flesh and blood, closer to me than even you are to her."

"Are you . . . ?" He tried to imagine what relation they could be, who were so alike in every feature. "Moon's aunt? Her father's—"

She shook her head; a creamy strand of hair came loose and uncoiled along her neck. "Moon has no father . . . any more. And we don't have her any more, you and I. I never even had the chance to meet her, but she was as important, as precious to me as she was to you. Perhaps even more so. I had hoped, in time, that we could have her with us here in the city." Her eyes left him, moving restlessly over the ornate, cluttered table along the wall.

"She wouldn't have come." His voice went flat. "Not after she was a sibyl."

126

"You think not? Not even for you?" The hand still rested sympathetically on his arm.

He sighed. "I wasn't ever as important to her as being a sibyl was. But why didn't you tell me about—her, and you, and—and us?" Somehow he was no longer speaking to the Queen, but to the one person who understood his own loss.

"I would have told you. I am telling you now. But I wanted to know what sort of lover my . . . kinswoman would choose over all the rest. I wanted to know you for myself first. And I approve of her choice, very much." The hand squeezed lightly, left his arm again; she brushed irritably at the loose strand of her hair, only setting more free. He had never seen her like this, weary and distraught and disappointed. So very human, so much like he was . . . so much like Moon.

"I'll never know Moon now, Sparks. I only have you to tell me about her, to remind me of her. Tell me what you remember most clearly, and feel the most deeply about her. What things did she love—what things about her did you love more than all the rest? Tell me how much you loved her. . . ."

The night of firelight and wind came back to him, overlaid by a thousand more images of Moon: the child whirling with arms outflung on the shining beach; the muffled girl hauling in a netful of coppery fish beside him on an icy deck; and again the lover, whispering soft words, warm against his heart. "I can't. I can't tell you about her . . ." His voice fell apart. "Not if she's gone."

"She is gone, Sparks." Arienrhod pulled the diadem from her hair, shook it free like a fall of water, down over her shoulders and her back, over the muted cloud-colors of her simple robe. "But you haven't lost her. Not if you don't want to." She leaned forward. "We are very alike, aren't we—she and I?"

He stared at her, at the fall of ivory hair, the slender girlish body and the soft stuff of the robe drawn tight across her small, high breasts . . . the lips, the moss-agate

127

eyes that asked the question, her face that was the answer: "Yes."

"Then let me be Moon for you." Her fingertips lifted a strand of his own hair in a hauntingly familiar gesture; he felt the pulse begin to beat in his temple. Inside his head he heard the voice of the Sea; but whether it blessed him or cursed him he did not know, or care, any more. He was on fire, and not even the Sea could quench the flame of his need. He reached out, touching her for the first time, let his hand fall along her bared shoulder down the cool, curving surfaces of her arm.

She leaned eagerly into his caress, drew him down onto the bed beside her, guiding his hands. "Show me how much you loved her. . . ."

Sparks lay with his eyes closed, absorbing the messages that reached him through his other senses—senses heightened by the grateful heaviness of his weary body. He inhaled the warm, musky scent of Arienrhod's presence beside him, felt the soft pressure of her body contoured against his own. There was no smell of the sea about her, but instead a fragrance of imported perfumes. And yet he felt the Sea's presence in her: she who was the Lady incarnate, robed in foam, seabirds flying from her hair, with lips like sunrise, like blood . . . who had lain waiting for him for centuries. He listened to the rhythm of her quiet breathing, opened his eyes to look over at her face. Her own eyes were closed; smiling in half-sleep as she lay beside him, she could even be the one he had named her at the moment when he lost control. . . .

Amazement touched him with a tingling hand as he realized again that he lay beside the Queen of Winter. But a profound tenderness filled him, he ached to give her the love, the loyalty, the life that he had pledged to her lost otherness. "Arienrhod . . ." He breathed the unfamiliar name against her ear. "Arienrhod. I want to be the only one with you."

She opened her eyes then, regarded him with gentle censure. "No. No, my love."

"Why not?" His arms closed her in, possessively. "I was the only one for Moon. Let me be the only one with you. I'm not just another fish in the net; I don't want to share you with a hundred others."

"But you must share me, Sparks. I am the Queen, the power. No one puts limits on me, no one commands me—I won't allow it, because it weakens my control. There will never be an only one, man or woman. Because I am the Only One. But there will never be another one like you. . . ." She kissed him softly on the forehead, her fingers closing over the offworld medal resting on his chest. "My star-child."

He shivered.

"What's wrong?"

"She used to call me that." He pushed up onto an elbow, looking down at her as she lay back smiling, caught outside of time. "If I can't be the only one, then I want to be the only one who counts." He saw in his mind the mocking figure dressed in black who stood always at the Queen's right hand, who baited him and bullied him at every private opportunity, with an evil enjoyment rooted in bitter jealousy. "I want to challenge Starbuck."

"Starbuck?" Arienrhod blinked at him with honest surprise, before she began to laugh. "My love, you're too new here to realize what you're saying—and you're far too young and alive to throw away everything. Because that is what you'd be doing, if you challenged Starbuck. I'm flattered by the gesture, but I forbid it. Believe me when I tell you that he counts for nothing in my heart. Since the first Festival night, when I put on the mask of the Winter Queen . . . so long ago . . ." her eyes changed, and she was no longer seeing him, "there has been no one in my bed, or in my life, who made me long for the time when I was only Arienrhod, and lived in a world that was ignorant but free; when wishes and dreams meant something, because they weren't always realized. You make me dream of lost innocence . . . you make me dream. There is no need for you to do, or be, anything more to make me love you—and want to keep you from harm. Starbuck could kill you with any

129

weapon you could choose, including bare hands. And besides, Starbuck must be an offworlder, he must have the knowledge and the contacts among his own kind to help me keep them at bay."

"I'm enough of an offworlder." He held out the medal, let it spin on its chain in the air above her. "And enough a part of this world to hate them like you do. I've listened and watched; I've learned a lot about the court, and the city too, how the offworlders use it. Anything I didn't know you could teach me...." He smiled, a smile that Moon would not have understood. "And I know the one thing I really need to know, even if you don't believe it—how I can challenge Starbuck and win." He stopped smiling.

Arienrhod studied him silently; he felt her measure and weigh with her eyes. He thought a shadow passed across her face, before she nodded. "Challenge him, then. But if you do, and fail, I'll call you a vain little braggart and make love to him on your grave." She caught the winking pendant and drew him down on top of her.

"I won't fail." He found her lips again, hungrily. "And if I can't be your only lover, I'll be the best."

This was the morning of the day. Starbuck prepared himself slowly, deliberately, in the innermost room of his private suite; reassuring himself with each precise movement and small decision that his control was absolute. He wore the utilitarian coveralls of his hunting clothes instead of the funereal foppery of his court clothing, for comfort and ease of movement. He pushed the black leather gloves down over each finger, settled the hooded helmet onto his head. It entered his mind that this might be the last time he would wear the mask, or perform this ritual, and his muscles tightened. He brushed the thought aside disdainfully— the way he would brush aside Sparks Dawntreader.

So that wet-eared Mother lover thought he could be Starbuck, had even gotten up the nerve to issue a challenge —and Arienrhod had accepted it. It would have smarted that she'd done this to him, except that the contest was such an absurd mismatch he couldn't believe she took it seriously. She wouldn't let an ignorant punk from the outback with a pawnshop medal claim to be an offworlder, unless she knew there was no chance in hell of his winning the contest.

No, she just wanted amusement; it was like her to come up with this. She hadn't been the same since she'd gotten the news about Dawntreader's cousin: moody and spiteful, even harder to live with than usual. He wouldn't have believed there was anything on this world that could pierce the armor of her supreme egotism or shake her unshakable arrogance. What had the girl been to her, that Arienrhod had had her watched all those years? He'd give a lot to know what made Arienrhod vulnerable. . . .

He knew already what the boy had been to her—that she'd finally gotten the elusive quarry bedded, after the longest pursuit he'd ever known her to need. The kid was either crazy or he'd played the reluctant innocent on purpose: It could have been either one, and either way it had worked too well. Arienrhod's face when she watched the boy had driven him to private fury, with a jealousy he'd never known toward any of her lovers in the past.

But none of that mattered now. It had been a waste of time to sweat over it; she was already bored with him. Once the excitement of the chase was gone and the unattainable object was just another lousy lay, it figured that she'd decide to get rid of this one like all the rest. That made sense. That fitted the Arienrhod he had always known. She would be his again, she would come back to him as she had always done; because he knew what she wanted, in everything, and he could give it to her.

And it was going to be a pleasure to take care of this

next piece of business for her, by killing that troublesome little son of a bitch. Arienrhod had granted the boy choice of weapons; that didn't bother him either, because he was good with any weapon, and the kid was a flute-playing sissy. It was almost beneath his dignity...but he planned to enjoy it anyway.

Starbuck studied himself in the long mirror and was pleased with the effect. He strapped on his weapons belt and left his chambers, heading for the Hall of the Winds, where Arienrhod had ordered them to meet. That had surprised him, but he hadn't questioned it. The nobility and servants he passed in the halls gave him a wide berth, stealing fleeting, nervous glances. (Even the nobility always treated him respectfully, to his face, pampered highborn weaklings that they were.) They all knew that there had been a challenge, and that this was the day, although none would ever know who the challenger was . . . or the outcome, although everyone would guess.

What weapon would the kid try? he wondered. An electric eagerness tingled in his hands; he flexed them. The challenges were the kind of thing no respectable Winter liked to admit still existed anywhere in their half of the world: something left over from the dim dark times before the Hegemony had brought enlightenment back to this lost world; a time when the Queen was the actual Sea Mother in her people's eyes, and men fought for her divine favors . . . just as they did now. The fact that it was a vestige of an uncivilized age did not bother him. He enjoyed testing himself against other men, proving to the world—to Arienrhod, to himself—every time he won that he was a better man than the ones who tried to bring him down. Not just the strongest, but the smartest, too. That was why he'd always won, and why he always would. Even if he had been born Unclassified on Kharemough, with the whole world on his back making him eat shit, he'd fought his way out of that sewer, and into a position of power the best-educated technocrat on Kharemough could not match. He had everything they had, and more—he had the water of life. How many of them squandered their lives' fortunes to

132

erase a day from every week, or month, that they aged? He drank from the fountain of youth every day—it came with the job. As long as he gave Arienrhod what she wanted, he would have everything he wanted, and he would never have to grow old. And as long as he stayed in his prime no challenger would ever take that away from him

He reached the audience hall. It was empty now, vast and still, as though it held its breath. He started across it, and his passage did nothing to disturb the stillness. He wondered what it would be like to hold power for one hundred and fifty years, as Arienrhod had. What would it be like just to be alive for that long; to have seen the return of the offworlders and the rebirth of Winter—to watch civilization reborn, and to have your pick of its pleasures? He would like to know how a man—or a woman—would feel after all that; and he wondered whether if he'd lived that long he might have begun to understand the involutions of Arienrhod's mind.

He'd lost count long ago of the women he'd known, from highborn tech to slave; he'd hated some of them and used most of them and respected one or two, but he'd never loved even one of them. Nothing had given him any evidence that love was anything but a four-letter word. Only weaklings and losers believed in love or gods. . . .

But he had never experienced anything like Arienrhod. She was not so much a woman as an elemental; her magnetism was created of all the things he found desirable. She had made him an unwilling believer in his own vulnerability; and that had made him half-willing to believe in the power of strange gods, too . . . or strange goddesses. And he wouldn't have one hundred and fifty years of youth and pleasure, one hundred and fifty years to work at unraveling her mysteries, even if he wanted to. He had only five years before he would have to leave this world forever—or die. In five years it would all end at the Change, and Arienrhod would die . . . and he would die with her, unless he cleared out in time. He loved her, and he had never loved anyone except himself in all his life. But he didn't think he loved her more than life.

She stood waiting for him on the platform as he entered the Hall of the Winds; the pit groaned and sighed its eager greeting at her back. Stray tendrils of wind lifted her milk-white hair, let it fall free over the enfolding whiteness of her ceremonial cape. The cape was made from the down of arctic birds, flecked with silver, the softness of clouds . . . he remembered the feel of it against his skin. She had worn it six times, at each of his previous challenges; she had worn it the first time, when he had been the challenger.

The Hounds stood off to the left, their skins glistening, their inner eyelids lying across their nacreous, expressionless eyes. They were here to pledge service to the winner—and to dispose silently of the loser's corpse. In ten years he had never fathomed their endless droning dialogues, or cared that he hadn't. He didn't know whether they had any sex lives, or even any sex. Their intelligence was supposed to be subhuman, but how the hell could you judge an alien mind? They were used on some worlds as slaves; but so were human beings. He wondered briefly what they were thinking as they turned to watch him; wondered if they ever thought about anything a man could relate to, besides killing.

He made his formal bows, to Arienrhod, to the boy. "I've come. Name your weapon." It was the first time that the naming had not been his to say. Arienrhod's eyes touched him as he spoke the ritual words; but there was no reassurance in her glance, only a reaffirmation of the coldness that had grown in her since the boy's arrival. Then was she really still infatuated with that Summer bastard? Did she really believe that he had a chance?

Starbuck kneaded one fist inside the other, suddenly thrown off-balance. Damn her, she wasn't going to get away with it! He was going to kill that kid, and then she'd have him back in her bed again whether she wanted him or not! He struggled to force his rising, murderous anger into a straitjacket of concentration. "Well, what's your choice?"

"The wind." Sparks Dawntreader smiled tightly, and swept his hand around, pointing. "We stand on the bridge there—and whoever controls the winds better will still be there when it's finished." He took his flute slowly from his belt pouch, and held it out.

Starbuck's voice caught on a single barb of startled laughter. So the kid had imagination to match his gall . . . and his stupidity. The nobles with their whistles could hold a quiet space of air around themselves while they crossed over the pit, but they couldn't manipulate two spaces at once. With his own control box, he could produce the chords and overtones that would keep him protected and still attack. If the kid thought that he was better equipped than a noble, with that shell flute of his, then he was in for the biggest surprise of his life—and the last.

Arienrhod moved back, her cape billowing like mist, like the translucent wind panels above the bridge, left the two of them alone facing one another. "May the best man win." Her voice was expressionless.

Without waiting for Sparks to move first, Starbuck walked past him and onto the bridge. He crossed it almost carelessly, his fingers pressing the singing sequence of buttons at his belt. Once the wind licked him and his breath caught, but he was sure no one had noticed. He stopped at last, more than halfway along the span, and turned; stood waiting with one hand on his hip and the other at his belt. He had never stood still above the abyss before; the groaning entrails of the city machinery seemed infinite beneath him, and the span on which he stood far too frail. He pressed the piercing tone-buttons automatically, massaged by the fluctuations of the pressure cell around him, very carefully not looking down.

Sparks lifted his flute to his lips and stepped out onto the bridge; the fluid purity of the notes reached Starbuck clearly. He saw with some surprise that it actually worked —the music wrapped the kid like a spell, he moved in quiet air, the blaze of his hair and the green silk of his shirt unruffled. He must have spent a lot of time analyzing this place. Not that it was going to do him any good.

Starbuck pressed a second button when the boy was barely out past the brink. The bellying translucent panels shifted in the air; wind swept up from an unexpected quar-

135

ter and struck like a snake at the boy's back. He staggered and went down on one knee at the lipless edge of the walkway; but his fingers never released the flute, and he countered the crossdraft deftly, throwing himself back onto his feet in the center of the path. He came on, sudden ruthless anger in his face; a rush of shrill notes danced ahead of him, guarding his advance, blurring the sounds of Starbuck's own feint and parry.

Starbuck stumbled, barely managing to keep his feet as the wind struck him hard across the face. His eyes watered; he blinked frantically, trying to see when he should have been listening. The wind caught him from behind and knocked him down. On hands and knees he found the controls again, stabilized his space of air with desperate skill as he climbed to his feet. The wind panels cracked and rattled as Sparks attacked again, grinning now with mirthless concentration. It staggered him, but he managed to counter, notes clashing in the air; realizing at last that the contest was not going to be one-sided . . . at least not in the way he had imagined. He had never paid enough attention to the boy's music to realize his virtuosity with that damned piece of shell. He could produce overtones with it, and his fingers were so quick that the notes came close to being chords—close enough. And the boy was playing this game as though he had prepared for the match with all the skill of his musician's ear and his would-be technician's mind.

But it was a game of death, and out of all the skills he, Starbuck, had that the boy could have chosen, manipulating the winds was the least exercised. He began to sweat; for the first time in longer than he could remember, he began to feel afraid for his own life. The wind batted him again when he thought he was safe. He struck back viciously, sending the wind in from three different quarters, heard the boy's shout of surprise as one arm of it caught him unawares and sent him reeling forward. But he stayed on the bridge and recovered his equilibrium before another sweep could finish him.

136

Starbuck swore under his breath. There were too many options, there was no way to predict what effect the mixing of their separate tone commands would have, even if they could outguess each other. He crouched low, started back toward Sparks across the bridge; concentrating grimly on keeping himself protected instead of on attacking. The closer they were to one another, the less the kid could afford to threaten his own stability by shifting the winds around them. If he could just get his hands on that flute and crush it, then he could still finish this—

A clout of cold force knocked him flat; he sprawled sideways, flailing desperately as his feet went off one edge and head and shoulders slid out over the other. For an endless moment he looked straight down into the black-walled pit, where the dim spirals of machine lights glittered like the endless lost fire of a Black Gate's heart; and the smell of the sea and the moaning dirge were strong inside his head. In that moment he lay still, waiting, hands clutching at the narrow edge of the arcing span, hypnotized by the immediacy of death.

But the final formless blow did not fall, or rise, to tumble him over the edge; the paralysis released him and he raised his head, saw Sparks Dawntreader standing frozen like himself, unable to make the kill.

He levered himself back onto the meter-wide solidity of the span, reacting instinctively now; flung himself up and into a protective hole in the air. He ran forward, almost in reach before the boy finally reacted, lashing out at him with a double buffet of wind. He countered it easily, and at the same time brought his booted foot up with all his strength to kick the boy in the groin.

Sparks collapsed with an animal cry of agony. The flute stayed in his fist, but it was no use to him now, no danger to his rival. . . . Starbuck backed slowly away, savoring his triumph, sorry only that the kid hurt too much to care about what was going to happen to him next. Starbuck lifted his head to look at Arienrhod, still standing on the brink, far away, like some unattainable dream. In another moment the road to her would be clear again. His hand moved at the controls on his belt; Arienrhod moved slightly where she stood.

Two discordant notes collided in the air. Astounded, he felt his own feet go out from under him as the wind struck him down. Not the boy, not the boy—himself! Falling—

"Arienrhod!" He screamed her name, a curse, a prayer, an accusation, as he fell; and it followed him down into darkness.

16

The Black Gate filled the shielded viewscreen that filled the center of the wall, a flaming whorl against the amber blackness of the distant starfield. In the heart of this stellar cluster there had once been a glut of cosmic flotsam to feed a black hole's hunger; through eons it had been mostly consumed, and the deadly excrement of the hole's gravitational radiation had dimmed. But it had also captured the star the Tiamatans called the Summer Star; held it prisoner on a narrow tether, siphoning away its chromosphere. The minutiae of dust and molecules blazed up, giving off their potential energy, as they were sucked down to destruction, as this ship was being sucked down. . . .

Elsevier felt the hunger of the Gate lick out at her, felt the first tingling of physical sensation, the slow, compulsive movement of her weightless body toward the image on the wall . . . felt it too in the depths of her mind, where it probed her secret terror of dismemberment. The firmly yielding cushion of the transparent cocoon that wrapped her held her back with gentle reassurance.

She glanced down past her drifting feet toward the ship's center of mass, where the girl Moon hung in another light-catching chrysalis. Moon shifted restlessly, like a firemoth impatient for birth; her luridly pink flightsuit caught reflections from the console suspended around her. A crown of silver mesh hung useless in the air above her silver-gilt hair—the crown that Cress should have worn, the symb helmet of an astrogator. Moon looked up to find Elsevier looking down, and Elsevier saw the emotions struggle on her face.

"Moon, are you ready?"

"No..."

Elsevier stiffened, afraid of what an outburst of rebellion from the girl could do to them. She thought she had convinced Moon that this trip was no more than a brief detour in her journey to find her cousin. But if she refused to begin a Transfer now—

"I don't know what to do. I don't understand anything, I don't understand how—"

Elsevier felt a feeble smile form as she realized that it was only doubt on Moon's face, and not refusal. She had only read her own guilty conscience there. "You don't need to, Moon. Leave that to me. Trust me, I'm not ready to meet the Render yet. Just input all the data the way I showed you."

Moon looked back at the screen wordlessly, her awe tempered by a half-formed comprehension of the Gate's terrible power. They were above its pole of rotation, already trapped in the undertow of its black gravitational heart: that force so inexorable that light itself could not break free of it. This hole, at twenty thousand solar masses, was large enough that a specially designed ship fell through the event horizon before it could be ripped apart by the tidal forces working on its mass. But only an astrogator trained in singularity physics, and in symbiotic linkup with the ship's computers, could maintain the critical balance of its stabilizers. Only an astrogator could make certain they entered the Gate at the precise point that would put them in the pipeline for their chosen destination. Only an astrogator—or an ignorant girl from a backward planet whose mind was already in symbiosis with the greatest data bank in known space and time. "Do you want me

139

to begin Transfer? Elsevier—?" Moon looked up at her again, face set in a shield of determination.

Elsevier took a deep breath, postponing the inevitable moment. But the inevitable moment had already passed, and now she must say it. "Yes, Moon. Keep your eyes on the viewscreen and begin Transfer." *And the gods forgive me, as they protect you, child. Because you'll never see your home again.* Moon's eyes closed for a brief moment, as if in a prayer to her own goddess, and then she focused on the shining vortex before them. "*Input.*" Elsevier pressed a button on the remote at her belt as the girl's slim body quivered into a trance state; the data concerning their entrance flashed across the image on the screen, and was gone again. If she was right—and she couldn't afford to be wrong—that should be enough to start the necessary information feeding back into the ship's guidance system. Without an astrogator's implants no human could make full use of the ship's computer symb circuits, but the sibyl Transfer would supply the information the computers could not.

"It done." Silky's voice, speaking broken Sandhi, reached her in a sibilant whisper across the control room's silence. "Is girl hurting?"

"How do I know?" sharp with the stab of her doubt. She frowned down across the open space at him. His amphibian body shone through its own cocoon, silken with the oils that kept him from dehydrating. He sounded strangely unsettled; it struck her that he must feel an empathy for this helpless innocent torn loose from the world she knew, at the mercy of betraying strangers.

"Could she die?"

"Silky, damn it!" Elsevier bit her lip and looked back at the spreading malignancy of the Gate. "You know I can't answer that . . . but you know I wouldn't have done it if I believed that she would. You *know* that, Silky. . . . But what choice did any of us have, except to try? I told her it would be a long trance; she accepted that."

"She too young. She not know. You lie to her," as close to reproach as she had ever heard him come.

140

Elsevier closed her eyes. "I'll make it up to her. I'll see that she has everything she needs to be happy on Kharemough." She opened them again, looking down on Moon. The girls pink-suited body was limp now, pressed softly against the walls of the cocoon. Was it barely four days tau since they had made that fate-cursed landing on Tiamat, fled back to the ship with nothing to show for it but Cress barely on this side of death, and a dazed stranger in his place?

And with time running out: The police would be searching Tiamat space for them, and they couldn't afford to be caught with a kidnapped citizen of the planet on board. The girl had wanted to go home... but there was no way to send her back. Cress needed a hospital... and the only ones that could save him were on Kharemough, beyond the Gate.

But only Cress could take them through.

And then she had remembered: Moon was a sibyl, and once TJ had told her of seeing a sibyl go into a trance and operate a field polarizer to save five people during an industrial accident. That sibyl hadn't been trained on sophisticated machinery; it shouldn't matter that this one barely knew what machinery was. She was only a vessel, just as she had said; and it was her duty to serve all who needed her—she could take them through the Gate to safety.

But when she had tried to explain it to Moon, she had run into a barrier as impassible as the Gate itself. Moon sat firmly strapped into her seat on the LB, refusing to set foot inside the greater ship. "Take me back. I have to go to Carbuncle!" Her face was like a clenched fist, and she had answered every imaginable argument with the same two sentences, immoveable and unmoved.

"But Moon, the offworlders will never let you go back if they find you with us. Your world is proscribed. They'll sentence us all to the cinder camps on Big Blue, and believe me, my dear, you'd be better off dead."

"It doesn't matter, if I can't go back. Nothing matters without him."

Oh, child, how lucky you are to believe it's that simple

141

... and how naive. And yet a part of her said it was true; that since TJ's death she had only lived half a life. . . . "I know, truly. I know it seems that way to you now. But if you won't think of yourself, then think of Cress." Her hand had moved along the cool, translucent shell beside her that breathed on the fragile embers of his life. "He'll die, Moon. Unless we reach Kharemough, he will die. You're a sibyl; it's your duty."

"I can't do what you ask!" Moon shook her head, her braids drifting with the motion. "I can't, I don't know how to do that. I can't fly a starship—" Her voice rose, "And I can't leave Sparks!"

"It's only for a few weeks!" The words had burst out of Elsevier in exasperation; but before she could take them back she saw the girl's head come up, the eyes fix on her quizzically.

"H-how long?"

"About a month, one way." *Ship's time.* And more than two years would have passed on Tiamat in the meantime. But Elsevier did not say that; inspiration took root in her need. "Only a month each way. Moon, if you'd taken a trader's ship from Shotover Bay to Carbuncle it would take you as long. Help us get through the Gate, help Cress . . . and if you still want to come back when we reach Kharemough, I'll bring you back. I promise it."

"But how can I? I can't fly a starship."

"You can do anything, be anything, answer any question except one. You are a sibyl, and it's time that you learned what it means, my dear. Trust me."

The words had choked her as she reached out to release the straps that kept Moon in her seat.

A loud *clack* echoed through the ship, jerking Elsevier back into the present. "Silky! What was that? Something's loose—" The protective counterbalances of the cocoon had immobilized her. She could not pull a finger free, or shift her head a fraction of an inch; there was nothing to do but gaze straight ahead toward the shining cancer that spread across the screen before them.

"Wristwatch."

She gave a small sigh of vexation and relief, seeing it stuck to a double star in the lower half of the screen. The images of the stars drained inward toward the center of the screen; the black hole wore a starry crown, symbol of its power over light itself. . . . *Careless!* Something larger than her watch left unsecured might have torn a hole through the hull in its urge to suicide. "I just got that watch! I've endured this trip too many times; I don't carry the years lightly, alone. TJ was my strength, Silky . . . and he's gone." She sensed a faint tremor through the fiber of the ship; looking up again she saw no starfield before them now, but only the film of reddening hellshine lighting their way to doom. "She's controlling the field stabilizers, Silky, or we'd be turning somersaults by now. I knew she could hold us!"

But what if it destroys her mind? If anything happened to the girl because of this, she would never forgive herself. Never. In the bare few days the girl had spent with them she had reaffirmed by her simple presence the things TJ had always believed. Flexible and independent, she had begun to recover from the shock of her abrupt transplanting, begun reaching out to the possibilities they offered in propitiation. In a cheerful, eye-stimulating jump suit instead of drab handmade clothing, there was no way a stranger could have known her for a second-class citizen of the Hegemony, one judged undeserving of a full share of its knowledge. And the sibyl-machinery of a civilization far more knowledgeable than their own had judged her and found her worthy.

TJ's dream had always been that all intelligent beings would someday have an equal chance to fulfill their potential. That was why he had begun running contraband shipments to Tiamat, against her own futile protests that he was becoming a common smuggler. "There are smugglers and smugglers, my heart," he had said, grinning; and by then she knew that no human protest could shout down the inner voice that drove him . . . not even hers.

The Hegemony held Tiamat back from developing a

technological base of its own by restrictions and embargoes (she still remembered how his lectures rang through their cramped apartment); kept the inhabitants at a level where they were only pampered children, given selected toys their parent-masters could later render harmless. And all for the sake of that precious obscenity, the water of life, that seduced the Hegemony's privileged and powerful with the hope of eternal youth.

If Tiamat developed a technologically-based world society of its own, if it were left to mature untended during the century that it was cut off from the Hegemony, who knew what they would find when they returned? A world able to stand up to them, one which no longer craved their technological toys because it could make its own—a world which had decided that it preferred to keep immortality to itself, and was tired of exploitation? Or a world which had decided that its own exploitation of mers was immoral... worse yet, one which had turned itself into a radioactive cinder the way Caedw had done. Tiamat had something that no other world could offer, and what it had was more of a curse than a blessing.

It was a situation that TJ had found intolerable. Knowing she couldn't stop him, she had gone with him again, as she had always gone with him, always been unable to refuse him any desire. And as always, she had been caught up in his passion in the end ... and after his death, she and Silky had carried on his crusade, the only thing in her life that had seemed to have any purpose after he was gone.

And now chance had swept the girl Moon into her life, as if to prove that it had all been worthwhile—the image of the child that she and TJ had never had. *He would have been proud.* It would be no burden to be guardian to Moon's new life; it would be a privilege. . . .

Elsevier felt a sickening vertigo as the irresistible force of the tidal stress sucked at her immobile body. Even with the protective fields functioning, the ship could not protect them entirely. She looked toward the glowing heart of blackness once again. *Oh, heaven, I'm not ready; it happens too fast, and lasts too long.* At least Moon was free of the heat and pain, with her mind held captive somewhere halfway across the galaxy. . . . *I wouldn't have done it, except for Cress. . . . It wouldn't have happened, except for Cress. . . . Oh, gods, let him be all right.* He still lay in the emergency prism; they hadn't dared to move him to a safer spot. But the whole of the ship and all its equipment had been designed to survive this passage; surely he would survive, too—if any of them did. . . .

She felt the sockets of her bones loosen and shift again, felt the less acute but growing discomfort as the temperature inside the ship rose. She imagined the outer hull incandescent now with stress as it plummeted toward the black hole's horizon, a part of the flaming distress call endlessly broadcasting as the damned were gathered in to their final reckoning. The ship was constructed of the strongest, most resilient materials known to man, and equipped with counterfields to protect and stabilize its descent into the maelstrom. It was as small in size as possible, and shaped like a coin; the stabilizers kept its flat broad face always aligned with the gravitational gradients as it fell. Because the walls of the black hole's gravity well in space were so steep, if the ship ever lost its stability and began to tumble it would be ripped apart in seconds by tidal stresses. Death would come to them all in an instant's blazing agony, and their death scream would echo in that well forever. Passage through the Black Gate taxed human and mechanical endurance, and the limits of Kharemough's technology. Only the symbiosis of a computer and the astrogator's human brain could hold them together and guide them down to the precise point of entry at the horizon.

And what if Moon held them together, but they missed the tiny opening to the hyperspace conduit that would spit them out two light-years from Kharemough? Kharemough had redeveloped the principle of Black Gate travel over a millennium ago, working from the Old Empire knowledge given to them by sibyls. The Old Empire had had a hyperlight stardrive that let it extend its control across distances still impossible for the Hegemony; but even it had used the

Black Gate as a local center for its far-flung communications. The Hegemony had used its cosmic shortcut to reestablish this small part of the Empire's network of worlds, and used its fossil wisdom to get them safely through. But they still had no real understanding of the forces they manipulated. . . . If this ship did not pass through the horizon at the proper coordinates, it might emerge in an entirely unexplored sector of space, with no system nearby and no coordinates for their return . . . or it might never emerge anywhere in the known universe. Ships had been lost before; and they had been lost forever.

Elsevier felt her eyes bulging against her closed lids, no longer able to watch the coruscating fire of the black hole's surface swallow her universe. She heard the ship groan, and her own groan as she felt herself coming apart at the seams. The rippling bright blackness echoed inside her as her consciousness gave way; she let all her doubts and fears fly up like a shower of sparks and surrendered herself at last, gladly, to oblivion.

The Black Gate opened.

It doesn't happen like that. Jerusha stood in the elegant den of the upper city townhouse, staring out through the diamond-patterned window, hands behind her back. Children danced among circles scrawled on the timeworn pavement, caught in some inscrutable childhood fantasy— children of wealthy Winters and wealthy offworlders together, oblivious to the distances of space-time and outlook that separated their parents. She tried not to think about the distances, the differences, the terrible— *It just doesn't happen like that!*

But even the furious denial couldn't keep it out of her mind, keep her from reliving the unexplained summons that had taken her away from the night duty desk at police headquarters, up into the darkened corridors on the second level. She couldn't keep from remembering the sounds that had drawn her—not human sounds but the sounds of some tortured *thing*—to open the final door and turn on the light.

She had not screamed in half a lifetime, but she had screamed that night. One raw cry of denial: that she did not see the bleating, bleeding animal that lay tearing at itself on the floor of that stinking room . . . the filthy, raving ruin of what had been a human being. Not just any human being, but the Commander of Police for all of Tiamat—who had burned out his brain with an overload of k'spag. Gods, if she lived to see the New Millennium she would never forget that sight! She blinked fiercely as the children swam out of focus. No matter how hard she tried to put it out of her mind, it clung like the odor of death, corrupting every emotion, every thought. She had seen enough ugliness in this job to harden the weakest woman; but when it happened to one of your own. . . . She had not liked much about LiouxSked, but no man deserved to suffer such degradation before the eyes of an entire world. Though he would probably be beyond caring, forever.

But that left his family. It had been her duty, devolved upon her by Mantagnes, the new Acting Commander, to help LiouxSked's wife make the arrangements for the family's departure from Tiamat. "Marika needs another woman's presence at a time like this, Jerusha," Mantagnes had said, quite sincerely. She had bitten her tongue. *Well, damn it, maybe she does.*

She had wondered how she would be able to face Lesu Marika LiouxSked and the two little girls, with the knowledge of what she had seen that night still branded on her memory. But she had kept control of her emotions with a success born of long practice, and it had seemed to have a good effect on the distraught and grieving woman.

Lesu Marika had always been distant and disapproving during their previous encounters—usually when LiouxSked had made her play glorified nanny on family expeditions into the Maze. But, like most of the force stationed here—like herself—LiouxSked and his family had come from Newhaven; and so now they spoke together in their own language of home, like strangers met in an alien land. Marika and the children were returning home to family and friends (and the Commander was returning with them, to spend the rest of his life in an insitution; but they did not speak of that). Jerusha encouraged safe, nonspecific recollections of the world they had all longed to see again: the sunbleached heat of the days; the vital, quicksilver people; the starport metropolis and trade center of Miertoles lo Faux—where she had first seen the glory of the Prime Minister's visitation, and been awed by its splendor. Where she had dreamed her own dreams of other worlds . . .

Jerusha felt someone come to stand silently beside her; glanced over and then down at ten-year-old Lesu Andradi, the younger of LiouxSked's two daughters. She was a bright, eager girl, very unlike her simpering older sister, and Jerusha had grown fond of her. And the gradual realization that the child hanging on her hand looked up at her uniform with the same near-awe that she had always felt toward her own uniformed father and brother had made the humiliation of her nursemaid duty bearable.

Now Andradi imitated her own pose at the window unthinkingly—a small, forlorn figure in a shapeless gray robe, her forehead smudged with ash. The family dressed for mourning, as though LiouxSked had actually died. But the gods weren't that kind. . . . *Gods, hell!* Jerusha's mouth thinned. The gods had nothing to do with it; this stank of human treachery.

Andradi rubbed her eyes surreptitiously with her fist as she watched the other children play, part of the world that she had suddenly been cut off from. "I wish I could say good-bye to Scelly and Minook. But Mamá won't let us, because—because of Da."

Jerusha wondered whether it was simply that her mother considered it inappropriate to mourning, or whether Marika was afraid of what the other children might say to her own. But she only said, "They'll understand."

"But I don't want to go away and not see them any more! I hate Newhaven!" Andradi had been born on Tiamat, and her image-conscious parents affected a pretentiously Kharemoughi life-style; her homeworld was nothing to her but a name, the symbol of all that had abruptly gone wrong with her life.

Jerusha put an arm out, circled the girl's narrow shoulders, glancing over her head at the sterile sophistication of the room behind them. She heard muffled echoes from the upper stories, where Marika and the servants were gathering together the last of the family's belongings. They were leaving behind most of the furniture—not because of the expense of shipping it, she suspected, so much as the painful associations of this place. "I know, Andradi. You hate Newhaven now. But when you get there you'll find new friends, and they'll show you how to climb up into prong trees, and weave the bark into hats. They'll take you out with a lamp to find flowers that only bloom at night; and in the rainy season water falls out of the sky like a warm shower, and all the vines in your courtyard will be covered with sweet berries. You can catch shiny wogs in a pool. . . ." Although she doubted very much that Marika would let her daughters catch wogs.

Andradi snuffled. "What—what are those?"

Jerusha smiled. "Little things like fish that live in the winter rainpools. In the summer they burrow down into the mud and sleep there until the rains come again."

"For a hundred years?" Andradi's eyes widened. "That's a long time."

Jerusha laughed as comprehension caught up with her. "No, not a hundred—just a couple. Winter and summer don't last as long there as they do here."

"Oh, double luck!" Andradi clapped her hands. "That'll be like living forever. Just like the Snow Queen!"

149

Jerusha winced, pushed the thought aside and nodded her encouragement. "There you go. You'll like growing up on Newhaven. I know I did." She was aware that she was ignoring the things she had come to hate once she was grown. "I wish I was going back myself." The words slipped out, unintended.

Andradi abruptly was clinging like a burr, her small face buried against Jerusha's tunic. "Oh, yes—oh, yes, Jerusha —please come! You can show me everything, you know everything; I want you to come with me." She trembled. "You're a good Blue."

Jerusha stroked the dark, curly head, speechless with the sudden comprehension of what she meant now to this child, whose rightful symbol of firm stability and trust had suddenly destroyed himself. She let herself realize, at last, how deeply Andradi's bewildered grief had penetrated her own defenses and tightened its grip around her heart.

She pried the girl's arms loose where they wrapped her waist above her equipment belt, and took the slim, warm hands in her own. "Thank you, Andradi. Thank you for asking. I wish I could go with you; but my job here isn't done. Your father . . . your father didn't do this thing to himself, Andradi. No matter what anybody says, don't you ever believe he did. Somebody did it to him. I don't know who yet but I'm going to find out. I'm going to make sure that person pays. And when I do, you'll get a message from me, so that you'll know he has—or she has. Maybe after that I'll be ready to go home myself."

"All right . . . " The curly head bobbed once, and then the somber, upslanting eyes found her face again. "When I'm grown, I'm going to be a Blue too."

Jerusha smiled, without irony or condescension. "Yes, I think maybe you will."

They glanced up together as Marika entered the den, veiled in gray; she gestured her daughter to her side, and Andradi moved away reluctantly. "Everything is ready, Jerusha." Her voice was as dreary and gray as she was. "You may see us to the starport now."

Jerusha nodded. "Yes, Madame LiouxSked." She followed them gladly out of the abandoned room.

Jerusha left the hovercraft to an attendant whose presence she barely registered, walked toward the heavy windowed doors that separated the cavernous garage from police headquarters on the other side. The whole of this alley was taken up by offices and detention cells and the court buildings, a drab stain of moral rectitude on the crazy quilt of the Maze. Officially it was the Olivine Alley; but everyone, including its inhabitants, knew it as Blue Alley.

She barely remembered to pause for the second it took the sluggish doors to snap open and let her pass through, into the anonymous hallway beyond. Her mind still lay on the trip she had just made, the reason for it, the whole incredible, ugly chain of events that had shaken everyone in this—

"Excuse me, patrolman. Excuse me, patrolman. Excuse me, patrolman."

Something clutched at her uniform sleeve as she pushed into the crowded ward room. She looked up distractedly into the faceless plastic shielding a head full of mechanical brains—a polrob, blocking her way with mindless urgency. "Inspector," she said, with something of the same robot monotony. Someone jostled her from behind.

"Excuse me, Inspector. I must make my report and return to work. Please authorize me." There was a hint of desperation in the mechanical inflections. "A man from Number Four has been making seditious remarks about the Hegemony in the Stardock Bar. He is also telling locals that sibyls have access to forbidden knowledge. He appears to be under the influence of drugs."

"Yeah, all right, authorization 77A. File an ident on him and we'll pick him up." *Drugs. Don't think about drugs.* She moved on across the room, concentrating on not looking toward what had been LiouxSked's private office until a month ago.

"Excuse me, Inspector!" This time from an apologetic

151

patrolman as he backed into her with an armload of holo files.

"My fault; I wasn't watching." Already the inundation of paperwork that marked the end of their stay on Tiamat was beginning to mount. Merchants and other resident aliens had already begun to worry about the future, or the lack of it; begun to plague the bureaucracy about the hundred different permits and forms and regulations it demanded of them before the final departure. And if she thought they were busy now, just wait another four years. *... Yes, busy, busy, have to keep busy; too busy to think about it....*

But nothing kept her mind clogged with interference loud enough to drown the images of horror and grief for long. She had not lied when she told Andradi that her father didn't make himself into a drooling vegetable. It made no sense—she knew that man, and whatever he might have been, or done, he was not the kind of man to play with drugs. Hell, he wouldn't touch a pack of iestas! But there were half a hundred dealers in Carbuncle who could arrange to have an overdose dropped into a cup of tea or a bowl of soup.

And one person who might want to see it happen— Arienrhod. Jerusha had seen the look on her face at the news of the girl Moon's kidnapping—the fury and despair. And suddenly she had known why Moon Dawntreader had looked at her from the face of another woman, the face of Winter's Queen. There was only one way a perfect stranger could be the Queen's double—and that was if that stranger was the Queen's clone. Arienrhod had had plans for that girl, plans that must have had something to do with the coming Change, when the offworlders would leave and turn this world over to the Summers again. Their records showed that every past Snow Queen had tried something to keep her power, and Winter's reign, intact when the Change came. Somehow that girl had fitted into this queen's plan; she was sure of it. But she had spoiled that plan inadvertently. And Arienrhod was not a woman to let an injury go unpunished. She had taken revenge on the force, on

152

LiouxSked; Jerusha was sure of that, too, just as she was sure that she would never be able to prove it. But she might be able to find out who had done the actual deed. . . .

If the Queen didn't take revenge on her before then. Jerusha swallowed the familiar lump of tension that formed in her throat. She was the one actually to blame; if Arienrhod wanted to punish anyone, it ought to be her. She had barely been able to eat or drink for a week, afraid that the thing that had happened to LiouxSked was waiting to happen to her. And maybe that was part of the punishment: the waiting. Gods, she couldn't stand it, to end up like that. . . .

"*Inspector.*"

She flinched with the shock of her return to the real world; blinked the corridor that led to her office, and Gundhalinu's worried face, into focus. "Oh . . . BZ, what are you doing here?"

"Waiting for you." He glanced over his shoulder in the direction of her office, back at her, concern spreading on his freckled face. "Inspector, the Commander's sitting down there in your office—and so is the Chief Justice. I don't know what the hell they want, but I thought you ought to have some warning."

"The Chief Justice?" Her voice echoed incredulously along the walls. "Shit." She shut her eyes. "It looks like the waiting is over."

Gundhalinu raised his eyebrows. "You know what it's about?"

"Not exactly." She shook her head, feeling cold despair settle in the pit of her stomach. The Chief Justice was at the pinnacle of the offworld judicial system on Tiamat, the only man who could give orders to the Commander of Police. There was no reason she could possibly imagine for his being in her office . . . no good reason. This was Arienrhod's revenge, then. Was she being dismissed, arrested, deported; charged with corruption, coercion, sex perversion? A thousand nightmares of unjust persecution peopled the silent hallway like a gauntlet of demons, waiting for her to pass. *Maybe I should have gotten on that ship this*

153

morning after all. "Thanks for the warning, BZ." Her voice sounded small and faraway.

"Inspector—" Gundhalinu hesitated, his eyes still asking the question he didn't have the nerve to ask aloud.

"Later." She took a deep breath. "Ask me later, when I know the answer." She went on down the hall, knowing as she took each step that it was the bravest thing she had ever done.

She saw them through the clear panel of the door before they noticed her standing outside it. Mantagnes, formerly Chief Inspector and now the Acting Commander, sat tapping on her desk terminal with ill-concealed discomfort; the aging Chief Justice sat in a chair, gaunt with dignity in his tight-collared official robes. She felt her hand slip as she turned the tarnished brass knob on the door.

Both men rose abruptly as she entered the room. The unexpectedness of it left her staring; she recovered in time to make her salute, a fraction of a second before Mantagnes began his own. "Commander . . . Your Honor." The Chief Justice acknowledged her; they both remained standing. She wondered whether they were waiting for her to sit down first out of some misguided sense of tribunal chivalry. She glanced at the emptiness behind her; if they were, then they must be expecting her to sit on the floor. "Please . . . don't stand on my account." The gracious tone rang very false in the small space. She didn't try to match it with a smile.

Mantagnes moved out from behind her desk, offered her her own seat with a silent gesture. The anger that she read in his eyes made her skin prickle. He was a Kharemoughi, like the Chief Justice—Kharemoughis tended to rise to the top in the foreign service; not surprisingly, since their homeworld dominated it. She knew that on Kharemough women enjoyed relative social equality, since their society valued skill and class status more than sheer physical strength. But the foreign service, which included a wide variety of recruits from less enlightened worlds, seemed to attract the most regressive and autocratic Kharemoughis as well—Mantagnes included. She didn't know anything about Hovanesse, the Chief Justice, but she could read nothing encouraging in his expression. She went to the desk and sat down, the feel of familiar territory easing her fear a little. She glanced from wall to wall, wished with more than usual feeling that the room had a window.

They were still standing. "You're probably wondering why we're here, Inspector PalaThion," Hovanesse said, with pitiless banality.

She fought down a sudden, monstrous urge to laughter. *If that isn't the understatement of the millennium.* "Yes, I certainly am, Your Honor." She folded her hands on the gray-lettered keyboard of her terminal, watched her knuckles whiten as they formed a hopeless prayer gesture. She noticed a battered parcel sitting at the corner of the desk, read her name; considered absently that she did not know the handwriting. Her name was misspelled. *I hope it's a bomb.*

"I understand that—former Commander LiouxSked and his family left Tiamat today. You saw them off?"

"Yes, Your Honor. They left on schedule."

"The gods go with them." He looked down grimly at the stained, ancient ceramic floor tiles. "How could he do such a thing to his family, and his good name!"

"Your Honor, I can't believe—" She felt Mantagnes's hostile gaze catch her, and faltered. *They want to believe it; he wasn't a Kharemoughi.*

The Chief Justice tugged sharply at his tailored doublet. Jerusha pulled surreptitiously at the collar of her own tunic. It secretly surprised her to see him looking so ill at ease. Kharemoughis were made to wear uniforms; it was the Newhavenese who were miserable in the formality of any clothing. "As you know, Inspector, Commander Lioux-Sked's . . . departure leaves us without an official head of the police force on Tiamat. Naturally, we need to fill the post as soon as possible, for reasons of morale. The responsibility for filling that post belongs to me. But of course it has always been the policy of the Hegemony to allow local rulers some say in the choosing of officials who will work most closely with them."

155

Jerusha leaned back into her chair as Mantagnes's expression darkened further.

"The Snow Queen has asked—has demanded—that I appoint you as the new Commander."

"Me?" She caught at the desk edge. "Is this . . . is this a joke?"

"A monumental joke," Mantagnes said sourly. "And we're the butt of it."

"You mean, you're going along with it? You want me to accept the position?" She could not believe the words when she said them.

"Of course you'll accept the position," Hovanesse said tonelessly. "If this is what she wants from the police force that protects her people, this is what she'll get," suggesting that he thought Arienrhod had chosen her own punishment.

Jerusha pushed slowly up out of her seat, leaned across the desk. "You're ordering me to become Commander, then. I don't have any choice."

Mantagnes put his hands behind him. "You had no objection to being made an inspector over men who deserved it, to please the Queen." It was the first time anyone had ever acknowledged it openly. "I'd think you'd jump at the chance to become Commander of Police just because you're female."

"It's better than never being promoted at all just because I'm female." She felt pressure growing in her chest, until she thought her heart would stop. "But I don't want this! Damn it, I don't like the Queen any better than you do, I don't want to be Commander—not if it only means being a puppet!" *A trap, this is a trap*—

"That isn't up to you, Commander PalaThion . . . unless of course you resign," Hovanesse said. "But I'll see that your doubts about your ability to do a satisfactory job as Commander are duly recorded."

She said nothing, unable to think of a single appropriate response.

Mantagnes reached up to his collar, unfastened the insignia he had plainly been expecting to wear forever. He threw them down on her desk; she put out a hand just in time to stop one of them from skidding over the edge. "Congratulations." He saluted with utter precision.

She bent her head stiffly. "Dismissed . . . Inspector Mantagnes."

The two men left the room without a word.

Jerusha sat down again in her seat. Her hands closed over the winged Commander's badges, felt them cut into her palms. This was Arienrhod's doing, Arienrhod's revenge. *Commander PalaThion* . . . The Queen had hung her up to twist in the wind, thrown a challenge at her that Arienrhod expected would ruin her career.

But by the Bastard Boatman, she hadn't gotten to be a Blue by being a weakling or a quitter. So she was Commander PalaThion now—well, damn it, she'd make the most of it! She reached up with great deliberateness and pinned the badges to her collar. "If you think you're going to ruin me, if you think I'm going to fail," she said aloud to the Queen of the Air, "then that's your second mistake." But her hands trembled. *I won't fail! I'm as good as any man!* feeling the pain of old, deep wounds that weakened her self-belief.

She pulled open the drawer in front of her, reaching for the pack of iestas. But the image of LiouxSked's agony crossed her vision, and her hand closed over itself instead. She shut the drawer. She had not touched the pack of iestas in all the time since his overdose.

Her glance found the mysterious parcel again; she pulled it across the desk instead, to give her hands and her mind a focus. She untied the twine, unwrapped the rough brown cloth that covered a crude box. It looked like something that had come from the outback on a trader's ship; and there was no one out there whom she could envision sending a parcel to an inspector of police.

She opened the box and lifted the contents out carefully: a shell the size of her two open hands, with one of the spiny fingers broken off of its fragile crest. It was the color of sunrise, and its surface had been patiently burnished until it glowed like the dawn sky. She had seen it

157

last, and admired it, on the mantel over the fireplace at Ngenet ran Ahase Miroe's plantation house . . . while she stood listening to the flames crack in the easy silence, sipping the strong black tea Ngenet had urged on her before she went on her way to Carbuncle. That surprisingly peaceful moment came back to her now quite clearly, soothing her. Ironic to think that the only pleasant social visit she could remenber since coming to this world ten years ago had been fifteen minutes spent in the company of a man who was probably breaking the law. . . .

She probed inside the shell with her fingers, dumped the packing out of the box; but there was no message for her. She sighed—not sure what she had been expecting, only disappointed that it wasn't there. "Congratulations on your promotion, Geia Jerusha," she said wearily. She picked up the shell again, closed her eyes; held it against her ear in the way Ngenet had shown her, listening for the voice of the Sea.

—— **18** ——

HEY SPARKS, DON'T LEAVE WHILE YOU'RE HOT. GIVE US A CHANCE TO BREAK EVEN.

The hologrammic torso above the ravaged city on the game table threw the protest at him as he removed his fragile headset. But he hung it up on the terminal, officially withdrawing.

"Sorry." He grinned with nonchalant smugness, making his answer more to the hostile stares of the other players than to the computer controlling the phantom croupier. "It's getting boring." He tapped his credit card into the slot, saw it pop out again with the new sum—more money than he had imagined existed in the world a few months ago. The idea that it all belonged to him had almost stopped impressing him now; now that he knew how much wealth circulated along the spiraling Street of Carbuncle. He was even getting a feel for how much money must flow through the Black Gates to the other worlds of the Hegemony . . . he was learning fast. But not fast enough.

He lurched away from the table, drunk on rose-colored Samathan wine, but not so drunk that he couldn't quit while he was ahead. That was one of the things he was good at, he thought, knowing the odds and his own limits —that was why he was winning more and more often at the games. Arienrhod kept him supplied with money, and he spent the time when he was free of Starbuck's official persona squandering it in the saloons and gambling hells up and down the Street; ingratiating himself with as many of his fellow pleasure takers as he could stomach. Listening, asking, watching the undercurrents shift: trying to get a feel for where the information came from and flowed to.

But he was struggling to climb out of a pit of abysmal ignorance, and when the wine and the drugged perfume of too many rooms like this one began to clog his senses, the frustration rose up in him until he ached. There was nothing about the city that gave him any pleasure any more: The things that had delighted a Summer boy might still exist here in the Maze's vibrant convolutions, but he no longer saw them. The longer he lived in Carbuncle, the more he despised the people who were its life.

He had begun to hate the sight of everything and everyone, without knowing why; the blackness stained his past and future, and even the sight of his own face. Everything—except Arienrhod. Arienrhod understood the blackness that lay like poisoned pools in the deepest places of his mind; knew how to bleed off his hostility; reassured him that every soul was black at the heart. Arienrhod comforted him, Arienrhod brought him peace, Arienrhod granted his every wish . . . Arienrhod loved him. And the fear that he might lose her love, make her regret that she had let him become Starbuck—see her cast him off, as she had cast off his rival—was a cloud always lying on the horizon of that peaceful sea.

159

She used her own extensive system of electronic spies and confiding nobles to augment the scraps of information he brought her; but offworlders who really had something to hide had effective countermeasures, and he knew that she missed the insider's knowledge of a real Starbuck, a man who had spent his life among them. The day would come when she would begin to resent his Summer ignorance. Maybe, drunk with the moment, he had lost sight of his own limits just once. . . .

Sparks pushed his credit card into the lining of his belt, felt his elation sour as he started away from the table. He wondered briefly, resentfully, whether he was really any good at these games; or whether Arienrhod watched him secretly even here and arranged the winning for him.

He shook the thought off, his hands bunching on his belt; glanced across the scape of turbaned heads, bare heads, caps, helmets, gem-woven coiffures, bowed in unholy worship within the flickering panoramas of their chosen games of chance. This was one of the high-class hells; more sophisticated, less luridly obvious than the cheaper joints in the lower Maze, which catered to a crowd made up largely of Winter laborers. But even here there was no honest joy. The players laughed and cursed with equal vindictiveness, oblivious to the glaring music that blurred conversation and muted the sounds from the next room. In the next room were the dream machines, where you could lock yourself into terrifying experiences on other worlds, commit any crime, experience anything up to the moment of death that you had the courage to endure. He used them more and more, and they gave him less and less.

He began to weave his way between the tables toward the entrance, moving with a purpose and assurance that belonged to another man: a man who wore a mask and an offworld medallion on his chest. Sparks Dawntreader wore a bright-banded imported tunic and high boots; his hair was cut short like a Winter's—but it was the unaware arrogance of Starbuck that made the other patrons step out of his way.

"You look like a man who knows what he wants." The one who didn't move aside stepped boldly into his path, the slitted silver of her long gown disguising nothing.

He looked, and looked away again, still less than comfortable with the publicity of sexual advances here in the city. "No, thanks. I just want to get out of here." The silver of her gown, for a flashing instant, made him think of silver-white hair.... He pushed on past, trying not to touch her. He felt no real desire for any woman except Arienrhod now: Arienrhod who was teaching him to desire things he had never even dreamed about. And the idea of sex for money seemed grotesque and perverted, even though he knew that half the women and men who offered their bodies in these places were Winters. Bored or money-hungry, they had adapted their normal easiness about sex to the offworlders' mercenary appetites.

There were offworlder prostitutes here, too, controlled by other offworlders higher up in the covert power web that covered the Maze. There were worlds in the Hegemony where slavery was an accepted fact or a tacit one—and Arienrhod did not interfere with the customs of her customers. Some of them looked no different from the local body sellers (only, to his eyes, more exotic); but there were the zombies, too, flesh-and-blood victims for hire who satisfied the kind of customers who weren't content with dreams. They moved nearly naked through the crowds, flaunting their scars—no, flaunting was the wrong word. They were the living dead, they moved vacant eyed, like sleepwalkers; theirs was the dream, and the nightmare. They were drugged, he had been told, or drugs had already destroyed their brains. He had been told by Arienrhod that they felt nothing. And once, when his own mood had turned especially black, he had almost . . .

But the memory of lying helpless in an alley while four slavers called him "pretty" had broken the black mood the way his shell flute had broken that night; left him wondering whether it was really the offworlders he despised, or the offworlder in himself.

But Arienrhod had eased his conscience again, brushed

161

away his questions, laughed gently and told him that there would always be evil, on any world, in any being, because without it there would be no measure for good. . . .

Sparks took a deep breath as the casino doors swept shut behind him, stood letting his lungs clear on the inset slab of rare metallic ore that served as a doorstep. A tawny cat slipped past his feet, disappeared into a hidden cranny in the wall, hunting.

". . . Come on, S'eing, gimme a break." Something familiar yet strange about the voice made him turn and look along the building front. "I'll do anything, for gods' sakes, anything to get out of this hellhole and back to someplace where they can help me! Sign me on—" The speaker was an offworlder, thick dark hair, brown skin, a sparse half-grown beard. He sat on a box, propped against the wall, wearing a stained crewman's coveralls with no insignia. He was a stranger; he looked like a strong man slowly starving to death, and Sparks began to turn away from the sight of him. But the voice . . . "You owe me, damn you, S'eing!" He watched the stranger push away from the wall with an awkward twist of his spine, catch the pants leg of the second man's flightsuit.

The second man was a freighter captain, he guessed, or something less official: a heavy man with a scarred face. He stepped back suddenly, jerking the seated man off-balance. Sparks watched the first man sprawl helplessly into the street, realized with a shock of empathy that the man's legs were paralyzed. The scarred officer laughed, the kind of laughter he'd never wanted to hear again. "I don't owe you shit, Herne, if you can't collect." Herne's curses followed him down the alley.

The man called Herne rearranged his useless legs laboriously, ignoring the subtle and the not so subtle stares of the passersby. Sparks stood staring like the rest, trapped in the voyeurism of pity. He moved forward at last, tentatively, as he watched the man try to drag himself back onto his seat. The man glanced up at him; slid back down onto the pavement.

"You!" Hatred followed recognition like night behind

162

day. "Did she send you here? Did she tell you where to find me?...Yeah, take a good look, kid! Fill up your eyes, fill up your brain; and then don't ever forget that someday she'll do the same to you." Herne's hand closed on a fistful of dust, flung it away.

"Starbuck." He was not sure he had even spoken it aloud, but he knew it for the truth. "She—she said you were dead." He had imagined she meant fallen thousands of meters into the sea. But there were platforms and machinery jutting out into the shaft. One of those must have broken his fall...and broken his back. And now he might as well be dead—but he was alive. Sparks felt the sudden release of an unconscious pressure somewhere in his chest, a thing he became aware of only in its absence. "I'm glad..."

Herne twisted in futile rage; his hand leaped out at Sparks's leg. "You son of a Summer slut! If I could get my hands on you I'd finish what I started!" He slumped back again, letting his hand drop. "Go ahead, enjoy it, kid. I'm still twice the man you are, and Arienrhod knows it, too."

Sparks stood just beyond reach, his face burning. The memory of what Herne had done to him, and failed to do, there in the Hall of the Winds drowned his compassion like a gnat in a bowl of bitterness. "You're no man at all, Herne, any more. And Arienrhod is all mine!" He turned and started away down the alley.

"You fool!" Herne's angry laughter beat at his retreating back. "Arienrhod is no man's! You belong to her, and she'll use you until she uses you up—"

Sparks walked on, not looking back, until he reached the corner of the Street. But he did not start uphill toward the palace; he stood while his anger drained away and left him purposeless, before he chose the downhill route. He walked aimlessly for a long time, moving into the heart of the Maze. He passed the bars and casinos that had become a second home to him; glanced desultorily at shop windows filled with imported spices and herbs, jewelry, paintings, caftans, terminals...and a hundred different technological toys: costly, sophisticated baubles spread out for the jostling freeport trade and the wondering eyes of the natives. Once every window had stopped him in his tracks, and a walk in the Maze had been like a walk through heaven. Now they barely caught his eyes; and somehow, without his being aware of it, time had coated his awe with a rind of disillusionment, and the wine of wonder had turned to vinegar.

Even the many-colored alleys, the fertile meeting ground where artisans of this world and seven more let their creativity bloom, had grown strangely dim and separate from his own reality. He was no longer drawn into the sight and fragrance and music as he moved along them; and now the vivid bruise left on his awareness by Herne's living death pressed painfully, acutely, against the walls of yielding glass that closed him in. Surrounded by the beating heart of the city he had come here to discover, he discovered instead that somehow the thing he had reached out for had slipped through his hands again. Like everything he had ever cared about, or counted on. . . .

His hand closed violently over the stem of a kinetic sculpture in the display stall he was passing; harsh notes clashed among its spines, leaping like cats. But the jangling isotonic music stopped at his skin, the cool metal stem swayed into another dimension. Or maybe he only imagined their unreality; but still it did not pass. . . . *Why? What's wrong with me? What's wrong?*

He let it go in disgust as the sculptor came indignantly to the door of his shop. He went on, realizing only now what alley he had come into: It was the Citron Alley, and ahead of him he could already see Fate Ravenglass sitting as she always did with her trays and trimmings on her doorstep. The place he had come to once before for shelter, and been taken in without question or demand. The place that he could always come back to, a haven of calm and creation in a universe of indifference and broken parts.

He saw that Fate was not alone, saw her visitor rise from the step in a cloud of midnight-blue veils embroidered with rainbows. He recognized her friend Tiewe—by the

164

veils, he had never seen anything more of her than her ebony hands. He heard the sweet song of her hidden necklace of bells. He had asked Fate why she never showed herself, thinking that she must be disfigured; but Fate had said that it was a custom of her homeworld. He had seen only one or two others like her since, carefully protected by chaperones. Tiewe was uneasy in the presence of men, and he felt a jealous gratification as he realized that she was leaving because she had seen him. Fate had many friends—but there were none who seemed to be anything more than friends to her. He had wondered from time to time about her celibacy.

As Tiewe moved away, trailing music, Fate's face turned to his approach: half a smile, half a frown of concentration. "Sparks—is that you?" Malkin the cat meowed affirmation from his crouching spot in her doorway.

"Yes. Hello, Fate." Sparks stopped in front of her, suddenly uncertain.

"Well, what a nice surprise. Sit down, don't be a stranger. You've been too much of a stranger these past months."

He grimaced his guilt as he sat down, carefully, among the trays on the stoop. "I know. I'm sorry, I—"

"No, no, don't apologize." She waved her hands, absolving him goodnaturedly. "After all, how often have I come to the palace to visit you?"

He laughed. "Never."

"Then I should be grateful you come here at all." She felt for the mask she had laid down. "Tell me gossip about the court—what they wear, how they play, what marvelous inconsequentialities they brood over. I need some cheering up. Tiewe is inspired with a needle and floss, but such a sad person. . . ." She looked away, frowning at nothing, reached out abruptly for a tray of beads and upset it. "Damn!" Malkin leaped up from the doorway and disappeared into the shop.

"Here, let me—" Sparks leaned out, barely catching a cascade of shimmering green as it poured over the step's edge. He righted the tray and refilled it patiently, soothed by the mindlessness of the task. "There." He handed her three beads at a time, falling back gratefully into the habits and the comfortable feel of his days with her.

"See how I've missed you." She smiled as the beads dropped into her palm. "But not just for your patient hands—for your lilting Summer songs and the freshness of your wonder."

Sparks let his fingers dig into his knees, said nothing.

"Will you stay and play for me awhile? It's been too long between songs in this alley."

"I—" He swallowed the stone in his throat. "I didn't bring my flute."

"No?" More incredulous than if he'd told her he wasn't wearing clothes. "Why not?"

"I—don't feel like playing, lately."

She sat leaning forward over the mask form, waiting for something more.

"I've been too busy," defensively.

"I thought that was what you did for the Queen—played your music."

"Not any more. I do . . . uh, other things, now." He shifted on the hard surface of the step. "Other . . . things."

She nodded; he had forgotten how disconcerting the gaze of her third eye was. "Like gambling and drinking too much wine at the Parallax View." It was a statement of fact.

"How'd you know—where I've been?" not quite willing to admit the rest of it.

"I can smell you. Their incense is imported from D'doille. Every place has its own identity, and so does every drug. And your voice is just a little slurred."

"Tell me if I won or lost."

"You won. If you'd lost you wouldn't sound so smug about it."

He laughed, but it was not an easy laugh. "You'd make a good Blue."

"No." She shook her head, and searched a bead for its hole with her needle. "To become a Blue a person needs a

166

certain sense of moral superiority; and I refuse to pass judgment on my fellow sinners. Ah—" as the bead slipped into place. "Some green feathers, please."

"I know you don't." He passed feathers to her.

"And is that why you've come here today?" She dipped her fingers in glue and dabbed the feather stems. "As long as you quit the tables while you're ahead, the Queen can't object to how you spend your free time and money, can she?"

"She wants me to gamble. She gives me the money." The words came out inexorably; he could feel the forbidden secret rise inside him, knowing that it was only a matter of time.

"She does? Are you that good?" Fate said it as though she doubted it.

"No. I do it to learn things, about how the offworlders think, what their plans are, so I can tell her. . . ."

"I thought that's what she has Starbuck for."

"It is." The invisible wall of his anomie seemed to close them into a place of utter silence, and his voice that should have been proud barely carried across it: "I am Starbuck."

The small sigh of her indrawn breath was all the answer she made, at first. "I heard that there was a new Starbuck. Is this true, Sparks? You, a Summer, a—" *A boy*, but she didn't say it.

"Half Summer." He nodded. "Yeah. It's true."

"How? Why?" Her hands lay motionless over the mask's gaping mouth.

"Because she's so like Moon. And Moon is gone." Arienrhod was the only thing that had not changed for him, the only thing whole and real, more real to him than his own flesh. "She knew about Moon, knew what she meant to me. She's the only one who could understand. . . ." The wounded words crept out, to tell her what (but not all) had passed between Arienrhod and himself after the news of Moon's kidnapping reached them. ". . . So I had to challenge Starbuck; because I love her. And she let me challenge him, because she loves me. And I won."

167

"How did you manage to kill a man like that?"

"I killed him with my flute . . . in the Hall of the Winds." *Only he didn't die.*

"And you haven't played it since." Fate shook her head, her thick braid rolled on her shoulder. "Tell me—has it been worth it?"

"Yes!" He flinched back in surprise from his own voice.

"Why did I think I heard 'no'?"

His fingers tightened over a tray of beads, his muscles tightened; she didn't see it. "I had to be Starbuck. I had to be the best, or I wouldn't be—worthy of her. I have to be the one who counts. But I thought once I won the challenge, the rest would be easy; and it's not. I thought it would be everything I ever wanted."

"And it's not."

He shook his own head. "What the hell's wrong with me, anyway! Everything always goes wrong for me . . . everything I do."

"Then maybe you weren't meant to do it. You could still go back to Summer; nothing's stopping you."

"Back to what?" He spat the words. "No. I can't go back." He had already asked it of himself, and been answered. "Nobody goes back, I know that now; we just go on and on, and there's never any reason. . . . I won't leave Arienrhod; I can't. But if I can't be what she wants me to be, I'll lose her anyway." *Herne knew; Herne knows everything. . . .*

"You'll find a way to take the offworlders' pulse. If you were smart enough to outwit Starbuck, you're smart enough to take his place. You'll get the feel of being him; you've already begun to."

Something in the words, a sorrow, surprised him. He made a fist, wrapped it in his hand. "I've got to. I've got to believe it—before the Hunt comes again."

"The Hunt that brings in the water of life? The mer hunt?"

"Yes." He stared down through the pavement, through the heart of the city and the world, toward the spaces of

the sea controlled by the Winter nobles. In his mind he
strewn over the open sea; the rhythm of the ocean swells
could see the Hunt again: the necklace of barren rocks
singing through the ship timbers, the song of the world he
had left behind. Remembering how he had searched the
horizon with sudden longing.... But if the Lady called
him home, he could not hear Her voice any more. Perhaps
because he had come to hunt mers; or perhaps because the
Sea was only the sea, a body of water, a chemical solution.

He had watched the shore of the nearest island, where
the dwindling colony of mers had lain along the black-
pebbled beach ... until the Hounds had driven them back
into the sea, and into the waiting nets that would entangle
and drown them. If they could not resurface twice in an
hour to breathe, they died.

No Summer would kill a mer; they were the Lady's
children, born to Her after stars fell into the sea and became the islands, her consorts, the Land. It was said that
the sailor who killed a mer by accident had no luck from
that day on ... the sailor who killed one intentionally was
drowned by the rest of the crew. He had heard a hundred
different stories of mers saving sailors gone overboard,
even whole crews of a ship that had foundered; seen the
mer that lived in the harbor at Gateway Island, its brindle
back stitching a track across the supple cloth of the harbor
surface as it guided ships safely through the treacherous
Gateway Reef. He remembered the mers that had greeted
them at the sibyl island. He had never heard of a mer
doing anything evil, or anyone harm.

But for the good they could do humans—the ultimate
good of eternal youth—they must die. He had always believed that the myth of mers being immortal, and granting
immortality to humans, was only an old tale ... until he
had come to Carbuncle. And then he had met the Queen,
who had reigned for one hundred and fifty years ... and
Arienrhod had placed the vial of viscous silver liquid into
his hands, and he had let the spray fall into his throat, and
realized that he too could stay young forever.

And so he had stood by, paying for his immortality with his presence, betraying all that he had ever been or believed in, while the Hounds netted and drowned their helpless victims somewhere below.

Then they had hauled the carcasses aboard the ship, and shoving him aside like the useless thing he was, they had squatted down with their knives to rip open the dappled throats. They drained away the precious mer blood while their tentacles reddened and the deck turned slippery under his feet.

And the red leaked back into the sea, and the mutilated bodies followed, their dark eyes still incredulous with death. *Wasted . . . all wasted!* He had turned away, sick at heart, long before the butchery was finished, trying to lose himself in the infinite vista of ocean and sky. But there was no escape from the splash of carcasses plunged back into the sea, *too late, too late*, or the savage lashing of the water as the scavengers gathered, defiling the green-blue purity with the ecstasy of their feeding. The Sea Mother in her pitiless wisdom wasted nothing, and cursed the wantonness of those who did. . . .

"Sparks?" Fate's voice called him back; the sheltering city closed around him, keeping him from the Lady's curses, denying that they even existed at all.

"It was so ugly—it was all wasted! I couldn't—" He shook his head. "But I'm going to do it right this time. I can gut a dead mer, I'm not some superstitious Mother lover any more." Remembering the disdain of the Hounds, which had been all too plain even without words; remembering Arienrhod's soothing condescension as she set free the devils of doubt and self-disgust he carried back with him to Carbuncle. And then she had handed him the gilded vial of the water of life, without comment.

"No, I suppose you're not, are you?" Again the regret. "Death is never an easy thing to face. That's why we all long to taste the water of life. And we take it for ourselves because our own death is the hardest thing of all. . . . We do what we think we have to." She reached out, searched the air for his arm.

170

"Uh, not to interrupt—" A stranger's voice came at them over his shoulder. "Got a delivery here."

Sparks turned, looking up with Fate at the two figures standing in the alley, one drab, one inhuman—"You!"

The faceless face of the servo Pollux regarded him with unchanging nothingness, but Tor's gray eyes registered along a scale from incomprehension to acute chagrin. "Dawntreader?" She shifted from foot to foot. "Hey, uh . . . Well, how've you been, kid? Looks like you've done all right for yourself," raising an eyebrow. "I hardly recognized you."

"No thanks to you if I have."

"Yeah, well . . ." She glanced away self-consciously. "Hi, Fate. Got your new load of trims together finally. You want Pollux to stack them for you?"

Fate began to push her trays aside, clearing a path to the door. "I'll show him where. I didn't know you were a friend of Sparks's, Tor."

"She isn't." Sparks stood up and stood aside as Pollux moved unconcernedly toward the step, towing the floating platform of containers. He watched Fate disappear inside, moving easily into familiar surroundings, and Pollux after her. But he blocked Tor as she tried to follow, with an arm across the doorway. "Uh-uh." He backed her around and up against the building wall. "Let's talk. About what you did to me at the starlbaiting. About what you did with everything I owned, after you cleaned me out."

Tor pressed back against the peeling paint, her eyes looking everywhere but at his face. "Listen, Sparks, I'm really sorry about that, you know? I really hated sticking you like that, I mean, you were so trusting . . . and so stupid. . . . But I owed my life to Hardknot over at the Sea and Stars; I lost part of the casino's daily take I was delivering up the line. If I didn't pay it back she'd've had it taken out of my hide, you know what I mean? It was either you or me, frankly. And I figured it'd teach you a lesson you needed, anyway." She shrugged, beginning to recover her nerve.

"What did you do with my stuff?"

"Pawned it, what do you think?"

He laughed once. "How much did you get for it?" almost casually.

"Birdseed, what do you th—" Her voice choked off as his arm came up and across her throat, pinning her against the wall again. "Ye gods!" She squirmed, trying to look away from something in his eyes. "What's gotten into you, kid?"

"I learned your lesson." He put more pressure against the arm, enjoying the expression on her face. "And now you owe me, Tor, and I could take it out of your hide right now."

"You—you wouldn't do that?" He felt her swallow in sudden fright; her hands came up, tightened over his arm. "What are you—"

"Sparks, what are you doing!" Fate's astonished voice.

He blinked as the haze of his wounded pride cleared, and let Tor go. "You aren't worth the trouble."

Tor sighed noisily, feeling her throat with her hands. "Just—just a misunderstanding, Fate. I'll get you the money, kid. I mean, come payday—"

"Forget it." He turned away, feeling his face hot with anger and embarrassment, wondering how much of it Fate could see. But something Tor had blurted in the diarrhea of her excuses caught in his mind, at the root of his bad humor, and he turned back again with calculated vengeance showing. "On the other hand—no, don't forget about it. You owe me, and I'm going to tell you how you can pay me back. And there might even be something in it for you, if you play it right." He pulled out his credit card, and held it up to her face.

Tor looked at it blankly, "Huh?" She reached for it, hesitant; he pulled it away.

"You're a runner for the Sea and Stars, you said. You must know plenty about who controls what here in the Maze, you must hear a lot of interesting gossip around . . .?"

"Oh, no—I don't know anything, kid, I keep my ears closed." She shook her head, shutting her eyes against temptation. "I just run a few errands on the side, for a little extra credit at the tables, that's all."

172

"Don't give me that." He frowned. "But maybe you don't know enough to find out the things I want to know." Inspiration struck him, blinding. "I know somebody who does, so it doesn't matter! You can get the information out of him, and I can't. You're going to take care of it for me, take care of him, understand?"

"No." She shook her head again. "What the hell have you gotten into, anyway? What're you trying to get me into?"

"I work for somebody too, somebody—up the line. Somebody who wants to know what the opposition's doing. And there's a man named Herne who knows it all, only he's down on his luck. You're going to pick him up and help him out; and he's going to be so grateful he's going to tell you anything you want to know."

"Ha! I know a Herne, a big spender, and if he's down on his luck now he can rot. Him and some of his buddies were drug ugly, and he tried to—" The word wouldn't come out; her hands tightened over the seal of her coveralls. "I had bruises in places I wouldn't show my own mother before Pollux pulled him off me and changed his mind." She glanced past Fate's silent witnessing at the phlegmatic metal being in the doorway. "He may be a dumb machine, but he's a damn sight more of a man than the ones who program him."

Sparks grinned at the borrowed vision of Herne's discomfiture. "He really must have been drugged out of his mind to pick on a—"

Tor's face reddened, her fists came up. "Listen, Summer, you don't joke about a thing like that with a Winter woman!"

His grin fell away abruptly. "By 'r—by the gods, that's not what I meant! If it's the same Herne, you've got nothing to worry about. He won't give you any trouble this time. You'll find him near the Parallax View. I'll pay the expenses, and make it worth your while; just make sure that he never knows why you're doing it. Don't ever mention me." He lowered his voice, turning away from Fate.

173

"If I don't get what I want, you'll regret it, and even Pollux won't be enough to keep you safe."

Tor's pallid face turned paler; he felt a brief surprise as he realized that she believed him. "Meet me back here at the same time in—one week."

"Yeah, sure," she said weakly, and oozed out from behind the barricade of his body. "Come on, Pollux, let's go."

"Whatever you say, Tor." He stepped down off the porch and followed her away. She hit him spitefully on the chest, went on down the alley rubbing her hand.

"Shut up, you damn junk pile; I'm going to trade you in on a dog."

Fate was sitting again, decorating the naked, gaping mask form as though it were the only reality in the universe. She did not speak to him, or look up with any of her eyes.

Sparks felt his elation implode as he saw her withdrawing from him—as though she too were setting herself apart from him; or as though he had done it for her.

"You said I'd find a way to solve the problem. And I've done it."

"Yes, I suppose you have." She picked up a piece of satin cloth.

"I thought you didn't make moral judgments."

"I try not to. We all choose our own paths to hell. But some of the choices are easier to watch than others . . . I don't like to watch my friends being hurt."

"I just said that. I wouldn't hurt her." But he knew that just for a moment he had been inches from it. And that was the moment that Fate had seen.

" 'Today's word is tomorrow's deed,' " she quoted softly. "And I consider you my friend, too."

"Still?"

"Yes, still." She looked up at him, but without smiling. "Take care, Sparks. Life isn't woven from a single thread, you know."

"All right." He shrugged, not really understanding. "I'll see you again, Fate."

174

She smiled at last, but it wasn't the smile he had been waiting for. " 'In one week, at this same time.' "

" 'Scuse me, buddy, have you seen a guy called H-Herne?" Tor broke off as the derelict's face looked up at her, glaring with the useless hatred of a chained animal, and she realized that she had seen it before. Gaunt and bearded, it was still the same face: a dark offworlder's face, a too-handsome face with eyes that were long lashed and beautiful and as cold as death. She stood for a moment staring down, pinched between the vise-fingers of the present and the past. This was Herne, the same Herne, whose eyes looking at her once had not seen a human being but a thing.

But there was no sign of recognition when he looked up at her now, no acknowledgment of the irony of their reunion. She backed up a step from the stink of him, his filthy coveralls, remembering the richness of his clothes the last time. Maybe the drugs had gotten the last laugh on him after all. . . . She almost smiled. There were a half-empty bottle and a dented can with a handful of coins in it sitting on the box beside him. As she came along the alley she had seen a Blue lieutenant with incongruous pink freckles give him a citation for begging. But the truculent expectation faded from his face as her question registered; he inventoried her, and Pollux with her, in a quick, expressionless glance. "Maybe I know a Herne. Can't seem to remember." His hand closed significantly around the can. "Why?"

She dug into a pocket, tossed her loose change into the can. "I hear he's down on his luck. Maybe I want to change it."

"You?" He took a swig from the bottle, wiped his hand across his mouth. "Again, why?"

"That's between him and me." She folded her arms, almost beginning to enjoy the game. "So where is he?"

"I'm Herne," grudgingly.

"You?" She echoed his incredulity; laughed, going it one better. "Prove it."

"You bitch!"

She leaped back from the memory of his brutal strength; but he only swayed forward on the box, would have fallen off it if Pollux had not put out a rigid hand to push him upright again. Tor stood staring, still beyond his reach, while she tried to assess what she had just seen. "So that's what he meant. You're a cripple!"

His mouth twisted. "Who? Who sent you here?"

"Nobody important." She shrugged awkwardly. "I'm the one that wants to see you, Herne. I'm the one you better worry about." She leaned against Pollux, ran a hand along the cool metal of his shoulder, smiling. "What do you figure you'd do to me, it our positions were reversed . . .?"

Startled doubt tightened the muscles in his cheek. He studied her again, and Pollux. For a moment she thought she saw recognition; or maybe it was only the fear of recognition. How many enemies did a man like that have in a place like this . . . how many real friends did he have in the whole universe? Herne slouched against the wall, resigned. "Do what you want, I don't give a fuck." He took another drink from the bottle.

"No." she shook her head, remembering Dawntreader and her own troubles with something nearing empathy. "Just asking. So how's business?" She peered into the can.

"Slow." She felt him refusing to ask her her own business; a subtle tension filled the half of his body that still responded. Patrons from the Parallax View passed them by with averted eyes.

"You've come a long way down, since the last time we met."

He didn't remember. She was certain now, not sure if she was glad or sorry. "I've begged before; it never killed me."

She shifted her weight against Pollux, looked him over slowly. "I think it might, this time."

He glanced up, down again; didn't answer.

"I hear you really knew your way around the Maze before your—uh, accident." She wondered what or who had done this to him. "I hear you really know which way

176

the power flows, offworld and on. Well, that's worth something to me."

"Why?" sharply.

"What's it to you?" She countered, not sure what reason was going to come off her tongue that wasn't the truth. "You ask a lot of questions for a beggar."

"I want to know why a Winter would want to know. There's only one Winter—" He frowned.

"There's thousands of us, and we're just as interested in making it big as you are, foreigner." She unfastened a pocket and pulled out her credit card, held it up in front of him as Sparks had held his up to her. "Maybe I don't want to be a loader forever. Maybe I want to get my slice before all of you go offworld and take the cake with you." She felt a dim surprise that the words made sense to her.

He nodded, noncommittal, as though they even made sense to him. "You said it's worth something. How much?" He squinted at the card face.

"I don't have much ... but it's more than you've got. You even got a place to stay?"

A single shake of his greasy, unkempt head.

She swore. "That's what I figured. You can stay at my place, for now. You need somebody around to feed you and clean up after you anyhow."

"I need money, not somebody to wipe my goddamn nose! Don't waste my time." He reached over his shoulder and scratched, grimacing.

She watched him scratch. "It's a wonder anybody gets close enough to put anything in that," she gestured at the can. "What are you going to do when your clothes crawl right off your back some night?"

"You want to take 'em off tonight, instead, sweetheart?" He leered.

Her mouth thinned; she forced it back into a smile. "You're not my type, cripple. Pollux here does all my dirty work for me. He's used to dragging around dead weights."

"Whatever you say, Tor," Pollux droned benignly. There was an indefinable suggestion of approval in the toneless voice. She stood away from him again, a little uneasily.

Sometimes it was hard to remember that he was nothing but a predictably programmed loading device.

"You can have food and shelter as long as you're worth it to me, Herne. Take it or leave it." *Take it or leave it, you bastard. I'm screwed either way.*

"I can't keep up with what's happening unless I get to circulate. I need money for that, I need a way to—"

"You'll get what you need—as long as I do." *As long as Dawntreader keeps his bargain with us.*

He leaned back, with a smile that was something ugly on his handsome face. "Then you've got yourself an advisor, sweetheart." He stretched his arms, carefully.

"I've got myself a big pain in the ass." She picked up his battered can and emptied the coins out into her hand. "All right, Polly, cart him home."

The limitless absence of light and life wrapped Moon's senses in a smothering shroud, deprived her of all sensation. Falling into a bottomless well, she knew herself for the last feeble spark of life in a universe where Death reigned undisputed . . . the consort of Death, whose intangible embrace sapped her of strength and sanity. She had come into this place outside life, searching for her lost love, by a gate she had passed through many times; but this time she had lost her way, and there was no one to answer her cries, no ear to hear them, no voice to carry. . . . *Let me go home. . . .*

"Let me go home!" Moon sat up in bed, her voice beating back at her from the tight walls of the tiny room.

"Moon, Moon—it's only a nightmare. You're safe with us now. Safe." Elsevier's arms were around her, gentling her, as Gran had comforted a child in the night; so long ago, so long ago. . . .

The room filled her wet blinking eyes with painful artificial day; the threedy set into the wall fountained noise and motion—just as they had before she slipped down into uncertain sleep. Since the ordeal of the Black Gate, she could not stay in a darkened room. She swallowed a knot of aching grief, rested her head against Elsevier's soft-robed shoulder, feeling the cool movement of air over the back of her own clammy nightshirt. The world slowly congealed around her, reaffirming her place in it; her heart stopped trying to tear itself out of her chest. She found herself listening for the sound of the sea.

"It's all right. I'm all right now." Her voice still sounded thin and unconvincing . . . the nightmare loss of strength and control had become a part of her waking existence. She sat up again, away from Elsevier's reassuring presence, pulling strands of damp hair back behind her ears. "I'm sorry I woke you again, Elsie. I just can't—" She broke off, ashamed of her helplessness, rubbing miserably at her eyes. They burned as though they were full of windblown sand. It was the third night in a row that her haunted dreams had carried through the thin partitions of the apartment. She saw weariness and worry settling deeper into the lines of Elsevier's face as each day passed. "It's stupid." Her hands clenched. "I'm sorry, keeping you up all night with my stupid—"

"No, Moon, dear." Elsevier shook her head; the tenderness in the indigo eyes silenced Moon with surprise. "Don't apologize to me. Nothing you could do would bother me. I'm the one who should be begging your pardon instead; it's my fault that you have these dreams, my fault that you can't wear your trefoil—" She glanced across the room at the sibyl sign lying alone on the single chest of drawers. "If I could take your fear on myself I'd do it gladly; it would be small penance for the wrong I've done you." She looked away, her fingers massaging her arms.

"It wasn't your fault. It was my fault; I wasn't strong enough to be a sibyl." Moon tightened her jaws until her

179

teeth hurt. Her fault that she had come through the Black Gate and out of her Transfer a stranger, haunted by a split reality. By the time they had reached Kharemough she had functioned again, was almost human again; but still, when she closed her eyes and left her mind unguarded . . .

She had worn her trefoil freely here in the orbiting spaceport city, gratified when total strangers from worlds she had never heard of acknowledged her with smiles and obeisances. But then a man had come up to her and asked her to answer a question. She had turned away from him in sick terror and refused—*refused*. Elsevier had driven him away; but she had known in that moment that she would never be able to answer another question. . . . "I'll—I'll be all right when I get home, to Tiamat." Where the sky at night was on fire with suns—not this black and bitter nothingness which consumed even the life force of a star, where even the stars were shrunken and icy and hopelessly alone. Where the only thing that mattered to her as much as the thing she had destroyed coming here still waited to be done, and the one person who would understand what it meant to lose her life's desire. Sparks—she had to find him. "How much longer—?" She had tried not to ask the question in the time they had spent here, afraid to; wanting to ask it every day, every hour.

"Then you really don't want to stay? Even after all you've seen?" The depth of disappointed hope that Moon felt in Elsevier's voice pinched her heart. She had seen how very hard Elsevier had tried to fill her time and her mind with the incredible wonders of this city, this starport that sailed through space on an invisible tether held by the world below. She had thought that Elsevier only did it to drive away her fears, but now she realized that there had been another reason. "You—really want me to stay with you forever?"

"Yes. Very much, my dear." Elsevier smiled, hesitant. "We never had any children, you know, TJ and I. . . ."

Moon glanced down, steeling herself to deliver another disappointment. "I know. If it was only me, if I was no one, I would stay with you, Elsie."

She realized that it was true, even though she was like a child lost at a Festival here in this incomprehensible, immaculate island wheeling in the sky. Elsevier had tried to make her a part of all she saw, until she had begun to feel the careless pride of the offworlders, who thought a starship was as natural as a sailing ship, who treated things that were awesome and miraculous as no more than their right. With each small technological marvel Elsevier's patience taught her to control, her awe of the greater ones faded, until she could stand on the balcony outside their apartment and look out over the Thieves' Market pretending that she was a true offworlder, a citizen of the Hegemony, completely at home in this interstellar community.

But then the thought would touch her that she finally understood what Sparks had always tried to make her feel; and she would think of how much it would mean to him to stand here where she stood—and she would remember that she had abandoned him when he needed her. "Sparks is still in Carbuncle; I have to go back to him. I can't stay here without him." *Exiled on an island surrounded by lifeless void.* "I can't be a sibyl here." She pressed a hand against the trefoil tattoo at her throat. "I left my own world when I should have stayed. I failed my duty, I failed Sparks, I failed. . . . The Lady doesn't hear my prayers. I'm lost, that's why I've lost Her voice." She pushed her bare feet off the edge of the bed, settling them on the cold floor. "It's wrong; I don't belong here. I won't be happy here. I'm needed on Tiamat—," feeling it with a peculiar intensity. She held Elsevier's indigo eyes, willing Elsevier to understand her need, and her longing—and her regret.

"Moon." Elsevier pressed her hands together, in the way she did when she was trying to make a decision. "How can I say this, except badly? . . . You can't go home."

"What?" Nightmare dimmed her vision of the room and Elsevier's anxious face. "I can!" She threw the light of her will against the shadow. "I have to!"

Elsevier held up her hands, half placating, half shielding herself. "No . . . no. I only meant—I meant that you can't go home until Cress is strong enough to astrogate again." The words faded like a lost opportunity.

Moon frowned uncertainly; a veil of doubt still clouded Elsevier's face. She rubbed at her own, her body sagging with fatigue and disappointment. "I know. I'm sorry." Her hand groped for the half-empty bottle of tranquilizers on the stand beside the bed.

"No." Elsevier's dark hand gripped her wrist, drew her arm back. "That isn't the answer. And you won't find the answer to your fears by going back to Tiamat; they'll follow you everywhere, forever, unless you learn what a sibyl really does. And I'm not wise enough to explain that to you, but there's someone who is. At the first good window we'll go down to the ground and see my brother-in-law." She reached out and took the bottle of pills. "It's something I should have done long before now . . . but I'm only a foolish old woman." She stood up, smiling down at Moon's incomprehension. "I think it will do us all a world of good just to set foot on a real planet again, anyway. Maybe Cress can join us. Rest now, my dear . . . and pleasant dreams." She touched Moon's cheek softly and left the room.

Moon pulled her feet up onto the bed again, smoothed the one thin cover that was all she needed here over her stomach. But there were no sweet dreams waiting in the lifeless night that surrounded this island city or its world. She lay staring at the half-intelligible action flickering eerily through the screen on the wall, her mind and body aching with their separate needs. There was no one in this alien place who could change any of her dreams from dark to light, unless they would let her go home . . . *home*. . . . Tears trickled down her cheeks as her eyelids slipped shut.

She rode through the Thieves' Market in the artificial day, jammed into the crowded spaceport tram with Elsevier and Silky and a rubber-legged Cress, and enough surly commuters to populate an island. The space station's orbit passed over a window—a transportation and shipping corridor down to the surface of Kharemough—every few

182

hours; but those were located hundreds or thousands of miles apart on the planet below. Someone who missed a stop would have to wait a full day for it to open again.

There had been no seats when she boarded the tram, but a man had risen from his as she passed and offered it to her inexplicably. She had smiled and given it to Cress when another man stood up for her in turn. Embarrassed, she had pulled Elsevier forward into the seat instead, whispering, "Do they think I'm so pale because I'm sick?"

"No, dear." Elsevier had frowned mock disapproval and tugged at the hem of her sleeveless, thigh-length yellow tunic. "On the contrary. You really should put on your robe." She touched the sedate wine-colored garment draped over Moon's arm.

"It's too hot." Moon felt the crisscross of braids she had woven out of the way on top of her head, remembering the voluminous robes and tight-fitting jump suits she had tried on and tossed away in the shops of the Center City Bazaar. She had tried to wear her own clothes, now that they were off the ship, but the air of the station was as warm as blood, and so she wore as little as Elsevier would allow.

"When I was a girl I went covered in veils from head to foot; it was part of a woman's mystery." Elsevier arranged the folds of her own loose, color-splashed caftan; her necklace of bells jingled sweetly. "And what I wouldn't have given to throw them all off and run naked down the street, in the steaming heat of summer. But I never dared."

Moon clung to the seat back, one step behind a silently miserable Silky, empathizing with his discomfort locked in a press of strangers. She looked out through the open sides of the tram as they passed avenue after avenue of the port's interstellar community, where Elsevier shared an apartment with Silky and Cress—and now her—in the elegant claustrophobia of Kharemough's offworld ghetto. Already she was lost; she could no more comprehend this city's pattern than she could the customs of the people who controlled it. All she knew was that it all fit into a hollow ring, with the starport centered in the gap. The Kharemoughis referred to the offworld community as the

"Thieves' Market," and its resident aliens accepted the name with amused perversity. Kharemough dominated the Hegemony because it made the most sophisticated technological items available, and Elsevier had remarked to her one day, not without pride, that "Thieves' Market" was more truth than slur.

"How did you become a—come to Kharemough, then?" as Elsevier did not go on with her thoughts. It had seemed more and more unlikely to her that this gentle, self-effacing woman would ever have chosen a career that defied anyone, let alone interstellar law.

"Oh, my dear, how I lost my veils and my respectability is a long, dull, involuted story." But Moon saw the smile that crept out at the corners of her mouth.

"False modesty." Cress slouched in the seat ahead of them, eyes closed, hands pressing his chest. He had been back from the port hospital for only two daylight periods.

"Cress, are you all right?" Elsevier touched his shoulder.

"Fine, mistress." He grinned. "All ears."

She nudged him, leaning back with a shrug of resignation. "Well. I come from Ondinee, Moon, which is a world that would seem even more incomprehensible to you than Kharemough, I'm sure; even though their tech level is not nearly as high. Women in my country were not encouraged—"

"*Allowed,*" Cress said.

"—to live full lives, the kind you've always known." Her voice drifted above the murmur of conversation like smoke rising into the city haze of another world, in a land dominated by the pyramidal temple-tombs of an ancient theocracy. It was a land where women were bought and sold like bartered goods, and lived in separate quarters within the family compound, apart from the men, who were not their partners but their jealous lords. Their lives followed narrow paths worn deep over generations; lives that were incomplete but reassuringly predictable.

A timid girl called Elsevier—*Obedience*—had followed the worn paths of tradition, swathed in veils that hid her humanity from view, stumbling often in the ruts of ritual

184

but never seeing her own life from enough of a distance to wonder why. Until one day in the temple square her curiosity had drawn her away from her offertory rounds at the shrines of her patron spirits, into the crowd gathered to hear a crazy offworlder shouting about freedom and equality. He climbed brazenly up the steps of the Great Temple of Ne'ehman, while a gang of radical local youths jammed leaflets into the hands and clothing of anyone who stood still. But the mob had turned angry and ugly, the ruthless Church Security had come to break it up, and in the panic that followed they had thrown everyone they laid hands on into the black vans together.

Elsevier had cowered, beaten down into a corner of the lurching van by the crush of bodies. Pawed and trampled, her veils torn, she had crouched there sobbing, hysterical with fear of defilement or death. But strong hands had seized her suddenly, dragging her to her feet, and held her up against the wall. Mindless with terror, she felt the world turn to water around her, and her body with it. . . .

"Don't faint now, for gods' sakes! I can't hold you up forever—" and a slap.

Pain punctured the wall of her madness like a spike. She opened her eyes, whimpering, to see in front of her the haggard, bloodied face of the crazy offworlder, the man who had caused this to happen . . . the one man she would love for the rest of her life. But at that moment nothing was further from her mind than love.

"You okay?" He grunted as someone jabbed him in the kidneys. He held his arms rigid against the walls, shielding her with his body. She shook her head. "Did I hurt you? I didn't mean to." He drew one hand in, touched her bare cheek softly. She shriveled away from his fingers, pulling the torn cloth of her veil back over her head. "Sorry." He glanced down, bracing again as the van swayed through a turn. "You weren't even there to hear my speech, were you?" He grimaced ruefully; suddenly he looked barely older than she was. She shook her head again, and wiped her eyes. He muttered something bitter in his own tongue. "KR's right; I do more harm than good! . . . Don't tremble,

185

they won't hurt you. Once we get to the inquisitory they'll weed out the bad seed and let you go."

Another shake. She knew the reputation of the Church police all too well. She felt her eyes fill with tears again.

"Don't. Please don't." He tried a smile on, couldn't keep it. "I won't let them hurt you." It was an absurdity, but she clung to it, to keep from drowning. "Listen," he groped for a change of subject, "uh, since you're—here, you want to hear my speech? This may be my last chance." Beads of sweat glistened in his wiry brown hair.

She didn't answer; and taking it for assent, he had filled the rest of their stifling journey to judgment with the sweet fresh air of his hopeless idealism—of all men living together like brothers, of women sharing the same freedoms with men, and taking the same responsibility for their own actions.... By the time the van lurched to a stop, throwing them back into the reality of their plight, she had become certain that he was utterly insane ... and utterly beautiful.

But then the doors banged open, letting in the harsh light of day and the harsh commands of the guards, who herded the miserable captives out into the walled yard of the detention center. They were the last ones down, and he had pressed her hand briefly—"Be brave, sister"—and asked her name.

She spoke to him at last, only to say her name, before the guards reached him. She heard him begin to protest her innocence as he was hauled out, heard it turn into a gasp. Groping heavy hands dragged her down and away so that she could not see what they did to him. She was herded into the station with the rest, and she didn't see him again.

But waiting inside the station was her father, who had come at a frantic call from her chaperone after she had been carried off in the van. She ran sobbing to him, and after many threats and a large payment to the Church missionary fund he had taken her away from that place of horror, before the Church's inquisitors could inflict any permanent damage to her reputation.

She had been at home for almost two weeks, barely

186

daring to leave the house while her fright slowly healed, before she could bear to think about the mad offworlder again... to wonder about his words, and his kindness to her in the midst of chaos... harder still, to wonder whether he was even still alive. Knowing that she would never know, never see him again, still she could not push his shining-eyed ghost out of her mind.

Even so, she did not recognize the stranger who sat self-consciously on the bench under the vine-covered courtyard wall, as her mother led her to "a suitor," and left her to stand awkward and uncertain in the man's eager scrutiny. He was conservatively dressed in a business suit and cloak; the shadow of a wide-brimmed hat half obscured his face. But what she could see of the face, dimly through her veil, was purple and green.

Apprehensively she threw back her dark blue head veil to let him see her own face, keeping her eyes averted. She curtseyed, her necklace of silver bells singing in the quiet air.

"Elsevier. You don' recognize me, do you?" The words slurred, but his disappointment reached her clearly. He pulled off his hat.

But she had recognized his voice, even distorted as it was, and sat down on the bench beside him with a small cry of astonishment. "You! Oh... hallowed Calavre!" barely aware that she swore. Her hand rose to, but didn't touch, his face; the warm brown of his skin was a tapestry of half-healed cuts and bruises, the sharp line of his jaw was still blurred and swollen.

"I tol' your fadder I was in an acciden'." He smiled with his lips and his eyes; pointed, "Jaw's 'ired shut," in explanation.

Her own face furrowed with empathy, she twisted her hands in her lap.

"It's awright. Hardly hurts at all now." The inquisitors had not given him to the Blues, but instead had taken turns beating him bloody in holy vengeance for a day and a night, finally throwing him out into the street at dawn, to crawl away as fast as he could. "I don't wanna think about

187

it eidder. . . ." He laughed once; but many years would pass before he even told her the smallest part of the truth. He fell silent, looking at her as though he expected something. "Is your jaw 'ired shut too, sister?"

"No!" She shook her head, jingling. "I—I have thought about you. Over and over. I thought I'd never see you again; I was afraid for you." She felt a sudden desire to cradle his bruised face against her heart. "Why did you come here?" She wove the cloth of her veil between her fingers. *Not as a suitor.* But she did not re-cover her face, or feel a need to, with him.

"I had to be sure you 'ere awright. You are awright?" He leaned forward.

"Yes. My father came. . . . You were so kind to me. My father would—"

"No. Blease don' tell him about me. Jus' tell me you listened to my ideas. Tell me I blanted a seed in your mind. . . . Tell me you want to know more."

"Why?" Of all the questions and answers that filled her mind, all that escaped her mouth was the one that told him nothing.

" 'Why?' " But she saw in his eyes that he understood. " 'Ell . . . because I 'ant to see you again."

"Oh! I could touch the sky with my fingers!" She giggled inanely; put her hands over her mouth at the look on his face. The woman who won this man's love would have to win his respect first. "Yes." She met his eyes boldly, impulsively, but with a muscle quivering in her cheek. "I do want to know more. Please come again."

He grinned. "When?"

"My father—"

"When?"

"Tomorrow." Her gaze broke.

"I'll come." He nodded his promise.

"H-how many wives do you have?" hating herself for asking it.

"How many?" He looked indignant. "None. On Kharemough we believe in one at a time. One is enough for a lifetime . . . if she's d' right one." He reached into his

188

jacket, pulled out a handful of pamphlets. "I brought you dese, 'cause I can't shpeak for myself yet. But I wrote dis one . . . an' dis one. Will you read 'em?"

She nodded, feeling as though a shock ran up her arm as they touched her hand.

"You have a beautiful garden here." A kind of longing crept into his voice. "Do you tend the flowers yourself?"

"Oh, no." She shook her head, a little sadly. "I'm only allowed to come here on special occasions. And I'm never allowed to do anything that would get me dirty. But I love flowers. I'd spend all my time here, if I could."

A look of peculiar resolution settled over his bruised face. Very deliberately he reached up to pluck a many-petaled lavender blossom from the vine above their heads. He put it into her hands. "We all die, someday. Better to live a free life than die on the vine."

She cupped the flower in her hands, inhaling its fragrance. She smiled at him more than at his words.

He smiled back. "Till tomorrow, den." He got stiffly to his feet.

"You're going—"

"Godda meeting at d' university over in Merdy, tonight." He beamed at her disappointment, and leaned down, conspiratorial. "I'm an outside agitator, y' know."

"You won't—?" She dared to touch him.

"Uh-uh." He pulled his hat down over his eyes. "No more shpeeches; at leas' till I can open my mouf again. . . . Good-bye, sister." He moved away across the courtyard with a rolling lurch, before she could realize that she still didn't know his name. She looked down at the stack of propaganda, read, *"Partners in a New World" by TJ Aspundh*. She sighed.

"What's that he gave you?" Her mother peered at the pamphlets suspiciously.

"Uh . . . l-love poems." Elsevier tucked them hastily into her waistband and pulled down her veil. "He wrote some of them himself."

"Hmm." Her mother shook her head, and bells sang. "But he's a Kharemoughi; he gave your father a videocom

189

outlet for the right to see you. My lord was very pleased. And it's up to him in the end, after all . . . not to us."

"Why?" Elsevier got up, crinkling with papers. "Why isn't it?"

Her mother took the flower out of her hand and led her back to the women's quarters.

TJ came faithfully to see her, a paragon of respectability before her parents, in private a headstrong dreamer falling in love not with the girl she was, but the woman she could be. He brought her more revolutionary literature disguised as love poems; but before she could begin to explore the new world whose horizons he widened every day, her halting attempts to assert herself with her family led to the discovery of her hidden cache of pamphlets, and he was banished from her life.

"But you didn't let them keep you apart." Moon leaned on the seatback. "Did you run away?"

"No, my dear." Elsevier shook her head, folding her hands with remembered obedience. "My father locked me in the tower room because he was afraid I would, before I even thought of it." She smiled. "But TJ was dauntless. He came back one night in a hovercraft, climbed in my window, and kidnapped me."

"And you—"

"I was frantic! I wasn't nearly as enlightened as he thought I was, or I did; in asserting myself I'd really only been pleasing someone else again . . . him. And now he'd ruined my reputation. I nearly died of shame that night. But by morning we'd reached the spaceport, and there was no going back." She looked out at the city, seeing another place and time. "We were always like that, all our lives, I suppose: him believing in 'Be certain you're right, and then go ahead,' me believing in 'Do what you must.' . . . But even that terrible night, there was no doubt in my mind that he'd done the deed with the purest of hearts, that he loved me in a way I had never dared to dream about being loved. I chided him—years later—for committing such a male-dominant act. He only laughed, and told me he was just trying to work within the system.

"We were married at the spaceport by one of those dreadful notary machines, and the passage to Kharemough was our honeymoon. Poor TJ! We were halfway across the galaxy before I let him touch me. But once I learned that all I'd been told about—my body all my life was a lie, it was easier to believe that I had a mind as well, and nourish it. We were different in many ways... but our souls were one." She sighed.

Darkness swallowed them unexpectedly as the tram entered one of the transparent spokes that spanned the starship harbor's vacuum to the spaceport hub of the city wheel. Moon lost the images of Elsevier's words as they flowed into a memory of her own, of firelight and wind, warm kisses, and two hearts beating together. The empty blackness seeped into the space in her own soul which should have been filled and hid her face, as her face turned as bleak as her heart.

"Wish I could have known him." Cress's face shone briefly as he lit one of the spicy-smelling reeds everyone here seemed to smoke.

"He gone," Silky said, pointlessly, remarking on the obvious. He spoke barely intelligible Sandhi, the international language of Kharemough, which Moon had been learning with Elsevier's help. But the thoughts behind his murky mutterings were as opaque to her as they had ever been.

"TJ would have driven you right up the wall, Cress," Elsevier said, fondly. "He was always switched on. You move through a much thicker temporal medium; you're much better suited to astrogation."

Cress laughed; it became a fit of coughing.

"You know they told you not to smoke!" Elsevier reached forward and took the glowing reed out of his hand; he didn't protest.

"Gone," Silky said. "Gone. Gone ..." as though he were obsessed by the feel of the word.

"Yes, Silky." Elsevier murmured. "The good always die young, even if they live to be a hundred." She stroked one of the maimed tentacles draped across the back of Cress's seat. "I never saw him as angry, or as fine, as the day he

191

took you from that street carnival in Narlikar." She shook her head, her necklace of bells rang silverly. "He suffered everyone's pain; and that was why he wanted to end it. Thank the gods he was so strong. I don't know how he lived with it. . . ."

Where is Sparks now, and who is hurting him? And why can't I help him? Moon's booted feet moved restlessly beside the seat; she stared at Silky with sudden, unwilling insight. *Oh, Lady—I can't wait longer!* Her knuckles turned white on the seat back.

"To think he cut all his radical ties because he was afraid for *me*—when I knew he would gladly have died for his beliefs himself. I was incensed; but I was glad, too: He was a pacifist, among people who were not." She took a puff from Cress's reed. "And then he took up smuggling! Oh—"

The tram burst into the light again, on the passenger level of the starport itself. Wallscreens were everywhere along their path, with changing scenics of other worlds; in the lower levels of the complex an unimaginable number of goods imported from all of those worlds waited shipment down to the planet's surface. Countless more shipments from Kharemough's sophisticated industries passed through the starport in the return trade: There were other scenics, designed to awe arriving visitors, that glorified the technological heights that could sustain major manufacturing processes in space itself. Moon had been told that this was the largest floating city, but not the only one, above Kharemough; there were thousands of other production stations and factories, whose workers spent most of their lives in space between the planet and its moons. The idea of spending a lifetime in black isolation haunted and depressed her.

The tram drifted to a stop, in the waiting area for travelers down to the planet's surface. Moon followed Cress and Silky wordlessly through the exploding crowds, to claim space on a lounge while Elsevier went to the ticketing machines.

"Ah . . ." Cress settled back, looking up at the omnipres-

192

ent video displays. Here they changed from scene to scene of the starport's exterior: now the hazy, cloud-dressed surface of Kharemough; now the surface of the nearer moon, an abstract painting of industrial pollutants; now the glaring image of an interstellar freighter, a chain of coin discs strung out on the matte blackness like a necklace of drilled shell beads. He sat on Silky's far side, protecting Silky from strangers by the barrier of their bodies; Silky gaped at the sluggish patterns of passersby, oil on a water surface. "That's what I like about Kharemough—they always try to keep your mind occupied." A false note sounded in the easy words as the starships flashed onto the screen. Elsevier had said that Cress had once been a journeyman astrogator for a major shipping line. "Too bad we can't see the Prime Minister's ships; but he's not due home for a couple more weeks. That's a sight to put your eyes out for sure, young mistress."

Moon glanced down from the screens. "Why do you always call me that? My name is Moon!"

"What?" Cress looked at her blankly, shrugged. "I know it is, young mistress," deliberate. "But you're a sibyl; and I owe you my life. You deserve to be addressed with honor. Besides," he smiled, "if I let it get too casual, I might fall in love with you."

She stared at him, taken by surprise, but his face refused to tell her whether he was making fun of her or not. She looked away again moodily, not knowing how to answer him; tried to watch the pictures on the screens.

Disembodied voices made announcements in Sandhi, and half a dozen other languages she didn't recognize at all. The ideographic symbols of written Sandhi were incomprehensible to her, but she was learning the spoken language from tapes that heightened recall while she listened. They opened her mind with music while they etched the words painlessly on her unconscious; and by now she could understand most of what she heard. But there were nuances within nuances to this language, just as there were to the relationships between the people who used it. A strict caste system controlled the people of this world, de-

193

fining their roles in society from the day they were born. Offworlders were immune to its restrictions, as long as they remained aloof from them—she had been given a ticket, over Elsevier's pleading, for addressing a shopkeeper by his Sandhi classification, instead of as "citizen." More serious breaches of conduct within the system were punishable by stiff fines or even loss of an inherited rating. There were separate shops, restaurants, and theaters for the Technical, Nontechnical, and Unclassified ratings, and the highest and lowest could not even speak to each other without an intermediary. She had wondered indignantly, clutching her ticket, why they put up with it. Elsevier had only smiled and said, "Inertia, my dear. Most people simply aren't unhappy enough with the known to trade it for the unknown. TJ could never understand that."

Moon leaned forward on the quilt-surfaced couch as Elsevier rematerialized out of the crowd mass.

"They're already boarding. We'd better go." Elsevier waved the ticket printouts toward the gateway at the far side of the waiting area, where passengers were funneling into the unknown. Cress stood up with Silky; Moon followed, resigned. "Don't look so glum, young mistress; you won't feel a thing. It's all in the hands of the traffic controllers, a shuttle's not like a ship. More like a crate."

"It's beautiful down there, Moon. Wait until you see KR's ornamental gardens."

"Gardens aren't what I need, Elsie." Her eyes went to the view of space again, like iron to a lodestone. "I need to go home."

Cress gave Elsevier an accusing, unreadable look; she turned away from it. "Wait until you meet KR, Moon. You'll understand everything then."

20

They boarded the shuttle at the tail of the crowd. Moon caught a glimpse of its tubby, boxlike exterior through the airlock's port: It was a crate, just as Cress had said, with no propulsion of its own. It was drawn down to the planet and shunted back up again just like any other piece of freight, clutched in an invisible hand of repeller—or tractor —beams from one of the planetary distribution centers. A shipping window was a column of no-man's space thirty meters wide, licking out into the zone of heavy industry between Kharemough and its moons.

On board they were led to tiers of seats above a central floor screen that showed her a view of the planet's surface, misty with blue and khaki; she tried to concentrate on the solid immensity of it, and not to remember that it was unspeakably far below them. No one drifted weightless out of a seat even here on board the shuttle; the Kharemoughis claimed, with unsubtle pride, that getting rid of gravity was the hard part; they could produce it whenever they wanted to.

The exits sealed, the shuttle broke free from the station's grasp and began its drop into the tube of force. Moon sat oblivious to the muted conversations, mostly incomprehensible, around her—oblivious to everything but the vision of the planet's surface rising up to meet them in midfall: An amorphorous, cloud-swirled plate widened into ever clearer detail, while Elsevier's hushed voice pointed out the burnished blue seas, and the green-ochre of this world's islands, so huge that they shouldered aside the sea itself. The island centrally below grew until it was all she could see, dividing and redividing into murals of mountain,

195

forest, farmland, all rolling inexorably into morning . . . and then, before she quite realized it, a slender ring of twilit city laid out in ripples concentric around an immense, shining, treeless plain.

". . . landing field," Elsevier said.

At the final moment she had the feeling that another giant's invisible hand plucked them out of the air, before they impacted on the glowing grid lines of the field. It swept them aside, into one of the stolid warehouse buildings that perimetered the landing area, and at last set them down.

The crowd of passengers left the warm-colored interior of the passenger terminal. Moon felt her feet tingle as she walked at the pressure of an alien world . . . or else they tingled with bad circulation. The artificial gravity of the space city was less than she was used to, and this was more; her feet came down like ballast no matter how carefully she moved.

It was barely dawn here on the planet surface, the air was still cool; Elsevier rubbed her arms inside her sleeves. Moon slipped on her own wine-red robe and belted it without protest. The Kharemoughis were a modest people, and Elsevier had warned her that the free ways of the Thieves' Market did not extend down to the ground. Sunrise opened like a flower in the east, the sky overhead would still be black and starless. . . . Looking up, her breath caught in her throat at the sight of the sky. Overhead the darkness was curtained with light, banner folds of green/rose, yellow/gold, icy blue; sighing bands of rainbow, rays of scintillating whiteness crowning an enchanted dreamland.

"Look at that, Silky." Elsevier lapsed into Sandhi as her gaze followed Moon's up; the words were not praise. "It's disgraceful."

"You can say that again, citizen." Three fellow shuttle passengers, dark, slender native Kharemoughis, stood beside them waiting for a taxi; one of them nodded his helmeted head in disgust. "Pollution—you'd think there no tomorrow was. Ye gods, the sheer tonnage of cast-off junk floating up there. I don't know how they expect us

196

our job to do. It's not traffic control any more, it's a demolition derby."

"SN—" The second of the three was a woman; she laughed lightly, tapped him not quite playfully on his uniformed shoulder. "These citizens aren't from around here," a significant lifting of the eyebrows. "They don't need by our petty complaints to be bored, do they?"

"Yes, old man." The third helmet bobbed. "You really do need this vacation. You're like a biopurist sounding."

The first man pushed his hands into his belt, looking annoyed.

"What's wrong with the sky?" Moon pulled her gaze down, reluctantly. "It's full of light." *The way it should be.* "It's beautiful."

The first man glanced at her with a frown starting, ended up smiling in spite of himself. He shook his head, more in sorrow than in anger. "Ignorance is bliss, citizen. Be glad you're not a Kharemoughi." A hovercraft slowed in front of them, and they climbed in.

"Welcome to Kharemough," Cress said pointedly in Tiamatan, "where the gods speak Sandhi." He grinned at her.

Elsevier claimed the next taxi; the Kharemoughi Nontech at the controls gave them a group stare of mild astonishment when she asked for the estate of KR Aspundh. She held up a graceful hand, showing him the ruby signet she wore on her thumb. He turned back to the controls without comment and began a long arc around the perimeter of the field.

"What's wrong with the sky, anyway?" Moon peered out through the taxi dome; the sky ws brightening, the aurora faded before the light of day.

"Industrial pollution," Elsevier said quietly. " 'Are we forever doomed to repeat the errors of our ancestors? Is history hereditary, or environmental?' "

"Nicely put," Cress said, glancing back from his seat beside the pilot.

"TJ's words." Elsevier brushed the compliment aside like a gnat. "Kharemough was fairly well-off even after the Old

197

Empire fell apart, Moon. They still had some industrial base—though hardship was great here, like everywhere, after they were cut off from the interstellar trade that had supported them. They learned to do things for themselves, but in ways that were cruder and infinitely more wasteful. They suffered the consequences of pollution and overpopulation; they almost destroyed their world over a millennium ago, before they got clean hydrogen fusion and moved most of their industry into space. But now they've exchanged their old problems for new ones—not such serious ones, at present, but who knows what they'll mean to future generations? Cause and effect; there's no escape from them."

Moon touched the tattoo hidden under the enameled sunburst collar, looked past Silky at the sea of green foliage beneath them. She leaned away from him as she looked down; knowing he was afraid of her touch, and still secretly repelled by his glistening alienness. They had drifted up and across the narrow band of city—mostly, from what she could see, warehouses and shops of every imaginable kind, not yet stirring to the day; but not many apartments or houses. Now they were rising over open woodland, broken by small parklike clearings holding private homes. "I thought you said there were still too many people here, Elsie. They aren't even as crowded as islanders."

"There are, my dear—but with so many of them and so much of their manufacturing out in space, the surface dwellers have all the room they want, and can afford. They gather around hubs like the one we just left, that distribute everything they need. The wealthier you are, the farther out you live. KR lives quite a way out."

"Is he rich, then?"

"Rich?" Elsevier chuckled. "Oh, filthy rich. . . . It all should have been TJ's, he was the oldest; but he was censured and stripped of his rank for his scandalous behavior. I'm sure he did it on purpose, he loathed the whole caste system. But not KR; he was always a supporter of the status quo. He and TJ didn't even speak."

198

"Then why would he want to see us?" Moon moved uneasily.

"He'll see us, have no fear." The enigmatic smile touched her face again. "Don't let me make you think badly of him; he's a very good man, he simply lives by a different set of values."

"All Kharemoughis are intolerant," Cress said. "Only they're intolerant about different things."

"KR came to TJ's funeral; and he told me that he knew he owed everything he had, and was, to TJ, who had given it all up. He said that if I ever needed anything, I had only to ask."

"How did TJ die?" hesitantly.

"It.was his heart. Passing through the Black Gates puts a strain on the human body, on the heart. And disappointment puts a strain on the heart." She glanced away, out and down, at the greens and the dusky reds of the rolling forest land. Immense knobs of gray rock pushed up through the trees now, like thick, stubby fingers; houses clung precariously to the tips and sides. "It was very sudden. I hope that I, too, may be taken by surprise."

They were dropping down again now, into the grounds of a large estate; skimming above paintings laid out on the land in beds of glorious blooms, shrubs trained to mimic strange creatures, fragile summerhouses wrapped in mazes of hedge. The pilot set them down on the flagstoned landing terrace before the main house, a structure the size of a meeting hall, but all curves and hummocks and gentle slopes covered with vines, imitating the land itself. There were many windows, many of them filled with colored glass, repeating the forms and hues of the art gardens. Gaping at the house, Moon saw the great frescoed doors begin to open.

"You want me to wait, citizens?" The pilot hung an arm across the edge of his seat back, looking skeptical.

"That won't necessary be." Elsevier passed him her credit card coolly; Moon climbed out with the others.

"Looks like just the spot for a day in the country." Cress stretched his arms.

"Many." Silky turned slowly where he stood, looking back and down over the tiers of gardens.

Elsevier led them to the entrance. A dignified middle-aged woman with pale freckles and a silver ring piercing one nostril stood waiting for them; she wore a simple white robe wrapped by a wide sash, covered by strand on strand of heavy turquoise jewelry. "Aunt Elsevier, what an unexpected surprise." Moon was not certain if the gracious smile that included them all went any deeper than her skin.

"Hardly unexpected," Elsevier murmured. "One of the inventions that made my father-in-law's fortune was a system that screens callers electronically. . . . Hello, ALV, dear," in Sandhi. "How nice that our visits coincide. I've a friend your father to see brought." She touched Moon's arm. "I hope he well is." Moon noticed that she did not use the familiar *thy*.

"Fine, thank you; but at the moment the physicist Dar-jeeng-*eshkrad* is him consulting." She ushered them into the cool interior, closing the doors. Light from the stained glass panels on either side fragmented Moon's vision, softened her sudden awareness of their group incongruity. "Let me you comfortable make until he's through." She gestured them on down the hall; Moon noticed that her fingernails were long, and had been filed into sculptures.

She took them through a series of rising rooms into one where the wide, color-banded window overhung the painted gardens. ALV pressed one of a series of controls in the wall inset by the door; a large painting of several Khare-moughis picnicking under the trees became a threedy screen full of arguing men. She nodded toward the mounds of red and purple tapestry cushions, the oases of low wooden tables inlaid with gold and amethyst. "Here you are. The servos will in and out be . . . in case you anything need. And now I hope you'll me excuse; I'm going over the tax data for Father, and it's a dreadful project. He'll you join, just as soon as he can." She left them alone with the declaiming debaters on the wall.

"My, my." Cress folded his arms, wheezed indignantly.

" 'Make yourselves at home; steal some silverware.' Family ties meant something on Big Blue. All my parents—"

"Now, Cress." Elsevier shook her head at him. "I've only met the girl—the woman—twice, once when she was eight, and once at TJ's funeral. She can't have heard much good about any of us in between. And you know how the highborns are about—" she glanced down at herself, "mixed marriages."

Cress shook his head back at her, nudged a table leg with his sandal. "This's fine workmanship, Elsie," loudly. "We could four digits for a couple of those stones upstairs get."

She hissed disapprovingly. "Control yourself. Moon?"

Moon started, turned back from the window.

"Didn't I tell you it was beautiful here?"

Moon nodded, smiling, without the words to say how beautiful.

"Do you think you could stay, and be a sibyl here?"

Moon's smile faded by halves. She shook her head, moved slowly back into the room and settled onto a pile of cushions. Elsevier's eyes followed her, but she couldn't answer them. *I can't answer any question!* She pointed at the screen, changing the subject, as Elsevier sat down beside her. "Why are they angry?"

Elsevier peered at the gesticulating speakers, concentrating. "Why, that's old PN Singalu, the Unclassified's political leader. Bless me, I didn't know he was still alive. It's a parliamentary debate; there's an interpreter, so that temperamental young dandy on the right must be a highborn. They can't speak directly to each other, you know."

"I thought the Unclassifieds didn't have any rights." Moon watched the two men face each other burning-eyed from their podiums, across the neutral ground of the droning, shaven-headed interpreter. They ran over the tail of his words to answer each other, while he repeated what they had already heard, like children arguing. Looking at them she couldn't tell one from the other, wondered how they knew for themselves which one was the inferior.

"Oh, they have some rights, including the right to representation; it's simply that everything not specifically given to them is specifically forbidden. And they aren't allowed enough representatives to change the laws. But they keep trying."

"How can they run a government at all; I thought the Prime Minister was out in space?"

"Oh, he's on another level entirely." Elsevier waved a hand. "He and the Assembly represent Kharemough, but they represent the days when Kharemough was first making contact with the other worlds that became the Hegemony." Kharemough had thought that it was rebuilding the Old Empire in microcosm, with the help of the Black Gate. But in fact they came nowhere near the Old Empire's technological sophistication, and they had learned in time that real control over several subject worlds wasn't practical without a faster-than-light stardrive. Their dreams of domination were swallowed up in the vastness of space; until they could regain a stardrive they would have to be content with economic dominance, a kind the rest of the Hegemony was willing to support. But the Prime Minister and his floating royalty continued as they had begun, a symbol of unity, although not the unity of empire. They traveled from world to world, accepting homage as virtual gods—seemingly ageless, protected by time dilation and the water of life from the precession of the universe outside.

"And they're always welcome, of course; because, ironically, they're nothing but a harmless fantasy." The voices of the debaters, and the tempers behind them, had been rising while Elsevier spoke; her sudden gasp echoed the stricken silence that suddenly fell, half a continent away, in the hall of government.

Moon saw the look of wonder that spread over the worn-leather face of the old man . . . and the utter disbelief on the face of the arrogant young Tech. Even the interpreter lost his glaze, sat openmouthed between them, looking left to right. "What?" she said, and Cress echoed it.

"He didn't wait; he didn't wait for the interpreter!" Elsevier pressed her hands against her cheeks with a cry of delight. "Oh, look at that old man! He worked all his life for a moment like this, knowing it would never come. . . . And now it has." There was a rising sigh of noise from the hall; the young Tech turned and walked off camera like a man caught in a trance. Someone wearing gray robes and a mantle of authority took his place, calling for order.

"What happened?" Moon leaned forward, hugging her knees with absorbed tension.

"The Tech forgot himself," Elsevier breathed. "He addressed Singalu directly—as an equal—instead of through an interpreter. And in front of millions of witnesses!"

"I don't understand."

"Singalu is now a Technician!" Elsevier laughed. "One way to rise in rank on Kharemough is for someone from a higher level to raise you to it, by addressing you as an equal before witnesses. And that's what happened."

"What if Singalu did it? Would the Tech become Unclassed?" Moon watched the wiry, feather-haired old man clutch the podium, weeping unashamedly, grinning through his tears. She felt her own throat tighten; beside her Elsevier wiped at her eyes.

"No, no, the Tech would merely have had him arrested . . ." Elsevier broke off as the man in gray crossed the platform to Singalu and embraced him stiffly, offered congratulations face to face. "Oh, if only TJ could have this moment seen, this shared—"

"And would he equally in the dark moment share, when the young man who it caused home tonight goes and poison takes?"

"KR?" They turned together toward the voice at the door. Moon saw a once-tall man, stooping now under the weight of years—even though Kharemoughis held off old age more skillfully than any people who didn't possess the water of life. She blinked, looked at him again, but a second look did not remove the brown parchment of his skin, and even his loose caftan could not disguise all the marks of age. But this was TJ's younger brother . . . how could he have aged so badly?

"Yes, KR," Elsevier sat back, smoothing her skirts. "He would that moment also share. Even though the young fool

203

brought it on himself; even though you people take 'death before dishonor' far too lightly. Do you share in old Singalu's joy, too?" The familiar *thou* did not replace the formal *you* with Aspundh, either.

He smiled, on the edge of good-natured laughter. "Yes, I do. He's himself both smart and capable proven, over the years—and this proves again that our system for intelligence and initiative selects; despite all that TJ did it upside down to turn, promoting every lowborn who at him smiled."

"KR, how can you that say? You know the highborns their purity like virgins protect! No one would your father raise up, one of the most brilliant minds of his generation."

"But I've raised up been." He shrugged benignly. "My father was satisfied; he knew it would come, in time."

"When there was enough credit in the bank to pay for adopting some respectable ancestors," Cress said.

Aspundh's expression remained placid; Moon guessed that he did not speak Tiamatan. "It's a highly scientific structuring of society, perfectly suited to our technological orientation. And it works—it raised us up out of the chaos of the prespace era forever. It's us a millennium of stable progress given."

"Of stagnation, you mean." Elsevier frowned.

He gestured indignantly. "You can still that say, after living on the most advanced world in the Hegemony?"

"Technically advanced. Socially you're hardly better than Ondinee."

He sighed. "Why do I feel that I've this conversation before had?"

Elsevier lifted her hands. "Forgive me, KR—I didn't come politics to argue, or your time or mine to waste. I've to you in your apolitical capacity come; and I've brought someone who your guidance needs." She got to her feet, drew Moon up from the cushions.

Moon stood numbly, staring as KR Aspundh came forward on slippered feet; staring at the darkly gleaming trefoil suspended on his chest. "A sibyl! He can't be!"

204

He stopped, with a solemn nod. "Ask, and I will answer."

Elsevier reached up and unfastened the enameled collar, slipped it from Moon's throat, uncovering the matching tattoo. "Your sister in spirit. Her name is Moon."

Moon's hands flew to her throat; she turned away, hiding the sign of her failed inspiration as though she had been caught naked in his presence. But Elsevier turned her back firmly, lifted her chin until she looked into his eyes again.

"You honor my house," Aspundh bent his head to her. "Forgive me if my behavior has you disappointed, and made you ashamed that you came."

"No." Moon dropped her eyes again, spoke awkwardly in Sandhi. "You have not. I'm not . . . I'm not a sibyl. Not here, this is not my world."

"Our vision is not by time or space limited; thanks to the miracle of the Old Empire's science." He came forward, searching her face as he came. "We can anywhere answer, any time . . . but *you* can't. You've tried, and failed." He stopped before her, gazing evenly into her astonished eyes. "Anyone could that much see; it doesn't any special insight take. Now why? That's the question you must for me answer. Sit down now, and tell me where you come from." He lowered himself onto the cushions, using a tabletop for leverage.

Moon sat down, facing him across the table; Elsevier filled in the circle with Silky and Cress. "I came from Tiamat."

"Tiamat!"

A nod. "And now the Lady no longer speaks through me, because I left my—my promises unkept."

"The 'Lady'?" He glanced at Elsevier.

"The Sea Mother, a goddess. Maybe I'd better how we came to be here explain, KR." She pressed her hands together, leaning forward, and told him how it had happened. Moon saw a furrow deepen between Aspundh's white brows, but Elsevier was not watching. "We couldn't her back take, and we needed an astrogator through the Gate to get. Because Moon was a sibyl, I—I used her," a slight emphasis on *used*. "She had only just a sibyl become, and since then she hasn't into Transfer been able to go." The fingers twined, twisted.

A high-albedo mechanical servant appeared in the doorway, moved to Aspundh's shoulder with a tray of tall glasses. He nodded, and it set the drinks down on the table. "Will there anything else be, sir?"

"No." He waved it away with a hint of impatience. "You mean you her in Transfer for hours left, unprepared? My gods, that's the kind of irresponsible act I'd of TJ expect! It's a wonder she's not a vegetable."

"Well, what were they supposed to do?" Cress interrupted angrily. "Let the Blues us take? Let me die?"

Aspundh looked at him, expressionless. "You consider her sanity a fair trade."

Cress's gaze dropped to the trefoil at Aspundh's chest, moved to Moon's tattooed throat, but not to meet her eyes. He shook his head.

"I do." Moon watched Cress's profile soften as she spoke the words. "It was my duty. But I—I wasn't strong enough." She took a sip from the tall, frosted glass in front of her; the apricot-colored liquid effervesced inside her mouth, making her eyes tear.

"Since you're me this now telling, I would you call one of the strongest-minded—or luckiest—human beings I've ever known."

"Am I?" Moon cupped her hands against the soothing burn of the cold glass. "Then when will I stop being afraid back into the darkness to go? When I feel it over me start to come, the Transfer—it's like dying inside." Another swallow, her eyes blurred. "I hate the darkness!"

"Yes, I know." Aspundh sat silently for a moment. "Elsevier, will you for me translate? I think it important will be that Moon every word perfectly understands."

Elsevier nodded, and began to give Moon the words in Tiamatan as Aspundh spoke again: "Tiamat is—undeveloped. Do you understand where you go when you're thrown into the darkness? Do you understand why sometimes you see another world instead?"

Elsevier shook her head at Aspundh as she finished. "That's why I her to you brought."

Moon looked toward the window, searching the air. "The Lady chooses . . . "

"Ah. So on your world your goddess is in charge—or you've always believed that she is. What would you say if I told you that your visions weren't a gift from the gods, but a legacy of the Old Empire?"

Moon realized that she had been holding her breath, let it out suddenly. "Yes! I mean, I—I expected it. Everyone here knows I'm a sibyl; how could they know? You're a sibyl; and you've never heard of the Lady." She had long ago stopped seeing the Sea Mother literally, a beautiful woman with seaweed hair, clad in spume, rising from the waves in a mer-drawn shell. But even the formless, elemental force she had sometimes felt touch her soul would not have left Her element or journeyed so far. If in fact she had ever even felt anything, beyond her own longing to feel. . . . "You have so many gods, you offworlders." She was too numbed by loss and change to feel one more blow. "Why do you have so many?"

"Because there are so many worlds; each world has at least one, and usually many, of its own. 'My gods or your gods,' they say, 'who knows which are the real ones?' So we worship them all, just to be sure."

"But how could the Old Empire put sibyls everywhere, if no god did? Weren't they only humans?"

"They were." He reached out to the bowl of sugared fruits in the table center. "But in some ways they had the power of gods. They could travel between worlds directly, in weeks or months, not years—they had hyperlight communicators and stardrives. And yet their Empire fell apart in the end . . . even they overextended themselves. Or so we think."

But even as the Empire fell, some remarkable and self-less group had created a storehouse, a data bank, of the Empire's learning in every area of human knowledge. They

207

had hoped that with all of humanity's discoveries recorded in one central, inviolable place, they would make the impending collapse of their civilization less complete, and the rebuilding that much swifter. And because they realized that technical collapse might be virtually total on many worlds, they had devised the simplest outlets for their data bank that they could conceive of—human beings. Sibyls, who could transmit their receptivity directly to their chosen successors, blood to blood.

Moon's fingers felt the scar on her wrist. "But . . . how can someone's blood show you what's in a—a machine on some other world? I don't believe it!"

"Call it a divine infection. You understand infection?"

She nodded. "When someone is sick, you stay away from them."

"Exactly. A sibyl's 'infection' is a man-made disease, a biochemical reaction so sophisticated that we've barely begun to unravel its subtleties. It creates, or perhaps implants, certain restructurings in the brain tissue that make a sibyl receptive to a faster-than-light communication medium. You become a receiver, and a transmitter. You communicate directly with the original data source. That's where you are when you drown in nothingness: within the computer's circuits, not lost in space—or with other sibyls living on other worlds, who have answers to questions the Old Empire never thought to ask." He lifted his glass to her with an encouraging smile. "All this verbalizing makes me dry."

Moon watched the trefoil turn against the rich, gold-threaded brown of his robe; saw her own turning silently, exiled, on a hook in an air-conditioned room somewhere high overhead. "Is it the disease that makes people go mad, then? It's death to kill a sibyl . . . death to love a sibyl—" She broke off, touching the cool stones along the table edge.

He raised his eyebrows. "Is that what they say on Tiamat? We have that saying too; though we don't take it literally any more. Yes, for some people infection with the 'disease' does cause madness. Sibyls are chosen for certain

208

personality traits, and emotional stability is one . . . and of course a sibyl's blood can transmit the disease. So can saliva—but usually the other person must have an open wound to become infected. Obviously it isn't 'death to love a sibyl,' with reasonable care, or you wouldn't have seen my daughter today. I suppose the superstition was fostered in order to protect sibyls from harm in less civilized societies. The very symbol we wear, the barbed trefoil, is a symbol for biological contamination; it's one of the oldest symbols known to man."

But she heard nothing after—"It isn't death to love a sibyl? Then Sparks . . . we don't have to be apart. We can live together! Elsevier!" Moon hugged the old woman until she gasped. "Thank you! Thank you for bringing me here —you've saved my life. Between the sea and the sky, there's nothing I won't do for you!"

"What's this?" Aspundh leaned on his fist, bemused. "Who is this Sparks? A romance?"

Elsevier pushed Moon away to arm's length and held her there gently. "Oh, Moon, my dear child," she said with inexplicable sorrow, "I don't want to have to hold you to that promise."

Moon twisted her head, not understanding. "We were pledged, but he went away when I became a sibyl. But now, when I go back I can tell him—"

"Go back? To Tiamat?" Aspundh straightened.

"Moon," Elsevier whispered, "we can't take you back." The words rushed out like a flight of birds.

"I know, I know I have to wait until—" She beat the words away.

"Moon, listen to her!" The shock of Cress's broken silence stopped it.

"What?" She went slack in Elsevier's grip. "You said we would—"

"We're never going back to Tiamat, Moon. We never meant to, we can't. And neither can you." Elsevier's lip trembled. "I lied to you," looking away, searching for an easy way, finding none. "It's all been a monstrous lie. I'm—sorry." She let go of Moon's arms.

209

"But why?" Moon brushed distraughtly at her hair, strands of cobweb tickling her face. "Why?"

"Because it's too late. Tiamat's Gate is closing, becoming too unstable for a small ship like ours to pass through safely. It . . . hasn't been months since we left Tiamat, Moon. It's been more than two years. It will be just as long going back."

"That's a lie! We weren't on the ship for years." Moon pushed up onto her knees as comprehension melted and ran down around her. "Why are you doing this to me?"

"Because I should have done it at the beginning." Elsevier's hand covered her eyes. Cress said something to Aspundh in rapid Sandhi.

"She isn't lying to you, Moon." Aspundh sat back, unconsciously separating himself from them. Elsevier translated his words dully. "Ship's time is not the same as time on the outside. It moves more slowly. Look at me, look at Elsevier—and remember that I was younger than TJ by many years. Moon, if you returned to Tiamat now you would have been missing for nearly five years."

"No . . . no, no!" She struggled to her feet, wrenching loose as Cress tried to hold her down. She crossed the room to the window, stood gazing out on the gardens and sky with her forehead pressed hard against the pane. Her breath curtained the glass with ephemeral frost, making her eyes snowblind. "I won't stay on this world. You can't keep me here! I don't care if it's been a hundred years—I have to go home!" She clenched her hands; her knuckles squeaked on the glass. "How could you do this to me, when you knew?" turning furiously. "I trusted you! Damn your ship, and all your gods damn you!"

Aspundh was standing now beside the low table; he came slowly toward her across the room. "Look at them, Moon." He spoke quietly, almost conversationally. "Look at their faces, and tell me they wanted your life to ruin."

She forced her unwilling eyes back to the three still sitting at the table—one face inscrutable, one bowed with shame, one winking with the track of acid-drop tears. She did not answer; but it was enough. He led her back to the table.

"Moon, please understand, please believe me . . . it's because your happiness is so important to me that I couldn't bring myself to tell you." Elsevier's voice was thin and brittle. "And because I wanted you to stay."

Moon stood silently, feeling her face as rigid and cold as a mask. Elsevier looked away from it. "I'm so sorry."

"I know." Moon forced the words out past frozen lips. "I know you are. But it doesn't change anything." She sank down among the pillows, strengthless but still unforgiving.

"The wrong has been done, sister-in-law," Aspundh said. "And the question remains—what will you do to repair it?"

"Anything within my power."

"Our power," Cress said.

"Then take me home, Elsevier!"

"I can't. All the reasons I gave you are true. It's too late. But we can give you a new life."

"I don't want a new life. I want the old one."

"Five years, Moon," Cress said. "How will you find him, after five years?"

"I don't know." She brought her fists together. "But I have to go back to Tiamat! It isn't finished. I can feel it, it isn't finished!" Something resonated in the depths of her mind; a distant bell. "If you can't take me, there must be a ship that can. Help me find one—"

"They couldn't take you either." Cress shifted among the cushions. "It's forbidden; once you leave Tiamat, the law says you can't go home again. Your world is proscribed."

"They can't—" She felt her fury rising.

"They can, youngster." Aspundh held up his hand. "Only tell me, what do you mean, 'it isn't finished'? How do you know that?"

"I—I don't know." She looked down, disconcerted.

"Just that you don't want to believe it's finished."

"No, I know!" suddenly, fiercely certain. "I just don't know—how."

"I see." He frowned, more with consternation than disapproval.

"She can't," Cress murmured. "Can she?"

"Sometimes it happens." Aspundh looked somber. "We are the hands of the sibyl-machine. Sometimes it manipulates us to its own ends. I think we should at least try to learn whether her leaving has made any difference, if we can."

Moon's eyes fixed on him in disbelief, like the rest.

Cress laughed tightly beside her. "You mean it—acts on its own? Why? How?"

"That's one of the patterns we're still trying to relearn. It can be damnably inscrutable, as I'm sure you know. But anything able to perform all its functions would almost have to possess some kind of sentience."

Moon sat impatiently, only half listening, half understanding. "How can I learn that—whether I have to go back?"

"You have the key, sibyl. Let me ask, and you'll have the answer."

"You mean . . . No, I can't! I can't." She grimaced.

He settled onto his knees, smoothing his silver-wire hair. "Then ask, and I will answer. *Input . . .*" His eyes faded as he fell into Transfer.

She swallowed, taken by surprise, said self-consciously, "Tell me what—what will happen if I, Moon Dawntreader, never go back to Tiamat?"

She watched his eyes blink with sudden amazement, search the light-dappled corners of the room, come back to their faces, to hers alone—"You, Moon Dawntreader, sibyl, ask this? You are the one. The same one . . . but not the same. You could be her, you could be the Queen. . . . He loved you, but he loves her now; the same, but not the same. Come back—your loss is a wound turning good flesh bitter, here in the City's heart . . . an unhealing wound. . . . The past becomes a continuous future, unless you break the Change. . . . *No further analysis!*" Aspundh's head dropped forward; he leaned against the table for a long moment before he looked up again. "It seemed to be—

night, there." He took a sip from his drink. "And the room was full of strange faces. . . ."

Moon picked up her own glass, drank to loosen the invisible hand closing on her throat. *He loved you, but he loves her now.*

"What did I say?" Aspundh looked toward her, clear eyed again, but his face was drained and drawn.

She told him, haltingly, helped on by the others. "But I don't understand it. . . ." *I don't understand it! How could he love . . .* She bit her lip. Elsevier's hand touched hers lightly, briefly.

" 'You could be Queen,' " Aspundh said. " 'Your loss is an unhealing wound.' I think you had a true intuition . . . your role in a greater play has been left unfilled. An inequality has been created."

"But it's already happened," Elsevier said slowly. "Doesn't that mean it was meant to happen?"

He smiled, shaking his head. "I don't pretend to know. I am a technocrat, not a philosopher. The interpretation is not up to me, thank the gods. Whether it's finished or not is up to Moon."

Moon stiffened. "You mean—there is a way I can go back to Tiamat?"

"Yes, I think there is. Elsevier will take you, if you still want to go."

"But you said—"

"KR, it isn't possible!"

"If you leave immediately and use the adaptors I'll provide, you'll get through the Gate safely, and before Tiamat is cut off for good."

"But we don't have an astrogator." Elsevier leaned forward. "Cress isn't strong enough."

"You have an astrogator." His gaze moved.

Moon stopped breathing as all their eyes reached her at once. "No!"

"No, KR," Elsevier said, frowning. "You can't ask her to endure that again! She couldn't if she wanted to."

"She can—if she wants to enough." Aspundh touched his trefoil. "I can help you, Moon; you won't have to go through it unprepared this time. If you want your old life back, and your power as a sibyl, you can—you must—do this thing. We can't face down all our night fears; but you must face this one, or you'll never believe in yourself again. You'll never use the precious gift you carry; you'll never be anything at all." The sharp voice stung her. He folded his hands, resting them on the table.

Moon shut her eyes, and the blackness swallowed her whole. *But it isn't finished yet. I was meant to be something more! And he was meant to be with me. He can't be lost, he wouldn't forget me; it isn't finished....* Sparks's face burned away the darkness like a rising sun. It was true, she had to do this; and if she did she would know that she had the strength to solve any problem. She opened her eyes, rubbed her trembling arms to still them. "I have to try." She saw the half-formed grief in Elsevier's deep-blue eyes—and the half-formed fear. "Elsie, it means everything to me. I won't fail you."

"Of course you won't, dear." A single nod, a ghost of smile. "All right, we'll do it. But KR—" she glanced up. "How will we back again without her get?"

His own smile twitched with secret guilt. "With false papers, which I shall also provide. In the chaos of the final departure on Tiamat, you'll never noticed be, I'm sure, even—Silky."

"Why, KR, you secret sinner." She laughed weakly.

"I don't it amusing consider." His face did not. "If I teach this girl all that a sibyl should know and then send her back to Tiamat, I will an act of treason be committing. But in doing this I obey a higher law than even the Hegemony's."

"Forgive me." She nodded, chastened. "What about our ship?"

"It will a fitting monument in space to my late brother's impossible—dreams be. I told you that you'd never for anything want, Elsevier. Do this thing, and you'll never again need to smuggle."

"Thank you." A spark of rebellion showed in her eyes.

"We were planning to retire, anyway, if this last trip hadn't such an utter disaster been. This gives us one more opportunity our wares to—deliver, after all."

Aspundh frowned briefly.

Cress unfolded his legs with leaden effort as the others began to stir. Looking at him, Moon found him looking at her; his glance hurried on, caught at Elsevier like an orphan's hand. He grinned, badly. "I guess this is good-bye, then, Elsie?"

Moon stood up, helped him to his feet while the realization registered around the table. "Cress—"

"Consider this my payment on the debt we owe you, young mistress." He shrugged.

Elsevier turned to Aspundh, but Moon saw his face tighten with refusal even before the question formed. "It won't be hard for him another ship to find; astrogators are highly in demand in your—trade, I'm sure."

" 'There are smugglers and smugglers,' KR," Elsevier said.

"You mean they might not all a ship with a man blacklisted for murder want to share?" Aspundh's expression turned to iron.

Moon let go of Cress's sleeve.

Cress flushed. "Self-defense! It's in the record, self-defense."

"A drugged-up passenger challenged him to a duel, KR. The man would him have killed. But the rules don't any exceptions make. . . . Really, do you imagine that I'd a ship with a murderer share?"

"I can't even why you married my brother imagine." Aspundh sighed in defeat. "All right, Elsevier; though you press my promise to you near the breaking point. I suppose I a shipping line somewhere own that can an astrogator take on."

"You mean that? Oh, gods—" Cress laughed, swaying like a reed. "Thank you, old mas—citizen! You won't sorry be." He glanced at Elsevier, a long, shining glance full of gratitude.

215

"I hope not," Aspundh said; he moved past Cress to Moon's side. "And you won't me sorry make either, will you?"

In his eyes she saw the grim reflection of what her failure would mean, not to herself alone, but to the others. "No," firmly.

He nodded. "Then stay with me for the next few days, while the ship is readied, and let me you all a sibyl should know teach."

"All right." She touched her throat.

"KR, must she—"

"It's for her own good, Elsevier—and for yours—that I her here keep." He lifted his head slightly.

"Yes . . . of course." Elsevier smiled. "You're quite right, of course. Moon, I—" She patted Moon's hand, looked away again. "Well, never mind. It doesn't matter. Never mind." She went on toward the door, not looking back to see Moon's outstretched hand. Silky followed her wordlessly.

"Well," Cress grinned, half at her, half at his feet. "Good luck to you, young mistress. 'You could be Queen.' I'll tell them I knew you when." He kept her gaze at last. "I hope you find him. Good-bye." He backed away, turned and went out after the others.

Moon watched the empty doorway silently, but it remained empty.

Moon sat alone in the garden swing, giving it momentum with the motion of her foot. Overhead the night sky sang, a hundred separate choirs of color transfiguring into one. Moon rested her head on the pillows, listening with her eyes. If she closed them she could hear another music: the sweet complexities of a Kharemoughi art song drifting out through the open doors onto the patio, the counterpoint of insects chirping in the shrubs, the shrill and guttural cries of the strange menagerie of creatures that wandered the garden paths.

She had spent this day like the ones before it, practicing

the exercises that disciplined her mind and body, watching the information tapes that KR Aspundh gave to her, learning all that was known to the Hegemony about what sibyls were, and did, and meant to the people of their worlds. The sibyls of this world attended a formal school, where they were sheltered and protected while they learned to control their trances—as she had learned, more uncertainly, from Clavally and Danaquil Lu on a lonely island under the sky.

But besides the rigorous basic discipline, Aspundh and the other sibyls of the Hegemony learned about the complex network of which they were a part, the vast reach of the Old Empire's technological counterspell against the falling darkness. They understood that the Nothing Place lay in the heart of a machine somewhere on a world not even a sibyl could name; and the knowledge gave them the strength to endure its terrifying *absence*, which had nearly destroyed her with her own fear.

They learned the real nature of their power: the capacity not only to ease the day-to-day burdens of life, but to actually better it; to contribute to the social and technological growth of their world more profoundly than even the greatest genius—because they had access to the accumulated genius of all human history . . . if only their people had the wisdom, and the willingness, to make use of that knowledge.

And they were taught the nature of their unnatural "infection," how to use its potential to protect themselves from harm, how to protect their loved ones from its risk. A sibyl could even bear a child. The artificial virus did not pass through the placenta's protective filters—ensuring the birth of children who might not share their mother's temperament, but who would have more chance than most of becoming sibyls to a new generation. To have a child . . . to lie in the arms of the only one she would ever love, and know that they could be all to each other that they had ever been . . .

Moon sat up, startled out of her reverie by the sound of

217

someone coming toward her across the patio. *But he loves another now.* The memory of the thing that separated them now, more than just a gap of distance and time, hurt her abruptly as she saw KR Aspundh approaching.

"Moon." He smiled a greeting. "Shall we our evening stroll take?" Every evening he walked down through his gardens to the small building of pillared marble in the heart of a shrubbery maze, where the ashes of his ancestors rested in urns. The Kharemoughis worshiped a hierarchy of deities, neatly extending their view of a stratified society into the realm of heaven, and incorporating the pantheon that watched over the Hegemony's other worlds. On its first tier were a person's revered ancestors, whose success or failure determined their child's place in society. Aspundh paid homage devoutly to his own ancestors; Moon wondered if a father's success made it easier to believe in his divinity.

She got up from the swing. Each evening she joined him on his walk, and in the privacy of the gardens they discussed the questions her day's studies had left unanswered.

"Are you warm enough? These spring evenings are chilly. Take my cloak."

"No, I'm fine." She shook her head, secretly defiant. She wore the sleeveless robe she had picked out on the threedy shopper's-guide show. She had the feeling that even the sight of a bare arm embarrassed these people; she resented being forced to wear more than she wanted to, and so she wore less.

"Ah, to have a hardy upbringing!" He laughed; she felt a small frown form. "You're not your lovely smile tonight wearing. Is it because tomorrow you back to the spaceport must go?" They began to walk together, Moon controlling her strides to match his slower steps.

"Partly." She looked down at her soft slippers, the pattern of the smooth stones underfoot. Silky would spend hours crouching over them in fascination. . . . She would even be glad to see him again, more glad to see Elsevier; to escape from the stifling perfection of this world's artificial

218

beauty. She looked forward to these evening walks, but during the day KR was preoccupied with business and ALV oversaw her studies, making certain that discretion was maintained while a young girl of questionable background stayed in her father's house. ALV treated her respectfully, because of the trefoil at her throat; but ALV's very presence could turn her every move into a clumsy stumble, a spilled bowl, a broken vase. ALV's relentless sophistication made mispronunciation fatal, questions gauche, and laughter unthinkable. This was a world afraid to laugh at itself, afraid of losing control—control of the Hegemony, control of Tiamat.

"Do you feel that you more time need? I think there's little more I can you teach ... and time is critical now, unfortunately."

"I know." A startled creature spread its ruff of winking scales and shrieked in their path. "I know I'm as ready as I can be. But what if I'll never ready enough be?" She had felt her belief in herself and in the trefoil tattoo she wore, the power that it represented, slowly re-form as she learned the truth; but still she had not been able to begin an actual Transfer, for fear that a failure now would mean failure forever.

"You will ready be." He smiled. "Because you must be."

She managed a smile of her own as affirmation echoed in her mind. There were some things about the sibyl network that even the Kharemoughis couldn't explain— anomalies, unpredictabilities—as though the all-knowing source of the sibyls' inspiration was somehow imperfectly formed. Some of its answers were so involuted that no experts had ever been able to make them clear; sometimes it seemed to act toward ends of its own, although ordinarily it only reacted. This time it had chosen to act, and chosen her as its tool. ... She wouldn't fail; she couldn't. But what was her goal, if Sparks no longer wanted her? *To get him back. I will. I can.* She tightened her fists, not letting it go. *We belong to each other. He belongs to me.*

"That's better," Aspundh said. "Now, what final questions will you of me ask? Is anything still unclear?"

She nodded slowly, asking the one question that had troubled her from the beginning. "Why does the Hegemony want it on Tiamat a secret kept, that sibyls everywhere are? Why do you the Winters tell that we evil are, or crazy?"

He frowned as though she had broken some particularly strong taboo. "I cannot that to you explain, Moon. It's too complicated."

"But it's not right. You said that sibyls vital were—they only did good things for a world." She realized suddenly what that said about the Hegemony's intentions; realized how much more she had learned here than simply what she had been taught.

Aspundh's expression told her that he realized it, too, and regretted it—because he was powerless to stop it. "I hope I haven't done, and shan't do, too great a harm to my own world." He looked away. "You must to Tiamat returned be. But I pray that it no grief to Kharemough brings."

She had no answer.

They left the fragrant pathway through the flowering sillipha, wound into the topiary maze until the marble shrine appeared, reflecting pastel skylight, at its hidden heart. Aspundh went on into the shadowed interior; Moon sat on a dew-damp marble bench to wait. The scent of propitiatory incense reached her on the rising breeze; she wondered what prayers KR Aspundh spoke to his ancestors tonight.

Birds whose colors would be strident in the daylight fluttered down into her lap, pastel and gray, murmuring placidly. She smoothed their delicate feathered backs, remembering that it was for the last time; that after tomorrow there would be no peaceful gardens, but only the Black Gate. . . . She rubbed her arms, suddenly feeling the night's chill.

21

"Citizen, *what* are you doing in my office?" Jerusha glared across the landfill of official refuse heaped by her terminal and mounting in drifts to the corners of the desk, in the corners of the room.

"I was told to come here. About my permits." The shop-keeper twisted his ties, midway between uncertainty and truculence. "They said you'd tell me why I haven't heard anyth—"

"Yes, I know that. And any sergeant could look it up for you, any patrolman with half a brain!" *Gods, if I could get through a day without raising my voice . . . if I could get through one hour.* She ran a hand through the tight red-black curls of her hair; tugged. "Who the hell sent you here?"

"Inspector Man—"

"—tagnes," she echoed him. "Well, he sent you to the wrong place. Go back to the front desk and tell the duty officer to find out."

"But *he* said—"

"Don't take no for an answer this time!" She waved him toward the door, already looking down at the half-read report still waiting her acknowledgment on the screen, reaching for the intercom button. "Sergeant, wake up your brain and screen these idiots! What do you think you're out there for?"

"Hell of a way to run a world, damn—" The invective was lost as the door shut behind the shopman.

"Sorry, Commander," the sergeant said, sullenly disembodied. "Shall I send in the next one?"

"Yes." *No. No, no more.* "And get me Mantag— No, cancel that." She let up on the speaker button. She could

bust Mantagnes right off the force for his harassment . . .
but if she did she'd have open mutiny on her hands, instead
of just open resentment. In the years since she had become
Commander her position with the force had gone from bad
to worse. *And he knows it. He knows it, the bastard.* . . .
She stared at the report printout blindly. Their main computer had crashed monumentally—months ago—and
thrown their entire records system into chaos. Even now it
barely functioned at half normal efficiency; even Kharemoughi expertise hadn't been able to put things right, because somehow they were missing the critical components.
. . . She had been trying to get their records back in order
for months; trying to get through this one report for an
hour, half a minute at a time, getting nowhere. She punched
APPROVED, and let it pass unread. *Getting nowhere.
Sliding backwards, being buried alive*— She rummaged
among the crumpled, empty packets in her desk drawer for
one with any iesta pods left in it. *Damn, almost gone—
how will I ever make it through the day?*

The door opened, not answering her question, and
Captain—*oh, gods, what's his name?*—entered and saluted.
"Captain KerlaTinde reporting, Commander," as if he
hadn't expected her to remember. She was used to the
coldness, and the insolent tone, by now. The force hated
her guts, almost every single man of them, and it was close
to mutual by now. Discipline had gone to hell, but she
couldn't demote everybody on the force—and she had tried
everything else. They would not obey her: because she was
a woman, yes (and damn the day she had decided to be
anything more) . . . but also because she had taken the
place that rightfully belonged to Mantagnes. And because
it had been the Queen's idea. They believed she was the
Queen's puppet; and how could she prove they were
wrong, when Arienrhod's strings had trapped her like
spiderweb, held her suspended here between heaven and
hell, draining away her will to continue?

"What is it, KerlaTinde?" unable to keep the sharpness
out of her own voice.

"The other officers have asked me to speak for them,

ma'am." The word was heavy with incongruity. "We want an end to enforced patrol duty by officers here in the city. We feel that the duty belongs to the patrolmen; it's damaging to the prestige of an officer to be forced to harass citizens in the street."

"You'd rather let the citizens harass each other?" She frowned, too easily, leaning forward. "What important duty do you feel you should be attending to instead?"

"Attending to our designated duties! We don't have time enough to get through all the filework as it is, without patrolling as well." His broad face matched her, frown for frown. He looked pointedly at the stacks of tape containers on her desk.

"I know, KerlaTinde," following his gaze. "I've cut out every piece of red tape I can." *And you should see the scars Hovanesse put on me for it.* "I know the computer crapping out made it all ten times worse; but damn it, our main job here is still protecting the Hedge's citizens, and it has to be done."

"Then give us something worth doing for once!" Kerla-Tinde swept his hand across the nonexistent view from her window. "Not picking up drunks out of the gutter. Let us go after the big-time criminals, get some convictions that would mean something."

"You'll never get those convictions. It's a waste of time." *Gods, am I really saying that? Am I really the one, the same one, who stood there where he's standing and said what he's saying to me?* She wadded an empty iesta packet into a painful ball below the desk edge. *No ... I'm not the same one.* But it was true, what she had just said to him. . . .

As soon as she became Commander, she had tried to crack down on the big operators she knew were controlling networks of interplanetary vice from right here in Carbuncle. But they had slipped through her fingers like water. Any illegal activity that they might conceivably be caught in here on Tiamat turned out to be technically under the control of a citizen of this world. And the Winters were under the Queen's law; she couldn't touch them without the Queen's permission.

223

"Commander LiouxSked didn't think that way."

The hell he didn't. But there was no point in saying it. Had LiouxSked faced the same infuriating impasse—or had Arienrhod restructured Carbuncle society just for her? She couldn't explain it to KerlaTinde, or any of the rest, anyway; they already knew she was in the Queen's pocket, and nothing she could say would ever make any difference. "You're patrolling the Street for a good reason, KerlaTinde; you know crimes of violence have soared"—she saw Arienrhod's hand behind that, too; saw herself taking the blame for it in KerlaTinde's eyes—"as we near the final departure. And we won't be getting any more replacements. So you'll go on patrolling the Street until I tell you to stop; until the last ship is ready to lift off this planet."

"Chief Inspector Mantagnes isn't—"

"Mantagnes isn't Commander, damn it! I am!" her voice slipped away from her. "And my orders stand. Now get out of my office, Captain, before I make it Lieutenant."

KerlaTinde retreated, his olive skin darkening with indignation. The door shut her off from one more unresolved confrontation, one more stupid mistake.

No wonder they hate me. Hating herself, she stared at the opacity of the polarized windows, her only shield against the radiation of hostility from the station beyond. The windows reflected her own image faintly, like a hologrammic transmission ghost, a flawed recreation of a false reality. There was no Jerusha, no woman, no solid human flesh, any more: only a nerve-racked, knife-tongued harridan with paranoid delusions. Who the hell was she kidding? It was her own fault, she couldn't handle the job, she was a failure . . . an inferior being, weak, overemotional, female. She leaned back in her chair, looking down along her body, knowing the truth that even the heavy uniform could never fully conceal. And she didn't even have the guts to admit that it was her own fault, not some wild plot of the Queen's. No wonder she was a laughingstock.

And yet—she *had* seen the Queen's face on a Summer girl. She *had* seen the Queen's fury at the girl's loss. And she *had* seen LiouxSked crawling in his own filth—for no conceivable reason, if not for Arienrhod's revenge. She wasn't losing her mind! The Queen was systematically taking it away from her.

But there was nothing she could do about it; nothing. She had tried everything, but there was no escape—only the awareness that her career, her future, her faith in her own ability were inexorably bleeding away. Her career was being ruined, the record of her command would be one long list of failures and complaints. The end of their stay on Tiamat would mark the end of everything she had worked toward or ever wanted. Arienrhod was destroying her, too, not swiftly, not like LiouxSked—but in a way that would let her perceive every agonizing nuance of her own destruction.

And best of all, Arienrhod must have realized that she would stay on, keep defying her own destiny—as she had always done, all her life. Because to quit now and leave Tiamat, give up her position, would be to admit that it had all been futile. It would all be futile yet, when they finished with this world; but in the meantime even this hellish charade of her dream was better than a life with no dream at all.

She couldn't strike back at the Queen, hadn't been able to cause her even the smallest inconvenience in return. Accidentally she had foiled one plot by Arienrhod to keep Winter in power. But it hadn't given her even a moment's satisfaction, the gods knew—and since then she had turned up no clue about what new webs the Queen might be weaving. There was no doubt in her mind that there would be another plan . . . but more than enough doubt that this time the Hegemony, in the person of herself, would be able to stop it. And that failure would be the crowning act in her own ruin.

But there was still time. The contest wasn't over yet, she had to turn herself around. . . . "Are you listening, bitch? I'll get you yet; by the Bastard Boatman, I swear it! I won't break, you can't destroy me before I—"

The door opened again, batting the words back at her; a patrolman entered, realizing with one swift look around

225

that she was alone. He set another stack of cassettes on her desk with a sidelong glance.

"Well, what are you staring at?"

He saluted and left.

With another choice one for the wardroom gossips. Her resolution crumbled. *How do you really know; how can you tell if you've really lost your mind . . . ?* She reached past the terminal toward the new pile of records, but her hand closed over a solitary printed sheet lying half-pinned beneath them. She pulled it free, read one line: LIST OF GRIEVANCES. She crushed the paper between her hands. *Who put it there? Who?*

The intercom began to chime; she hit the go-ahead mutely, not trusting her voice.

"Radiophone call from the outback, Commander. Somebody named Kennet or something. Should I put it through?"

Ngenet? Gods, she couldn't talk to him now, not like this. *Why the hell does he pick the worst times, why does he even bother any more?*

"And Inspector Mantagnes is here to see you."

"Put the call on my line." *But what will I say? What?* "And tell Mantagnes to—" She clenched her teeth. "Tell him to wait."

She heard storm static crackle from the speaker, and the familiar distortion of a familiar voice. "Hello? Hello, Jerusha—"

"Yes, Miroe!" Remembering with a sudden rush of pleasure what it was like to hear a human being speak to her willingly, gladly . . . realizing suddenly how much more than simple humanity his friendship gave her. "Gods, it's good to hear from you again." She was smiling, actually smiling.

"Can't hear you . . . reception's lousy! How'd you . . . come out to the plantation again . . . day or so? . . . of a long time since we've had a visit!"

"I can't, Miroe." How long had it been? Months, since she had accepted an invitation, even spoken to him— months since she had spent a day or an hour selfishly on something that made her smile. She couldn't, she couldn't afford to.

"What?"

"I said, I—I . . ." She saw herself reflected in the wall, the face of a jailer, the face of a prisoner in a cell. Panic touched her with a dim finger. "Yes! Yes, I'll come. I'll come tonight."

22

"All right, suckers. You're on your own again." Tor moved back, hoping for sinuous grace, hoping against hope. Inadvertently revealing more flesh than she had intended to, she bowed her way out of the eerily glowing obstacle course. Hologrammic coin ships and a meteor swarm tangled intangibly in the golden crocheted cap that held her midnight wig under control. The drapery of her silken overalls flashed the blue flame-color of a welding torch; the expanses of skin they left uncovered were a deathly lavender against the darkness.

Whistles and protests followed her in a crowd; she had been gambling with the patrons, as ordered, losing just enough, winning back just enough more to convince them that the games were honestly run. *Suckers.* The games were honestly run, for the most part—much to her surprise. They were simply so complicated that the ordinary human being couldn't hope to outwit them. When she thought about the hours and the money she had thrown away, as wantonly and stupidly as any of these drugged-up boobs, she shook her ebony-frizzed head in disgust. Still, it wasn't so bad now; now that she knew the codes that let her secretly control the outcome of the plays.

No, it wasn't so bad at all, not any of it: running a

casino, taking care of business as the front woman for the Source's own on-planet interests. She was the Hostess, the titular owner, of Persiponë's Hell, unquestionably the finest gambling hell in Carbuncle. And on the side she tended to whatever other discreet dealings the Source—the head man of the offworld criminal subculture on Tiamat—told her to tend to. It was a part of the Queen's policy to provide capable Winters to act as a screen for offworlder illegalities, so the vice lords themselves could operate with virtual impunity, free of harassment by the Hedge's police. She had been picked up four times by the Blues as she was working her way into the Source's favor; but they had had to turn her over to the Queen's guard, who had simply let her go.

"Hey—" She squinted through the dance of shifting bodies, saw more clearly the offworlder who had just come through the curtain of tiny, shimmering mirrors with a zombie in tow. "Pollux!" She pressed the caller on her bracelet as a secondary summons as she shouted into the throbbing music around her. Pollux appeared at her shoulder with the reassuring solidness of steel. "That pervert who just came in the door; show him out again. We don't need his business." She pointed, trying not to see whether the zombie was male or female, or any detail of its form. The very sight sickened her, and the sight of a man or woman who enjoyed using a living body that way.

"Whatever you say, Tor." Pollux moved away with single-minded inevitability. He made a better bouncer than any of the humans who worked in this place; she had bought out his rental contract for the duration.

It had all worked out so perfectly . . . funny how it had. Even Herne . . . She turned back, leaning an elbow on one end of the coal-black, curving bar. The strange light-absorbing material sucked the warmth out through her skin; she shivered and straightened up. Farther down the way Herne sat in command of the banks of automated drink and drug dispensers, an outrageously popular anachronism. Putting him in charge of the bar, where customers gathered to lose their inhibitions along with their good credit, had been her most inspired move. They spilled their guts to each other, and better yet to him; and she fed what he learned to Dawntreader, who still lapped it up like an addict after all these years.

Who would ever have dreamed, that day in Fate's alley when Dawntreader had nearly strangled her, that his bad temper would lead her to this? But between Herne's savvy and Dawntreader's contacts with somebody up the line, she had risen higher and faster than she had ever dreamed of doing.

"Hey, Persiponë, baby, the Source wants you." Oyarzabal, one of the Source's lieutenants, was abruptly behind her. His hands settled on her waist, got dangerously personal under the bib of her sensuous evening suit.

She controlled the unsubtle urge to dig an elbow into his ribs. She had learned tact and sophistication of a sort, painfully, since leaving the loading docks; getting mauled came with the territory. "Careful. You'll set off my burglar alarm." She pushed his hands away, but not too far. Oyarzabal was a jerk, proven by the fact that he seemed to prefer her to his choice of the easy, chic women who flowed through this place; but she didn't work too hard at discouraging him. He was a onetime farmboy from somewhere on Big Blue, and attractive in a loutish, overgrown sort of way. She had gone to bed with him a few times, and hadn't been too disappointed. She'd even toyed with the idea of getting him to marry her before the final departure, and getting off Tiamat for good.

"Hey, sweeting, how about later on you and me—"

"Tonight's taken." She started away before he could get his hands on her again; glanced back, relenting a little, enough for a smile. "Ask me tomorrow."

He grinned. His teeth were inlaid with rhinestones. She turned away again, shaking her head.

She made her way through the crowd, through the forbidden door that led her to the Source's private suite of offices and guarded meeting rooms—guarded not only by hidden human eyes, but also by the most elaborate anti-snoop devices money could buy. When she had learned that Herne was a Kharemoughi, she had asked him about the possibility of using his legendary technical prowess to let her eavesdrop on the Source's private dealings. But he was no match for the electronic guards, and she had finally realized that all Kharemoughis weren't born knowing how to turn ore into computer terminals. So she had had to be content with noticing who called on the Source, and when, and only suspecting why.

She didn't much like being the caller herself. The door to his office opened as she reached it, with the prescience she had learned to expect, and let her in to her audience. She blinked compulsively and slowed as she entered; the room was dark to the point of blindness for her, as it always was. Incense clogged the air with an overwhelming sweetness. She lifted a hand to rub her eyes, stopped it just short of ruining the perfect flowers painted over her lids. She let her hand drop again, resigned, as a dark form began to coalesce against a dimly reddening background: the Source, in silhouette, the only way she had ever seen him.

She had been told by Oyarzabal that the Source had some disease that made his eyes unable to stand the light. She didn't know whether to believe it, or just to figure that he liked to keep his face hidden. Sometimes, as she adjusted slowly to the dull wash of red from the wall behind him, she thought there might be a distortion about his face. But she could never be sure.

"Persiponë." His voice was a rasping whisper, and again she didn't know whether it was the real one. He spoke with an accent she couldn't identify.

"Here, master." His chosen form of address took on new and sinister meanings here in the blackness. She pushed uneasily at her wig, her scalp itching with sudden tension. He saw perfectly well in the darkness, she knew, and at each visit she was forced to endure his scrutiny.

"Turn around."

She circled on the deep carpet pile, wondering pointlessly what color it really was, or whether it was simply black.

"Better . . . yes, I like it better. You'll never be beautiful, you know; but you're learning to disguise the fact. You've come a long way. I didn't think you would come such a long way."

"Yes, master. Thank you, master." *You're telling me.* She didn't tell him that she had begun to let Pollux pick her clothes for her. His totally impartial judgment topped her own uncertain taste in choosing the styles that made the most of her flawed body; with the wig and the paint she could, as the Source said, disguise her unrelenting plainness.

"But then, how could anyone be compared to the ideal, and not suffer by the comparison . . . ?" His voice sighed away, he was silent again through seconds that hung on like hours. Once, when she had been allowed a small red-tipped pencil of light to read a list of directions, she had glimpsed a picture-square on the desk, a woman's face. A woman of striking offworld beauty, with a fog of ebony hair netted in gold. And she had understood with abrupt discomfort why she was wearing the same hair, and why her predecessors had worn it too; and why this place was Persiponë's, and why they all were, too. It had surprised her that a man like the Source might have loved or even hated one woman enough to be obsessed by her; and it gave her the creeps to be window dressing to the obsession. But the rewards had been enough to keep her from saying so.

"How is business tonight?"

"Real good, master. It's payday over at the starport, we've got a big crowd."

"Was the latest deal successful? Have you got sufficient —variety on hand to satisfy certain private customers?"

"Yeah, Coonabarabran was right where you said he'd be, and everything on him. We can handle any pleasure tonight." She was sure he already knew the answer to the questions, and so she always answered honestly. He did not ask her to handle all his requests—she didn't mind fronting on drug transactions, because she could keep herself mentally clear of the consequences. The Source oversaw, and dabbled in, numerous other illegal transactions, and there

231

were some she couldn't stomach. But there was always someone else around who could.

"Good . . . I'm expecting a particularly important visitor tonight. Make certain the inner meeting room is secure, and prepared appropriately. She will be at the side entrance at midnight. See that she isn't kept waiting."

"Yes, master." *She?* There were not too many women in the underworld society who rated such solicitude in an audience with the Source.

"That's all, Persiponë. Go back to your guests."

"Thank you, master," meekly. The door opened and she escaped, blinking again, into the white glare of the hall beyond. She sighed as the door clicked securely behind her; not offended, as she walked away, that he found her unattractive—only relieved. He was completely off her scale of ambition, and in her private heart she was very much afraid of him, for all the rational reasons—and for all the reasons a child fears the dark.

Arienrhod followed the lurid figure of Persiponë through the private passageways to the Source's inner meeting room. The sounds of the casino reached her distantly through the barrier of separating walls, a deep throbbing that was more vibration than true sound, that reached into her chest like death's hand. It was more than appropriate, she thought, that the heartless merriment of the gaming crowds should show its real nature here in the shadowy halls of the Source's hidden power. Persiponë stopped ahead of her, before a sealed doorway that looked like any other they had passed, and beckoned to her. She moved forward, and Persiponë pressed her hand against a panel in the door—the arrival signal, as though they were not already being observed. She nodded to Arienrhod with self-conscious deference, and went away down the hall. Arienrhod was certain that the woman recognized her; wondered what she would think if she realized that Tor Starhiker/Persiponë was equally well-known to her Queen as Sparks Dawntreader's pawn.

But the door was opening before her, opening on darkness, and she put all other thoughts out of her mind. She pushed back the hood of her shadow-colored cloak and walked boldly forward, without waiting to be summoned. But as she crossed over the threshhold the door sealed again behind her, sealing her into utter lightlessness. Panic seized her with heavy hands, as it always did. Suddenly it was hard not to believe that she had stepped into another plane, into the merciless unknown of an interstellar vice network—out of the world she knew and controlled. That she was lost. . . . Her mechanical spies peered into every corner of this city, but they could not penetrate this place: It was guarded by even more powerful and sophisticated technology . . . this all-pervasive darkness that tried to smother her will and swallow her self-control. She stood rigidly still, until the moment passed and she recaptured her perspective. *Darkness . . . it's a damn good trick. I wish I'd thought of it.*

"Your Majesty. You honor my humble establishment." The Source's ruined voice (like the voice of a corpse; or was that just an effect, too?) hissed the welcome, oddly accented. "Please take a seat, make yourself comfortable. I would hate to keep the Lady standing."

Arienrhod noted the intentional play on words, the reference to her barbarian heritage. She made no response, but moved forward confidently to take the deeply cushioned seat across the empty table from him. Ever since their first meeting, where she had been forced to grope humiliatingly through the dark, she had been certain to wear light-enhancing contact lenses when she came to call on him. As her visual purple built up she could actually make out the general form of the room's contents, and the uncertain outline of the Source himself. Try as she would, she could not fill in the features of his face.

"What is your pleasure, Your Majesty? I have a full store of sensory delights, if you care to indulge." A broad hand gestured, vaguely misshapen.

"Not tonight." She gave him no title, refusing to acknowledge the one he demanded of his other clients. "I never combine business with pleasure, unless it's absolutely

233

necessary." She felt the heightened intensity of her other senses in the darkened room, and how her crippled sight still struggled to dominate them.

A hoarse chuckle. "Such a pity. Such a waste . . . don't you ever wonder what you may be missing?"

"On the contrary," refusing to be condescended to. "I miss nothing. That's why I'm the Queen of this world. And that's why I'm here. I intend to stay Queen of Tiamat after you and the rest of the offworld parasites abandon it again. But in order to do that, I'll need to employ your questionable services on a much bigger scale than I've done in the past."

"You put things so delicately. How could a man refuse you anything?" iron on cement. "What did you have in mind, Your Majesty?"

She rested an elbow on the sense-absorbing chair-arm. *Like flesh. It feels like flesh.* "I want something to happen during the Festival, something that will create chaos—at the expense of the Summers."

"You had in mind, perhaps, the sort of accident that befell the former Police Commander? But on a much larger scale, of course." His voice betrayed no surprise at all; something she found both reassuring and disturbing. "Drugs in the water supply, perhaps."

But why should it disturb me? It was my idea. "No drugs. That would affect my people too, and I don't want that. We have to remain in control. I had in mind an epidemic, something most of Winter has been vaccinated against. The Summers would have no protection."

"I see," A dim nod. "Yes. It can be arranged. Although I would be betraying the Hegemony in a great way, if I gave you the means of retaining power. It's very much in our interest to leave the savages in control when we depart."

"The Hegemony's best interests are hardly yours. You're no more a loyalist than I am." The smell of incense in the air was too strong, as though it were hiding something.

"Our interests coincide in the matter of the water of life." She heard his smile.

"Name your price, then. I don't have time to wade in the shallows." Sharpening her own voice, she jabbed at his smug formlessness.

"I want the take from three Hunts. All of it."

"Three!" She laughed once, not admitting that it was no more than she'd expected him to ask for.

"What is the price of a queen's ransom, Your Majesty?" The darkness around them settled into his voice almost tangibly; she was aware again of how much more she heard, trying to compensate for not seeing his face. "I'm sure the police would be more than interested to learn what you have in mind for this world. Genocide is a serious charge—and against your own people. But that's what comes of letting a woman rule. . . . Women don't rule the Hegemony, you know. There are many places, on many worlds, where even your arrogance could be broken, Arienrhod."

Arienrhod's hands tightened at the unexpected eagerness of his hatred, a terrifying crack of white-hot damnation between the shielding curtains of the darkness. She became aware of a peculiar odor underlying the perfume of incense in the air . . . an odor of disease, or decay. *But he doesn't dare!* "Don't threaten me, Thanin Jaakola. You may have been a slavemaster on Big Blue, and you may be responsible for the majority of the misery on seven different worlds," letting his comprehension of her own private knowledge harden. "But until the Change this is *my* world, Jaakola, and you exist here only because I permit you to. Whatever becomes of me becomes of you, because if anything happens to me you lose your protection from the law. I'm sure there are many places that you would find a humbling experience yourself." *And I'm sure you never forget that for a moment.* "What I'm asking of you is risky, yes, but simple. I'm sure it's nothing you can't handle easily, given your resources. I'll give you the entire take of Starbuck's final Hunt . . . and that is worth a Queen's ransom, to you or anyone."

The darkness magnified his separate breaths, and his silence. Arienrhod held her own. At last she detected the faint inclination of his head, and he said, "Yes. I'll handle the matter, for the agreed payment. I'll enjoy thinking of you ruling Tiamat after we're gone, without the water of life to keep you young. Ruling in Carbuncle after we're gone . . . it won't be the same place without us, you know. It really won't be the same." His laughter tore like rubber.

Arienrhod stood up without further comment, and only after her back was to him and she was crossing the room to the door did she allow herself to frown.

"Where the hell are you going?"

Tor started guilty as the voice caught her from behind in the corridor—Herne's voice; she was just past the room she had arranged for him to use here in the casino. Most of the other rooms along this corridor were used by prostitutes and their clients. But a new day was dawning somewhere in the outer world, and the hall was empty; the casino was closed for a brief span of rest and recovery.

Tor turned back with deliberate slowness to study Herne. He leaned heavily against the door frame, his useless legs wrapped in the clumsy, powered exoskeleton that let him get around on his own after a fashion. A short, slashed robe thrown on carelessly over his head left him just short of indecent. She frowned. "I've got a heavy date. What's it to you, grandmother?"

"Dressed like that?"

She glanced down at her coveralls; saw her face in the mirror of memory stripped of its painted persona—her own dreary, genuine self, tired of pretending to be someone she was not, glad just to see her own lank and mousy hair emerge from underneath the gold-capped wig. "Why not?"

"Only you would ask a question like that." He sneered his disgust, tugged at his robe. His eyes were bloodshot, his face heavy with fatigue, or drugs, or both.

"If I dressed to turn you on I wouldn't get much return on the investment." She watched his mouth thin; satisfied. Time had not made her like him. *And it never will.* She was bound for a meeting with Sparks Dawntreader, not a rendezvous with a lover; time had made her like him even

236

less than Herne. It was hard to remember that he had ever been the frightened Summer kid she'd found cowering in an alley. She had changed outwardly since that day, until sometimes she hardly recognized her own face; but she knew that when she threw off the trappings, she would always find herself. But she had watched the inner thing that had made Sparks Dawntreader himself slowly suffocated by something inhuman. . . . "What are you standing around the hall like a hooker for, anyway, for gods' sakes? You spy for me, not on me, remember? Sober up and get some sleep; how do you expect to do your job if you stay up all day?" She wished that she were safely asleep in her elegant rooms upstairs, and not starting out for a thankless confrontation at dawn.

"I can't sleep." He bent his head, rubbed his face on his arm against the doorjamb. "I can't even sleep any more; it's all a stinking—" He broke off, looked up at her abruptly, looking for something he didn't find. His face hardened over again. "Get off my back!"

"Lay off the drugs, then." She started on down the hall.

"What was *she* doing here last night?" His voice caught at her.

Tor stopped again, recognizing the emphasis, his recognition of the Source's midnight caller who had passed this way, too. Arienrhod, the Snow Queen. The Queen had been muffled in a heavy cloak, like her bodyguard; but Tor was a Winter, and she knew her Queen. It surprised her that Herne would know her, too, or care what she was doing here. "She was here to see the Source. Your guess about what they were doing is as good as mine."

He laughed unpleasantly. "I can guess what they weren't doing." He glanced away down the hall, back in the other direction. "It's getting close to the final Festival; close to the end of everything, for Arienrhod. Maybe she's not ready to give it all up to the Summers, after all." He smiled, an iron smile, full of pointless amusement.

Tor stood still as the idea struck her that the Change was not an inevitability. "She has to. That's the way it's always been; otherwise there might be a—a war or something. We've always accepted that. When the Summers come . . ."

He made a derisive noise. "People like you accept the Change! People like Arienrhod make their own changes: Would you give up everything, after being Queen for one hundred and fifty years? If you could get hold of official records, I'll lay odds you'd see every Snow Queen before her tried to keep Winter here forever. And they all failed." The smile came back. "All of them."

"What do you know about it, foreigner?" Tor waved a hand, brushing off the idea. "It's not your world. She's not your Queen."

"It is now." He looked up, but there was only ceiling above them. He turned away, dragging his legs inside their steel cages, turning his back on her. "And Arienrhod will be Queen of my world forever."

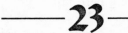

Time is flowing backwards. Moon hung suspended where she had hung suspended before, in the cocoon surrounded by controls at the coin ship's heart. Everything the same, just as it had been . . . even the thundering image of the Black Gate on the screen before them. As though her passage through the Gate had never been; as though she had never set foot on another world, never been initiated at its springs of knowledge under the guidance of a stranger, a sibyl who had no right to exist in her universe at all. As though she had never lost five years of her life in a single, fatal moment.

"Moon, dear." Elsevier's voice touched her hesitantly from above; gently urging, full of quiet tension. The invisible web of the cocoon had closed her in already until she could not look up at Elsevier's face; it was becoming hard to breathe, or maybe it was simply her own tension closing around her. She shut her eyes, felt a tremor thread through the ship; sealing the inevitability of their destruction, unless *she*— She opened her eyes again, to the dreadful face of judgment.

But the Black Gate was not the face of Death—only an astronomical phenomenon, a hole in space punctured at the beginning of time, falling in and in on itself. The singularity at its heart lay now somewhere in another reality, in the endless day she imagined must be heaven for the dark angels of this night's dying suns. But around that unknowable heart, the fabric of space turned inside out in the maelstrom of the black hole's gravity well. Between the outer reality of the universe she knew and the inner one of the singularity lay a zone where infinity was attainable, where space and time changed polarity and it was possible to move between them unfettered by the laws of normal space-time. This strange limbo was riddled by wormholes, by the primordial shrapnel wounds of the universe's explosive birth and countless separate corpses of dying stars. With the proper knowledge and the proper tools a starship could leap like thought from one corner of known space to another.

Even the starships of the Old Empire, traveling faster than the speed of light, had used this Gate, because they could not cross direct interstellar distances instantaneously. And now, when the nearest source of the rare element needed for those stardrives lay in a solar system a thousand light-years from Kharemough, its ships could not cross them directly even in weeks or months. They would do so again only when the ship that Kharemough had sent to that system to bring it back returned, and brought the New Millennium with it.

Even with only a fraction of the black hole's total radiation showing on the screen before her, she could catch no glimpse of what lay at its secret heart; because once light fell into that hole, it never came out again. The blinding glare she saw was an image frozen at the limit of this universe's perception: All journeys of all things that had

239

ever entered this Gate—ships, dust, lives—were suffused there into a red smear on the horizon of time, a scream of despair echoing all across the electromagnetic spectrum, echoing and reechoing through eternity.

Like a prayer she repeated the litany of all she had learned: She did believe that sibyls were a universal truth; she did believe in the skill and the wisdom of the Old Empire; she did believe that the Nothing Place was not the land of Death, that it was no more frightful than the lifeless halls of a computer's brain.

She was meant to do this thing; she would not fail. No gate was impassable, there was no gulf of space or time that could not be crossed, no gulf of misunderstanding or of faith, as long as she held to her goal. She fixed her gaze on the image on the screen, absorbed it into her consciousness. She spoke the word at last that came so familiarly/ strangely to her lips, "*Input . . .*" And fell into the darkness.

No further analysis. The sibyl's cry, the end of Transfer, came to her distantly, rising on golden wings through a spiraling tunnel whose other end was utter blackness. The voice went on, sounds that would not coalesce into meaning; a high, thin, witless song. She raised her hands to her lips, pressed—only with the movement aware that her hands were free to move—squeezing her face, astonished by sensation and silence. With the awareness of feeling she was aware of its savage intensity, the red-hot filaments of muscle and tendon put on the rack by their passage . . . by their passage. The Transfer had ended, ended!

She opened her eyes, starving, craving, dying for light. And light rewarded her with a crescendo of brilliance, inundating her retinas until she cried out with joy/pain. Squinting through her fingers, wetting them with squeezed tears, she found Silky's face hanging in front of her like a distorted mirror, the milky opacity of his eyes darkening with inscrutable interest.

"Silky." There was no cocoon separating them. "I thought I might see Death. . . ." She pressed her fingers into her flesh, devoured the sensation of her own substantiality. There in the sourceless halls of the Nothing Place she had hallucinated again, as she had before, consumed by her most primitive fears. Deprived of all her senses, her body was made of void; flesh, bone, muscle, blood . . . soul. And Death had come to her again in a dream of deeper darkness and asked her, *Who owns your body, flesh and blood?* And she had whispered, "You do." *Who is stronger than life, and will, and hope, and love?* "You are."

And who is stronger than me?

With trembling voice, "I am."

And Death had moved aside, and let her pass—

Back through the tunnels outside of time, and into the light of day.

"I am!" She laughed joyously. "Look at me! I *am* . . . I am, I am!" Silky's tentacles clutched the control panel between them as she destroyed their precarious equilibrium. "Nothing is impossible now."

"Yes, my dear . . ." Elsevier's voice drifted down to her, lifting her eyes. Elsevier rested on air above her, also free of her cocoon, but not moving freely. "You've found your way back. I'm so glad."

Moon's eager face lost its celebration at the feebleness of Elsevier's voice. "Elsie?" Moon and Silky rose like clumsy swimmers, pushing off from the stabilized panel; stabilizing themselves again by the suspended controls above Elsevier's head. "Elsie, are you all right?" She reached out with a free hand.

"Yes, yes . . . fine. Of course I am." Elsevier's eyes were shut, but a silver track of wetness crept out from under each lid as she spoke. She brushed away Moon's hand almost roughly; and Moon could not tell whether the tears were from pain or pride, or both, or neither. "You've begun to set things right, by your own courage. Now I must find the courage to see that we finish what we've begun." She opened her eyes, wiping her face as though she were rousing out of her own black dreams.

Moon looked down through a sea of air, away at the screen, where no Gate lay before them now, but only the

241

ruddy candleglow of a thousand thousand stars, of which the Twins were only two . . . the sky of home, of Tiamat. "The worst is behind us now, Elsie. Everything else will be easy."

But Elsevier made no answer, and Silky looked only at her.

24

"BZ, I wish I didn't have to hand you this duty; but I've put it off as long as I can." Jerusha stood at the window of her office, looking out, confronted by the sight of the blank wall that was all her view. *Boxed in. Boxed in . . .*

"It's all right, Commander." Gundhalinu sat at attention in the visitor's chair, the benign acceptance in his voice warming her back. "To tell you the truth I'm glad to get out of Carbuncle for a while. Certain people have been leaning a little hard on 'shirkers' . . . it'll be a relief to breathe fresh air, even if it turns my lungs blue." He grinned reassurance as she turned back to him. "They don't bother me, Commander. I know I'm doing my job . . . and I know who uses personal incompetence as an excuse to make you look bad." Disapproval pulled his face down. "But I have to admit sharing the company of inferiors— wears on one."

She smiled faintly. "You deserve a break, BZ, the gods know it; even if it's only to waste your time chasing thieves across the tundra." She leaned against her desk, carefully, trying not to dislodge a heap of anything. "I just wish I didn't have to send you to oversee starport security because I don't know how the hell I'm going to manage here, without your support." She glanced down, a little ashamed to be admitting it; but her gratitude at his unshakeable loyalty would not leave it unsaid.

He laughed, shaking his head. "You don't need anybody, Commander. As long as you've got your integrity, they can't touch you."

Oh, but I do ... and they do, every day. I need that encouraging word, like life needs the sun. But he'd never really understand that. Why couldn't she have been born with the sense of supreme self-worth that seemed to be bred into a Kharemoughi? Gods, it must be wonderful, never having to look to anyone else for the reassurance that what you did was right! Even when she had promoted him to inspector, he had never questioned that it might be for any reason other than his competence as an officer. "Well, it's only a matter of—months, anyway."

"And only a matter of months until it's all over, Commander. Come the Millennium! Only months until the Change comes, and we can clear off of this miserable slush-ball and forget about it for the rest of our lives."

"I try not to think that far ahead," dully. "One day at a time, that's how I take things." She rearranged a stack of petition cards absently.

Gundhalinu stood up, concern coming vaguely into his eyes. "Commander ... if you need somebody who'll support your orders while I'm gone, try KraiVieux. He's got a hard shell, but he's got at least half his mind working—and he thinks you're trying to do an honest job."

"Does he?" surprised. KraiVieux was a veteran officer, and one of the last she would have expected to feel even the slightest willingness to accept her. "Thanks, BZ. That helps." She smiled again, only straining a little.

He nodded. "Well. I suppose I'd better start packing my thermals, Commander. . . . Take care of yourself, ma'am."

"Take care of yourself, BZ." She returned his salute, watched him go out of the office. She had a sudden, wrenching premonition that it was the last time she would ever see him. *Stop it! You want to wish him bad luck?* She reached into her pocket for a pack of iestas as she moved back around her desk; answered the chiming intercom with an unsteady hand.

Arienrhod sat patiently, resting her hands on the veined marble of the wide desktop, as the latest in the day's progression of local and offworld petitioners stated his proposals and laid down his plans. She listened with half an ear as he mangled the language—a native speaker of Umick, from D'doille, she decided—without letting him lapse into his own. She knew Umick, among the nearly one hundred other languages and dialects she had absorbed over the years; but she enjoyed forcing the offworlders to speak her own when they came to court her favor.

The merchant droned on about shipping costs and profit margins, gradually becoming invisible. She found herself looking through him, back along an endless procession of echoes, others like him—different, but the same. *How many?* She wished suddenly that she had kept count. It would give the past proportion, a sense of the absolute. It all became gray with age, dust-gray with disuse; a blur, stultifying and meaningless. Just once she would like to have brought into her presence a new offworlder who did not look at her and see a woman before he saw a ruler, a barbarian before an experienced head of state....

" . . . time in—uh, *sallak*—transit. That means I couldn't much make a good profit on the salts, anyway, which is why I cannot offer but only—"

"Correction, Master Trader." She leaned forward across the desk top. "The transit time from here to Tsieh-pun is in fact five months less than you claim, which puts you exactly in synch with their collody cycle. That makes the shipping of our manganese salts to Tsieh-pun extremely profitable."

The merchant's jaw twitched. Arienrhod smiled sardonically and popped the presentation disc out of her tape reader. She tossed it out, letting it slide across the polished marble into his outstretched hands. They might come to her expecting a naive weakling once; but they never did it again. "Perhaps you'd better come back when you've got your facts straight."

"Your Majesty, I——" He ducked his head, afraid to look her in the eye: an arrogant aging whelp with his tail abruptly between his legs. "Of course, you're so right, it was a stupid—uh, oversight. I can't think how I could do such a mistake. The terms you offer would be—agreeable, now that I see my mistake."

She smiled again, with no more kindness. "When you've seen as many 'mistakes' made as I have, Master Trader, you learn not to make many of your own." She looked back into the distant beginning, when she had stumbled over every lying "mistake" the offworlders had thrown in her path—when she had had to consult her Starbucks about every decision, no matter how great or small, obvious or obscure. And the kind of information they had brought her was not always the kind she needed. . . . But as the months, years, decades went by, she had seen the cost of her mistakes; and the lessons she had learned from experience she never forgot, the mistakes were never repeated. "Well, since you've seen the error of your calculations, I'm inclined to go against my judgment and grant you the shipping and trade agreements. In fact—" she waited until he was looking directly at her again, hanging on each word, "I might even have a little added business I could direct your way, now that I think of it. To our mutual benefit, of course. I know of a trader just in who has a small hoard of ledoptra that he intends to carry to Samathe." *But only as a last resort.* "Ledoptra would bring a much higher price on Tsieh-pun, as you know." *And so does he, but he doesn't know you're in port.* "For a reasonable commission, I'd be willing to convince him that you'll gladly take the ledoptra off his hands."

Greed licked the trader's face, and doubt. "I am not sure I have enough—cargo stabilizers for such a soft—uh— *fragile* load, Your Majesty."

"You would if you left the computerized library system you're transporting to Tsieh-pun here on Tiamat instead."

He gaped. "How did you . . . I mean, that would be— uh, unlawful."

All the more reason why such a resource belongs here, where it's really needed. "An accident. An oversight. It happens all the time in shipping goods across a galaxy. It's happened to you before, I'm sure," insinuating more than she was sure of, following his face.

He didn't answer, but a kind of wild panic showed, far down in his dark eyes.

Yes, I know everything about you . . . I've seen your echoes for a hundred and fifty years. "The ledoptra is by far the more profitable cargo. And once you reach Tsieh- pun, and the mistake is discovered, it will be too late to do anything about it—the Gate will have closed. It's all very simple, you see. Even simple enough for you. Profit—that's all that really matters, isn't it?" *A profit in knowledge for Winter; a reward that money can't buy.* She smiled in- wardly, at the secret knowledge of all the similar profits she had accumulated, in similar ways, down the long years; quietly stockpiling technology and information against the coming time of famine.

The trader nodded, his eyes still searching the corners of the room furtively. "Yes, Your Majesty. If you say so."

"Then I'll see that it's arranged. You may go."

He went, without further urging. She looked down, speaking reference notes into her desk recorder.

When she looked up again Starbuck stood in the door- way, bemused admiration showing in his eyes.

"I see. . . . Well, is that all, then?" Arienrhod leaned against the cushioned back of the chair at her desk, lis- tened to it sigh familiarly as she set it gently rocking.

" 'Is that all?' " Starbuck laughed, with an aggrieved

edge on it. "I've been out on the Street all day long busting my ass to please you. Don't I bring you a big enough load of rumors? Doesn't that bitch Blue have more trouble than she can handle already, without me buying her more? Doesn't—"

"There was a time, you know, when that question would have cut you to the quick." Arienrhod leaned forward again, into the cup of her hands. "Sparks Dawntreader used to sail on my smile, and quiver at my frown. If I had said 'Is that all?' he would have gone down on his knees and begged me to set him another task; anything, if only it made me happy." She set her lips in a petulant pout, but the words wrapped razors, and cut her inside.

"And you laughed at him for being a sap." Starbuck's black-gloved fists rested on his hips defiantly. But she sat without responding, letting the words do their work; and after a moment his hands dropped, and his gaze with them. "I am what you wanted me to be," softly, almost inaudibly. "I'm sorry if you don't like it."

Yes . . . and so am I. Once she had known the warmth of a forgotten summer when she looked at him, when he held her. But he had forgotten Summer, and she saw no past in his changeable green eyes; not hers, not even his own. Only her own reflection: the Snow Queen, eternal Winter. *Why must I always be too strong for them? Always too strong . . . send me someone I can't destroy.*

"Are you sorry? Sorry you let it happen—let me become Starbuck? Haven't I done the job?" He was not defiant any more.

"No, I'm not sorry. It was inevitable." *But I am sorry that it was inevitable. . . .* She found a smile, an answer for the insecure boy who had stolen away his voice. "And you have done very well." *Too well.* "Take off your mask, Starbuck."

He reached up and pulled the black helmet off, held it under his arm. She smiled at the blaze of hair spilling out, the fair face still the same, fresh and youthful . . . no, not really the same. Not any more. Not any more than her own

247

was. Her eyes stopped smiling behind her smile; she watched his smile fade in response. They looked at each other for a space of time, silently.

He broke free at last; stretched, struck a pose with feline self-awareness. "You mind if I sit? It's been a long day."

"By all means, sit, then. I'm sure it must be enervating to wallow in depravity day after day as diligently as you do."

He frowned as he settled into one of the matched wing-form chairs, across the intimate gulf between desk and doorway, and himself and her. "It's boring." He leaned forward suddenly, reaching across the space with his voice. "Every minute seems like a year, it bores the hell out of me when I'm away from you." He sat back again, restlessly, hopelessly, fingering the offworlder medal that dangled in the silken gap of his half-open shirt.

"You shouldn't find it boring to make trouble for the Blues—for the woman who lost Moon for us both." She forced her tone to stay businesslike, shaping her emotion into a weapon to punish . . . *whom?*

He shrugged. "I'd enjoy it more if I could see some results. She's still on top."

"Of course she is. And she'll stay there to the bitter, bitter end. And every day of what should have been sweet victory she'll spend walking barefoot over broken glass. . . . Stay here in the palace tomorrow, and I'll let you watch her."

"No." He looked down at his feet abruptly. She saw with some surprise that his face burned. "No. I don't want to see it, after all." His hands felt along his studded belt for something that wasn't there, had not been there for a long time.

"Whatever you want. If you even know what you want," half critical, half concerned. But he was unresponsive, and so she went on, "I must say PalaThion's held together more stubbornly than I'd expected. Brittle as she is, I thought she'd be showing deeper fractures by now. She must be getting support from somewhere."

"Gundhalinu. One of the inspectors. The others hate

him for it; but he doesn't give a damn, because he thinks he's better than they are."

"Gundhalinu? Oh, yes . . ." Arienrhod glanced down, at the note recorder. "I'll keep that in mind. And there's another offworlder, Ngenet is his name; he has an outback plantation down along the coast. She's been out to visit him there, I understand. A friendship with questionable roots . . ." She smoothed her hair, gazing at the mural behind Starbuck's head, the white blackness of a winter storm roaring down out of the ice-crowned peaks, obliterating the valley and the world around a solitary Winter holding. "His plantation has never been harvested, has it?"

Starbuck straightened up in his chair. "No. He's an offworlder. I thought we couldn't, unless he—"

"That's right. And I understand that he strictly forbids it; he's hostile to the whole idea. Now what would happen, I wonder, if you hunted his preserve, and PalaThion couldn't punish you?"

He laughed, none of the old reluctance showing now. "A good Hunt. And the end of an affair?"

"All in a day's work." She smiled. "The final Hunt will net us some souls."

"The final Hunt . . ." Starbuck leaned into a wing of the chair back, playing with his fingers. "You know, I heard something interesting on the Street. I heard the Source had a midnight visitor a few nights back. I heard it was you. And the word is that maybe you're not ready to see the end of Winter come." He glanced up. "How's my hearing?"

"Excellent." She nodded, listening to the silence keep them company. Surprised, yes—but only a little. She knew his sources of information, that he used Persiponë to use Herne. She even approved of his resourcefulness. It only surprised her a little that her intentions were quite so obvious to them all. She would have to keep closer watch on Persiponë.

"Well?" Starbuck pressed his knees with his fists. "Were you going to tell me about it? Or were you just going to let me go on thinking we were both going into the sea together at the next Festival?"

"Oh, I would have told you—eventually. I just rather enjoyed hearing you swear to me that you couldn't, wouldn't, live without me . . . my dearest love." She stopped his anger with three words that came unexpectedly from her heart.

He stood up, came across the room and around the silver-edged curve of desk to her. But she put up her hands, holding him back with quiet insistence. "Hear me first. Since you've asked, then I want you to know. I have no intention of going meekly to the sacrifice, and seeing all that I've struggled to make of this world thrown into the sea after me. I never had. This time, by all the gods who never belonged here, this world is not going to sink back into ignorance and stagnation when the offworlders go!"

"What can you do to stop it? When the offworlders go, we lose our support, our base of power." It pleased her to hear his unconscious pledge of allegiance. "They'll see to it that we do. And then we can't hold back Summer, any more than we can hold back the seasons. It'll be their world again."

"You're brainwashed." She shook her head, gestured with a ring-heavy hand at the city beyond the walls. "The Summers will gather here in the city for the Festival—here on our ground. All we need is something that will take them unawares . . . like an epidemic. One that we Winters are fortunately immune to, thanks to the miracle of offworld medicine."

Starbuck's face twisted. "You mean . . . you could do that? Would—?"

"Yes, and yes! Are you still so bound to those ignorant, superstitious barbarians that you aren't willing to sacrifice a few of them for the future of this world? They play right into the hands of the offworlders; there's a conspiracy between them to oppress us—Winter—the people who want to make this world a free partner in the Hegemony. And they've succeeded, for a millennium! Do you want them to go on succeeding, forever? Isn't it time we had our turn?"

"Yes! But—"

"But nothing. Offworlders, Summers—what have they

250

ever done for you, either of them, but betray you, abandon you?" She watched the words work in the dark corners of his soul that she had probed so thoroughly.

"Nothing." His mouth was like a knife slash. "You're right . . . they deserve it, for what they've—done." His hands closed over his belt, like claws sinking into flesh. "But how can you arrange a thing like that, without the Blues finding it out?"

"The Source will handle it. He's arranged other accidents of fate for me; even one that happened to the last Commander of Police." She watched Starbuck's eyes widen. "This is on a somewhat larger scale; but then, for the possession of your take from this final Hunt, I'm sure he'll see that the task is done efficiently. He's an honorable man, after his fashion."

"But it'll have to happen before the final ships go. Won't the Blues still try—"

"With the Prime Minister here, and the Gate closing? They'll run; they'll leave us in chaos, thinking that without them we'll end up in the sea anyway. I know them . . . I've studied them for a century and a half."

He let his resistance out in a sigh. "You know them better than they know themselves."

"I know everyone that way." She rose from her chair, letting his arms come around her at last. "Even you."

"Especially me." He breathed the words against her ear, kissing her neck, her throat. "Arienrhod . . . you have my body; I'd give you my soul if you'd take it."

She touched a button on the desk, opening a door into a more appropriate room. Thinking, with sorrow, *I already have, my love.*

26

"Got warm bodies registering down there someplace, Inspector." The pilot, TierPardée, roused from his usual truculent silence with rare animation. "Looks right for humans. Along that rift to the left; there's bush for cover."

"Using any power?" Gundhalinu stuck the Old Empire novel into a pocket of his heavy coat, leaned forward in his seat, the patrolcraft's shoulder harness pressing the side of his throat. *At last, some action* . . . He peered out through the windshield, scanning with inadequate human eyes for a trace of what their all-seeing equipment saw. They had been tracking this party of thieves for a day and a half after the raid on the starport. The trail had been muddled at the start, but it had been steadily getting fresher. The list of things missing included a crate containing a portable heavy-duty beamer that belonged to the police; he wondered how in hell they had managed to get access to that. The nomads were not usually well armed, which was why their raids depended on stealth and avoided confrontation. But they were as pitiless and unsubtle as the stark black-and-white land that sheltered them, and they had killed almost casually the handful of offworlders who had gotten in their way. He meant to make sure this acquisition didn't change their method of operation.

He glanced down at the readout on the panel again, to make his own assessment, as TierPardée sang out, "Yes, sir! We've finally nailed 'em, Inspector, they've got snowskimmers down there." TierPardée laughed gleefully. "I'll take us in low and scare the piss out of them; ought to be no trouble picking the Mother lovers off after that, right, sir?"

Gundhalinu opened his mouth to make a skeptical response just as his eyes found the next readout, just as it suddenly glared red—red warning—"Get us the hell out of here now!"

He reached across TierPardée's amazed and sluggish body, jerked the control bar back and around into a steeply climbing turn. He felt the bar tremble and fight his control. "Come *on* . . ."

"Inspector, what the—" TierPardée never finished it, as the hidden bolt of directed energy caught them from below and punched them out of the sky.

Gundhalinu had a brief, whorled image of black-white-blue photoprinted indelibly on his brain; giddy freefall spun him like a lottery wheel before the craft's stabilizers reintegrated and stopped their nightmare tumbling. But not their fall—they were dead in the air, dropping down like a stone through a soundless dive that would end with them dead on the ground. His hand stretched instinctively to press the restart button; he pushed it again and again, his numbed brain acknowledging at last the reason why there was no response: the beamer had slagged the shielding on the power unit, and there was nothing he could do. *Nothing*— TierPardée sat gaping like a plastic dummy, making a sound that at first he mistook for laughter. The sky disappeared, he saw the rumpled cloud-surface of the snow and the jutting black fangs of the naked cliff leap up to meet them. . . .

They hit the snow before they hit the cliff, and that was all that saved them. The snow plowed up in a cushion of blinding white, absorbing the impact that still threw him forward so hard his helmet warped the pliant windshield.

For a long time he lay without moving, doubled over in the embrace of the harness; listening to bells, unable to focus his eyes or even make a sound. Knowing that there was something important he must say, must warn—but it wouldn't take form in his mouth or even his mind. The cabin felt hot to him, which struck him as strange because they were buried in snow. *Buried. Buried. Dead and . . . ?*

He shut his eyes. Something stank. His eyes hurt. . . . The air. The air was going bad, smelled like buried—like burning.

His eyes watered; he opened them again. Burning insulation. That was it. The avalanche of snow was slushing, slipping down outside the windows. " 'Pardée. Overload. Gedoud." The words were unintelligible even to him. He shook TierPardée, but the patrolman's eyes stayed shut, and he hung forward across the straps unmoving. Gundhalinu struggled with his own harness latch, finally set himself free. He tried the door; it was still blocked shut by snow. He beat against it with his fist, uselessly, while every blow fed back through his bones into his throbbing head. At last he wedged himself sideways and shoved with his feet, threw all his returning strength and his fear into it. The door began to give, a centimeter at a time, until at last it sprang upward on its own, half dumping him out into the snow.

He landed on his knees in a puddle of slush, shocked by the sudden assault on his aching body of painful heat and cold. He pulled himself up the side of the craft, forcing his rubber legs to lock and support him, separating the sinister heat of the power unit going critical from the icy embrace of the wind. He had to get TierPardée out and as far away as he could before the patroller turned into a star.

He leaned into the cabin; but something caught his collar, jerked him away and back into the snow again. Not bells, this time, but the ugly music of human laughter echoing off the cliff face; ugly, because he knew it was directed at him. He rolled over, pushed up onto his knees to face his tormenters—saw with no surprise at all the white parkas and leggings, half a dozen pale, amorphous faces half obscured by slitted wooden goggles, like the bulging eyes of a family of insectoids. But these were human, all right—nomadic Winter pfalla herders turned thieves by opportunity, who had shed their bright, traditional clothing for the antiseptic camouflage of arctic commandos. A blow on the back ended his assessment as he sprawled forward into the snow; he felt someone roll him onto his side and deftly disarm him. There was a whoop of triumph as the bearded male held his stunner up like a prize.

Gundhalinu sat up, wiping snow from his face, forgetting the indignity of his position in the urgency of his need. "That's going to blow—!" He pointed, not sure how much they would understand. "Help me get him out of there; there's not much time!" He climbed to his feet, relieved at the murmur of consternation that ran through the group. He started back toward the patrolcraft, but another of the nomads had gotten there first, and straightened holding TierPardée's gun, grinning satisfaction. "He's good for nothing, that one—this's all I found. It's too hot in there; forget about it." The roving muzzle of the stunner suddenly targeted Gundhalinu's chest. "Zap, you're paralyzed, Blue!" A high-pitched adolescent giggle escaped from the muffled figure.

Gundhalinu stopped, looking past the teenager and the filamented muzzle of the gun. "He's not dead, he's hurt! He's alive; we've got to get him out of there—" His breath rose up white in his face.

But the man who had taken his own gun and another man caught him by the arms at a sharp command. They began to drag him back away from the craft. The teenager strutted behind him, on snowshoes like the rest, giggling again as his boots broke through the snow crust and he floundered.

"No! You can't do this; he's alive, damn you, he'll be burned alive in there!"

"Then be glad you're only watching, and not joining him." The first man grinned at his side. They forced him to go with them as far as the outcropping of fallen rock where they had hidden their snow skimmers. They all stopped then, and turned back, crouching down to watch. The two men still held his arms locked between them, forcing him to keep his feet as they made him turn with the rest. He could see the distant patrolcraft melted clear of snow now, and a dull glow spreading over its crumpled frame. He looked up into the sky, filling his eyes with the

255

blue of heaven, and prayed to the gods of eight separate worlds that TierPardée would never know what was happening to him now.

But the sky was empty, and in the empty white silence of the frozen Winter world a sunball of searing light burned his sight away and the blast that followed obliterated all his other senses.

Consciousness followed pain back into his aching body; he lay propped against a boulder while the nomads shuffled and muttered and pointed past him in subdued awe. One of them laughed nervously. Memory came back to him and he remembered why they were laughing . . . he leaned over and vomited into the trampled snow.

"They send you to kill us, and you can't even stomach the sight of death!" One of the nomads stood over him and spat. The spittle landed on the heavy cloth of his uniform coat; he watched it begin to freeze. He looked up, aware of how the cold air burned as his lungs sucked it in, aware of the fact that he had just been spat upon by a barbarian, by an old hag with a face like fishnet, who wasn't fit to touch the lowest Unclassified on Kharemough.

He pulled himself up the rock, clumsy with stiffness and cold, until he could stand looking down at her. He said, his voice brittle with fury, "You are all under arrest, for murder and robbery. You will return with me to the starport to face charges." Hearing the words, he could not quite believe that he had really said them.

The old woman stared at him incredulously, burst into obscene, frost-clouded laughter, wrapping her arms around her. The rest of the bandits began to close in around him, having lost interest in their first victim now that he no longer existed. "You hear him?" She poked an arthritic claw at his face delightedly. "You hear what this sniveling foreigner with the dirty skin says to us? That he thinks we're under arrest! What do you think of that?" She swept her hand away again.

"I think he must be crazy." One of the men grinned; Gundhalinu thought that there were three men and one other woman . . . guessed that the adolescent was female,

256

too, but he wasn't sure. This damned world turned civilized behavior upside down until he couldn't judge anything by standards he knew.

But there was one thing he understood clearly enough— that he was not going to get out of this alive. They were going to kill him next. The realization made him dizzy; he pressed back against the rock for support. He watched them push up their goggles to get a better look at him, and saw no mercy in the pale-ringed, sky-colored eyes. One of them fingered the sleeve of his coat; he jerked his arm away.

"What're we going to do with this one, huh?" The teen-ager elbowed one of the men aside for a better look. "Can I have him? Oh, let me have him, Ma!" The stunner pointed him out again. He realized she was speaking to the old woman. "For my collection."

He had a sudden vision of his own mutilated head jammed on a stake, like a piece of meat in some grisly charnel-house freezer. His stomach knotted again; he pressed his tongue against the roof of his mouth. *Gods! ... oh, gods, not like that. If I have to die let it be clean ... let it be quick.*

"Shut up, brat," the crone said sharply. The girl made a face behind her back.

"I say kill him now, shaman," the other woman said. "Kill him ugly. Then the other foreigners will be afraid to come out here any more."

"If you kill me they'll never stop coming after you!" Gundhalinu took a step forward, saw two knives come out of hidden sheaths. "You can't murder a police inspector and get away with it. They'll never stop until they find you." He knew he was saying it only to comfort himself, because it wasn't true. He felt the lameness of the lying words, knew that the others felt it, too. He began to shiver.

"And who's ever going to know what happened?" The old crone grinned again; her teeth were flawless, as white as the snow. He wondered, absurdly, whether they were false. "We could throw your corpse down a crack and the ice would grind up your bones. Not even all your gods will ever find where you lie!" Abruptly she brought up the thing hanging at her back and jammed it into his chest, driving him back against the boulders with a grunt of surprise. "You think you can hunt us down on our own land, foreigner? I'm the Mother. The earth is my lover, the rocks and the birds and the animals are my children. They speak to me, I know their language." The opacity of madness made porcelain of her eyes. "They tell me how to hunt a hunter. And they want an offering, they want a reward."

Gundhalinu looked down at the long, bright metal tube that pinned him against the icy rock, recognized a police-issue electron torch before his eyes blurred out of focus again. He stood up with rigid dignity, controlling his physical responses by an effort of will, as the old hag backed slowly away. The others moved with her, out of range of the energy backwash; leaving him alone in a circle of eddied snow. His mouth hurt, his lungs ached from the frigid air. Every breath now might be his last, but in his mind he saw no playback of life scenes, no profound revelation of universal truth . . . in this final moment nothing; there was nothing at all. . . .

The old woman raised the torch, and pressed the trigger.

Gundhalinu swayed with the shock of the blow that did not fall; opened eyes that he didn't remember closing, in time to see the woman press the trigger again and again, with no result. She muttered furiously, shaking it; curses of frustration circled the fence of leering witnesses.

He moved forward unsteadily, holding out his hands. "Here—let me fix that for you."

Amazement came back into the washed-out blue eyes; she jerked the torch out of his reach.

He stood patiently with his hands extended, palm up. "It's jammed. Happens all the time. I can fix it, if you'll let me."

She frowned, but her expression shifted subtly again, and she made a small gesture with her head. He was aware of two stunners directed at him now, aware that he would never get away with an escape attempt. She thrust the torch into his hands. "Fix it then, if you're so eager to die."

The tone suggested that she thought he had lost his mind; he wondered if he had.

He kneeled down, sinking back, feeling the bite of the snow as it soaked through the cloth of his pants leg. He balanced the torch across his thigh, pulled off his gloves and unsnapped the tool pouch he wore at his belt. He withdrew a hair-fine magnetized rod and inserted it into the opening at the base of the torch handle, began to probe the hidden mechanisms with gentle confidence. His sweating hands stuck to the frozen metal as he worked; he scarcely noticed. Feeling his way along unseen paths, he came at last to the crucial crossroads and separated the two components that had locked together. He withdrew the probe again carefully, grateful that the problem was only what he had expected. He put the probe away in its place, wondering why he bothered, and held the torch out to the old woman. He met her eyes without expression. "That ought to do it. You shouldn't steal our toys unless you know how to take care of them."

She jerked the torch out of his hands, taking a layer of epidermis with it. He grimaced, but his hands were like wood, senseless, useless already. Like his face; like his brain. He got up, letting his gloves drop at his feet. At least he had proven his superiority over these savages, at least now he could die cleanly, with honor, executed by a superior weapon.

But she did not aim the torch at him this time. Instead she turned, bracing it against her, and took aim at the stand of evergreen shrubs below the cliff wall. She fired; he heard the electric crackle of the beam and a small explosion as a solitary tree-shrub burst into flame. Shouts of approval rose around him, and the eagerness for death came back into the wild, pitiless faces.

The crone shuffled around toward him with the torch. "You did a good job, foreigner," smiling without any humanity.

He watched the blazing tree from the corner of his eye. The smoke collected against the cliff wall; the smell of the burning wood was pungently alien. But burned human

259

flesh smelled like any other seared meat. . . . "I'm a Kharemoughi. I can repair any piece of equipment made, blindfolded. That's what makes us more than just animals."

"But you'll die like any of us, foreigner! Do you really want to die?"

"I'm ready to die." He stood straighter; his whole body seemed to belong to someone else now.

She raised the torch, her arms trembling faintly with the effort of supporting it. Her hand closed over the trigger and her eyes probed his face, wanting him to break down and beg for his life. But he would die before he gave them that satisfaction . . . and he knew that he would die anyway.

"Kill him. Kill him!" The voices began to rise with the watchers' impatience. He glanced distractedly at the ring of faces, saw on the teenager's face an expression he couldn't name.

"No." The old woman let the tube drop, grinning with hideous spite. "No, we won't kill him; we'll keep him. He can repair the equipment we steal from his people at the starport."

"He's dangerous, shaman!" one of the men said, angry with frustration. "We don't need him."

"I say he lives!" the hag snarled. "He wants to die—look at him! A man who's not afraid to die is crazy, and it's bad luck to kill a crazy man." She still grinned at him, with self-aware mockery.

Gundhalinu felt his fatalistic stupor clear as he finally understood: They were not going to give him a clean death. They were going to make him their slave. . . . "No, you filthy animals!" He threw himself at the old woman, at the torch. "Kill me, damn you! I won't—"

She brought the tube of the torch up instinctively and hit him in the face with it. Gundhalinu fell back into a snowdrift, blood burning on his skin, pain rattling in his head like a scream. He spat a mouthful of blood and a tooth into the snow, sat moaning behind his frozen hands as the nomads began to drift away from him. He heard the old woman giving orders, but not what she said; not caring, not caring about anything.

"Here . . . put on your gloves, stupid." The teenager stood over him; waved them in his face. He pulled back, tried to ignore her as he scooped up a handful of snow and packed it into his torn mouth.

"Blue!" This time it was TierPardée's stunner shoved into his face. "Blue-boy, you better listen to me!" She tossed the gloves onto his stomach.

He pulled them on slowly, over senseless fingers iced with blood. The thought of being stunned helpless, dragged to a sled and dumped aboard like a crate of spare parts was unendurable. He must bear himself with all the dignity he could, until he found a way out of this nightmare . . . some way, any way.

Something dropped over his helmet, slithered down his face like a snake to settle around his neck. He looked up, startled, and the noose tightened against his throat. The girl laughed at his expression; the other end of the rope wrapped her mittened hand. She let it swing loose, standing arrogantly akimbo in front of him. "Good boy. Ma says she wants your hands. But she says I get the rest of you, for my zoo." She pushed her goggles down, half hiding her narrow, knobby face. "My pet Blue." She laughed again, jerked suddenly on the rope. "Come on, Blue! And you better come quick."

Gundhalinu climbed hastily to his feet, floundered after her through the snow to the waiting skimmers. Knowing that even though they hadn't killed him he was still a dead man; because in that moment his world had come to an end.

261

27

Moon looked past the back of Elsevier's heavily padded seat, straining against the arm of her own seat to see out of the LB's shielded window. Tiamat lay in their view like a rising moon, but infinitely more beautiful to her inner eye. Home—she was coming home, and it was hard not to believe that time had turned itself inside out: that she would find everything as it had been, even as it should have been, when that circle of cloud-limned blue below her expanded and filled once more with the endless sea. But even if it was not the world she had lost, she knew now that she would find the way . . . she would find the way to change it back.

"Shields green?"

"Ya."

She listened to Elsevier's murmured queries, Silky's monosyllabic responses, the comforting rhythm of a ritual repeated countless times before. Their entry into Tiamat's atmosphere was neither as painful nor as terrifying as their leaving of it; that outward journey seemed now as though it had happened to someone else. She listened with only half her mind, the other half roaming from past to future, sidestepping the uncertainty of their perilous present. Nothing could go wrong now, nothing *would*. She had passed through the Black Gate; she was meant to do this.

But Elsevier had radioed an incredulous Ngenet before they broke orbit, only to learn that he could no longer meet them at Shotover Bay; that he had lost his hovercraft five years ago, after their last abortive landing. This time they must take the greater risk of approaching his own plantation on the coast south of Carbuncle; there was no one else to whom Elsevier would trust their final landing.

262

Elsevier had been—fading, it was the only word Moon could put to the subtle metamorphosis she had witnessed since they had come through the Gate. She had tried to learn what was wrong, but Elsevier had refused to answer; and without any lessening of tenderness, withdrawn into herself and closed Moon out.

Moon was hurt and puzzled, until the time when the Twins began to dominate the ship's viewscreens. And then she saw at last that this was what Elsevier had been looking toward, preparing for: The end that would come with Moon's fresh beginning. The final parting from the life she had known, the final parting from the ship that held half a lifetime's bittersweet memories. The final parting from the surrogate daughter who could have given her a new life to replace the one she was leaving behind, but who instead had only given her a deeper loss to endure.

A vast pseudo-sea of boundless cloud was blanketing their view of the sea now, as they dropped lower and lower, plummeting through the sapphire upper air. Soon . . . soon they would break the cloud surface, soon she would see their destination, the long unbroken line of the western continental coast where Ngenet's plantation lay—and Carbuncle.

". . . Ratio is up one and a—Silky! We're in the spotlight! Shift power to rear shields, there's lightning com—"

A blaze of blue-white light put out the sky ahead, sent daggers into Moon's eyes; the metal pod shuddered around her, jarring her teeth. *No, no; it can't be!*

"Oh, gods!" Elsevier cried out, in something that was closer to anger than despair. "They've tracked us down! We're locked in, we'll never get—"

Another explosion burst around them . . . a stretch of silence followed. It was broken as the radio abruptly came to life on its own. ". . . Surrender now or be destroyed. We have you in our beam. You will not escape."

"Losing—" The third explosion tore away the name of what had been lost, and Moon's own questioning cry. The fourth gave them no more time; the instrument panel sparked and shrilled abuse, overloading their dazzled senses.

263

"Cutting power!" She heard Elsevier's voice break; the words barely penetrated her ringing ears. ". . . only hope . . . think we're already dead—" The cabin went black with the suddenness of death, but Moon's blinking eyes recaptured the light of the outer air; saw the limitless blue, white, and golden fantasy fields of heaven obliterate as they broke into the surface of the clouds. She clung to the edge of her seat, counting every beat of her heart; realizing with each reaffirmation of her own life that there had not been another explosion yet—the one that, utterly defenseless now, they would never even see.

They fell out of the clouds again, as abruptly as they had fallen into them. She saw the sea at last, rolling beneath them, an ocean of molten pewter. Raindrops spattered and blurred across the wide window, smearing the view of sea and sky like tears. And they were still alive. The LB dropped through a flattening arc, like a slingstone skimming an infinite pond. Elsevier and Silky worked in silence at the controls. Moon kept silence with them, her voice cowering in her throat, making the only contribution she could.

"Now, Silky; emergency systems on—"

The smoke-gray cone above Moon's seat dropped unexpectedly over her, cutting off Elsevier's voice beginning a distress call, and her last view of the rising sea surface, ice-white and iron-gray. She was immobilized against her seat by a cushion of expanding air, lay unresisting—unable to resist—as her helplessness became total. After an eternity of anticipation, the coming together of metal sphere and iron-gray sea rang dimly through her, like a blow falling on someone else, in astounding anticlimax.

And after another brief eternity the cushion shrivelled away from her, the smoky pod lifted. She threw off the restraining straps and pulled herself forward out of her seat to stand between the pilots' couches. The gray shield was still rising above Silky's seat; he shook his head in a very human gesture of befuddlement. Before her the sea butted against the port with furious indignation; droplets of icy

264

water seeped through the shatter-frost that impact had etched over the reinforced transparent wall. The very structure of the LB heaved under her feet, and the crash of the angry water was loud around them.

The hood hung firmly in place above Elsevier's seat; as though it had never— Moon looked down suddenly at Elsevier's face, afraid to see, unable to look away.

A track of red traced the ebony of Elsevier's upper lip, but she looked up, resting her head against the seat back. "It's nothing, my dear . . . only a nosebleed . . . I had to finish my message. Ngenet's coming." She shut her eyes, gasping shallowly, as though gravity's heavy hand still crushed her . . . had already crushed her. She sat motionless, making no effort even to raise a finger; like a woman who had all the time in the world.

Moon swallowed, choking on a smile, touched her shoulder with frightened tenderness. "We're down, Elsie. You saved us. Everything's all right now! It's over."

"Yes." A strange surprise filled the violet-blue eyes; Elsevier looked out in astonishment at something beyond their view. "I'm so cold." A spasm worked the muscles of her face.

And as suddenly the eyes were empty.

"Elsie. Elsie?" Moon's hand tightened over her shoulder, shook her . . . released her, when there was no response. "Silky—" half turning, not willing to turn away, "she's not . . . Elsie!" pleading.

Silky shouldered her aside in the cramped space between the seats. He reached out with the cold snake-fingers of his gray-green arm to touch the warm flesh of Elsevier's face, her throat. . . . But she did not flinch under his touch, only went on gazing at something beyond view, until the flat strips of gray passed over her eyes, closing them forever. "Dead."

The LB heaved and settled, throwing them off-balance; Moon looked down distraughtly as her feet did not respond. Water lapped the legs of her pressure suit, sea water, rolling into the cabin. "Dead?" She shook her head. "No, she's not. She isn't dead. Elsie. Elsie, we're flooding! Wake up!" shaking the limp, unresponding body. Tentacles wrapped her arms, jerked her away unceremoniously.

"Dead!" Silky's eyes were the clearest, the deepest she had ever seen them. He pressed a sequence of buttons on the panel, repeated it. "Hatch sprung. Sink. Out, go—" He shoved her toward the lock; she staggered as a new, knee-deep surge met her halfway in the aisle.

"No! She isn't dead. She can't be!" furiously. "We can't leave her now." Moon clung to a seat back.

"Go!" Silky struck at her, driving her away, back toward the lock. She stumbled and fell, another surge covered her and brought her up gasping with salt fire burning her eyes. She struggled on to the lock entrance, caught hold of the doorway, turning to look back once more: to see Silky kneel in the swirling water by Elsevier's side and bow his head, rest it briefly against her shoulder in tribute and farewell.

He climbed to his feet again, waded down the aisle to Moon's side. "Out!" The tentacles wrapped her arm again as he dragged her on into the lock.

She let go of the door frame, unable to resist, and plunged after him. She saw the hatchway agape, swallowing the sea, like a helpless drowner.... "My helmet! I'll drown—" She turned back to the inner cabin, but the waist-deep surge wrapped its own arms around her, dragged her off her feet. Icy water doused her again; she struggled upright, half swimming, gasping as the frigid runoff sluiced in around the neck of her suit. The LB tilted with the heaving of the sea swells, canted the floodwaters back toward the hatch, sweeping her with them. She slammed into the edge of the hatch opening, cracking her head on the metal, before the LB spewed them both out into the open ocean.

Moon's cry extinguished like a flame as the sea closed over her head. She kicked her way to the surface, broke out into the air, where wind-driven sleeting rain beat her back against the water surface. Fingers of blinding hot and cold mauled her inside her clumsy suit. "Silky!" She

266

screamed his name, and it was torn away by the wind, as lost and desolate as a mer's cry.

But then as suddenly, Silky's spume-splashed face and torso were beside her; supporting her as she fought to keep herself afloat, dragged down by the waterlogged pressure suit. He had shed his own suit, swimming freely, in his element. She felt him jerk at the seals of her suit front, trying to strip it from her.

"No!" She clawed at his slippery tentacles, but they escaped her like eels. "No, I'll freeze!" Her struggles drove her under, she came up again gagging and spitting. "I can't live in this—without it!" knowing that she would not survive anyway, because the suit was filling with liquid ballast to drag her down. She understood at last, in the way that would only come to anyone once in a lifetime, the full and poignant irony of the Sailor's Choice: to freeze, or to drown.

Silky left her suit alone, only trying now to help her stay afloat. Already the first shocking agony of cold had blurred to a bone-deep ache that sapped her of strength and judgment. In the distance between the shifting molten mountains, for a moment she glimpsed the foundering LB—and then nothing where it had been but the flowing together of sea and sky. *Elsevier*. A sacrifice to the Sea. . . . Moon felt the salt water of her own grief mingle with the sea's and the sky's.

And after an uncertain length of time she realized that the squall was passing: The sky dried its tears and lost its anger, the swollen wrath left the sea's face, exhaustion dried her own tears as a wan, ice-splintered sun blinked down at her through the opening clouds. Silky still held her firmly from behind, helping her stay afloat; her body was convulsed with uncontrollable shivering. Sometimes she thought she could see the shoreline, unreachably far away, never sure it was more than a phantom of the mists or of her mind. She had no strength left to speak, and Silky spoke only with the wordless reassurance of his presence. She felt his alienness more vividly than she ever had, and the knowledge that it made no difference. . . .

She should tell him to let her go, save his strength, there was no hope that Ngenet would ever find them in time. It would still come to the same thing in the end. But she couldn't form the words, and knew in her heart that she didn't want to. To die alone . . . to die . . . to sleep here forever. She thought she could feel the marrow congealing in her bones. She was so tired, so achingly weary; and sleep would come, rocked in the Sea Mother's inexorable cradle. The Lady was both creator and destroyer, and with dim despair she knew that the single lives of woman or man were no more important in Her greater pattern than the life of the tiniest crustacean creeping through the bottom mud. . . .

Something broke the water's surface in front of them, sending cold spray into Moon's face. She groaned as Silky's arms tightened around her chest, squinted with ice-lashed eyes at a shining brindle face gazing back at her. Two, then three more inhuman faces surfaced, behind and beside the first, to lie like fishing balls on the brightening water. Recognition rose slowly, like a bubble rising out of the depths, penetrating her anesthetic stupor: *mers.* . . .

They closed in around her, prodding her insistently, urgently, with their webbed fore-flippers. Her mind could not form an image of what they wanted from her; but she knew, with the unquestioning trust of her childhood, that they were the Lady's own children come to save her if they could. "S-Silky," chewing the words to pieces between her chattering teeth, "let me—g-go."

He released her; she sank like a stone beneath the surface. But before she could react, the sleek, buoyant shapes were raising her again. Web-fingered flippers enfolded her like the petals of a closing flower, drawing her up into the air—over onto her stomach on the soft, broad breast of a mer at rest in the water. She lay sputtering and amazed, held barely clear of the lapping surface of the sea, her feet still trailing in its insatiable cold. But the mer—it was a female, she could tell by the necklace of golden fur it wore—wrapped her in its flippers like a nurseling cub, feeding her its body heat as it would warm and feed its own young one. It began a deep toneless crooning, in rhythm with the rocking of the sea. Too exhausted to wonder, Moon lay her head on its silky breast, hands beneath her, feeling the toneless song penetrate her shuddering body. Silky and two of the other mers still hovered nearby; but she did not remember them now, did not remember anything past or future as her existence telescoped down to the present moment.

How long in the time of the greater world she drifted, held in the mer's embrace, she never knew, or wanted to know. The sun had crossed the sky, rolling down the farther slope to its own rendezvous with the sea, before another change came over the face of the water: the long shadow of a ship reaching ahead to greet them, the distant heartbeat of its engines breaking their silence more and more insistently.

"Moon. Moon. Moon." Silky spoke her name, wreathing her neck with dripping tentacles as he tried to make her hear.

But there was no Moon, no moon above, only the sea, the Sea, to answer him . . . the Sea reclaiming Her own.

"Moon . . . can you hear me?"

"No—" It was more a protest against the intrusion on her mindless peace than an answer to a demand. The world was a watercolor painting formlessly flowing. . . .

Something jarred her lip against her chattering teeth; hot, viscous liquid spilled into her mouth and trickled down her throat like flaming oil. She whimpered in pleasure and denial, feeling the watercolor world congeal, take on a form that was without reference in her grayed memory—except for the face centering above her, pulling past and present into a single double-image. "M-M-Miroe?"

"Yes," with infinite relief. "She's coming back to us, Silky. She knows me." Beyond him she made out Silky crouched patiently, watching, and the round unblinking eye of a cabin porthole.

"W-where?" She gulped the peppery-sweet syrup convulsively as Ngenet pressed the cup to her lips again. Her shivering, shriveled body was bare of the waterlogged suit and bundled in heated blankets.

"On my ship. Hauled in safe on board at last, thank the gods. We're going home." He replaced a hot compress across the bridge of her nose, over her cheeks.

"H-home . . . ?" Past and present lives ran together again.

"To my plantation, to safe harbor. You've spent enough time walking the star road, and enough time in the arms of the Sea Mother, mer-child . . . almost a lifetime." He brushed her sodden hair back from her forehead with a callused, gentle hand. "Time to be grateful for solid ground, now."

"El-Elsie . . . " The word hurt her throat like bile.

"I know." Ngenet straightened up from the edge of the bunk. "I know. There's nothing you can do for her now but rest, and heal." His voice and the cabin space faded into the unreachable distance.

Moon huddled deeper inside the nest of blankets as her awareness shrank inward, dwindled down to the sensation of hot needles penetrating her cold-deadened flesh, turning ice-locked veins to spring, unbinding her muscles; setting her free. . . .

Jerusha left the empty rooms of her townhouse behind, left the bread and fruit of her unwanted evening meal half-eaten on the table, and went out and down into the Maze. The twilight beyond the walls at the alleys' ends marked the end of one more unbearable day that she had borne, somehow—and the promise of another to be borne tomorrow, and another, and another. Her job had been her life, and now her whole life had become hell. Sleep was her only escape, but sleep only hastened the coming of the new morning. And so she walked, aimlessly, anonymously, through the dwindling crowds, past the shops—half of them empty now, half still clinging tenaciously to life and profit, hanging on until the bitter end.

The bitter end . . . Why? Why bother? What's the point? She drew the hood of her coarsely woven striped caftan further forward, shadowing her face, as she turned into the Citron Alley. Midway to twilight was a botanery she frequented: herbal remedies and spices, cluttered shelves full of household saints and charms against ill fortune; all imported from home, from Newhaven. She had gone so far as to buy the most potent amulet she could find and wear it around her neck—she who had sneered at her elders back home for wasting blind faith and good money on superstitious nonsense. That was what this job had driven her to. But the damned charm hadn't done her any more good than anything else she'd tried in all this time. Nothing had done any good, held any purpose, had any effect.

And now the one person who had supported her, kept her from believing that she was a complete and utter failure, was gone. *BZ . . . Damn you, BZ! How could you do this to me? How could you—die?* And so she had come here again, telling herself that she did not know why. . . .

But as she neared the shop she caught sight of a familiar face—a familiar shock of flaming-red hair—Sparks Dawntreader coming toward her, dressed like a sex holo. She had seen him only rarely over the past few years, during her infrequent official visits to the palace. It surprised her now, seeing him again, to realize that he didn't look a day older than the first time she had seen him, sprawled in that alley almost five years ago. But then, it had surprised her that Arienrhod kept him (in every sense of the word, she supposed) at the palace . . . had she kept him young as well?

Her interest became self-interest as their trajectories closed; with guilty preoccupation she assumed that he would see her, assumed that he would recognize her even in this disguise, and read her hidden motives in her restless eyes. She slowed, trying to keep her destination obscure until he passed. *Gods, am I skulking like a criminal now?*

"Hello, Dawntreader." Defiantly she acknowledged him first; saw by his start of recognition that he would not have looked at her twice if she hadn't spoken.

But the expression that showed next was none she would have expected, none that she deserved—a smile that held his flawless youth up like a mirror to show her how painfully she was aging, when every day passed like a year. His eyes were a disturbing echo of the Queen's: too knowing, too cynical for the face that held them. They moved to the display of god-figures and charms in the botanery window, back to the amulet hanging at her throat. He pulled uneasily at the multiple collars of his skintight shirt; the gesture shouted hostility. "Save your money, Commander PalaThion. Your gods can't reach you here. All the gods of the Hegemony couldn't stop what's happening to you— even if they cared." A mouthful of gall.

Jerusha fell back a step as the words struck at her like vipers, poisoned with the venom of her own deepest fears. *Does he want it? Even him? Why?* "Why, Dawntreader? Why you?" whispered.

Hatred smouldered. "I loved her; and she's gone." He dropped his gaze, pushed on by her, not looking back.

Jerusha stood still in the street for a long moment before she realized that he had given her the reason why. And then she went on to the botanery entrance, dazed, like a woman caught in a spell.

She stood in the cramped aisle before the dusty shelves that held what she had come for; blind to the bittersweet nostalgia of the place, the stubborn refusal of Newhaven tradition to conform to the standards of a new age or another world. She ignored the clusters of dragonsfoot, the festoons of garlanded herbs, the wild tangle of odors in caressing assault on her senses; was deaf to—

"Were you speaking to me?" She became abruptly, resentfully aware that she was not standing there alone any longer.

"Yes. They seemed to have moved the powdered louge.

Would you know where—?" A dark-haired, fair-skinned, middle-aged woman; probably a local. Blind—Jerusha recognized the light-sensor band she wore across her forehead.

Jerusha glanced over the shelves, saw the shopkeeper caught up in animated gossip with some other Newhaven expatriate; looked back. "It's by the rear wall, I think." She stepped toward the shelves to let the blind woman pass.

But the woman stayed aggravatingly in the aisle, her head bent slightly as though she were still listening. "Inspector . . . PalaThion, isn't it?"

"Commander PalaThion." She returned contempt with barely concealed contempt.

"Of course. Forgive me."

When the sun turns black. Jerusha looked away.

"The last time I heard your voice you were still Inspector PalaThion. I never forget a voice; but sometimes I forget my manners." She smiled in good-humored apology, radiated it, until unwillingly Jerusha felt her own habitual frown letting go. "It's been nearly five years. My shop is next door . . . I came to your station one time with Sparks Dawntreader."

"The maskmaker." Jerusha pinned an identity on the woman at last. "Yes, I remember." *I remember, all right. Saving that little bastard was the second biggest mistake of my life.*

"I saw you talking to him outside." (*Saw?* Jerusha experienced a moment's disorientation as it registered; tried to conceal her obvious irritation.) "He still comes to see me now and then; when he needs shelter. There aren't many people he can talk to any more, I think. I'm glad he talked to you."

Jerusha said nothing.

"Tell me, Commander—have you been as sorry to see the changes happening in him as I have?" She bridged the void of Jerusha's silence as though it did not exist.

Jerusha refused to face the question, or the questioner; touched the hollows of her own changed face with morbid fingers. "He hasn't changed at all as far as I can see. He

273

doesn't look a day older." *And maybe he isn't, damn him.*

"But he is, he has. . . . " heavily. "He's aged a hundred years since he came to Carbuncle."

"Haven't we all." Jerusha reached out and took a small dark plastic bottle of viriol oil off of the shelf, hesitated; took another one. She thought suddenly of her mother.

"Sleeping drops, aren't they?"

Jerusha's hand knotted possessively, defensively, over the bottles. "Yes."

A nod. "I can smell them." The woman grimaced. "I've used them; I had insomnia terribly, before I got my vision sensors. I tried everything. Without sight I didn't have any guide to the pattern of day and night . . . and I'm not properly tuned to Tiamat's rhythms. I suppose none of us are, really. We're all aliens here in the end—or the beginning."

Jerusha glanced up. "I suppose so. I never thought of it that way. . . . Maybe that's my whole problem: Wherever I go, I'm an alien." She heard herself say aloud what she had only intended as thought; shook her head, past caring. "The more I want sleep the less I get it. Sleep is my only pleasure in life. I could sleep forever." She turned, tried to move past the woman to the shopman at the door.

"That isn't the way to solve your problems, Commander PalaThion." The maskmaker blocked her path without seeming to.

Jerusha stared, felt her legs turn to soft wood. "What?"

"Sleeping drops. They only make the problem worse. They take away your dreams . . . we all have to dream, sometime, or we suffer the consequences." She reached out; her touch wavered toward the handful of bottles Jerusha held, pushed them away. "Find a better answer. There must be one. This will pass. Everything passes, given enough time."

"It would take an eternity." But the pressure remained against her hand . . . against her will . . . she felt her hand give way and the bottles go back onto the shelf.

"A wise decision." The maskmaker smiled, looking through her, into her.

Jerusha made no answer, not even certain how to answer.

The woman stood aside at last, somehow releasing her as she had somehow held her prisoner; moved past her toward the shelves at the rear of the store. Jerusha went on to the door and out, without buying anything, or even speaking to the shopman.

Why did I listen to her? Jerusha reclined, motionless, on an elbow on the low serpentine couch. She absorbed the sensation of cotton-wrapped twigs that crept inexorably from hand to wrist to elbow as her arm went to sleep. Each time she entered this place a paralysis seemed to overcome her, destroying her ability to act or even react, to function, to think. She watched the seconds blink out on the sterile clock face embedded in crystal in the sterile matrix of empty shelving that cobwebbed the room's far wall. Gods, how she hated the sight of this place, every lifeless centimeter of it— It was just as it had been when the Lioux-Skeds departed, the same facade insulating its occupants from the timeless reality of the building and the city that had surrounded them.

They had affected a Kharemoughi lifestyle with excruciating dedication: a sophisticated, refined, and soulless imitation of a lifestyle she found obscure and unappealing to begin with. The patina of her own possessions scarcely altered it. She fantasized an overlay of ornate, rococo frescoes and molding, the unashamed warmth of a palette of garish colors everywhere . . . closed her eyes with her hand as the unrelenting subtlety of the truth seeped through like water, to make the colors blur and bleed.

This place hung with ugly memories had been forced on her—a part of her burden, her punishment. She could have struck back, cleared this mausoleum of its morbid relics and replaced them with things fresh and alive . . . she could even have gotten rid of it entirely, gone back to her old, cramped, comfortable set of rooms down in the Maze. But always, when her day's work was through, she had returned

275

here and done nothing, one more time. Because what was the point? It was useless, hopeless . . . *helpless* . . . . She lifted her locked hands to her mouth, pressed hard against her lips. *They're watching, stop it—!*

She sat up, pulling her hands away, bowing her head so that the caftan's hood fell forward about her face. The Queen's spies, the Queen's eyes, were everywhere—especially, she was sure, in this townhouse. She felt them touching her like unclean hands, everywhere she went, everything she did. In her old apartment she had been free to be human, free to be herself, and live her own heritage . . . free to strip off her chafing, puritanical uniform and go easily naked if she wanted to, the way she had been able to do on her own world, the way her people had done for centuries. But here she was always on display for the Queen's pleasure, afraid to expose herself, physically or mentally, to the White Bitch's unseen scorn.

She picked up the tape reader that had dropped to the floor, gazed at without seeing the manual on ultrasound analysis that she had been trying to study for a week . . . two weeks . . . forever. She had never been one to enjoy fiction, in any form: she heard too many lies on the streets every day, she had no patience with people who made a living doing it. And now she could no longer concentrate on facts. But still she could not let go and allow herself to escape into fantasy . . . the way BZ had always done, so easily, so guiltlessly. But then, to be a Kharemoughi Tech was to live in a fantasy world anyway, one where everyone knew his place, and yours was always on top. Where life functioned with perfect machinery . . . only this time the machinery had broken down, and the chaos that waited outside had rushed in to destroy him.

She imagined the patrolcraft vaporizing, releasing two spirits from this mortal plane into—*what?* Eternity, limbo, an endless cycle of rebirth? Who could believe in any religion, when there were so many, all claiming the only Truth, and every truth different. There was only one way she would ever learn for herself . . . and a part of her own spirit had already passed over that dark water without a

276

ticket, gone with the Boatman, and with her only friend in all this world of enemies. Her only friend ... *Why the hell did I listen? Why did I leave those bottles on the shelf?* She stood up, the tape reader falling from her lap to the floor again unnoticed. She took one step, knowing that she was starting for the door; stopped again, her body twitching with indecision. *Motivation, Jerusha!* desperately. *I wanted to leave those bottles there, or she'd never have changed my mind.* Her muscles went slack, she slumped where she stood, her whole body cotton-wrapped with fatigue. *But I can't sleep here!* And there was no escape, no haven left, no one. . . .

Her searching eyes stopped on the dawn-colored shell that lay like an offering on the Empire-replica shrine table beside the door. *Ngenet ... Oh gods, are you still a friend of mine?* The solid peace of the plantation house, that inviolable calm in the storm's eye, crowded her inner sight. She had seen it last more than a year ago; had been both consciously and unconsciously separating herself from even the loose and superficial ties of their infrequent visits as her depression deepened, as her world shrank in and in around her. She had told herself she did not want him to see the knife-edged harridan she had become ... and yet perversely, at the same time she had begun to hate him for not seeing that she needed his safe haven more than ever.

And now? *Yes ... now!* What kind of blind masochism had made her wall herself into her own tomb? She crossed the room to the phone, punched in one code, and then another and another from memory, putting through the outback radio call to his plantation. She marked the passing seconds with the beat of her fingertips against the pale, hard surface of the wall, until at last a videoless voice answered her summons, distorted by audio snow. *Damn this place!* Storm interference. There was always storm interference.

"Hello? Hello?" Even through the interference, she knew that the voice was not the one she needed to hear.

"Hello!" She leaned closer to the speaker, her raised voice echoing from room to silent room behind her. "This

277

is Commander PalaThion calling from Carbuncle. Let me speak to Ngenet."

"What? . . . No, he isn't here, Commander . . . out on his ship."

"When will he be back?"

"Don't know. Didn't say . . . leave a message?"

She cut off the phone with her fist; turned away from the wall shaken with fury. "No message."

She crossed the room again to pick up the dawn-pink shell, held it against her while she traced its satin-rubbed convolutions with unsteady fingers. She touched the flawed place where one fragile spine had snapped off. Her fingers closed over the next spine, and broke it. She broke another, and another; the spines fell without a sound onto the carpet. Jerusha whimpered softly as they fell, as though she were breaking her own fingers.

"Everything we do affects everything else."

"I know. . . ." Moon walked beside Ngenet down the slope of the hill that lay ochre and silver with salt grass, rippling like the wind's harp below the plantation house. The house itself melted into the sere, burnished hills beyond; its weathered stone and salt-bleached wood were as much a part of this land as—*as he is.* Moon studied his profile moodily from the side of her eye, remembering how strange it had seemed to her the first time, the last time, she had seen it. Five years ago . . . it was true, she could see five years of change in his face; but not in her own.

And yet she had changed, aged, in the moment that she saw the lifelight go out of Elsevier's eyes. Death had let her pass . . . but Death had not been denied. Grief lifted her and dropped her, the storm tide of mourning trapped in a

278

bottle. If she had not willfully challenged Death, this death would not be on her soul. "If Elsevier hadn't brought me back to Tiamat, she'd still be alive. If I'd stayed on Kharemough with her, she would have been . . . happy." Suddenly she was seeing not Elsevier, but Sparks. *No one's dreams ever mattered as much as mine.* Moon's legs trembled under her.

"But you wouldn't have been." Ngenet looked down at her, steadying her with a firm hand as the slope steepened. "And knowing that you were unhappy, she'd have been unhappy too. We can't spend our lives living a lie for someone else; it never works out. You have to be true to yourself. She knew that, or you wouldn't be here now. It was inevitable. Death is inevitable, deny it though we will." She glanced up at him sharply, seeing him distorted by her own grief, and away again. "After TJ died, she was never the same. My father always used to say that she was a one-man woman. For better or worse." He pushed his hands into the pouch of his parka, gazing northward, following the coastline into the white-hazed distances where Carbuncle lay. "Moon, everything affects everything else. I've lived this long without learning anything, if I haven't learned that. Never take all the credit . . . or all the blame. You weren't to blame."

"I was!" She shook her head disconsolately.

"Then start thinking about what you can do to repay her!" He waited for the question in her eyes. "Don't let your grieving turn sour. Don't be so damned selfish about it. You said yourself a sibyl told you to return to Tiamat. And that your own mind told you to."

"To help Sparks." She followed the line of his northward gaze. *A one-man woman . . .*

"Only a circuit in a greater machinery. The sibyl mind doesn't send messages across half a galaxy to comfort a broken heart. There's more to your destiny than that." He stopped suddenly, facing her.

"I—I know." She moved her feet in the tangled grass, suddenly afraid; watched her shadow like a cloud looking down on the face of the land. "I understand that now," not really understanding, or believing it. "But I don't know why, if it's not to help Sparks. Something did tell me to come—but it didn't tell me enough."

"Maybe it has told you. What did you learn by going to Kharemough that you wouldn't have learned here?"

She glanced up, startled. "I learned . . . what it means to be a sibyl. I learned that there are things on Kharemough that we have a right to have here, but they keep them from us." She heard her voice turn cold like the wind. "I understand what Elsevier believed in, and why. . . . All of that is part of me. No one can make me forget it. And I want to change it." Her mouth twitched; her fists tightened in her pockets. "But I don't know how." *Sparks. Maybe Sparks knows. . . .*

"You'll discover the way, when your reach Carbuncle."

She smiled. "The last time we talked about that, you didn't want me to go at all."

"I still don't," gruffly. "But I'm not talking to the same woman. Who am I to argue with destiny? My father taught me to believe in reincarnation—that what we are in this life is the reward or punishment for what we did in the last one. If I wanted to play philosopher I'd tell you that when Elsevier died her spirit was reborn into you, there in the sea. A sea change."

"I want to believe that—" She closed her eyes; smiled at last, opening them again, as belief metastasized. "Miroe, do you ever wonder who you were before? And whether, if we were born knowing what we had to make up for instead of crawling blindly through a penance, anything would be different?"

He laughed. "That's the kind of question I should be asking you, sibyl."

Sibyl. I belong again. I am whole again. Wholer. Holy. . . . The cold air burned in her lungs. She pressed the spot beneath her parka where the trefoil lay hidden; found herself looking to the north again, longing for a glimpse of what lay beyond sight. It was nearing the time of the final Festival, when the Prime Minister came to Carbuncle for the last time. She felt a stirring of curiosity at the thought that he was following her here from Kharemough. But it would be another fortnight before a trader's ship put in here to take her to Carbuncle. Only a fortnight until she would know— She was suddenly aware of her heart beating hard in her chest, and did not know whether she was feeling anticipation or fear.

They passed the outbuildings where he kept his peculiar workshops, kept going downhill toward the vast flooded fields that embroidered the narrow coastal plain, north- and southward to the limits of his land grant. In his workshops Ngenet tinkered with an incredible variety of obsolete engines and primitive tools—things that would have seemed marvelous to her short months ago, but that simply seemed pointless to her now. She had asked him why he bothered with them, when he had things from the city that could do everything they did, and much better. He had only smiled, and asked her not to tell anyone else about his quirks.

Winter laborers strolled past them on stilts through watery beds of seahair—a staple crop for human and animal here in the harsher northern latitudes. The workers glanced up in respectful greeting; a man here, a woman there gave Moon an extra, fleeting smile. Ngenet had told his household staff only that she was a sailor saved from drowning by the mers. But the outback Winters, who lived with the Sea, were not as far removed from belief in the Sea Mother as she had always heard. They had nursed her with all the solicitude due the object of a small miracle. The field hands had taught her to walk on stilts one sunny afternoon: Balancing precariously, taking awkward, stumbling strides on the dry land, she knew ruefully why they wore watertight suits when they worked in the tangle of inundated grasses.

She followed Ngenet along the raised stone walkways that netted the fields, passing through a tunnel of time, the sight and the smell of the sea harvest carrying her home to Neith: to Gran, to her mother, to Sparks—to the lost time. To the time when the future had been as certain as the past, and she knew that she would never have to face it

281

alone. *The lost time.* Now she had heard the voice of the new future, and it called her from star to star, to the City in the North. . . .

Their boots rattled on the wooden pier that sat in the sheltered inlet which served as the plantation's harbor. The waters of the half-bay, held in safe arms away from the constant wind, lay blue and silver under the sky. She could still look at the Sea without being swept back into the nightmare of the Lady's ordeal by water; it had surprised her to find that she could. But stronger than the memory was the knowledge that the Sea had spared her in the end. She had survived. The Sea gave and She took away, an elemental manifestation of a greater, universal indifference. And yet twice she had faced that indifference, with her mind and her body, and been spared. A nameless counter-fate was alive inside her, and while it lived in her, she would not be afraid.

The far blue surface of the water fountained white as a tandem of mers shattered its peace with the perfect arc of their bodies. She watched them rise and fall again and again through the surface of the bay; disappear once more into the watery underworld. Another track, less obtrusive, veered toward her across the water as she stood leaning on the splintery rail: Silky, who had spent most of his time since their arrival here in the bay. "What's he going to do, Miroe? He doesn't have anyone, any home." She remembered how Elsevier and TJ had found him.

"He's welcome here; he knows that." Ngenet gestured across his land, smiled at her concern.

She smiled back at him, looked out over the water again. The irony of Silky's presence among the mers struck her deeply now, as she watched them together: The humans of the plantation hated and distrusted all his kind—not simply because they were alien, but because they were the Snow Queen's Hounds, who hunted and killed the mers. And she had learned that not only did Ngenet hate the slaughter and protect the mers within his boundaries, but he had sur-rounded himself with workers who felt the same way.

Ngenet had known Silky as a comrade of Elsevier for years enough to trust him; his people had not.

But the mers, who should have been the most mistrustful, accepted him; and so he spent his time mainly in the sea. She could glimpse his emotions only through the narrow window where his perception and her own looked out briefly on the same world; he was more taciturn and less communicative than ever, and it was only from her memory of the last moments on the LB that she could guess that he mourned. He joined them now on the hinged, sighing dock, pulling himself fluidly up and over the rail to stand dripping beside them. His wet, sexless body was bare of any trappings of the world of air, beaded with the ephemeral jewels of the water world. (It had seemed odd to her that Elsevier and the others regarded him as male, when to her mind his smooth body could as easily have been female.) His eyes turned back their own merging reflections, keeping them from any penetration of his inner thoughts. He nodded to them and leaned on the rail, tentacles trailing.

She looked past him at the bay, where three more mers had joined the first pair in a flashing ballet, an outward image of their selfless inner beauty. Every afternoon when she walked down this way, the mers performed a new quicksilver dance on the water, almost as though they celebrated her return to life. Their grace caught her up in a sudden passion to be as they were, as Silky was: a true child of the Sea, and not forever a foster-daughter. . . . "Silky, look at them! If I could change my skin for yours, for even an hour—"

"You're wanting to go back into the sea, after I fished you out of it ice blue and rattling only a fortnight ago?" Ngenet looked down at her with disbelief or indignation. "I think you suffered some mental impairment after all."

She shook her head. "No—not that way! Lady, not ever again." She winced, rubbing the muscles of her arms through her heavy parka. The spasms of her hypothermia had wrenched every muscle in her body, and left her disoriented and crippled. Now that she could think and move again, she walked longer every day in Ngenet's patient company, stretching the knots out of her body, trying to remember what it felt like to move without hurting all over. "All my life my people have belonged to the Sea. But to *really* belong to the Sea, like they do, for even a little while; long enough to know—" She broke off.

The mers had ended their dance and disappeared beneath the waters again; now, abruptly, three slender heads with runnelled fur emerged in the half-shadow below her. Their sinuous necks bent back like sea grass flowing, the eyes of polished jet looked up at her together. Protective membranes slid smoothly over the obsidian surfaces; the ridge of feather-tipped bristles above their eyes stiffened upright, giving them a look of amazement. The one in the middle was the mer who had held her like its own child when she was lost at sea.

Moon hung over the rail, stretching down with her hand. "Thank you. Thank you." Her voice was strong with feeling. One by one the mers rose in the water, butted briefly against her downreaching hand, and submerged again. "It's almost like they know." She straightened away from the railing, feeling cold bite her dripping hand. She pushed it back into her glove, and into a pocket.

"Maybe they do." Ngenet smiled at her. "Maybe they even realize somehow that they've rescued a sibyl, and not just another unlucky sailor. I've never seen them dance like that for a stranger, or linger here the way they've done. They're remarkable beings," answering the question in her eyes.

"Beings?" She realized how much he had said and denied in one word. Since her rescue she had learned many things about Ngenet, about his relationship to the mers, his respect for them, his concern for their safety. There was even a rudimentary communication of sign and sound that passed between mer and human; that had sent them searching for her, and led Ngenet to the crash site in time. But she had not suspected . . . "You mean—human beings?"

284

She blushed, shook her head. "I mean, intelligent beings, like Silky?" She glanced from face to face and back.

"Would that be so hard for you to believe?" Half a question, half a challenge. His voice held her with an odd intensity.

"No. But, I never thought . . . I never thought." *Never thought I'd ever meet a stranger from another world; never thought he might not be human; never thought a sibyl would have to answer any question like this one.* "You— you're asking me—to answer . . . ?" Her voice was high and strained, she felt herself slipping. . . .

"Moon?"

Slipping away . . . *Input.*

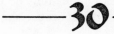

"What did I say?" She had asked him, afterwards.

"You told me about the mers." And Ngenet had smiled.

Moon repeated the words in her mind as she moved through the blue-green water world with sinuous undulations. The liquid atmosphere resisted and yielded, resisted and yielded, to the pressure of her hands. This was Ngenet's gift to her, for answering his unspoken question, for affirming his belief: She knew at last what it was like to be of the Sea, wholly, exuberantly; not forever balanced on the precarious tightrope between sea and sky, on the thin edge between worlds.

She listened to the rhythmic, reassuring hush of air that answered every demand for breath; savored its warm faintly-staleness feeding in through the regulator valve. In the distance the boundless spaces of the sea were curtained by a mist of sand in solution. But here in this shallow bay she could see clearly enough—see the flawless beauty of

285

the mers and Silky, her companions, their streamlined forms suspended by unseen hands.

"This is why you sing!" Her voice went out to them on a cloud of laughter through the mouthpiece speaker; undistorted, although it meant no more to them than a cloud of bubbles. *Because you can't hold in your joy.* In the spaces between her breaths the mer songs reached her, the siren songs she had heard only in legends and dreams: a tapestry of whistles and wails and bell-like chimings, sighs and cries —forlorn, abandoned sounds heard separately, but weaving together into a choir that sang hymns of praise to the Sea Mother. Their songs continued sometimes for hours— and they were songs in the truest sense, songs that were sung again and again by their ageless creators, unchanging over centuries.

She knew that; although their complexity was beyond her ability to separate one song from another, although she was not sure they had any meaning in the sense that a human song did. . . . She knew because she had told herself so.

When she had come out of her unexpected Transfer she had found Ngenet pinioning her hands, his bronze face crumpled with emotion. When she knew him again, he had raised her gloved hands and kissed them. "I believed . . . I always believed, hoped, prayed—" his voice broke. "But I never would have dared to ask you. And it's true. I don't know whether to laugh or cry!"

"What—what is?" Shaking herself out, mentally, physically.

"The mers, Moon! The mers . . ."

. . . an intelligent, oxygen-utilizing mammalian life form; artificially created through genetic manipulation, designed to serve as host for experimental virusoid longevity factor, special class IV. . . . The Old Empire biological specifications had run on endlessly, all but meaningless to her. But Ngenet had made her listen to every detail that had been burned into his memory, the words rough-edged with feeling. *Intelligent life form . . . intelligent . . .*

Moon felt her arms wrapped by Silky's tentacles as he

286

drew her up and over in a somersault, into the pattern of spiraling bodies; caught her up in creating the moment's image. She saw the blue-shafted ceiling of the bay slide by far overhead, and the shadowed sandy bottom latticed with colonies of brachiform crenolids, polka-dotted with lurid crustaceans. On every side of her slow-motion helix was life, singly or in schools, familiar and unknown, hunters and hunted . . . and she passed freely among them all in the company of mers, whose ancestral territory she had traveled to this place to see—who were a threat to few and feared none, here in the ocean depths . . . who feared nothing except the Hunt.

Stunned, she had asked Miroe how the offworlders could justify the water of life if they knew that the mers were more than just animals. "They must know it, if the sibyls know."

"Human beings have been treating each other like animals forever. If they can't recognize an intelligent being in the mirror, it's not so damn surprising that they treat nonhumans even worse." Ngenet had glanced down at Silky, crouched pensively by the rail watching the water surge and retreat. "And even if the mers were no more than animals, what right does that give us to murder them for our vanity? The mers were genetically synthetic. They must have been meant as a test case; the Old Empire must have collapsed before anyone could generalize their 'benign infection' to give perfect immortality to a human being. But killing mers for the water of life goes back into the chaos at the Empire's end—when the ones who took immortality for themselves didn't care what it cost in lives. The truth was probably suppressed a millennium ago, when the Hedge first rediscovered this world. So now they only have to worry about what it costs, period."

"But—why did the Old Empire make mers intelligent at all?"

"I don't know. And neither do you." He had shaken his head. "There must have been a reason, but why? I only know that they weren't given intelligence in order to become victims of the Hunt!" He had told her then about

why he had had use for a smuggler's services, and his
father before him: A tradition had been passed down from
his grandfather, the first native-born ancestor, who had
come to love the mers as he loved this world, and made his
lands a sanctuary. But later generations had not been satisfied with a passive role as protector, and had begun secret
hostilities against the exploiters—with warnings, interference, sabotage—until . . . "that day the Blues burst in on
you at the inn, and tore a hole in all our lives." And he had
looked northward again with a quizzical frown that had
nothing to do with the words.

But now, after another one hundred and fifty years of
exploitation, the offworlders were about to leave Tiamat
again; the injustice he had tried to stop was almost at an
end . . . and the time of regression and ignorance almost
returned, another half-revolution on an endless wheel of
futility. At least Summer would give the mers an inviolate
space in time—time to replenish their numbers with painful slowness, inevitably righting the hideous wrong their
creators had done them.

But wrong and right, time itself, meant nothing to the
mers, formed no concept that Moon could recognize in
their scheme of things. Unmolested they lived for hundreds, perhaps thousands, of years. A different set of
parameters took precedence in their brain: They lived for
the moment, for the ephemeral beauty of a bubble rising
into the light and vanishing—for the act of creation, of
becoming. There was no need, and no purpose, to a lasting
artifact; for the song, the dance, the act, was in itself a
work of art, like a flower or a life, made more beautiful by
its impermanence. The tangible, the material, were of no
more use or consequence to them than time itself. Their
lives were endless by human standards, and they lived them
hedonistically, absorbed in the sensuous caress of their passage through the supple water, the flow of heat and cold,
current and surge—the stunning schism between water and
air, the fluid heat of desire, the soothing pressure of a
clinging child.

There was little she could have shared in words with

them, if there had even been a translator to cross the barrier of incomprehension. And yet here and now among them, even enclosed in the insensate skin of her diver's drysuit, she could feel the rigid mind-skin of her perceptions, values, goals, dissolving. She could put aside the memories of what had just passed, and the uncertainty ahead, letting now become forever and the future melt into foam. She saw the mer who had been a mother to her circling her exuberantly; knew them all as friends, family, lovers, felt herself become a part of their timeless world. . . . Softly, tentatively at first, she began to blend her voice into the harmony of the mer song.

She felt Silky come up close behind her, felt his tentacles slide over her slick-suited shoulders, circle the air hose of her oxygen pack, pull— "Silky!" The angry protest garbled as she sank her teeth into the regulator, to keep him from jerking it out of her mouth. She brought up her hands, felt more tentacles twine around them as she tried to protect her air supply; pulled her fin-awkward feet up to kick him away. And then she realized that two Silkys struggled beside her; saw the sheathed knife come free from behind the false one's shoulder, swaying among tentacles like a fanged snake, caught between victims. She kicked out, thrusting him away with her feet, but not before the blade chose a victim and she saw the dark cloud of blood at Silky's shoulder.

She caught Silky in her arms, trying to swim them both out of reach of the killer; but the quiet waters suddenly boiled with forms as the mers from the shore colony poured into the sea, were herded together with the rest into a panic-stricken mass. They thrashed around her, crowded her heavily, flipper, head, body, banging and bruising. She clung grimly to Silky's sluggish, grasping tentacles, struggling upward through the chaos. But the brightening water above showed her the silhouette of the heavy net settling toward them, the black stain of a strange ship's double hull breaking the surface of the bay. More figures that should have been Silky but were not guided the net's fall as it settled on her like a shroud, dragging her back down in

289

wild claustrophobia.... *The Hunt! No—it can't be! Not here, not here....*

But it was useless to deny that the impossible had its fingers at her throat; that the mers below her were maddened by the pain and disorientation of alien sonics ... that they would all die. She let go of Silky, keeping close by him, saw him nod and weave his tentacles through the netting as she bent double and pulled the diver's knife from the sheath on her leg. She began to slash with all her strength at the strands of the net; it tore under the angry attack of her blade, left her a space wide enough for them to slip through.

She swam through the gap, drawing Silky after her, just as the net forced them down into the maddened mers. But she clung to the opening, still slashing, ripping, widening the gap, "Here! Here! Get out, get out, get out!" shouting into the ululation of their cries, half sobbing with furious rage. But the mers' panic was deaf to coherent thought, and the handful who tumbled through were only driven out by the heaving turmoil beneath them. She searched them for her mer mother, but did not find her. She went on slashing, cursing; gasping with the effort of pulling in air. But the mers were drowning, helplessly drowning themselves for their murderers, and she could not save them....

Silky hung at the net beside her, moving clumsily, stunned by his wound or by the sonics that had dazzled the mers. Looking up at him, she saw two of the Hounds fall out of the heights and bind him in tentacles, breaking his hold on the netting as—

More tentacles wrapped her from behind, half blinding her, wrenched the knife from her grasp as she tried to turn it on her attacker. Like flailing snakes they covered her face mask, found her air hose again, tore the regulator out of her mouth. Icy water squirted in through the mask's seal, and panic gave her the strength of two. But the Hound's bonds of flesh gave her no leverage, and it was only the strength of two women drowning....

Not until her head broke the surface, not until her bursting lungs opened at last to pull in air and not the final, agonizing liquid breath, did she realize that they had not held her under to drown; that they were not finished with her yet.

She stumbled, incredulously, as her fins caught in bottom-weeds; she squeezed the ocean's fiery tears out of her eyes, saw the lapping water's edge and the shore rising ahead. Two Hounds propelled her out onto firm ground; half dragged, half carried her up the stony beach of the mer rookery. There were no mers left on it now, and the Hounds let her fall untended, to lie coughing and choking. She heard another body drop beside her on the hard stones, saw Silky sprawled next to her. She levered up on her elbows to reach him, tried to see his wound but could not; squeezed his nearer shoulder with feeble encouragement.

She sat up, every breath crawling down her raw throat into her congested lungs; pulled off her fogging mask and felt the bitter wind stun her face. After a time more figures emerged from the water down the beach, hauling an unwieldy harvest of mer corpses into the shallows for the final processing. Moon ground her fists into the beach cinders, whimpering softly, but not for herself.

Standing nearer on the shore, watching them work, was a strange apparition in black, with a man's form and the spiny head of a totem creature. She saw him wave and gesture, his toneless voice came to her half-inaudibly over the wind—a human voice. The first mers were dragged up onto the shore; she watched a Hound kneel by each, saw the knife flash, and the blood spill over the fur as soft as sighs, into the collecting bucket. And then, its grace gone, its life stolen, its joy and beauty torn away, the Hound left the body to rot on its ancestral beach and make a feast for the carrion birds.

Moon's eyes swam, refusing to see more. Sickness rose in her, and a murderous hatred. Her hand closed over a heavy cobble, tightening and tightening; she got to her knees. Beside her Silky pulled himself up, climbed to his feet in one abrupt motion, leaning on her shoulder. She heard him speak, not understanding the words, but feeling the deeper wound he had taken to watch his brothers slaughtering his friends. He went forward, staggering a little, before she could follow. He started toward the inhuman being in black and the cluster of Hounds around him.

"Silky—" She struggled to her feet, kicking off her fins, cradling the stone as she started after him.

The man in black barely glanced their way. "Stop them." He gestured indifferently, and three of the Hounds left his side to block Silky's advance, surrounding him without hesitation. There was a burst of alien speech, and a muttering; and then she saw them struggle. Tentacles whipped at heads and silvered eyes, she saw a silvery knife bared again—

"No! Silky!" She ran forward. The third Hound broke away and caught at her, threw her aside—as she saw the serrated blade sink home. She screamed, as though she had taken the blow herself. Silky fell like a stone among the stones. The man in black turned at her scream, but even as he did she struck the third Hound with all her strength, clubbing him down. The others grabbed her, held her struggling between them as the third staggered, bleeding, to his feet and ripped off the hood of her suit, baring her throat. Her hair spilled loose over her shoulders, tentacles tangled in it, jerking back her head.

"Stop!" Someone shouted the word. But she had no voice and no time at all, only a last kaleidoscope of clouds and sky as the dripping blade bit her throat—

A shock of violent motion hurled the Hounds away from her, knocked her to the ground. "Get away from her! What the hell do you think you're doing?" The heavy boots of the man in black straddled her, sheltering her like a tree in the face of a storm. She looked up and up, seeing only his shadow silhouette against the desolate stone-washed shore. ". . . Because she's a sibyl, goddamn it, that's why! What are you trying to do, contaminate me? Get the hell away, and throw that knife into the sea!" He waved them off, stepped clear of her as they left, and squatted down beside her.

Moon pushed herself up warily, felt a thin warm necklace of blood trickle down over the tattoo in the hollow of her throat, creep on into the neck of her suit and down between her breasts.

The man in black . . . she was sure it was a man now, hidden behind a mask. His eyes were all that she could see of him, and they were gray-green. He stretched an uncertain glove toward her throat. She cringed back, startled, but he wiped the blood from her tattoo with a sudden sweep of his hand. She saw him shudder at the sign of the trefoil; he rubbed his gloved hand convulsively on the stones. "Gods! Am I going crazy?" He looked away, searching the shore for a denial, an affirmation. "You aren't real. You can't be! What are you?" His hand rose again, caught her chin to hold her face in front of him; let it go, slipping across her cheek, along her hair almost like a caress. "Not her . . ." It was almost a plea.

She lifted her own gloved hand to her throat, where pain was spreading from ear to ear, chin to breastbone; shielding her wound, shielding the trefoil from his gaze. "Moon," she whispered, not sure why she gave her name, but grateful that she still had a voice left to speak it. "Sibyl—" her voice roughened, "yes, I am! And I tell you that you've committed murder. You have no right to hunt these lands. And no man has the right to murder an intelligent being!" She swept a hand toward the carnage on the beach, not following it with her eyes. "It's murder, murder!"

His eyes followed, came back as green and hard as emeralds. "Shut up, damn you—" But they stayed on her face, incredulous, demanding, and his hands knotted on his knees. "Damn you, damn you! What are you doing here? How could you come *here*, to see me like this? After you left me—I could kill you for this!" He twisted his head, wrenching his eyes away, throwing the words into the wind.

"Yes! Yes! Kill me too, mer slayer, sibyl slayer, coward —and damn yourself!" She bared her throat to him again, grimacing with the motion. "Spill my blood, and take its curse on you!" She stretched out her bloody fingers, trying to reach him, wound him, infect him—

But her hand lost its strength, fell from the air forgotten, as she saw at last the symbol that gleamed on his black suit: the circle sign crossed and recrossed, the sign of the Hegemony; the medal that she had seen every day of her life in Summer. . . . Her hand rose again, and he did not stop her from touching it. Slowly, slowly, she lifted her eyes, knowing that in another moment she would—

"No!" His fist came at her without warning and crushed her into blackness.

31

"Hello, Miroe." Jerusha climbed out of the patrolcraft, wearing her uniform and her best imitation smile. The wind clapped its chill hands on her shoulders, tried to jerk her half-sealed coat open for ruder intimacies. *Damn this weather!* Her smile struggled.

"Jerusha?" Ngenet came striding down the slope from the outbuildings, summoned by field hands who had seen her coming in. His own widening smile of welcome looked real to her, and hers began to warm. But she read ambivalence in the glance that took in her uniform before it met her eyes. "It's been a long time."

"Yes." She nodded, an excuse to look down, wondering if time was all that lay behind his hesitation. "I know. How—how've you been, Miroe?"

"About the same. Everything's about the same." He pushed his hands into his parka pockets, shrugged. "It usually is. Is this official business, or strictly a social call?" He peered past her into the empty patrolcraft.

"A little of both, I guess," trying to make it sound casual. She saw his mouth tighten ever so slightly, twitching his mustache. "That is, we had a report on a techrunner downed near here"—*fully two or three weeks ago*—"and since I was in the area checking it out . . ."

294

"The Commander of Police chasing down strays in the outback? Since when?" amused.

"Well, I was the only one they could spare." She grinned ruefully, stretching the unused muscles in her cheeks.

Laughter. "Damn it, Jerusha, you know you don't need an official excuse to come by here. You're welcome any time . . . as a friend."

"Thank you." She understood the qualification and was grateful for it. "It's nice to be singled out as a human being for a change, and not as a Blue." She plucked at her coat, suddenly embarrassed by it. *My shield, my armor. What will I do when they take it away from me?* "I . . . I tried to call you, a couple of weeks ago. But you were gone." It occurred to her suddenly to wonder why he hadn't returned the call. *Gods, who could blame him, when I never returned any of his?*

"I'm sorry, I couldn't—" He seemed to reach the same question, without finding an answer either. "You've been—busy, I suppose."

"Busy! Oh, hell and devils, it's been . . . sheer hell, and devils." She leaned against the patrolcraft, pulled down the door and slammed it. "BZ is gone, Miroe. Dead. Killed by bandits outside the city. And I just can't . . . I can't stand it any more." Her head bowed in invisible bondage. "I don't know how I'll be able to stand going back to Carbuncle again. When all I can think of is how much better it would be for everyone, how glad everyone would be, if I never came back at all. How much better it would be if I'd been the one who'd been lost."

"By all the gods, Jerusha—why didn't you tell me?"

She turned away from his outstretched hand, leaning on the hood, looking desperately out to sea. "I didn't come here to—to use you for a garbage can, damn it!"

"Of course you did. What are friends for?" She heard his smile.

"I did not!"

"All right. Then why not? Why not?" He pulled at her elbow.

"Don't touch me. Please, Miroe, don't." She felt his

hand release her, felt her arm still tingling with the contact. "I can handle it. I'll be all right, I can handle it alone." Her control hung by a thread.

"And you feel like dying is the way to do it?"

"No!" She brought her fist down on the cold metal. "No. That's why I had to get away . . . I had to find some other way." She turned back, slowly, but with her eyes shut.

He was silent for a moment, waiting. "Jerusha—I know the kind of screws they've been putting to you, all this time. You can't handle that kind of pressure by holding it all back. You can't do it alone." Suddenly almost angry, "Why did you stop calling? Why did you stop—answering? Didn't you trust me?"

"Too much." She pressed her mouth together, stopping an absurd giggle. "Oh, gods. I trust you too much! Look at me, I haven't been here five minutes and already I've spilled my guts to you. Just seeing you breaks me down." She shook her head, keeping her eyes closed. "You see. I can't lean on you, without becoming a cripple."

"We're all cripples, Jerusha. We're born crippled."

Slowly she opened her eyes. "Are we?"

He stood with hands locked behind him, looking out toward the sea. The wind stiffened, whipping his raven-feather hair; she shrank down inside her heavy coat. "You know the answer, or you wouldn't have come. Let's go up to the house." He looked back at her; she nodded.

She followed him up the hill, making hesitant small talk about crops and weather, letting all her resistance flow out of her and down to the sea. They passed the creaking windmill that stood like a lonely sentinel over the outbuildings. He used it to pump water from his well; it occurred to her again, as it had occurred to her before, that it was an absurd anachronism on a plantation that functioned on imported power units.

"Miroe, I've always wondered why you use that thing to power your pump."

He glanced back at her, away at the windmill, said good-naturedly, "Well, you took away my hovercraft, Jerusha. You can never tell when I might lose my generators."

It was not the answer she had been expecting, but she only shook her head. They reached the main house, went in through the storm-shuttered porch, into the room she still remembered perfectly from the first time; and from the handful of stolen evenings in the years since then that she had spent cross-legged before the fire, wrapped in warmth and golden light, caught up in a game of 3D chama or feeding Miroe's quiet fascination with her reminiscences about another world.

She pulled off her helmet, shook out her dark curls. She let her eyes wander over the comfortable junk-shop home-liness of the room, where relics of his offworlder ancestors, heirlooms by default, kept uneasy truce with rough-hewn native furniture. Moving to the broad stone hearth she turned to face him, letting her back begin to thaw. "You know, after all this time I feel like I haven't even been away. Funny, isn't it, how some places are like that?"

He looked up at her from halfway across the room; didn't answer, but smiled. "Why don't you take your things upstairs? I'll get us something to eat."

She picked up the shoulder bag she had half filled with a change of clothing, climbed the worn staircase to the second story. It was a large house . . . filled with echoes of children and laughter . . . filled with memories. The banister under her hand was worn smooth by the polishing of countless hands; but the halls, the rooms, were empty and silent now. Only Miroe, the last of his line, alone. Alone even among the Winters who worked for him here. She sensed the bond of trust and respect that seemed to exist between them, a stronger bond than she would have expected between owner and workers, natives and offworlder. But there was always an intangible field of reserve surrounding him, keeping him separate, self-contained. She felt it, sometimes, striking sparks against her own.

She entered the room she had always taken, threw her bag and her helmet down on the rumpled bed, watched them sink into the comforters. The wooden-framed bed itself was as hard as a board—was a board, for all she knew—but she had never lain awake here for half the night, praying for sleep while her eyes burned a hole through her lids in the dark. . . .

She unfastened her coat, took it off, started toward the massive wardrobe with it. Stopped, as her gaze landed on the eye-stunning chartreuse flightsuit lying in a heap on the wardrobe's floor. She hung her coat on a hook mechanically, picked up the jump suit and held it against herself. Held it at arm's length again, studying the contours. Then, slowly, she took her coat back and hung the flightsuit in its place.

She went back to the bed, looked again at the rumpled covers; picked up the brush lying on a stool at bedside, fingered the strands of long, fair hair. She put it down again. She stood silently, suddenly in her mind seeing a small, solitary, curly-haired child, in threadbare underpants and sandals, who crouched to watch silvery wogs flit in a dying pool. The sunlight poured over her like hot honey, suffocating all sound, and the stone-studded, blistered moraine of the dry riverbed stretched away forever. . . .

Jerusha took back her helmet and her bag from the bed, and went quickly down the stairs.

"Jerusha?" Miroe straightened away from the low planked table near the fire, frowning his lack of comprehension. "I thought you were—"

"You didn't tell me you had—other guests." The word took on meanings she hadn't intended. "I won't stay."

His face changed, like the face of a man who had just been caught in a terrible oversight. Her own face seemed to have frozen to death.

He said quietly, "Aren't you ever off duty?"

"Your morals are no aff—concern of mine, even on duty."

"What?" Another expression entirely. "You mean— Is that what you thought?" His relief burst out in deep laughter. "I thought you were looking for smugglers!"

Her mouth opened.

"Jerusha." He picked his way across the cluttered room to her. "Ye gods, I didn't mean it like that. It isn't what

298

you think; she's only a friend. Not a romance. She's young enough to be my daughter. She's out on a boat right now."

Jerusha looked away, down. "I didn't want to—intrude."

He cleared his throat. "I'm not a plastic effigy, gods know—" He picked up a flabby, faded cushion, put it down.

"I didn't expect you were." She knew she was saying it badly.

"I . . . you said once that I wasn't a stupid man. But in all this time, all the visits you've made here, I never realized . . ." his hand rose to touch her in a way he had never touched her, ". . . that you wanted something more."

"I didn't want you to." *Didn't want to admit it, even to myself.* She tried to move, tried to step away from his hand, tried, tried—trembling like a wild bird.

He took his hand away. "Is there someone else? In the city, back on your world, another—"

"No," her face burning. "Never."

"Never?" He held a long breath. "Never? . . . No one has ever touched you like this—" along the nape of her neck, her earlobe, the line of her jaw "—or like this—" tracing the seal of her tunic down over her breast "—or done this—" slowly surrounding her with his arms, tightening her against him until she felt the lines of his body melt into hers, and his mouth was on her mouth like nectar.

Murmuring, "Yes . . . now . . ." as his kiss released her. She found his lips again, demanding.

"Beg your pardon, sir!"

Jerusha gasped, breaking his hold in reflex; saw the ancient cook with back turned to them in the doorway.

"What is it?" Miroe's voice was frayed around the edges.

"Midday, sir. Midday meal is ready . . . but it'll keep until you are, sir." Jerusha heard the knowing smile as the cook shuffled back into the pantry.

Miroe sighed heavily, his face trying to smile and frown but only managing to look aggrieved. He reached for her hand, but she slipped it through his fingers before they closed. He looked at her, she saw his surprise.

299

"You asked the question eloquently." Her own smile wavered with the static of her emotions. "But you should have asked it another time, Miroe." She shook her head, pressing her hands to her lips for a moment. "It's too close to the end for me now . . . or not close enough."

"I understand." He nodded, suddenly noncommittal; as though the moment that had just been between them, the moment she had waited so long for, meant nothing to him.

Disappointment and sudden shame pinched her chest. *Is that all it would have meant to you?* "I'd better be getting back to the city." *So you can tell your Winter doxies how you almost had the Commander of Police for lunch.*

"You don't have to go. We can—pretend it didn't happen."

"Maybe you can. But I can't pretend, any more. Reality is too loud." She pulled on her coat, began a crooked course to the door.

"Jerusha. Will you be all right?" The concern caught at her.

She stopped, turned back, under control. "Yes. Even a day outside Carbuncle is like a transfusion. Maybe . . . will I see you again, at the Festival—before the final departure?" She hated herself for asking, when he would not.

"No, I don't think so. I think this is one Festival I want to miss. And I'm not leaving Tiamat; this is my home."

"Of course." She felt an artificial smile starting again, like a muscle cramp. "Well, maybe I'll—call, before I go." *Go to pieces, go to hell. . . .*

"I'll walk you out."

"Don't bother." She shook her head, settled her helmet on, pulling the strap down under her chin. "No need." She opened the dark, ironhinged door and went out, putting it between them as quickly as she could.

She was halfway down the hill when she heard him calling her name. She looked back to see him come running down the slope after her. She stopped, her hands making awkward fists inside her gloves. "Yes?"

"There's a storm coming."

"No there isn't. I checked the weather bulletin before I left Carbuncle."

"The hell with the forecasts; if those bastards would get off their simulators and look up at the sky—" He swept a hand from horizon to zenith. "It'll be here by daybreak tomorrow."

She looked up, seeing nothing but scattered clouds, a pallid double sundog haloing the eclipsing Twins. "Don't worry. I'll be home by dark."

"It's not you I'm worried about." His eyes were still on the northward horizon.

"Oh." She felt her face lose all expression.

"The girl who's staying here, she's up the coast in a small boat. She's not due back before late tomorrow." He faced her grimly. "I've fished her out of the sea half-frozen once already. I might not be so lucky again. I'll never reach her in time, unless—"

She nodded. "All right, Miroe. Let's go find her."

He hesitated. "I—don't know how to ask you for this kind of favor; I have no right to ask you. But—"

"It's all right. It's my duty to help."

"No. I'm trying to ask you to be—off duty, when you do this. To—forget that you ever met whoever you meet." He smiled, or grimaced. "You see. I trust you far too much, too." He began to rub his arms; she realized he had come after her without a coat.

And she remembered his unease at her arrival, and understood it, at last. "She isn't a mass murderer or any-thing?"

He laughed. "Far from it."

"Then I've got a terrible memory. Come on, let's go before you freeze. You can fill me in on the conspiracy charges on the way."

They went on down the hill, into the wind's teeth. Jerusha took them up in the patroller, heading north along the sere ribbon of the coast. "All right. I guess I can let myself put the parts together now. You did have something to do with that techrunner they zapped out here a fortnight or so ago. Your guest is a smuggler." She slid back with a kind of relief into familiar patterns, familiar habits, their old uncomplicated relationship.

"Half-right."

"Half?" She glanced at him. "Then explain."

"You remember the—circumstances of our first meeting."

"Yes," with a sudden image of Gundhalinu's face, full of righteous indignation. "He really had you nailed."

"Your sergeant." She felt him smile, and then remember. "I'm sorry about—what happened. For your sake."

"At least it was quick." *And that's all the mercy we can hope for in this life.* "The girl—?" with a growing prescience.

"Is the Summer girl who broke your arm; the one who went offworld with the smugglers."

"She's back? How?"

"They brought her back with them."

Jerusha felt the patrolcraft buck and swoop in a strong downdraft, reset the controls. "Which means she's an illegal returnee." *And maybe a whole lot more.* "Where's she been in the meantime?"

"Kharemough."

She grunted. "Wouldn't you know. Tell me, Miroe—are you sure her being taken offworld was an accident?"

His brows tightened. "One hundred percent. What do you mean?"

"Hasn't it ever struck you that Moon Dawntreader Summer bears a remarkable resemblance to the Snow Queen?"

"No." Utter blankness. "I haven't even seen the Snow Queen in years."

"What would you say if I told you the Queen knew who she was—was furious over her disappearance? If I told you all my troubles started because I let her get away. What would you say if I told you that Moon Dawntreader is the Queen's clone?"

He stared. "You have proof?"

"No, I don't have proof! But I *know* it; I know Arien-

302

rhod had plans for that girl . . . plans for making her other self the Summer Queen. And if she finds out that Moon is back—"

"They aren't the same person. They can't be." Miroe frowned out at the sea. "You've forgotten something about Moon."

"What?"

"She's a sibyl."

Jerusha started, as memory doubled the words. "So she is. . . . But that still doesn't mean I'm wrong. Or that she isn't a danger to the Hegemony."

"What are you going to do about it?" Miroe twisted in his seat until he was facing her.

She shook her head. "I don't know. I won't know until I get there."

"Get those hides stripped off, there. Hurry up . . . a white one coming . . . shelter by dark . . ." Dogs barking.

Moon felt the words ebb and flow, like the cold tongue of the tide licking her feet, her ankles, her legs. She opened her eyes, to the memory that she did not want to open her eyes and see— But all she saw was the sky, meaningless cloud flotsam drifting. She did not move, afraid to.

"This one's dead."

". . . is luck, praise the Mother! . . . never found so many hides . . ."

"Praise the Snow Queen." Laughter.

"This one's not." A face blotted out the sky, shrouded in white. It knelt, dragged her up to sitting.

"Black." Moon heard her own voice mumbling like a madwoman's. "In black. Where . . . where?" She reached out; dug her fingers into the thick white shoulder for support, as she saw the body that lay beside her own—"Silky!"

The figure in white shoved her away, getting to its feet. "One of those mer-loving bleeders, I guess. Must've killed the Hound. Hounds left the job half done on her." The voice was male, young.

"Silky . . . Silky . . ." Moon stretched to reach the ends of inert tentacles.

303

"Finish it." A harsh, timeworn voice.

Moon struggled back onto her side as the youth squatted, picking up a rock. She clawed at the fastening of her suit, jerked it open halfway down her stomach as the rock arced over her head. "Sibyl!" She threw the word up like a shield.

The boy dropped the stone from twitching fingers, pushed back his hood. She saw his face lose its inhumanity, saw his confusion follow the track of dried blood upward to her wounded throat.

"Sibyl . . ." She pointed at the tattoo, praying that it was clear enough, and that he would understand.

"Ma!" The boy sat back on his heels, shouted over his shoulder. "Look at this!"

Other ghost-white figures materialized around her like a spirit tribunal, doubling and shining in her uncertain focus.

"A sibyl, Ma!" A slight female figure danced with eagerness beside her. "We can't kill her."

"I'm not afraid of sibyls' blood!" Moon identified the crone's voice among the glaring whites as the old woman struck herself on the chest. "I'm holy. I'm going to live forever."

"Oh, the hell you are." The girl shoved her brother aside, bending over to peer down at Moon's throat. She giggled nervously, straightening up again. "Can you talk?"

"Yes." Moon sat up, put a hand to her throat, one against her swollen face, hoarse with trying not to swallow. She looked across Silky's sprawled body, saw beyond it more white figures using their skinning knives, mutilating the bodies of the dead mers. She swayed forward, clutching her knees, hiding from the sight of them. *I didn't see him. I didn't. It was someone else!* She moaned; her voice was the desolate mourning of a lone mer song.

"Then I want her." The girl turned back to the old woman. "I want her for my zoo. She can answer any question!"

"No!" The old woman slapped at her; she ducked her head. "Sibyls are diseased, the offworlders say they're diseased. They're all deceivers. No more pets, Blodwed! You stink the place up with them already. I'm getting rid of those—"

"You just try!" Blodwed kicked her viciously. The old woman howled and stumbled back. "You just try! You want to live forever, you old drooler, you better leave my pets alone!"

"All right, all right . . ." the crone whined. "Don't talk to your mother like that, you ungrateful brat. Don't I let you have anything you want?"

"That's more like it." Blodwed put her hands on her hips, looked down at Moon's huddled grief again, grinning. "I think you're going to be just what I need."

"Gods! Oh, my gods," more a curse than a prayer.

Jerusha stood silently beside Miroe on the lifeless beach, listened to the far, high skreeling of the displaced scavenger birds. Her eyes swept the death-littered field of stones restlessly, not wanting to settle anywhere, register any detail of the scene, but unable to look back at Miroe ashenfaced beside her. Unable to speak a word or even touch him, ashamed to intrude further on a grief past comprehending. This was the Hunt, the mer sacrifice—this stinking abattoir on the barren shore. This was the thing she had resented in principle, without ever trying to approach its reality. But this man had hated the reality.

Miroe moved away from the patrolcraft, began a path through the mutilated corpses of the mers, inspecting each hide-stripped, bloody form with masochistic thoroughness. Jerusha followed him, keeping her distance; felt her jaws tightening until she wondered whether she would ever be able to open her mouth again. She saw him stop and kneel down by one of the bodies. Moving closer, she saw that it was not a mer. And not human. "A—a dead Hound?"

"A dead friend." He picked the dillyp's limp body up like a sleeping child, she saw the dark stain that it left behind on the beach. She watched uncomprehendingly as he carried the body to the edge of the water, entered it without hesitation, wading further and further out until the frigid sea lapped his chest. And then he let the exile go quietly home.

As he came out of the water again Jerusha took off her coat and threw it around his shoulders. He nodded absently; she almost thought that the cold did not reach him. She remembered suddenly that one of the techrunners five years ago had been a dillyp.

"She must be dead, too." His voice was like steel. She realized that there was no sign of Moon Dawntreader. "Starbuck, the Hounds, did this." He gestured; the word was a curse. "The last Hunt. On my land." His hands coiled into fists. "And leaving them like this, mutilating them, this—flaunting. Why?"

"Arienrhod ordered it." The simple statement seared her like a beam of light, as she saw the only conceivable reason that Arienrhod might have for lashing out at an offworlder, a total stranger. *Because of me? No, no . . . not because of me!*

Miroe turned as though her guilt shone out like a beacon. "This is a crime against a citizen of the Hegemony, on his granted land." His voice accused her without needing to say the words. "You've seen it with your own eyes, you have the jurisdiction. Do you have the control to charge Starbuck with murder—Commander?"

She stiffened. "I don't know. I don't know any more, Miroe . . ." touching the badges on her coat collar. She took a deep breath. "But I swear to you, before your gods and mine, that I will do anything in my power to make it happen." (*seeing the ruined bodies*) "She destroys everything she touches, goddamn her—" (*BZ's life gone up in a ball of flame*) "—and I'll make her pay, if I have to die to do it! She won't get away with it—" (*LiouxSked's life ruined*) "—she thinks she's untouchable, she thinks she'll be Queen forever; but she won't get away with it—" (*her own life ruined*) "—if I have to drown her myself!"

"I believe you, Jerusha," Miroe said, unsmiling; she heard the cold accusation fade from his voice. "But there isn't much time."

"I know." She looked away, deliberately imprinting her

mind with the gaping ruin of a creature whose only crime was life. "I've never seen a mer—" She pressed her lips together.

"You haven't seen one here, either." His voice was unsteady. "Not those mounds of dead flesh—those are nothing at all. You haven't seen the mers until you've seen them dance on the water, or heard their song. . . . You haven't understood the real crime until you know the truth about what they are. They're not just animals, Jerusha."

"What?" She turned back. "What are you saying?" *No, don't tell me this; I don't want to know.*

"They're intelligent beings. There weren't two murders on this beach today, there were half a hundred. And over the last millennium—"

She swayed, shaken by the wind. "No . . . Miroe, they're not. They can't be!"

"They're a synthetic life form; the Old Empire gave them intelligence as well as immortality. Moon Dawntreader told me the truth about them."

"But why? Why would they be intelligent? And how could the Hedge not know . . . ?" Her voice faded.

"I don't know why. But I know the Hegemony has to have known the truth, for a millennium. I told Moon when I heard it that I didn't know whether to laugh or cry." Muscles twitched in his face. "I do now." He turned his back on her.

Jerusha stood without words, without motion, waiting for the brittle bowl of the sky to crack open and fall, waiting for the weight of injustice to crush this eggshell world of lies and bring it crashing down on her. . . . But there was no change in the sea, in the air, no difference in the profile of the cliffs or the suffocating awareness of death, waste, mourning. "Miroe . . . come back to the patroller. You'll—you'll catch your death."

He nodded. "Yes. The survivors will return, in time. I have to leave them to—to their own. I can't help them, I can't help my own, any more." He looked toward the small outrigger beached at the water's edge, its sail flapping mournfully. "She gave me the most important gift anyone could have given me, Jerusha: the truth.... She said she was told to come back here; she'd had a sibyl's sending. I don't understand, I can't believe it was meant to end like this for her. What does it all mean?"

"I don't know. Nothing." Jerusha shook her head. "Maybe everything we do is meaningless. But we have to try, don't we? We have to go on looking for justice ... and settling for revenge." She started back toward the patrol-craft, her arms wrapped around her. As they passed the abandoned outrigger it occurred to her that Arienrhod's Hounds had destroyed Arienrhod's clone child ... and Arienrhod would never know it.

32

"I was worried about you when they reported the storm."

"It was nothing. We just rode it out," listlessly.

Soft laughter. "How many of my Starbucks could say that without lying?"

Sparks did not answer, lying motionless on the bed, watching himself in the mirrors, watching her watch him watch, into infinity. Arienrhod lay beside him; the curving lines of her body were the folds of a continent rising from the sea, cloaked in the snowfields of her hair. Strands of thread-fine silver chain spilled down from her waist like a river of light. She massaged the fragrant oil into his skin with slow, exploratory fingers; but his body did not respond. Would not respond, to her most intimate touch, her most knowing suggestions. *Like a corpse ... gods, help me, I'm buried alive.*

Arienrhod's hand slipped from his thigh as his muscles hardened, *rigor mortis.* She rolled onto her stomach, resting across his chest as she looked down at him with concern in her agate-colored eyes. The wrong eyes—as he saw the shadows that lay just below the surface, the depths of wisdom without mercy . . . the eyes of a changeling who had made him a prisoner locked in his own mind. He closed his own eyes. *But I did it all for you, Arienrhod.*

"Are you so tired, then, after all?" She lifted the off-worlder medal from his chest, turning it idly between her fingers; he heard the undercurrent of cool resentment below the shallows of her solicitude. "Or so bored? Shall I make it a threesome——?"

"No." He put his arms around her and pulled her down on him, filling his hands with the silken cloth of her hair, kissing her lips, her eyes, the hollow of her throat . . . and feeling nothing. Nothing. The ghost-girl who had come to him out of the sea would lie between them whenever they lay together from now on, and he would see her eyes—the right eyes, the only eyes. They would accuse him, weeping tears of blood, forever. . . . "Arienrhod," despairingly. "Damn it, you know I love you! You know you're everything to me, everything she ever was, and more——" But the word was a moan. His hands fell away from her.

Arienrhod turned rigid on top of him. " 'She'? . . . What are you talking about, my love? Our Moon?" Her voice was soft and clouded-over. "Does she still come back to haunt you, after so long? She's gone. We lost her a long time ago; you have to put her out of your mind." She stroked his temples with her fingers, in slow circling motions.

"By all the gods, I thought I had!" He rolled his head from side to side, trying to look away from his own reflection, but it followed him inexorably.

"Then why? Why think about her now? Are you afraid of the Change coming? I promised you it would never come."

"I don't care about that." *About killing my people . . . then I don't care about anything at all.* He shifted her carefully off of him, rolled over onto his stomach and propped his head in his hands. She sat up beside him, the girdle of silver threads whispering over her skin.

"Then what——?" a wildness in it. Her hands closed over

his shoulders. "You're mine, Starbuck; you're all that I love in this world. I won't share you with a Summer dream. I won't lose you to a ghost ... even my own."

"She wasn't a ghost! She was real." He bit down on his fist.

Arienrhod's fingernails bit his flesh in turn. "Who?" knowing who.

"Moon." Something shook him, close to a sob. "Moon. Moon, Moon! She was there, at the Hunt; she came out of the sea with the mers!"

"A dream." She frowned.

"No dream, Arienrhod!" He threw himself onto his back, feeling her nails rake him. "I touched her, I saw the sign on her throat—and the blood. I touched her blood ... she cursed me." *Death to kill a sibyl ... death to love a sibyl ...*

"You fool!" But not for his foolhardiness. "Why didn't you tell me about this immediately?"

He shook his head. "I couldn't. I—"

She slapped him; he fell back on the pillows in disbelief. "Where is she? What happened to her?"

He rubbed his hand across his mouth. "The Hounds—would have killed her. I stopped them. I—I left her there on the beach."

"Why?" A world of loss in one whispered word.

"Because she would have recognized me." He tore the words out by the roots. "She would have known ... she would have seen what I am!" His reflection pinwheeled him, around and around and around.

"So you're ashamed to be my lover, and the most powerful man on this planet?" She tossed back her hair.

"Yes," ashamed to look at her, too, as he said it. "When I was with her, I was ashamed."

"But you left her alone on the shore with a blizzard coming, and you're not ashamed of that." Arienrhod wrapped herself in her arms, shivered as though it was herself he had abandoned.

"Damn it, I didn't know about the storm, there wasn't any report!" *You only needed to look up at the sky to know*— But he had shut himself into his cabin to hide his trembling loss of control from the Hounds; and he had come out again only when the storm was already sweeping down on them, when it was too late to think of anything but their own survival. And afterward—it was too late for anything at all. He looked up angrily into Arienrhod's anger. "I don't understand you! Why does she matter so much to you? Even if she is your kinswoman, you were never close to her. Not like I was. . . ."

"No one in this world is closer to her than I am." Arienrhod leaned toward him. "Haven't you realized that? Haven't you seen by now—*I am Moon*."

"No." He pulled away from her; she caught the chain of his medal and held him tethered.

"Moon is my clone! I had her raised as a Summer to take my place as Queen. We're identical in every way— *every* way." She took his hands and ran them down along her body. "And we both love you, above all others."

"It isn't possible . . ." He touched her face and knew that it was. They were night and day, iron and air, gall and honey. . . . *Then why do I love you both?* He bowed his head. *Because I do love you both; gods help me!*

"Anything is possible. Even that she's come back to me." Arienrhod looked through him, through time. "But do I still need her . . . do I still want her?" Her focus narrowed to him again. "And do you, my love?"

He sagged against her; felt her arms circle him, her hands stroke him lovingly, possessively. "No." *No more than I ever wanted her, only her.* "Only you, Arienrhod. You made me everything I am. You're all I need." *And you're all I deserve.*

311

33

"Come on, sibyl! Come meet my other pets." Blodwed's sharp, high voice pricked Moon like a goad, started her through the crowd of gawkers gathered at the entrance of the cavern. They had all come forward to stare at her, pointing and muttering, calling out vulgar questions that she ignored with all the restraint left in her dazed body: a prize fish, dangling on the pier. But none of the nomads would get close enough to touch her, and they parted before her stumbling progress like grasses before the wind. Even Blodwed had never actually touched her; but Moon recognized the stunner hanging from the girl's belt.

And even if she dared to break free from her captors, there was nowhere to go. They had traveled for two days on snowskimmers, climbing into the icebound highlands of the interior, to get to this isolated nomads' camp. She had no strength left to carry her alone through the Winter wilderness . . . barely the strength to carry her on across the immense floor of the rock shelter. Dogs barked and bayed at her passing, chained among the bright-colored synthetic tents, the patterned gray-and-brown ones made from hides—the tents dotted the cavern like grotesque fungal growths. Dozens of perpetual-radiance heaters and lanterns filled the looming space with warmth and light, as the voices of the booty-haggling kinsmen behind her filled and refilled it with echoing noise. Moon slowed, holding out her mittened hands to one of the heaters as she passed. But Blodwed's impatience radiated like heat—"Come on, hurry up!"—and she moved on, too numb with exhaustion and cold to protest.

Blodwed herded her into a narrow, downsloping passage half in shadows at the rear of the cave; she saw light dimly,

312

on ahead. A miasma of strange smells prickled like smoke inside her head as she went forward, to find her way barred by a gate of wood and twisted wire. Blodwed pushed past her, pressed a thumb into the bottom of the heavy lock. The lock opened, and she waved Moon through.

Moon went ahead, hearing Blodwed come through behind her; stood still in place as she took in the details of her new prison. The rock chamber was twenty or thirty feet in diameter, with a ceiling almost as high, and an incandescent heater sat in its center like a sun. Around the perimeter, locked in cages, tethered by rope or chain, were creatures of half a dozen unidentifiable species, furred, feathered, covered with scales or masses of naked wrinkles. She covered her nose and mouth with her hand as the smell of their squalid misery struck her full force. She saw them cringe, saw them snarl; saw the ones that lay sullenly apathetic with no response at all . . . saw the human being lying on a bare cot by the far wall, as far from the gate, as far from the rest, as possible.

"Damn her! Damn her!" Blodwed shouted suddenly. Moon jerked around, the menagerie hissed and yowled and clamored, as Blodwed turned and ran back up the passage. The gate banged shut behind her. Moon turned back, looking across the room toward the figure still lying unresponsive on the cot. She went forward slowly, limping as sensation began to burn in the soles of her feet again. The frightened animals cowered back from her.

She reached the stranger's side without waking him, seeing as she approached that it was a man, an offworlder . . . a Blue. His heavy uniform coat was splattered with dark stains, and he wore the dingy white leggings and boots of the nomads. Looking down at his face she saw the finely-drawn features she had seen so often on aristocratic Kharemoughis; but this face was like cut crystal, the skin strained over the hollow bones. And still he did not wake. His breathing was labored, wrong. She put out a hand uncertainly, touched his face; pulled it back from the burn of fever.

She let her quivering legs go out from under her, sank

313

down beside his cot on the cold floor. The animals had grown quiet, but she felt their frightened eyes still on her, and their misery overwhelming her, until her own cup of misery overflowed. She let her head fall against the cot's edge, hard dry sobs shaking her apart. *Help me, Lady, help me . . . everything I touch I destroy.*

"What's . . . wrong?" A feverish hand ruffled her hair; she jerked upright, swallowed her sobs. "Are you . . . for me crying?" The words were in Sandhi. The sick man struggled to lift his head; his eyes were red and crusted, she thought he barely saw her.

"Yes." Her answer was scarcely louder than his question.

"No need—" A fit of coughing knocked the breath and the words out of him.

"Look at this! Look at it!" Moon stiffened back and around as Blodwed burst into the chamber again, dragging a larger girl after her. "Smell it! I told you to keep them right while I was gone!"

"I did—" The older girl cried out as Blodwed caught her by the braid and yanked.

"I ought to rub your face in it, Fossa. But I won't, if you get this place clean before—"

"All right, all right!" The older girl backed toward the gate, wiping away pain-tears. "You snotty little wart."

"Wait. What's wrong with him?" Blodwed pointed past Moon at the offworlder.

"He's sick. He tried to get away when we let him out to take a piss; he ran right out into the blizzard, you know? He went in circles and we found him right outside." She made the crazy sign, and shook her head, backing up the passageway.

Blodwed came on across the chamber, crouched down beside Moon, looking at the sick man's face. "Ugh." She clamped his jaw roughly in her hand as he tried to turn his head away. "What did you do that for?" His eyes closed.

"I don't think he hears you." Moon put a hand over his, squeezed his fingers lightly before she let go. "He needs a healer, Blodwed," tentatively.

314

"Is he going to die?" Blodwed sat back on her knees, the truculence unexpectedly melting out of her voice. "There's no healer here. Ma used to do it, but she's not right in the head. She never taught anybody else. Can't you help him?"

Moon glanced up at her. "Maybe I can. . . ." She began to put her hair into braids. "Do you have any offworlder medical supplies?" Blodwed shook her head. "How about herbs, anything?"

"I can steal Ma's. They're old—" Blodwed stood up expectantly.

"Just get them." Moon watched her go, confused by her willingness. She lifted the offworlder's hand again, feeling for the pulse in his wrist; caught her breath as she saw the inside of his arm, crisscrossed with ragged scars. She stared in silent disbelief, lowered his arm again carefully, wrist down. She kept her hold on his hand as she sat waiting, and kept her mind empty.

"Here they are." Blodwed came back through the gate at last, carrying a skin-wrapped bundle beaded with tiny bones and bits of metal. She opened it, spread it out on the floor between them. "Neutron activation," she said, waving her hands. "Ma always says power words. Do you say power words, sibyl?" There was no taunt in it.

"I suppose so." Moon picked over the leafy bundles of dried plants, sniffing at clear plastic bags of seeds and flower heads. Her hope faded. "I don't know any of these."

"Well, that one's—"

She shook her head. "I mean, I don't know how to *use* these." KR Aspundh had told her about the Old Empire's exploration service, that before they opened new worlds for human colonists they had seeded them with a panacea of medicinal plants, different series for different ecosystems. "In the islands we used a lot of sea plants for curing." *And called them the Lady's gifts.* "I'll have to ask—*you'll* have to ask for me, input me; will you?" Blodwed nodded eagerly. "Ask me their uses," Moon gestured. "Remember what I say—exactly, or it won't do any good. Can you?"

"Sure." Blodwed grinned arrogantly. "I can sing all the

315

landmarks of the trail song. Nobody else can, any more. I can sing any song I ever heard on the radio even once."

Moon managed half a smile, stopped by the stiff bruise on her cheek. "Then prove it. Ask, and I will answer. *Input....*"

Blodwed cleared her throat, sat up straighter. "Oh, sibyl! Tell me ... uh, how to use these magic plants?"

Moon took up a bundle of herbs in her hand, felt herself begin to fall backwards down the well of absence....

...Clavally. She came into the light again, to find a face she knew, Clavally's flushed and startled face, tousled hair, bare shoulders as close to her as *...Danaquil Lu.* She saw Clavally pull a blanket up to cover herself hastily. She thought, uselessly, *Danaquil Lu, I'm sorry ... Clavally, it's only Moon....* But she could not affect their lives even while she intruded on them so profoundly, to share her apologies or her happiness at even this reunion; to ask their help, or to communicate in any way at all.

But a tentative smile formed at the corners of Clavally's wide mouth, as though she saw a message fill the window of Danaquil Lu's eyes. She touched his cheek tenderly, still smiling, and with knowing patience lay back on the bed to wait....

"*...No further analysis!*" Moon slumped forward, drained, felt Blodwed's quick hands catch her and keep her upright.

"You did it! You're not a fake—" Blodwed propped her against the cot and took her hands away, suddenly leery. "Wake up! Are you awake? Where did you go?"

Moon nodded, let her forehead rest on her knees. "I ... visited old friends." She wrapped her arms around her shins, holding on to the memory: the only warmth, the only happiness she could remember.

"I know all the herbs now, sibyl." Blodwed's voice pawed at her. "I'll show you. Are you going to cure him?"

"No." Moon raised her unwilling head, opened her eyes. "I'm going to bring a real healer to use the herbs. But you'll have to help me, give me whatever I need." A nod. Moon readied herself, knowing that if she simply had the

316

strength to begin, the Transfer would take her through to the end. Her body rebelled, refusing to gather for another ordeal, but she new that if she surrendered to exhaustion now, it might be too late for the offworlder by the time she could start again. And she was not going to watch another person die because of her. She focused her attention on his face.

"All right, ask me how to treat him. *Input!*" and she flung herself through . . .

. . . Into a white-walled anti-gravity chamber, where she watched a cluster of men clad in pastel and transparent suits drift weightless, tethered to a table, arguing an incomprehensible medical procedure. Beyond them, beyond the reinforced glass of a wide window, she saw thick fingers of ice depending beneath an eaves, and floodlights illuminating a field of drifted snow. . . .

". . . *analysis!*" She came back into herself, barely hearing the dry rattle of the end sign inside her head. She smelled the pungent reek of half a dozen strange herbs on her hands and clothing as she crumpled forward. Mind fog haloed her view of Blodwed's peering face and the inert blanket-bundle of the sick offworlder, turning them to a holy vision. Reassured, she found her hands and knees and crawled toward the heater in the room's center. When the cloud of energy became so intense that her body could not endure more, she let herself down at last, and slept.

Moon came awake with the urgency of terror, stared at the unexpected walls that closed her in. Stone walls—not the endless desolation of sky above a lifeless, stony beach, where an executioner in black wore a medal as familiar as the face of her only love. . . . She hid from the phantom behind a wall of fingers, pressing the swollen soreness of her face. *No, it isn't true!*

A soft trilling intruded on her, expanding her awareness, pulling her back into the stone-walled chamber. She lowered her hands, seeing the cluster of cages across the room, and felt time's flood sweep her into the present. Someone had moved her to a pad of blankets. The animal stench had

317

cleared, as though someone had cleaned the cages out as well, and the air was strong with the smell of herbs. No sounds reached her from beyond the locked gate; she guessed that it must be far into the night. The animals stirred and rustled, tending to their own lives, watching her with only half an eye now. "You know I'm just another pet." She climbed uncertainly to her feet, swayed a moment, seeing stars, before she could cross the room.

The offworlder lay under a half-tent of blanket, wrapped like a swaddled infant in more covers. A pot of pungent herb-brew steamed on a hotplate by his head. She kneeled down by the cot, put her hand against his face. *Cooler*, not really sure that he was. "Please come back. . . ." *Prove I have a right to be alive, and be a sibyl.* She bowed her head, pressed her forehead against the hard frame of the cot.

"Have you . . . back for me come, then?"

She looked up, saw the offworlder struggling to open his eyes. "I—I never left you." He frowned, shook his head as though it didn't make sense. "I've never away gone." She repeated it in Sandhi.

"Ah." He watched her through slitted eyes. "Then I'm not afraid. When . . . when will we go?"

"When? Soon." She smoothed his wiry hair, and saw him smile. Not knowing what he was asking, she said, "When thou art stronger." She used the familiar form unthinkingly.

"I didn't think you so fair would be. Stay by me . . . until then?"

"I will." Glancing down, she saw the untouched mug of thick medicine broth on the floor by her knee. She picked it up. "Thou must this drink." She put her arm under his shoulders, rolled him onto his side. He worked a hand free obediently, but it could not hold the cup; she saw the livid scars along the inside of his wrist again. She held the cup for him, helped him drink it down. Coughing took him as he finished it, rattling in his chest like stones. The plastic mug slipped from her hand and rolled under the cot. She

318

held him tightly in her arms, sharing her own strength with him, until the attack passed; and then a little longer.

"Thou feel . . . so real." He sighed against her shoulder. "So kind . . ."

She let him slip back onto the cot, already asleep. She sat for a long moment watching him, before she settled against the cot frame, resting her head on her arm, and closed her eyes again.

"You are real."

The words greeted her like old friends as she woke again, slowly raised her head from her sleep-deadened arm. She sat back, disconcerted, blinking.

The offworlder slumped against the wall, propped into place by a knot of blankets. "Did I it dream, or . . . did you to me in Sandhi speak?"

"I did," in Sandhi. Moon worked her fingers, felt the needles starting as circulation stirred in her arm. "I—cannot it believe. You were so sick." She felt a shining warmth fill her. *But the power came through me, and I healed you.*

"I thought you the Child Stealer were. When I was young, my nurse said she as pale as aurora-glow is. . . ." He leaned more heavily on the heaped blankets. "But you're no ghost. Are you—?" As though he still half doubted his senses.

"No." She massaged her twisted neck muscles with her other hand, wincing. "Or I wouldn't so much hurt!"

"You're a prisoner too, then." He leaned forward slightly, squinting; his eyes were still inflamed. She nodded. "Your face. They didn't you . . . molest?"

She shook her head. "No. They haven't me hurt. They—fear me; so far."

"Fear you?" He glanced toward the gate, and what lay beyond it. The distant sounds of a new day out in the camp reached them like an echo of another world.

She lifted her chin, saw him grimace at the wound on her throat, before his face went slack: "Sibyl?"

319

She lowered her head again.

"Gods, this moves too fast." He lay down again, resting on his side through another attack of coughing.

Something out of place caught the corner of her eye. She twisted, found a pile of blue-black cloth trimmed with braid behind her, a jug, and a bowl of dried meat. "Someone brought us food." Her hands were reaching for it even as she spoke. "Food—" not even knowing how long it had been since she had eaten anything.

"Blodwed. Hours back. I pretended to sleep."

Moon took a long drink from the pitcher, a creamy blue-white liquid that slid down her parched throat into her shriveled stomach like ambrosia, "Oh—" Suddenly ashamed, she lowered the pitcher, pushed up onto her knees. "Here." She filled the plastic mug, held it up to him.

"No." He put an arm across his eyes. "I don't it want."

"You must. To heal, you need strength."

"No. I don't—" The arm came down from his eyes, he lifted his head to look at her. "Yes . . . I guess I do." He took the drink in his good hand; she saw scars on that wrist, too. He caught her looking at him, raised the mug to his mouth without comment and sipped slowly.

Moon chewed a mouthful from a strip of dried meat, swallowed it whole before she asked, "Who are you? How did you here get?"

"Who am I . . ." He looked down at his uniform coat, touched it; his face changed with a kind of wonder, like a man coming out of a coma. "Gundhalinu, sibyl. Police Inspector BZ Gundhalinu—" he grimaced, "from Kharemough. They shot down my patroller, and took me."

"How long have you here been?"

"Forever." He opened his eyes again. "And you? Did they you from the starport kidnap? Where are you from— Big Blue, or Samathe?"

"No, Tiamat."

"Here? But you're a sibyl." He lowered the cup from his lips. "The Winters don't—"

"I'm a Summer. Moon Dawntreader Summer."

"Where did you Sandhi learn?" Something darker than curiosity shadowed it.

Moon frowned uncertainly. "On Kharemough."

"You're proscribed, then! How did you back here get?" His voice broke, too feeble to support the weight of an authoritarian demand.

"The same way I left—with techrunners." She slipped into her own speech without realizing it; taken by surprise, indignant at his indignation. "What are you going to do about it, Blue? Arrest me? Deport me?" She put her hands on her hips, clenched with resentment.

"I'd do both . . . if I were in any position to." He followed her doggedly from language to language. But the righteousness drained out of him and left him limp on the cot. He laughed, a hoarse, hating sound. "But don't worry. Flat on my face . . . with the cosmic crud, and living in a kennel . . . I'm not in any position." He finished the liquid in the mug, let it hang empty from a finger over the cot's edge.

Moon refilled the mug and put it into his hand again.

"A smuggling sibyl." He sipped carefully, watching her. "I thought you were supposed to be serving humanity, not yourself. Or did you have that tattoo . . . put on purely for business reasons?"

Moon flushed with fresh anger. "That isn't allowed!"

"Neither is smuggling. But it's done." He sneezed violently, spilling his drink on himself, on her.

"I'm not a smuggler." She flinched, brushed droplets from her parka. "But not because I think it's wrong. You're the ones who are wrong, Gundhalinu, you Blues— letting your people come here and take what they want, and give us nothing in return."

He smiled mirthlessly. "So you've swallowed that simplistic line bait and hook, have you? If you wanted . . . to see real greed and exploitation, try a world that didn't have our police force to keep the peace. Or to keep . . . people like you from coming back to make trouble, once you've been offworld."

Moon settled back on her heels, saying nothing, holding

the words prisoner. Gundhalinu matched her silence; she sat listening to the breath wheeze in his throat. "This is my world, I have the right to be here. I am a sibyl, Gundhalinu, and I'll serve Tiamat any way I can." Something harsher than pride filled her voice. "I can prove my claim any time you ask. Ask, and I will answer."

"No need, sibyl." A whisper of apology. "You already have. I ought to hate you, for curing me—" He rolled onto his stomach, looking down at her; she blinked at his expression, her hands closed over her own wrists. "But knowing I'm alive and not alone, seeing your face . . . hearing you speak a civilized language, my own language: Gods, I never thought I'd ever hear it again! I thank you—" his voice broke. "How long . . . how long were you on Kharemough?"

"Almost a month." She put another piece of dried meat into her mouth, let the juices begin to dissolve, easing a throat closed by sudden empathy. "But—I might have stayed longer, maybe all my life. If things had been different."

"Then you liked it there?" There was no sarcasm now, only a hunger. "Where were you? What did you see?"

"The Thieves' Market, mostly. And the starport city." She sat crosslegged, pulling her feet into place, and let her mind see only the days that had feasted her eyes; see Elsevier and Silky and Cress alive and sharing her feast; the journey down to the planet surface, and KR Aspundh's ornamental gardens. . . . "And we drank *lith* and ate sugared fruits. . . . Oh, and on the screen we saw Singalu raised to Tech."

"What?" Gundhalinu sat against the wall, gasping with incredulous delight. She noticed that he was missing a tooth. "Ye gods, I don't believe it! Old Singalu? You're making that up, aren't you?" Laughter was the best medicine.

She shook her head. "No, really! It was an accident. But even KR was glad." And she remembered tears welling in Elsevier's eyes, in her own. . . . Tears rose again suddenly; tears of grief this time.

"Dropped in on KR Aspundh." He shook his head, wiped his own eyes, still grinning. "Even my father didn't just drop in on KR Aspundh! Well, go on, what next?"

Moon swallowed. "We . . . we talked. He asked me to stay a few days. He's a sibyl, you know—" She broke off.

"And I know there are a lot . . . of things you're not telling me," Gundhalinu said quietly. He shook his head. "No. I don't want to know. I don't even want to know why the hell KR Aspundh has techrunners to tea. But you could have had anything you wanted there—the life, all the things you couldn't have here. Why? Why did you leave all that, and risk everything to come back here? I can see it in your eyes, you wish you hadn't."

"I thought I had to." She felt her broken nails dig into her palms. "I never wanted to go offworld in the first place. I was going to Carbuncle to find my cousin. . . . But when I got to Shotover Bay I met Elsevier, and then the Blues tried to arrest us—"

"Shotover Bay?" A peculiarly chagrined expression settled over his face. "It's a small universe. No wonder I keep thinking . . . I've seen your face somewhere."

She leaned forward with a smile starting, studied his face in turn. "No—I guess I was too busy running."

He twitched his mouth. "No one's ever called it memorable. So you were going to Carbuncle. But after five years, you aren't still going there? Whatever happened to your kinsman is ancient history, by now."

"It's not." She shook her head. "While I was on Kharemough I asked, and the Transfer told me I had to return, that it wasn't finished yet." The cold silence of the void grew loud inside her, squeezed her breath away. "But ever since I've come, everyone I've cared about I've destroyed, or hurt . . ." She hunched over, pulled herself into a hiding place.

"You? I don't—understand."

"Because I came back!" She let the words come, making him see her for what she was, every act and every retribution that had brought her relentlessly to this place. . . . "I

323

made it happen! I made them do it, it was all for me. I'm a curse—none of it would have happened without me, none of it!"

"You wouldn't have seen it happen; that's all. Nobody rules anyone else's fate—we don't even control our own." She felt his hand hesitantly on her shoulder. "We wouldn't be prisoners here; I wouldn't be alive now to say . . . you're wrong to blame yourself, if we did. Would I?"

She raised her head. "But the mers, Lady, even the mers . . . they were safe on Ngenet's land, until I came!"

"If Starbuck and the Hounds were poaching, it was no fault of yours. It was nobody's doing but the Queen's. I'd say you must be thrice blessed, not cursed, if all you got . . . out of an encounter with Starbuck was a sore throat." He began to cough, pressing his own throat.

"Starbuck?" Slowly she uncoiled, stretching her legs, gathering the courage to ask: "Was he—the man in black? What is he?" Not asking, *Who is he?*

Gundhalinu raised his eyebrows, took his hand away from her softening shoulder. "You've never heard of Starbuck? He's the Queen's consort: her Hunter, her henchman, her chief advisor when she deals with us . . . her lover."

"He saved my life." She traced the scab of the healing wound across her neck, finding the strength to ask, "Who is he, Gundhalinu?"

"No one knows. His identity is kept secret."

He loved you once, but he loves her now. The words of the Transfer reverberated. "Now I understand. I understand everything! . . . It's true." She looked away, and away; but the emerald eyes behind the black executioner's mask followed her, followed—

"What is?"

"My cousin is Starbuck," whispered.

Gundhalinu said calmly, "He can't be. Starbuck is an offworlder."

"Sparks is one too. His father was one. He always wanted to be like them, like the Winters. . . . And now he is." *A monster. How could he do this to me?*

"You're jumping to conclusions. Just because Starbuck was afraid . . . to kill a sibyl—"

"He knew I was a sibyl before he ever saw my sign!" She struck back at his insufferable conviction. "He knew me; I know he did. And he was wearing the medal that was Sparks's." *And he was killing mers.* She pressed her knotted fist against her mouth. "How could he? How could he change into *that*?"

Gundhalinu lay down again, uncomfortably silent. "Carbuncle does that to people. But if it's true, at least he had enough humanity left to spare your life. Now you can forget about him; forget about . . . one problem, at least." He sighed, staring up into shadows.

"No." She pushed herself to her feet, moving in a stiff circle beside the cot. "I want to get to Carbuncle more than ever. There has to be a reason for what he's done; if he's changed, there's a way to change him back." *Win him back. I won't lose . . . not after I've come so far!* "I love him, Gundhalinu. No matter what he's done, no matter how he's changed, I can't just stop loving him." *Or needing him, or wanting him back. He's mine, he's always been mine! I won't give him up—no matter whose he is, or what she's made him into. . .* appalled by the truth, made helpless by it. "We pledged our lives to each other; and if he doesn't want that any more, he's going to have to prove it to me." One hand made a fist, the other clung to it.

"I see." He smiled, but there was uncertainty behind it. "And I always thought you natives led dull, uncomplicated lives," unwitting condescension crept back, making him comfortable. "At least on Kharemough love has the courtesy to know its place, and not tear our hearts out of us."

"Then you've never been in love," resentfully. She crouched down by the pile of bright-and-dark cloth Blodwed had left them; picked up a piece distractedly. It was a tunic, sewn with wide bands of woven braid.

"If you mean all-consuming, sense-clouding, lightning-struck love—no. I've read about it. . . ." His voice softened

325

at the edges. "But I've never seen it. I don't think it exists in the real universe."

"Kharemoughis don't exist in the real universe." She took off her parka, pulled open the seal of her drysuit and climbed out of it, rubbing her skin-sore, abraded arms, scratching her back. Letting him watch, aware that he tried not to; taking perverse pleasure in his discomfiture. She pulled the soft, heavy tunic on over her skimpy undersuit, struggled into the leggings and fur-lined boots, buckled the wide painted-leather belt around her hips. She touched the handwoven braid that ran down the tunic front, along the hem—all the colors of sunset against the night-blue wool. "This is beautiful...." Astonishment pushed up through her darker preoccupation. She realized suddenly that the braid, the garment, were very old.

"Yes." Gundhalinu's expression was not the one she had expected. But she saw the embarrassment lying below it, and felt a pinprick shame at his shame.

"Gundhalinu—"

"Make it BZ." He shrugged away his self-consciousness. "We're all on a first-name basis here." He gestured at the animals.

She nodded. "BZ. We've got to find—" She broke off again, hearing someone enter the passageway. The lock rattled and the gate swung back. Blodwed came through it, trailed by a small, rosy-cheeked child and carrying a box. She pulled the gate shut with her foot. The animals stirred and peered out at her all along the walls; tension made their movements furtive. The toddler wandered toward the cages, sat down unexpectedly on the floor in front of one. Blodwed ignored him, coming on across the room.

Moon glanced at Gundhalinu, saw the life go out of his eyes and the animation out of his face, leaving bleak resignation. But Blodwed beamed as she dropped the box, stood before him, inspecting him like an inquisitor. "I don't believe it, he's all right! See—" She caught his sleeve, tugged on his arm. "I got a real sibyl just to keep you alive, Blueboy." He pulled free, sitting up. "Now you can finish reading to me."

"Leave me alone." He put his feet over the cot's edge, propped his head on his hands. He began to cough, sullenly.

Blodwed shrugged; looked back at Moon, scratching her beaky nose. "You okay too? I thought you were both dead this morning." A bare hint of deference crept into her voice.

Moon nodded, controlling her own voice, picking the words cautiously. "I'm all right. . . . Thank you for bringing me clothes to wear." She touched the front of the tunic. "This is very beautiful." She couldn't keep the incredulity out of it.

Blodwed's sky-blue eyes were full of pride for an instant; she glanced down. "They're just old stuff. They belonged to my great-grandmother. Nobody wears those things any more; nobody here even knows how to make them." She tugged at the hem of her dirty white parka, as though she really preferred it. She rummaged in the carton, pulled out a fist-sized cube of plastic. Unintelligible noise filled the air like rain. Blodwed began to hum a tune, and Moon realized that she was picking it out of the radio static. "Reception really stinks back in this cave. Of course it didn't help that old Blue-boy here tried to take this apart and make a transmitter." She made a face at him. "Here's your dinner," tossing a can onto the cot. A sudden shriek behind them jerked Moon around. The toddler stood wailing, waving his hands by the cages. "Well, don't stick your fingers in there, damn it! Here's yours."

Moon caught the can as it arced into her hands, sat down and pulled the lid up. It vaguely resembled stew. She watched Gundhalinu open his own can, with a twinge of relief. "Is . . . he your brother?" to Blodwed.

"No." Blodwed moved away, carrying handfuls of meat and a box with an animal's picture on it. She made the circuit from tethered creature to caged one, giving them each their evening meal. Moon watched them flutter up or cringe away from her rough movements, slink forward again after she passed.

Blodwed came back, scowling, sat down with her own

327

can. The little boy appeared beside her, pulling at her jacket and whining. "Not now!" She pushed a spoonful of stew into his mouth. "You know anything about animals?" She glanced at Moon, looked back over her shoulder at the cages.

"Not these." Moon looked away from the boy, whose face was as perfectly pink and white as a porcelain figurine.

"Then you're going to do what you did yesterday again —only this time tell me about the animals." She glared, expecting a refusal. "I think some of them are sick too. I—I don't know how to take care of them either." Her gaze broke. "I want to know how."

Moon nodded, swallowing the last of her stew, and got slowly to her feet. "Where did you get all these animals?"

"Stole them from the spaceport. Or got them from traders, or out trapping . . . the elffox, and the gray birds there, and the conies. But I don't even know the names of the rest."

Moon felt Gundhalinu's eyes trail her with dark accusation, ignored it as she walked toward the closest of the animals, the hardest one to face—the shivering pouch of wrinkles that squatted on a nest of dried grass. It blubbered obscenely, showing her a wide sucker-mouth as she opened the cage door. Biting back her disgust, she crouched before it, offered it a handful of food pellets at arm's length, holding very still.

Its burbling hysteria gradually died away, and after another endless moment it floundered forward, inch by inch, to touch her hand tentatively with its mouth. She shuddered; it scuttled back, worked its way forward again. It took the pellets one by one from her palm with great delicacy. She dared to stroke it with her free hand; its brainlike convolutions were smooth and cool to her touch, like the surface of a smocked satin pillow. It settled contentedly under her hand, making a sound like bubbles popping.

She left it slowly, went on to the pair of lithe, pacing carnivores in the next cage. Their ears flattened, their tusks showed white against the black-on-black patterning of their fur. There was something feline about them, and so she began to whistle softly, creating the overtones that had made cats come purring into her lap at home. The long, tufted ears flicked, swiveled, tuned like radar ... the animals came toward her almost reluctantly, drawn by the sound. She offered them her fingers to sniff, felt a thrill of pleasure when an ebony cheek brushed her hand in a gesture of acceptance. The cat creatures sidled along the bars, demanding her touch with guttural cries.

She moved on more confidently to the leather-winged reptile with a head like a pickax; the feather-soft oblongs with no heads at all; the bird with emerald plumage and ruby crest that lay listlessly in the bottom of its cage. She lost track of time or any purpose beyond the need to communicate even to the smallest degree with every creature, and earn for herself the reward of its embryonic trust.... Until she reached the end of the circuit at last, found the little boy lying asleep on Blodwed's knee, and Blodwed staring up at her in silent envy.

Moon glanced away, understanding the look in one final moment of empathy. "I—I'm ready to begin Transfer, Blodwed; whenever you say."

"How did you do that?" Blodwed's words struck her like blows. "Why do they come to you, and not to me? They're my pets! They're supposed to love me!" The boy woke at the sound of her anger, and began to cry.

"That should be obvious," Gundhalinu muttered sourly. "She treats animals like human beings, and you treat human beings like animals."

Blodwed stood up furiously, and Gundhalinu stiffened; but no words came out of her, and she did not bring up her white-knuckled fists to strike him.

"Blodwed ... they're afraid of you. Because ..." Moon struggled, fitting reluctant words to her thoughts. "Because you're afraid of them."

"I'm not afraid of them! *You* were afraid of them."

Moon shook her head. "Not that way. I mean ... I'm not afraid to let them see I care about them." She twisted a braid.

Blodwed's mouth worked, her scowl faded. "Well, I feed them, I do everything for them! What else am I supposed to do?"

"Learn to be—gentle with them. Learn that . . . that gentleness isn't . . . weakness."

The little boy clung to Blodwed's leg, still crying. She looked down at him, put her hand on his head hesitantly, before she followed Moon back to the cages.

Moon began the circuit again with the brain creature, luring it into her hands, making it the focus of her senses. "Ask me about them. *Input*—" She heard Blodwed's question and carried it down. . . .

". . . *analysis!*" She found herself sitting on the floor, exhausted, with the snub-nosed elffox cub suckling her braid. She smoothed its thick white crest, removed the braid from its mouth and its pinprick claws from her tunic with great care, held it out to Blodwed in both hands. "Here," faintly, "take him."

Blodwed reached out, uncertainty slowing her movements; the cub did not struggle or protest as Moon slipped it into her waiting hands. Blodwed settled it against her stomach, held it there almost timidly. She giggled as it worked its way in through the opening of her parka and settled against her side. The toddler sat at her feet reaching up after it with one hand, his thumb in his mouth.

"Did I tell you—enough?" Moon glanced away, along the circle of bare cages, still overlaid by the shadowy green and gold of an imported-pet shop somewhere on another world. *So far away . . . all of us so far away from home.*

"Lissop, starls, batwing . . ." Blodwed named them all. "I guess I even know what's wrong with those," pointing. "I don't have the right food." Her face pulled down. "But you did good," encouraging again. She held the cub close. "Didn't she, Blue?"

Gundhalinu smiled, grudgingly, and made a salute. "A noble—" He broke off.

Three pairs of eyes looked up together at the sound of someone else entering the passageway. The gate swung open, and a bearded, heavy-faced man entered. The animals shrank back along the walls.

"What do you want, Taryd Roh?" The surliness was back in Blodwed's voice.

"The shaman wants this fixed." He held out a fragile-looking instrument that Moon did not recognize. "Tell the Tech there to get started earning his keep."

"He's too sick." Blodwed stuck out her chin.

"He's alive." Taryd Roh grinned, swiveling his gaze to Moon. "And this pretty little doll you brought him would put life back in the dead. How'd you like to visit my tent, little sibyl?" A rough hand brushed her bruised cheek, hurting her.

Moon backed away, filled with disgust. He laughed and went on past her.

"Listen, Turd," Blodwed said, "you keep away from her! She really has the power—"

He sneered. "Then what's she doing here? You don't believe that superstitious crap, do you, Tech?" He set the broken instrument down in front of Gundhalinu, and a set of tools. "Just don't have too much fun. Because if this isn't working by tomorrow, I'll make you eat it." He flicked the tarnished insignia on Gundhalinu's collar; Moon saw Gundhalinu's thin face go gray and slack.

Taryd Roh turned away from him, strolled back across the chamber to the gate like a killer skule moving through a fish trap.

Blodwed threw an obscene hand-sign after his retreating back. "Gods, I hate him, that bastard!" She winced as the elffox pup woke inside her jacket, squirming and scratching. "He thinks he's the Prime Minister or something, just because he's Ma's favorite. He's been to Carbuncle, and he's crazy too—that's why she likes him so much."

Moon watched Gundhalinu stretch out on the cot, moving like an aged cripple, and turn his face to the wall. She said nothing.

Blodwed pulled the wriggling cub out of her parka and thrust it back into its cage, almost angrily. Moon felt Blodwed search the room with her eyes for something that

331

had disappeared; she kept her own eyes on Gundhalinu. Blodwed dragged the babbling baby to his feet and went out the gate, leaving them to smother in silence.

Moon made her way through the heaviness of the air to Gundhalinu's side, kneeled down. "BZ?" Knowing that he did not want her to ask, knowing that she had to. She touched his shoulder. She felt the trembling of his body even through his heavy coat. "BZ . . ."

"Leave me alone."

"No."

"I'm not one of her animals, for gods' sakes!"

"Neither am I. Don't shut me away!" Her fingers dug into his arm, forcing him to acknowledge her.

He rolled onto his back, lay staring up at her with bleak eyes. "And I didn't think things could get any worse."

Moon looked down, nodded. "Then maybe they'll start getting better."

"Don't." He shook his head. "Don't tell me there's going to be a future. Just facing tomorrow is all I can stand."

She saw the broken instrument that Taryd Roh had left for him on the ground beside her knee. "You can't fix this?"

"Blindfolded," with a broken smile. He lifted his hand. "If I had two good hands. But I don't."

"You have three." Moon clasped his hand like a pledge.

He brought his other hand up, laid it clumsily over hers. "I thank you." He took a long breath, and sat up. "Taryd Roh . . ." he swallowed. "Taryd Roh caught me recircuiting Blodwed's radio. After he'd finished working me over, I couldn't walk for two days. And gods, he *enjoyed* it." He ran his hand through his hair; Moon saw it tremble again. "I don't know what he did while he was in the city—but he was good at it."

Moon shuddered, wiped the memory of Taryd Roh's touch from her face. "Is that—why?" She glanced at his hands, his scarred wrists.

"Everything! Everything was why." He shook his head. "I'm a highborn, a Tech, a Kharemoughi! To be treated like a slave by these savages—worse than a slave! No one

332

with any pride would go on living that way: without honor, without hope. So I tried to do the only honorable thing." He said it with perfect evenness. "But Blodwed found me, before it was—finished."

"She saved you?"

"Of course." Moon heard hatred in it. "What's the point in humiliating a corpse?" He looked down at his useless hand. "A cripple, though. . . . I stopped eating; until she told me she'd let Taryd Roh feed me. Fifteen minutes and he could have me eating shit." He tried to get up, fell back onto the cot, coughing until his eyes ran. "And then there was the storm—" He spread his hands helplessly, as though he wanted her to know how hard he had tried to do the right thing.

Afraid that she did understand, she only said, "And now?"

"And now everything's changed. I . . . have to think about someone besides myself again." She didn't know whether he was glad, or only resentful.

"I'm glad you failed." She looked down. "We'll get out of here, BZ. I know we will." *It isn't finished.* Suddenly certain of it again.

He shook his head. "It doesn't matter to me any more. It's too late, I've been here too long." He lifted her chin with his fingers. "But for your sake, I'll hope."

"It isn't too late."

"You don't understand." He pulled at the seal of his uniform coat. "I've been here for months, it's all over! The Festival, the Change, the final departure . . . everyone's gone offworld by now, they've left me behind. Forever." His gaunt face twitched. " 'In dreams I hear my homeland to me call; and I cannot answer. . . .' "

"But they haven't! It hasn't happened yet."

He gaped as though she had struck him. He pulled her up onto the cot beside him, almost shaking her. "Truly? How long? How long? Oh, gods, tell me it's true!"

"It is," breathlessly, stumbling. "But I don't know h-how long . . . I mean, I'm not sure . . . a week or two, I think, until the celebrations."

"A week?" He let her go, slumping back against the wall. "Moon . . . Damn you, I don't know whether you're heaven or hell: a week." He rubbed his hand across his mouth. "But I think you're heaven." He embraced her, briefly, chastely, his face averted.

She lifted her hands as he pulled away, clung to him with sudden gratitude. "No, don't. A little longer. Please, BZ; I need a little longer. . . . Hold me just for now." *Until everything isn't drowning in ugliness. Until I believe in hope, and feel his arms holding me again. . . .*

Gundhalinu stiffened with surprise and a strange reluctance. But his arms circled her, almost mechanically, and pulled her to him again, sheltering her, answering her.

So long . . . remembering Sparks's tender hands as though it had been only yesterday . . . *it's been so long.* She rested her head on his shoulder, let herself dissolve, mindless, timeless, against the solidity of his flesh; let it give substance to the phantom of another flesh, and strike the chains of bitter knowledge from the future. After a time she felt Gundhalinu's arms tighten, felt his breathing change; felt her own heartbeat quicken unexpectedly with answering emotion.

"Wilt thou . . . to me in Sandhi sometimes talk?" hesitantly.

"Yes." She smiled against his sleeve. "Though I—do not it well speak. . . ."

"I know. Thy accent is terrible." He laughed softly.

"So is thine!" She felt his head rest on her own shoulder; she rubbed his back with slow, peaceful motions, heard him sigh. Gradually his arms loosened and fell away from her; she felt his breathing change again. She lifted her head, saw his face half smiling, asleep beside her own. She lowered him carefully onto the cot, lifted his legs up and covered him with blankets. She kissed him gently on the mouth, and went to her own pad on the floor.

"You fixed it, huh? Lucky for you, Blue-boy." Blodwed stooped down as she entered the chamber, picked up the broken distance-finder, which Gundhalinu and Moon had repaired working together through the new morning. Her voice barely disguised relief; but Gundhalinu heard only the threat, and frowned. "Hey, what did you do that for?"

White birds fluttered up from Moon's shoulders; the pair of starls slunk under the cot at the sound of her voice. "To give them a little freedom," Moon said, more confidently than she felt.

"They'll get out! That's what I keep them in cages for— they'd run away if I didn't, the stupid things."

"No, they won't." Moon held out her palm, filled with bits of bread. The birds circled down again onto her arm, jostling for position. She stroked their curling feathers. "Look. This is all they really want. Keeping them in a cage won't make them yours; not if you know you can't ever open the door."

Blodwed came toward her across the room, the birds flew up again. Moon put the crumbs into Blodwed's hand; but the hand made a fist and she dropped them onto the floor. "Screw that. I don't want that. I want a story, Blue." She moved on across the room to Gundhalinu, sat down on the cot beside him. "About the Old Empire, some more."

He moved away from her pointedly. "I don't know any more stories. You know them all."

"I don't care. Just do it!" She shook his arm. "Read that book again. Read it to her, she's a sibyl too."

Moon glanced up from watching the birds peck at crumbs around her feet.

"Sit, sibyl." Blodwed gestured imperiously. "You'll like this. It's all about the first sibyl that ever was, and the end of the Old Empire. It's got space pirates, and whole artificial planets, and aliens, and superweapons, *zap!*" She disintegrated Moon with her finger, laughing.

"Really?" Moon said, looking at Gundhalinu. "Do they really know about the first sibyl?" He shrugged.

"He said it was all true." Blodwed's enthusiasm and her

voice rose. "Come on, Blue. Read the part where she saves her True Lover from the pirates."

"He saved *her*." Gundhalinu coughed his indignation.

"Look, just read it." She leaned over, the starls scuttled out with clicking claws as she groped under the cot. She found the battered book, tossed it at Gundhalinu. "And in the end, she thinks he's dying, and he thinks she's dead; it's so sad." She grinned ghoulishly.

"Blodwed, I'll tell you a story," Moon said suddenly, clutching inspiration's key. She sat down cross-legged; the starls came to her, scattering the birds, and laid their pointy muzzles in her lap. "About me . . . and my True Lover, and techrunners, and Carbuncle." *And you will listen, and understand.* She felt the strength of the inspiration suddenly take hold of her, almost as though she were compelled.

She told the story again; letting down the barriers that kept her emotions back, letting herself see Sparks's face laughing in sunlight, hear his music drifting over the sea, feel the fire-bright nearness of him . . . feel his going away as it wrenched a part of her soul out of her. And she left nothing out, of the things she had seen and done—

("You mean you didn't even know it'd take five years to go to Kharemough? You really were stupid!")

("I'm learning.")

—the people who had tried to help her; the price they had paid for it. "And then on the man in black, who was killing the mers, I saw the medal, his medal. . . . It was Sparks, I f-finally found him." She looked down, pressing a hand against her purple cheek; remembering only his caress.

"You mean . . . he's Starbuck?" Blodwed whispered, awed. "Holy shit. Your own True Lover killed the mers. . . . And—and you still love him?"

Moon nodded silently; her mouth trembled. *Damn everything, I do!* She held a long breath, fighting for control; struggling back into the present to measure Blodwed's reaction.

Blodwed wiped her eyes surreptitiously, scratched her

head, her cropped-off hair standing out like straw. "Oh . . . it's not fair. Now he's going to die, and he'll never even know."

"What?" Moon stiffened.

"The Change," Gundhalinu said. "The last Festival, the end of Winter. The end of the Snow Queen—and Starbuck. They drown together." He looked back at her with unspoken understanding. "It's the end of everything."

Moon rose up on her knees, pushed the starls away, breaking the spell that had held her holding Blodwed. "Mother of Us All—there's hardly any time left! Blodwed, you have to let us go! I have to find him, I have to get to Carbuncle before the Change."

Blodwed stood up, her face turning hard. "I don't have to do anything! You just made all that up, so I'd let you go. Well, I won't!"

"It's not a lie! Starbuck *is* Sparks, and he'll die . . . I can't have come all this way just for that!" She struggled to keep panic from taking the rest of her voice. "If I can get to Carbuncle, BZ can help me find Sparks in time. And if he doesn't get back there in time, his own people will go offworld and leave him behind. There's not even a fortnight left—"

"Then in a fortnight it'll all be over, and you won't even care about it any more, either of you. So you can stay here with me, forever." Blodwed folded her arms, her eyes fierce with betrayal.

"In a fortnight my life will be meaningless. . . ." Moon got up, feeling the walls of stone close in on her. "Please, please, Blodwed! Help us!"

"I don't care if it's all true! You don't care about me; why should I care about you?" Blodwed caught the sleeve of Moon's tunic and jerked at it, ripping the fragile cloth halfway up her arm. She went out, slamming the gate behind her.

"I don't understand it," BZ murmured, between irony and despair. "The stories I read always have happy endings."

* * *

337

Lying sleepless far into the night, she felt the starls wake suddenly beside her, listening. Listening with them she heard the covert sound of footsteps coming back from the silent camp beyond. She sat up, blinking in the heater's glow. BZ sat up on his cot; she realized that he must have lain awake with her in silent misery half the night. *Oh, Lady, she's changed her mind. . . .*

But the gate swung open, and the figure that took form in the light was not Blodwed. Moon heard Gundhalinu's indrawn breath. She sat as still as death, paralyzed.

"Wake up, little sibyl. I've come for a few of your tricks . . . and to teach you a few of mine." Taryd Roh came on across the chamber, shrugging off his parka.

Moon struggled to her feet, moving in slow motion. *He doesn't believe. . . . Mother, please Mother, let me wake up!* She stumbled back as the dream did not dissolve and her prayers flew up unheeded. She felt Gundhalinu's hands grip her shoulders and pull her to him.

"Leave her alone, you son of a bitch, unless you want to lose what mind you have."

Taryd Roh laughed. "You don't believe that, any more than I do! Keep out of it, Blue, or this time I'll show you what real pain is."

BZ's grip lost all strength on her shoulders. His arms dropped, he backed away. Moon clenched her teeth on a cry. But as Taryd Roh lunged across the gap between them, Gundhalinu moved forward, struck at Taryd Roh's throat with a well-trained blow.

But there was no strength behind it, and Taryd Roh blocked his arm, twisted it, threw him aside into the cages. Gundhalinu pushed away from the wall, but before he could recover his balance Taryd Roh's heavy fist clubbed him to his knees, and a boot knocked him sprawling. And then Taryd Roh had reached her again, his arms were around her. His mouth covered hers; Moon twisted her face frantically until she found his lip. She sank her teeth into it, tasted his blood mingling with her saliva.

He knocked her away with a shout of pain. She half fell, staggering up again as she tried to keep beyond his reach.

338

"You're cursed, Taryd Roh! You have the sibyl-madness now, Motherless, and there's no hope for you!" Her voice shrilled like the screech of the white birds beating above her head. But he still came after her, blood shining on his face and another kind of madness in his eyes. Moon clung to the wire of the locked gate, screaming, "Blodwed! Blodwed!" His hand closed on her neck, she gasped and lost her voice as pain leaped out along her arms, paralyzing her. He jerked her away.

A starl attacked his leg, sinking its thick claws into the cloth of his legging, and on into his flesh. Tusks locked in his calf; he dragged her around, kicking viciously until he threw it off into its circling mate. But as his hands closed around her throat again he suddenly staggered back, losing all his strength. "You bitch!" thick with fear. He put his hands to his head, swaying; toppled and fell, sprawled motionless on the floor.

Moon stood over him, her voice raw. "I'll teach you some tricks, unbeliever." She stepped across his unconscious body, ran back to where Gundhalinu was getting to his feet uncertainly. She tried to steady him with tingling, heavy hands, saw the livid bruise swelling on his forehead. "BZ, are you all right?"

He looked at her incredulously. "Am *I* all right?" He cupped her face in his hands for a long moment, before his arms went around her, holding her close to his heart; she pressed her face against his neck. "Thank the gods . . . thank the gods, we both are."

"All right, what do you think you're—doing?" Blodwed burst in through the gate, stopped short at the sight of Taryd Roh's body on the floor. The starls circled it like hunters over prey, growling threats. She looked up at Moon and Gundhalinu together across the room; Moon saw the question that came into her eyes, and the answer she got without asking. "Did—you do that to him?" Half-afraid.

"I did." Moon nodded, surprised at the calmness of the words. "I infected him."

Blodwed's mouth fell open. "Is he dead?"

"No. But when he wakes up tomorrow he'll—he'll start to go mad. Madder." Moon swallowed suddenly.

Blodwed looked down into Taryd Roh's slack face. She glanced up again, her own face filling with a strange mixture of emotions, anger slowly separating and rising. She reached inside her parka, took out her stunner and adjusted the dial. She leaned down and put the muzzle close to his temple. "No he won't." She pressed the stud; his body jerked.

Moon flinched, felt Gundhalinu stiffen beside her. But she felt no pity, or remorse.

"Good riddance." Blodwed stuck the gun away. "I told him he'd be sorry if he tried to hurt you." She lifted her head, looked back at them with something deeper than possessiveness, and stronger than frustration. "Damn you, now you really did it! When Ma finds out what happened she'll want you skinned alive; and she gets what she wants around here, I can't stop it. Everybody thinks she's holy, but really she's just crazy." She wiped her nose. "All right! All right, don't look at me like that! I'm going to let you go."

Moon swayed as reaction caught her, and slid down to her knees.

The carnivorous predawn cold gnawed Moon, even through the insulated clothing, the gray-brown woolen mask pulled down over her face. The stars crackled on the black dome of sky, the snow lay silvered under a gibbous moon beyond the gaping cavern mouth. "I never saw such a beautiful night."

"Nor I. Not on any world." Gundhalinu shifted beneath the thermal blankets, among the lashed-on supplies at the front of the loaded snowskimmer. "And I never will again, if I live until the New Millennium." He took a deep breath, coughed rackingly as the frigid air assaulted his healing lungs.

"Shut up, will you?" Blodwed reappeared beside them for a last time. "You want to wake up the whole camp? Here." She thrust something into Gundhalinu's lap; Moon recognized three small carrying cages. "Take these back to the starport. They're sick. I can't keep them here." Her voice was as tight as a clenched fist. Gundhalinu worked the cages in under the blankets beside him.

Blodwed moved away to the other animal cages she had piled by the cave entrance. She picked up the first one, unfastening the lock. "And I'm dumping all these damn wild ones, they don't even like *you*," defiantly. Gray-winged birds fluttered out, tumbled astonished to the ground. They picked themselves up from the snow and flew away, crying their freedom. She jerked open a second cage; white-furred conies leaped out in a mass, tumbling over their snowshoe feet, and bounded into the moonlight making no sound at all.

She opened the last cage, shook it; the elffox cub rolled out, spitting its indignation. She pushed it with her foot out into the snow. "Go on, damn it!" The cub sat bleating in confusion, its silver-limned fur standing on end; picked itself up again, shuddering, and struggled back toward warmth and shelter. It found Blodwed's foot in its way, crawled up onto the fur-and-leather of her boot, whimpering.

Blodwed swore, bent down to pick it up. "All right, then . . ." her voice cracked. "I'm keeping the rest!" She looked back at Moon. "But I know how to keep them better now. They'll want to stay with me."

Moon nodded, not trusting her own voice.

"I guess you got everything." Blodwed stroked the cub's head self-consciously. "Even the distance-finder. You better hope you fixed it right, Blue."

"What are you going to do now?" Gundhalinu said. "When you don't have anybody to fix these things—or any way to get more? You've forgotten how to live like real herders and hunters any more—like anything besides parasites."

"I haven't." Blodwed tossed her head. "I know the old ways too. Ma's not going to live forever, no matter what she thinks. I can take care of myself—and everybody else, once I'm in charge. I don't need you, foreigner!" She

341

rubbed her eyes. "Or you." She threw her arms around Moon suddenly. "So you better get out of here. You better go find him, before it's too late!"

Moon hugged her, all wrongs forgotten, all forgiven; felt the elffox squirm between them. "I will!"

Together they pushed the sledge out onto the open snow, and Moon settled behind the controls. She started the power unit, following Gundhalinu's grudgingly surrendered instructions.

"Hey, Blodwed." Gundhalinu twisted to look over his shoulder at her. "Here." He tossed her the battered novel. "I don't expect I'll ever want to read that again." He didn't smile.

"I can't read it either, it's in your language!"

"That's never stopped you before."

"Get out of here, damn you." She waved the book like a threat; but Moon saw her smile.

Moon switched on the headlamp, and they began the final journey northward.

Arienrhod sat enthroned in the audience hall, where before another fortnight had passed she would be receiving the Prime Minister of the entire Hegemony on his last official visit. She wondered idly whether he would pity her. But today it was merely the Commander of Police, and it did not require much imagination to guess the reason for her visit. It must be a sign of how well Starbuck had succeeded that PalaThion had come here herself.

PalaThion left her escort among the gossiping nobles at the far side of the hall, presumably so the two men would not be required to kneel. She was no longer willing to kneel herself, now that she had become Commander—a small victory she had won, the only one. Arienrhod smiled to herself as PalaThion removed her helmet and bowed formally before her. "Your Majesty."

"Commander PalaThion. You look terrible, Commander —you must be working too hard. Your people's departure from Tiamat isn't the end of the world, you know. You should take care of yourself, or you'll be old before your time."

PalaThion looked up at her with ill-concealed hatred, and barely detectable despair. "There are worse things than growing old, Your Majesty."

"I can't imagine one." She leaned back. "To what do I owe this visit, Commander?"

"Two things which I consider worse, Your Majesty: murder, and the illegal slaughter of mers." She sounded as though she believed there shouldn't be any distinction. "I've come with a warrant for the arrest of Starbuck, on charges of murder and of killing mers on land belonging to an offworlder named Ngenet. He has forbidden the Hunt on his plantation, as you know." Her eyes snapped with accusation.

Arienrhod raised her eyebrows, not entirely feigning surprise. "Murder? There must be some mistake, some other explanation."

"I saw one body myself. And the bodies of the mers." PalaThion blinked as the memory came back to her, and her mouth pulled down. "There was no mistake, and there's no other explanation. I want Starbuck, and I want him now . . . Your Majesty."

"Of course, Commander. I want to question him about the charges myself." She had not learned any more about Moon's fleeting reappearance in the short time since it had happened. But now— "Sparks!" She looked away across the whiteness of the room, to where he stood among the nobles who had been displaying their Festival costumes for her perusal. With the resourcefulness of the rich, they had already managed to claim the most beautiful and elaborate specimens of the maskmakers' art, and had costumes designed to match. They stood together like a gathering of

343

beautifully misbegotten beasts, their mutant totem-faces gazing at her impassively, creatures out of a drug fantasy.

Sparks came quickly at her call. She watched him move, seeing how his blue sleeveless jerkin and tight-fitting pants accentuated the litheness of his movement. But his expression was a false face, his listless mourning made him as much of a stranger as any festival mask. He kneeled before her with silent subservience, ignoring PalaThion utterly. She was not certain whether his rudeness was calculated or only guilty; knowing that he felt guilt toward the woman but never understanding why. "Yes, Your Majesty." He looked up.

She gestured for him to rise. "Where is Starbuck, Sparks?"

He gaped at her, recovered himself hastily. "I—uh, I don't know, Your Majesty. He's left the palace. He didn't tell me when he'd be back." He showed her a sardonic hidden smile, and his curiosity. "He doesn't talk to me."

"Commander PalaThion has come to arrest him for murder."

"For murder?" Sparks turned to PalaThion.

Poison showed in PalaThion's eyes as she looked back at him; the poison was still there as she lifted her head again. "How very well he timed that."

"Come now, Commander," irritably. "Do you think I'm a mind reader? And I don't condone murder among my subjects." PalaThion's expression said that she wouldn't be surprised at either one. "I want to know more about this. You said you saw the bodies yourself? Whose bodies?"

"I saw one body—if you don't include the corpses of the mers." PalaThion swallowed, as though it was more to her than simply an unpleasant memory. Sparks toyed with the agates at his belt ends, striking them against his thigh like a whip, grimacing at each blow. "It was the body of a dillyp."

"A Hound!" She couldn't keep the disdain out of her relief.

"No, Your Majesty," coldly. "A dillyp. A free citizen of the Hegemony, a guest of Citizen Ngenet. He had been stabbed. According to Ngenet another of his guests was missing, and she is also presumed to be dead. She was a citizen of this world, a Summer woman named Moon Dawntreader. The mer bodies had been mutilated." She made it as ugly as she could.

"Mutilated?" Sparks said, too loudly.

Arienrhod felt the spotlight of PalaThion's gaze on her as she spoke Moon's name: *She suspects*. But she was prepared for this, and she kept her polite disgust unchanging. "The name is vaguely familiar to me. . . . Is she a relative of yours, Sparks?"

"Yes, Your Majesty." One hand closed over his other wrist; Arienrhod saw his nails bite into his flesh. "If you remember, she was—my cousin."

"You have my condolences." She gave him no warmth.

PalaThion was watching her with something that was neither amazement nor disappointment, but some of both. "She was an illegal returnee. She disappeared about five years ago." Something grated.

"I think I recall the incident." *And I thought it was the end of everything; but it wasn't.*

"What do you mean, the mers were—mutilated?" Sparks said again. "Mutilated how?"

"I have a filmed record of it at headquarters, if you enjoy that sort of thing, Dawntreader."

"Goddamn it, I didn't mean—I want to know what happened to Moon!"

"Sparks." Arienrhod leaned forward in quiet warning. "It's his cousin, after all, Commander. Of course he's concerned about what happened." *Damn him . . .* seeing just how concerned he was.

"They had been—skinned, Your Majesty." PalaThion still frowned tightly.

"Skinned?" She glanced at Sparks with veiled disbelief, saw incomprehension in his eyes. "Starbuck would never do something like that. Why should he?"

"You'd know his reasons better than I would, since he's your man." PalaThion toyed with her weapons belt, coming treacherously close to arrogance. "Who else would have the resources to drown so many mers at once?"

I don't like this. I can't see far enough into it. Arienrhod
probed the transparent convolutions of the throne's arm.
"Well, frankly, Commander, even if he did do it, I don't
see why you're so concerned. He'll be dead soon enough,
when the Change comes." She shrugged with fatalistic acceptance, and a trace of smile.

"The law can't count on that, Your Majesty." PalaThion
looked at her pointedly. "And besides—that would be too
easy on him."

Sparks turned back; stopped himself, running a hand
through his hair.

Arienrhod felt the blood sing unexpectedly in her ears.
"Speak for yourself, offworlder! I suggest you concern
yourself with your own fate after the Change, and leave
ours to us."

"Your fate and mine are bound together, Your Majesty,
since Tiamat belongs to the Hegemony." Arienrhod thought
there was a subtle emphasis on *belongs*. But PalaThion's
confidence cracked even as she made the bluff, and drove
her back into her place. PalaThion knew—yes, knew—that
Winter had plans; but she knew just as surely that she was
helpless to stop them. "In any case, I want Starbuck for
questioning, and I expect that you will cooperate," expecting nothing of the kind.

"I'll do what I can to get this unpleasantness straightened out, of course." Arienrhod untangled the free-falling
collar of crystal beads that cascaded down her silver shirt.
"But Starbuck is his own man, he comes and goes as he
pleases. I don't know when I'll see him next."

PalaThion's mouth twisted skeptically. "My men will be
looking for him too. But of course it would help me more
if you'd tell me his name."

Arienrhod gestured Sparks up onto the dais, stroked his
bare arm with her hand. She felt it quiver as though her
touch burned him with cold fire. "I'm sorry, Commander. I
can't reveal his identity to anyone; that would be a viola-
tion of trust, of the whole concept of his position. But I
will keep my eyes open for him . . ." She reached up to
touch a lock of Sparks's hair, curled it around her finger;

346

he only looked at her with sudden apprehension. She smiled, and he smiled, uncertain.

"I can find it out for myself. And when I do, I'll get him!" PalaThion bowed with all the appearance of propriety, and strode away.

Sparks laughed tightly, a release of tension. "Right in front of her eyes!"

Arienrhod allowed herself to join him, without any real pleasure; remembering a time when laughter was a simple thing, with its roots in joy, not pain. . . . "What a shame she'll never appreciate what she missed." *But I need to make certain of that.* "Starbuck will have to wear the mask of Everyman for a while."

Sparks nodded, suddenly sober. "That's all right with me," as suddenly bitter.

"What happened on that beach?" She leaned toward him, holding him with her eyes.

"I told you everything I know, everything I saw! We killed the mers in the usual way, and we left them for Ngenet to find. We didn't do anything else." He folded his arms in front of him. "I don't know what happened after that. By'r Lady, I wish I did. . . ." a miserable prayer of loss and longing.

She looked away from him, feeling her face pinch with an unnameable emotion. *Do you? Then by all the gods, I hope you never find out!*

"Lady's Eyes!" The snowskimmer slewed to a halt.

Gundhalinu echoed the muffled curse of Moon's exasperation silently. A new stretch of bare, stony ground blocked their path up the exposed face of another hillside. He had never seen, or expected to see, the land beyond the spaceport when it was not covered by meters of drifted snow. But Tiamat had reached orbital summer again while he had been held prisoner; and it was entering the high summer of the Change as well—when the Twins reached the periapsis of their path around the Black Gate. The Gate's gravitational influence was increasing the solar activity of the twin suns; slowly thawing this frozen world, gradually turning the equatorial regions insufferably hot.

In the past few days, as they made their way down out of the black and silver wilderness where the bandits camped, the weather had smiled on them. The vast, shining solitude had stretched a pristine carpet below the glacier-bitten volcanic peaks, beneath the flawless purity of the sky, day after day. And with every passing day, although they journeyed northward, the temperature edged up and up toward freezing, and passed it at the suns' zenith. Their gratitude had turned to curses of frustration as more and more patches of naked stone and tundra blocked the snow-skimmer's way.

He crawled out from under the pile of skins and blankets, trudged to the front of the sledge and leaned down to lift the runners and the fragile underside clear. Moon threw her weight against the rear of it, and together they dragged it up the endless slope. He watched the sun-cast giants that mimicked their stumbling progress, trying to ignore the bands of red-hot metal tightening in his chest— and the awareness that his weakness forced a girl to do all the heavy work; the awareness that she did it quite adequately alone, and without complaint.

They reached the crest of the hill, the snowy downslope, at last. He let out the breath he had been holding, and the spasm of deep coughing he had held in with it. He felt Moon come up beside him, pulling him back to his seat on the sledge.

"How much longer, BZ?" She frowned, pulling furs up under his chin again like a fretful nanny. She had no herbal medicines now, and he knew that she knew the cough was worse again.

He smiled briefly, shook his head. "Soon. Maybe an-

other day, we'll be there." *The starport. Salvation. Heaven.*
He didn't admit that he couldn't remember now whether it
had been five or six days that they had been journeying. He
never let himself believe that it had been too long, or that
his calculations might be wrong.

"I think we should make camp down there." Moon
pointed; he saw her shiver as an ice-barbed lash of wind
struck the spine of the hill. "The suns are setting already."
She looked out across the infinity of hills falling toward the
distant sea, looked up into the deepening indigo sky. "It's
getting too cold for you to travel." He heard her sudden
indrawn breath, louder than the wind's sigh. "BZ!"

He looked up, following her hand, not knowing what he
expected, but only that it was not what he found.

Out of the blue-black zenith stars were falling. But not
the broken-glass stars of this winter world—these were the
stars that shone in dreams, stars that a man would die for,
the stars of empire, grandeur, glory . . . the impossible
made real.

"What—what are they?" He heard in Moon's voice the
awe and the dread of countless natives on seven separate
worlds down through a millennium, as they witnessed what
she was witnessing now.

The five starships grew against the sky with every heartbeat, the harmonies of color and intensity shifting and
reordering as parallaxes changed, building complexity on
complexity like light poured through prisms of flowing
water. He watched the five ships slowly realigning, moving
into a cross pattern; saw the lightning-play of their cold fire
spreading, coalescing, into one immense star, the sign of
the Hegemony. The colors blazed with a music he could
almost hear, filling the sky with all the hues, all the impossible permutations of an aurora-filled night sky on his
homeworld. . . .

"The Prime Minister? Is it the Prime Minister?" Moon's
words came to him muffled by her protective face mask,
and her upraised hand.

He swallowed, and swallowed again, unable to answer.

"They're ships!" She went on answering her own questions. "They're only ships. How can they be real, and be so beautiful?"

"They're Kharemoughi." He might have said "the Empire"; he might have said "gods." He did not say that they were only coin ships wrapped in cloaks of hologrammic projection to astound a subject world. He looked back at her, glory blind, and took her smile at face value.

"Are they?" She touched his cheek, turned back to the sky as the formation split apart again, the flames died away and embers fell to earth . . . behind the hills, scarcely two ridges away. "Look!" She shook off her wonder. "That must be the starport! BZ, we're almost there. We could reach it tonight." Frost clouds feathered around her cheeks. "We're on time!"

"Yes." He took a deep breath. "Plenty of time. Thank the gods." He watched the last of the ships snuff out behind the snowy hills. *Tonight.* . . . "There's no need to push on tonight. One more day won't matter. Tomorrow is soon enough."

She glanced at him, surprised. "It's only a couple of hours. It's as easy as if I set up camp."

He shrugged, still looking into the distance. "Maybe so." He began to cough, smothered it behind his hand.

She put a mitten to his forehead, as though she were feeling for a fever. "The sooner you see a healer—a medic —the better," firmly.

"Yes, Nanny."

She poked him. He grinned, eagerness coming back into him, as she started the power unit. The snowskimmer slipped quietly over the ridge and into the valley, blotting out even the afterglow of the ships' landing. Hours . . . only hours, until he would rejoin the living, regain the life he had almost lost forever, the only life worth living. Gods, yes, he wanted to reach the starport tonight!

Then why had he said "tomorrow" to her? *Tomorrow is soon enough.* He moved his hands under the blankets, shifting Blodwed's caged pets that shared the warmth of his body—only two of them now. The green bird had died, three or four nights ago. In the morning they had made a small grave in the crusted snow. *There but for you go I. . . .* He had spoken those words aloud to her, kneeling in the snow beneath the silent witness of heaven.

And he had spoken them with his eyes at every new dawn's light, when he woke to find himself a free man, and see her beside him in the bubble tent—close enough to touch, but never touching, since that one night. He had watched her unguarded sleep, the dreams that moved across her face . . . the fair face and the snowy tumbled hair, the wild, unnatural paleness of her, more familiar to him now than his own darkness, suddenly grown beautiful and right. In his mind he had held her again, kissed her lips to wake her to the day . . . and in this timeless wilderness he was free in a way that he had never been free, from his past and his future, the rigid codes that defined his existence. Here he drifted formlessly, an embryo, and he felt no shame at his yearning for a barbarian girl with eyes like mist and agate.

And he had seen her wake from troubled dreams to his imaginary kiss, lie looking back at him with a drowsy smile. He had seen the awareness fill her eyes, knew the hesitant answering desire that filled her, too. But only his eyes had asked, and only her eyes had answered him. And now there would never be one more morning. . . .

They crested a final hill, cold and aching, and the starport's muted dawn-glow opened out before them like a midnight sun rising. The low dome of the subterranean complex was a vast bruise on the seaward plain, almost a city in its own right; unearthly light suffused its curving surface. There was no sign now of the starships' landing: the dome's impervious surface was unbroken by any opening. Away on the sea's horizon he saw the winking shell-form of unsleeping Carbuncle.

Gundhalinu sighed, easing the painful tightness in his chest. Moon sat silently behind the controls; he wondered whether awe at the sight of the first starport she had ever

351

seen had put her into stasis—until he remembered that it was not her first starport. Her hand reached out suddenly and pressed his shoulder, in a gesture that asked reassurance more than offered it. He lifted his own hand to cover hers; found that it would not close. He dropped it again. "Don't worry," woodenly, inadequately. "We'd better angle left, make the approach toward the main entrance. Security will be upped a mag for the state visit—I don't want to be a casualty to caution."

She obeyed, still without answering him. Caught in his own sudden inability to reach her, to reassure her or even himself, he watched the dome grow ahead.

They were still a hundred meters out from the main surface entrance when light flooded around them and a disembodied voice ordered them to a halt. Four men wearing the blue uniform he'd almost forgotten the look of approached cautiously; he knew that more were observing the snowskimmer from inside. The face shields on their helmets were down; he couldn't recognize any of them. But the knowledge that they were his own people did not comfort or reassure him. Instead he sat frozen with guilty unease, as though he had been a criminal and not a victim.

"You're trespassing in a restricted area." He recognized a sergeant's insignia, but not the voice. "Clear out, Mother lovers, and if you brought more of your thieving clan along, take 'em with you, before we use you for target practice."

Gundhalinu stiffened. "Who the hell taught you procedure, Sergeant?"

The sergeant drew back in mock surprise. "Who the hell wants to know?" He gestured with his hand. Two of his men closed in around Moon, the third dragged Gundhalinu up from his place on the sledge. His legs gave way and he sat down unceremoniously in the snow.

"Leave him alone, damn you!"

"Get your hands off her!" His own angry protest overran Moon's as she started toward him and the two men jerked her back. He pushed down his hood, peeled off the scratchy

352

weather mask that disguised his face. He spoke deliberately in Klostan, the primary language of Newhaven: "I tell you 'who wants to know,' Sergeant. Police Inspector Gundhalinu wants to know."

The sergeant pushed back his helmet shield, staring. "Ye gods—"

"Gundhalinu's dead!" The third patrolman looked down into his face. "Millennium come, it is him!"

Moon pulled free, came forward and helped him up. Gundhalinu brushed off his leggings, straightened with slow dignity. "The reports of my death were premature." He put his arm around her, leaning heavily on her shoulder.

"Inspector." The sergeant jerked to attention. Gundhalinu put a name to his face, TessraBarde. "We thought the bandits got you, sir. Give him a hand there—"

"I'm fine." Gundhalinu shook his head as Moon's grip tightened protectively, defensively, refusing to separate herself from him. "I'm just fine now," suddenly oblivious to cold and fatigue, warm and strong with relief.

"Welcome back, Inspector! You made it just in time." One of the men gripped his hand, peered curiously at Moon: Gundhalinu felt implications forming. "Who's your Mother loving friend?"

"It's good to be back; you can't imagine how good." He glanced at Moon's unmasked face, saw the frightened question on it, and understood at last that a part of her silent uncertainty had centered on him. He smiled a promise, felt her grip on him ease. "My companion was a prisoner along with me. And before I say anything more about either of us—" postponing the moment when he knew he would have to lie, "we could use a hot meal and a chance to sit down." He coughed rackingly, making his point.

"Inspector, as you know, sir—" he heard TessraBarde's emphasis, "the, uh, locals aren't permitted in the complex."

"By all the gods, Sergeant!" He had no patience left. "If Winter bandits weren't getting into the goddamn complex I wouldn't be standing here half-dead! And if it wasn't for this woman I wouldn't be standing here at all." He started

353

toward the tunnel entrance, Moon supporting him. "Bring our sledge."

There were no more objections.

Jerusha rubbed her eyes, stifled a yawn with a quick shifting of her hand. The drone of half a hundred conversations rolled over and around her, rose to the ceiling and were deflected back in a numbing assault. She had been awake for twenty hours already today, after another night of broken sleep; even this position of honor, seated at the head table in the hall among the demigods of the Hegemonic Assembly, had turned into just one more test of endurance. By the shipboard time of the Prime Minister and the Assembly, this was the middle of the day and not the middle of the night; and so it became for everyone delegated to welcome them as well.

She had shaken hands with Prime Minister Ashwini himself tonight, wearing the dress uniform of a Commander of Police, weighted down by enough glorious braid and brass to give the sun competition. Or so she had thought, until she had seen his own state garments, gembrocaded, exquisitely tailored to show every line of his still-youthful body.... How old was he, in real time? Four hundred? Five hundred? Even Arienrhod must feel a jealous twinge at the sight of all he represented. (It filled her with secret pleasure that Arienrhod was not permitted to attend this banquet.) Prime Minister for life, he had succeeded his father as a Hegemonic showpiece in the centuries after Kharemough's dreams of dominating its fellow worlds had been laid low by the ultimate indifference of galactic space-time. He had greeted her with polite gallantry, in which she had read his private incredulity at finding her to be a woman. Chief Justice Hovanesse was seated beside him now, but she was almost indifferent to the sort of reports he was hearing about her.

A servo eased in beside her, deftly removed the sixth or seventh untouched course of her meal and put down another in front of her. She sipped at her tea, watching the oils eddy on its steaming reddish-black surface. It had steeped until the spoon must be ready to dissolve, and she hoped that it would be enough to keep her awake.

"Be we keeping you from an honest night's sleep, Commander?"

Jerusha turned guiltily to look at the man on her right, the First Secretary, Temmon Ashwini Sirus, a natural son of the Prime Minister. He was a handsome man, fair skinned and large boned for a Kharemoughi, and just about entering middle age. The latter surprised her, because the Prime Minister himself looked younger. But it was hardly as surprising as finding a halfbreed among the members of the Assembly, that ultimate repository of Kharemoughi arrogance. Apparently he had earned considerable fame as a warrior-statesman on his homeworld, and that had moved the Prime Minister to break with tradition and 'elect' him to a vacant Assembly post. She had made banal conversation with him for the first hour or so, and with the royally dressed Speaker on her left, whose heavy cologne had started her sneezing. But the talk had died a self-conscious death, and she had been grateful when they let their attention be drawn elsewhere. "No, of course not, Secretary Sirus," remembering her manners at last. She ran a finger along under the braid-rough edge of her high collar.

"You hardly touch your meal. And after all the trouble your finest chefs go to to please us. This canawba rind be excellent." He spoke Klostan easily; an accomplished linguist, like most Kharemoughi Techs. *But what else has he got to do with his time?*

She smiled insipidly. *Gods, get me out of here—* "I not eat many twelve-course dinners in my line of work." Her own language felt more foreign on her tongue than Tiamatan, after so many years. "I guess I not be up to the challenge." *Any challenge, any more.*

"Try the melon, Commander." He nodded as she picked up her serrated spoon obediently. "To enjoy good food be the only way to survive the excruciating boredom of these state affairs, I say. And to drink good liquors—"

So that's what loosened your tongue. She ate another

355

spoonful of melon, suddenly realizing that against her will she had enjoyed it. *Oh, what the hell—live in a dream world for an hour; it'll have to last you a lifetime. Pretend that it's all turned out the way you wanted it to, that it won't all end with the final departure.* She looked out across the windowed hall, into the awesome, red-gold pit of the landing field, where the ships of the Assembly had come to rest like dim cinders, like a thousand other battered coin ships, after the fiery splendor of their descent. The energized grids of the field and its peripheral bays were crusted with light, like the congealing surface of a lava flow. And for a moment she felt a surge of pride and pleasure at the sight of humanity's most incredible accomplishments, at her presence among its first citizens, at the ever more glorious future that lay ahead . . . the siren promise that had lured her away from her homeworld. *And for what . . . ?* She looked back again along the tree-form of the banquet tables, the faces like animate leaves shifting in a wind, to Sirus's face, thinking suddenly, painfully, *BZ . . . this moment should have belonged to you, not me.*

"Tell me, Commander, how happened you to—"

"Excuse me, Commander." The sergeant of the guard intruded on their space with apologetic effrontery. "Excuse me, sir," to the First Secretary.

"What is it, TessraBarde?" Jerusha couldn't recognize the peculiar urgency in his tone.

"I'm sorry to interrupt you, ma'am, but I thought you'd want to know—we just got Inspector Gundhalinu back."

Jerusha's spoon clattered on the petals of her flower-form dish. "He's dead."

"No, ma'am, I saw him myself. Some native woman brought him in. We've got a medic checking him over now, down in the hospital—"

"Where is he?" Jerusha threw the question at the nearest technician as she entered the examining room from the hall of the hospital wing. She had left TessraBarde to make an explanation to the First Secretary, hoping but not really caring if her apologies had been sufficient. "Inspector Gundhalinu—"

"In there, Commander." The woman pointed with her chin, hands full of equipment.

Jerusha went on through the second doorway without stopping, still only half believing that the room would not be empty. "Gundhalinu!" It was not empty, and his name burst out of her with more feeling than she had intended.

He turned to look at her from where he sat, feet hanging over the edge of the examining table, stripped to the waist while a blue-clad med tech ran a diagnosticator down his chest. She counted each and every rib standing out like staves along his side. She saw his face, felt disbelief as it registered: gaunt, unshaven, gap toothed. She saw him grope for a shirt that wasn't there as she came to a stop before him. He waved the medic away, moved his hands in the air, and finally folded them across his chest like an embarrassed little boy. "Commander—"

Yes, by all the gods; it is you, BZ. . . . She controlled the urge to ruin his dignity and her own completely by embracing him like a mother. "If you aren't a sight for sore eyes, Gundhalinu," grinning until she thought she couldn't stand it.

"Gods! Excuse me, Commander; I didn't mean to see you looking like this . . . that is, I meant, presentably—"

"BZ, all I give a damn about is whether that body's the real thing. If it is, then this celebration upstairs isn't pointless after all."

His face fumbled with a smile. "As real as they come." He slouched forward, putting up a hand to catch an ugly cough.

"Are you all right? What's wrong with him, medic?" Jerusha turned to the technician, realized for the first time that there was a fourth person in the room, sitting quietly in the corner.

The medic shrugged. "Exhaustion. Walking pneumo—"

"Nothing a couple of antibiotic lozenges can't take care of," Gundhalinu said abruptly, cutting him off. "And a hot meal for my friend and me." He glanced at the silent fourth party with a quick smile, focused official disapproval on the medic like a gun.

"I'll see what I can do, Inspector." The technician left the room, his face utterly expressionless. Jerusha wondered whether he was hiding irritation or simply laughter.

"If I'd known, I would have brought you my leftovers. The first half of my state dinner would have fed the starving masses of a planet." Curiosity pulled her around even as she spoke, looking past sinks and shelves filled with medical obscurities, to study their silent observer. A fair-skinned girl draped in a white parka, with a yellowing bruise on her face; *a native?* Jerusha frowned. The girl looked back at her, not with the cowed timidity she had expected, but with a measuring stare. And there was something familiar—

Gundhalinu followed her gaze, said almost too quickly, "Commander, this is the Summer woman who saved my life, who got me back in time for the final departure. Moon, come and meet Commander PalaThion; if there's anyone on this planet who can help you reach your cousin, she can." He looked back. "I was taken prisoner by bandits, ma'am, and so was she. But she—"

Jerusha let his words roll over her unheeded. *Moon . . . Summer . . . Moon Dawntreader Summer!* The kidnapped innocent, Ngenet's murdered guest, the Queen's lost clone . . . *the Queen's clone.* Yes, she knew that face now, now that she saw it clearly at last. A cold tremor fell through her: *What is she doing here? How can she be here, how can she be the one who brought him back? Not her—* The girl came to stand beside Gundhalinu; his hand closed over hers protectively. *Doesn't he know she's proscribed; doesn't he remember her?* "Commander PalaThion?" Moon smiled with subtle anxiety.

"What are you doing—"

"Commander, I take responsibility for bringing her—" Gundhalinu broke off as a crowd of voices filled the outer room. Jerusha saw his face light up, and then flash panic, as he realized what language they spoke. "Sainted—!

358

Commander. . . . Moon," jerking the parka off her back, "I need your coat."

Moon let him take it, even helped him struggle into the sleeves as though she somehow understood his embarrassment. He slid to his feet alongside the table, sealing the jacket up the front as the First Secretary and the Speaker entered, trailing an exquisite wake of half a dozen banquet guests and their companions. Jerusha saluted them, saw Gundhalinu salute in a rictus of pride.

"Commander." First Secretary Sirus acknowledged them with a nod. "When we learned that the lost officer was one of our own people, we decided that we ought to come and congratulate him ourselves on his safe return." He looked at Gundhalinu, and at Moon; back at Gundhalinu again, as though he couldn't believe a Kharemoughi had ever looked like that.

"Inspector BZ Gundhalinu, *sadhu*." Gundhalinu saluted again as though he had to prove it. Jerusha was suddenly glad that she had spent the last month of sleepless nights listlessly learning spoken Sandhi for this occasion. She still could not sort out the convolutions of the rank forms. "Technician of the second rank. *Sadhanu, bhai,* I—I thank you all for coming. This is the greatest honor, the highest moment of my life."

"Gundhalinu-*eshkrad*." Sirus's expression eased at the compliment, and at the reassurance that they were, at least, in the presence of a highborn. "You bring your class and family prestige, at such a young age already an inspector to be."

"Thank you, *sadhu*." Gundhalinu's freckles reddened. He tried to hold back a fit of thick coughing, failed; they waited with polite sympathy.

"He has my best officer been. I've him sorely missed." Jerusha took pleasure in Gundhalinu's swift glance filled with surprise, at the tribute, at hearing it in Sandhi. Moon stood silent between them, with a private smile on her face. Jerusha noticed for the first time the tunic the girl was wearing; its colors heightened the alienness of her pale skin and light-silvered hair. It was the traditional costume of the

Winter nomads; she had seen one once displayed as a rarity in the window of an antique shop in the Maze. *Who are you, girl?*

But she heard only Secretary Sirus introducing himself, holding up a palm for the Kharemoughi equivalent of a handshake. Moon went unexpectedly rigid at the sound of his name. Gundhalinu stepped forward, raising his own hand. A second of discomfort passed like an electric spark between them before their palms met: She saw that Gundhalinu's hand would not open fully; the fingers were drawn up like claws. She saw the pink-white scars ridging his inner wrist next. *Oh, gods, BZ—*

Sirus went on with the introductions. Gundhalinu kept a straight face as the perfumed Speaker refused to touch his hand. *Does he think it's catching?* Jerusha frowned. She knew a slashed wrist when she saw one, knew the Kharemoughis, being what they were, would recognize it, too.

"You—must terrible hardships have suffered, lost in the wilderness after your patrolcraft crashed, Inspector Gundhalinu." Sirus's words were a springboard for an explanation.

"I—I wasn't in the wilderness lost, Secretary Sirus," Gundhalinu said woodenly. "I was by bandits prisoner made. They treated me—badly." He looked down under the weight of their combined gaze, pressed his wrists together. "If not for this woman here, I would never back have gotten. She saved my life." He reached out, caught Moon's elbow and drew her forward. "This is Moon Dawntreader Summer." His expression as he glanced at her told her the honor she was being paid. She smiled at him, looked back at Sirus with sudden intentness.

"A *native*?" the Speaker said, loud with drink. "An ignorant barbarian girl has a Kharemoughi inspector rescued? It doesn't me amuse, Gundhalinu-*eshkrad*, not at all."

"No humor was intended." Gundhalinu raised his head, his own voice suddenly soft and cold. Jerusha looked a warning at him, but he didn't see it. "She's no ignorant savage. She's the wisest, the noblest human being in this room. She is a sibyl." He pulled aside the collar of her

360

tunic carefully; she lifted her chin with pride to expose a half-healed knife wound and a trefoil tattoo. Jerusha grimaced. *By the Boatman, now you've done it!*

Caught off guard, instinctive reaction filled their watching faces; but the Speaker was too deeply in his cups for respect or even good manners. "What does that on this world mean? Put her in a robe and call her *eshkrad*, but that won't her a Technician make. A sibyl on this world ..." He choked off as someone seized him from behind, muttered sharp, unintelligible words at his ear.

But Jerusha was watching the girl, and saw her cheeks color as if she had understood every word. She stepped away from Gundhalinu, her arms stiffly at her sides, and said in stilted Sandhi, "I am only a cup that knowledge holds. It does not to knowledge matter how poor the cup is. It is the wisdom of those who drink of me that me wise makes. Fools make a sibyl foolish, wher*ever* she is." Jerusha flinched at the irony.

The Kharemoughi expressions rippled with astonishment. "We meant you no offense," Sirus said swiftly, placatingly. "Since you are a holy woman to your own people, you deserve our respect as well, sibyl." A small, self-deprecating smile. "But where did she Sandhi learn, Commander?"

"I taught it to her," Gundhalinu said, before Jerusha could fill her mouth with the obvious response. Gundhalinu put his arm around Moon's shoulders, drew her back to him, closed her in. "And with due respect to the honorable Speaker, I wish to say that if I her Gundhalinu-*eshkrad* made, if she my wife were, she would the honor of my entire class raise."

The astonishment verged on horror this time. Jerusha stared with the rest. "—appalled"—a woman's voice from somewhere in the rear among them.

"Gundhalinu-*eshkrad*," Sirus shifted position uncomfortably, "you have a great hardship endured, we understand that. ..."

Gundhalinu faltered under the unanimity of their censure. His arms loosened, but his hands still rested on

361

Moon's shoulders. "Yes, *sadhu*," apologetically. "But I will not her insulted hear. She saved my life."

"Of course." Sirus smiled again. "But you don't her intend to marry—" He glanced from side to side.

"She loves another," almost sadly. Moon turned under his hands to look at him.

"Then you would her marry?" the Speaker said indignantly. "Have you no pride left? Are you so degenerate? To say such a thing without shame! You're already a failed-suicide!" The word also meant *coward*.

Gundhalinu sucked in a breath, coughing. "I attempted the honorable thing. It isn't my fault if I failed!" He held out his hands.

"It is always the fault of a truly superior man when he fails." Another official, one Jerusha didn't recognize. "A failed-suicide doesn't deserve to live."

Gundhalinu's battered shield of self-worth fell apart entirely; he stumbled back the few steps to the examining table, clung there as though the very words were a mortal blow. "Forgive me, *sadhanu, bhai*, for—for disgracing my class and my family." He could not even look at them. "I never deserved the honor of your respect, or even your presence. But I deserve your scorn and your execration fully. I am no better than a slave, a crawling animal." His arms trembled; Jerusha moved quickly to support him before he collapsed.

"What's the matter with you people!" She threw the accusation over her shoulder, heedless. "What do you want from him? Do you want him to slash his wrists again, do you want to watch his 'honor' drain into the sink?" She waved a hand. "One of your own people, a brave, decent officer, has gone through hell and was strong enough to survive; and all you can say to him is 'drop dead'!"

"You're not one of us, Commander," Sirus said quietly. "Gundhalinu . . . understands. But you never could."

"Thank the gods for that." Jerusha helped Gundhalinu up onto the table, not acknowledging their departure as the muttering officials began to leave the room. She heard the Speaker's voice rise to the surface of sound deliberately, to

362

call Gundhalinu by a form of address reserved for the lowest Unclassified. Gundhalinu's mouth quivered; he swallowed convulsively.

"Citizen Sirus!"

Jerusha found Moon's voice an excuse to turn away while Gundhalinu got control of himself. She saw Sirus hesitate in the doorway, and the girl's struggle to curb her own white anger as she looked at him. It was successful; Jerusha saw the anger submerged by another more urgent emotion.

"I—I must to you speak."

Sirus raised his eyebrows, glanced toward Gundhalinu. "I think that too many words already have been said."

She shook her head with stubborn resolution, her lank, pale hair flopping. "About—about someone else."

"Do you as a sibyl ask?"

Another shake. "I ask as your niece." His limbs stopped trying to move him through the doorway. The rear guard of the departing Kharemoughis looked back, tittered scandal as they went on out into the hallway. Jerusha blinked, felt Gundhalinu straighten up beside her. "About your son. From the last Festival."

Sirus's eyes looked briefly into the past. He nodded once, and with another glance their way beckoned Moon into the other room. She went after him, looking back.

Gundhalinu's eyes followed her, as though to lose sight of her now would be more than he could endure; but his face was hopeless.

"BZ . . . Inspector Gundhalinu." Jerusha demanded his attention with a sharpened voice.

"Ma'am." His head swung back obediently, but his attention did not come with it.

Jerusha hesitated, suddenly unsure of what she was about to do. "BZ . . . you aren't really in love with that girl, are you?"

His throat worked. "And what if I am, Commander?" too evenly. "It may be a scandal, but it's not a crime."

"BZ, don't you realize who she is?"

He glanced up, and she read his guilt. He didn't answer.

363

"She's the girl we lost to the techrunners five years ago," telling him what he already knew, hoping that would be enough. "She's proscribed, an illegal returnee. She'll have to be deported."

"Commander, I can't—" His good hand tightened on the padded tabletop.

"If you're really in love with her, BZ, then it doesn't have to be a problem." She smiled encouragingly. "Marry her. Take her off as your wife."

"I can't." He picked up a spine-sharp probe from the tray at the end of the table, tested it against his palm.

She said hastily, "You're not going to let those hypocritical snobs—"

"It's not that." He stiffened. "And you will not speak of the Hegemony's leaders in such a manner. They had every right to criticize me."

Jerusha opened her mouth, closed it again.

"Moon wouldn't marry me." He put the probe down again. "She's—uh, pledged," as though that unofficial bond was still improper in some part of his mind. "To her cousin ... First Secretary Sirus's son." He looked toward the doorway again, incredulously. "She's in love with him. She's been trying all this time to get to Carbuncle to look for him." He spoke the facts flatly, like someone reading a report. "His name is Sparks Dawntreader."

"Sparks?"

"You know him?"

"Yes. And so do you. We saved him from slavers once, the day of your last visit to the palace. After that Arienrhod picked him up; he's been one of her favorites at court ever since. And it's turned him rotten."

Gundhalinu frowned. "Then it's possible. . . . "

"What is?"

"Moon thinks he's become Starbuck."

"Starbuck!" Jerusha put a hand to her forehead. "Yes—yes, it does fit. Thank you, gods! And thank *you*." She turned back to him grimly. "I've been trying to learn who Starbuck is, so I can nail him for murder, and illegally killing mers."

364

"Murder?" Gundhalinu started.

She nodded. "He murdered a dillyp, or let his Hounds do it. And I thought he'd murdered Moon too . . . but it's still enough. This time I'll sting Arienrhod where it hurts!" *So you've gone rottener than I ever dreamed, Dawntreader.* She saw in her mind a battered boy with a smashed flute, a killer in black against the image of a corpse-strewn shore. *Never in my wildest nightmares did I imagine you'd fall so high.*

"I—promised Moon that we'd find him . . . help him, if we could. The Change will get him anyway, if we can't."

"Don't be so sure of that. So Moon still wants him back, even after what she must have seen him do on that beach?" Jerusha was struck by the sudden disconcerting realization that Sparks had belonged to both Arienrhod and Moon . . . and still did. *Arienrhod's clone.*

"How did you know about that?" Gundhalinu said.

"Never mind." Jerusha reached out, touched a conical metal device attached to sensor pads.

"She says she still loves him. You don't simply stop, after years. . . . She only wants to know whether he feels the same way about her." A glimmer of lost hope surfaced. *Is that really all she wants?* "I can't let her loose in the city, BZ." Jerusha shook her head, fingering brass on her collar. "I'm sorry. But I can't risk it."

"I don't understand. She's not going to contaminate anyone. I'll stay with her until we find him."

"And then what?"

He lifted his hands, dropped them again. "I don't know. . . . Commander, the Change is almost here, and when it happens it's not going to matter whether she's been offworld or not. The Summers hate the whole idea. She was only on Kharemough a few weeks. What harm can she do?"

"You're asking me what harm a sibyl can do here, when she knows the reason for her existence?" almost angrily. "If we manage to pick up Starbuck, she can share a cell with him. But otherwise, believe me, it's better for all concerned if she never sees him again, and he never sees her."

"I can't believe I'm hearing that from you." The words were heavy with sullen accusation.

"And I can't believe I'm hearing you say she's no threat, Gundhalinu! What the hell's gotten into you?" *Don't push me, BZ. Be a good Blue, and accept it; don't make me hurt you now.*

"I care about her. It seems to me that ought to mean something." He began to cough, pressing his chest.

"More than your duty to the law?"

"She's just one innocent Summer girl! Why the hell can't we leave it alone?" It had the sound of a man in torment; Jerusha realized that he was his own most unforgiving inquisitor.

"She's not just another Summer, BZ," she said with heavy reluctance. "Haven't you ever noticed how much she resembles Arienrhod?"

His expression said that she was out of her mind.

"I'm serious, Gundhalinu! I have every reason to believe the Queen got herself cloned somehow. And the only reason she could possibly have for that would be that she doesn't want Winter to end." She told him everything, every detail of the circumstantial evidence. "So you see— Moon is a sibyl. I can't risk letting Arienrhod get her hands on—on *herself*, carrying a deadly weapon like that. She's doing all she can to hold on to her power." *And go on corrupting everything she touches on this world.* "But I'm doing anything I can to make sure she doesn't get away with it. And that includes keeping Moon out of her hands."

"I can't believe that." Gundhalinu shook his head, and she realized that he couldn't. "Moon—Moon is like no one I ever met. She's nothing like Arienrhod! She cares about everyone, everything—and they feel it in her. If there's a spark of decency in a man or woman she makes it catch fire. They fall in love with her . . . they can't help it." An inane smile turned up the corners of his mouth.

Jerusha grimaced. "For gods' sakes, BZ, nobody's that wonderful."

"She is. Just talk to her."

"I'd better not even look at her, if she's all you claim.

No wonder they say 'love is blind,' " gently. She felt her own apologetic smile grow as healthy resentment turned his mouth into a line. "Your perspective is out of synch, BZ, that's all. You need a good meal and a lot of sleep, and time to believe you're back in the world you belong to."

"Don't patronize me!" He hit the instrument tray, things leaped and glittered. Jerusha winced. "I know where I am, and I don't belong here any more! I'm not fit to be a police inspector, I'm not fit to belong to the human race. All I want is to keep the one promise I'm still capable of keeping, to the one person who doesn't give a damn what I've become. And now you're trying to tell me she's a monster; and that I have to keep her from the one thing she wants when it's almost in her hands!"

"I'm telling you it's your duty as a police officer to protect the Hegemony! That has to come first. You can't start bending the law to fit your personal tastes. It doesn't work that way." *I should know.*

"Then I resign."

"I don't accept your resignation. You're in no state to offer it—and you're too valuable to me. I need every man I've got until that final ship goes up." She knew as she spoke that there was infinitely more at stake: a career, a man's self-respect, maybe even his life. "Listen to me; please, BZ. You know I wouldn't have told you all this unless I believed it. Arienrhod is a threat!" *And a monster and a disease.* "She's a danger to the Hegemony, and that makes Moon a danger," *whatever she is.* "And Starbuck is a vicious murderer, who's killed whatever Sparks Dawntreader once was as surely as he's killed a thousand mers. Think, Gundhalinu, think about it! You're still a good officer—you can't deny that you're neglecting your duty. And you're not doing Moon a favor to turn her over to them." Reason began to seep back into Gundhalinu's eyes, and a dark resolve. *Stay with me, BZ.*

Moon reappeared in the doorway, looking back over her shoulder, her face pinched with frustration and disappointment. Beyond her, Sirus was leaving the outer room.

Damn, not when I've almost won! Jerusha turned back to Gundhalinu, saw with abrupt relief that his expression had not changed. "BZ," she whispered, "you don't have to be the one. I'll have her taken in by someone else. Stay here until they've treated you. You need rest and—"

"I'll do it." He spoke as though she did not exist. He pushed himself off of the table, stood down unsteadily, gathering himself to his duty. "They've already treated me, Commander. I'm fine," absently. "I have to do this; have to do it now, before I change my mind." His freckles stood out like stars, anemic white against the darkness of his skin.

Moon looked at him, stopped where she was across the room. "BZ?"

Gundhalinu said quietly, "Moon, you're under arrest."

Moon huddled at the very edge of the seat, pressed against the curving window, as the shuttle car began to move soundlessly out of the starport's station. There was a handful of other people in the car, mainly technicians going off duty, going to join the Festival crowds in the city. *Carbuncle*—she had reached the end of the journey that had taken so long, and cost so much. She looked ahead into the sucking blackness through a progression of pulsing golden rings, blinking each time the car threaded a ring like a silent needle . . . blinking and blinking, to keep her vision clear. Betrayed. *Betrayed. . . .*

She twisted her hands again with impotent fury, feeling the cold, unyielding binders bite into her wrists. Gundhalinu sat beside her, separated from her by an unbridgeable gap of betrayal and Duty. What had that woman said to him? Or had he always meant to do it? She glanced at him, looked away again abruptly when she found him still watching her. Misery was in his eyes now, soft and yielding, not the unforgiving iron of Inspector Gundhalinu that she could beat against with honest rage. She could not look at his misery, afraid of becoming lost in it; drawn down into the memory of those all-too-human eyes touching her face in the dawn-light, needing her, wanting her, asking but never demanding ... the memory of how she had almost answered them ... almost....

Let him suffer! ... Damn you, you liar, you bastard; I trusted you. How could you do this to me! Her head bumped the window in rhythmic frustration. He was taking her to jail; and in a few more days his people would take her from this world again forever, abandon her to a lifelong exile on some other planet. He had even lied to Pala-Thion, telling her that the medics had treated him so that she would let him do this job himself. And she had heard him volunteer—*volunteer*—to bring in Sparks as well; to do his penance by letting her lover be charged with murder and sent away to some hellworld prison colony for the rest of his life ... if he could be found in time. And if he couldn't be found ...

She had told First Secretary Sirus everything, trying not to hate him, and she had seen the light-echo from a distant time in this same place shine out in him as she told him of the medal that bore his name, and his son.... "He always wore it; he always wanted to be like you, to learn the secrets of the universe."

He had laughed with startled pleasure, wanting to know where his son was now, and whether they could meet. She had told him, hesitantly, that he could and would see Sparks at the Snow Queen's court. Sirus had been born, like Sparks, after the celebration of an official visit by the Assembly on Samathe; at the Prime Minister's next visit he had taken his nearly middle-aged son with him on a whim. She saw the possibilities for his own son registering in Sirus's mind, and with suddenly tangling hope and fear she had told him the rest:

"... and Starbuck will be sacrificed with the Queen at

the end of the Festival, unless someone saves him." She had waited for the shock to register, and then, turning all her willpower on him, "You can save him! He's the Prime Minister's grandson, your son, no one would dare execute him if you ordered them to let him live!"

But Sirus had stepped back from her with a smile of grief. "I'm sorry, Moon... niece. Truly I am. But I can't help you. As much as I want to—" his fingers twitched. "There's nothing I can do. We're figureheads, Moon! Images, idols, toys—we don't run the Hegemony; we simply decorate it. You'd have to change the Change itself, and the ritual of the Change is far too important to be disrupted at my whim." He looked down.

"But—"

"I'm sorry." He sighed, and shrugged, hands empty. "If there's anything I can do to help that's within my power, I'll do it; just contact me, and let me know. But I can't perform miracles... I wouldn't even know how to try. I wish you'd never told me this." He had turned away and left her standing alone.

Alone... In all her life she had never felt so alone. The shuttle car slowed, coming into the light at the tunnel's end, and brought them to a sighing stop. Looking out she could see an immense manmade cavern, a wide, harshly lit platform. Its walls were painted with lurid stripes, a heartless, futile attempt at celebration. The platform was deserted, except for three well-armed security guards; access to the starport was even more strictly limited tonight than usual. They had reached Carbuncle, but she had no impression at all of its real identity.

The technicians left the car in a laughing, elbowing knot; one or two glanced back briefly before they went on across the platform. Gundhalinu stood up, coughing heavily, and gestured her to her feet, still without speaking to her. She followed the technicians' path, head down, lost in the silence of questions without answers. At the far side of the platform were elevators of various sizes. The technicians had already disappeared into one. Gundhalinu still wore his blood-stained coat, and a borrowed helmet; the

370

guards studied his own identification more closely than they looked at his prisoner.

The lift took them up, and up and up, until Moon felt her empty stomach turn over in protest. There were no stops along the way. The elevator shaft rose through the hollow core of one of Carbuncle's supporting pylons, into the heart of the lower city—where goods had come from and gone to the entire Hegemony . . . but would no longer.

The doors slid open as they reached the city level. Noise and color and raucous celebration rushed in to overwhelm them like a joyous madman. Men and women danced past them to the glaring music of an unseen band; locals and offworlders together, filling the bare, littered loading docks with motion and every imaginable contrast of clothing and being. Moon shrank back, felt Gundhalinu recoil beside her, as the cacophony shattered senses attuned to the fragile silence of the snow.

Gundhalinu swore in Sandhi, breaking his own silence in self-defense. But he took her arm, pushed her out of the elevator before the doors could close again. He led her along the edges of the mauling crowd, navigating the interminable gauntlet to the warehouses where the crowded Street began. At last he stopped her, finding shelter in a pool of quiet, the corner space between two buildings. He backed her resolutely up to the wall. "Moon—"

She turned her face away, drowning his face in images. *Don't tell me you're sorry—don't!*

"I'm sorry. I had to do it." He took her hands in his. His thumb pressed the hollow lock on the crosspiece of the binders, they snapped open. He took them off and tossed them away.

She looked down at her wrists in disbelief, shook them, looked up into his face again. "I thought—I thought—"

"It was the only way I could get us here to the city, past security, once the Commander recognized you." He shook his head, wiped his face with the back of a hand.

"Holy Mother! BZ—" She took a deep breath, clenching her hands. "You lie too well."

His mouth quirked. "So much for Good Blue Gundhalinu." He reached up and took off his borrowed helmet, patted it almost reverently. "Nobody understands that it doesn't fit any more." His voice turned harsh with self-recrimination. He bent over and set the helmet down on the pavement.

"BZ, no one needs to know." She pulled at his arm with sudden understanding. "Can't you say I slipped away in the crowd?"

He straightened up, his mouth like a knife cut, his eyes like cinders; and she saw that this was not the catalyst, but only the precipitate of his change. "The Commander told me what she knows about your cousin. We can't get at him in the palace, but she said he visits a woman named Raven-glass sometimes, in the Citron Alley. That's as good a starting place as any." He stood away from her, and away from himself, retreating onto safe ground. "I guess we can go as we are; nobody will look at us twice in this mob." He frowned abruptly, looking at her. "Braid your hair. It's too much like—it's too obvious."

She obeyed, not understanding.

"Hold on to me, and whatever you do, don't get separated in this crowd. We've got half a city to go, and it's all uphill." He put out his good hand; she clasped it tightly in her own.

They made their way up the Street, assaulted by the appalling intensity of Carbuncle's high spirits. The Winters celebrated with a kind of uninhibited desperation, because it was the last Festival they would ever know; the Summers celebrated the coming of the Change that would set their world right. The sight of kleeskin boots and slickers, the weather-burned faces of the countless islanders who had made this pilgrimage, filled Moon's eyes and clogged her throat with longing. She found herself searching the faces for one she knew, always disappointed—until she glimpsed a red head bobbing, a youth in a slicker moving away. She struggled to break Gundhalinu's grip, but he would not let her go. Shaking his head, he towed her up the Street, until she realized for herself that there were half a hundred redheaded Summers adrift in this sea of faces.

372

Vendors cried their wares, people danced in human chains, performers and musicians climbed boxes and stairs to win the fickle worship of the passing crowd. It was the middle of the night, but no one seemed to know it from the middle of the day—Moon the least among them. The Prime Minister had arrived, and from now until the night of masks the revels would only grow wilder.

Offworlder storekeepers sold the last of their stock for near-nothing, or gave it away, piled clothes and food and unrecognizable exotica in their doorways, TAKE IT AWAY. Winters wrapped in yards of family totem-creatures paraded along the street-center, alight with holo-grammic cold fire. Moon yelped as a firecracker burst beside her, wrote her name in the air with an incandescent sparkler she found unexpectedly in her hand. Fistfights and worse fights broke out along the alleys as the electric tensions that lay beneath this Festival's melting valences exploded in sudden, petty violence. Moon had to struggle to keep her own hold on Gundhalinu as a fight broke out beside them and his instincts started him toward it. But a regulation Blue in a shining helmet had claimed it for his own, and Gundhalinu changed direction again with wrenching urgency.

As they went on up the Street, Moon felt the crowd spirit infect her with giddy optimism, pummeling her with the absolute awareness that she was here at last—this was the city, this was Carbuncle, and it was a place of unimaginable delight. She had come in time, she had come in the time of Change, when probabilities broke down and anything became possible. She had come to find Sparks, to change the Change, and she would.

But more and more she found herself leading Gundhalinu, pulling him against the current of humanity, his own senses and endurance failing him as hers heightened. She looked back at his sweating face, falling from the heights as she heard him cough and remembered that he had thrown away rest and treatment to help her. But he shook his head as she slowed, pushed her on again, "Almost there."

They reached the Citron Alley at last. Moon found a store that was still open, asked the shopman eagerly for Fate Ravenglass. He looked at her face with peculiar surprise; she drew the neck of her tunic together over her tattoo. "Fate's right next door, little lady—but you won't find her in. She's seeing to her masks, all around the city. Come back tomorrow, maybe you'll have better luck."

She has to be in! How can she be gone—? Moon nodded, speechless with disappointment.

Gundhalinu leaned against the peeling building wall. "Do you—have anything for a cough?"

The shopman shrugged. "Not much now. An amulet for good health."

Gundhalinu gave a grunt of disgust and pushed away from the wall. "Come on, let's ask around the hells."

"No." Moon shook her head, caught his arm, stopping him. "We'll—we'll find somewhere to sleep first. And come back here tomorrow."

He hesitated. "You're sure?"

She nodded, lying, but knowing that she would be utterly lost here in the city, if she lost him now.

They found refuge at last with his former landlady: a pillowed, mothering woman who took pity on him, once she believed that he was more than a ghost. She put them in the rooms that belonged to her grown son. "I know you won't steal anything, Inspector Gundhalinu!"

Gundhalinu grimaced wryly as the door clicked shut, granting them privacy at last. "She doesn't seem to care whether I brought you here for immoral purposes."

Moon bent her head. "What does that mean?" blankly.

His smile grew wryer. "Nothing, I suppose, in this town. Gods, I want to see hot, running water again! I want to feel clean again." He turned away and went into the bathroom; after a moment she heard water running.

Moon ate her share of the fisherman's-pie they had panhandled on the street, sitting by the window with her back to the room's self-conscious schizophrenia—a room like all of Winter, caught between the Sea and the stars. The rooms were on the second floor, and she looked down on the Festival from above, watching humanity course like blood through the arteries of the city. *So many . . .* there were so many.

Cut off from the life support of its artificial vitality, she felt her endurance break down again, lost her confidence that she would ever find that one face in the thousands. The sibyl machinery had brought her to Carbuncle; but what did it expect of her now? Aspundh had not been able to tell her anything about the way in which it acted; only that it was the most unpredictable and least understood of the things a sibyl might experience. She had believed that it guided her; but now that she had come to the city there was no blinding revelation to help her: Had it abandoned her, forgotten her, left her to count grains of sand on the endless shore? How would she find Sparks without its help?

And what if she did find him? What had he become—a cold-blooded killer, doing the dirty work of Winter's Queen, even sharing her bed? What would she say to him if she found him; what could he say to her? He had rejected her twice already, on Neith, and on that hideous shore . . . how often did he have to tell her that she was no longer his love? Had she really gone through so much, just to hear him say it to her face? Her hand rose to her cheek. *Why can't I let go? Why can't I admit it?*

The curtain at the bathroom doorway pushed back and Gundhalinu came out, clean and freshly shaven, but modestly redressed in the same filthy clothes. He stretched out on the bed-sofa with a sigh, as though it had taken the last bit of his strength. Moon shut herself into the tiny washroom in turn, to hide from him the doubts that she could not speak and could not disguise. She showered; the steaming water soothed her crippling tension, but it could not wash her guilt away.

She came out into the larger room again, wearing only her tunic, drying her hair and her eyes; expecting to find Gundhalinu asleep. But he stood at the window as she had stood.

She joined him. They stood side by side, not touching, in silent communion before the diamond panes, watching the street below, listening as the Festival rattled against the glass.

"Why did I come here? Why did it make me come, when there wasn't any reason?"

Gundhalinu glanced at her, frowning in surprise.

"What am I going to do, even if I find him? I've already lost him. He doesn't want me any more. He has a Queen—" she pressed her hand against her mouth, "and he's willing to die for her."

"Maybe he only wants Arienrhod because he doesn't have you." Again Gundhalinu searched her face, looking for something she didn't understand.

"How can you say that? She's a Queen."

"But she'll never be you." Hesitantly he touched her fingers. "And maybe that's why he doesn't want to go on living."

She caught his hand in hers, pressed it to her cheek, kissed it. "Thou makest me—valued feel, when I wind-drift am . . . when I lost have been, for so long." She felt her face burn.

He freed his hand. "Don't speak Sandhi! I never want to hear it again." He pulled clumsily at the sleeve of his rough shirt. "I'm not fit to hear it. Wind-drift . . . that's what I am, not what you are. Spume on the sea, dust in the wind; dirt under the feet of my people—"

"Stop it!" She stopped his words, aching with his pain. "Stop it, stop it! I won't let you believe that! It's a lie. You're the finest, gentlest, kindest man I ever knew. I won't let you . . . believe . . . ." as he turned to her, his dark eyes drawing her, and his hands pressing her back, and his need . . .

He bent his head slowly, almost in disbelief, as her mouth rose to his kiss. Moon shut her eyes, kissing him again with tremulous hunger, feeling his astonished hands begin to caress her as she answered his unspoken question at last.

"How did I come to this place?" he murmured. "Is it real? How can you—"

"I don't know. I don't know, don't ask me." *Because*

there is no answer. Because I have no right to love you, I never meant to . . . and I do. "BZ . . . this may be all there is, this could end tomorrow." *Because you give me the strength to go on searching.*

"I know." His kisses grew more reckless. "It doesn't matter. I'm not asking forever of you . . . just let me love you now."

37

"Starbuck!" Arienrhod called his name again, when he did not look up from his work table.

He raised his head slowly, his face elusive and shadowed as he acknowledged her at last. He pushed aside contraband tools, the half-disassembled piece of hardware he had been peeling down layer upon fragile layer; his workroom was choked with technological stormwrack, some of which he actually claimed to understand. His native technical ability had always pleased her, until now. Since he had returned from the final, fateful Hunt, he had lost himself in this sterile fantasy of machinery, to hide from himself and from her. "What do you want?" His voice was neither curious nor hostile; it was nothing at all, and nothing showed on his face as he spoke.

She tried to curb her irritation, knowing that only patience and time would bring him out of his despondent brooding. But it had been weeks since he had acted like a man; since he had tried to make love to her, touched her, even smiled at her. Her resentment smouldered, leaving her with no stomach for coddling his sullen bad temper. "I want to know when you'll be finishing your duty as Hunter."

"My duty?" He shifted in the swivel seat, his eyes leaping like a hart, searching for cover in the wilderness of electronics gear. "I've done it all," bitterly.

"You haven't made the payment. The Source is waiting for the water of life. I'm sure I don't need to remind you that unless he gets it Winter will end—and so will our lives."

"And half of Summer will die . . . Summer will end forever." His green eyes met hers again, dull with anguish.

"So I hope." She forced her gaze past the barriers and into his unwilling mind. "You aren't pretending this is the first time that's occurred to you, are you?"

"No." He shook his head; his red hair brushed the links of silvered chain that caught the shoulders of his loose-hanging shirt. "I've thought about it every day, and dreamed it—"

"Pleasant dreams," she said sardonically.

"No!" She remembered the nightmares, the ones that he had refused to discuss with her. "Get someone else to make the delivery. I've done my duty, I'm choking on Winter's dirty work. I draw the line at giving that rotting offworlder slug eternal life for destroying my own people."

"You're no Summer! And you're paying for your own life, and mine." Arienrhod leaned across the work table, reaching out. "You can't crawl back into a Summer shell; you outgrew that long ago. You've killed your sacred mers, you've left your Summer love dead with their corpses. You abandoned your people and your goddess years ago—for something better! Remember that! You are an offworlder now, and my lover. And like it or not, you will be until you die."

Starbuck pushed to his feet, sweeping the clatter and blink off of the table with his fist. Arienrhod stepped back as she realized he had only just kept that rage from striking out at her.

"Then I'd just as soon die now." He clenched his hands on the table edge, leaning forward with his head down. "And finish what I've started."

"Sparks." His name rose out of her deepest heart, where the hot pain of his suffering reached her dimly. But he did

378

not respond. She could not reach him any more; he had shut her out. "Starbuck!" The suffering became her own, and the pain became her anger. He did look up this time, with his face hard and clenched. There was nothing of Sparks in the look; only a ghost lying behind it: the ghost of lost Moon, her own lost otherness. Moon, whose death was his fault, and who had taken his love for the both of them with her into the grave. Arienrhod felt his reality, shrouded by the ghost of Moon, become the focus for failure's burning glass: *failure*. The word left a smoking track across her inner sight. "You will deliver the water of life, and I want it done soon. Your Queen commands it."

His mouth thinned. It was the first time she had ever commanded him; the first time he had ever forced her to. "And if I refuse?"

"Then I'll give you to the offworlders." Refusing to let him defy her, she pulled at the sliding reins of her control. "And you'll spend the rest of your life in a penal colony wishing that you had died at the Change."

Starbuck's mouth dropped open. His eyes felt her face like a blind man's hands, until at last he knew that she meant every word. He bowed his head in surrender, helpless under the weight of his own self-hatred.

She knew then that she could make him do anything . . . and that in winning this victory she had lost him forever.

—— 38 ——

Moon woke suddenly with a sigh in the warm embrace of someone's arms. *Sparkie, I had such a strange dream.* . . . She opened her eyes, jerked at the unexpectedness of the room opening out before her. And remembering, she looked

379

down along her side to find a warm brown arm freckled with pink secure beneath her own. For just a moment pain caught inside her; but then she smiled, without guilt or regret, twining her fingers in his. She shifted carefully on the narrow bed-sofa to study BZ's sleeping face, remembering how he had watched over her in the silent dawns. Remembering the poems of his heart that he spoke to her wondering ears, as he gave himself to her at last, *my star, white bird, wildflower garden* . . . until she had cried out the words that she had no right to say, and no power to deny, *I love you, I love you.* . . .

She stroked his cheek, but he did not stir; rested her head on his shoulder. Here in this room, this space apart from their separate lives, they had shared love, and they had given each other something else as precious—an affirmation of their own value.

The sounds of the Festival still reached her, muted but unchanging; the level of light flowing in through the window had not changed either. ("I've never done this in the light," he had murmured. "We're so beautiful . . . Why was I ashamed?") She had no feel for whether it was night or day, or how long they had slept. Her body was sluggish and unwilling, telling her it had not been long enough. But she couldn't afford any more time. BZ still slept like the dead, and she moved out from under his arm as quietly as she could, without trying to wake him; certain that she could find her way as far as the maskmaker's alley alone. She dressed and slipped out the door.

The crowds seemed as vibrant, as endless, as before, as though one shift of revelers merged imperceptibly into the next, an infinite wheel. She kept as close to the building walls as she could, forcing her way through the eddying backwaters around vendors' booths and outdoor cafes. She grabbed a piece of spiced meat from a table as she passed, choked it down, her throat tight and her mind sparking with the feedback of sheer energy from every side.

At last she broke through into the Citron Alley, where the crowd current slowed and grew less deep. She found her way to the botanery entrance, went one more shop to the maskmaker's. Its yellow-green double door was firmly shut; she beat on the upper half with her fist, throwing all her frustration and urgency into it. "Open up! Open up!"

The top half of the door opened, catching her in mid-cry; she ended with a laugh of triumph. A middle-aged woman with dark hair in a heavy plait looked out at her, through her, with eyes sleep reddened . . . with eyes that did not see her. "Yes, who is it?" wearily, a little impatiently.

"Are you—are you Fate Ravenglass, the maskmaker?" She wondered what she had been expecting, relieved that this woman wasn't it.

"Yes." The woman rubbed her face. "But all my masks are gone. You'll have to go to one of the displays to look at them. There are warehouses and vacant stores full of them all over the city."

"No, I don't want a mask. I want to ask you about— Sparks. Sparks Dawntreader."

"Sparks?" The reaction she had waited for, prayed for, filled the woman's face. She opened the bottom of the door. "Come in then! Come in."

Moon entered the shop, blinked with the dimming of light. As her eyes readjusted, she saw boxes and baskets piled in precisely ordered confusion in the room's four quarters—remnants of cloth, face forms, feathers, bangles, beads. Her foot skidded on a bead as she moved forward; she picked it up carefully and held it in her hand. The walls of the room were empty now, but they bristled with hooks where a hundred masks must have hung like rare flowers until only two or three days ago. . . . The last wall-space was not empty. On it hung one mask all alone, and she stood staring, transfixed by the shimmering vision of a summer's day: mist-rainbows reflecting in pied pools, emerald-velvet moss underfoot and the green-gold silk of new grasses springing up on the hillsides; hoards of wild-flowers, fragant with life, berries and birds' wings dappled with shadow; and in their midst a face of radiant innocence captive to wonder, crowned by the rays of the twin suns. "Is that—the Summer Queen?" she whispered, awed.

381

The woman turned to face it instinctively. "That is her mask. Who she will be, herself, is still a mystery known only to the gods."

"To the Lady," Moon said, without thinking.

"Yes, of course." The maskmaker smiled a little sadly; Moon realized all the things this mask would mean to a Winter, and that none of them were the same things that moved her.

"You've made her so beautiful; when she's come to take your life away."

"Thank you." The woman smiled again, proudly this time. "But that's the price any artist pays—to lose a part of herself each time she creates something she hopes will live on after her. And perhaps if I make her fair and kind, the Summer Queen will fulfill the prophecy, and be those things to us."

"She will," Moon murmured. *But she won't understand you—so how can she be?*

"Now, tell me, Summer girl"—Moon glanced around in half-surprise—"why you've come asking about Sparks Dawntreader."

"I'm his cousin, Moon Dawntreader."

"Moon!" The maskmaker frowned at nothing. "Wait, wait just a minute." She went surely through a doorway into another room, and was back in a moment wearing a peculiar headband. "He told me so much about you, the two of you. Come over by the door, where I can see you better with my 'third eye.' "

Moon obeyed. The woman held her with her face to the light, slowly grew rigid. "Sparks said that you were like her . . . like her. . . ." She seemed to shiver suddenly.

"Like who?" Moon forced the words out through stiff lips.

"Like Arienrhod, like the Snow Queen. But I've seen you, another time, in another place, somewhere. She lifted her hand to map Moon's face with sensitive fingertips, keeping her from asking another question. Fate led her back inside to the one round, glue-dribbled table with chairs that was all the room's real furniture. "Where have I seen you, Moon?" A large gray cat appeared out of nowhere on the tabletop, came to sniff questioningly at Moon's hands. Moon scratched him absently under the chin.

"I—I don't think you have." Moon sat down, following Fate's motion, unclenched her fist and laid the single red bead on the table.

Fate's breath caught. "Yes. You're a sibyl."

Moon's hands flew to her throat. "No—"

"Your cousin told me; it's all right." Fate shook her head reassuringly. "Your secret is safe. And it means I can trust you with mine now." She pulled down the high neckline of her sleeping gown, exposing her throat.

Moon felt her own breath stop. "You're a sibyl, here? But how? How do you dare?" She remembered Danaquil Lu, and the scars he wore as a warning.

"I have a very—select clientele." Fate turned her face away. "Maybe that's selfish of me, maybe I'm not doing all I can with the gift, but . . . I feel that there is a *need* for me to be here, somehow. As an . . . outlet, if nothing else." Her hands found a stray feather on the tabletop. She picked it up, running it between her fingers. The cat watched her, its ears flickering. "I have strange ideas about sibyls, you see; maybe they're absurd, but . . . " Her shoulders twitched.

Moon leaned forward. "You mean, you think there might be sibyls on other worlds than this one?"

The feather fluttered down, the cat pounced. "Yes! Oh, by the gods, have you felt it too?" Fate reached out for reassurance.

"I've seen it." Moon touched her hand. "I met a sibyl on another world. There are sibyls everywhere, part of an information network the Old Empire left to help us now. The Hegemony lies to us."

"I thought as much—I knew there was something more! Yes, it makes so much sense." Her smile was a candle being lit in darkness. "Is that where I saw you, then? On another world? Asking about him . . . "

"I did ask about him! That's why I came back. Then it

was you who told me about him. . . . " *That he loved someone else.* "That it wasn't finished yet, that he needed me," raising her voice to drown out doubt's. "But how do you know that? Can we remember what we say, and see? I've never been called."

"Yes, you remember it. Clearly." Fate smiled at the memory of clear sight. "It happens to me rather often, and that's why I feel I'm needed here. I may be the only answer there is to questions about Carbuncle. And that's why I began to suspect there was more to us than anyone pretended to know. How could the Hedge *not* know what we did was real?"

"There are a lot of things they lie about." *The mers . . . is that the real reason they don't want us in Carbuncle—so no one can prove that they've lied about the mers? And about how many other things?* "But we could change that, now that we know the truth. When the offworlders go—"

"Then Summer will reign, and they won't listen."

"*I* listened." Moon felt her gaze drawn away to the mask on the wall. *Would they listen to a sibyl Queen?* A tingling excitement ran along her nerves from spine to fingertips. "Fate, in Transfer you said . . . you said I could be the Queen. What did it mean?"

"That was years ago. . . ." Fate pressed a hand over her sensor eye. "I suppose I meant that you looked like Arienrhod." She took her hand away, looking toward the mask on the wall. "But—maybe not. I called you back; it seemed important. If you ran the race with the others on the day of choosing, who can say? You could be chosen Queen."

"How long is it until they choose?"

"It's the day that leads into the Mask Night—the day after tomorrow."

Moon wove her tingling hands together, completing the circuit, felt the current of terrifying certainty surge through her. *This is the reason. This is why I've come. To make this a real Change, to open the circle. . . .* "Yes, I can; I know I can! I was meant to!" Possibilities exploded inside her eyes.

But it won't save Sparks. The fire of revelation drowned in the cold waters of truth. There would be no rebirth without death; she would have no power until the Snow Queen died.... "But that's why I came!" She shook her head angrily; Fate's face turned quizzical, listening. "Fate, I came to find Sparks, I want to help him, if I can. If he still needs me, if he even wants me.... " She faltered.

"You know—what he's become?"

"Yes. I know. I know everything." She pulled on a braid, hurting herself. "Starbuck."

Fate nodded, her face drawing down. She pulled the cat into her lap. "He isn't the boy you knew any more. But you aren't the girl he left in Summer either. And he does need you, Moon, he needs you desperately; he always has, or he would never have turned to Arienrhod. Find him, and save him if you can. It matters very much to me."

"And to me." Moon jarred the table. "But I don't know how to find him. That's why I came to you. Can you help me find him, can you bring him here? There's hardly any time." *Today and two more days, until he dies—three days to search a whole city.*

"I know." Fate shook her head, looking down. "But he comes here at his whim, not mine. And I don't know.... Wait." Searching, she found the red bead, picked it up. "There is someone else who sees him more than I do. Her name is Tor Starhiker, and she runs the casino called Persiponë's. She calls herself Persiponë; ask for her by that name. Are you here alone?"

"No." Moon smiled. "I have someone," realizing that she had been away from him far longer than she had meant to be. "I'd better get back and tell him what I've learned." She stood up, hesitated. "Thank you for helping me. And thank you for being Spark's friend when I couldn't be." She longed for the time to hear all that had passed between them through that long/brief gap of years. "May the Lady smile on you," shyly.

"May She smile on us all. But especially on you, now." Fate smiled.

Moon looked a last time at the mask of the Summer Queen before she went out the door.

She reached the rooming house where she had left BZ at last, burst in through the windowed door, breathless with elation and relief.

"Moon!" BZ stood in the narrow hallway, the tail of his ragged shirt half tucked in. His landlady stood beside him, overpowering his frail official presence with her own, midway through a shrug of denial. BZ pushed past her, ran to catch Moon in his arms, lifting her off her feet. "Gods! Where the hell have you been? I thought—"

"I went to the maskmaker's." She laughed her surprise as he set her down again. "Stop, you shouldn't—"

"The maskmaker's? Alone? Why?" He frowned disapproval, but his face showed her only concern.

"I knew the way. You needed the rest." She smiled until he smiled with her. "I found her. And BZ, you won't believe this—" She broke off, remembering the landlady still listening intently behind his back. BZ glanced over his shoulder, cleared his throat.

"All right, all right, Inspector." The woman raised her hands in good-natured surrender. "I can take a hint." She eased past them toward her own apartment door. "You had him worried." She winked unsubtly. "Keep him worried and he won't go offworld without you, child!" She opened her door and went in; it closed behind her.

BZ glanced ceilingward, away from Moon's embarrassment and his own. He moved them further down the hall. "Now tell me. You found her?"

"Yes! And BZ—when KR Aspundh went into Transfer, she was the one who told me to come back."

It took a moment to register. "She's a sibyl? Here?"

Moon nodded, missing the undertones of his incredulity. "The only one, for the whole galaxy—"

"What did you tell her?" He was suddenly angry.

This time she understood; old resentment and fresh disappointment darkened her eyes. She stepped back, away from him. "I told her I wanted to find Sparks." *And that's all you have the right to know.*

"I didn't mean that." He muffled a cough, muzzling his bad temper. "I—I was afraid you'd left me," ashamed and awkward, "without even saying good-bye."

Knowing that he knew it wasn't the whole truth, she accepted it; because she knew that he wished it were. "BZ, how could I ever . . . not to you. Not to you." She took his hands in hers, in promise, and kissed him with gentle grief.

He let her go reluctantly, suddenly obsessed with the disorder of his shirt. "So what did you find out? Has she seen him?"

"Fate doesn't know how to reach him." Moon saw his head come up. "But she told me about somebody who might: Her name is—Persiponë; she runs a casino."

She thought he was disappointed. But he nodded. "Right. I know the place. Uptown, one of the biggest. We'll try it next." He glanced toward the spidery stairway that helixed to the upper floors, and to the room that had been theirs for a night. "Just let me . . . get my coat."

"Hi there . . . hello, sexy . . . welcome to hell, big spender . . ."

Tor leaned languidly against a pillar, greeting the faceless mob that poured through the wall of tinkling mirrors with soulless monotony. She bit down on a yawn, her mouth crinkling with the effort, trying to keep her makeup intact. They had just reopened after being closed for a few hours of rest and recovery, and they would not be closed again until the night of masks was over and the day of Change had come. She had been gulping uppers until they barely gave her a jolt, and her flower-lidded eyes were ready to sink into her skull. Like somebody about to begin a life of unwilling asceticism, the Festival crowd was insatiable in all its appetites, and the Source wanted them squeezed to the last drop.

And whatever the Source wanted, she meant to give him. He had touched the bureaucratic mountain of permission forms with his omnipotent, distorted finger, and it had melted into an unobstructed plain: He had given his blessing for her marriage to Oyarzabal, her escape from this world before the offworlders slammed the lid on Winter's coffin and nailed it down tight. In just a few more interminable hours, this casino would close forever—well, forever as far as she was concerned. It struck her that she was going to miss this place, and that surprised her. But this casino had been filled with people who *lived*, people who weren't afraid to take chances, people from a collection of worlds so diverse she could barely begin to fathom them; worlds she wanted to get her hands on, and would, thanks to Oyarzabal and the Source.

She experienced a moment of fleeting doubt at the thought that she would actually be Oyarzabal's wife. The offworlders' legal marriage seemed as heavy and ugly as a length of chain. To be chained to Oyarzabal forever . . . Oyarzabal, who was in lust with Persiponë, not Tor Starhiker. Would she have to wear this damned wig, this painted, phony shell, forever, until it became the reality? *Oh, the hell with it.* If she got sick of Oyarzabal she could lose him fast enough: Chains were made to be broken. " . . . You look like a real winner . . . hello there—" She stopped in mid-drone, her mouth hanging. "Your Majesty?"

The white-braided girl in a nomad's tunic looked at her in strange confusion, and the look was enough to convince her that she was wrong. But the girl stayed put in front of her, oblivious to the crowd's jostling as it eddied past. "Are you Persiponë?"

She smiled garishly. "Only a cheap imitation, kid. But by the gods, you're a high-priced copy of the Queen."

"I . . . uh—" The girl didn't seem very flattered at the comparison. "Fate sent me."

Tor laughed nervously. "Gods, I hope not. . . . Oh! You mean Fate Ravenglass?"

The girl nodded. "My name is Moon Dawntreader. She said you know my cousin Sparks."

"Sparks! Yeah, I certainly do." She felt an irrational relief rush her, pushed away from the pillar. *Hell and devils, I'm way too high tonight.* "Come on, let's get out of the stampede." She realized for the first time that the girl wasn't alone; a scarecrow Kharemoughi stood behind her like a shadow, wearing a Blue's jacket with inspector's insignia. Her heart leaped into her throat, irrationally again, before she saw that the rest of him was strictly nonregulation, saw the stains on his jacket front. The stains looked like dried blood. The possibility did not reassure her. *Don't ask; just don't ask.* She pointed, led them on through the casino. Moon Dawntreader gawked like a rube at the game effects drifting through her in the air, at the astounding extremes of clothing and the extremes of behavior that went with them; at the blaring, mind-battering totality of a gambling hell being experienced by a virgin soul. She heard the girl's half-shout thinned by the throbbing music: "Look at us!" They were passing through the spillover of a hologrammic Black Gate, engulfed in flaming flotsam. "I never saw anything like this on Kharemough, not even in the Thieves' Market!"

Tor looked back in surprise; the fallen Blue said, feelingly, "And you never will!" Tor shook her head and went on.

She led them through into the dim, gossamer-draped hallway where the prostitutes took their clients—the quietest, most private place she could think of offhand. Looking fruitlessly for an unoccupied room, she saw that Herne had still not come out of his own room and gone on duty at the bar. She pounded on his door with the flat of her hand. "Hey, beautiful, your fans are waiting for you! Let's go!"

The door opened. Herne's corroding pretty-boy face

glared at her and past her with undifferentiated loathing. "Why don't you take a—" His gaze landed on Moon; his expression changed and changed and changed again. "My gods!" The final change was pure fury. "What are you doing here? You bitch, you goddamn back-stabbing bitch! I knew you'd come someday—you couldn't enjoy destroying me unless you saw it for yourself—"

"Herne!" Tor blocked him as he would have gone for the girl. "What the hell's wrong with you, are you sky-wheeling? She's a total stranger."

"You think I don't know Arienrhod when I see her? I know your Snow Queen, I slept with her for years! Didn't I, you white whore?"

"I'm not the Queen," Moon said feebly.

"She's not, Herne!" Tor cut him off before he could start again. "Shut up and use your bloodshot eyes, you jerk. She's only a Summer, come looking for her cousin. You never saw her before; and I bet my life you never saw the Queen, either, let alone laid her. She's got better taste."

"What do you know about it?" Herne said. "You don't know a damn thing about her, or me!" He straightened up against the door frame, smoothed the wrinkles out of his garish overshirt, trying to stand with some dignity. "I was Starbuck—until she sold me out for that weakling, Dawntreader."

"Dawntreader!" Tor gaped at Herne. "I don't believe it!" That punk extortionist—had he been bleeding information out of her for five years to stay in good with the Snow Queen? Was it possible? Was it possible Herne wasn't lying about himself, either; had Dawntreader been using her just to use him? She rubbed her face, dislodging a sequin, smearing the tendrils painted on her cheek.

"Sparks Dawntreader is my cousin," Moon said, ignoring Herne's fierce scrutiny. "I know he's become Starbuck; I want to find him before it's too late."

"Your cousin?" Herne frowned, ignoring the rest. "Yeah . . . there's something about you: You disappeared. . . ." He scratched his side, as if he could scratch the memory loose. The drugs he used for the boredom and

390

pain were turning his brain soft. "And you're like her." His eyes held hungry demons. "Just like her."

"Don't waste your breath on that drug-soaked liar," the renegade Blue said impatiently. "He's insane. No Kharemoughi lowborn has enough talent to make himself Starbuck."

Herne seemed to notice him for the first time, stared at him while an ugly grin spread wider. "I remember the day I taught you how to kneel to your betters at the Queen's court, Blue." The other man jerked with recognition. "You were too good for her, for me, then, weren't you, Gundhalinu-*mekru*? And look at you now!" He waved a hand at the Blue's disreputable clothing. "You must have been crawling on your belly, *mekritto*. You're not fit to speak to me!"

The Blue struggled to keep the words in, but they got past him. "I'm still a better man than you'll ever be, you dungheap bastard!"

"You're still a bigger ass. Thank the gods for that!" Herne spat, just as the next door down the hall opened.

"Hey, watch it!" The prostitute led her aggrieved client past them quickly, glaring.

"Well, are you going to get to work, or not?" Tor put her hands on her hips, feeling them slide on the silky cloth of her bodywrap, adding her own withering stare.

"Not. Not till I hear more about this." He bent his head at Moon. "Why Arienrhod's double has come looking for Arienrhod's lover." He backed clumsily into his room, a travesty of gracious invitation. Tor followed with the others.

She had never seen the inside of his room before, and she had the feeling that she still wasn't seeing it. The room held a bed and a storage cupboard, like any other room on this hall, and that was all. A few dirty clothes thrown into a corner, nothing more. No picture on the wall, no books or tapes, no radio or threedy. It was a room for a night—worse, a prison cell. Herne collapsed onto the bed, his steel-wrapped legs protruding. No one made a move to join him there; Moon and Gundhalinu looked at his legs while trying not to. "So what do you want with Sparks Dawn-treader after so long, pretty cousin?"

"We're pledged." Moon faced down the dark insinuation in his eyes. "I love him. I don't want him to die."

Herne laughed. "Oh, yeah. Arienrhod found his vows of faithfulness a real challenge; you ought to be proud. But she always gets what she wants in the end. How about you?"

Moon stiffened, clutching her belt. "I'll get my way. But I have to find him first. Fate said maybe you'd know how—" She turned back to Tor.

Tor shrugged, apologetic. "You just missed him; he came to see the Source." *And I wondered why. Why would Starbuck come? Why would the Queen . . . ?*

"Her plot gets thicker and thicker." Herne grinned obscurely.

And he knew Sparks was Starbuck. . . . Tor frowned inside her thoughts. *What else does he know that he never told me?*

"What do you mean, I just missed him?"

She refocused on Moon's frustrated face. "He came from the palace with a message, about an hour ago."

"And he left again with a couple of Blues on his tail," Herne said smugly.

"What?" Tor raised her silver-dusted eyebrows.

"The Commander," Gundhalinu said. "She must have put out an alert on him, now that she knows who he is."

"What happened to him?" Moon's fists twisted the painted belt-leather. "Did they catch him?"

Herne grunted, amused. "Hah. Those suckers couldn't catch cold," for Gundhalinu. "He got away into the crowd. But if he's a smart boy he'll stick to the palace where Arienrhod can protect him from now until the Change."

"He can't! He can't do that. . . . Damn her!"

Tor saw the Blue try to comfort Moon, saw her twitch his arm off her shoulders, and the look on his face. Herne saw it, too, and smiled. Skeptical, Tor said, "Listen, if you

392

were so devoted to him, kid, why did it take you five years to get around to this in the first place?"

"It hasn't been years, just months!" Moon shut her eyes, head back. "Why couldn't it have been the other way around? Why does it just keep getting harder?"

"Because you're approaching Arienrhod," Herne muttered, "and she's the speed of light."

"She was kidnapped offworld by smugglers five years ago," Gundhalinu ran over Herne's words irritably. "She just got back. She nearly died trying to get to Carbuncle to find him. Is that devoted enough for you?"

Tor quirked her mouth, softening against her will. "It seems to be good enough for you, offworlder." *You poor lovesick bleeder.* "And good enough for Fate. But she's going to have to go to the palace if she wants to find him now."

"She can't," Gundhalinu said.

"Why not?" Moon looked at him. "I can slip into the palace and find him. If that's what I have to do, I'll do it." Her eyes changed, grew dim and unseeing, as though she were having a seizure; when they cleared again resolution glittered. "It's right—I will go there! I have to. I'm not afraid of Arienrhod."

"And why should you be?" Herne stared at her, not really seeing her but something else.

"Shut up, pervert! I'll tell you why." Gundhalinu caught Moon's arm. "Because Arienrhod—because she . . . because she's—dangerous," stupidly. Tor wondered, and Moon half-frowned. "She's got guards all over the palace, and if she caught you trying to come between her and Starbuck . . . damn it, she'd stop you! How the hell are you even going to find him, you can't just go asking who's seen him!"

"Why can't she?" Herne grinned, hell's advocate. "She's got the best disguise anybody could ask for—Arienrhod's face. She can do anything, and nobody'll question it."

"What about the real Queen?" Tor said.

"She'll be entertaining the high lords of the Hedge, if

you time it right. And I've got the thing that'll make you perfect in the part."

"What is it?" Moon moved forward, bright with hope. Gundhalinu looked knives over her shoulder.

But Herne's gaze never left her; it moved slowly down her body and rose again to her face. Tor felt the static charge building between opposite poles inside him. "Spend an hour alone with me, Arienrhod, and it's yours."

Moon paled into an alabaster statue. Gundhalinu's freckles turned scarlet with outrage.

"What are you going to do, Starbuck?" Tor jabbed vindictively. "Teach her how to play cards?"

Herne's head swung toward her. When she saw what had happened to his face, she came closer to pitying him than she had ever come. "For gods' sakes, Herne—don't be a crud, for once in your life! Do something to prove you've got a right to be alive."

Herne's upper body quivered with pent emotion; but she saw it drain away, and he looked back at Moon again. "In there." He pointed at the storage cupboard. "Open it."

Moon went to the cupboard and pulled open the door. Tor saw clothes, and drugs, and half-empty bottles, and one shelf that was entirely empty except for a small black object.

"That's it. Bring it here."

Moon took it to him, handed it over, keeping her distance. He held it in the palm of his hand almost as if it were alive, stroking its surfaces with uncertain fingers. He touched a colored key, and then another, and another. Three changing notes sounded, loud in the cramped room's silence.

"What does it control?" Gundhalinu asked.

"The wind." Herne looked up at them all with defiant pride. "In the Hall of the Winds at Arienrhod's palace. She has the only other one of these there is now. You'll be able to get into the heart of the palace this way without anybody suspecting anything," watching Moon again. "I'll teach you how to use it, and where to look for Starbuck."

394

"In return for what?" Moon's hands closed over the desire to hold the box again, but her face was set for refusal.

Herne's mouth twisted. "No strings. It's yours by right ...and when could I ever refuse you anything you wanted? Or give you anything you wouldn't have, no matter how hard I tried. ..."

Gods, he really thinks it's the Queen. Tor shook her head.

But a trace of sympathy crept into the mock-Queen's eyes, and she said quietly, "If there's ever—anything else I can give you ... "

Herne glanced down at his atrophying legs. "No human being can give me that."

"Well, look, if you're going to the palace you can't go looking like a refugee." Tor pointed. "Come with me, I'll find you some royal rags, or at least something that'll cover up those."

"Moon, you can't go to the palace! I forbid it." Gundhalinu blocked her way as she turned, desperately officious.

"BZ, I have to. I *have* to," undaunted.

"You're wasting your time; you're risking your—soul, if you go there. He's gone rotten, let him go, forget about him!" Gundhalinu held out his hands to her. "Just this once listen to me! You're obsessed by a dream, a nightmare—wake up, for gods' sakes! Believe me, I'm not asking this out of selfishness, Moon. You're all I care about; your safety ... "

She shook her head, looking away. "Don't try to stop me, BZ. Because you can't." She went past him, and he made no move to hold her. Tor led her out of the room.

Gundhalinu stood looking after her, sealing his coat against a sudden chill; feeling Herne's eyes boring into his skull, with no strength to turn back and face them.

"You know the truth about her, don't you?" Herne's voice pulled at him. "You know they're the same, Arienrhod and her."

"They're not the same!" Gundhalinu turned back, stung by his own guilty knowledge.

Herne smiled, believing the answer his eyes gave away. "That's what I figured. She's the Queen's clone, it's the only thing she could be."

"Are you sure?" He asked the question compulsively, not wanting to, not even meaning to.

Herne shrugged. "Arienrhod's the only one who's sure. But I'm sure enough. It's not her daughter—she never misses taking the water of life. And she'd never let a man get that hold on her."

"It makes you—sterile?" Gundhalinu blinked, taken by surprise.

"While you use it . . . maybe forever, after a hundred and fifty years. Who knows? That's a joke, isn't it? It makes you slow to heal, too. It's even killed a few people." Herne chuckled, pleased at the idea. "Makes some people go a little crazy too, 'personality distortion' or some crap like that. That's what the whiners claim, anyhow—the have-nots. It's the power that warps you, not the drug. How's it feel to be a have-not, Gundhalinu-*eshkrad*?"

Gundhalinu ignored him, an image of Sparks Dawn-treader in a helmet of spines suddenly blotting out his sight. He started forward. "Give me the control box, Herne. You aren't sending Moon into that snakepit."

Herne moved slightly, and there was a stunner in his hand. "Hold it, Blue. Suppose you just stand up against the wall, unless you really want what you're asking for."

Gundhalinu backed away again, his own forgotten stunner weighing like lead on his hip, under his coat. He leaned against the wall, coughed with grueling helplessness until his head swam. "Do you mind . . . if I sit?" He slid down the wall without waiting for an answer, sat on the floor.

"You ought to see a medic," Herne said unsympathetically. "When a Tech sits on the floor he's as good as dead."

"I can't." Gundhalinu pulled open his coat again, abruptly too hot. *Not until this is finished.*

"You mean they're hunting you too." A statement, not a

question. "All your old true-Blue buddies. You're on the run with a proscribed Mother lover, you don't have a friend in the world; you've thrown away your job and your position and dragged your highborn honor in the gutters. And all for love."

Gundhalinu looked up, his face burning, opened his mouth.

"I can two and two add." Herne grinned, dripping vitriol. "I'm a Kharemoughi." He shook his head, leaning back on an elbow. "She's really sticking it to you, boy. . . . What did she promise you? Her body?"

"Nothing, *mekru!*"

"Nothing?" Herne leered. "You're a bigger ass than I thought."

"Anything that's happened to me I've done to myself." Gundhalinu sat up straighter, struggling against his fury, against the galling truth that roused it. "It was my decision; I accept the consequences of a rational act."

Herne burst out laughing. "Sure, she can make you believe that! That's her power. She could make you believe you can breathe vacuum. It makes a lot of sense, doesn't it, you rational brainwipe— You want her so much nothing else matters; you could have her under your thumb, a deportee. But instead you're helping her find another lover! Gods, that's Arienrhod down to the ground. And they want the same man; the only one she'll ever want enough to make her hate herself. The ultimate incest. If that isn't enough proof they're the same . . . if that isn't the hell of it." He sat forward, his fingers lacing in the mesh of his caged legs, his head down.

Gundhalinu felt disgust rise in his throat. "That's what I'd expect of you—that you'd drag everything down to your own level, and smear it with filth. You're incapable of anything better; of even understanding what it is you degrade and destroy."

"How would you know?" Herne raised his head.

Gundhalinu frowned. "Because you can't see why I want to help Moon more than I want to help myself. Because you can't feel what it is about her—" He closed his eyes,

397

looking back. "Yes, she made me love her. But she didn't mean to. She took by giving . . . and that makes all the difference."

Herne held up the control box, a challenge. "Why do you think I'm giving her this?"

"Revenge."

Herne looked down again, without an answer.

"No clone ever made is a perfect image of the original. Even identical twins aren't the same, and they're not created by a middleman. The control in cloning isn't nearly that precise, all you ever have is an imperfect recreation."

"A flawed copy," Herne said harshly.

"Yes." Gundhalinu pressed his mouth together. "But why couldn't it be better for the things that were changed—lost, or gained, inadvertently?"

Herne seemed to consider the possibility. "Maybe . . ." He scratched his jaw. "If you're so sure Moon's not the same, why don't you tell her the truth?"

Gundhalinu shook his head. "I tried to." He looked down at his wrists, traced the scarring with unresponsive fingers. "How can I tell her a thing like that?"

"Failed-suicide," Herne whispered.

Gundhalinu stiffened, pushed up onto his knees. But then he saw that Herne was not trying to bait him.

"Did she drive you to that?" with bald curiosity, without rancor. Herne plucked at his braces like a harpist.

"No." Gundhalinu shook his head, sinking back again. "She made me see that there might be some reason to go on living." It struck him as strange that it did not seem stranger to be telling this to an Unclassified, sitting on the floor in a brothel. "All my life I never imagined it was possible to survive without the armor of one's honor intact. And yet, here I am—" not quite a laugh, "—naked to the universe. And it hurts like hell . . . but maybe that's only because now I feel everything more clearly." *And I don't know yet whether I want it like this or not.*

"You'll get used to it," Herne said sourly. "You know, I never used to be able to figure that at all—how you Techs swallowed poison any time life gave you a kick in the butt.

398

You'd be dead a hundred times over if you'd been through my life—a thousand times!"

"You're right." Gundhalinu cringed at the idea of being trapped inside Herne's mind. "Gods, that would be a fate worse than death."

Herne looked at him with bleak disgust, with the unrelenting hatred of half his world's people, until he felt his brittle arrogance crumble, and his gaze broke. "Yes. 'Death before dishonor' is a rich man's privilege. Just like the water of life. . . ." *But nobody really owns Life, or Death.*

"I used to think there was nothing more important to me than my life, there was nothing that could ever make me understand weaklings like you who'd throw it away. Survival was all that was important, it didn't matter how you survived—"

"Was?" Gundhalinu rested his head against the wall, catching the past tense. His tongue absently explored the place where a tooth had been. He followed Herne's glance down the exoskeleton that encased his lower body, realizing all that it implied the loss of—all that had made Herne a man in his own eyes, in the eyes of the world he belonged to. "You don't have to stay here, you know. You could get that fixed on Kharemough."

"After five years?" Herne's voice rose, ready with all the arguments, all the answers he must have gone over and over endlessly in his own mind. "Nobody has that kind of money. I sure as hell don't . . . I don't even have enough to get off this goddamn spitball!"

"Go to the authorities. They aren't going to leave any offworlder behind who doesn't want to stay."

"Yeah, sure." Herne pulled a bottle out from under his bed, unstoppered it and drank without offering to share it. "You have any idea, Blue, of how many outstanding charges I got against me back home? And a lot of other places. If you think I'm going to sweat blood in some penal colony for the rest of my life, you're crazy." He drank again, deeply.

"Then it doesn't look like you've got much in the way of open options." *And you probably don't deserve any.* But he

399

felt an unexpected prick of empathy. *Sainted ancestors—what if I had been born in his body, and he in mine....*
"I'm—sorry."

"Are you." Herne wiped his mouth. "What about you, are you gonna go back, let them bust you off the force, throw you in prison for this? No. Hell, no, you'll probably plead insanity: A crime of passion—you did it for love. Love—love is a disease!" His hand trembled around the bottle neck.

Death to love a sibyl ... death not to. Gundhalinu let himself cough, postponing the need to answer. *What am I going to do? I don't know.* The future opened like an infinite sea. "Ask me tomorrow...." He glanced toward the doorway as someone entered the room—Persiponë, and a second figure cloaked and hooded.

Persiponë moved aside to let the other step forward, drew the hood carefully back from her face.

"Moon?" Gundhalinu got to his knees, pulled himself up the wall, staring. Moon stood before him, her face subtly altered by cosmetic art—not painted with the tasteless gaud of Persiponë's, but heightened to a luminous, mother-of-pearl beauty that blinded his memory of the plain-pale, open face of an outback native girl. Her upswept hair was caught in a net of silver braids interwoven with golden beads, convolutions his eyes couldn't follow. Tor pulled the cloak from her shoulders, revealing a honey-hued gown that flowed along her body like a field of wind-rippled grasses, that clung to her everywhere without seeming to, falling away from a bodice of ivory lace melting sensually against her skin. A collar of opalescent beadwork hid the secret sign at her throat.

BZ stood speechless, watched her radiance shine as she absorbed his admiration.

"BZ, I feel like a fool." She shook her head; but she brightened still.

"My lady—" Like a starlord of the Empire he took her hand, bent above it, touched it briefly to his forehead. *And every centimeter a queen.* "To thee would I gladly kneel."

400

Moon smiled freely, not understading—her own smile, and not Arienrhod's.

"What do you think, Herne?" Persiponë beamed, carrying Moon's nomad tunic under her arm. "Will she pass?"

"Did you do that to her?" Herne asked.

She twitched a shoulder modestly. "Well . . . Pollux gave me a hand. He's got good taste, for a machine."

"Arienrhod doesn't like that color." Herne set the bottle on the floor. "But she'll pass. . . . Gods, yes—she'll pass! Come here, Your Majesty." He held out his hands.

Gundhalinu frowned, kept his own hold on Moon's hand, felt her grip tighten as she looked back at Herne. "Don't call her that," warning.

"She'd better get used to it. I won't hurt you, damn it! I won't even touch you." Herne let his hands drop. "Just let me look at you awhile."

Moon let go of Gundhalinu, went to stand before him. She turned slowly, uncertain of her skirts, but no longer uncertain under his gaze. He devoured her with his eyes, consumed her, but she stood with patient dignity, without censure; allowing, not enduring. Gundhalinu watched her watch Herne through the endless moment, his own feelings unanalyzable. He tensed as Herne pushed himself abruptly to his feet, swaying . . . stayed where he was, as Herne dropped clumsily, jarringly, onto one knee before Moon. "Arienrhod . . ." He murmured something, inaudible to any ears but hers. Gundhalinu glanced at Persiponë; her flower-lidded eyes widened, answering his amazement with her own. She made a crazy-sign in the air, shook her head.

"I know, Starbuck. . . ." Moon nodded, hiding pity. She helped Herne up onto the bed again with an unqueenly hoist.

Herne glanced away from her, suddenly remembering that he had an audience; let his face harden over again. "Your mistake, Dawntreader . . . when I was down you should have kicked me. Arienrhod hates losers." He leaned on the rowelled word with masochistic pleasure. "Now listen good, while I tell you the rest."

"You still mean to help her try this?" Gundhalinu said, indignant.

Herne smiled cryptically. " 'The prey is safest at the hunter's door.' You ought to know that, Blue."

Moon turned back, caught between expressions. *Or is it just that you're afraid to refuse her?* Gundhalinu sighed; it hurt his chest. "Then it'll be because I'm the doorkeeper." Moon smiled, and was all that he could see.

"Oh, my aching back!" Tor stretched to her limits in the privacy of the casino's storeroom. The words rebounded from the exposed walls; the room was almost empty of supplies, and the patrons were doing their best to finish the job. "Come on, Pollux, get this last container of tlaloc out front for me before their tongues turn black." She yawned, hearing the crack of her jaw echo inside her head. *Empty?* "Lost my mind at last."

"Whatever you say, Tor." Pollux moved stolidly across the room, following her point like a faithful hound.

She giggled, giddy with exhaustion. "I swear you do that on purpose! Don't you? You can tell me—"

"Whatever you say, Tor." Pollux connected with the crate.

Her mouth fell, her emotions avalanched from the heights. "Oh, hell, Polly . . . what am I going to do without you? I'm really going to miss you, you greasy hunk of junk." She straightened her wig. "There's only two things Oyarzabal can do for me that you can't, and once I get off this rock it'll be down to one—and I can get that from any man. No wonder he's jealous." She laughed glumly. Oyarzabal had told her that she would become his wife only if she agreed to get rid of Pollux first. She had agreed, and felt another link soldered onto the chain he was forging to turn her into his slave. *He wants what I am . . . so why does he try to change it?* She pushed her wig crooked, straightened it again. "Damn it, who's going to keep me neat, anyway? Hauling crates and turning Summer fish-eaters into queens—all in a day's work for you, isn't it? Don't you ever wonder about yourself, Pollux? Can you really do all that and not ask yourself how, or why?" She trailed him back across the room. "Or whether the kid's going to save her lover from the Queen, or whether she's crazy to want a crud like Sparks Dawntreader at all?"

His faceless head regarded her with imitation attention, but he said nothing.

"Aagh—" She shook a hand at him. "I really must be sold out of brains. You don't even know I'm here; how're you going to give a damn when I'm not? So why should I worry?" She kicked an empty carton spitefully out of their path. "When you finish with this, come back and get the last barrel of that fermented sap, and hook it up for Herne." *For Starbuck. Old Starbuck, and New Starbuck; I know them both. And the Queen's twin. Thank the gods I'm leaving Carbuncle soon—before I meet myself walking backwards.*

She reached the doorway, heard voices drifting out of the room across the hall, the one with a door that was unobtrusively as secure as the vault of the Bank of Newhaven; the one she had never seen unlocked before. But just now its seals were green, it stood unguarded and ever so slightly ajar, and she recognized one of the voices from behind it as Oyarzabal's. Pollux clanked away down the hall toward the casino, oblivious, but she crossed to the door impulsively and pushed it open.

Half a dozen heads turned to look at her, all male, all offworlders. Three she recognized immediately as the Source's lieutenants; Oyarzabal came toward her, annoyance and subtle panic showing in every move.

"I told you to secure that door!" one of the strangers said murderously.

"It's all right—she runs the place, she knows everything,"

Oyarzabal called back. "What the hell are you doing here?" whispered.

She threw her arms around his neck, smothered his protests under a wet kiss. "I'm hungry for my man, that's all." *And if it's one thing I can't stand, it's a locked door.*

"Hell, Persiponë!" He pulled away. "Not now! We got a big job to take care of for the Source here in the city. Later I—"

"Something for the Queen?"

His hands brushed her bare upper arms. "How did you know that?"

Wild guess. "Well, you just said I know everything." She mugged a hidden face at him. "I don't want to make a liar of you. I saw Starbuck come to see the Source today, and I figured the Queen must have sent him," scoring another point.

"You know who Starbuck is, too?"

"Sure. I'm a Winter, aren't I? And I do the Source's business, just like you." She looked him brazenly in the eye. "So what's the rest of it, huh? What's the Queen buying, one last surprise for her farewell party? You can tell me, I'm you're wife, almost." She stood higher on her platform shoes, peering over his shoulder at the knot of gesturing men around a sterile slab of table. Looking past them she realized that the place was a fully equipped laboratory. She had always wondered how the Source managed to keep such a variety of illegal pleasures stocked here, even when they couldn't be gotten from the regular suppliers. . . . Glancing back, she saw on the flawless surface of their meeting table a single heavy metal carrying case. On the lid, on its sides, WARNING . . . and the barbed trefoil of a sibyl. Her skin began to prickle.

"Well, yeah, you could say she's planning kind of a surprise for the Summers." He grinned. "But you don't need to worry your pretty head about it. You've had your shots; and you're going offworld with me, anyway. You don't care what happens here after you're gone, do you?"

She twisted uncomfortably in his grasp. "What do you

mean? . . . Hey, why is there a sibyl sign on that box, huh? That means—" *contamination*. "'Biological contamination'?" as the fine print suddenly slid into focus. "What's in that—germs? Disease, poison?" her voice rose.

"Hey, shut up, will you? Keep your voice down—" He shook her ungently.

"What are you going to do?" She struggled, her panic rising now. "You're going to kill people! You're going to kill my people!"

"Just the Summers, goddamn it, Perse! Not the Winters, they'll be safe; the Queen wants it this way."

"No, you're lying! It's going to kill Winters too, the Queen wouldn't let you kill us! You're crazy, Oyar, let me go! Pollux, help me, Pollux—" The other men were up from the table, coming toward her, and Oyarzabal's heavy hands still held her prisoner. Desperately she brought up her knee; he doubled over with a howl and she was abruptly free to—

The stunner beam caught her from behind, and she fell against the door, knocking it shut as she slid helplessly down to the floor.

41

"You'd better wait for me here, BZ." Moon stopped in the middle of the courtyard that formed a wellspring for the Street at the palace entrance. It was night again beyond the city storm walls, but even here there were revelers laughing and dancing, musicians playing. The people at this high end of the Street were more dazzling and exotic, crusted with jewels, dusted with powder-of-gold; the imported splendors of half a dozen worlds clamored for her wonder. Her own imitation royalty seemed almost drab, and she

kept it hidden, along with her face. BZ's disreputable
clothes were more and more grotesquely out of place, but
he clung to his uniform coat with irrational stubbornness.

"I'm not letting you go in there without me." He shook
his head, his breath rasping after their climb up the long
spiral to Street's-end. "The Queen—"

"*I* am the Queen." She looked at him with mock disdain.
"You forget yourself, Inspector. . . . By'r Lady, what's she
going to do, chop off my head?" She grinned, trying for
whimsy, but not getting any feedback. "BZ, how could I
explain you, in there?" She glanced toward the guarded
palace entrance, feeling her chest tighten.

"I've got these." He held out his identification and his
stunner. "They make me look considerably more regulation." He sealed the open collar of his coat.

"No." She felt the tightness turn to pain. "I'm going in
there to find Sparks, BZ." She forced his shadowed brown
eyes to keep hers when they tried to slip away. "However it
turns out, I have to do that alone. I can't do it . . ." *in front
of another lover.* Her mouth quivered.

"I know that." He did look away now. "And I—I
couldn't watch it happen. Moon, I want the best for you,
believe me; I want whatever happens to be what will make
you happy. But damn it, that doesn't make it any—easier."

"Harder." She nodded. "It makes it harder."

"The entrance . . . let me take you that far. The guards
would ask questions if you didn't have some kind of escort.
And I'll stay here at Street's-end until you come out of
there—or I'll learn the reason why."

She nodded again, not trying for words. They waded the
whirlpool of the circle-dance; she felt her hopes and her
regrets sucked down into a vortex of agonizing anticipation. . . . *You are the Queen; be the Queen, stop shaking!*
She held her breath as the guards at the massive doors
focused on their approach. The guards wore stunners, as
Gundhalinu had predicted. *Oh, Lady, do you hear me?* remembering that it was not a goddess who would guide her
now, but only a machine; a machine that had told her she
must come.

406

At the moment she was certain the guards would challenge her she threw back her hood, keeping her head high, trying to believe strongly enough to make them believe.

"Your Majesty! How did you—" The man on the left remembered himself, brought his hand up to his chest, bowing his head. The woman on the right joined him, their offworlder-style helmets gleaming whitely. The immense, age-darkened doors began to open.

Moon turned quickly as her face began to fall apart, to Gundhalinu's face taut with dutiful respect . . . with a frustrated loss that only she could see. "Thank you for your—cooperation, Inspector Gundhalinu."

He bent his head stiffly. "My pleasure . . . Your Majesty. If you need me again, call me," emphasizing each word. His hands twitched uncertainly in front of him; he saluted, and turned away to lose himself in the crowd.

BZ! She almost called after him; didn't, as she looked back toward the open doors, the darkly shining hallway beyond, beckoning her on to journey's end. The guards glanced surreptitiously past her at Gundhalinu's seedy, retreating back. Wrapping her cloak close around her, Moon entered the palace.

She moved like a ghost along the empty hall, her soft shoes' passage belying her substantiality. She put blinders on her senses, afraid of stopping, of losing herself in the crystalline hypnotic wilderness of purple-black peaks and snow-burdened valleys, Winter's domain that muralled the endless walls of the corridor. And ahead of her, gradually, her straining senses caught the murmur of the Hall of the Winds. Her hand gripped the control box Herne had given her; her palm was moist and cold.

Herne had broken out in a sweat and his own hands had shaken while he told her what she would find there—the captive wind, the billowing cloudforms, the single vaulting strand of walkway above the Pit. The Pit that he had almost made the grave of Sparks, his challenger; the Pit that had destroyed him instead—because of Arienrhod. Arienrhod had defied her own laws to intervene, to save

407

Sparks, and left Herne a prisoner in a broken body, while pitiless love-hatred ate away his soul.

Moon reached the end of the hall where it opened out on the air—vast, moaning reaches of restless air above her, pale cloud-wraiths swelling and shuddering under the caress of an unearthly lover. She felt herself dwindle and diminish as the frigid backflow of the outer air discovered her solitary intrusion, swept hungrily around her, pulling at her cloak. Beyond the breached walls the thousand thousand stars lay white hot on the ruddy forge of night; but there was no warmth here, no light except the haunted green glow of the gaping service shaft below her ... no mercy.

She took one step forward, and then another, toward the thin span of utter blackness silhouetted above the abyss. *He didn't tell me it would be dark!* Fear made her falter, her fingers playing over the sequence of buttons on the control box at her wrist—the sequence Herne claimed would unlock a safe tunnel through the air. *Did he lie about everything?* But she wasn't the object of Herne's twisted passion, only its surrogate. If her presence here was anything to him it was only as a tool for his revenge.

She took another step, and another, until she came shivering to the brink of the Pit. The sudden damp updraft rising out of the shaft caught her by surprise, butting her back on the platform. And with it came the smell of the sea, pungently sweet-sour, fish and salt and moldering pilings. Moon cried out in amazement, her voice swallowed by the wind. "Lady!" The breath of the Sea blew her back again, stumbling over her unaccustomed skirts; she caught her balance, instinctively, a sailor on a pitching deck ... only a sailor, not a Queen.

She lifted her head, saw the shuddering ghostly curtains not as clouds now, capricious and uncontrollable, but as flapping sails untended under the sea wind. And in her hand, in this palm-sized box, were rudder and line to set a course across this well of the Sea. The updrafts beat her back again, in final warning.

"I *will* go." She touched the first button, heard the first tone in the sequence, felt the air grow quiet around her.

And with the skill of a hundred generations before her, a people who had dared the sea and the stars before that, she stepped out onto the rimless span and began to walk. Every third step she sounded a new note, being sure each step was neither too short nor too long, holding her concentration locked into the sequence, the pattern, the rhythm.

And as she passed over the center of the bridge, the greenish glow intensified and she felt a nameless presence, a soundless voice, an echo from a distant place and time . . . the song the sibyl cave had sung to her. She moved more slowly, until she could not move at all; mesmerized by its inhuman beauty, imprisoned in the moment. Her fingers relaxed on the control box, its shrill intruding tone grew thin and faded. . . . A sudden clout of wind knocked her to her knees, the sound of her own scream shattered the prism of spell and set her free. She scrambled up again, recapturing the control note with frantic hands. She hurried on, reckless with panic, feeling the call still tendriling through her mind, but ever fainter.

She reached the far rim, stood sobbing for breath on solid ground, dazed and uncomprehending. This wasn't a choosing-place! How could it know her? . . . She remembered dimly that somewhere in this city Danaquil Lu had been called by the sibyl machine. Was this the same well of the Sea that had sung to him? She shook out her cloak, backing away from its rim in silence; turned away from the sight of the abyss, and left the Hall.

She chose another corridor, tracing the arteries of the palace diagram Herne had drawn on paper and graved into her memory. She began to hear music again—mortal music this time, the sounds of a graceful Kharemoughi art song played by a string quintet. She saw in her mind's eye Aspundh's gardens, the shimmering splendor of the aurora dancing into dawn across a velvet sky. She reached the wide, carpeted stairway leading to the vast hall that was half the palace's second story; met the music drifting sedately down it, and two startled servants who bowed their heads and hurried on past her.

She hurried on, too, climbing past the landing that gave

409

entrance to the grand hall, where tonight the Queen was holding a reception for the Prime Minister and the Assembly members. She went on to the third level, where Herne had told her Starbuck's chambers were, knowing that he would probably still be in the crowded hall below, but knowing that she did not dare enter the place where Arienrhod herself was the center of attention.

But as she left the stairway, she heard the music beckon unexpectedly, found a tiny, half-hidden alcove overlooking the hall below. She wondered whether it was a watchman's perch—but there was no one watching from it now. She tiptoed forward to the railing, looked down out of the shadows, her skin crawling with the certainty that all eyes would be on her like searchlights.

But as the hall opened out under her gaze she forgot herself, no more than an insect on the wall to the mass of royal guests below: Pale Winter nobles and dark-skinned Kharemoughis mingled freely, the eye-dazzling spectrum of their dress diminishing the contrast of their origins. They feasted desultorily at buffet tables spread with the last of Winter's culinary art, the eclectic delights of native and imported cuisines. Moon swallowed, her mouth suddenly full of saliva, remembering the one inadequate meal she had eaten in the casino, hours ago. Mirror-faceted balls suspended in the air above her eye level turned silently, perpetually, sending a snowfall of fractured light down over the crowd.

Moon let her eyes rove, noticing the security force of offworld police stationed unobtrusively around the perimeters of the hall. She wondered whether the Police Commander was here tonight, thought a curse at her for what the woman's untempered justice had done to BZ; what it would have done to her own life, and Sparks's. Once she thought she glimpsed First Secretary Sirus, but lost the face again as a cluster of guests gathered for a toast.

But nowhere in the vast hall could she see a woman who looked like a Queen . . . or one who looked like her. And nowhere a man in black who masked his face like an executioner . . . or a red-haired boy whose face she would

410

know anywhere, no matter how it had changed. Wasn't he here, then? Had he left the hall already; would she find him in his chambers?

She moved back from the balustrade, her heart beating like a caged bird's wings. *I will find you. I will—*

"So there you are. Can't you resist spying on your guests, even tonight?" A man's voice directly behind her, slurred and full of teasing hostility.

Moon froze, feeling her face turn crimson with betraying guilt. She pulled her mouth into a line, clenched her teeth to hold it there, hoping her blush would seem to be anger. She turned, picking up her skirts, holding her head high. "How dare you speak to—" Her gown slipped through senseless fingers. "Sparks?" She swayed.

"Who else?" He shrugged, and hiccupped. "Your faithful shadow of a man," bowing precariously.

"Sparks." She brought her hands up, locked them together to still them, to keep from reaching out. "It's me."

He frowned, like someone hearing a tasteless joke. "I hope to hell so, Arienrhod; or I'm not drunk enough to save me from real-time nightmares. . . ." He peered at her, bleary eyed, rubbing his arms through his slitted shirtsleeves.

"Not Arienrhod." She struggled to pry words out of her dust-dry mouth. "Moon. It's Moon, Sparkie—" She touched him at last, felt the contact climb her arm like a shock.

He wrenched free, as if the contact burned him. "Damn you, Arienrhod! Leave me alone. It isn't funny; it never was." He turned away down the hall.

"Sparks!" She followed him into the light, struggling with the clasp of her necklace. "Look at me!" It came undone, she caught it in her hands. "Look at me."

He swung around truculently; she raised her hand to touch her throat, lifted her head higher. He came back to her, squinting—she saw all the color go out of his flushed face at once. "No! Gods, no . . . she's dead. You're *dead*. I killed you." He pointed at her, accusing himself.

"No, Sparks. I'm alive." She seized his hand in both of hers this time, pulled it to her against his resistance, ran it

411

along her shoulder. "I'm alive! Touch me, believe me. . . . You've never hurt me." *Or if you have, I can't remember now.*

His muscles stopped fighting her grip; his hand closed slowly over her shoulder, slid down her sleeve to her wrist. His head fell forward. "Oh, my thousand gods . . . why did you come here, Moon? *Why?*" fiercely, in anguish.

"To find you. Because you needed me. Because I need you . . . because I love you. Oh, I love you. . . ." She let her arms go around him, buried her face against his chest.

"Don't touch me!" He pried at her arms, pushed her roughly back. "Don't touch me."

Moon stumbled, shook her head. "Sparks, I . . ." She rubbed her face, felt the pain of his bruise stir dimly in her cheek. "Because I'm a sibyl? But that doesn't matter! Sparks, I've been offworld since then; I learned the truth about sibyls. I won't contaminate you. You don't have to be afraid to touch me. We can be together the way we always were."

He stared at her. "The way we were?" flatly, disbelievingly. "Just two simple Summer folk, stinking of fish, with our nets drying in the sun?" She nodded, faltering, feeling her neck resist the lying motion. "And I don't have to be afraid of you contaminating me." A shake, sincere. "Well, what about my contaminating you?" He struck his chest with his open hand, forcing her to see him as he demanded: the shirt of flame-shaded satin tatters showing ribbons of flesh between ribbons of cloth; the heavy jewelry that hung like golden chains of bondage from his neck and wrists; the skintight breeches that left nothing to her imagination.

"You're . . . you're even more beautiful than I remembered." She told the truth; felt a sudden rush of desire, was frightened by it.

He put his hand up, covering his eyes. "Don't you know? Why won't you understand, damn it! That was me you saw on that beach, killing the mers! I'm Starbuck— don't you know what that means; what that makes me?"

412

"I know," catching at the fragments of her breaking voice. *A murderer . . . a liar . . . a stranger.* "I know what it means, Sparks, but I don't care." Because the price she had paid for this moment was too high a price for ruins and ashes. "Can't you see that? It doesn't matter to me what you've seen, or done, or been—now that I've found you it doesn't matter to me any more." *There is no time, or death, or past; unless I let them come between us.*

"It doesn't matter? You don't care if I've been another woman's lover for five years? You don't care how many of the Lady's sacred mers I've butchered just so I can stay young with her forever? You won't care, when you find out where I went today with the take from our last Hunt, or what's going to happen to your fish-stinking kin and mine in a few more hours because of it?" He grabbed her by the wrist, twisting her arm. "It still doesn't matter that I'm Starbuck?"

She pulled back, half in revulsion, half in anger, unable to answer or even struggle as he began to lead her down the hall.

He reached a door, hit the lock with his palm and kicked it open, dragging her after him into a room. Light flared, hurting her eyes, as he shut the door again behind her, and sealed them in with his fingerprints. Moon found her own reflection gaping at her in every wall. She looked up at the ceiling to find herself looking down; looked down again too quickly, and staggered sideways into Sparks's waiting arms. He smiled at her, but it was no smile she had ever seen on his face, and it turned her cold inside. "Sparks . . . what is this place?"

"What do you think it is, Cuz?" He twisted her in his arms until she saw the wide bed in the center of the room. His arms locked around her as she began to squirm; his hand groped her breast. "It's been a long time for you, hasn't it, sweeting? I could tell when you looked at me out there. So you've come all this way to be Starbuck's lover, huh? Well, any way you like it, honey—" He jerked open his shirt front, she saw scars like thin white worms along his ribs. "I can oblige you."

"Oh, Lady, no—" Her hand covered his side, shutting them away from her eyes.

"No? Then we'll make it fast and uncomplicated, the way Summer girls are used to it." He hauled her to the bed and threw her down across it, pinning her there with his body. She kept her mouth clamped tight against his rough kisses, bit back her cry as his hand squeezed a breast hard enough for pain. "This shouldn't take long." He fumbled with his pants, his eyes never leaving her face.

"Sparks, don't do this!" She worked a hand free, stroked his face with desperate gentleness. "You don't want it to happen, and I don't—"

"Then why don't you fight back, damn it?" He shook her, with a kind of wildness in it. "Contaminate me, sibyl! Prove you're something I can never be. Kick me, bite me, make me bleed—make me crazy."

"I don't want to hurt you." Staring up at her own face in the ceiling, Sparks's fiery hair, his body obliterating hers, she saw only the image of Taryd Roh's face going slack and mindless, the image of Sparks's the same way . . . *too easy, too easy!* She sucked in a harsh breath. "I can! Believe me, I can do it! I can make you mad. But I don't want to hurt you." She shut her eyes, turned her face away, feeling the weight of his breathing body press the air out of her lungs. "She's hurt you enough, because of me."

His eyes were a wall. "Don't waste your pity on me, sibyl, because you won't get any back." He gripped her jaw with his hand, turned her face to him. "You're with Starbuck—you wanted Starbuck, and there's nothing lower on this world than he is." But it was his gaze that broke under hers this time; and she realized suddenly that even if he had wanted to go on with it, his body had refused him.

"I wanted Sparks! And I've found him. There's no crown of spines on you, no black hood, no blood on your hands. You aren't Starbuck! Throw them away, Sparks— you don't have to wear them any more."

"I'm not Sparks! And you're not even Moon. . . ." He shook his head, she felt a tremor flow through their bodies.

"We're ghosts, echoes, lost souls; caught in limbo, damned in hell." He let her face go.

"Sparks . . . I love you. I love you. I've always loved you." Wincing, murmuring the breathless words like a charm to bring calm seas. "I know what you've done, but I'm here. Because I know you. I *know* it was meant to be. I wouldn't be here if I didn't believe we could make up for the time and the wrongs between us. If you don't believe it's true, then send me away. . . . But first look at yourself, look in the mirror! It's only you there, only me beside you. We're the waking, not the nightmare."

He rolled off of her slowly, staring at her. "What—what happened to your cheek? Did I do that to you?"

She lifted a hand to the smudged yellow remains of the bruise, nodded.

He got up from the bed, his face pale and expressionless, went toward his reflection waiting impassively in the wall. Their hands met at the interface; he pressed his forehead against its image, and Moon saw his body tighten like a coiled spring.

"Sparks—"

His hands turned into fists, and he smashed them into the mirror; sent his reflection clamoring down in a hail of splintered ice. He backed away, turned . . . she saw blood trickling down his hand like zigzag lightning.

She pushed herself up and went to him, closing his hand in hers, staunching the wound.

"No, don't!" he cried. "Leave it, let it bleed!" eagerly, almost joyfully. She looked up at him, sickened, but he shook his head. "Don't you see? I'm alive! I'm alive, Moon . . ." He made a sound that was like laughter, but wasn't. She saw his eyes become the color of emeralds; and tears overflowed with the flicker of the lids. He raised his wet hand to his wet face. "Moon. My Moon." His arms went around her again; but this time there was nothing hurting about his embrace except the pain of rebirth and release. "Alive. Alive again. . . ."

She felt sudden fire pass into her through her skin and

kindle at his nearness. She reached up to unfasten her cloak, let it fall, pressing herself even closer. Her fingers found the slashes of his shirt; she felt his flesh, warm and smooth, his muscles sliding under her touch. His own hands slipped down along her sides, rose again, tracing the line of her back. He began to lead her to the bed, moving with her, drawing her down beside him on the cool sheets, this time with infinite tenderness. "No, let me ... just let me ..." He kissed her softly. He slipped her dress down over her shoulders, along her body to the floor, with hands that sang against her skin. He removed his own clothes, self-consciously; she tried not to see the scars on his body.

They lay back together, and now looking up she saw nothing but the moment reflected, and her heart's desire. They began to touch each other again; slowly, almost shyly, rediscovering the secret joys that had been theirs in Summer. Time began to spiral toward infinity, and her body became the source point of the universe as he brought every part of his own body to the realization of her pleasure. He took her to the brink of ecstasy with a skill that had never been his before, holding her there, circling in the air ... with a motion letting her fall in glorious flames, to rise again like a phoenix ... again and again. Swept out beyond the depths of her anticipation, lost in time, she answered him as best she could, murmuring the breathless love words that could not tell him enough about her joy, filling her own instinctive response with the passionate energy of her pent-up longing set free. And at last they fell together, consumed in fire; lay as soft as ashes in each other's arms. Complete in their love, complete in each other, they slept.

42

"Moon . . . Moon, wake up."

Moon sighed, dreaming in the warm embers. "Not yet." She kept her eyes closed, half-afraid to open them.

"Yes. You have to." Sparks's voice stirred her gently, insistently. "We can't stay here much longer. The reception will be over soon. We've got to leave the palace before Arienrhod comes looking for me." Fear closed the words in. "But the police are looking for me too."

"I know." She nodded. "We'll find a place where you can stay until after the Change."

"The Change!" He turned rigid under her hand. "Oh, my gods . . . oh, my Lady!" He sat up, his fists clenched.

"What is it?" Moon sat up beside him, abruptly awake, and afraid.

He faced her, pale with anguish. "There won't be any Change, if Arienrhod has her way. She's going to start a plague that'll kill most of the Summers here in the city."

Moon shook her head. "How? Why?"

"She's hired an offworlder to do it, a man called the Source. He does a lot of her dirty work; he even had the old Commander of Police poisoned. I paid him today with the water of life." He bit his lips. "She wants to stay Queen, and keep Winter here forever; that's why!"

Moon shut her eyes, concentrating on the enormity of horror so that she would not see his hand in it. "We've got to stop it!"

"I know." He threw the covers back. "Go to the Blues, Moon, and tell them everything. They can stop it, if it isn't too late already." He twisted the covers between his hands. "Mother's Eyes! How could I—?"

Moon felt panic clog her throat as she remembered why

417

she could not go to them either. "Sparks, I've been off-world. And they know that, too."

He looked up sharply. "They'll deport you."

She nodded, pushing back her hair. "But they have to be told."

"Then we'll both go. Maybe . . . they'll let us stay together." He let his hand fall along her back.

She felt her skin turn to gooseflesh. "Yes." She pushed herself up and off the bed, knowing that if she hesitated she would never be able to separate herself from him again. "We'd better go now." She remembered abruptly that BZ would be waiting; she closed her eyes again, blotting out their reflections.

They dressed in silence and left the mirrored chamber; she glanced back one last time through the closing door, as the mirror-light winked out. They moved along the empty corridor quickly and still silently, in their silence discovering that the reception hall below had grown dim and silent, too. She watched Sparks's face turn tense and furtive. "Sparks—remember that we belong here!" She pulled her hood up, half covering the ruin of her disheveled hairdo, and made her movements regal.

He looked at her. He nodded, but his expression was equally troubled. They went on down the stairs, slipping unobtrusively past the reception hall where weary servants circled, clearing away the remains of the banquet. They reached the Hall of the Winds at last, shadowy and moaning as she remembered it, with the ghost ships eternally adrift.

"How did you cross the Pit?" He whispered it, and she could not help whispering her answer.

"With this." She held up her wrist, letting him see the control box.

He started. "Only Arienrhod—"

"Herne. Herne showed me how to use it."

"Herne?" Disbelief. "How?"

She shook her head. "I'll tell you—everything, later." The memory of the calling spell as she crossed the bridge came back to her vividly. "Just help me cross back now . . .

don't let me stop, whatever happens." She took a deep breath.

"All right." Worry touched his dim face again, without any understanding of why she was afraid.

They started toward the lip of the Pit, toward the bridge. Moon felt the Sea breathe, coid and damp against her flushed face; raised her hand to press the first tone of the calming sequence. But Sparks turned back, for one last look into the dark past. She reached out, her doubt quickening as he turned.

And then the rattling air filled with light, the hall was transformed. They shrank together, blinking, uncomprehending; shielded their eyes.

They were not alone. "Arienrhod!" Sparks gasped. Moon saw a woman standing where they had stood at the entrance to the hall, around her a gathering of richly dressed nobles—and palace guards. Glancing back over her shoulder, she saw more figures waiting across the bridge.

The Queen. The woman Sparks had named Arienrhod came toward them slowly; slowly coming into focus. Moon saw the hair, milk white like her own, twisted into an elaborate sculpture and crowned with a diadem . . . saw Arienrhod's face—her own face, as though she were moving into her own reflection. "It's true. . . ."

Sparks didn't answer, not looking ahead but only from side to side, searching for an escape.

Arienrhod stopped in front of them, and Moon lost track of everything but the fascination that locked the moss-agate eyes of the Queen with her own. But there was none of her own amazement in the Queen's gaze. She almost thought that Arienrhod had been waiting for this moment forever. "So you've come at last, Moon. I should have known you would survive. I should have known *you* wouldn't let anything keep you from your goal." She smiled, and there was pride in it, but curiously wrapped with envy.

Moon met the gaze steadily, expressionless, not understanding its implications. But at a deeper level she felt their vibration like a sonic field, disorienting her. *She expected me . . . how could she know that I had to come?* "Yes, Your Majesty. I've come for Sparks." She made it a challenge, knowing instinctively that it was something this woman would appreciate.

The Queen laughed, a high sharp sound like wind rattling ice-coated leaves; but with disconcerting echoes of her own laughter. "You've come to take my Starbuck away from me?" Sparks glanced up at her, and past her at the waiting nobles, as she let his secret out; but they were too far away to hear what was said over the sighing of the Pit. "Well, you're the only one who can." Again Moon heard the ache of secret envy. "But you wouldn't keep him long. You saw him hesitate. You don't really believe that he could be content in Summer after he's belonged to Carbuncle, do you? You don't really believe he'll be satisfied with you when he's belonged to me?" almost sadly. "No, child of my mind . . . you're still only a child. An incomplete woman; a pitifully inadequate lover."

"Arienrhod!" Sparks cried out, his voice raw with anguish. "No—"

"Yes, my love. I was moved. You were very tender with her." She smiled. Moon felt her face flush, felt outrage and humiliation throb like poison in her blood. "You see, I do know everything that happens in my city." The words glinted. "I'm disappointed in you, Starbuck. Although I can't say that I'm surprised. But I'm willing to forgive you." She reached out to him with the words, softly, without sarcasm. "You'll realize this was a mistake when you've had time to think it over." She raised a hand, and the guards came toward them, semicircled them at the Pit's edge. "Escort Starbuck to his chambers . . . and see that he stays there."

Sparks stiffened. "It's finished, Arienrhod! You know that. I'm free, no matter what you do to keep me here. I'll never change back. You'll never touch me again—" He took a long, unsteady breath. "Unless you let Moon go. Let her go away now, and I'll do anything you want."

Moon opened her mouth, starting forward; but he froze

420

her with a look. She followed his urgent glance across the bridge—*to warn them....*

"After we've talked together, alone. If she still wants to go then, I promise you I won't stop her." Arienrhod held out her hands to them, empty of deceit.

"Whatever she says, don't listen to it. Promise me, promise me you won't believe what she'll tell you." Guards closed in on Sparks. Moon felt her own hands try to reach him. But Arienrhod stood watching, as she had watched.... Sparks reached out, but the same unspoken knowledge stopped him, and his hands dropped to his sides. The guards took him away.

Moon stood alone between the Queen and the abyss. The wind lapped her, her shivering loss intensified; she kept it hidden under her cloak. "I have nothing to say to you." The words fell from her mouth like stones. She turned her back on the Queen, took a step toward the bridge's beginning. *Don't think, don't think about it. You have no choice.*

"Moon...my child. Wait!" The Queen's voice caught her like a fishhook. "Yes, I saw you, but you no more need to feel ashamed of that than you would of seeing your own reflection."

Moon turned furiously. "We aren't the same!"

"We are. And how often does a woman have the chance to watch herself make love...?" Arienrhod held out her hands again, with a kind of longing. "Didn't he tell you, Moon? Couldn't he?" Moon stared, uncomprehending, saw Arienrhod begin to smile. "Well, it's better this way; if I explain to you myself.... You're mine, Moon. You're of me. I've known about you since the day of your conception, watched over you all your life. I wanted to bring you here to me years ago; that's why I sent you that message about Sparks. Then you disappeared, and I thought I'd lost you forever. But you've come at last."

Moon stepped back from Arienrhod's intensity, felt the wind warn her. *Lady, is she insane?* She tugged the cloth of her cloak. "How do you know so much about me? Why would you even care? I'm no one."

421

"Moon Dawntreader is no one," Arienrhod said softly. "But you are the most important woman on this planet. Do you know what a clone is, Moon?"

Trying to remember, Moon shook her head. "A . . . a twin." She felt a peculiar prickling begin just under the surface of her skin. *But you've been the Queen forever.*

"More than a twin, closer than a twin. An ovum, a set of genes, taken from my body and stimulated to reproduce an identical person."

"From your body," Moon whispered, touching her own, looking down at it as though it had suddenly become a stranger's. "No!" raising her head again. "I have a mother . . . my grandmother saw me born! I'm a Summer!"

"Of course." Arienrhod said. "You are a Summer . . . I wanted you to be raised as one. I had you implanted in your mother's womb at the last Festival, along with other clones in other hosts. But you were the only one who survived, and was perfect. Come away from the edge. . . ." She moved forward to take Moon's arm and draw her away from the brink of the Pit.

Moon tried to pull free, but her body belonged to the Queen . . . and she felt it obey, stiffly, liquidly; a thing made of technology and magic. *We're so alike . . . everyone sees it, everyone.* "Why—why did you want so many— copies; Summers, not Winters?" Refusing to include herself.

"I only needed one. It was my dream, then, to replace myself with you, when I died at the Change. With myself —but raised to understand the Summer mentality, and how to manipulate it. I would have brought you here, explained it all to you years ago—so that you would have had time to adjust to your true heritage. But then I thought you were lost to me . . . and I found Sparks, instead." Moon grew rigid; but Arienrhod was looking inward. "And I decided that I didn't have to die—that I could live on, myself, and let Winter live on with me. I made another plan, to let me do that; I didn't need you any more. But I still want you—I've always wanted you here by me: my own fair child; and no one else's." She lifted Moon's face, with fingers under her chin.

No one else's . . . Moon felt her eyes lock with Arienrhod's, her mind shifting heights—the voice that spoke to her like a mother, the face of a girl, the face in the mirror; the eyes that call her down the endless spiral of time. . . . *Who am I? Who am I?* "I'm a Summer! And you're trying to kill my people."

Arienrhod recoiled, the moment shattered. "He told you that . . . he's a fool. He can't see that they're not his people, or yours. Moon, Myself, you are a Winter in your heart, just as Sparks is an offworlder!" She gestured at the stars. "You've been offworld, you know how the Hegemony oppresses us—you've seen what they keep from us, and keep for themselves while they exploit us. Haven't you?" demanding an answer.

Moon stood looking up. "Yes, I know it. And I hate it." She saw the death of countless mers among the countless stars. "The Change has to be changed."

"Then you understand how the absurd, tech-hating superstition of the Summers keeps us in chains while the offworlders are gone. We'll never break free from their control unless we have the time to start developing a technological base of our own. How else can we keep even what little the offworlders leave to us, unless we destroy the Change pattern?"

"Not by destroying our people!" *My people; they are my people!* Blotting out Arienrhod's mirror image with the memories of her family, her childhood, her island world.

"Then how?" Arienrhod's voice lost its patience. "How else will you ever convince them, or convert them?" But she stood as though she were actually listening, expecting a genuine alternative.

"I'm a sibyl." Her heart lurched as she confessed it to the Queen of Winter, but she knew that Arienrhod must already know it, too. "When I tell them the truth about what I am, when I prove it, they'll listen."

Arienrhod frowned her disappointment. "I thought you'd have lost your obsession with that religious mummery, after what you've seen offworld. There's no Sea Mother filling your mouth with holy drivel; any more than

423

the other ten thousand gods of the Hegemony exist in any way except as straw men for the offworlders to curse at." A gust of wind poured out of the Pit, smelling of seaweed; Moon shivered inside her cloak, in spite of herself. But Arienrhod, wrapped in fog layers of filmy cloth, laughed at her mirror's reflection of fear.

"Sibyls aren't a—" But Moon broke off again. *She doesn't know the truth. She can't know* ... suddenly aware that she held a hidden weapon, and that she had almost given it away. She felt her broken confidence begin to mend itself; tried to keep the knowledge from showing in her eyes, afraid that in some way Arienrhod would be able to read her every secret.

But Arienrhod was caught in the machinery of her own design. "I know why you wanted to be a sibyl ... because you couldn't be a queen. But you can be, now—" A light behind the agate translucency of her eyes.

"Forget Summer! You can share a whole world with me, a Winter world forever. Throw away your trefoil and wear a crown. Cut the strings that tie you to those narrow-minded bigots, and be free to think freely, and dream." She cast an invisible sign into the abyss. Moon felt the wind's blade at her back. "They'll never accept you as one of them, or trust what you are now. It's too late to save them, anyway. The wheels have been set in motion. You can't stop their fate, you can't change it. . . . Accept it. Rule with me, as you would have ruled after me. We'll build our dream of a new world together. We can do it together, we'll share it all—" She held out her hands, shining with passion. Moon lifted her own hands, spellbound by the nearness, the undeniable reality of her own self, her original self ... formed in the image of her creator. . . .

"Arienrhod," Arienrhod said.

Moon pulled back, smarting: Realizing that Arienrhod did not see her at all, had no understanding of why words meant to win and seduce battered and bruised her other self like stones. Arienrhod's egotism saw only the thing she longed to see ... only Arienrhod. *And you're wrong.* A deep and unshakeable certainty that was more than her own relief moved in Moon, as though she had somehow been tested without knowing it, and had proven her worth. "What about Sparks?" She heard her own question, brittle ice to match Arienrhod's expectations. "Will we share him too?"

Arienrhod's placid face flickered, but she nodded. "Why not? Could I really be jealous of my . . . self? Could I refuse myself anything? He loves us both, how could he help it? Why should he have to deny it?" as though she had to make herself believe it.

"No."

Arienrhod's head gave a curious twist. "*No*? No what?"

"No more." Moon drew herself up, feeling the limitless strength the word released in her. "I'm not Arienrhod."

"Of course you are," Arienrhod said placatingly, as to a stubborn child. "We share the same chromosomes, the same body—the same man and the same dream. I know this must be difficult for you to accept, when you never suspected. . . . I would never have had it happen like this. But how can you deny the truth?"

Moon wavered, felt a deeper certainty harden her resolve. "Because I know that what you plan to do is wrong. It's wrong. It's not the way."

"Why is it wrong to change the world for the better, when you have the power to do it? The power of change, of birth, of creation—you can't separate those things from death and destruction. That's the way of nature, and the nature of power . . . its inexorability, its amorality, its indifference."

"Real power," Moon lifted her hand to the sign at her throat, "is control. Knowing that you can do anything . . . and not doing it only because you can. Thousands of mers have died so that you could keep your power while the offworlders were here; and now thousands of human beings are going to die so that you can keep it when they're gone. I'm not worth a thousand lives, a hundred, ten, two —and neither are you." She shook her head, seeing the face before her, seeing herself. "If I have to believe that being what I am means I'd destroy Sparks, and destroy the

425

people who gave me everything, then I should never have been born! But I don't believe it, I don't *feel* it," fiercely. "I'm not what you are, or what you think I am, or what you want me to be. I don't want your power . . . I have my own." She touched her throat again.

Arienrhod frowned; Moon felt her anger like sleet. "So they were all imperfect, failures . . . even you. I always believed I could supply the thing you lacked . . . but no; no one can give you that. You're a gutless weakling—thank the gods I don't have to depend on you now to achieve my goals."

Moon looked down at her hands, at white fists. "Then we really have nothing to say to each other, after all. You told me I could go." She took a step toward the bridge, her heart leaping ahead.

"Wait, Moon!" Arienrhod caught up to her again, drawing her back and around. "Can you really leave me like this; so soon, so easily? Isn't there some way for us to share something more than our stubborn pride? You above all should have been the one, the only one, who would understand the things no one else could ever reach in me, the things that I've never been able to give to anyone else." Her voice, her touch, softened. "Give me time, and perhaps I can learn to reach what lies unreachable in you."

Moon swayed: a fatherless, motherless child hearing her own voice crying a lifelong loneliness; reaching out to embrace her own strength, and redouble it, parent and child in one. But her inner eye showed her Sparks, scarred in body and mind, and what his final silence had sworn her to. "No. No, we can't." Her gaze fell. "There's no time left."

Arienrhod flushed; softness fell away from her face, left unforgiving iron. Her hand rose as if to strike Moon's face; but it caught the beaded choker instead and jerked, breaking the threads. "You think you can stop me. Then leave, if you can. My nobles know that you're a Summer sibyl." She waved at the Winters still standing patiently beyond the bridge and behind them. "And they know that you came here disguised as me, to commit some treachery. If

426

you can make them believe you're not those things, then you deserve to go free—and to be a part of me." She turned away abruptly, striding back toward the palace halls alone.

As she went toward them the waiting nobles advanced, bowing as they passed her, and ringed Moon in at the foot of the bridge. Moon watched Arienrhod go on, never turning back, until she lost sight of her beyond the shifting wall of vengeful faces.

43

"Well, Commander. I hope you enjoyed the Queen's banquet." Chief Inspector Mantagnes broke off his conversation with the sergeant, hoping nothing of the kind, as Jerusha entered the hollow quiet of headquarters from the clamoring streets. Virtually everyone on the force was out, either protecting the Prime Minister or patrolling the festivities. The two men made a desultory salute; she returned it perfunctorily. Mantagnes eyed her dress uniform enviously. She knew that he must have spent the evening brooding because he wasn't at the reception in her place, strutting in front of his fellow Kharemoughis in the position that was rightfully his.

"I don't enjoy wasting my time, when there's still so much work to be done." She looked pointedly at the two of them; pulled off her scarlet cloak, opening her collar. "You're relieved as acting commander, Inspector."

"Yes, ma'am." He saluted again, his eyes reminding her that she wouldn't be hearing that for much longer. *Yes, you son of a bitch, you'll have your turn.* The Chief Justice's damning, unfavorable report on her and Mantagnes's own ambitious backbiting would ensure the record of her command here was painted as black as the void. Her career

427

would be finished with this post, her seniority and rank swept under the carpet of official censure. She would never have a chance at a command again; she would be shipped off to some godforsaken outpost on the back side of nowhere (acknowledging grimly that there were worse places than Carbuncle). And there she would rot for the rest of her natural life.

Gods, I'm sick of Kharemoughi arrogance! She bunched her cape between her hands as she started toward her office. *If I have to see one more damned, supercilious Technocrat face* . . . BZ Gundhalinu's face came suddenly into her mind, slowing her. *One more face.* That face she would give anything to see, right now, right here. But he had never arrived with his prisoner. She should have known— but how the hell could she know that Gundhalinu of all men would run off with the girl instead? *Because it was obvious!* She had put into her report that he was ill, unaccountable for his actions; and the gods knew it was probably truer than she wanted to admit.

And tonight she had seen Sparks Dawntreader, openly flaunting his sanctuary there at the banquet, drinking himself into a stupor. And Arienrhod, serenely beautiful as always, serenely unconcerned about her upcoming fate as she moved among her subjects and her supposed masters— far too unconcerned. *Damn it! What's she planning?*

"Damn it, what's this doing here?" She stopped, glancing away at Mantagnes, and back at the polrob standing as immobile as a tree in front of her office. "Why aren't you on duty?" addressing it directly. It made no response, and she realized that its power was off.

"It's malfunctioning," Mantagnes said irritably. "Came in here a while ago with some garbled story about its Winter lessor being mugged by the Queen's men. Probably just maudlin with lease-lapse syndrome. Needs a complete system wiping—letting ignorant natives do even partial maintenance on sophisticated hardware like that is absurd."

"Even 'ignorant natives' would wonder, if they had to bring their brainless servomechs to the police for every loose screw." She threw the power switch on the polrob's

428

chest, more out of aggravation than interest, watched the light sensors brighten inside its steel and plastic skull. She glanced at its identification plate. "Unit 'Pollux.' Who's your lessor?"

"Thank you, Commander!"

She stepped back, startled.

"Please hear me, Commander. It is urgent, and I cannot—"

"Yeah, yeah—just answer the questions." She would never get used to their voices.

"My lessor is one Tor Starhiker Winter, Tiamatan female, titular owner of Persiponë's Hell." It radiated impatience.

"You said she was attacked by the Queen's guard? That's no business of ours."

"No, Commander. By offworlders. By her fiancé—"

"A lover's quarrel?"

"—one Oyarzabal, a casino employee, and his companions. She called to me for help, and was stun-shot by them. I could not reach her because the door was locked. So I came here for help."

"You know why they attacked her?" Jerusha felt her interest stirring.

"Not clear, Commander. Perhaps she interfered with an illegal activity."

"Who controls that casino?"

"One Thanin Jaakola, male, native of Big Blue."

"The Source?" She felt even Mantagnes begin to listen behind her.

"Yes, Commander."

"Repeat everything you heard them say."

"OYARZABAL: Just the Summers, goddamn it, Perse. Not the Winters, they'll be safe; the Queen wants it this way. STARHIKER: No, you're lying. It's going to kill Winters too, the Queen wouldn't let you kill us. You're crazy, Oyar, let me go. Pollux, help me, Pollux."

Jerusha listened, her skin crawling at the nasal dirge of words, until their meaning coalesced in her mind, catalyzed by two: *the Queen.* "Holy gods—I've found it! I've found

429

it! Sergeant!" Shouting as she turned, she found him already standing at her elbow. "Contact the dozen men closest to Persiponë's—tell them to get over there immediately and seal that place off! Mantagnes—"

"What's this all about, Commander?" She couldn't decide whether he was indignant or frightened.

"It's about life and death." She dropped her cloak on the floor, reaching to check her stunner. "It's about Arienrhod buying her own life with the death of half this city, or I'm not the Commander of Police." She watched his jaw fall. "Unit Pollux—your prayers and mine have been answered." She clapped its metallic shoulder. "Gods, just let it be in time!"

"Please help Tor, Commander. I have grown—attached to her."

She nodded, not quite believing she'd heard that. "Mantagnes, you're always bitching about how you want more action. Let's go find it."

"You're going up there yourself, Commander?" more astonished than critical.

Grinning now, she said, "I wouldn't miss this for sainthood."

44

"So, sibyl, you've threatened our Queen." A man spoke at last; Moon felt the group stare of the angry nobles burn the tattoo into her throat like a brand. "And you're forbidden to come into the city. We have been given the privilege of seeing that you never do either of those things again."

Moon backed toward the bridge span, fighting the memory of what had happened here in the city to Danaquil Lu. "I'm going to leave the palace. If you touch me, I'll contaminate you. Don't try to stop me—" Her voice slid.

"We won't try to stop you, sibyl," he said, his voice hungry and blurred. "Cross the bridge; go ahead." He grinned, and it turned his thin face into a death's-head. They were all smiling suddenly, with drug-drunken, heedless malice—people who had been celebrating the end of their world, and knew who to blame for it. He took something out of a hidden place in his long outer robe and held it up; it looked like a dark finger. "Cross the Pit."

Moon covered her control box with her hand, staring at the thing he held; not sure what it was, but only that it was a threat to her. But she had to cross the bridge; she had to try. There was no other way. With clumsy hands she reached up to unfasten her gold-stitched velvet cloak. She folded it in threes, which was the Lady's sacred number, and stepped toward the windy lip of the abyss in a defiant ritual. The cape was only a hindrance on her back; but it was a worthy gift to the Sea Mother, if She lay hungry below. Hungry for tribute, or hungry for sacrifice . . .

Lady, guide me! Moon pitched the cloak outward with a prayer, heard the laughter of the nobles behind her. It bellied out in the crossdrafts, drifted and circled like a plummeting fisher bird into the shaft's green darkness.

Moon pressed the first button in the sequence at her wrist, and started out onto the bridge. The Winters watched and muttered, but did nothing. Moon sounded another note, walked on, not even breathing. At the far end of the bridge more nobles waited; she tried not to see them clearly . . . not to look down, not to listen to the demon dirge around her or the clamoring of fears inside her head. . . .

But as she neared the center of the span the catch-spell of the sibyl's song invaded her again, slowing her, lulling her fears, dulling her instinct for survival. *No!* She froze, letting her terror rise up and counterattack before the song could snare her mind again. But even as she stopped moving, she saw the Winters ahead all holding the same hollow fingers, raising them to their lips—*whistles!* To control the winds. . . . And now at last she understood: They were turning the winds against her; this was how she would die, without a human hand shedding her blood.

431

Moon threw herself flat on the bridge span as the choir voice of the whistles collided and smashed her circle of quiet air. The winds swept over her, tearing at her. But in the middle of the wind lay the sibyl song—like the clear air in a hurricane's eye, the clarity of a strange madness filling her mind. Hypnotized, paralyzed, she plunged through into a refuge that lay in some other plane of existence. . . .

Why? Why does it call me here? "What's the answer?" she heard her own voice screaming wildly. "What's the answer?" *You can answer any question, except one,* Elsevier had told her. Not *What is Life?*, not *Is there a God? . . .* The one question she was forbidden to answer was *Where is your sourcepoint?* And in this moment, teetering at the eternity's edge of insanity or death, she knew that at last it had been answered, that she had been chosen again by the power that lived in her mind: *Sourcepoint, fountainhead, wellspring . . . here, here, here!* Below this shaft that plunged into the sea, below this pinpoint city driven into a map of time, as secret as stone beneath the guardian seaskin of this water world, lay the sibyl machine. And she alone would know. She felt her mind give way under the final assault of knowledge, and fall into the well of truth; cried out as she felt her body lose control to follow it down. . . .

Like a startled dreamer she came into herself again, lying on the bridge span, gasping loudly in the quiet air. *The quiet air. . . .* She pressed her hand over her mouth, pushed up slowly onto her knees. There was no wind at all; only a peaceful stirring and sighing around her. The Winters stood gape-faced on the far edge of the abyss, their whistles dangling from strengthless fingers. She dared to look away, past the wind curtains hanging slack in a becalmed sea, to the storm walls beyond. The walls were closed, shutting off the flow of the cold crosswinds from the outer world, sealing off their only access to the well at Carbuncle's heart, and to her. She sank forward again, pressing her forehead against the surface of the span in silent gratitude.

432

She climbed unsteadily to her feet, made her way on across the bridge. She moved slowly, for the sake of the watchers, for the sake of her uncertain legs. The Winters' expressions mixed awe and terror now; she set her face in grim defiance, willing them to let her pass.

And some fell back, but there were some who turned angrier, more hate-filled and reckless at the sight of a Summer wearing the face of their Queen, wielding the power of a goddess. And among them she saw the iron pole crowned with a halo of metal thorns, the witch collar that had torn open Danaquil Lu's throat. The collar came forward to meet her and keep her from stepping off the bridge. "Kneel down, sibyl, or go into the Pit!" The jewel-turbaned woman who held it thrust it at her; she took a step back, her hands knotting at her sides.

"Let me past or I'll—" As she spoke she saw them turn, heard the precessing echoes of many footsteps coming down the entry corridor toward the hall. And as suddenly the crescent of space behind the nobles began to fill with human figures—but this time they wore homespun and kleeskin: *Summers!* Their faces were as murderous as any Winter face had been until a second before; they carried knives and harpoons, and the faces looked at her, alone on the bridge, without changing.

"There she is! It's the Queen!"

Moon saw the one face that didn't belong with the rest, one man working his way forward among them with desperate determination. "BZ!" She shouted over the rising noise as the mobs met, caught his searching gaze and felt it embrace her.

Gundhalinu elbowed aside a final Summer, making himself a space to draw his weapon and let the crowd see it clearly. "Hold it! Hold it!" He jerked the thin-mouthed woman holding the spined collar half around and wrenched it out of her startled hands. He hurled it over the edge into the Pit. "That's gone far enough, Winter. Get back— clear away, all of you!"

"What right have you got to interfere with us, foreigner? This is Winter business, Winter law—"

433

"That's for damn sure," BZ muttered, his eyes coming back to Moon even as he cleared a path for her through the human wall. "This woman's under arrest; she's mine." Moon caught the wink of an eye in it, and smiled in spite of herself.

"That's the Queen, Inspector Gundhalinu!" one of the Summers said angrily. "And she's ours. She's not going anywhere until the Change." The words were as deadly as frost.

"She isn't Arienrhod. She's a Summer, a sibyl! Look at her throat." BZ waved a hand. "If you want Arienrhod, you'll have to cross that—" Following his own gesture, he looked out across the windless hall for the first time, and his face turned blank. "What—?"

"What business do you have with our Queen, fish farmers?" The jewel-turbaned woman who had lost control when she lost the sibyl collar tried to take it back again. "You're not welcome in this palace while it still belongs to Winter."

"Your Queen has business with us!" a Summer shouted. "She's trying to kill us all, and we've come to make sure she doesn't get away with it. And to make sure she goes down to the Lady for the third time."

Moon listened without moving, overwhelmed with aching, irrelevant joy at hearing a voice speak with a Summer burr. "I'm Moon Dawntreader Summer—" Her voice was in rags. "The Queen is inside. Cross the bridge now! As long as I stand on it you'll be safe." She waved them forward, felt BZ's astounded eyes on her.

The mob came more confidently as they saw her trefoil and put their trust in it. Her own belief wavered as the first of them joined her on the bridge; but the air lay resting, and the Summer smiled briefly and bent his head as he passed. One by one the others followed, treading nervously but driven by the furious need to reach their goal. Moon waited until the last Summer had stepped safely onto the ledge at the far side of the hall before she took the final steps onto solid ground. The Winters backed away, sullenly watching her and Gundhalinu. She turned as she reached his side, hearing a tremulous sigh behind her. She saw the storm walls open like langorous wings spreading, felt the chill winds rise again, the curtains shudder into life. The Pit groaned and stirred, reeking of the sea.

"Gods! Father of all my grandfathers," BZ whispered. "It was you, holding back the wind. How—how did you do it?" He kept distance between them.

"I can't tell you," hugging herself. *That it's Carbuncle. I can never tell anyone; never.* "I don't even know." *Must never let anyone know.* She followed the Pit down in her mind, down, down to the sea and below it, into the timeless bedrock of the planet itself, where the ultimate receptacle of human wisdom lay in secret omniscience. "Take me away from here, BZ. This is no place for a sibyl; the Winters are right. It's too dangerous." She felt the hostile, disbelieving stares of the nobles crawl over her.

BZ led her from the Hall of the Winds with regulation propriety, back down the corridor past the scenes of Winter's reign. No one followed them. BZ still kept a small distance between them as they walked. Shaking out her mind, she picked through the dazzling fragments of her last hours for the terrible secret that had been uppermost until she stepped out onto the bridge: "What were they doing here, the Summers? Did they tell you what Arienrhod—" *who almost killed me;* she was suddenly dizzy, "what she had done?"

He shook his head, his concentration fixed on the motion of his feet. "I couldn't make anything of it; they were in too much of a hurry. I don't think they even knew. All a mob needs is a crazy rumor."

"It's not a rumor. It's true. And they won't stop it by holding her prisoner. She's hired offworlders to start a plague." Moon threw the words out at him heedlessly.

"What?" He stopped, stopping her. "How do you know—?" breaking off as the possibilities registered.

"Sparks told me."

"Sparks." He looked down again, nodding to himself. "So you found him, then. And it—you and he, still . . ."

"Yes." Her hands locked in front of her.

435

"I see. Well." He sagged against the wall, kept his face averted for a long moment, with his coughing as an excuse. She realized that his reluctance to touch her wasn't all because of what he had seen in the Hall of the Winds. "He didn't come out with you."

"The—Arienrhod caught us. She took him back." She looked back along the hall, felt herself tearing inside. But the spur of alien prescience goaded her again: *Leave him, leave him. Leave now. . . .* "He'll be all right, now that the Summers have come to guard the Queen. They don't know him," trusting the power that protected her to guard him too. "I have to stop the plague. I know who's behind it; Sparks told me everything. I've got to tell someone, the police . . ."

"He didn't turn you over to the sibyl baiters, then?" BZ said, as though his mind couldn't leave the idea alone. He wiped his forehead on his sleeve, pulled open his coat.

"No. Arienrhod did it."

"Arienrhod! But I thought she—" He didn't finish it, didn't need to. She felt his wordless compassion reach out to her.

She wrapped a strand of hair around her finger, looked at it, pulled on it. "There were nine of us, BZ . . . and none of us suited her. We weren't what she wanted us to be. So she—she abandoned us, she threw us away." Moon lifted a hand, a farewell to her own lost soul. But sudden sun shafts penetrated her clouded sight. "You knew. You knew about me too. Why did you trust me here, if you knew all along?"

"I knew all along that she'd never make you into her image. Do you think I could spend—so much time with you, and not feel the difference between you?" He shook his head; his smile grew stronger. "And it won't be long now before she'll damn her haste in getting rid of you. Come on, and tell me what you know about this plot."

Moon walked with him again, holding the healing warmth of his trust against the scars of grief as they went on toward the looming palace entrance, moving toward the end of Winter. She told him everything she knew, forcing herself to keep her mind on the narrow path through wild-lands. The doors opened, letting in the life force of the city, sucking them back into its vortex of vitality. There were no royal guards at the entrance now, but instead a knot of belligerent Summers squatting in a watch of their own. Moon stayed close in BZ's shadow, until she realized that they had no more idea of what the Queen looked like than she had had. She saw one or two spot her trefoil tattoo instead, and look their surpise at her. "BZ, how did you know to come after me? How did you know I needed you?"

"I didn't. When the Summers showed up, I decided I'd waited long enough. So I flashed my ID and made myself into a police escort." He nodded left and right as the Summers let them by. "I'm going to miss that badge . . ." There was nothing to support the lightness in his tone, and it collapsed. He began to cough again, the ugly coagulation rattling deep in his chest. He stopped moving as they reached the no-man's-land between the Summer guards and the milling onlookers. "Now . . . listen, Moon." He wiped at his eyes, struggled for a breath. "I've got to face charges . . . sooner or later anyway. I've got to go back, I might as well get it over with now. I'll report everything you've told me to the first patrolman I see. There's no need for you to risk turning yourself in. Your people are here; tell them about you and Sparks before they learn he's Starbuck. They can help you where I can't." His mouth pulled into a tight line, as though he couldn't trust himself to say more.

"BZ." She covered her mouth with her hand. "How can I—"

"You can't. Don't try." He shook his head. "Just let me go. . . ." He began to turn away, but she saw his knees turn to water. He collapsed in slow motion and lay senseless on the white stones.

——45——

Tor sat in the corner, propped against the wall like a spine-
less rag doll; the laboratory's white, formless light drove
spears into her watering eyes. Beyond the wall behind her
back she knew there was a whole city full of people oblivious to her folly or her doom—oblivious to their own
doom. But no sound of the celebration reached into this
sterile room, no laughter, no music, no shouting. The wall
was sound sealed, and no sound of hers would ever escape
it, if she had even had the power to make one. She struggled futilely, silently, against the invisible bondage of her
paralysis. It would be nearly an hour before her voluntary
nervous system would have the control to move even a
finger again; and she was sure there wasn't that much time
left in the rest of her life. *Oh, gods, if I could only scream!*
The scream echoed inside her head until she thought her
eyes would explode ... and she whimpered, a thin, miserable thread of sound, the most beautiful noise she had ever
made.

Oyarzabal glanced over at her from the table, where he
sat in the hot glare of disfavor's spotlight. His broad face
with its leonine brush of side-whiskers showed discomfort
approaching her own; he looked away again hastily. The
casually surreal debate about the most effective means of
starting an epidemic here in the city droned on, the buzz-
ing of a ghoulish hive. One of the others had gone to talk
to the Source. *Oyarzabal, you lousy bastard, do something,
do something!*

Oyarzabal suggested that they pollute the water supply.
It was rejected as ineffective.

Hanood, who had gone to the Source half an eternity

ago, came back into the room, relocking the door behind him with exaggerated care.

The insect drone fell silent. Tor watched heads turn to the judge's verdict, not even able to roll her own eyes. "Well?" One of the men she didn't know asked it.

"He says get rid of her, naturally." Hanood bent his head in her direction. "Dump her body into the sea; nobody'll be able to figure out where she disappeared to in all this." He waved a hand toward the unreachable reality beyond the wall. "They say, 'The Sea never forgets' . . . but Carbuncle will."

Tor moaned, but the sound stayed trapped inside her.

"No, damn it, I don't believe it!" Oyarzabal stood up to a confrontation. "I'm going to marry her; I'm going to take her away. He knows that, he wouldn't say to get rid of her!"

"Are you questioning my orders, Oyarzabal?" The Source's hoarse, disembodied voice descended on him from the air; all of them looked up involuntarily.

Oyarzabal hunched under the weight of it, but his resolution held. "You don't need to kill Persiponë. I can't just stand here and let that happen." His eyes searched the walls, the corners of the ceiling, uncertainly. "There's got to be some other way."

"Are you suggesting I should have them kill you, too? Your incompetence caused this situation, after all. Didn't it?"

Oyarzabal's hand slid toward his gun under the tail of his long leather vest. But it was five to one against him, and Oyarzabal never took suicidal odds. "No, master! No— But . . . but she's going to be my wife. I'll make sure she's not going to talk."

"You think now that Persiponë knows what you're doing here she'll still want to marry you?" The voice turned colder. "Amoral animal that she is, she still hates you for this. You'll never be able to trust her."

Oh gods, oh Source, just let me talk! I'll promise him anything! Sweat trickled maddeningly down her ribs.

"And I'll never be able to trust you again, Oyarzabal,

unless you prove your loyalty is still to me." The voice paused, seemed to smile; Tor shuddered inside. "But I'm not totally unsympathetic to your position. So I'll give you two choices: Either Persiponë dies, or she lives. But if she lives you'll have to take measures to make sure she can never testify against us."

Oyarzabal's sudden hope went behind clouds. "What do you mean?" He dared to glance at her, looked away again.

"I mean I want her unable to tell what she knows to anybody, no matter what they do to her. I think an injection of xetydiel would be effective enough."

"The hell! You mean turn her into a zombie?" Oyarzabal swore. "She won't have any brain left!"

One of the others laughed. "What's wrong with that: mindless and yours. Since when did a woman need a brain, anyhow?"

Oh, Lady, help me . . . help me, help me! Tor called on the faith of her ancestors, abandoned by the thousand uncaring gods of the betraying offworlders. *I'd rather die. I'd rather die.*

"You see the trouble women cause when they take too much freedom on themselves, Oyarzabal—see the trouble this stupid female's curiosity has brought on you. And think of the trouble her Queen is about to cause her own world." The Source's voice was a rasp wearing down metal. "Then make your choice: dead or brainwiped. And choose for yourself, when you choose for her."

Oyarzabal's hands clenched and opened at his sides as he swept the room and the five other faces, seeing what was obvious. "All right! But I don't want her killed, I don't want to watch her killed. I want her alive."

Tor whimpered again, felt a dribble of saliva ooze out at the corner of her mouth. A tremor ran up her legs out of her toes—*Move, move!*—but no further.

"Then I can take care of the lady's needs." The spokesman for the group of technicians—a man she had finally recognized as C'sunh, a biochemist, an expert on drugs—stood up from the table and moved to one of the sealed cabinets beyond her cone of sight. She listened to him sorting bottles and utensils, listened to the hissing cloud inside her head begin to drown out every other sound.

Oyarzabal shifted from foot to foot, his head down, as though he hadn't expected things to happen so suddenly, so irrevocably. Tor murdered him with her eyes.

"Shall I go ahead and inject her, master?" The biochemist came back into her line of sight, holding a syringe.

"Yes, take care of it, C'sunh," the voice said softly. "You see, Persiponë, you never win. It always turns out the same."

Tor watched C'sunh come toward her, watched everything within her sight turn golden; the static in her head deafened her. Oyarzabal watched him, too; watched her, his hands at his sides, his eyes glazing.

A heavy pounding sounded through the sealed door. The chemist froze in midstep as a muffled voice shouted, "Open up! Police!" The men at the table leaped to their feet, looking at each other and up into the air in disbelief.

"Blues!"

"Master, there's Blues in the casino! What'll we do?"

But no answer came, and sensation too excruciatingly high to register as sound drilled into Tor's brain. The men covered their ears with their hands. "They're cancelling the seals! Do something, for gods' sakes! Finish her, C'sunh!"

The chemist came toward her again, his face contorted with pain, the thin plastic cylinder still in his hand. Oyarzabal went after him abruptly, grabbed his arm. But then the others were on Oyarzabal, and C'sunh was bending over her.

"No!" Tor gasped the word, her last—

The door burst open and her vision filled with fluid blue: the room filling with half a dozen uniformed police. "Hold it!" Weapons trained everywhere; two or three found C'sunh's back and face. He straightened slowly away from her. "Drop it." The Blue stared him down. He let the syringe fall; she cringed as it landed centimeters from her unprotected leg.

"Doctor C'sunh, as I live and breathe!" Tor saw the Commander of Police herself materialize out of the

441

amorphous wall of blue tunics. "You've been in our files for as long as I can remember—it's a real pleasure to finally meet you in the flesh." She grinned with the pleasure of it, and clamped binders on him. Her men were doing the same for Oyarzabal and the rest. She leaned over, searching Tor's face, glancing aside at the fallen syringe. She smiled again. "Well, Tor Starhiker. You look like you've got something you just can't wait to tell us. And I can't wait to hear it. Hey, Woldantuz! Get over here and give this woman a shot. The right kind." She winked reassurance as one of the patrolmen appeared at her side and kneeled down.

Tor barely registered the burn of the antidote as the Commander's space was filled by an even more unexpected face. "Pollux!" The word didn't quite form, but control was coming back to her; she felt it climb through the levels in her mind like a drug rush.

"Tor. Are you all right?"

"What . . . what . . . did you . . . say?" She gulped and gasped.

" 'Tor. Are you all right?' " he repeated, as tonelessly as before. He bent forward, offering her his arm as she tried to get her feet under her. She took the arm gratefully, hauling herself up.

"Whoo." She put a hand to her head, dizzy with relief, leaning heavily against him. Her fingers sank into the soft frizz of her skewed wig; she pushed at it absently . . . hearing again the last words the Source had spoken to her. She closed her hand, jerked the wig off her head and threw it down. "Since when have you had a vocabulary, you can of bolts?" She leaned back, staring into Pollux's inscrutable nonface; felt a grin of triumph spread across her own. "Hellfire . . . I was right about you. You old fraud! Why didn't you ever talk to me before, damn it?"

"Just a little joke, Tor." Deadpan.

"Hah. That's the kind of laughs you'd expect from a machine. How long've you been able to talk like that?"

"Since I was programmed at the police academy on Kharemough."

"The what?"

"Cancel that, Pollux." The Commander reappeared on his other side, frowning. "You really do need work. . . . You can thank Pollux for your timely rescue, Starhiker. And I think I can thank him for a lot more—if you'll tell me I'm right in what I figure was going on here." She pointed a thumb at the lab and the captives behind her.

"Thanks, Pollux." Tor burnished his chest softly with her hand. "They were going to start a plague," she felt her legs weave under her again, "and kill all the Summers with it."

PalaThion nodded as if it was what she'd expected to hear. "Who put them up to it?"

Tor looked down.

"The Snow Queen?"

Startled, she nodded, feeling inexplicable shame at admitting it to an offworlder. "That's what they said."

"That's what I thought." PalaThion smiled cold-bloodedly, no longer seeing her. "I've beaten her at last! Unless . . ." She shook her head, glancing away as another Blue entered the room, an inspector this time. "Mantagnes?" she said eagerly.

But the inspector shook his head grimly. "We missed him, Commander."

"Jaakola? How the hell could you possibly—"

"I don't know!" He met her anger with his own. "When we broke into his office, he was gone. We searched everywhere—a fly couldn't have hidden in there! They're still searching . . . but he had a way out, and we haven't traced it yet."

"He won't get off-planet." PalaThion pulled at the empire sign on her belt buckle. "We'll get him."

"Don't bet on it." Mantagnes studied his feet, disgusted.

"Then let him try finding a hiding place from charges of attempted genocide." She waved a hand. "Woldantuz, let's put these other beautiful people in the bottle where they belong. At least we've got all the evidence. And a witness. Starhiker, I'll need your testimony."

"Count on it, Blue." Tor nodded, feeling her urge for

revenge blaze up as C'sunh was led past her. Two of the others followed him before she saw Oyarzabal.

"Persiponë?" He pulled his guard to a stop. "I guess I won't be takin' you with me after all. Not where I'm bound now."

"You wanted to make me into a vegetable, you lousy bastard! That's all you ever wanted!" She pushed past Pala-Thion to stand in front of him. "I hope you stay there until you rot. I hope you never even see another woman——" She remembered suddenly that he had tried to stop it at the last; and that the few seconds he had won her had made all the difference.

"I didn't want you dead, that's all! Even havin' you like that was better than havin' you dead." He leaned toward her; the Blue held him back.

"Speak for yourself." She folded her arms. "Since you're the only one you seem to think about."

He looked away, at PalaThion. "If you want what I know about this, just ask. I'll tell you anything." PalaThion nodded, and one of the other men swore under his breath. Tor realized that Oyarzabal's life wouldn't be worth a drunkard's damn from now on, no matter where they sent him.

And there would be no getting off this world for her now, no matter what she did. *Oh, gods, why can't I ever do anything right?* She hugged herself tightly, because there was no one else left to hold her, or to hold. She felt PalaThion look at her, found an unexpected sympathy in the woman's eyes. PalaThion's head moved imperceptibly, until she was looking at Oyarzabal, and past him.

Tor stepped forward, still holding onto herself, protecting herself, as she closed with Oyarzabal. She kissed him briefly on the mouth. She stepped back again, and they wouldn't let him follow. "So long, Oyar."

He didn't answer her. The Blues led him out of the room. Tor moved back to stand beside Pollux. *Why is it? Why is it? That you never want what you've got till you've thrown it away?*

444

——— 46 ———

Jerusha leaned forward across the duty desk, craning her neck to follow the sight of Dr. C'sunh and his fellow would-be genocides being led away into the detention wing. *Oh, sweet revenge!* There was nothing sweet in her smile. She had broken Arienrhod's plot at the last possible moment; and even though she couldn't touch Arienrhod herself, she had set the Summers on her, and they would keep her safe until the day of her execution. *Maybe there is some justice in the universe, after all.* "Starhiker!"

Tor Starhiker glanced through the thinning screen of self-congratulatory blue uniforms; she sat drinking strong tea under the watchful gaze of Pollux. She got up from the bench, came striding through the patrolmen toward the desk. Jerusha watched her come with bemused interest. Her clinging bodywrap left considerably more of her chunky body uncovered than it covered; she walked like a dockhand, oblivious to the casual ogling of the men she passed. A plain, pragmatic face was emerging through the smeared makeup, and her lank mouse-colored hair was chopped off bluntly at ear-length. *Ye gods, there's a human being in there.* Jerusha remembered abruptly that one of the men she had just sent away seemed to be in love with that human being. *Damn it, why can't right be right and wrong be wrong . . . why can't it be simple, just once? I'm sick of gray.* She shook it off as the woman stood before her. "How are you doing?"

Tor shrugged, lost a drape of cloth and pulled it back onto her shoulder. "All right, I guess. I mean, considering . . ." She looked away at the doorway to the detention block.

"Well enough for a monitored testimony?"

445

"Sure." Tor sighed. "I guess I don't get to appear at the trial, huh?" She rested her hands on her hips.

The trial would be held on some other world now. Jerusha smiled, understanding the irony. "Consider yourself lucky. Dr. C'sunh has a lot of friends, and they're all out there." She gestured at the ceiling. Tor made a face. "At least once we're gone from Tiamat, you'll be safe from them. Your statement will do all the damage that you could, as long as it's properly recorded; and I'll make damn sure it is, believe me. I just hope it'll be enough to drag in the Source. If the—" She broke off as a fresh clot of strangers entered the station. No, not strangers. She stood up, saw everyone else in the room turn to stare with her.

"What the—"

"Arienrhod?"

"Moon!" She heard herself say it, heard Tor echo it, without taking time to wonder. She saw two sturdy Summers behind the girl, carrying Gundhalinu's body. "Shit . . . !"

Moon hesitated as she saw Jerusha move out from behind the desk, but she stood her ground resolutely as the handful of patrolmen gathered around them.

"Who's that?"

"Gundhalinu!"

"I thought he was—"

"Is he dead?" Jerusha caught Moon by the shoulder, all her perspective gone.

"No!" Jerusha saw the anguish on the girl's face as she wrenched her around, and she let her go in surprise. "He isn't dead. But he's sick, he needs a medic." Moon's hand reached out toward him, couldn't quite touch him.

"That didn't matter much to you two days ago, did it?" Jerusha looked past her at Gundhalinu's lolling head and closed eyes, his gaunt, sweating face. She gestured for two of her own men to take him away from the Summers. "Get him over to the med center; hurry. And carefully, damn it! He's worth more than diamonds to me."

They carried him away, carefully. The two Summers nodded at Moon, almost making obeisances, and went

446

back out into the alley. Moon didn't try to follow them, or Gundhalinu, with more than her eyes. She had gotten herself a long golden gown somewhere; even with her hair straggling down around her face her resemblance to Arienrhod was incredible.

"And you're under arrest, Dawntreader, in case you'd forgotten." *My gods, this is too much for one day.* She lifted her hand, summoning another officer.

Moon grimaced. "I haven't forgotten you, Commander. BZ . . . Inspector Gundhalinu . . . I escaped. He found me again. He was bringing me in when he collapsed." She said it all unblinkingly.

"Sure he was." Jerusha unhooked the binders from her belt, said very softly, "That's the biggest crock I ever heard. Fortunately I choose to believe it, for Gundhalinu's sake." She saw the girl's marked throat, remembering abruptly that she was a sibyl. Jerusha lowered her hands with the binders toward her belt again, grudgingly. "I suppose these aren't necessary, sibyl. But you didn't come here to tell me that. Why the hell did you come?"

Moon smiled briefly, ironically; the expression looked alien on her face. She stopped smiling. "I came because the Queen wants to cause a plague to kill all the Summers in the city, and I know who's going to start it."

"You're too late." Jerusha grinned with self-satisfied triumph, until she saw Moon's reaction. "No—I mean we've already stopped it. We've got the guilty parties, they're our permanent guests right now." She gestured toward the lockup, mellowing in the warmth of fortune's smile.

"Already? It's over? They didn't—" Moon glanced over her shoulder at the station entrance. She looked back at Jerusha again, stricken, abruptly realizing that she had sacrificed her freedom for nothing.

"They didn't. The Summers are safe. Arienrhod has failed, and she's under house arrest. She won't get away from your Lady." A passing patrolman called congratulations to her; she nodded.

Moon's face twitched as though she didn't know what to feel, as though there were more layers to the knowledge

447

than even she could penetrate. "How . . . how did you find out?" wearily.

"By chance; with unintentional cooperation from—" She turned to Tor Starhiker, eavesdropping behind her.

"Hey, kid," Tor raised a hand, and Moon blinked with recognition. "Hey, Pollux, come here!"

"Persiponë?" Moon half frowned at Tor's unglamorized face, still only half-sure. She looked past her as the polrob came toward them.

"What's she under arrest for?" Tor jerked a thumb at Moon, indignantly, a little too impressed with her own role as key witness. "It's not against the law to impersonate the Queen, is it? Not your laws, anyhow."

"That depends on how well you do it," Jerusha said. She shifted her weight from one foot to the other. "You know each other?"

"Since today. That seems like forever." Tor shook her head, strained for a smile. "Look what she's done to your hairdo, Polly. . . . So what happened, cousin? Did you find him? Did you get him out of the palace? Did you see the Queen—did she see you?"

"You were in the palace?" Jerusha demanded. The clear wall of official accusation turned the girl into a prisoner again. "To meet the Queen—"

Moon felt the change, and defiance beat back at her. "To find my cousin!" She glanced quickly at Tor, nodded, blushing. "You know what . . . who I am, don't you, Commander?"

Jerusha nodded, keeping her distance mentally. "I've known for a long time." Tor looked blank beside her.

"So has everyone; except me," Moon murmured bitterly. "I was the last to know."

"I still don't know," Tor said.

"Did Gundhalinu tell you?"

"No, Arienrhod did." Moon twisted a strand of hair.

Jerusha started. "You saw her?"

"Yes," almost a whisper. "She wanted me with her to share . . . everything. Even Sparks," coldly. Moon reddened again; angry, not ashamed. "She wanted me to forget that

I'm pledged to him; forget that I'm a Summer; forget that I'm a sibyl. And when I wouldn't forget, she tried to kill me." The bitterness increased a magnitude. Jerusha frowned as her own surprise deepened. Moon rubbed her eyes, swaying where she stood; Jerusha remembered all that she had been through, and how much of it had been for Gundhalinu's sake.

"Sit down. Pollux, bring us some tea." Jerusha dismissed the waiting guard, touched Moon's elbow, turning her toward the seat along the wall. Moon looked surprise at her; Jerusha felt a twinge of surprise at herself. Pollux moved away obediently through the trajectories of official activity. Tor included herself in the rest of the invitation: "Get me a refill, Polly."

"You said Arienrhod tried to kill you?" Jerusha sat down.

Moon dropped heavily onto the seat, a little away from her; Tor stretched out fluidly at the bench's end. "She told the nobles I was a sibyl, and they tried to throw me into the Pit."

Tor sat up straight, speechless for once.

"Her own clone?" Jerusha felt her incredulity fade even as she said it. *Yes, that's the Arienrhod I know. No competition.*

"I'm not Arienrhod!" Moon's voice shook with denial. "I'm wearing her face, that's all." She pulled a hand down over her own, her fingers clawing, as though she wanted to strip it off. "And she knows it."

Pollux returned and passed around tea with the silent propriety of a butler. Jerusha took a sip from her bowl, letting the scalding heat rise inside her head. *It could be a trick, another trick, her coming here.* But for the life of her she couldn't imagine what purpose could lie behind it.

"They tried to throw you in the Pit?" Tor prodded, staring at Moon's throat. "What happened?"

"It wasn't hungry." Moon drank her tea, a strange emotion moving across her face. Tor looked pained. "BZ—Inspector Gundhalinu came in with the Summers and made them let me go."

449

"You mean that fishing pole with you was a real Blue?" Tor asked.

"He was once." Jerusha rested her heavy-helmeted head against the wall. "I hope he will be again."

"He never stopped wanting to be anything else," Moon said quietly. "Don't let him give it up, and throw everything away. Don't let him blame himself for what happened." She gulped tea.

"I can't keep him from doing that." Jerusha shook her head. "But I'll make sure no one else blames him for it." *I can save his career; but I can't save him from himself . . . or from you.* "Tell me," her resentment crystallized into accusation, "by all the gods, what do you see in Starbuck, that bloody genocide—"

"Sparks isn't Starbuck . . . not any more." Moon set her empty cup down on the bench, rattling it as the *genocide* registered. "And he never knew about the mers. But you do."

From you. Jerusha glanced away abruptly. "Yes. Your friend Ngenet—told me the truth about them." *My friend Ngenet . . . who trusted you, and trusted me to know about you.*

"Ngenet?" Moon shook her own head, rubbed her face again. "You must have known it before. Any sibyl knows the truth, you can't deny that," including the whole of the Hegemony in the accusation. "You want to punish Sparks for killing mers on offworlder land—for splattering blood on you while you stand and watch them die, with your hands out begging for the water of life! And you want to punish me for knowing the truth—that you're punishing my world for your own guilt."

Tor sat listening with wide ears, but Jerusha made no move to get rid of her. She made no move even to answer, cupping the Hegemonic seal of her belt buckle with cold fingers; Moon watched her intently through the long moment. Jerusha frowned. "I don't make the laws. I just enforce them." Wishing, as she said it, that she hadn't said that much.

Disappointment showed in Moon's eyes, but she didn't

450

press the argument. "Sparks isn't Starbuck! He wasn't Starbuck in Summer; and there won't be a Starbuck any more, when Winter's gone. Arienrhod did it to him, and he only let her do it because—because she was so like me." Moon glanced away. Jerusha felt a pang of sympathy at the girl's sudden shame and confusion. She stared at the trefoil tattoo. "Sparks was the one who told me about the Queen's plot. He was coming here when she caught us—he didn't care what you did to him, or me, as long as you kept our people from dying." She looked up.

"If he wants to make up for the last five years, it'll take more than that. It'll take him the rest of his life." Jerusha tasted venom.

"Do you hate him that much?" Moon frowned. "Why? What did he ever do to you?"

"Listen, Moon," Tor said. "Everybody in Carbuncle has a reason to hate either Sparks Dawntreader or Starbuck. And that includes me."

"Then you gave him a reason to hate you."

Jerusha looked away. "He repaid us all a hundred times over."

Moon leaned forward. "But at least you owe him a chance to prove he doesn't belong to the Queen now. He knows everything about the Source's plan—couldn't he testify for you? He knows other things about the Source, things you could use—"

"Like what?" interested in spite of herself.

"What happened to the former Commander of Police? He was poisoned, wasn't he?"

Jerusha felt her mouth fall open. "The Source did it?"

"For the Queen." Moon nodded.

"Gods . . . oh, gods, I'd like to get that on tape!" *With a spare to play every night, to sing me to sleep.*

"Enough to drop the charges against us?"

Jerusha refocused on Moon, saw determination running swift and deep in her strange eyes; realized suddenly that she had been led blindfolded to this point—that the girl was still fighting for her lover's life, and her own. *You've learned the rules of civilization well, girl.* Resentment

451

struggled inside her, died stillborn. She looked at the trefoil tattoo again. *Hell and devils, how long can I go on hating her face, when there's no proof she ever deserved to be born with it?*

"Will you let me go and bring him here?" Moon half rose, anticipating her surrender.

"It may not be that easy."

Moon sat down again, her body taut. "Why not?"

"I let it be known all up and down the Street that Sparks was Starbuck, when I learned about it. The Summers must already know who he is." *And I'd be a hypocrite if I didn't know that I wanted it to happen that way.* "They won't let him leave the palace now."

"He was supposed to be all right! That's the only reason I left him there!" Moon cried her betrayal to the air; faces turned to stare at her across the room. Her eyes glazed suddenly, vacant windows. Jerusha edged away from her, away from contamination. "No, no!" Moon's hands clenched into fists. "You can't use him and let him die! I did it all for him—you know that's why I came here. Not for you, not for the Change. . . . I don't care about the Change, if it means he has to die!" It had the sound of a threat. "Sparks isn't going to die tomorrow—"

"Someone has to," Jerusha said uncomfortably, uncertainly, trying to pull her back into the real world. "I know he's your lover, sibyl—but the Change is bigger than any one person's wants or needs. The Change ritual is sacred; if the Sea Mother doesn't get her consort, there'll be hell to pay from the crowds that came to see it. Starbuck has to die."

"Starbuck has to die." Moon echoed it, getting slowly to her feet. "I know. I know he does." She put her hand to her head, her face drawing pain, as though she struggled against some compulsion. "But Sparks doesn't! Commander." She turned back, her face still strained. "Will you help me find First Secretary Sirus? He promised me," she smiled suddenly, sardonically, "that if there was anything he could do himself to help his son, he'd do it. And he will."

"I can contact him." Jerusha nodded. "But I want to know why."

"I have to see someone, first." Moon's determination faltered. "Then I'll tell you, and you can tell him. Persiponë, where's Herne now?"

Tor raised her eyebrows. "Back at the casino, I expect— By all the gods," with a kind of wonder, "I think *I* finally understand something in this conversation." She grinned congenially at Jerusha. "Eat your heart out, Blue."

Jerusha lay sprawled on the low couch in the den of her townhouse, one foot hanging, tethering her to the floor, *or I might just float up to the ceiling.* She smiled, watching the past day's events replay again on the inside of her eyelids; listening with half an ear to the noisy celebration out in the alley, and letting herself believe that it was all for her. *Well, hell, at least half of it ought to be.* She loosened the seal of her uniform tunic a little further. For once she had not taken it off immediately when she got home . . . for once it felt too good to be a Blue, and the Commander of Police.

She heard Moon Dawntreader moan and sigh in her sleep in one of the darkened spare rooms. Even as tired as the girl must be, she didn't rest well in this place either. Jerusha had not slept at all, and another day had begun already, somewhere beyond the time-stopping walls of the city. But it didn't matter; in another few days she'd be gone from this place forever. And for once she didn't mind reliving over and over the day just past, or anticipating the new one to come: There was a message on her recorder asking—not ordering, asking—her to a meeting with the Chief Justice and members of the Assembly. After breaking up Arienrhod's plot and capturing C'sunh, after making the Source too hot for any world . . . after all that, her black-and-blue career was alive and well again, and so was she.

Then what was she doing with a criminal asleep in her guest room? She sighed. By the Bastard Boatman, the girl was no more a criminal than she was. And no more Arienrhod than she was. Who cared if Moon had seditious thoughts about the Hegemony? Gundhalinu was right—what could she do about them, once the offworlders were gone? And although she wanted to deny it even to herself, the memory of the mers and what the girl had said about punishment and guilt still gnawed at her like an ulcer. Because it was true—it was, and she would never be able to deny that again, or deny the hypocrisy of the government she served. *Well, damn it, what government was ever perfect?* She had stopped Arienrhod, and she could tell herself that looking the other way about Moon was her payment of conscience to Tiamat's future. She could even let it go for Sparks, let him be Moon's grief, if he delivered the testimony she wanted. And if she let him go, her conscience damn well ought to be clear forever. . . . But she knew it wouldn't be. She had seen too many things she should never have seen here, and had too many people she had tried to categorize slip out of her psychological shackles and overcome her resistance. *Some of my best friends are felons.*

She smiled painfully, pinched by sudden regret. *Miroe . . . good-bye, Miroe.* She had not heard from him since that last death-cursed day they stood together on the bloody beach. . . . *But that's no good-bye. Not remembering that scene.* She sat up on the couch, shaking out cobwebs. *No—I can tell him that I've found Moon, that she's all right, and that Arienrhod is going to pay.* Yes, she should call him now, while she had the time, before they cut communications, before it was too late. *Call him, Jerusha, and tell him . . . good-bye.*

She got up, moved stiffly across the room to the phone, unexpected flutterings in the pit of her stomach, as though

454

she had swallowed moths. She punched in the code, cursing the adolescent attack of nerves under her breath as she waited for the call to go through.

"Hello? Ngenet Plantation here." The voice was absolutely clear, for the first time she could ever remember. It was a woman's voice; Jerusha heard the coldness come into her own:

"This is Commander PalaThion calling. Let me speak to Ngenet."

"I'm sorry, Commander, he's gone."

"Gone? Gone where?" *Damn it, he can't be smuggling now!*

"He didn't say, Commander." The woman sounded more embarrassed than conspiratorial. "He's had a lot on his mind lately—we've all been getting ready for the Change here. He went on board his boat a few days ago and left. He didn't tell anyone why."

"I see." Jerusha exhaled gradually.

"Is there any message?"

"Yes. Three things: Moon is safe. Arienrhod will pay. And tell him I—tell him I said good-bye."

The woman repeated the message carefully. "I'll tell him. A good voyage to you, Commander."

Jerusha glanced down, glad that her face didn't show. "Thank you. And good fortune to all of you." She switched off the speaker and turned away from it—seeing the shell on the shrine table by the door, still sitting where it always had, its broken spines a mute testimony to what had been, and was not to be. *It's better this way . . . better that he was gone.* But her eyes were hot and brimming suddenly; she did not blink until the reservoir of tears subsided, so that none escaped her control.

She turned back to the phone, changing the subject with an effort of will. Gundhalinu . . . should she call again about him? But she had already called the city medical center twice, and they had told her the same thing: He was delirious, she couldn't talk to him. They didn't know how he'd managed to stay on his feet, the shape he was in, as sick as he was; but they didn't expect it would kill him.

455

Reassuring. She grimaced, leaning against the wall. "Well, maybe by the time she got back from the meeting with the Chief Justice. . . . Yes, she'd have everything to tell him, then. And in the meantime she'd better wash up and get back to headquarters again before it was time for her audience.

She pulled a pack of iestas out of her pocket, went into the bathroom to wash up and change. Moon slept on, restlessly, exhaustion setting her free from her fears about whether Sirus would get her cousin out of the palace. Jerusha still could not really believe that the First Secretary of the Hegemonic Assembly had ever agreed to attempt such a thing, even if Sparks Dawntreader was his son—a son he had never seen, and could hardly be sure was even his. But he had come willingly to meet with Moon, and he had gone away willing to try.

More inexplicable to her was how Moon had gotten the crippled Kharemoughi bartender from Persiponë's to agree to take Spark's place. Gods, the girl had barely been in the city two days! If she really believed Moon's personal magnetism was enough to make men willing to die for her, she'd lock that kid up so fast her head would spin—But there had been undercurrents in the conversation between the girl and the two men that told her there was more to Herne's going than just the way he looked at Moon . . . and one glance at his legs gave her a good reason. In her own private judgment Herne looked like a man the Hegemony would be better off without; and in any case, she had asked no questions, for fear of getting an answer she couldn't ignore.

Jerusha heard someone stirring in the next room, looked out the refinished doorway to see Moon stumble foggily into the hall. "You might as well go back to bed, sibyl. Time passes faster when you aren't watching it. For better or worse, Sirus won't be back for a while yet."

"I know." Moon rubbed her sleep-blurred face, shook her head. "But I have to get ready if I'm going to run in the race." Her head came up, and her eyes were not soft with sleep.

456

Jerusha blinked. "The Summer Queen's race? You?"

Moon nodded, daring her to try to stop it. "I have to. I came here to win the race."

Jerusha felt someone step on her grave. "I thought you came for your cousin Sparks."

"So did I." Moon looked down. "It lied to me. It never meant for me to save him; it only used him, to make me follow its plan. But it can't keep me from trying to save him anyway. . . . And I can't keep it from making me Queen."

Millennium come. Jerusha breathed unspoken relief, felt her pity stir. *Gods, it's true—sibyls are a little crazy. No wonder Arienrhod didn't want her after all.* "I appreciate your being honest about it with me." She pulled a fresh tunic on over her damp skin, and sealed it up the front. "I won't stop you if you want to try." *But if you win, don't tell me; I don't want to know.*

Moon would not have believed it was possible to clear a space as long as her arm and keep it clear for even a moment in the quicksand shifting of the Festival mobs. But somehow order had been created out of chaos; somewhere in the seemingly formless superentity that was the Festival an underlying structure existed. A course had been cleared along the Street's upper reaches for a mile below the palace, and eager spectators lined the way like the elegant townhouse walls at their backs. Most who had a viewing place had been holding it for hours, and the Blues who patrolled casually up and down before them had little trouble keeping them there. They had come to watch the beginning of the end, the first of the ancient ceremonies of the Change: the footrace that would thin the numbers of

457

the women who had come to compete for the mask of the Summer Queen.

Moon had come out into the Street as soon as the nucleus of Summer women began to form around an elder of the Goodventure family, who carried in her the blood of Tiamat's last line of Summer Queens. Members of that family were forbidden to become Queen at this Change, but instead bore the honored responsibility of seeing that its rituals were faithfully preserved and carried out. She had pulled a colored ribbon from one of their sacks to tie around her head—the ribbon that would give her a place at the front, middle, or back of the starting mass. The band she drew was green, the sea: the color that put her in the front, ahead of brown for the land, blue for the sky. She tied the ribbon across her forehead, her face palely expressionless against the triumph and the disappointment around her. Of course it had been green . . . how could it not be? But a tension born of certainty wrapped her, tightening like tentacles; she pushed toward the front of the forming field of runners to escape it.

She looked around her as she struggled to hold a new equilibrium in the jostling mob of colored ribbons and eager Summer faces . . . in this crowd of strangers. Most of the women who had come to the Festival intending to run in the Summer Queen's choosing had brought with them traditional-style holiday garments: soft wool shirts and trousers dyed sea-green, summer-green, to please the Lady. They were all elaborately sewn with designs made of shell and bead and traders' baubles, ribbons that dangled fetishes of their family totems. But she wore the nomad's tunic she had brought back with her from Persiponë's, the only clothing she owned, its gaudy color as alien as she suddenly felt herself, among the people who should have been her own. She had covered her hair with a scarf, to hide her resemblance to the Queen. Some of the Summers had challenged her right to run because she wore no totem or proof that she was even a Summer. But then she had shown them her throat, and they had backed away. She felt the irony of wearing a Winter's clothes today, and not ones

458

that were rightfully hers; and yet somehow it was appropriate.

She had not seen anyone she knew, either among the runners or in the crowd of spectators beyond. Even though she knew that she could hardly expect to find anyone from Neith or its few island neighbors in these hundreds, in the thousands that filled Carbuncle, still she searched, and was disappointed. The sights and the sounds and the smells of her home surrounded her here; but her grandmother was far too old to make this voyage, and her mother— "Festivals are for the young," her mother had said to her once, with pride and longing, "who don't have ships to tend and mouths to feed. I had my Festival; and I hold the precious memory of it close beside me every day." Her arm had gone around her daughter's shoulders, steadying her on the rolling deck. . . .

Moon whimpered, seeing the ugly truth hidden in her mother's merrybegotten memory. The woman next to her apologized and edged nervously away. Moon looked down at herself as the half-fearful sibyl-space opened around her again; suddenly glad that her mother had not come, would not watch her in the race today, whatever its outcome was. Her mother and Gran must think she was dead, and Sparks, too, by now; and maybe it was better that way. Their time of mourning must be long past. Was it better never to let them know the truth, or to always be afraid that once they had learned part of it they would somehow learn the whole, terrible truth about their children? She swallowed her grief, choking on it, turned her vision outward again.

She was not her mother's child . . . and not Arienrhod's, either. *Then what am I doing here?* She looked around her in sudden doubt. She was the only sibyl she had seen here anywhere. Was she the only sibyl among all the Summer people who wanted to compete? Was it really the Queen's ambition running in her blood that made her want to be a queen herself? *No, I didn't ask for this! There must be a change; I am only a vessel.* Her fists tightened as she repeated the vow. If no other sibyl ran in this race, maybe it was only because none of them knew the truth.

None of them know. She could read on the faces around her the spectrum of motives and gradations of desire that had brought the runners here: some of them hungry for the power (although the power of a Summer Queen had always been more ritual than secular), some for the honor, and some for the easy life of being worshiped as the Lady incarnate; some simply for the sheer joy of competing, a part of their celebration, with no cares at all about winning or losing. *And none of them knows why it really matters, except me.*

She kept her fists tight as tension wound its springs inside her, pushed forward again until she could just see the piece of weighted ribbon that marked the course's start. The Goodventure elder was shouting for quiet and announcing the rules. She did not have to be the first in this race, she only had to be among the sacred first thirty-three—and the course wasn't long, it was meant to give some besides the strongest a chance. But there were a hundred women behind her, two hundred more . . . she couldn't even see them all from where she stood.

The voice of the Goodventure elder called them all to the mark, and Moon felt her self-awareness slipping, caught in the swell of many moving forward as one. Through a gap between heads and arms she watched the fragile bunting that held back their tide—saw it fall at a signal. The mass of runners surged, sending her forward, helpless to resist if she had wanted to, and the race of the Summer Queen began.

She danced like a reef spotter through the first hundred yards, needing all her concentration just to keep on her feet in the crush before the knot of bodies began to loosen. As spaces opened she broke between, not always easily, feeling elbows bruise her sides in retribution. She couldn't keep track of how many were ahead in the shifting field; she could only weave and sprint and try to put as many of them behind her as her feet could overtake.

A mile was nothing, a mile was hardly enough to quicken her heartbeat when she and Sparks had raced along the endless gleaming beaches of Neith. . . . But this mile ran

460

uphill, on hard pavement, not yielding sand. Before she had reached halfway her breath rasped in her throat and her body protested with every jarring step. She tried to remember how long it had really been since she had run on that shining sand; couldn't even remember how long it had been since she'd had enough food or sleep to satisfy the body of a bird. *Damn Carbuncle!* There were only a dozen women ahead of her, but they were slowly gaining ground. New runners began to come up on her and pass her from behind. She saw with a kind of dread that one of them wore a brown ribbon, not green—the second group of runners was overtaking the first starters; and she stumbled as her mind left her straining legs unguided.

Two thirds of a mile, three quarters, and there were more passing her all the time, easily thirty ahead of her now, and a cramp in her side that took her breath away. *They're passing me . . . and they don't know, they don't even know what they're reaching for!* Reaching after it with the last of her strength, she saw the final distance hurtle past; suspended all other awareness until the white stone courtyard of the Winter palace was under her feet, and the next-to-last winner's garland had fallen around her shoulders.

Laughing, gasping, dazed, she was swallowed by the ecstasy of the waiting crowd, joyously praised with hand-clasps, kisses, and tears. She made her way through them, took her place in the circle of winners that was forming at the very center of the courtyard. Looking back, she heard and then saw the group of musicians dressed in white, draped in garlands like her own, and wearing black chimney hats with Winter totem crests. Behind them came a small procession of Summers—more Goodventures, bearing a canopy of ornamental net woven with shells and sprays of greenery, held aloft on oars delicately carven with a fantasy of sea beasts.

And beneath the canopy came the mask of the Summer Queen. She heard the sighs and cries of admiration, like a wind through the crowd; felt her own wonder rise again at the sight of its beauty . . . *and its power, the face of*

461

Change. Her gaze moved to the one who carried it, and she jerked with recognition: Fate Ravenglass. The circle parted to let Fate through alone; the rest of the procession circled outside, mingling its music with the crowd's.

The Goodventure elder bowed before her, or before the strength of her artistry. "Winter crowns Summer, and the Change begins. May the Lady help you to choose wisely, Winter woman; for your sake as well as for ours." She stood serene in her faith in the Lady's judgment.

"I pray that I will." Fate bowed in turn, her white gown all but hidden by the mask's trailing sunbeams as it rested on her arms.

The Lady will choose. . . . Why had Fate Ravenglass been picked as Her representative, if not to choose in turn the one face, the one heart and mind behind it that knew the secrets she knew about this world? *But she's almost blind.* Could she even tell one face from all the rest? How would she know?

The Goodventure elder began to sway from foot to foot; the lacy drape of beaded network that covered her clothing clattered and chimed. She began to sing the ancient feast-day invocation, and the ring of women began to circle slowly, stepping foot across foot, drawing Moon along. The words of the litany and response came to her easily, almost hypnotically, rooted as deeply in her memory, wrapped as profoundly around its most primitive images, as anything she still remembered. It had no true rhyme, like most of the holy songs, because the language it had once been shaped from had lost its own shape down the years; its tune fell strangely on her ears. She sang with the rest, but a part of her mind held separate, watching the pageantry that the rest of her flowed into unquestioningly: the part of her that was no longer certain Fate would choose her, blindly, unaided. *Does the sibyl mind really control what happens here? It twists me in its own directions—but can it reach beyond my hand, can it really move anything that it doesn't hold on strings?*

"... Who suckles us upon Her breast
And makes Herself our grave?"

462

"The Lady gives us all we need.
We give her all we can."

Moon watched Fate begin to drift out in a countercircle, bearing the mask, her expression intent but formless. *She won't recognize me.*

"Who fills our nets and pools and bellies,
Who fills our hearts with grief?"

"The Lady gives us all we need,
And asks for all we have."

Moon bit her lip against panic, against more words, the urge to cry out, *Here, here I am!* Wanting to believe that it was predestination, but no longer certain that anything was predestined. She couldn't leave it to chance—not after she had come this far, and seen so much. *She has to choose me. But how—?*

"Whose blessings cause the sky to weep,
Whose curse melds sea with air?"

"The Lady gives us all we need,
And makes us what we are."

Moon's memory leaped forward to the next verse, and the two levels of her consciousness fused: *"Input!"*

"Who knows the one that She will call,
Or what their fate will be?"

The refrain faded as she fell into Transfer, came back with a sudden intensity that deafened her. She felt herself lurch with the shock, tried to open her eyes. But her eyes were open, and still the world she saw was barely brighter than moonlight, its edges blurred and indistinct. Her other senses fed her perception all out of proportion . . . because she was blind! In another second she had passed through terror to the understanding that she was—Fate Ravenglass. And that somewhere in that dimly seen line of figures circling past her immobile body was one that must be caught at the other pole of this Transfer. . . .

463

She watched the dim figures pass, and pass, wondering what she would find, if she would even be able to tell what was taking shape. And then she made out the one figure that stumbled in line, supported, half-carried, on the arms of the indistinguishable women at either side: herself—she was seeing herself. And Fate Ravenglass looked back with her eyes; each of them seeing her own face and knowing they did. . . . Abruptly Moon felt her borrowed body unlock and move forward freely toward her real one, the mask held out before her in her hands. As she closed with herself she could see at last that the face was really her own. It stared at the mask, back at her, with wonder and wordless fascination. She lifted the mask with Fate's trembling hands, moved again by its beauty as she set it firmly on her own shoulders.

As the mask settled in place she felt herself wrenched back across the Transfer gap, into her rightful mind, and heard her cry as she ended the trance. Looking out now through the eyeholes of the mask, she saw Fate standing dazed before her, felt her own arms still supported by the women beside her, heard the roar of the crowd's jubilation. But all that she remembered of the moment was Fate touching the face that was her own again: "My face—I saw my face. And the mask of the Summer Queen . . ."

The crowd began to close in around them, smashing the fragile circle of hands, sweeping away the also-rans. Moon's support broke away as she regained her equilibrium; she reached out and grasped Fate's hands, holding her steady, face to face. "Fate—it's happened! I did it! I am the Summer Queen!"

"Yes. Yes, I know." Fate shook her head, tears putting light in her darkened eyes. "It was meant to be. It was. It must be the first time two sibyls ever looked out of each other's eyes, and saw themselves—" She smoothed her collar of white feathers distractedly. "You'll be everything as Queen that I made your mask to be."

Moon felt her heart squeezed by a sudden, heavy hand. "But not alone. I'll need help. I'll need people my people can trust . . . and yours can. Will you help me?"

464

The feather collar rustled with Fate's nod. "I'm in need of a new career. Whatever I can do to help I'll do gladly. Moon ... Your Majesty."

The netted canopy shadowed them, and the Goodventure elder came up between them, gravely gay. "Lady!" The other Goodventures bowed around her. "Your duties today are three: To go among the people and show them that the Mask Night has begun. To be carefree. To rejoice. And your duties tomorrow are three: To go down to the docks when dawn comes beyond the walls. To deliver Winter to the Sea. To rule in her place as the Lady wills."

To deliver Winter to the Sea. Moon looked toward the palace. "I ... I understand."

"Then come with us, and let the people see you. Until tomorrow we are all between worlds, between Winter and Summer, between the past and the future. And you're the harbinger." The Goodventure woman gestured Moon under the waiting canopy.

"Fate, will you come with me?"

"Oh, yes, I'll be along." Fate smiled. "This may be the last time I have a chance to see my fellow human beings in all their glory, and I want to make the most of it." She touched her artificial eye with a loving fingertip, and sorrow. "All my masks, a lifetime's work, will bloom and fade in this one night ... and soon my sight will go into the sea with the rest of Winter's bounty, good and bad together."

"No!" Moon shook her head. "I swear to you, Fate— this will be a real Change!" The crowd began to pry between them.

"Moon—what about Sparks?" Fate called it across the widening gap.

Moon stretched her hand fruitlessly, losing control, lost in the mob. "I don't know! I don't know—" Strong arms lifted her up onto a garlanded litter, and she was borne away beneath the canopy down the Street, a leaf swirling on the stream.

Everywhere as she was carried along she saw masks appearing as the revelers hid their faces, cast off their own identities; becoming their fantasies, as the Summer Queen

465

had—as she had done. Tonight there would be no Winter or Summer, offworlder or native, right or wrong. Everywhere costumes blossomed, music played, masked faces laughed and sang and shouted for the Queen. Everywhere people followed alongside her litter, offering her food and drink and gifts, trying simply to touch her for luck. It was her duty today, tonight, to be the merry mayfly, symbol of life's fleeting joy; because not until tomorrow would her rule and the world become genuine again. . . .

And she was grateful for the mask she wore that was all those things to them, that let her hide the truth that whenever she became a part of the moment time leaped ahead again for her, and tomorrow took away her laughter. Because if her plan had failed, if Sirus had failed her, tomorrow she would speak the words and give the sign as Summer Queen, and Sparks would drown. . . .

So she actually believes she's going to be chosen Summer Queen. She hears voices telling her she'll win. Jerusha paced slowly in the rattling emptiness of the Chief Justice's antechamber, too nervous to sit still on the forlorn assortment of abandoned furniture. Against odds of hundreds to one? No, Jerusha, the universe doesn't give a damn what she believes . . . or you do, or anybody else. It doesn't matter.

There was nothing to distract her mind but the fuzzy negatives of places where things had been and no longer were in this sad, anciently naked room. But a new set of things, and people, would be back in their place when the Change came again to enduring Carbuncle. Things change all the time; but how much of it is real? Does any choice any of us ever makes, no matter how important it seems,

466

really cause a ripple in the greater scheme of things? Passing the window, she saw herself superimposed on the image of the metamorphosing city, studied the reflection silently.

"Commander PalaThion. It was good of you to come. I know how busy you've been." Chief Justice Hovanesse stood in the doorway, held up a hand in courteous welcome, and she managed to forget that she had been kept pacing out here well past the appointed time of the invitation.

She saluted. "I'm never too busy to discuss the Hegemony's welfare, your honor." *Or mine. Or to watch a man eat his words. . . .* She touched his hand politely, and he gestured her ahead of him into the inner room. It was a meeting room, with a long table built out of smaller tables and cluttered with portable terminals. The usual assortment of local Hedge bureaucrats she had come to know and loathe sat around it, intermittent with actual assemblymen, mostly strangers to her. They had, she supposed, been making the last of the obligatory reports on every imaginable aspect of their occupation of Tiamat. Even on a world as unpopulated and underdeveloped as this one the process of departure was leviathan. The few Kharemoughi faces she could see clearly looked exceedingly bored. *Thank the gods I'm only a Blue and not a bureaucrat.* She remembered that since she had become Commander she had hardly been anything else. *But yesterday I was a real officer again.*

She stood listening to the patter of their applause, of palms against the table surface, absorbing their reception while she compared it mentally to the one she had been anticipating until yesterday. Most of the civil officials assigned here on Tiamat were from the same part of Newhaven, like most of the police; the Hegemony felt that cultural homogeneity made for more efficiency. And today, at least, the fact that she was one of their own being honored in the presence of Kharemoughis seemed to outweigh the fact that she was only a female. She bowed with dignity, acknowledging their tribute, and took a seat in the mismatched chair at the near end of the table.

467

"As I'm sure you all have heard by now," the Chief Justice stood at his own place, "Commander PalaThion uncovered, and at virtually the last moment thwarted, an attempt by Tiamat's Snow Queen to retain her power...."

Jerusha listened covetously to the report, savoring every flattering adjective like the scent of rare herbs. *Gods, I could get used to this.* Even though Hovanesse was a Kharemoughi himself, he was aware that as Chief Justice he reflected her glory today, and he was laying it on thick. He sipped frequently from a translucent cup; she wondered whether it was really water, or something to numb the pain of paying her compliments. "... Even though, as most of us here are aware, there was a certain amount of—controversy about appointing a woman Commander of Police, I think she has proved that she is capable of rising to a challenge. I doubt if our original choice for the post, Chief Inspector Mantagnes, could have handled the situation any better if their positions had been reversed."

That's for damn sure. Jerusha glanced down in false modesty, hiding the glass fragments in her smile. "I was just doing my job, your honor; as I've tried to do it all along." *With no help from you, I could add.* She bit her tongue.

"Nevertheless, Commander," one of the Assembly members stood up expansively, "you'll finish your service here with a commendation on your record. You're a credit to your world and your gender." One or two Newhavenese coughed at that. "It just goes to show that no one world, or race, or sex, has a complete monopoly on intelligence; all can and shall contribute to the greater good of the Hegemony, if not equally, at least according to their individual abilities...."

"Who writes the graffiti inside his braincase?" the Director of Public Health muttered sourly.

"I don't know," behind her hand, "but he's living proof that living for centuries doesn't have to teach you anything." She saw his mouth twitch and his eyes roll in a fleeting moment of comradely aggravation.

"Would you care to say a few words, Commander?"

468

Jerusha flinched, until she realized the assemblyman hadn't even been aware of anyone speaking besides himself. *Don't let me choke, gods.* "Uh, thank you, sir. I didn't really come here planning to make a speech, and I really don't have the time." *But wait a minute—* "But since I've got you all here listening to me, maybe there is a matter important enough to spend our time on." She stood up, leaning forward on the slightly uneven tabletop. "A few weeks ago I had a very disturbing question put to me: a question about the mers—the Tiamatan creatures we get the water of life from," for the benefit of any assemblyman who was or pretended to be ignorant of it. "I was told that the Old Empire created the mers to be creatures with human-level intelligence. The man who told me this had the information directly from a sibyl Transfer."

She watched their reactions spread like ripple rings colliding on a water surface; tried to guess whether it was genuine—whether the Assembly knew, whether the civil officials did, whether she was the only human being in this room who had been blind to the truth. . . . But if any of them were faking their amazement, they were good at it. The murmurs of protest rose along the table.

"Are you trying to tell us," Hovanesse said, "that someone claims we've been exterminating an intelligent race?"

She nodded, her eyes downcast as she spoke, treading lightly. "Not knowingly, of course." In her mind she saw the bodies on the beach: *but killing them just the same.* "I'm sure no one in this room, no member of the Hegemonic Assembly, would let anything like that go on." She glanced deliberately at the oldest Wearer of the Badge among them, a man in his sixties who just might be left over from long enough ago. "But someone knew once, because we know about the water of life." If he did know, he wasn't letting her see it on his face; she wondered suddenly why she wanted to.

"So you are suggesting," one of the other Kharemoughis demanded, "that our ancestors consciously buried the truth, in order to get the water of life for themselves?" She heard the extra grimness that weighed down *ancestors*, and

469

realized that she had made a misstep. Criticizing a Kharemoughi's ancestors was like accusing one of her own people of incest.

But she nodded, firmly, stubbornly, "Someone's did, yes, sir."

Hovanesse took a sip from his glass, said heavily, "Those are exceptionally ugly and unpleasant charges to bring up at a time like this, Commander PalaThion."

She nodded again. "I know, Your Honor. But I can't think of a more appropriate audience for them. If this is true—"

"Who made the accusation? What's his proof?"

"An offworlder named Ngenet; he has a land-grant plantation here on Tiamat."

"Ngenet?" The Director of Communications touched his ear in derision. "That renegade? He'd claim anything to make the Hegemony look bad. Everyone in the government knows that. The only attention he deserves from you, Commander, is a jail cell."

Jerusha smiled briefly. "I once considered it. But he claims this information was given to him by a sibyl; it would be easy enough to corroborate by asking another one."

"I wouldn't degrade the honor of my ancestors by such an insulting act!" one of the assemblymen murmured.

"It seems to me," Jerusha leaned forward again, "that the future of this world's people, human and nonhuman, ought to be a lot more important than the reputation of Kharemoughis who were dust a millennium ago. If a wrong's being done, let's admit it and correct it. If we wink at mass murder here we're as bad as the Snow Queen herself. Worse—splattered with the blood of innocent beings by the slaves and lackeys who only obey our demands, while we punish them for our guilt by keeping them in the Fire Age!" Stunned by the words she heard come out of her own mouth, she remembered abruptly who had put them into her mind.

The silence of the grave met her on every side, and bore her back down into her seat. She sat still, very aware of her

own breathing, and of their goodwill draining away, empty-
ing out of this husk of a room. "Sorry, gentlemen. I guess
I—spoke out of turn. I know this is a hard accusation to
face; that's why I've had so damn much trouble knowing
what to do about it myself, whether to file a report—"

"Don't file a report," Hovanesse said.

She looked up at him, questioning; back along the table's
length at the brittle anger of the Kharemoughis, and the
resentful anger of the Newhavenese. *You damn fool! What
made you think they'd want to look Truth straight in the
face, any more than you did?*

"The Assembly will take up the matter after we leave
Tiamat. When we've made our decision, the Hegemonic
Coordinating Center on Kharemough will be notified of
any policy change that needs to be made."

"You will question a sibyl, at least." She twisted her
watchband below the table's edge, longing for a handful of
iestas.

"We have one among us, on the ships," not entirely
answering the question.

I pity the poor bleeder, with a clientele like that. She
wondered in her heart whether this one question worth
asking would ever be asked again.

"In any case," Hovanesse frowned at her silence, "whatever is decided won't have to concern you, Jerusha; you'll
spend the rest of your career, and your life, light-years
away from Tiamat. Just like we all will. We appreciate
your concern, your honesty in speaking your mind. But the
question and Tiamat become purely academic for us from
here on."

"I suppose so, Your Honor." *And even the rain doesn't
fall if it doesn't fall on you.* She got to her feet again and
saluted them all stiffly. "Thank you for your time, and for
asking me here. But I've got to be getting back to my
duties before they become academic, too." She turned
without waiting for a sign of dismissal and went quickly
out of the room.

She had gotten as far as the hallway before Hovanesse's
voice called her to a stop. She turned back, half hot and

471

half cold, saw him coming after her alone. She couldn't quite read his face.

"You didn't give the Assembly the opportunity to give you your new assignments, Commander." His eyes castigated her for her tactlessness and ingratitude before the Assembly members; but he said nothing more.

"Oh." She took the printout automatically from his hand, with fingers that felt nothing. *Oh, gods, what's my fortune to be?*

"Aren't you going to look at it?" It was not a casual inquiry, or a friendly one, and she felt the numbness spread.

She almost refused, but some perverse part of her would not ignore the challenge. "Of course." She unsealed the flimsy paper and let it fall open, her eyes striking the page randomly. The Tiamatan force was being split up, as she had expected, reassigned to several different worlds. Mantagnes had been given another chief inspectorship. And she . . . she . . . her eyes found her own name at last and she read. . . .

"There's been a mistake." She felt the perfect calm of perfect disbelief. She read it again: a sector command, almost the equal of her position here. But at Paradise Station, Syllagong, on Big Blue. "There's nothing there but a cinder desert."

"And the penal colony. Extensive mineral mining goes on there, Commander. It's of considerable importance to the Hegemony. There are plans for starting an additional colony; that's why they're expanding the force there."

"Damn it, I'm a police officer. I don't want to run a prison camp." The paper sighed as her hands tightened. "Why am I being given this? Is it what I just said in there? It isn't my fault if the—"

"This was your original assignment, Commander. But because of your accomplishments, your rank has been raised to a sector command."

He said the words deliberately, oozing the smugness of a man who lived by influence and prior knowledge. "Rehabilitating offenders is just as important as apprehending them,

472

after all. Someone has to do it, and you've proven you can handle a—difficult position."

"A dead-end position!" To argue was only to humiliate herself further, but she fought a losing battle with her temper. "I'm the Commander of Police for this entire planet. I've just been given a commendation. I don't have to stand by and let my career die!"

"Of course you don't," he patronized. "You can take it up with the Assembly members—although you probably won't earn much sympathy after the disgusting and outrageous charges you just made in there." His dark eyes grew darker. "Let's be blunt about this, shall we, Commander? You and I both know you owe your place at the top to the Queen's interference. The only reason you were made an inspector in the first place was merely to humor her. This new position is more than you deserve. You know as well as I do that the men under your command here never accepted taking orders from a woman." *But that was Arienrhod's doing! And it's changing now, changed already*— "Morale was terrible, as Chief Inspector Mantagnes frequently reported to me. You are neither needed nor wanted on the force. Whether you take this assignment or resign is up to you, but it's all the same to us." He locked his hands behind his back and stood before her, as immovable as a wall. She remembered the glowing platitudes he had mouthed about her so short a time ago.

You set me up for this, you bastard. I saw it coming. I knew it was coming, but after yesterday I thought—I thought— "I'll fight this, Hovanesse." Her voice trembled with rage, half the rage turning back on herself for letting it happen. "The Queen couldn't ruin me, and neither will you." *But she has, Jerusha; she has. . . .* She turned and walked away from him again, and this time he did not call her back.

Jerusha left the Court Building and started back down the uncongested Blue Alley toward police headquarters. (Even in Festival time, the carousers avoided this piece of the city.) Her first and only thought was to go to her men, tell them her problem, see if she could get their support. It

473

was true, their feeling toward her was changing, because of yesterday; she had seen it in almost every face. But had it changed enough? If she had the time now, she might be given a fair chance to prove that she could hold their respect as well as any man. But she didn't have that much time. Did she even have time to try to get them behind her now? And even if she did . . . was it worth it?

She found herself standing alone in the alley before the station house: that ancient, hideous fossil which had grown so familiar. No other building, no other post would ever be quite so hated—or, she suddenly realized, quite so important—in her life. But wherever she went, if she went in the uniform she wore now, she would always be an outsider, would always have to be fighting not simply to do a good job, but to prove that she even had the right to try. And there would always be another Hovanesse, another Mantagnes, who would never accept her, and try to drive her away. Gods, did she really want to spend the rest of her life that way? *No* . . . not if she could find something else to do with it that meant as much to her as this job, something she believed in as much. But there was nothing else . . . nothing. Beyond this job she had no life, no goal, no future. She went on past the station house, on to the alley's end, and out into the river of celebration.

Sparks moved through the dimly lit rooms of Starbuck's suite like a stranger, sleepless, aimless. No longer a part of them—but no longer free to leave. Both the public and the private entrances to the suite were watched now—not by the Queen's guards, but by Summers furious over her attempt to stop the Change. They were guarding Arienrhod, too—and somehow her plot had been overthrown. But when he had tried to ask them about Moon, and whether she had been the one who told them, they didn't know, or wouldn't tell him. And when he had tried to get them to let him out, or to convince them that he was only a Summer like they were, they had laughed at him, and driven him back into the room with harpoons and knives: They knew who he was; Arienrhod had told them. And they would keep him here until the sacrifice.

Arienrhod would not let him go. If her dreams were ruined, then his would be, too. He would die tomorrow if she died; she had bound him to her as inescapably as they would be bound together when they were thrown into the sea. She was the Sea incarnate, and Starbuck was Her consort, and they would be reborn on the new tide . . . but as new bodies with fresh, untainted souls—Summer souls. That was the way it had been since the beginning of time, and even though the offworlders had twisted it to suit their own purposes, it had endured, and always would. Who was he to change Change? Moon had tried to save him from it, but his fate had been stronger than them both. He tried not to think about what had happened between Arienrhod and Moon after he had been taken away—when Moon must have learned the truth about herself at last. Even if Moon had somehow escaped Arienrhod, there was no way she could come back to him now. He could only be grateful that he had been given one last hour with her, a condemned man's last comfort . . . and the final irony of a wasted life.

He rummaged in a gilded chest, found the bundle of clothes he had worn when he first came to the palace, and brought them out. He spread them carefully on the soft surface of the carpet, finding at their core the beads he had bought himself on his second day in the city . . . and his flute. He laid the flute aside, took off the clothes he wore, and pulled on the loose, heavy pants and the rainbow shirt that belonged with the beads, dressing as though for a ritual. He took up his father's medal from the dresser top when he finished, hung it about his neck in completion. He picked the flute up gently and sat with it on the edge of the heavy-legged reclining couch.

Sparks raised the flute to his lips, lowered it again, his mouth suddenly dry, too dry for song. He swallowed, feeling the pulse in his temple slow. He raised the fragile, hollow shell again. Positioning his fingers over the opening, he breathed into the mouthpiece. A tremulous note filled the air around him, like a spirit amazed to find itself free from the silence it had thought would be eternal. The breath clogged in his throat and he swallowed again; melody after melody filled his head, trying to escape into the air. He began to play, haltingly, with wrong fingers responding to memory's patterns, shrill overtones stabbing his ears. But gradually his fingers loosened, the water of song poured sweet and pure from the depths of his being again and carried him back to the world he had lost. Arienrhod had tried to ruin his last meeting with Moon, to take away even that, as she had taken away his pleasure in any beauty or joy that was not of her; but she had failed. Moon's passion and belief were as pure as song, and the memory of her carried away all shame, healed all wounds, righted all wrongs. . . .

He looked up, the song and the spell broken, as the guarded door to the suite unlatched and opened unexpectedly before him. Two figures hooded and robed entered. One moved slowly, grotesquely. The door closed again behind them. "Sparks Dawntreader Summer . . ."

Sparks squinted, reaching up to brighten the suspended lamp. "What do you want? It isn't time—"

"It's time . . . after twenty-odd years." The first man, the one who moved easily, came forward into the globe of light and pushed back his hood.

"What?" Sparks saw the face of a man on the young end of middle age, an offworlder. A Kharemoughi, he thought at first, but with paler skin and a heavier frame, a rounder face. That face . . . something about it he knew. . . .

"After twenty-odd years, it's time that we met, Sparks. I

476

only wish the setting were more appropriate to a joyful reunion."

"Who are you?" Sparks rose from the couch.

"I am your first ancestor." The words registered, without meaning; he shook his head. "Your father, Sparks." Something in the *your* was incomplete, as though the stranger could not express all that he really felt by it.

Sparks sat down again, dizzy, as the blood fell away from his head.

The stranger—his father—unfastened his cloak and shrugged it off onto a chair; under it he wore a plain silver-gray jump suit, and the ornamental badge and collar of a member of the Hegemonic Assembly. He made a small, formal bow, somehow awkward for all its grace, as though he were equally uncertain about how to begin. "First Secretary Temmon Ashwini Sirus." The second man—a servant?—turned and shuffled away, disappearing into the next room without comment, leaving them alone.

Sparks laughed, to cover another sound. "What is this, some kind of joke? Did Arienrhod put you up to this?" He covered his offworlder medal with his hand, wrapping his fingers around it, tightening his fist until it whitened . . . remembering how she had teased him and tormented him, telling him she knew who it belonged to, the name of his father; telling him lies.

"No. I explained to the Summers that I had come to see my son, and they showed me where you were."

Sparks jerked the medal off over his head. He threw it out to land at Sirus's feet, his voice harsh with disbelief. "Then this must belong to you, hero—it sure as hell doesn't belong on Starbuck. It took a lot of guts to come here and stick a knife into me . . . here's your reward. Take it and get out." He shut his eyes, trying not to look for resemblances. He heard Sirus lean over and pick up the medal.

" 'To our noble son Temmon . . .' " The resonant voice grew transparent. "How is your mother? I gave her this on the Mask Night . . . your legacy."

477

"She's dead, foreigner." He opened his eyes deliberately to watch Sirus's face. "I killed her." He let the shock recoil. "She died the day I was born."

The shock turned to grief, disbelief. "She died in childbirth?" as though he actually cared whether it had happened.

Sparks nodded. "They don't have all the modern conveniences in Summer. They won't have them here either, after the Change." He ran his hands along the rough cloth of his pants. "But that won't matter to me. Or you."

"Son. Son . . ." Sirus turned the medal over and over between his fingers. "What can I say to you? The Prime Minister is my own father, your grandfather. When he came back to me, it was all so simple. His blood in my veins made me royal in the eyes of my league—it made me a leader; gave me a right to rule, nothing but success and happiness. When he returned again to Samathe, he gave me this medal with his own hands, and took me into the Assembly." He let the medal slip through his fingers. It circled on its chain, catching light, like a fiery wheel. "I gave this to your mother because she was so like my mother's people, with her eyes as blue as a woodland lake, and her hair like sunlight. . . . She carried me back to my homeworld for a night, when I was lonely and it was far away." He looked up, offering the medal from his outstretched hand. "This was hers, yours, and it always will be."

Sparks felt his bones dissolve and his body turn to smoke. "You bastard . . . why did you come here now? Where were you then, years ago, when I needed you? I waited for you to come back, I tried to do everything to be what I thought you'd be, so you'd want me when you saw me." He spread his hands, surrounded by the technological mysteries he had solved so painstakingly, so pointlessly. "But now, when it's all gone, and I've ruined my life . . . you come and see me like this!"

"Sparks, your life isn't ruined. Your life isn't over. I've come to—to make amends." He hesitated; Sparks turned back to him slowly. "Your cousin Moon told me about you. It was Moon who sent me here."

478

"Moon?" Sparks swallowed his heart.

"Yes, son." Sirus's smile filled with encouragement and reassurance. "Her mind is behind this reunion, and her heart, I think, is waiting for another one. . . . Having met your cousin, I know that you come from a fine family line." Sparks glanced away, silent. "And having collided with her belief in you," ruefully, "I don't think there could be anything that would make me ashamed to have you for a son." Sirus gazed past him and around him at the instruments and machines, the silent testimony of their common blood, their shared heritage.

Sparks got to his feet as his father came toward him. Sirus hung the medal around his neck again, looking at his face and deeply into his eyes. "You favor your mother more . . . but I can see that you have a Technician's need to know *why*. How I wish there were an answer for every question. . . ." He put his hand on Spark's shoulder tentatively, as though he was not sure that it would be allowed to stay.

But Sparks held his father's eyes, absorbing the moment and the touch, as the cold empty cell where a part of his wholeness had been captive for years was thrown open at last, to let light and warmth pour in. "You came. You came for me—Father . . ." He spoke the word he had never expected to hear from his own lips; put his own hands over Sirus's hand on his shoulder, clinging to it like a child. "Father!"

"Very touching." The second man shuffled back into the room, breaking apart the moment. "Now, if you don't mind, Your Holiness, I want to get this over with."

Sparks released his father's hand, turned resentfully to see the other man unfasten his cloak and take it off. "Herne! What—?"

Herne grinned darkly. "The Child Stealer sent me. I'm your changeling, Dawntreader." His paralyzed legs were meshed in a clumsy exoskeleton.

"What's he talking about?" Sparks looked back at his father. "What's he doing here?"

"Your cousin Moon brought him to me. She said he was willing to take your place at the sacrifice of the Change."

"Take my place?" Sparks shook his head. "Him? You? . . . Why, Herne? Why would you do that for me?" Not letting himself hope—

Herne laughed once. "Not for you, Dawntreader. For her. They're more alike than you know. More than you know . . ." His eyes turned distant. "Moon knew. She knew what I needed, and wanted: Arienrhod, my self-respect . . . and an end to it, the last laugh. And she's given it all to me. Gods, I want to see Arienrhod's face when she learns she's been cheated in everything! I'll have her to myself forever, after all . . . that should be enough of hell, and heaven, for both of us." His vision telescoped back to their faces. "Go to your flawed copy, Dawntreader, and I hope you're satisfied with her. You never were man enough for the real thing." He held out the cloak.

Sparks took it from him, threw it around his own shoulders. "That's one way of putting it, I suppose." He fastened the catch at his throat.

His father held out a small jar of brownish paste. "Stain your face and hands, so that the guards will take you for a Kharemoughi."

"One of the galaxy's Chosen." Herne smirked.

Sparks went to the mirror, smeared the stain over his skin obediently, watching himself disappear. Behind his own reflection he saw Sirus waiting, and Herne searching the room with eager possessiveness—saw Starbuck in his element, and a son with his father . . . and they were two different men. Two different men, who had been the same man; who had loved the same woman who was not the same woman, and loved her now for the ways in which she was different. One of them ready to return to life, and one of them ready to die. . . .

He finished coloring his skin and raised his hood, went back to Sirus's side. "I'm ready," smiling at last at his father's smile.

"Son of a First Secretary, grandson of a Prime Minister

. . . you suit the role admirably." His father nodded. "Is there anything you want to take with you?"

Sparks remembered his flute lying on the couch, picked it up. "This is all." He glanced at the clutter of hardware briefly, and away again.

"Herne—" Sirus said something humbly in Kharemoughi, and for Sparks repeated it: "Thank you for giving me my son."

Sparks took a deep breath. "Thank you."

Herne folded his arms, enjoying something that Sparks did not fully understand. "Any time, *sadhu*. Just make sure you remember that you owe it all to me. Now get out of my chambers, you bastards. I want to start enjoying them, and I don't have much time left."

Sirus tapped on the door; it opened. Sparks looked back quickly at Herne standing in his element, taking his own place. *Good-bye, Arienrhod. . . .* Sirus went out with his shuffling servant, leaving Starbuck alone.

Moon was swept on the crowded tide from one end of the Street to the other, down to the creaking docks of Carbuncle's underworld where the city waded in the sea. There the procession made offerings to the Sea Mother and set her free at last, after an eternity compressed into hours, to spend her own Mask Night however she chose until dawn. *Until dawn.*

She made her way back up the Street toward Jerusha PalaThion's townhouse, fending off giddy worshipers and eager would-be lovers in the crush of costumed bodies, feeling all around her the quickening pulse, the rising passion of the night's promise. But the electric energy all around her only made her more sharply aware of her own solitary journey through it, and that she might spend the rest of her life alone if she spent the rest of tonight that way.

Night was bluing into black at the alley's end when she reached PalaThion's townhouse at last and banged on the door. PalaThion opened it, wearing a shapeless robe instead of her uniform; started, at the face of the Summer Queen confronting her.

Moon lifted the mask from her shoulders, held it in her arms, saying nothing.

"My gods . . ." PalaThion shook her head, as though this were only one more blow in a beating that had already left her dazed. She stood aside, letting Moon escape into sanctuary, out of the mauling mobs beyond her door.

Moon went on through the atrium and into the living room, her heart in her throat, searching—

"No. Nothing yet." PalaThion followed her in. "He hasn't come back."

"Oh." Moon forced out the word.

"There's still time."

Moon nodded silently, laid the Summer Queen's mask across one end of the reclining couch.

"Is that too heavy for you already?" PalaThion's voice grew less kind.

Moon glanced up, saw the weary disillusionment that turned the woman's eyes to dust. "No. . . . But tomorrow at dawn, if Sparks isn't—isn't—" looking down again.

"Did you win that mask honestly?" PalaThion asked bluntly, as though she actually expected an honest answer.

Moon reddened, smoothing its ribbons. *Did I?* "I had to win it."

PalaThion frowned. "You're telling me that you really believe it was fore-ordained . . . sibyl?"

"Yes. It was. I was meant to do this, if I could. And I did. The reason for it is more important than either one of us, Commander. I think you know what the reason is . . . do you still want to stop me?" She held the challenge out in her open hands, watching the unnameable uncertainty on PalaThion's face.

PalaThion rubbed her arms inside the sleeves of her caftan. "That depends on the answer you give me next. I have a question, sibyl."

Moon covered her surprise, nodded. "Ask, and I will answer. . . . *Input.*"

"Sibyl, tell me the truth, the whole truth about the mers."

Moon's surprise followed her down, into the black void of the Nothing Place, as the computer's brain replaced her own to tell another offworlder the truth.

But behind the truth there lay a deeper truth, and as she floated formlessly in the darkness the vision came to her, and spoke to her alone. She saw the mers, not as they were—innocent, unknowing playthings of the Sea—but as they had originally been created: pliant, intelligent beings that carried the germ of immortality. The first step toward immortality for all of humankind . . . and still more than that. They had been given immortality for a reason, intelligence for a reason. And the reason was one that she alone knew: the sibyl machine, the secret repository of all the sibyls' guidance that lay here on Tiamat, below Carbuncle, beneath its sea. She saw the mers reigning peacefully over this water world—guardians of the sibyl mind, possessing the knowledge that would maintain it and allow it to function. The Old Empire scientists whose plan this had been had hoped the sibyl network might even buy them time enough to perfect immortality for human beings; or that it would at least halt the spreading decay that ate away the Empire from within.

But the decay had reached this world first, in the form of petty kingdoms broken loose from the atrophying higher order, whose shortsighted freebooters wanted imperfect immortality for themselves now, if perfect immortality wasn't available. The Empire's own subjects began a slaughter of the mers that destroyed their ability to perform their duties, crippling the potential sibyl network before it had really taken hold. The Old Empire fell com-

483

pletely, irrevocably, of its own weight . . . but the deadly open secret of the water of life hung on in informational stasis into the present, resurrected with the Hegemony's rise, and the cycle of slaughter had begun again. But by this time the mers had lost all understanding of their purpose here and fallen back into primitive, unquestioning unity with the sea. The refugee human colonists, struggling to make a new home here, no more understood the secret beneath the sea than the mers themselves did; but they paid its vestigial memory homage as the Sea Mother, and called its immortal children sacred.

The sibyl network continued to function, dispensing its knowledge to the crippled cultures picking themselves up out of the Old Empire's ruins; but its answers had grown obscure and exasperating through lost potential. . . . And Moon saw at last that it had lost an even more profound aspect of its power. The fumbling manipulations it had used to guide her in doing its will were not a fluke, were never meant to be a rare or erratic phenomenon. Sibyls had been designed as more than simply speakers of secondhand wisdom—they had been designed as agents of social change, to bring stability and humanity back to the cultures they were born a part of. And their function had almost been lost, along with much of the clarity of the original data files.

But she, Moon, had become the Summer Queen—as the sibyl mind had meant her to. And now that she was Queen, she would begin the task of rebuilding all that had been destroyed. She was the last hope of the sibyl mind; it had put all of its faltering resources into guiding her quest. Only if she could reverse its disintegration could it begin to function again fully—and only then could it help her put an end to the cycle of offworld exploitation forever. It would continue to guide her while it could; but she would carry the burden of making the ideal real. . . .

"No further analysis!" Moon swayed on her feet as the Transfer set her free. PalaThion supported her, let her down safely onto the couch.

"Are you all right?" PalaThion searched her face for a reassuring sign of comprehension.

She shook her head, sagging forward under the weight of her final revelation. "Oh, Lady . . ." A moan, as she realized at last to what she made her prayer. "How? How can I change a thousand years of wrong? I'm only one, only Moon—"

"You're the Summer Queen," PalaThion said. "And a sibyl. You have all the tools you need. It's just a question of time. . . . Do you have enough of that, before the Hegemony comes back again?"

Moon lifted her head slowly.

"No," PalaThion looked away. "I'm not going to stop you. How could I live with so much death, and live with myself? And for what—?" Her hands tightened.

It took Moon another moment before she understood that what PalaThion had heard was only what Ngenet had heard, and not what had been whispered in her own mind there in the secret darkness. What PalaThion saw as the challenge was not the real challenge—not a match of sheer technological strength, but a challenge on a far different level, with far greater repercussions—a change that would ripple across a galaxy. But PalaThion had understood that there *was* a challenge, and that its outcome could be measured in suffering and death; and that had been enough. Moon nodded. "This means more to more people than I can ever tell you."

PalaThion smiled tightly. "Well, that's some consolation." She moved away, across the room, to the shell sitting on a table by the doorway. She picked it up, held it for a long moment with her back to Moon.

Moon stretched out on the couch, her body leaden, her mind numbed with overload; wondering how she would get past tomorrow dawn to face the long years of the future.

"I have to be getting back to—" PalaThion glanced up as another knock sounded at her door. Moon sat up, her hands twisting on her belt as PalaThion disappeared into the atrium.

She heard the sound of the door opening, of people entering the hall. . . .

"You!" A voice sick with betrayal. A voice she knew—

Moon pushed herself up, started across the room. She saw three figures silhouetted in the light from the open door, red hair limned with gold.

"Hold it. Don't be in such a hurry, Sparks." PalaThion caught his arm in a steel grip as he tried to bolt back out into the alley. "If this was a trap you'd be in my jail, not my parlor."

"I—I don't understand." Sparks eased under her hand, confusion showing.

"I'm not sure I do, either." PalaThion let him go. His father stood beside her, smiling reassurance.

"Sparks—"

His head came up. "Moon!" He started toward her.

She put out her arms. He came into the room where she stood waiting; the rest of the world ceased to exist beyond the meeting point of their hearts.

"Oh, Moon! Moon . . ." Sparks breathed the words against her ear, stopped her own words with another kiss.

"Sparkie . . ." She tasted tears.

"Sparks." They looked up together, at Sirus's voice. "I must be leaving you now. Now that you're in—safe hands." He smiled his sorrow.

Sparks nodded, separated himself from Moon slowly and went back to his father's side. Moon watched them embrace for a last time, feeling her own heart torn, before his father went back out into the alley noise. PalaThion closed the door, looked at Sparks expressionlessly.

He forced himself to meet her eyes. "I'll tell you what I know about the Source. That's what you want, isn't it, to let me go . . . that's all you want?" as if he didn't really believe it.

She nodded, but her face was strained.

"Look, Commander—" He shut his eyes. "I don't know why you're doing this . . . except I know it's not done for me. But I want you to know I'm sorry—" Hastily, "I know

486

it doesn't do any good, it doesn't change anything, it doesn't even mean anything. But I'm—sorry." He spread his hands.

"It means something, Dawntreader." PalaThion looked as though she were surprised to realize that it actually did.

"There's one thing I can do for you, anyway," abruptly. He strode to the far end of the room, pried the ugly geometric clock-face out of the wall. Moon watched, incredulous, as he threw it to the floor and stepped on it. He smiled, rubbing his hands together. "If you've hated this place for no reason—that was the reason: a subsonic transmitter in the clock." He came back to Moon's side, hung onto her hand as though he were afraid she would disappear. "There might be others I don't know about."

The awareness of years of needless agony, of questioning her own sanity . . . the awareness that it had finally come to an end, filled PalaThion's face. "I always meant to make this museum into a real room again. But somehow I just never got around to it. . . ." Dreary disillusionment settled in again, as if it had never really left her. "Well, Moon. You got everything you came here to get; I'm glad, for somebody's sake. After Sparks gives his testimony, the two of you cease to exist as far as I'm concerned. That'll be the end of the problems you've caused for me. . . . I just hope you can solve your own now." She went past them and into the back rooms of the apartment.

"What did she mean?" Sparks turned back.

Moon shook her head, not meeting his eyes. "All that happened in the last year, I suppose." *Five years.* "And all that's going to happen, after the Change." She looked away at the mask of the Summer Queen.

"What's that?" He followed her glance.

"The mask of the Summer Queen." She felt him stiffen and pull away.

"Yours? You won it?" His voice thickened. "No! You couldn't have—you couldn't have won, unless you cheated."

487

Moon saw herself reflected, saw Arienrhod reflected in his eyes. "I won because I was meant to! I had to win—and not for myself!"

"I suppose you did it for Tiamat! That's what she always said, too." He stood away from her.

"I'm a sibyl, Sparks, and that's why I won! And yes, I care about Tiamat—and Arienrhod does too. She's seen more of what this world was, and became, and will stop being again, than anyone else has. . . . And she cared about you; you can't deny that."

Sparks looked down abruptly; Moon felt different kinds of pain start in her chest.

PalaThion came back into the room wearing her uniform; went on past them and out, without saying anything more. The door opened and closed behind her, cutting them off again from the celebration of the world outside. Moon fingered the trailing streamers of the Summer Queen's mask. Her mask . . . *my mask.*

"Sparks, please, believe that it's right. My becoming Queen is part of something much greater, much more important, than either you or me. I can't explain it to you now—" She knew, with misery, that he had never been meant to know; that he had always been the enemy to the shapeless sentience that guided her. "But we have to stop the offworld exploitation of Tiamat. When I was offworld, I met a sibyl on Kharemough; I learned that there are sibyls on all the worlds of the Old Empire—the whole reason they exist is to help worlds rebuild and relearn. I *can* answer any question." She saw his eyes widen, and change.

"And while I was on Kharemough I began to see what you always saw, about progress, technology, the—magic of what the offworlders do, and how it isn't magic to them. They understand so much more . . . they don't have to be afraid of disease, or broken bones, or childbirth. Your mother wouldn't have died— We have a right to live that way too, or there wouldn't be sibyls on this world."

She saw hunger in his eyes, for what she had seen that he would never see. But he only said, "Our people are happy the way they are. If they start reaching for power, wanting what they don't have, they'll end up like the Winters. Like us."

"What's wrong with us? Nothing!" She shook her head. "We want knowledge, we're asking for our birthright. That's all. The offworlders want us to think it's wrong to be dissatisfied with what we have. But it's no worse than being self-satisfied with it. Change isn't evil—change is life. Nothing's all good, or all bad. Not even Carbuncle. It's like the sea, it has its tides, they ebb and flow. . . . What you choose to do with your life doesn't matter, unless you have the right to choose anything. We don't have any choice. And the mers don't even have the right to live." *And they have to live . . . they're the key to everything.*

Sparks grimaced. "All right, you've made your point! Someone should try to change it. But why us?" His hand closed over his medal. "You know . . . my—father said he could get us off Tiamat. He could arrange for us to go to Kharemough. It would be so easy. . . ."

"They don't need us on Kharemough. They need us here." Seeing Kharemough, the Thieves' Market, the night sky: *It would be so easy. Even if we can plant the seeds here, we'll never see the final harvest, we'll never know whether we lost or won. . . .* "And we owe something to both places that we can only pay back here." Her voice grew dark.

"Some things can never be repaid." Sparks moved to the window; Moon saw someone outside wave in passing. "And having to stay here, in Carbuncle, in the palace—" He broke off. "I don't know if I can stand it, Moon. I can't start over, in the same place where I was—"

"Look at the people out there. This is the Mask Night—the night of transition. No one is what they were, or will be . . . we're not anything, our potential is infinite. And when the masks come off, they peel away the layers of our sins, and leave us free to forget, and start over." *And to prove to the sibyl mind that you are as I see you, and not wearing a death mask.*

She went to stand beside him. "After tonight nothing

489

will be the same. Not even Carbuncle. The Summers are coming here, and the future is trying to. It will be a new world, not Arienrhod's." *But it will be hers too; it always will be.* Knowing it, she didn't say it. "And I promise you I'll never set foot in the palace again." *And I'll never tell anyone why.*

He looked over at her in surprise; when he believed what he saw, relief freed his face. But still he sighed, and still she felt the space between them. "It's not enough. I need time—time to forget; time to believe in myself again ... and believe in us. One night isn't enough. Maybe a lifetime won't be enough." He turned to the window again.

Moon looked with him, not able to keep looking at him, letting the crowd blur and swim out of focus, oily colors on a water surface. *It never rains here. It ought to rain ... there are never any rainbows.* "I'll wait," biting off the words, to keep from choking on them. "But it won't take that long." She found his hand on the windowsill, squeezed it. "Tonight it's my duty to be happy." Her mouth quirked at the irony. "This should have been our Festival, to carry with us in our memories forever. It's the last Festival; and we will remember it. Do you want to go out there and end our lives the way we were meant to? Maybe, if we tried, we could make tonight one we want to remember forever."

He nodded; a smile teetered on his face. "We could try."

She looked back at the Summer Queen's mask, saw it overlain by faces, all the many lives that had sacrificed so much to make it hers. One face—"But first . . . I have to tell someone good-bye." She bit her lip, a counterpain.

"Who?" Sparks followed her eyes.

"A—an offworlder. A police inspector. I escaped from the nomads with him. He's in the hospital now."

"A Blue?" He tried to take back the tone of his voice. "Then he's more than just a Blue: a friend."

"More than just a friend," faintly. She faced him, waiting for him to understand.

"More than ... ?" He frowned suddenly, and she saw his face flush. "How could you—?" His voice broke, like a

490

stick snapping. "How could you ... How could I. We. Us ..."

She looked down. "I was lost in the storm, and he was my sea-anchor. And I was his. When someone loves you more than you love yourself, you can't help—"

"I know." He let his anger out in a sigh. "But what about—now, you and him? And me?"

She ran her fingers down the colored front of her nomad's tunic. "He didn't ask me for forever." *Because he knew he couldn't.* "He always knew that no one would ever come before you, or come between you and me, or take your place for me." *Even though he would have tried; wanted to try; did.* She felt his face trying now to come between Sparks's pinched face and her own. "No one!" blinking hard. "He—helped me to find you." *He gave up everything, gave me so much; and what did I give him? Nothing.* "Then he left me, asking nothing else. I have to know, to be sure, he'll—be all right, when he leaves here."

Sparks laughed; the sound was raw in his throat. "What about us? Will we be all right, when they're gone? When we're the ones who get stuck, when we have to live on with their memories looking over our shoulders, reminding us how we broke our pledge, our promise—and broke it, and broke it?"

"We'll make another. For our reborn souls—tomorrow." *After tonight.* She picked up the Summer Queen's mask. *After the dawn.* "But I think we never broke the old one, in our hearts."

He kissed her once before she put the mask on again.

"What about a mask for you?"

"No." He shook his head. "I don't need one. I've already taken mine off."

52

"Well, this sure's hell's not how I imagined spendin' Mask Night." Tor interrupted herself to fill her mouth with another sugary, alcohol-soaked drunken-cake from the sack in her hand, doing her best to deaden body and mind against the coming end of the world. She pulled her mask back into place, hanging onto Pollux's stalwart bulk, an island of comfort in the thinning Festival crowd. "Not with nothin' but a hunk of cold metal to cozy up to, and a future of cleaning fish. Hell, I get seasick in the bathtub. And I hate fish, goddamn it!" Shouting it.

"You're not the only one, sister!" A masked figure waved mutual disgust, disappeared after its chosen through a battered warehouse door, searching for a little privacy. Tor looked after them enviously; Pollux stared noncommittally down the Street. Nearly everyone who was going to had paired off for the night by now.

"I'm sorry things turned out badly for you, Tor," Pollux said unexpectedly. "If you want to spend your time with a person, I do not mind."

Tor glanced back at him, with the slightly irrational conviction that he would mind very much. "Nah. I can do that any night . . . but this's the last night I'll see you." He didn't answer.

They had made a sentimental journey down to the docks and warehouses of the lower city, because she had decided that she would rather spend the last night of her world in the places of her childhood, her origins: remembering her youth, reliving the days when she had never even aspired to the things she had ultimately become. Hoping that if she could remember when they didn't exist, they might not matter so much when they were gone.

She wondered who was running the casino tonight—
Who's left?—or whether anyone was. Even Herne had disappeared, by Moon Dawntreader's strange magic. *The hell
with it.* She had gone back just long enough to collect the
few things she wanted to hold on to from her time as
Persiponë, and left them at her half-brother's. She hadn't
seen her brother in a long time, and she hadn't seen him
tonight either—he'd already gone out on the town. But
they'd never been exactly close, anyway.

"You're the closest thing to a frien' I've got tonight,
Polly." She sighed. "Maybe you always were." She sat
down on an abandoned crate, in a pile of departure rubbish, comfortable in her old coveralls and her old surroundings. "You never bitched, no matter how hard I worked
you, or how much crap I gave you. . . . 'Course, I guess
you can't complain, anyhow, so what does that prove?"
She ate another cake. Pollux sat patiently on his tripod
before her. She saw a red light begin to blink on his chest;
the information short-circuited in her mind, and went un-
acknowledged. "Don't your feelings ever get hurt, really,
down inside someplace? Didn't I ever insult you, or offend
you, or something? Ye gods, I hope I never offended you,
when you've been nothin' but good to me. . . ." She snuffled
maudlinly.

"You could never offend me, Tor."

She looked up at his inscrutable face, trying to interpret
the meaning of the toneless words. "You mean that? I
mean, do you *mean* that? You mean you—like me?"

"I mean 'I like you,' Tor. Yes, I do." The faceless face
looked at her.

"Well, what do you know?" She smiled. "I thought you
weren't supposed to. I thought you couldn't. Feel anything,
I mean. I always thought you were—uh, dumb. No offense," hastily.

"I contain a sophisticated computer, Tor. I am programmed not to judge, except for legalities. But not to
judge is hard at my level of complexity. I need constant
readjustment."

"Oh." She nodded. "I guess I always knew you were

more than jus' a loadin' device. I mean, where would a loadin' device learn how to fix my hair? Or . . ." She faded, as she remembered. "Or squeal to the Blues about every wrong word somebody says on the Street." She shrugged. "Or save my life; huh, Polly . . . ?" reaching out to pat him on the chest. "Oh, hell—we had some good times, didn' we? You remember when old Stormprince assigned you to me? Gods, I was proud of myself! I thought bein' in charge of you was gonna be the high point of my life, you know? Who'd've figured . . . But in a way, maybe it was. I didn't have any regrets, then. I dunno." She ran a hand freely through her own limp hair. "I think it's gonna take me a long time to figure out what bein' Persiponë was." She looked at her hands, which had not had a trace of callus for a long time now. "What's that light flashing on you for? Did I forget to do somethin' for you?" She stood up unsteadily.

"No, Tor. That means my contract is expiring."

Surprise smacked her. "Oh. I know . . . I mean, I know it runs out tonight. But I . . ." *I just thought maybe nobody'd notice.* She gulped down the last of the drunkencakes, crumpled the sack spitefully and threw it away. The trash precipitate of the Festival littered the Street for as far as she could see. "Do you want to go now?"

"No, Tor." Pollux looked at her expressionlessly. "But if I am not at police headquarters soon I will stop functioning and be paralyzed."

"Oh," again. "I didn't know that. Maybe we better get started, then." She took his thick, angular arm as they moved back into the street, to keep their trajectories on the same course uphill. She looked back as they went; until it made her too dizzy, and she had to look ahead again. "What's gonna happen to you now, Polly? Where you gonna go next?"

"I do not know where I will be sent, Tor. But I will be reprogrammed first with new information. I will forget everything that happened here."

"What?" She pulled him to a stop, digging in her heels.

"You mean you're gonna forget all about Carbuncle? All about me?"

"Yes, Tor. Everything nonessential. Everything. Everything." He turned toward her. "Do you like me, Tor?"

She blinked. "Well, sure. How'd I ever have got along without you all these years?" But it wasn't enough, and somehow she could see that as she looked at him, although there was nothing of his face to see. "I mean . . . I really like you. Like a real friend. Like a real person. In fact, if you weren't just a machine, y'know, maybe I could even've . . ." She laughed self-consciously. "You know."

"Thank you, Tor." He made a movement that was almost a nod, and they started on again.

When they had nearly reached Blue Alley they passed a small crowd of masked revelers going downhill as they climbed, trailing music and laughter. "Look, Polly, there's the Summer Queen! There's the future passin' us by." Among the menagerie of masks, she glimpsed one face that wasn't hidden, a strangely familiar face under a crown of fiery hair . . . *Sparks Dawntreader?* She tried for a clearer look at the face, but it was hidden again in the crowd going away. *No* . . . She shook her head, refusing to believe it. *Couldn't be. Couldn't.*

Pollux slowed, and turned them toward the entrance to Blue Alley.

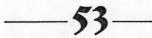

Jerusha sighed, leaning back in her chair at the night-duty desk, as her eyes wandered the nearly deserted room. Virtually all of the force were out patrolling the last night of the Festival; their final, most enervating duty on this world. Having nothing she wanted to celebrate, she had no heart for watching the rest of the world celebrate without her, and so she had stayed at headquarters. There had been few major problems: She had been surprised at how excruciatingly long and empty the night had been. *Empty. . . . that's the word for it.* She sighed again, turning the radio up a little louder to drown out the future. *Gods, was it worse not knowing what was going to happen to me, or knowing it for certain?*

Tor Starhiker stirred and rubbed her eyes, on the lonely bench along the wall where she had fallen asleep a couple of hours ago. *Passed out, more likely.* Jerusha could smell her clear across the room when she had brought the Pollux unit in . . . or it had brought her in, reeking and full of slurred, sloppy sentiment. The polrob stood motionless at the end of the bench, looking for all the world as though it were watching over her. Jerusha found it hard to believe that anyone could feel that maudlin about a robot, drunk or not. *But who knows? She's lost more than a robot in the past few days, I suppose.* If she wanted to spend these last hours holding its mechanical hand—or drugged to oblivion —that was her business.

Jerusha took out a pack of iestas, the strongest thing she'd had the nerve to touch in five years. She was sending a message to LiouxSked's family back on Newhaven, telling them what she's learned, at last. . . . *May it do them more good than it's done me.*

"What—?" Tor started and sat up abruptly, yawning. "Ohhh." Her hands pressed her head and her stomach indiscriminately. "I may not even live till Summer gets here."

Jerusha smiled faintly, leaning across the computer console. "If you're going to throw up, use the facilities; don't do it out here."

"Sure." Tor propped her head on her hands. "What time's it, anyway?"

Jerusha glanced at her watch. "Nearly time for me to start down toward the docks." She typed a summons on the comm frequency, to bring back a few more men to watch the station while she was gone, and to accompany her to her final duty on this world.

"You mean, for the—sacrifice?" Tor looked up. Jerusha nodded. "Hm. Well, you know, I just want to say ... thanks for letting me keep Polly here until the end of his contrac'. I mean, I know you knew I heard—you know." She shrugged.

"Don't remind me." Jerusha pushed herself to her feet, stretching. *Lax, PalaThion, you were lax,* taking a spiteful pleasure in acknowledging it.

"Well, still, Polly an' I—" Tor broke off, turning toward Pollux as someone else entered the station: a tall man, an offworlder.

Jerusha caught at the corner of the duty desk. "Miroe!"

He stopped across from Tor in the middle of the room. "Jerusha." His voice sounded as stupified as her own. "I didn't think I'd find you here ... but I didn't know where else to look." He looked as though he hadn't known what he would say to her when he did find her. He was dressed like any Winter sailor, and showing a stubble of beard.

"Yes, still on the job, Miroe. Until the New Millennium," bitterly inane.

"I was afraid I wasn't going to reach Carbuncle in time; the weather was bad down the coast." She realized that he looked very tired. "One more day and I would have been too late; you'd all have been gone."

She shook her head, keeping her face and her voice even. "No. Tomorrow we cease to exist here technically; but it takes a few days to make sure nothing critical gets left behind. What are you doing here, Miroe? Your people said—they said they didn't even know where you'd gone."

"It was a spur-of-the-moment decision." His eyes searched the empty corners of the room. "I didn't plan on making this trip. The gods know I couldn't afford the time. There's too much—preparation left to do, showing my people how to do things in new ways ... new old ways." Jerusha had the feeling that she was hearing more than she understood; perhaps more than she wanted to know.

"You going offworld?" Tor said with sudden interest. Ngenet glanced at her as though he had only just noticed there was someone else in the station. "Looking for a wife, handsome?"

Ngenet looked only mildly incredulous. "Maybe. But not one who wants to leave Tiamat. Because I'm not leaving Tiamat." He glanced at Jerusha again and came on across the room.

"Oh." The word was full of disbelief more than disappointment. "Thanks for warning me. Who wants to marry a loony. Right, Pollux?" She nudged him.

"Whatever you say, Tor."

She laughed loudly, for no obvious reason.

Jerusha leaned against the desk. "So you're really staying here for the rest of your life, then. Forever." The disappointment was all hers, although it had no right to be. "You didn't come here to be taken off."

"No. Tiamat is my home, Jerusha. Nothing has changed my feelings about that. And I don't expect anything has changed your feelings about leaving Tiamat either," as though it were a foregone conclusion.

"No." She heard the weakness, the moment of hesitation that should have been certainty. But he was expecting what he heard, and did not. He nodded, resigned; not taking it any further, simply accepting her decision without question —the way he had done before, at their last meeting. As though it didn't matter. "Then why did you come?" with a little too much force. "You said that you didn't want to see this Festival."

"I didn't." He matched her sharpness with his own. "I came to say good-bye to you. That was the only reason."

The only reason? She felt her face turn hot with surprise and embarrassment. *Damn it, Ngenet! I don't understand you at all!* But she didn't question his failure to question; couldn't bring herself to ask, if he would not. "I . . . uh, I'm glad that you came. I'm honored, that you've come so far just to say good-bye." Glancing at Tor, she caught hold of the gap between them again, and pulled it together.

"Because this way I can tell you the news in person: Your young friend Moon is alive."

"Moon?" He shook his head, pushed back his hair. "How? I can't believe—" He laughed, and she saw something alive in him again that she thought had been torn out of him forever that day on the beach.

"She was picked up by Winter nomads; but she got away from them, along with one of my inspectors they'd been holding."

"She's here, in the city, then?" Jerusha saw him glance away suddenly, toward the unseen interior of the station. "Where is she?"

"Not in a cell, Miroe." Jerusha straightened away from the desk. "As far as I know she's reigning over the Festival along with her cousin Sparks. She's the Summer Queen."

He looked astounded, and so did Tor, standing behind him. But his expression changed again to something more private and prescient. "And a more perfect Queen could not have been chosen. . . . Thank you, Jerusha." He nodded.

"Me? I had nothing to do with it."

"You had everything to do with it—you could have stopped it."

She almost smiled. "No. I don't think anyone could have stopped it, somehow."

"Maybe not." He did smile. "And she found her cousin Sparks, then? After all this time?"

"And yanked him out of the Snow Queen's boudoir. He was Starbuck."

"Gods—" His face emptied. "Starbuck." The word turned as ugly on his tongue as it had on hers. "And— Moon?"

She nodded, her mouth tight. "I know. Strange bedfellows; a sibyl and a monster. But I knew that boy before Arienrhod got her claws in him—and so did Moon. And that's still the boy she sees, even knowing the truth about him. Maybe she's right, maybe she's not; who knows? That's not up to me to judge, thank the gods."

499

"Then you've let him go? That doesn't erase what he's done. That doesn't change it!" Revenge rose in his voice.

So even you would take revenge over justice, if the wound went deep enough. Even you. And I thought you were a goddamn saint, all these years. Not disappointed, but only relieved to understand finally that even he was human, with a right to human emotions, human failings. "I know, Miroe. . . . And they'll know it, too. The best day of their lives, it'll come between them like an open grave, it'll carry away their happiness like the smoke of a funeral pyre." She saw the knowledge of what Starbuck had done to the mers struggle with his feelings for Moon.

He looked down at last; his head jerked once, accepting it.

"And Miroe, I've got the one who's really to blame . . . Arienrhod, that's who I'm talking about. She's the one who put him up to it. And she tried to take over the city by starting a plague among the Summers. But she didn't get away with it; and at dawn this morning her unnaturally prolonged reign comes to an unnatural end."

Ngenet looked up again. "She tried to do that? The Winters' Queen?"

"I told you what she was. And I told you I'd see that the guilty party paid. So now I've kept all my promises here." *Except for the ones I made to myself.*

"Then I owe you my thanks again, for seeing that justice was done. Real justice, not blind justice." He smiled, barely. "At our last meeting, as at our first. . . . Where are you going next, Jerusha? Where's your new assignment?"

She pushed away from the desk abruptly. "I'm being sent to Big Blue." She moved in a tight, restless circle, tugged at her jacket sleeves.

Ngenet raised his eyebrows when she didn't say more. "Whereabouts? Not the cinder camps, I hope," reaching for a joke.

"Yes." She turned on him, stung. "That is where I'm going. I'm in charge of the penal colonies there."

"What?" He laughed uncomfortably, not able to believe it wasn't a joke in return.

"It's no joke," flatly.

The laughter stopped. "You . . . running a place like that?" He looked at the desk, as though he expected it to give him an explanation. "Do they think so little of Tiamat that a penal colony is considered a step up?"

"No, Miroe." *They think so little of me.* She covered the Commander's insignia on her collar with the fingers of a hand. "You could say it's a case of blind justice."

"Do you want the job?" He stroked his mustache.

"No." She frowned. "It's a dead end, an insult—" She caught her breath.

"Didn't you complain, then? After all, you're a Commander of Police—" trying to comprehend the suddenly incomprehensible.

It was her turn to laugh without meaning. "I am a joke, that's what I am." She shook her head. "I either go where I'm assigned, or I quit."

"Quit, then."

"Damn it, that's all I ever hear from a man! Give up . . . give in . . . you can't handle it! Well, I can! I expected more from you, but I should have known better—"

"Jerusha," shaking his head, "for gods' sakes. Don't turn me into a thing."

"Then don't treat me like one."

"I don't want to see you turn yourself into one! And you will, running a place like that . . . when you treat another human being like something less than human, you make yourself less than human. Either it'll destroy your humanity, or it'll destroy your sanity. And I don't want to remember you going toward that; or imagine you—" He moved his large hands futilely.

"Then what else am I supposed to do? All my life I wanted to *do* something with my life—something worthwhile, something important. And becoming a police officer gave me that. Maybe it hasn't exactly been everything I thought it would be—but what ever is, anyway?" *If only there was something.*

"You consider what you'll be doing there worthwhile?" thick with sarcasm. He pushed his hands into his pockets.

501

"I already answered that." She turned away. "In time, maybe I'll be able to get a transfer. And besides, what else can I do? There's nothing else."

"You could stay here," an uncertain invitation.

She shook her head, not looking at him. "And do what? I'm not cut out to be a fishwife, Miroe." *Tell me there's something else.*

But if there was an answer, he was kept from making it by the arrival of two of the officers she had called in. They had Festival confetti in their hair and faintly martyred expressions on their faces, but they saluted her with reasonable deference.

She returned the salute, tugged her uniform and her thoughts into order. "Make yourselves official; you're going to the Change ceremony with me as soon as Mantagnes gets here."

They brightened some at the prospect of getting front-row seats for the human sacrifice; stole curious glances at Tor Starhiker as they moved away. Jerusha recalled her presence with belated chagrin, until she saw that Tor had fallen asleep again.

Miroe stood broodingly beside her, his gaze on the floor. "You're attending the—sacrifice?" He seemed to have a hard time getting the word out, just as Tor had. "The Snow Queen's death?"

She nodded, feeling uncomfortable with the thought despite having lived with the prospect of it for so long. *The Snow Queen's death. A human sacrifice. My gods.* And yet she wondered why the prospect of the clean, public execution of a woman who richly deserved it should seem more terrible than the living death of punishment at the place she was going to. The gods knew, a society that could undergo a total restructuring with only two executions as a result was better off than most. "It's my last official act as a Hegemonic representative; we turn over to the new Queen the keys to her kingdom, so to speak." *And watch Arienrhod drown in regret.* She glanced down, faltering. "Will you come, Miroe? I know it's not a thing you want to see—so I don't ask it lightly."

502

He shifted his weight, shifting his emotions. "Yes, I'll come. You're right, it's not a thing I ever thought I'd want to see. But knowing what I know of her now . . . They say it's supposed to be a catharsis, to watch the living symbol of the old order die: something that everyone needs, to clean the ugliness out of their souls. Well, I never thought I'd need it . . . but maybe I'm not so much better than anyone else, after all."

"Welcome to the club," not quite smiling. "I'll be right back." She went to her office for her cloak and helmet.

When she returned she found Mantagnes waiting, with supercilious aloofness, in answer to her call. She returned his salute without expression and ordered him to take her place in the station.

She stopped again on the way to the entrance and shook Tor awake. "Wake up, Winter. It's nearly dawn."

Tor sat up, rubbing bleary misery over her face.

"I'm going down to the Change ceremony now." Jerusha gentled her voice. "I didn't know whether you wanted to be there. If you do, you can come with us." *Though I wouldn't blame you if you wanted to sleep through it.*

Tor shook her head, stretched out her arms; her eyes cleared. "Yeah . . . I guess I will, after all. I can't stay here forever, can I?" rhetorical. She stood up, turning to Pollux, who still stood in the same place beside her. "I'd better go see the end of the world, Polly; there won't be another one. And if I don't see it, I might not believe it."

"Good-bye, Tor." The voice sounded thinner and even more dreary than Jerusha remembered. "Good-bye."

"G'bye, Polly." Her mouth worked. "I won't forget you. Trust me."

"I trust you, Tor." The polrob raised its hand, imitating a farewell.

"Good boy." She backed away slowly.

Still watching, Jerusha saw Tor wipe briefly at her eyes as she followed them out of the station.

503

Arienrhod took her place on the thick pile of white furs that draped the ship-form ceremonial cart in the palace courtyard. She entered her role in the ritual calmly, with perfect control, with the royal presence of nearly one hundred and fifty years. The cheers and the jeers of the gathered Summers closed around her, as inescapable as death; and the wailing grief of the waiting Winters. Their combined dirge was like the moaning hunger of the Pit, where the sea lay waiting . . . as the Sea lay waiting today. Her hunger would be satisfied, at last.

Starbuck was already seated among the silver-tipped furs, sitting like a figure chipped from obsidian in his mask and black court garb. She was surprised to find him here before her. *You were always so impatient, my love. But I didn't think you'd be impatient for this.* She felt a cold weight drop inside of her. *Because I'm not. I'm not.* "Good morning, Starbuck. I hope you slept well."

He turned his face away as she tried to look him in the eye, and said nothing.

"So you think you'll never forgive me? Forever is a long time, Sparks. And forever is how long we'll be together." She put an arm lovingly around his shoulders and felt him shudder, or quiver. His shoulders through the heaviness of cloth and leather felt broader than she remembered. *Only a boy, with a man's strength . . . and weakness.*

At least we'll spend it forever young, trying again to believe as she had once believed, that she would sooner die than live in a world where she would have to be poor, and sick, and old. . . .

The escort of Winter nobles gathered around the cart, all clad in formless white, amorphous in white-on-white masks

that mimed their family totem creatures. Half a dozen of
them picked up the traces to draw the cart forward, starting it down the hill; the rest, all bearing some precious
offworlder thing, formed a human curtain around it to
shield her at least partly from the view, the insults, the
occasional pieces of garbage flung by the Summers in the
crowd along the way. Their positions, this menial labor,
were both an honor and a kind of penance.

She arranged the fall of her own ancient feather cloak,
melting into the whiteness of the furs: the cloak she wore
on all ceremonial occasions, the one she had worn at every
challenge to Starbuck through a century and a half. Beneath it she wore only a simple white gown. White, the
color of Winter, and of mourning. Her hair fell free down
her back like a veil, netted with diamonds and sapphires.
She wore no mask—she was the only one who wore no
mask—so that all the world could be certain that she was
really the Snow Queen.

I am the Snow Queen. She watched the richly decorated
townhouses of the nobility passing for the last time; imag-
ining how they would look bare of their offworld elegance,
remembering the loyal service she had been given by their
many occupants who had been members of her court down
through the years. *And even today.* She glanced from side
to side at her retinue, listening to the defiantly offworld
song they sang to honor her and to drown out the crowd.
A handful of the masked honor guard were nearly as old as
she—although none were quite as well preserved. They had
proven their loyalty and their usefulness again and again,
and they had always been rewarded, while the less useful
and less pliant grew old and were banished to the country-
side. They grieved sincerely today, she knew, like all the
weeping, wailing Winters—and like all the Winters, grieved
mainly for themselves. But that was only human. There
was no one among them that she really regretted leaving
behind: many whom she had enjoyed and even respected,
but none for whom she had ever felt any real personal
warmth that hadn't paled again like infatuation over the
long reaches of time. There was only one whom she really

505

loved—and she was not leaving him behind. She put a hand on Starbuck's cape-covered knee; he brushed it away before it could settle. But after a moment, as though in apology, his own hand slipped across her back beneath her cloak, his arm circled her waist. She smiled, until a fish-head thumped into the furs behind her.

They had come to the edge of the Maze already. *Is this city really so small?* She glanced down the flotsam-full alleys, their throats choked with crowd; met the abandoned eyes of the empty storefronts directly. Seeing it all for the last time . . . which shared something with the first time, every image as perfect and fresh as a walk through new-fallen snow. The first and the last were the same, and had nothing in common with all of the countless passages in between.

And they shared things in common in a literal sense: the Festival crowds, the abandoned and half-empty buildings. But the first time she had seen Carbuncle it had been at the end of Summer's reign, when she had come here from her family's plantation to the first Festival in a hundred years, to see the return of the offworlders and to compete in the choosing of the new Queen. Although she had come from a noble Winter family, growing up at the end of Summer had meant growing up barely more civilized than the Summers themselves were. All of the offworld artifacts that were so commonplace to her now had seemed as strange and marvelous to that naive country girl as they must seem to any Summer.

But she had learned quickly enough the usefulness of the gifts the offworlders brought to this world—the strange magic of technology, strange customs, strange vices. And she had learned, too, what their patronizing lords wanted from her world in return, and from her as its inexperienced representative—begun to learn, painfully, how to take without giving, how to give without surrendering, how to squeeze blood from a stone. She had taken her first Starbuck, a man whose alien features she couldn't remember, whose real name she had long since forgotten. Dozens more had followed, until she had found the one. . . .

506

And meanwhile she had watched Carbuncle transformed into a thriving starport; she had kept learning, year upon year, more about the usefulness of technology, more about the frailty of human nature, more about the universe in general, and herself in particular. Ten lifetimes would barely begin to teach her all that she could have learned, and she had barely been given two. But she had realized at last that this world was an extension of herself, and immortal in a way that no human body could ever be. She had made plans to leave it a legacy when her own reign had to end—to set it free to go on learning and growing when she could not.

But she had failed. Failed to hold onto the key to Tiamat's future; failed to carry out her altered plan of guiding Tiamat's future herself; failed again to keep her hold on Moon, when Moon would have been her last hope. . . . And somehow, in the meantime, she had lost her perspective about her own future. She had lived the way the Summers lived, once, but it had been far too long ago now. She could not even imagine going back, doing without, living like a barbarian again. And even if the Summers weren't allowed to destroy every bit of technology they found remaining in Carbuncle, the city and all of Tiamat would still cease to be even a blurred hologram of the thriving interplanetary stopover that it had been.

She had believed once—secure in her faith that Moon, her clone, would reincarnate her—that she would go willingly to sacrifice. She would play out the traditional role to the end; and death would be one final new experience for a body that had experienced every other imaginable sensation. She would not regret leaving her life behind, because life as she knew it would have ceased to exist.

But after she had lost Moon, and found Sparks instead, after she had begun to build new plans whose foundation lay in herself, she had lost sight of all that. She had forgotten that she and her lover would have to grow old and endure hardship to keep Winter and its heritage alive. No, not forgotten—she had ignored it, because the greater goal,

507

and the greater chance for immortality, had so outweighed it.

But now—now she had failed, utterly, completely. She would end here in this dawn forever; become one more in an endless chain of forgotten Queens who lived and died without meaning. And she wasn't ready to die that way! No, no—not without leaving her legacy to the future! Damn them, damn the bastard offworlders, who had ruined her plans for the future to keep their own intact. Damn the miserable stupidity of the Summers, those jeering, stinking imbeciles who would cheerfully carry out their purge of knowledge. . . . She looked from side to side, radiating her useless fury.

"What's wrong, Arienrhod? Did you finally realize this is the end?"

She froze, her gaze on Starbuck. *"Who are you?"* Whispered, it was louder in her mind than all the shouting of the crowd. "Who are you? You aren't Starbuck!" She wrenched herself free from his encircling arm. *Sparks— Oh, gods, what have you done with him?*

"I am Starbuck. Don't tell me you've forgotten me already, Arienrhod." He caught her hand in a vise grip. "It's only been five years." He turned his black-helmeted head until she could see his eyes, pitiless earth-brown eyes with long, dark lashes. . . .

"Herne!" shaking her head. "It can't be—gods, you can't have done this to me! You cripple, you dead man—you can't be here, I won't permit it!" *Sparks . . . damn you, where are you!* "I'll tell them you're the wrong man!"

"They won't care." She felt his grin. "They just want an offworlder body to pitch into the sea. They don't care whose it is. Why should you?"

"Where is he?" frantically. "Where is Sparks? What have you done to him? And why?"

"So you really love him that much." Herne's voice rasped. "So much that you want him in your grave with you?" Black laughter. "But not enough to let him live on without you . . . or with your other self instead: greedy to the end. I traded places with him, Arienrhod, because he

508

doesn't love you enough to die for you—and I do." He pressed the hand he held to his forehead. "Arienrhod ... you belong with me, we're two of a kind. Not with that weakling; he was never enough of a man to appreciate you."

She buried her hands beneath her cloak as he let her go. "If I had a knife, Herne, I'd kill you myself!" *I'd strangle you with my bare hands—*

"You see what I mean?" He laughed again. "Who else but me would want to spend forever like this? You tried to kill me once already, you bitch, and I wish you'd finished the job. But you didn't, and now I'm going to get my wish, and my revenge too. I'll have you forever now, all to myself; and if you spend forever hating me for it, all the better. But like you said, love, 'forever is a long time.' "

Arienrhod wrapped herself in her cloak, shutting herself away, shutting her eyes against the sight of him. But the singing of the nobles was not enough to stop her ears against the wailing and taunting of the crowd; it seeped in through her pores and gave her despair a killing weight and substance.

"Don't you want to know how I did it? Don't you want to know who put me up to it?" Herne's mocking voice tangled in the voice of the crowd. She didn't answer him, knowing that he would tell her anyway. "It was Moon. Your clone, Arienrhod, your other self. She arranged it— she took him away from you after all. She's your clone, all right ... no one else gets her way quite like you do."

"Moon." Arienrhod clenched her jaw, keeping her eyes shut. For the first time in more years than she could remember, the fear of losing control in public came back to her. Nothing, nothing short of this could break her—nothing short of losing everything that had any meaning at all. And to know that the last blow had been delivered by herself! *No, damn it, that girl was never me—she's a stranger, a failure!* But they had both loved him—Sparks with his summer-green eyes, with his hair and his soul like fire.

And not only had that defective image of her own soul

defied her will, and escaped her curse, but she had stolen
him back. And replaced him with this—this— She glanced
again at Herne, her nails marking her arms. She caught a
hint of sea tang in the air; they were in the lower city
now. The end of her life's journey was almost in view.
Please, please, don't let it end like this! Not knowing whom
she asked it of—not the hollow gods of the offworlders,
not the Summers' Sea . . . yes, maybe of the Sea, who was
about to take the offering of her life, whether she believed
in the old religion or not. She had not put her faith in any
power beyond her own since she had become Queen. But
now that that power had been taken from her, the awareness of her own complete helplessness closed over her,
suffocating her like the cold waters of the sea. . . .

The procession reached the final slope at the Street's
foot, and started down the broad ramp to the harbor that
lay below the city. The ubiquitous mass of humanity was
even more tightly crowded here, a wall of solid flesh, a wall
of grotesque beast-faces. The cheering and the wailing rose
from below to greet her as the cart rolled forward, echoing
and re-echoing through the vast sea-cave. The dank chill
air of the outer world flowed around her. Arienrhod shuddered secretly, but pride masked her face.

Ahead, below, she saw stands draped in red clustered at
the far end of the pier, tiers filled with offworlder dignitaries and influential elders of Summer families. On the
best-placed viewing stands she saw the Prime Minister and
the Assembly members—already unmasked, as if it were
beneath their dignity to participate in this pagan ritual—
gaping without seeming to at her approach. Shimmering
déjà vu overtook her at the sight of them. She had seen this
tableau before, half a dozen times or more, but only once
that was like this time: the first time, when she had been
the new Queen who stood below on the pier and watched
the last of the Summer Queens pass this way—and sent her
predecessor triumphantly into the icy water.

All the rest, all the other Festival pageants, had been
only dress rehearsals for the next Change, this Change.
They had chosen the Queen for a Day by the same ancient

ritual rules, to reign over the Mask Night and make this journey at dawn. But only a pair of effigies had been given to the sea at her command, and not human lives.

And only she and the Assembly members had remained unchanged, like the ritual itself, through all of those Festivals, all the long years. But this final time would see the end of her and all her efforts to break free of them, while they went on and the system they symbolized went on forever. Her hands clenched on the soft cloth of her gown, *If I could only take them all with me!* But it was too late, too late for anything at all.

She saw the Summer Queen at last; standing on the pier in the open space between the red-robed stands, with the bitter-colored water lapping below her. Her mask was a thing of beauty that stirred unwilling admiration in Arienrhod's heart. *But it was made by a Winter.* And who knew what homely, undeserving islander's face was hidden beneath it; what sturdy peasant body and dull-witted mind were wrapped in the glistening fish-net cocoon of silky green mesh. The prospect of that face, that mind, taking the place of her own made her stomach twist.

Herne was silent beside her, as silent as she was. She wondered what his own thoughts were as he looked on the waiting elite of his homeworld, and the waiting sea. She could tell nothing about the expression beneath his mask. *Damn him.* She prayed that he was regretting his suicidal impulse now; that he felt even a fraction of the despair and regret that she knew, standing here in the ruins of her life's ambition. *Let death be oblivion, then! If I have to spend it with this symbol of all my failures, knowing that I did would be worse than all the hells of the god-damning offworlders combined!*

The cart had gone forward as far as it could into the open space along the pier's edge. The escort of her nobles slowed, stopped, let the traces settle. They circled slowly three times around her, casting their offworld offerings into the back of the cart, as they sang their final song of farewell to Winter. They bowed to her at last, and she could hear their individual weeping and lamentation above the crowd's cries as they began to file away from the cart. Some touched the hem of her cloak to their lips as they passed her for the last time. Some even dared to touch her hand—some of the oldest, the faithful followers of a century and a half—and their grief touched her suddenly, unexpectedly, deeply.

Their place was taken by a circle of Summers, also masked, also singing, a paean to the coming golden days. She closed her mind and did not listen to it. They, too, circled her three times around, throwing their own offerings into the cart—clattering primitive necklaces of shell and stone, colored fishing floats, sprigs of wilted greenery.

When they had finished their own song, a greater silence fell over the waiting crowd; until she could hear clearly the creakings and groans of shifting moorings, made aware of the greater alien crowd of ships that covered the water surface; a near-solid skin of wood and cloth and clanging metal. Carbuncle loomed above them like a gathering storm, but here at this edge of the city's understructure she could see beyond its shadow, out across the gray-green open sea. *Endless . . . eternal . . . is it any wonder that we worship you?* Remembering that once, in a faraway time, even she had believed in the Sea.

The mask of the Summer Queen came between her and her view of the sea, as the woman came up between the cart's traces to stand before her. "Your Majesty." The Summer Queen bowed to her, and Arienrhod remembered that she was still the Queen, until death. "You have come." The voice was strangely uncertain, and strangely familiar.

She nodded, regal and aloof, in control again of the one thing that was still within her power. "Yes," recalling the ritual response, "I have come to be changed. I am the Sea incarnate; as the tide turns and the world has its seasons, so must I follow to lead. Winter has had its season . . . the snow dissolves on the face of the Sea, and from it soft rains are reborn." Her voice rang eerily through the underworld. The ritual was being recorded by hidden cameras, broadcast sight and sound over screens set up throughout the city.

512

"Summer follows Winter as night follows day. The sea joins the land. Together the halves become whole; who can separate them? Who can deny them their place, or their time, when their time has come? They are born of a power greater than any here. Their truth is universal!" The Summer Queen lifted her arms to the crowd.

Arienrhod started slightly. She had never said that last line, never heard it before. The crowds murmured; a prickling unease crept in her.

"Who comes with you to be changed?"

"My beloved," keeping her voice even, "whose body is like the earth, coupled with the Sea. Together beneath the sky, we can never be separated." The cold wind burned her eyes. Herne said nothing, did nothing, waiting with appropriate stoicism.

"Then so be it." The woman's voice actually broke. She held out her hands, and two of the attendant Summers placed a small bowl of dark liquid in each. The Summer Queen offered a bowl to Herne; he took it willingly. She offered the other to Arienrhod. "Will you drink to the Lady's mercy?"

Arienrhod felt her mouth stiffen against the reply; said, finally, "Yes." The bowl held a strong drug which would dull her fear and awareness of what was coming. Beside her Herne lifted his black mask and raised the bowl to his lips, grimaced. Arienrhod raised her own. She had always intended to refuse it; rejecting the idea of dimming her awareness of the moment when her triumph would have been clear. But now she wanted oblivion. "To the Lady." She sniffed the pungent fragrance of the herbs, felt their numbing gall burn inside her mouth. She swallowed the liquid, deadening her throat; the second swallow, and the third were as tasteless as water.

As she finished it and returned the bowl she saw Summers approaching, carrying the ropes that would bind them to the cart, and to each other, inescapably. Terror congealed in her chest, panic darkened her sight. *Deaden me, for gods' sakes!* trying to feel the numbness spread. Herne almost resisted as the Summers laid hands on him; she saw

513

his muscles twist and harden, and his weakness gave her strength. She sat perfectly still and pliant as the Summers bound her hands, her feet, bound her body tightly against Herne's and fastened the ropes to the cart itself. Even though the cart had the form of a blunt-nosed boat, she knew that its bed gaped with holes beneath the heaps of furs and offerings, and that it would sink almost immediately. She couldn't keep her hands from straining at their bonds, or her body from trying to pull away from Herne's. His masked face turned toward her, but she would not look at him.

The Summer Queen was back in place before them, but turning to face the water as she recited the final Invocation to the Sea. As she finished, the silence that had fallen over the crowd continued, the silence of anticipation now. Now, at any moment, she would give the sign. Arienrhod felt a dreamlike lethargy creep along her limbs, along her spine; but her mind was still far too clear. *Is it meant to work that way?* At least now her body was becoming too leaden to betray her, granting her dignity in death whether she wanted it or not.

But instead of moving aside, the Summer Queen turned back to face her again. "Your Majesty." The urgency of the muffled voice caught at her. "Would you—look on the face of Summer's Queen before you die?"

Arienrhod stared uncomprehendingly, felt Herne stare, too. Tradition said that the new Queen did not unmask, casting off her sins, until the old one had gone into the sea; giving the sign for the crowd to follow. But this woman had stumbled off the ritual path once already. *Is she so stupid?* Or was it something else? "I would see your face, yes," forcing the words out between numb lips.

The Summer Queen moved closer to the cart, where the crowd could not see her clearly. Slowly she put her hands to the mask, and lifted it off her head.

A cascade of silvery hair tumbled out and down. Arienrhod gaped at the face that the mask revealed. The ring of Summers surrounding the cart gaped, too. She heard their

514

voices murmur as the wonder spread, as they all saw what she saw . . . face to face with her own face.

"Moon—" barely even a whisper to betray her. Her body sat perfectly still, as though it saw nothing unusual, nothing remarkable, incredible, impossible. *Not in vain. It was not in vain!*

"Gods," Herne mumbled thickly. "How? How'd you do it, Arienrhod?"

She only smiled.

Moon shook out her hair, meeting the smile with forgiveness, and defiance, and compassion. "Change has come . . . because of you, in spite of you, Your Majesty." She lowered the mask over her head again.

The Summers around the cart drew away, looking from face to face, their own expressions caught between amazement and fear. "The Queen! They're both the Queen—" *an augury, an omen.* The sibyl tattoo was clearly visible on Moon's throat; they pointed at it and murmured again.

Herne chuckled with difficulty. "The secret's out . . . it's out at last. She's been offworld; she knows what she is."

"What? What, Herne?" trying to turn her head.

"Sibyls are everywhere! You never knew, did you; you never even suspected. And those stuffed dummies—" glancing toward the offworlders in the stands, "they don't suspect a thing." His mangled laughter left him gasping.

Sibyls are everywhere? . . . Can they be real? No, it isn't fair, there's so much left to learn! Closing her eyes, unable to focus her inner sight. *But it wasn't in vain.*

The chorus of wailing and execration began to press again, inexorable like the process of change, impatient for the sacrifice. All of the crowd's overflowing grief, all of its blame, all of its hostility and resentment and fear poured into this fragile boat, onto the helpless beings of herself and Herne, to be taken down with them at the ritual's culmination. She no longer strained against the contact between her body and Herne's, grateful at last for someone to share the trial, and this last moment, with her . . . the passing through into another plane. She had seen too many

515

visions of heaven, too many hells, to choose among them. *I hope we make our own.*

She turned her gaze outward a last time, to see Moon standing aside from the cart's path: Her body was taut with strain, as though she were about to speak an unforgivable curse, one that she could never take back. *Why should it hurt her? I would rejoice—* Not able to remember why she would rejoice, or even whether it was true. She rallied her mind one last time, before Moon could speak the fateful words, to speak her own last words. "My people—" half obliterated by their cries. "Winter is gone! Obey the new Queen . . . as you would your own. For she is your own now." She dropped her head, catching only Moon's eyes. "Where . . . is he?"

Moon moved her head slightly, a twinge of jealousy in it, but granting her clone-mother's last request. Arienrhod followed her glance to find Sparks standing among the honored Summers, by the empty place that was the Summer Queen's own in the stands. But he stood with his eyes closed against the parting moment; or against the chance that she might look up and see him one last time. . . . *He cares . . . he does care.* She looked back again at Moon. *They both do.* In that moment infinitely surprised, eternally confounded, by life's imperviousness to reason or justice.

Herne's smoldering stare lay waiting for her when she turned her head back again—knowing whom her thoughts belonged to in this final moment.

"Forever . . . Herne."

He shook his head once. "We're forever. This is. Death is. Life's . . . what doesn't last."

"We live while someone remembers us. And they'll never forget me now—" Because her reincarnation already stood in her place. She had no will left to let her look back at Moon once more, or at Sparks. *Never look back.*

Moon raised her hands to the Sea, crying like a gull into the storm of the crowd's anticipation. "Lady Sea, Mother of us all, accept our gifts and return them ninefold, accept our sins and bring us renewal, accept the soul of Winter and let it be—reborn." She faltered imperceptibly. "Let spring come to Summer!"

Arienrhod felt the cart lurch as the Summers pushed it forward, watched the oily water surface draw near. The tide was at full, and it lay below the pier's edge like a distorted mirror. *Let it happen. It was not in vain.* The howls and moans of the crowd were a hymn to the future, praising her memory. The cart began to tilt under her; she leaned forward, looking for her reflection as it slipped. . . .

Moon saw the cart strike the water, plunge and reemerge; heard it, felt its impact vibrate in her bones. The crowd's roaring went on and on, hideously. The boat form drifted away from the dock, lowering in the water, swinging slowly until she could see Starbuck's hidden face and the face of the Snow Queen, Arienrhod . . . herself: serene with drug stupor, bound to her impotent lover in a grotesque parody of an embrace. The boat began to spiral more rapidly as it filled with water. Moon tried to shut her eyes, but they would not close against the hypnotic final movement of the death dance on the water. She remembered her own ordeal by sea, remembered all that had brought her to this place, again, sacrifice upon sacrifice. And still she could not look away—

The boat lurched suddenly, as the faces revolved again toward the crowd, and in the blink of an eye it was gone. Moon blinked again and again, but it did not reappear. The sea surface lay in unperturbed undulation, with only a telltale litter of boughs to mark Her acceptance of Her peoples' offering. The crowd's roaring was like a storm, and the underworld trembled. Moon watched the lazy motion of the swells, standing as fluid and unresponsive as the Sea Herself.

One of the Summers came forward at last, touched her arm hesitantly. Moon shuddered under the touch, and breathed again. "Lady?" He bowed as Moon turned at last. The Summers acknowledged their Queen's role as the Sea Mother incarnate, and did not use the artificial offworld form of royal address. "The unmasking—"

"I know." She nodded, looking back over her shoulder at the sea even as she spoke. *Fair voyage, safe haven.* She moved away from the edge of the dock, into the crowd's eye once more. *"Lady"* . . . *I am the Queen.*

"The Queen . . . the Queen . . . the Queen is dead. Long live the Queen!" The shouts of the Summers echoed inside her, a mockery.

She placed her hands on her mask, hands that felt damp and chill like the wind through the underworld. "My people—" She felt her body resist the motion of exposing her face again; suddenly, disconcertingly aware of the danger she had only glimpsed in the eyes of the Summers who stood here on the pier around her. Now her resemblance to Arienrhod would be obvious to everyone—and especially to the offworlders. If they even suspected the truth. . . . She shook her head, shaking the rest of the words loose that she must say to the waiting crowd: "Winter is past, Summer has come at last. The Lady has taken our offering, and will return it ninefold. The life that was is dead—let it be cast away, like a battered mask, an outgrown shell. Rejoice now, and make a new beginning!" She lifted the mask from her head.

All of the crowd together—Winters, Summers, even offworlders—became one in this one moment. Their shouts of joy and the rustle of countless masks being torn from countless heads crescendoed—baring faces freed for that moment from all past sorrows, sins, and fears. Their celebration and adulation lifted her up onto its shoulders, swept into her heart. *This world will be free!*

But as she spoke the words, holding her mask high, the crowd's voice changed; the cavernous underworld reverberated with the cries of a people who saw a thing beyond their understanding, and could not deny it. . . . "Arienrhod —Arienrhod!" Moon felt the Summers' superstition curdle, felt the disbelief spreading like paranoia through the crowd, imagined it echoing through the entire city. Knowing that she must stop it now—stop it before she lost everything without ever having had it. *How . . . how do I stop them?* like a prayer, pressing her hand to the sign at her throat. The sibyl sign . . .

"People of Tiamat, children of the Sea!" She reached up, pulling at the neck of her clothing, to bare the trefoil tattoo. "I am a sibyl! See my sign—I serve the Lady faithfully and truthfully. My name is Moon Dawntreader Summer, and I will do the same as your Queen. The keeper of all wisdom speaks through me, but only to you. Ask and I shall answer, and I will never speak falsely."

A hush fell, went on falling as the echoes died; all eyes throughout the city were on her throat, or on its image on some screen. The Winters were speechless with uncertainty, the Summers were speechless with reverence, at the undeniable proof of their Queen's transmutation, the symbol of her rebirth and holy status. And from the corner of her eye Moon saw the strange look that passed over the faces of the offworlder officials in the viewing stands, to see that sign, below that face. . . .

As she went on watching, her breath aching in her chest, she saw the look separating again into a natural spectrum of expressions: horrified amusement, fascination, disgust at the spectacle they had all just witnessed . . . but still a lingering unease and uncertainty. Nowhere among them did she see any guilt, any respect, any real understanding of what they had seen. *Next time—next time whoever stands here will see those things.*

Letting her gaze go on, she followed it, walking back toward her own place in the stands among the Summer elders. Sparks stood waiting in the place reserved for her consort; his flaming hair was a beacon to sign her place . . . his face was tight, like a drawn bow. She took her place silently beside him, looked away from the crowd again to

519

the spot where branches drifted on the sea. The crowd still waited, murmuring and uncertain.

"They expect a few words from you, Lady." One of the Goodventures who had been her ceremonial guides leaned toward her. She sensed a fog of unease among the Summers, too.

She nodded, wondering again, as she had wondered all through the mind-numbing song and celebration of the Mask Night, what the words would be that could make her people listen: How could one transform so many, and still keep their trust? But somehow, somewhere, there had to be the words. . . .

The words came to her suddenly, not from the strange guardian of her mind, but from the strength of her own feeling. "People of Tiamat, the Lady has blessed me once, by giving me someone to share my life with me." She looked at Sparks beside her; her hand touched his, hanging cold and strengthless at his side. "She has blessed me twice, by making me a sibyl, and three times, by making me a Queen. Since yesterday I have thought a great deal about my destiny, and this world's, which all of us will share. I've prayed that She will show me the way to do Her will and be Her living symbol. And She has answered me." *In a way that I never dreamed She could.* Moon glanced toward the sea, and the secret that lay beneath the dark waters.

"I know there is a reason why She has shown herself to you as a sibyl, through me. I don't know yet the full pattern of the future, but I know that to create it fully I must have help—help from all of you, and especially from other sibyls. Summer has come to Carbuncle, and this city is no longer closed to sibyls—more than anyone, more than anyone can know, sibyls belong here! Islanders, when you go back to your homes, ask your sibyls to make the journey here if they can—not to stay, but to come to me and learn their part in the future's design."

She paused, hearing the crowd's voice whisper, trying to judge whether it was accepting her words, and her. She stole glances at the Summers in the stand around her, relieved to find a benign surprise looking back at her. The

Winters would resent it, she knew instinctively, remembering their fear and scorn firsthand. She had to give them something of their own, a part in the future. She glanced again at the waiting offworlders, knowing the risk she took in this offering, the delicate balance she had to maintain while they still walked this world.

"If I—if I seem to stray out of tradition's shallows as Summer's Queen, and into uncharted depths, have faith in me. Try to remember that I am the Lady's chosen, and that I only follow Her will . . ." secure in the knowledge that she told the truth. "She is my navigator, and She charts my course by strange stars," *stranger stars than the ones that lie above us.* She glanced at the offworlders again. "My first command as your new Queen—" the potential of power sang in her head, potential energy, "is that all the offworld possessions of the Winters will not be thrown into the sea. Hear me!" before the crowd could drown her out. "Things made by the offworlders offend the waters, they choke the sea with filth. Three things from each Winter are all She demands—and the Winters will choose what offerings they make. Time . . . time will take care of the rest!" She braced herself against the rise of Summer outrage.

But there was only a rippling water of dismay, here and there a shining drop of laughter or applause from an astonished Winter. Moon took a deep breath, hardly daring to believe— *They trust me! They listen; they'll do whatever I say. . . .* realizing at last what Arienrhod had known—and how easily power, like fire, could break its bonds and destroy what it had been guardian to. Her hands tightened over the rail. "Thank you, my people." She bowed her head to them.

The Summers in the stands shifted into deferential resignation around her; but Sparks watched her like a cat, with suspicion and unease, as he sensed her sense of power.

She looked away quickly, struggling to keep her expression even as she saw the Prime Minister himself begin to descend opposite them, to start the final, official acknowledgement of her rule, to pay the hypocritical homage of one figurehead ruler to another. Watching him descend, she saw First Secretary Sirus among the Assembly members, caught his own eyes on her with a dubious foreboding. She nudged Sparks, led his gaze to his father's; saw him struggle to meet his father's sudden smile. Sparks looked down again silently at his grandfather, as the Prime Minister began his salutation.

The speeches of the Prime Minister, the Chief Justice of Tiamat, half a dozen other dignitaries whose function she had never even heard of, were brief and patronizing. She stood patiently through them all, shielded from their arrogance by her secret knowledge, but seeing in each face suspicion and mistrust stirred by her own speech to her people. The Chief Justice looked at her too long and too piercingly; but he only mouthed congratulations like the rest, praised the traditional and ritual, her peoples' smooth backsliding into ignorance. He urged her not to stray from tradition's path too strongly—to beware the consequences. She smiled at him.

As he left his place before her, the last of her tribute-bringers approached, and she saw that it was the Commander of Police. As PalaThion passed the Chief Justice, she glimpsed a silent exchange between them, saw the dullness of PalaThion's eyes as she came on.

"Your Majesty." PalaThion saluted with formal precision, and the dullness sharpened and brightened as she took in Moon's actual presence above her at the red-draped rail. "I congratulate you." Incongruity pricked every word.

Moon let her smile widen. "Thank you, Commander. I think I'm as surprised to find myself here as you are." She felt suddenly awkward, as though she were speaking through someone else's mouth.

"I doubt that very much, Your Majesty. But who knows . . . ?" PalaThion shrugged imperceptibly. She raised her voice, "The recognition of your position as the Summer Queen ends my duties here, Your Majesty, and all police responsibility for what happens on Tiamat. And all official rule by the Hegemony for a hundred years, until we return again at the next Change. Keeping order will be your responsibility from now on."

Moon nodded. "I know, Commander. Thank you for your service to my people . . . and especially to Summer, for saving us from the—the plague. I owe you a debt that I can't repay—" *two debts*, leaning forward against the rail.

PalaThion glanced down, up again. "I was only doing my duty, Your Majesty." But a surprising gratitude showed on her face.

"Tiamat regrets losing a true friend like you, and so do I. We don't have many true friends in this galaxy. We need them all."

PalaThion smiled thinly. "Friends turn up in the most unexpected places, Your Majesty. . . . But sometimes you only know it when it's too late. The same goes for enemies." She lowered her voice. "Walk softly, Moon, until the last ship is gone from the starport. Don't try to make the future happen yesterday. More than just your own people are wondering what you really are. You'd be in a cell right now if the Chief Justice didn't know it would cause a riot. . . . The only reason you'll get away with changing the ritual is because it won't make any difference."

Moon blinked, her hands white against the red cloth. "What do you mean?"

"The Hedge has its way of dealing with tech hoarders when it goes. Never underestimate them—not for a second. That's the best advice a friend can give you now."

"Thank you, Commander." Moon straightened her shoulders, trying to hide her dismay. "But even that won't stop me." *Because the mers are the real key*.

PalaThion started to turn away, looked on across the Pier toward her own people. She hesitated. "Your Majesty." She stood close in front of Moon again, speaking softly, almost inaudibly. "I believe in what you want to do. I believe it's just. I don't want anything to stop it." She seemed to reach out, without moving, "In fact, I want to help you make it happen," in a frightened rush. "I'm—offering you my services, my knowledge, my experience, the rest of my life, if

523

you'll take them. If you'll let me use them for something I can believe in."

Moon felt PalaThion's urgency reaching higher, further, deeper; beyond the thing she asked. "You mean . . . you want to stay? On Tiamat?" Her whisper sounded stupid and unqueenly. Sparks glared his disbelief.

But PalaThion, lost in her own inner vision, didn't hear, or see. "Not on the Tiamat that was. But on the one that could be." Her dark upslanting eyes asked, and demanded, a promise.

"You're the Commander of Police—the Hegemony's fist . . . Why?" Moon shook her head, certain that PalaThion was sincere, trying to re-form the slipping sands of reality.

"This is the time of change," PalaThion said simply.

"That's not enough." Sparks leaned forward over the rail. "Not if you want to spend the rest of your life interfering in ours."

PalaThion rubbed her face. "How much is enough? How much proof did I ask of you, Dawntreader?"

He looked away, and didn't answer.

"To tell you what caused the change in me would take me a lifetime. But believe me, I have reasons." She turned back to Moon.

"And you'll have to spend the lifetime here, regretting it, if you change your mind. Are you sure?"

"No." PalaThion glanced again at the offworlders waiting in the stands, light-years distant from the world she stood reaching out to. "Yes! What the hell have I got to lose? Yes." She smiled, finally.

"Then stay." Moon smiled, too. *If this world changed you, then it can change itself . . . we can change it . . . I can.* "Everything you want to give I'll need, Commander—"

"Jerusha."

"Jerusha." Moon stretched out her hand; PalaThion gripped her wrist, the handshake of a native.

"I won't be free of this," gesturing at her uniform, "till the last ship is gone from here; but neither will any of you.

After that I'll be finished with the Hegemony, and ready to belong wholeheartedly to the future."

Moon nodded.

"And now, with your permission, I'll leave you, Your Majesty. While I have the guts to change my old mistakes for new ones, I'm going to say some things that need to be said to a man who can't speak for himself."

Moon nodded, blankly, and watched her lonely journey back across the open space to the ranks of the offworlders. Moon raised her voice again as Jerusha disappeared among the stands, to pronounce the end of the ceremonies, of the Festival, of Winter . . . but only the beginning of the Change.

Cold twilight moved on wind wings through the oozing underworld of docks and moorages, where cold dawn had seen the Change come to Carbuncle. Moon walked with Sparks, trailed by a discrete retinue, among the creakings and sighings of the restless ships, the dim, echoing voices of their weary crews. The jam of Winter and Summer craft that had clogged every open patch of water surface had thinned by half already, as Summers and Winters alike began their post-Festival exodus from the city.

The Summers would be returning before long; the Change was the sign for them to begin their northward exodus, leaving the equatorial ranges of the sea to fill the interstices of the Winters' range. As Tiamat approached the Black Gate and the Twins' solar activity intensified, the lower latitudes would become uninhabitable—the sea would turn against them, its indigenous life retreating to the depths or the higher latitudes, forcing them to do the same.

The Winters would have to share with them the scattering of islands and the vast reaches of ocean that had been theirs alone, and share as well a new, hand-to-mouth existence without offworld sustenance. The nobility now would be going out of the city to relearn the task of making their plantations, which had been little more than boundaries for the Hunt, into a base that could support the precarious balance of life the offworlders had left them to.

And in the middle of this cyclical chaos, somehow she, Moon, had to begin a new order. "I thought that once I got to Carbuncle all my problems would be over. But they're just beginning." Her plaintive breath frosted. Even here, while they walked together, soothed by the presence of the sea, she felt the burden of the future bear down on her like the weight of the city overhead. She leaned on a time-grayed railing, looking down at the mottled, green-black water. Sparks leaned beside her, silent, as he had been all day: trying to make the best of what he could not change —to accept that change happened indiscriminately, and made its favorites and its victims one.

"You've got supporters now. And you'll get more. You won't have to carry it all alone. You'll always have them around you." A sullen note crept into his voice, and he moved slightly away from her. She knew that all of the people that she would be depending on knew what he had been; and even if they didn't still hate him for it, they would always remind him of it, and let him go on hating himself. "No one rules all alone . . . not even Arienrhod."

"I'm not Arienrhod!" She stopped, realizing that he didn't mean it that way, but too late. "I thought you—"

"I didn't."

"I know." But knowing that a part of him would always see Arienrhod when he looked at her—because Arienrhod would always be there for him to see; always there, making them afraid to meet each other's eyes. She wiped the twilight dampness from her face. Beyond the city's looming edge she could see the band of sunset in the west, a dying rainbow. "When will we ever see another rainbow now? Will we have to live all our lives without one?"

Something broke the water surface below them, a soft intrusion on the words. Looking down, Moon saw a sleek, brindled head rising sinuously to meet her gaze. She felt her own breath catch, heard Sparks's involuntary protest—

"No!"

"Sparks!" She caught his arm as he would have pulled away from the railing. "Wait. Don't." She held him.

"Moon, what are you trying to do to me?"

But she didn't answer, crouching down, drawing him with her, the beadwork of her gossamer green shawl rattling on the wooden pier. She put out her arm, reached until the mer's dark silhouette met her outstretched hand, becoming real under her touch. "What are you doing here?" The lone mer looked at her with ebony, expressionless eyes, as though it didn't have the answer even in its own mind. But it made no move to leave them, its flippers stirring the flotsam-littered water at the dock's edge rhythmically in place. It began to croon forlornly, a single voice from a lost chorus of patterned song. *The songs . . . why do you sing? Are they more than songs? Could they tell you your purpose, your duty, your reason for existence, if you only understood?* Excitement tingled in her. *Ngenet.* Ngenet could help her learn. And if she was right, learn to teach them—

She had seen him in the crowds today, seen the pride and hope on his face, but hadn't been able to reach him. And she had also seen the unforgiving memory as his eyes found Sparks beside her. She kept Sparks's hand locked in her own, holding on against his trembling resistance; forced it out over the water. He groaned, as though she were holding his hand over a fire. The mer looked cryptically from her face to his, and sank slowly back into the dark water without touching him.

Moon let his hand go, watched it stay outstretched above the water of its own accord. Slowly Sparks drew his hand back to himself; crouched, staring at it, bracing against the rail.

Behind them Moon heard the incredulous mutterings of her Summer retinue—the omnipresent Goodventures, who had seemed to follow while trying to lead her all through the day. She had antagonized them by her willful disobedience of their ritual expectations, and she knew that because of their royal background they could be dangerous enemies to the future. She resented them even more now, when she

527

needed this moment alone with Sparks in the intimacy of his grief. She understood at last that becoming Queen did not mean absolute freedom, but the end of it.

"The Sea never forgets. But She forgives, Sparkie." Moon reached to touch his hair, cupped his chill, tear-wet face between her chill, wet hands, feeling his shame like one more icy splinter of doubt. "It just takes time."

"A lifetime will never be enough!" A dagger, driven by his own hand. He would never belong, here, anywhere, until he found peace within himself.

"Oh, Sparks—let the Sea witness that you hold my willing heart, you alone, now and forever." She spoke the pledge words defiantly; the only words that filled her need to fill the need in him.

"Let the Sea witness . . . " He repeated the words, softening as he spoke, his strength, his resistance, melting away.

"Sparks . . . the day's finished out there, even if it never ends in Carbuncle. Let's find our place for tonight, where you can forget I'm a queen, and I can forget it. . . ." She glanced over her shoulder at the Goodventures. *But what about tomorrow?* "Tomorrow everything will start to fit into place. Tomorrow we'll be free of today; and then on the day after . . ." She brushed her hair back from her eyes, looking out across the darkening waters again, where no trace lay at all of the sacrifice they had given to the Sea this dawn. The Sea rested, sublime in Her indifference, an imperturbable mirror for the face of universal truth. *Today never ends in Carbuncle . . . will tomorrow really ever come?* She saw the future that lay dying beneath the dark waters: the future that would never come, if she failed, if she stumbled, if she weakened for a moment— She whispered fiercely, close by his ear, "Sparkie, I'm afraid."

He held her tightly and did not answer.

Jerusha stood in the fiery hell-glow of the red-lit docking bay, beneath the vast umbrella of the suspended coin ship. The final ship, taking on the last of her police officers—the last offworlders to depart from Tiamat. In the frantic finality of the past few days the ships of the Assembly had already lifted into planetary orbit, into the company of the other coin ships already there to take on shuttle-loads of die-hard merchants and exhausted Festival refugees.

She endured the inventories patiently, checked and re-checked the data from reports and records, trying to be certain that no one was left, nothing vital left undone, unsalvaged, unsealed. It was her responsibility to make certain that the job was thorough and complete. She had done the job to the best of her ability, making certain that her men left no power pack in place, no system unstripped, no outlet accessible. And all the while she had known, with a strange double vision, that tomorrow she would be trying to undo again everything that she had just undone today.

But by the gods, I won't make it easy on myself! Knowing that if she finished the career that had meant so much to her once with an act of betrayal, she would never be able to build a new life on its foundation that would have any meaning. *Nothing worth having is easy to get.* She looked away from the loading of miscellaneous supplies, away from the cluster of blue uniforms and containers by the coin ship's suspended loading foot. The ship, the docking bay, beyond it the spaceport's throbbing complexity that was almost like a living organism—all that they symbolized, she was giving up. Not in a year, or a week, or even a day—in less than an hour, all that would be behind her, would be leaving her behind. She was giving it all up . . . for Cabuncle. And before the last starship left Tiamat space, it would send down the high-frequency signal that would demolish the fragile microprocessors that made virtually every piece of technology left on the planet function. The tech hoarders would hoard in vain, and Tiamat would be returned to technical ground zero. She remembered with sudden incongruity the sight of a windmill on a lonely hilltop on Ngenet Miroe's plantation. *Not quite ground zero.* Remembering that she had had no idea of what use he could possibly have for a thing like that. *There are none so blind as those who will not see.* She smiled, as suddenly.

"Commander?"

She pulled her eyes back to the space around her, expecting one more request or verification. "Yes, I'm—Gundhalinu!" He saluted. His grin highlighted the spectral gauntness of his face; his uniform hung on him like something borrowed from a stranger.

"What the hell are you doing out here? You shouldn't be—"

"I came to say good-bye, Commander."

She broke off, set down the computer remote on the makeshift desk of empty shipping containers. "Oh."

"KerlaTinde told me—that you were resigning, that you're going to stay on Tiamat?" He sounded bewildered, as though he expected her to deny it.

"It's true." She nodded. "I'm staying here."

"Why? Your reassignment? I heard about that, too." His voice turned flat with anger. "Nobody likes it, Commander."

I can think of one or two who were overjoyed. "Only partly because of that." She frowned through him at the idea of the force chewing gossip about her resignation like old men in the town square. Having decided that it would be useless to complain, she had kept her anger in; but there was no way she could keep the fact of her humiliation from the others. And she had refused to discuss her decision or her resignation with anyone—whether out of fear

530

that they would try to change her mind, or fear that they wouldn't, she wasn't sure.

"Why didn't you tell me?"

Her frown faded. "Ye gods, BZ. You've had trouble enough without me giving you another load."

"Only half the trouble I'd have had if you hadn't covered for me, Commander." The point of his jaw sharpened with feeling. "I know if it weren't for you I wouldn't still have the right to wear this uniform. I know how much it's always meant to you . . . a lot more than it ever meant to me, until now; because I never had to fight for it. And now you're giving it up." He looked down. "If I could, I'd do my damnedest to help you get this assignment changed. But I . . . " He was looking at his hands. "I'm not my father's son, any more. 'Inspector Gundhalinu' is all I have left. I'm ten times as grateful to you that I still have that much." He looked up at her again. "But all I can do in return is ask you, Why here? Why Tiamat? I don't blame you for resigning—but hell, any world in the Hegemony is better than this one, if you want to make a new life for yourself. At least if you don't like it you can leave it."

She shook her head, with a small, resolute smile. "I'm not a quitter, BZ. I wouldn't be doing this if I didn't have something better I was going to. And I think I've found it here, unlikely as that sounds." She glanced up and away, toward the line of high windows overlooking the field—the empty hall where Ngenet Miroe kept unseen watch on the Hegemony's departure, waiting for the moment when she would become wholly and irrevocably a part of this world at last.

Gundhalinu followed the line of her glance, puzzled. "You always hated this world, even more than I did. What in the name of ten thousand gods could you have found—?"

"I'll be swearing by just one, now." She shook her head. "And working for Her too, I suppose."

He looked blank. Comprehension came back into his eyes: "You mean . . . the Summer Queen? You mean Moon . . . you, and Moon?"

"That's right." She nodded. "How did you know, BZ? That she'd won."

"She came to me, in the hospital; she told me." The color faded from his voice. "I saw the mask of the Summer Queen. It was like a dream." His hands moved in the air, touching something out of memory; his eyes closed. "She had Sparks with her."

"BZ, are you going to be all right?"

"She asked me that, too." He opened his eyes. "A man without armor is a defenseless man, Commander." He smiled, bravely, barely. "But maybe he's a freer man for it. This world . . . this world would have broken me. But Moon showed me that even I could bend. There's more to me, more to the universe, than I suspected. Room for all the dreams I ever had, and all the nightmares . . . heroes in the gutters and in the mirror; saints in the frozen wasteland; fools and liars on the throne of wisdom, and hands reaching out in hunger that will never be filled. . . . Anything becomes possible, after you find the courage to admit that nothing is certain." His smile twitched self-consciously. Jerusha listened in silent disbelief.

"Life used to look like cut crystal to me, Commander— sharp and clear and perfect. My fantasies stayed in my pockets where they belonged. But now . . ." He shrugged. "Those clean hard edges break up the light into rainbows, and everything gets soft and hazy. I don't know if I'll ever see straight again." A forlorn note crept back into his voice.

But you'll be a better Blue for it. Jerusha saw his eyes search the vastness of the sunken field, settle on the nearest exit, as though he expected that somehow his new vision would grant him one last glimpse of Moon. "No, BZ. She isn't here. The starport is forbidden ground to her."

His gaze sharpened and cleared abruptly. "Yes, ma'am. I know the law." But it told her he understood now that even the laws of nature were imperfect; that the laws of men were no less flawed than the men who made them; that even he could realize what Moon was and what she,

Jerusha, intended to help her do ... and look the other way. "Maybe it's for the best." Not even believing that.

"I'll do my best to take care of her for you, BZ."

He laughed shyly, the echo of a caress. "I know, Commander. But what force in the galaxy is stronger than she is?"

"Indifference." Jerusha surprised herself with the answer. "Indifference, Gundhalinu, is the strongest force in the universe. It makes everything it touches meaningless. Love and hate don't stand a chance against it. It lets neglect and decay and monstrous injustice go unchecked. It doesn't act, it allows. And that's what gives it so much power."

He nodded slowly. "And maybe that's why people want to trust Moon. Because things matter to her, and they do; and when she touches them they know they matter to themselves." He held his hands up in front of him, stared at the scars still waiting to be erased. "She made my scars invisible. . . ."

"You could stay, BZ."

He shook his head, let his hands drop. "There was a time ... but not now. It wasn't just my life that was changed. I don't belong here now. No," he sighed, "there are two worlds I don't ever expect to see again, barring the Millennium. This one, and my own."

"Kharemough?"

He sat down unsteadily on the stack of crates. "My own people will see my scars forever, even when they're gone. But what the hell, that still leaves six to choose from. And who knows what I'll find where I'm going?" But his gaze returned to the empty exit, searching for the thing he would never find again.

"A distinguished career." She flicked a switch at her throat as her communicator began to buzz again.

Gundhalinu sat on the crates, patiently watching while the final cargo was loaded, the final report given to her, the confirmation relayed to the heart of the looming ship. They stood together as the last of her men saluted her for the

533

last time and self-consciously wished her well before heading back to the cargo lift.

Gundhalinu nodded after them. "Aren't you coming aboard to give your final report?"

She shook her head, feeling her heart suddenly squeezed by a relentless hand, the moment of schism. "No. I can't face that. If I set foot on that ship now, I don't think I'd be able to leave it again, no matter how sure I was that this is right." She handed him the computer remote. "You can give them the all clear for me, Inspector Gundhalinu. And take these." She reached up to her collar again, unfastened her Commander's insignia. She handed them to him. "Don't lose them. You'll need them someday."

"Thank you, Commander." His freckles crimsoned, making her smile. His good hand closed over the pieces of metal like rare treasure. "I hope I wear them with as much honor as you did." He held up his twisted hand in an instinctive Kharemoughi gesture; she pressed her own against it in farewell.

"Good-bye, BZ. The gods smile on you, wherever you go."

"And on you, Commander. May your many-times-great grandchildren venerate your memory."

She glanced toward the distant, darkened windows where Ngenet waited; smiled privately. She wondered what those many-times-great grandchildren might say to his, on the day of their return.

Gundhalinu drew his healing body up with an effort, and made a perfect salute. She returned it—the final salute of her career, the farewell to a life and a galaxy.

"Don't forget to turn out the lights." He started away to where the other patrolmen waited, already in the lift and holding it for him. She turned her back on the sight of them, of the lift like an open mouth calling her, calling her insane. . . . She went as quickly as she could without running to the nearest exit from the field.

She found Ngenet watching the doorway for her as she entered the deserted auditorium. She joined him at the wall of shielded glass, looking down across the field at the inert mass of the solitary coin ship, alone in the vast, ruddy pit, as they were alone. Miroe spoke quietly, complimenting her competence, asking innocuous questions; his voice was hushed, as though he were experiencing a religious event. She answered him distractedly, barely hearing what either of them said.

The ship lay in its berth for a long time—made longer by her straining anticipation—and she let him listen over her headset to the last drawing-in of cranes and equipment, the ship's officers going through their final checks and tallies.

"Are you clear, Citizen PalaThion?"

Jerusha started as the captain's voice addressed her directly. "Yes. Yes, I'm clear." *Citizen.* An irrational disappointment stirred in her. "All clear, Captain."

"You're sure you want to stay behind here?"

Miroe looked up at her, waiting.

She took a deep breath, nodded . . . said, as an afterthought, "Yes, I'm sure, Captain. But thanks for asking."

Life and noise continued at the other end of the gap for a few seconds longer, and then her communicator went dead. She stood very still for a long moment, as though she had heard herself die, before she pulled off the delicate spider's web of the headset.

Below them she saw the hologrammic lights of the ignition sequence play across the ship's hull and fade, mute warning. She stared until her eyes ached, searching for motion.

"Look. They're lifting."

Now she saw the motion, too, saw the ship's structure tremble—as the grids of the starport repellers engaged and it began to rise—and the faint distortion of the air. It drifted up and up, toward the portion of the starport's protective dome opening like a flower on the deeper, ruddy field of the star-choked night. It passed through into the outer darkness where, somewhere far above, it would join itself to a convoy of a dozen others, in a fleet of dozens and dozens more. And from there their fusion drives would

535

carry them on to the Black Gate and they would pass through, and never in her lifetime would they come back to this world again.

The dome resealed far overhead, blotting out the stars.

Jerusha looked down, across the glowing gridwork of the field, down at herself standing in this dark, empty hall, alone, like a cast-off stick of furniture. *Oh, my gods* . . . She covered her face with a hand, swaying.

"Jerusha." Miroe steadied her hesitantly. "I promise you, you won't regret it."

She nodded, pressing her lips together. "I'm all right. Or I will be, when I catch my breath." She lowered her hand, tracing the seal of her jacket down. "Like any other newborn." She smiled at him, uncertainly; he fed her smile with his own until it grew strong.

"You belong here, on Tiamat. I knew it from the first time I met you. But I had to wait until you knew it too. . . . I thought you'd never see." He was suddenly embarrassed.

"Why didn't you say something, anything, to help me understand?" almost exasperation.

"I tried! Gods, how I tried." He shook his head. "But I was afraid to hear you tell me no."

"And I was afraid I might say yes." She looked out the window again. "But I've belonged to this starport, too. And so have you. . . ." She sighed, looking back. "Neither of us belongs here now, Miroe. We'd better get out of here before they seal it up like a tomb."

He grinned, easing. "That's a step in the right direction. We'll take the rest as it comes; step by step." He turned solemn again. "Whenever you're ready."

"I'm as ready as I'll ever be, Miroe. For whatever comes." She felt her excitement and her courage coming back to her. "It's going to be interesting." She felt her face warm as he touched her. "You know, Miroe—" she laughed suddenly, "among my people, 'May you live in interesting times' is not exactly a benediction."

He smiled, and then he began to laugh; and together they started back through the abandoned halls—returning to Carbuncle, going home.

536